The Independent Bookworm

About the Series

For twenty centuries the Lands of Hope prospered from their Heroes' peace, but suffer now from their absence. Chaos slowly grows in the central kingdom of the Lands of Hope known as the Percentalion. It no longer permits safe or reliable travel in or out.

Even the bravest adventurers, who for centuries made a living foraying into its midst after lore and treasure, seem unable to do so anymore. The sundered populations of the Percentalion are trapped there, beyond communication and without hope.

Worse yet, the liche Wolga Vrule plots escape from his extra-worldly prison to unleash a tide of undeath, and enlists the Earth Demon Kog, who ruled the Percentalion millennia ago, as an uneasy ally.

About the Author

Will Hahn has been in love with heroic tales since age four, when his father read him the Lays of Ancient Rome and the Tales of King Arthur. He taught Ancient-Medieval History for years, but the line between this world and others has always been thin. The far reaches of fantasy, like the distant past, still bring him face to face with people like us, who have choices to make.

Will has written about the Lands of Hope since his college days (which by now are also part of ancient history). He chronicled the adventures of Solmn Judgement dilligently in two tomes of over 1000 pages each. It is now being published as an eBook series and in print. His Shards of Light series, a sword and sorcery story, begins with "The Ring and the Flag" and continues with "Fencing Reputation". The concluding volumes "Perilous Embraces" and "Shards of Light" will be published soon. He also chronicled stand alone stories like "The Plane of Dreams" or "Three Minutes to Midnight." More of Will's tales of Hope are available at several online retailers.

Find out more on his website: www.WilliamLHahn.com

Judgement's Tale

The Complete Omnibus

William L. Hahn

Judgement's Tale: Complete Omnibus
published by the Independent Bookworm, USA und D
this book is also available as eBook at various retailers

If you find typos or formatting problems in the book, please contact the publisher (www.IndependentBookworm.de).

editor: Ethan James Clarke
printed On-Demand Publishing LLC, 100 Enterprise Way, Suite A200, Scotts Valley, CA 95066, USA, www.createspace.com

ISBN-13 978-3-95681-027-5

Find more information on the publisher's website:
http://www.IndependentBookworm.de

To my father, William A. Hahn
I remember his face

To my good friend, colleague and supporter Katharina Gerlach
Who has always shown such conviction about my efforts

To my lovely wife Dorie
Who has read not one word, yet knows the tale entire

For my miracle daughter Genevieve Celeste
Whose will to thrive and see joy has overcome all opposition
and inspires the same in me

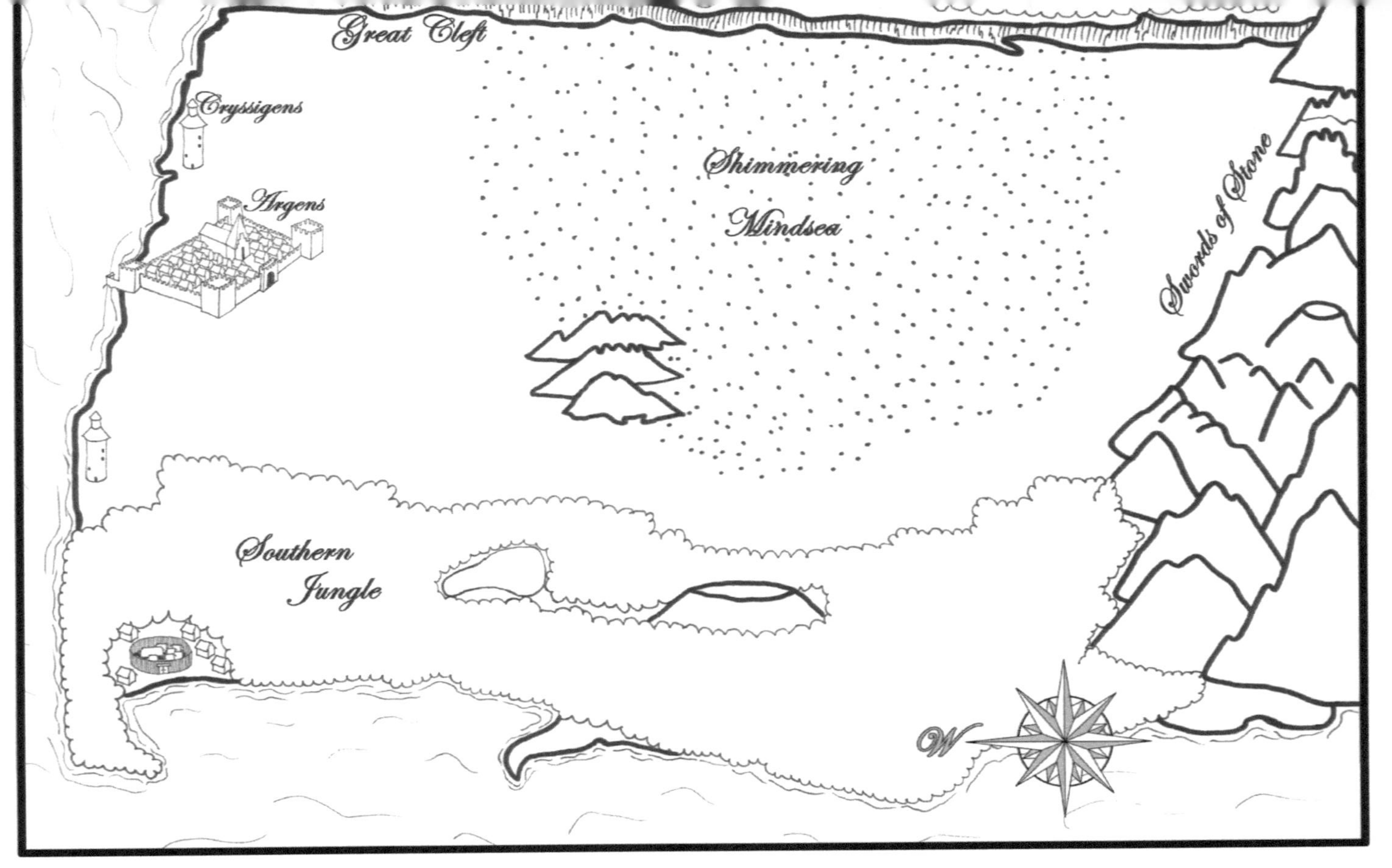
Great Cleft
Cryssigens
Argens
Shimmering
Mindsea
Swords of Stone
Southern
Jungle
W

The Lands of Hope
Northern Wastes
Novar
Conar
City of Wonders
Trainertown
Halfwoods
Stream Crossing
Cil-Ciluion
Shilar
Plains of Bordbeyonds
Percentalion
Skysword
River Sweeping
Eldaport
Araluntir
Mendel
Mendel
Great Cleft

Table of Contents

Beginnings

Hawk, 1995 ADR

As Areghel's line sits the Kingdom's throne
Ways keep straight, Kog's day is done.
But failing the seat, hell's place repeat,
And no child of Hope alone
No branch of Conar's bone
May demon cheat, his eye align,
Or Tridium seat, till the heir assign
The fivescore castles his own.

Ancient Prophecy

At forest's edge, the gypsy band huddled and watched a boy on the seashore burying his father.

Clouds ripped overhead in shreds of slate; below, the endless Western Sea reflected leaden chop without a white edge to relieve the monochrome sense of threat. Yet the boy outdid them both. He laid his father's corpse in a pose of dignity, and stubbornly hacked a fire-trench behind the tide-line scrub. All the while his posture, his pace, his entire demeanor radiated a total lack of color. The gypsies could have explained the ashen tint of his tunic, the dusty charcoal of his breeks and high leather boots. Salt water might have bleached his long, straight hair to dark silver, as well. But they could all sense it was otherwise — the boy was grey, through and through. And they came no closer yet, though the Rom were a hospitable people by nature.

"Grandmother, can they really have sailed from the West?" said Yellin the knife-thrower to the troupe's leader. The thin, tightly-wrinkled woman shrugged for answer, in annoyance, not indecision. He continued, "But no one has crossed the ocean to the Lands since…"

"Since the advent of Hope, if we are to believe the stories," said Mari the tambour-player; and at this everyone nodded, for to the gypsy a story is the blood of life.

"Yet see you the skiff," insisted Yellin. "Well-made and trim, to be sure, but so small, and with a crew of only two."

Now the leader bestirred herself and pointed with her stick to the skies, where a lone hawk circled and cried. "We have had strange storms this month," said Grandmother Valeria, "lightnings of many colors and winds that blew in circles, it seemed. And the hawk portends long journeys, the lone hunter who rules the signs of the Air. I think this young man comes from a land farther, yet not the same, as those our heroes set out from."

The band stood in silence after the grandmother had spoken — a new story unfolded now and none would interrupt it. Instead they watched as the young man completed the trench, then faced the skiff with arms akimbo. After three moments, he decided; bracing his leg under the mast-board for leverage, he hauled hard and began to break up the beautiful craft for firewood.

The gypsies watched him still an hour later near dusk and by the light of the burning pyre. Munching apples and crusts, they took in his every move, like watching a play: the boy piled the planks in a half-pyramid, put his father's body on the keelboard, and hauled it to the top with driftwood-rollers and all his strength. He had set the flame and now stood leaning on a half-length of the skiff's mast, serving him as a thick quarterstaff.

"He is not a man," said Mari. "Not fifteen, I bet."

"Old enough to see his father die, perhaps," Yellin said, nodding. "But to bury him… and now?"

"Now he is alone in all this world," said Grandmother Valeria. "For he is not of the Lands, I can feel it."

Again no one answered her, and the story continued in silence. The son had put aside some of his father's belongings, and with the funeral flame fully set he knelt briefly, then rose to take them. As the flicker-toothed fire ate the setting sun, the grey stranger put on the iron-hued broad-brimmed hat, hung the silver symbol around his neck and donned the full-length charcoal cloak, with all the gravity of a man putting on armor. He took up the staff and faced the fire on the beach once again. For a moment, he seemed to sag, as if under some nameless weight. The wind died down, but a single report of thunder signaled it was merely the quiet before the storm.

"He is a castaway, an orphan now," said Geltar the fire-eater.

"And so he is one of us," finished Valeria, and before anyone could stop her, she stepped from the edge of the trees and into the story, gesturing to the boy on the sand. At first he appeared not to notice, but after dipping to one knee a final time in a gesture of respect, he turned and strode steadily in her direction. From that moment, he never looked back at the fire or the sun, the father or the sea. The rest of the gypsy band shuffled from cover in response, and before long they were together. At this close range, the Rom could see that his eyes were large gems of silver, gazing hawk-like from beneath his ashen brows.

"Do you speak the Common Tongue, boy?" Valeria asked, holding her hand palm-up in a gesture of friendship.

For a moment, it was as if she spoke to a statue of a boy, his body unmoving and his face yielding no more comprehension to her speech than that of an animal. But as she prepared to try again, the grey youth said "Aye, though thy tongue is somewhat odd, I trow I do gain the meaning of thee, mistress." It was Common, as the gypsies knew it, but of an older dialect, such as the scholars in Conar might speak.

"Do you know any other speech, then?" Valeria asked, and in response the stranger tried first a smooth-flowing tongue, which had no meaning for any of the band, and then another, somewhat harder and more clipped. He spoke with fluency to judge from his ease; but on his third try, every tone hummed like a rung bell, and some of his listeners actually stepped back a pace from the resonance and strength of it.

"Those words!" started Yellin, "Is he singing? I never–"

But the leader of the band interrupted him, her face shining with wonder and fear. "It is Ancient, I'll be bound. I know it not but I've heard enough before, in the courts and at trials. This boy speaks the tongue of power like a native."

The stranger stopped to hear this dialogue, a puzzled expression on his face. "Ye know somewhat of those last words? I have little training in them–"

"And you should not speak it again, except at need," returned Valeria. "It is the Ancient speech, which our heroes used, the tongue of dragons and other beings of power, and one cannot lie while speaking it."

The boy raised a single brow. "Or in any other tongue, certes."

After a moment, a quiet chuckle made its way among the gypsies, the first hint of levity these entertainers had felt this day. Valeria too smiled, and said, "Assuredly. We have seen you from afar, traveler, and we welcome you to our band for as long as you may wish to stay. Tell us, what are you called?"

The young stranger stood even taller than before as he swept off his hat and answered in the manner of a captive soldier. "Mine name be Solemn Judgement, mistress. Son of… of Final Judgement, once of…" and here for a time the boy could not continue. As he stood in silent struggle, the weather broke and a storm came lashing down on him. The gypsies stood just under the lee of the forest and were mostly untouched, but the grey stranger's face was soon speckled with rain. Valeria scrutinized him closely, yet saw nothing but sky-water on his cheeks: the heavens granted a sign of grief he could not provide himself. "He was my teacher, mistress. Every day, as we sailed, he taught… I seek knowledge," he finished stiffly.

Valeria stepped forward then, and as her band gasped she reached for the young man with both arms. The same stick-hand which had just yesterday cracked Geltar's skull when he offered an impertinence in jest, the fingers which had turned the tarot cards in merciless judgment of her own people over the decades she had ruled the clan, these same limbs she now used to enfold the stranger, holding him close as if she would shelter him from the rain. And for all he bent in any human reaction to her welcome, she may as well have embraced his staff. But when she turned and led him by the arm, Solemn Judgement went along with the gypsy band, stepping east with them into the forest, further into the story, and fully onto the Lands of Hope.

Many leagues above the Lands of Hope the light of the sun is powerfully intense, a physical thing, like blinding water. As many leagues below, there is blackness wrapped thick, a shadow that has never felt the tinge of radiance. Long ago, as far back in time as distance away, these primal powers of sun and shadow met without making war upon each other, as was their nature. Suspended there between these two sharp-edged poles, the Hopeward broods, a silent pile of stonemetalearth, unformed yet regular, massive and elegant, open to the mute thundering fall of light through its milk-crystal roof, and enveloped by the intangible ocean of ebon surrounding its walls.

Within the Hopeward, beyond the maze-halls and their shifting doors of glass, past basalt guardians and broken bodies of the ages-slain, on the central bridge that forms its purpose and sustains the rules allowing it to exist, here waits a being near-made of evil, drenched in time and sodden with Despair. The liche Wolga Vrule was merely wicked, fifty centuries ago. Of unspeakable cruelty and bent beyond thought, yet he was a man, of human stock. Now, he breathes only when he speaks aloud, and there is nothing sentient here to speak to. His heart is still. No flow of fluid informs his nerves or bones, and all his contents softer than bone have shriveled. He shall exist forever, draining other life to continue, and with that he is content. But Wolga Vrule was tricked into serving as the keeper of the Hopeward, and with that he is far from content.

Near the center of his vast prison, a dais of twisted ores and minerals rises directly from the stone, topped with a flat, distinctly fleshlike surface. Enchanted and honed with centuries of Vrule's sorcerous energy, the dais-face bears an image of the Lands, as if drawn on an enormous vellum map. Vrule traces its surface with nail-hard fingers, viewing its faithful reflection of the kingdoms governing the present world and the unworthy races living there.

The hot southern empire below the Great Cleft and the frozen northern wastes he ignores — the game of empire had always been played in the center of the board. From the Western Sea to the kingdoms beyond the Marble Swords, the Hopelord Conar and his descendants long ago seized control from the Men of Despair, the race of Wolga Vrule. Where once Mauglir had been Liege (with Vrule as a chief among his thanes) the lands now bear the names of Conar and his vassals, the heroes of Hope.

The liche taps the center of the map, his dried-black pupils glazed with a hungry light. A murkish fog hangs over the Percentalion, through which even enormous Skysword pokes as a lonely peak. Long the main battleground between Hope and Despair, it had fallen in ancient times to Conar's vassal Areghel. That was three thousand years ago, long even as Wolga Vrule would reckon it; in recent centuries the chaotic nature of the powerful Earth-Demon who once ruled it for Mauglir is reasserting itself. The Land of One Hundred Castles, under Vrule's careful guidance and the inattention of his foes, is returning to its proper state. Soon it shall become again as it was in the before-times when Despair ruled all this world, a hell on earth, and Vrule intends to hasten the day.

Wolga Vrule has grown to despise them all, insects on two legs playing dress-up in the roles of their ancestors. He was of royal blood himself, and served Mauglir in person, even before his transformation to immortal undead. And, Vrule recalls with a shudder, he had seen Conar the Hopelord, the Law-Giver in the flesh as well, across the battle-lines of those early wars. To contest with one of the ancient race of heroes, such as the Hopelord of Men — now there, his cunning brain flirts, would have been a challenge. But these pale races so distantly descended from that stock; there will be no bar to his power arising from them. The moment for his escape draws near, and only the rules constrain him.

So much for the board; now the liche looks to the playing pieces presently on it. The mystic map shows pulsations where sentient beings live. Vrule sees Conar the City of Wonders, an offensive glow denoting the peaceful, happy lives of over a million beings living undisturbed and undeservedly happy under the Law. Other cities of lesser population are more vulnerable; the powerful mages in Araluntir, City of Glass, do not stir more now than they have over the endless years of Vrule's confinement. He fears their power, but has come to scorn their isolation. All the kings of Hope in fact, as in many games, rest impotent off in protected corners, never suspecting that this reign would require action, or a break with their beloved customs. One white queen, in particular, will serve his ends against her will.

But now is the time to look in on his own red rook. Vrule's vision veers from the sunlit lands shown on his mystic map, beneath seven leagues of the earth of the Percentalion, to a titanic chasm where air is flame and time is agony. Of the teeming, torturing thousands who crawl there, one vast spirit looms and towers; Vrule feels the endless power, the almost complete lack of volition, and in his mind he calls the horror by name. "Kog."

"Vrule? Every time you speak to me I am still a prisoner."

"The kingdom will be yours again soon."

"Always soon, never now. You bore me."

"The door opens. The queen will not disappoint," the liche assures the demon. "She needs to see her lover again" — and he gazes a moment at the man — "and when she returns in less than six months, I shall be free, as will you."

"A month, a decade. *Freedom.*" The strength of the demon's desire washes over Vrule and he nearly staggers. "Give me the Eye!"

"It is here, and I shall send it. The rules require–"

"Rules?" The mind-voice of the demon takes a dangerous change of course. "Who speaks?" Vrule bites back his frustration. The chaos being cannot be held to any consistent course, beyond his own will.

"I speak of your freedom, Kog. And when you are free, you will do a deed for me in return."

"I know of no deal," the demon grinds back.

"We have a pact! I am Vrule!"

"Nor do I bow to any mortal. Begone."

"You swore in blood with me."

"I drink blood, sometimes when I am bored. I am so often bored." Vrule can feel the demon losing all interest, again, and his bile rises to think that so much depends on this guideless leviathan. Mastering his fury, he tries again.

"Freedom, Kog. I have your eye here with me."

"You? Are you Vrule, then?"

"You remember when you care to. And remember, also, the pact we have made."

"You… seek to bind me." For just an instant the demon toys in his mind with the idea of destroying Wolga Vrule. The liche feels, even across the measureless leagues, a surge of strength and hatred so mammoth, it raises fears he has not felt since… since the last time they had spoken. A moment later, Kog's mind turns to something closer, and Vrule can sense the death-spasms of a score of beings.

"I– I seek to free you, Kog. We are allies, and soon you will be whole. The line that opposed your rule is gone–"

"There is one more. One left." This blunt assertion startles Vrule, but the present conversation is no place to show indecision.

"Aye, and his death will adorn your ascension. With the Percentalion again under your control, you can easily grant the access I need to the caverns under Skysword. A few small items there, for my further researches–"

"What of the Prophecy?" For a second time the liche jumps at the demon's insight. Was this all just a game he played?

"That ensures your success," he soothes, "for it clearly states that once the seed of Areghel is dead, none can stand before you."

"No child of Hope. Not the same."

"Leave the Prophecy to me, mighty Kog. And be ready. You will sense when you are free to return. Remember then who freed you."

"I accept your servitude, human," Kog responds with glee.

Vrule champs back the temptation to rejoin, knowing full well it does not matter what the demon thinks, so long as he can access the caverns beneath Skysword when both are back in the Lands. After that, there will be less question which of them governs. He smiles in his mind to cover his loathing and turns away the contact. Just as the malavert brain of the Earth-Demon becomes inaudible to him, Vrule hears him muse, "Why have a prophecy if it won't come true?"

The liche begins to wonder, but then dismisses any doubt with his characteristic air. Vrule turns his enormous mind to other matters. Striding to face the double-row of relics, his eyes trail absently across priceless treasures as they stand on their podiates; the black-bladed sword, the red armor, the sole gauntlet, the ruby gem. Such power, so casually arrayed, and how completely useless here in the prison of rules. Only his will and genius can release them, and make them serve his purpose.

The contact with Kog has proven draining; it always does, yet Vrule has risked it so many times since that day four years ago, when the wheels of his escape began to turn. He stands now at the magma-cleft, gazing almost fondly at the inferno below and catching just a glimpse of the behemoth within it. Even its scorching heat cannot revive his lost life energy; for Vrule, food gives no strength and rest no restoration.

But life so casually lost is easily regained. With a small gesture, he summons one of the faithful from beyond the maze to his chamber. It appears, and writhes and scuttles closer, its head ducked in obeisance that its beak cannot utter. The trembling thing even dares to lay a ropy arm upon his side, as he reaches to touch its middle. The thing cackles and chokes while its vital force drains away to him, until its husk falls into the cleft leaving only a slight cloud of *miasma* behind for Vrule to savor. The long days will pass and the Hopeward will divulge three treasures soon, counting as the greatest, of course, himself.

Excerpt from The Kingdom Chronicle 1994 ADR

… thus closed the year of Elosira in the Lands, on balance another of continued peace and stability for the Children of Hope. The major seats of power in Conar, Shilar, Mendel, and Araluntir remained secure as they have for centuries. From Argens, the news grew regrettably less, but no worse as the Empire of the Sun thrived under Viridian XXVII (in what would be the final year of that reign). Most bracing, the colony of Novar reported solid gains in its census and a quiet year, if not a fully peaceful one, with the neighboring Northern tribesmen.

Admittedly, piracy in the Bay of Mendel continued unchecked, as the captains raided merchant shipping and avoided capture on their undiscovered island lair. And the plight of the central kingdom, the Percentalion, only deteriorated as merchant trade or contact nearly dissolved entirely. Efforts to reach any surviving larger towns within the kingdom, or of their inhabitants to escape, found no success. Without an heir to the throne in Reghalion, the country fell increasingly back towards its condition from ancient days, when the Earth-Demon ruled. Sages of all nations regularly confer to find a solution, and have come away empty beyond adventurers' tales and wild prophecies. Of these, admittedly, there has been no shortage. Small parties of warriors, mages and assorted non-noble folk continued to enter, and occasionally leave the Land of One Hundred Castles. Of late itinerant preachers were heard in Shilar, speaking in mead-hall and market of the changing of the age, a coming day of great tumult, of ruin and heroism, heralded by various signs from the earth's creatures and in the sky.

In fine, however, the year passed without such signs; and it may earnestly be Hoped that the upcoming year of the Sun will bring to light more stability, peace and safety for the Lands.

Diary of Valenthur the Sage

Fourth Serpent, Sun Year 1995 A.D.R.

I realized today why it is that I like the typesetting so well.

The Chronicle of 1994 is at last done–the current year already halfway past!–which of course brings a tremendous sense of accomplishment. But now the master needs to be printed out, five and twenty copies to be sent from here in Trainertown, one to each of the great libraries of the Lands, and this is truly a labor. Were it not for my waning hand-strength, which causes the quill to shake sooner and sooner each year, I would be tempted to scribe-copy all of them as I did in my youth. Of course with age come changes: an acolyte to assist me, and now this marvelous press, a gift of the Conarian Guild where I hear of wonders untold, of a fleet of such presses that run day and night. Anteris has nimble hands of course, and a marvelous facility with thinking in reverse; the wooden letters must be set in place backwards in order for the printed page to come out properly, so he works from the right to left on each line. I find myself thinking that this is indeed the way the chronicle is written; we take notes as the year passes, but then we must look back and set things in their proper order after all is done. At first, it seems to make no sense. Finally, the product reaches the paper and it is once again seen in the right order. Were I to look back in ten more years, what of the details we set down today would truly survive, be thought of importance? But then, ten more years I will not likely see, so that will be someone else's puzzle.

Perhaps his. I watched Anteris today while pretending to rest my hands, and I see in him such love; he desires to learn and is obedient to any chore I set him. He enjoys the hard work of setting type, sharpening quills, sweeping, clearing dishes; there is no task he does not hop to with a ready will. And yet, for all his good cheer and the sunlight it lets into my life, I know the boy's heart is elsewhere. All these things, the slow steady compilation of knowledge he assists with, is just the first course in his ravenous appetite to hear tales of adventure. Truly, he is a child of this city, but I had hoped to draw him away with age to more serious pursuits. Even today, as his fingers moved so deftly across the plate, I could see his foot begin to fidget, and now and again he would check the sunlight outside the window. He knows when the time is near. Not that he minds the work, but Anteris will not be late to the far south walls for any bribe or threat.

I expected nothing else from the pack of ne'er-do-wells that sit there each day, watching for the first sign of a returning party of would-be heroes. But Anteris sits and searches and swaps tales with the rest of them, as if all these histories he has himself put to paper had never been written.

He has gone now, racing off to be the first, a flash of white I have seen from this window; he'll be there until past the sunset as every day, and never a word of complaint next morning if he misses his sleep from staying late to catch one more glimpse. Such a good, even noble lad; may the heroes cushion the blow of disappointment that is sure to fall on his heart, and soon.

Just four adventuring parties have set out from this town in the past half a year, and none have returned. The way is closed now, surely; except of course for wily Pelian, who leads a caravan more and more heavily armed each trip out. He, admittedly, has always come back, though how long he has been gone this time I cannot well recall; perhaps eight months? The folk murmur that he has some mystic spell, or a wand that guides him. But he is a merchant, no adventurer, and finds his happiness in trade rather than empty glory. Once, this city had more than plenty of each; now, the ways of the Percentalion have become too tangled, the cursed creatures too strong, and the would-be heroes to challenge them have died out altogether.

And better that way, though it means the death of this place: Trainertown as a simple way-station for Conarian messengers and the trade with Shilar were a happier, aye, more honorable course than the low and immoral custom it carried on in supporting that worthless, dangerous class of being the tales call adventurers. I well recall as a young man avoiding the central streets after sunset, when their carousing, their arguments over women or maps or treasure were the terror of right-thinking folks. We had twelve taverns then, instead of three, to stoke their moods and leech their funds; more guards to quell them, more comfort-folk to attend them in their wicked loneliness. The Guilds thrived on their trade in magic and weaponry; the smiths rang at all hours with special orders for this handle or that barding. Trainertown is better unknown today, rather than infamous as it was.

Still, Anteris will watch and hear the tales from Calper and the other broken old men who sit with them. They'll dream of something, and may Conar forbid but some of his friends will likely slip off one day to try for an untouchable glory on their own. Let the blacksmith's boy, or that wiry girl who runs for the tanner, try their hand if they're fool enough. I would spike Anteris' foot to the floor before I let him go on a fool's mission to the Percentalion. May the heroes have mercy on any benighted child of Hope who still languishes there. The way is closed now. With time, the lad will learn where his heart truly lies.

Games of Chance

The number of shaggy creatures ranged around them was not the problem. In the moonlit darkness, Treaman counted only five as they spiraled closer, covering a semi-circle and slowly backing the party towards the stream. Their size, admittedly, was disconcerting; the smallest, across from Linya on the other end of the party-line, was a hand taller than a mastiff; the largest in the center – furiously snapping at his pack-mates when they came too close – was the size of a pony. That, Treaman reasoned, was what leaders like Haltar were for. But the truly troubling thing about the half-ring of fangs and talons now close enough to feel the heat from their breath, lay somewhere unnamed. It was between each creature's six legs, the way their eyes stood completely out from their heads, the trampled arrows that had bounced off their hides, and the row of saw-toothed, palm-wide teeth running down their spines. In short, this pack of monsters had never been seen on earth before, outside the Percentalion. The nameless death, Treaman thought, was what made it so hard to bear.

The pack proceeded very deliberately; the creatures were heavy and slow, and without the deep stream behind them, the party might have risked running. Treaman took a hard jab at one with his spear, trying to hit an exposed eye but glancing off the bony skull when it jerked back to bite at the point. Haltar advanced with his bastard-sword whistling in a savage arc, feinting at the largest in front of him and then turning to land a perfect blow on the neck of the one next to it. It would have decapitated a horse, but the blade barely cut, and the strapping foot-knight hauled desperately back to retrieve the weapon from its hide. Too late – the jaws of the leader closed around his exposed bicep. The last trick was Haltar's, however, for this was the arm he kept covered in plate and chain. The teeth raised only flesh-wounds as he transferred his blade to the free hand and battered the leader over the skull with its pommel, whereupon it released his arm with a roar. The monster he first struck staggered and gave an awful shriek, but clearly more from anger than pain; the thinnest trickle of yellow blood was scant reward for such maneuver and risk.

To Treaman's right, Mhoral held his flail aloft, chanting, "Kaannn-yeeee-dar!" and delivered a grand sweep, his weapon suddenly glowing with mystic energy. It nicked the beast before him, which snarled and retreated as the weapon came so close to its eyes.

"No magic until command!" Haltar bellowed, but the helmed elf was committed; Mhoral continued forward and connected on a backswing, coming in low and breaking a foreleg. Haltar and Linya stepped up to cover his sides, but the pack-leader's bite clenched the chains of the flail. The monster tugged the weapon neatly from Mhoral's grasp and flung it into the brush followed by the elf's torrid curse. Scrambling back, the party remade its line while the beasts roughly ejected the wounded member, limping back and howling in pain. Mhoral drew his second weapon, a narrow-edged wooden club with an angle above the haft.

"Mhoral, cover Linya! Linya, step center, prepare for fire." Treaman heard the peremptory tone Haltar seemed born to use, all the while keeping both eyes on his enormous foe, certain he was being obeyed. Treaman poked ineffectually at his opponent as they gave ground, until his left foot landed in the water of the stream's edge. This was the end of the line. Why were they still alive?

Even with his death so near, the young woodsman could not shake his fascination with these strange creatures; they snapped at each other jealously and moved with all deliberation despite provocation from their human prey. "Each one wants us all to himself," he called out, and Haltar nodded, having had the thought. "Something more, though, I'm sure of– ho, back there!" Haltar took two more quick swings at the one to his right which was edging too close. "Something else, Treaman. Why so slow?"

"I don't–" the woodsman began, and then bit off his rejoinder with a muttered curse. Haltar was not being fair, but there it was; someone needed to figure this out, and fast. Treaman watched as a beast on the opposite end of the line dropped out, moving back towards the wounded one with clear intent. Three left for us, he thought. Still too many. His mind raced frantically as he tried to ascertain a weakness, a habit, something he could tell Haltar to pull them out of this.

Treaman's beast got hold of his spearpoint in its teeth briefly and worried the head until the young woodsman yanked it loose. Even with its breath on him, he was distracted by the death-dance of the wounded monster and its former pack-mate in the back. Snarling and biting, neither one wasted much effort on a full attack; but the wounded one constantly circled away from its foe, who switched directions to make it limp towards its broken limb, harder going and slower. It was relentlessly gaining ground, getting closer to…

"The gut!" he screamed, so loud the beast across from him snapped back. "The vitals, underneath, the hide is thinner there!" Haltar was nodding vigorously as it all made sense now. They had been maneuvered so slowly because the creatures did not want to expose their weak spots. The knight whistled sharply once, and from a tree several rods behind the beasts something the size of a human child dropped to the ground.

The party crowded the shore of the stream now, and as Haltar called out orders, the lead beast howled an interruption. Treaman saw everything happening at once.

The front three monsters gathered their legs to pounce heavily on their doomed human prey.

The execution-beast in back nosed beneath and ripped out a section of its victim's vitals the size of a small shield.

A buzzing sound ended with a sharp *twack*; one monster snapped at its own ear in sudden pain, and turned to look behind it.

Linya gestured and intoned what sounded like nonsense and the ground in front of the pack-leader suddenly ignited.

The behemoth already in mid-leap sailed through flame, and its fur sparked brightly and emitted an awful stench that made Haltar gag, even as it bore him down to the shore with four legs, driving his head underwater.

Treaman, still held rapt by the death-howls of the wounded beast in the back, let his creature past the guard of his shield; it sunk its teeth into his shoulder and he screamed, staggering fully down into the water as he tore free. Sputtering, he surfaced and tried to keep one hand on the spear as he gathered his legs.

The current had carried him downstream out of reach for the moment; the magical fire summoned by Linya illumined the carnage and confusion too well. Mhoral was clubbing his foe ineffectually over the head and only another invisible *twack*, this time on its hindquarters, was distracting the beast enough to keep the elf alive.

The lead beast, crackling with flame and surrounded by smoky stench, was apparently too angered to finish the fallen knight beneath its fore-paws; Treaman feared he was drowned in any event. Treaman's former foe, no longer able to get at him downstream, turned to try for Haltar's body instead; the central monster roared its fiery defiance and attacked its pack-mate. He saw Linya standing on the other side of Haltar's downed form, paralyzed with fear and just staring at the awesome hulk four feet from her.

Treaman raised his spear for a desperate heave, trying to steady his feet against the mud of the streambed. His shoulder burned and his body chilled at the same time. It was no doubt futile, and most of his mind assured him he would not live out the minute, much less the night. But something nagged at him deep inside, and he realized, even as he let the spear fly, that it was too much to die without knowing the creatures' name.

"Are you certain then, Grandmother?" Solemn Judgement asked.

"It is the judg– eh, the decision of this clan, young one," Valeria answered in the presence of the entire troupe. Her voice sounded serious, even grave; by the campfire's unsteady light, it was impossible to tell if the edge of her mouth held steady or quivered a bit.

The sea-borne stranger's last night among the Rom reached a peak with the pronouncement. By dawn the next day, the gypsies and the Man in Grey had to part company at last. The band would change course, while Judgement would keep to his. But no one among them knew that yet.

"Before you leave this band of entertainers," Valeria intoned the verdict, "you must play." All the heads around the campfire's edge nodded at this decision; to judge from the smothered grins and chortles, a popular one too. Nothing on the face of the young stranger betrayed his reaction; he sat still as if uncomprehending.

"Play," he said, as one who is trying out a new word in a foreign tongue.

"Aye, play. Something, anything!" put in Yellin, clearly one of the ringleaders in this rump-court. "For one hour in your young life, boy, do some frivolous, joyous, time-wasting thing."

"I have not finished the foraging," Solemn said, pointing, "There is work–"

"He works, all he does is work," Mari exclaimed. "He is up before the sun, he cooks food, he wrangles the wagons, he carries wood. He eats almost nothing, and then he sleeps."

"Have you seen him sleep, even?" Yellin shouted back across the fire. Mari looked confused a moment, and the knife-man hooted in triumph. "He's an elf, that's the secret! But I catch your meaning, lovely Mari – you wish you had seen him sleeping, and close in by you, aye!"

The general roar of amusement crested higher as a tamboor chittered through the fire's smoke to strike Yellin full on the chest. Even Valeria allowed herself a chuckle at this ribaldry, for the Rom are not a jealous or straight-laced people by any stretch. In the midst of the riot, Solemn Judgement sat unaffected, as the only one in a tavern who does not understand the joke. When at length things quieted down, everyone looked at the guest.

Once again, he said only, "Play."

"He could sing," said Valeria. But as the grey youth drew breath, Yellin interrupted loudly, "No, it won't do, Grandmother. We've heard him sing, and it's not right."

"He sings well enough," Crass put in from over by the horse-line.

"Aye," returned Yellin readily, "he sings on occasion, and his voice is fine. But it isn't *play*. He sings the hero-rhyme, the child-song we taught him, to keep the names straight. He sings the Song of the Silvertongue, so that he can recall the order of the fighting during the Battle of the Razor. He's learned every song we sing that *taught* something, and he memorizes them so that he can add to his store." Yellin stepped up closer to the seated grey guest now, and looked down on him in accusation. "But he does not *play*."

"Well let him dance then," one of the others offered, and there was a chorus of assent to this. At once the sound of the hand-keys and the recovered tamboor began, and several members of the troupe whirled into the steps from wherever they were. This continued for several moments, till Mari broke away from her playing to run to the stranger, reaching out a hand and inviting him to dance in the most winning way. Judgement stood, but only held her hand briefly, as one would greet a visiting dignitary, nodding his head in courtesy before taking his seat once more. The dancing continued awhile beneath the tribunal. Yellin was the merciless interrogator now, standing arms akimbo and practically touching the defendant at the knees.

"Fine, our young fire-guest will not dance. But it must be something, young Judgement, and it must be done by the dawn." The gaze the grey stranger returned to the knife-thrower was almost mild, and yet there was the quality of steel beneath the surface. At last, the dance ended and in the silence that followed, Judgement spoke.

"It may be any kind of play? In any form?"

"So long as it serves no purpose but your own amusement, aye."

"Not sparring, then? You and I could bout–"

"Nay, stripling. That's training for war, and we both know it," Yellin said, shaking his head. "You've done it hour by hour, dripping sweat after the work of the day is done."

"And aside from that," yelled a voice in the back, "he'd beat you hollow, Yellin!" More laughter and a clenched grin from the knife-thrower was the result.

"So," Judgement continued, as if musing about the weather, "perhaps a… game of some kind?"

There was a moment's silence from the gypsies, which seemed to give assent, but Yellin was suspicious.

"Not gambling, no game for money; that has too much purpose to it. Just a game."

"Certes, just a game, then. And may I use anything here?" the young man said, sweeping with his arm to indicate the entire camp.

Yellin shrugged, and for a time the Man in Grey remained still. Then, rising, he announced, "I must ponder this verdict, awhile." As he walked around the edge of the campfire, it seemed he was window-shopping the clan, seeking with his eye through their effects for a suitable object of frivolity. The clan was agog with anticipation, and several showed him juggling pins and hoops in hopes of being chosen. Little Tretha, only four years old, had always been shy of the grey stranger, but now she caught the general mood and pushed forward her corn-silk doll: Judgement thanked her gravely for this gesture but refused, and she ran back to her mother squealing at her unaccustomed and ephemeral bravery. Turning aside from all these alike, the young man walked past the fire circle and beyond the edge of the encampment, leaving them to wonder in his absence.

"Can this be so hard for him?" Mari asked. "He has seen our ways, and has lived among us with no complaints, and yet, he seems…"

"Pure stubbornness," put in Crass as he turned back to finish brushing down his horses. "Thinks he's too good for us, a band of beggars and entertainers. His sire was likely a knight or some such, and he won't put off his airs, orphan though he is."

"That's the truth of it, I'd bet all I have," said Yellin, "And we won't be put down, not by him, see? We'll watch some speck of our ways rub into that grim face before he goes, I swear it."

Grandmother Valeria listened to the discourse and said not a word, but only looked over her shoulder to see the straight slim form at the northern edge of the band, looking further north across the grassy sward of the inner kingdom coastlands. By the light of moon and stars, the white hill on the distant bay was still visible to his gaze, the young man's destination. Valeria remembered their conversation earlier that day, from the camp when Judgement had first caught sight of it.

"That hill, does it have a name, Grandmother?" he had asked.

"That is Conar," she had replied.

"They gave the mountain the same name as the hero-city? Is it nearby then?"

"Those are its walls. That is the City of Wonders itself."

He had gulped hard then, to realize the staggering size of what he was seeing from almost a league away. She recalled also the blaze of fire that had flared up in his eyes, and how his mind moved so quickly with the barrage of questions that followed. Libraries? Yes, the largest in the Lands of Hope, and sages in guilds to copy and study their tomes. The oldest city in all the kingdoms, and lore beyond measure. How easy it was to catalogue its miraculous attractions, and how hard to explain why the troupe would not accompany him there. The Rom would head north-by-east in the morning, taking a smaller and worse-kept road through poorer villages, in order to remain who they were.

Only one traveler would continue directly north, on the straight stone highway, into the capital of Hope, where the Law had never once been broken. Valeria knew it was his path, to find the power that was beating inside his chest like a panicked bird in a wicker cage. He had turned to her at last and uttered an apology in his usual sparse prose. "I follow his teaching, Grandmother. I must learn." She had nodded, knowing he meant the father who had spent his last breath to deliver him an orphan to the shores, and to her. Now the boy would leave so soon, to enter the City of Wonders. What sort of man would come out of Conar, she thought, and would she live long enough to see?

It was only a short while before Judgement returned to the band. He walked around the campfire to where the leader sat, bowed and said, "May I borrow your cards, Grandmother?"

For a few moments, it seemed as if the campfire had stopped crackling: all the clan caught their breath and watched Valeria to hear how she would respond. Yet the aged woman took a page from her guest's book, and said not a word. Slowly and deliberately, she produced the velvet pouch that held the thick, over-sized tarot deck and handed it to the Man in Grey. Judgement bowed to her and turned to sit on a stool near the backboard of her wagon, gently pulling the deck from its sheath before clearing a space and shuffling the cards. All the time, his eyes never left Yellin's, and about his mouth there was, if not a smile, a fleeting hint that it could be done.

The clan crowded around, blocking the firelight and cursing quietly and holding up lanterns and jostling for a view. Yellin the inquisitor was still suspicious.

"No magic tricks now. No sleight of hand, it won't do to insult the grandmother's cards–"

"No tricks," Judgement assured him.

"And we won't be gambling here," Yellin pursued. "No money at risk, that's not frivolous enough."

"What does he need with money, anyway?" said Crass. "Every town we stop in, he labors for the smith, he hustles for the inn-keep, and I'm damned if he hasn't kept every silver bit they tip him."

"Jealous, then, Crass?" threw out Mari from the back. "You'll have money enough next month, when you sell that fine horse you 'found' in the village back there!"

The response now was that classic, rising groan of 'trouble-coming,' but the Rom knew this was merely the way. They were still within the law, so long as Crass said the right thing now. And he did.

"Why, this animal wandered into my *keran* last night," Crass declared in a voice just a shade rehearsed. "We all know, once an animal comes within the stakes it belongs to the owner. I've no idea what village it may have come from, if it was in that last one I did not notice." His flashing smile produced smaller copies around the circle, as with a familiar tale. When the drover's gaze took in the stranger, however, he saw something less than friendly and his smile died.

"The black-and-white stallion, half a hand taller than any other in the village, that one?" the Man in Grey inquired. Even by firelight, the wonderful riding horse was easily visible on the edge of the camp, and so his question required no answer. Everyone knew that an accusation of theft was a dance on the edge of a knife, among the Rom. Death for the convicted, yet the curse for one who accused without proof. Now Crass stood defiant, daring the stranger to step in. Solemn's silver eyes seemed to say that some nameless fact was obvious, but when he spoke, his mouth said only, "A fine animal. And costly to care for, surely?"

"As to that," Crass said, now warming to his role, "it does indeed pull at my meager resources to shelter this orphan for long. It may be, someday soon, I will have to sell him."

Judgement nodded at this. "What would you expect to get in return? Someday, of course."

Crass seemed puzzled by this for a moment, and was telling more than half the truth when he exclaimed, "As to that, I– well, I hadn't considered it yet. That is, I hope to keep- well, at least fifty silver pieces, I should say. If I can bear to part with him at all, that is."

"Oh, aye!" was the general response, and more chuckles now as the drover stretched his credibility to the utmost with his clan.

"And may Conar grant, in his wisdom," the drover finished, "that if this horse should leave my care, he will one day find the path back to his previous owner."

There was a patter of applause, and one voice muttered, "For another fifty silver, no doubt." Then all eyes turned back to the Man in Grey. He had finished shuffling the deck and was now turning over the cards in order.

"No tarot, now!" cried Yellin. "You have no right, no matter what Grandmother says–"

At this, the clan leader at last spoke, cutting off debate. "Enough, Yellin. The boy does not throw the tarot. Though he knows how."

Now the clan looked to her in something like horror. Most had never seen another set of hands laid upon these tarot cards in their lifetimes, and many could not say from whom Valeria had inherited them. To see them in the unwrinkled hands of the strange young man who had spent less than a season among them was cause enough for grumbles in the back. Now, Crass and some others heard that this outsider had been taught the art of divination, and considered in their hearts it was just as well he would be leaving.

None of this quiet tumult seemed to bother the accused in the least, as he turned the cards to lay them face-up and half-atop each other. As the clan watched, Judgement laid out eight columns of cards and dealt them down, putting the Trumps aside as they turned up and using only the forty cards with numbers and their matching sets of faces, sixteen more. When the last card was laid, his hands were empty and he folded them to look upon the board in contemplation.

Everyone watched without a sound, long enough for some to suspect that it was a weak joke of the stranger's. Then he reached for a card at the bottom of one column, and put it atop another two columns over. The young man repeated this sort of movement twice more, once placing a bottom card above the card-grid and on the left. Then he lifted an exposed card, the ace of staves, to place it also above but on the right-hand side. Murmurs and whispers gave chase around the circle; none of the gypsies had ever seen this curious behaviour before.

"What is this?" Yellin asked, but the stranger gave no answer. Trying again, the knife-thrower demanded, "When is it my turn, then? How do you win?" Judgement looked up at Yellin on this, his eyes reflecting firelight and something more. "Hast not seen, then? Tis new to thee?" His turn of speech did not go unnoticed by Mari; it was his wont when he became more excited. But Yellin was taken in by the mystery, and shook his head in answer.

"Behold, then!" said Judgement, waving his hands over the board. "Here is an entire kingdom, taken prisoner. Defeated in war, all its population, from the lowliest servant"– here he tapped the recently moved ace– "to the nobility"– here a face-card back amidst the pack– "are all thrown into a common cell to rot. They must escape, but how?" Judgement sat back then with an expectant demeanor, and the gypsies shifted their feet as they realized an answer was truly expected of them.

Crass, rubbing his face with one hand, finally ventured, "They could bribe the guards?"

The boy-teacher nodded once, and said, "Ah yes, but the guards are aware of this, and watch for just such a thing. In fact, the leaders, the Marks, Baronesses and Knights, are watched most closely. So they must be the last to go, or else the entire enterprise will fail."

"Dig a tunnel," suggested Yellin.

"Exactly right, and one has been dug, as you can see by the ace's escape. Yet the tunnel is very narrow, and the cell is packed with prisoners. There are but four spaces free for them to move about." Here Judgement gestured to the left-hand top spaces. "And further, there are all races, classes and genders among the kingdom, and naturally everyone wishes not to be left behind, so there must be strict alternation. Thus they can be arranged in order by number, a four below a five, a three below a four, but only if the even numbers be men and the odd numbers women, or vice versa."

This last statement lost the audience completely, except the owner of the cards who smiled as she saw the puzzle. "The suits of the tarot lean towards the two genders," Valeria explained, and, rising, she moved to tap the spot where Judgement had already started a small row of order among the suits. "Nobles are of the earth, and speak to females; the suit has no men in its face-cards, only Handmaiden, Dame, Baroness and Marchess. Staves, otherwise, are of the air, and are male, with the Squire, Knight, Baron and Mark. The same with Vessels for water, and Swords for fire."

"Just so, Grandmother," said Judgement. "Thus, with the four spaces only to maneuver, the people must arrange themselves so that the lowest ranked can escape first, in alternation of genders and vocations, on up to the royalty who will escape last."

The clan looked down on the random cards in growing discontent. Finally, Yellin voiced what most of them felt. "It can't be done."

"On the contrary," Judgement returned in good cheer but deadly earnest, "I believe that no matter how the cards are laid, it is possible to win, though I admit that in some layouts even a single false move may doom the attempt. Wilt thou try it, sir?" Yellin looked around to both sides like the soldier who had not realized he had volunteered, and then shrugged aggressively and bent over the table. First he moved a six down upon a seven, but Judgement held up a finger reprovingly. "Ah no, sir, the stave can only go upon a vessel or a noble." Yellin replaced it, then glanced around, grunted in triumph and quickly put two more cards up to the left, then moved the exposed two of staves up upon its escaped ace. He looked to Judgement who nodded but did not smile; back on the board, Yellin's grin quickly died as he half-reached to the cards three times, but never picked one up.

"There are no moves, I can do nothing," he said, and Judgement nodded again.

"Aye, the tunnel is too narrow, you must pull these back and try again."

"But I– I don't remember where they were!" the gypsy cried. "Have I lost already?"

For answer Judgement only leaned forward eagerly to say, "Lost at what, sir?" Silence. "Lost this *game*, then?"

A murmur of assent rose behind them as the Man in Grey turned back to the board. Quickly pulling all four cards down to where they had been, he began to move them laterally, in a steady pattern, never putting more than two cards up on the left. The cards seemed a loom, and Judgement the weaver moving them back and forth, producing order from chaos as if by spell.

"Well," said Yellin reluctantly, "it's deuced head-heavy, and not very much fun…"

But he was drowned by a roar of disapproval from the clan, who were losing patience with the teasing now that Judgement had answered it. Hearing defeat, Yellin threw up his hands and shouted, "Aye, very well! It is a game. And see, our young guest is at last–"

Looking to the board, the Rom saw only four neat stacks of cards on the upper right, with two Marks and two Marchesses atop each one in alternation.

"Playing?" Judgement finished for him. "Aye, if you say so, Yellin. Shall I play again, then?"

"You must have cheated!" the knife-thrower shouted with heat. On that, all pretense of good humor drained from his enemy's frame, and Judgement slowly stood. Three of the acrobats moved between them, and a hush fell over the clan. "Dost wish to watch closely, this next time? Mayhap t'will be the game wherein I do fail: ye may like to see that."

Yellin knew he was beaten now at every turn, so he simply spat his refusal to one side into the fire. "And how did your dear dad react, when he caught you playing that game, eh? Tan your hide to see you fooling about when there was work to be done?"

Judgement only shook his head to this, quietly putting the tarot deck together and returning it to the bag. Everyone could see the tension in his shoulders, and they knew it was not over.

"You got away with it? He never caught you?"

Judgement handed the bag back to Valeria, then turned to face Yellin again. "I caught him."

At this, the knife-thrower's jaw fell completely open, and some of the clan laughed nervously to see it.

"I saw him use a deck of cards in this wise, three times from behind a crack in the wall, of an evening. I could not tell all the rules from watching, and so I asked him to show me. And he taught me the moral of the story."

"What?" Yellin roared. "He taught you, even in this! And what, be so good to tell us, is the moral of a card game!" He laughed loud, but alone at this.

Judgement took only a single step closer to Yellin, and when he spoke his voice was low. Around the campfire, men drew their weapons and Valeria in her chair gripped her cane and nearly stood.

"Aye, Yellin, he did teach me, in sooth. He taught me the moral of the game as a child, as a child I learned it. Canst not see it thyself, then?"

Yellin spat again to spite the notion. Judgement took another step closer, till his face and Yellin's were like the doors on a tavern. "When a nation's in chains, the most powerful cannot retreat first. The great, the leaders, must sacrifice for the good of all. Tis a lesson every child learns, in my country."

He paused one second for emphasis. "Either the least among us are free, or none of us are."

Yellin's fists were clenching and releasing as if he yearned to do murder. "You are no Rom," he ground, hurling the worst insult he knew.

"Enough," said Valeria, "Solemn is our guest, and he leaves us in the morning."

"He leaves now," Yellin growled, and gasps broke out around the fire.

"You dare," Valeria said quietly, and it was as if Yellin awoke from a dream.

"Grandmother, I was– I spoke wrongly! But he has insulted us, he has shown no respect for our ways-"

"Verily, I remember mine father," cried the Man in Grey, and every muscle on his frame betrayed his boiling fury. "I remember his face, Yellin. Dost thou?"

Now Yellin was hit from the other side and he stepped back, confused to think his foe could be as angry as he. Another step back, and with a scorching oath, Yellin spun on his heel and stalked beyond the fire's light. Judgement took one deep breath, and then a second, as if winded, and sat again, trying without success to show that nothing had happened.

No one spoke; there was no song or dance though the night was hardly old. Judgement wrapped his cape around him and stared into the fire as though he might see through it. The clan drifted off by ones and twos, and the last Mari looked back, Judgement was still sitting there alone. Though the night was far from cold, she thought possibly he shivered.

In the early morning, the Man in Grey was gone.

The first anyone knew was when Yellin roared, "He has taken my knife!" and came storming through the camp. Yet there, on the side of Valeria's wagon under the sign of the tarot, Yellin's blade pinned a parchment and a small leather pouch in place. Valeria was the only one who knew how to read, but the well-formed letters spelled nothing to her. In the pouch was the sum of fifty silver pieces and one extra silver bit, in various coins. Crass's fine new horse was missing, and no one doubted but that it was back in its village stall already.

Trainertown could no longer boast more than twelve thousand souls, a far cry from its glory days of the previous century. But it had a clock-tower finer than any east of the Marble Swords. Everyone in the South Mall near mid-afternoon knew just what time it was, except the preacher fresh off the road from Shilar and haranguing the crowd.

"We live at the end of the empty years, children of Hope," he thundered, his voice easily reaching across the square and informing those who still bought and sold at its edges, as well as the considerable crowd gathered nearer. "Nearly twenty centuries since the Battle of the Razor, barely less since our heroes left us, and these kingdoms have slumbered. *Slumbered*, keeping to ancient ways and seeking nothing from destiny. No longer. The sleepers shall be awakened, children, and a rude awakening it shall be."

Merchants transacted with familiar customers by points and nods, signaling the price with fingers while looking over to the church step where the preacher spoke. Across the square a hundred knots of people, adults and the very young, were all served by a single speech as they went about their lives. A few looked up from time to time at the clock-tower, as the hands moved towards the hour, and then gave him their attention once more. There was still time.

"An end to surrender! The death of the curse that lies across this land. Crowns will be overset, and every form of perilous beast will issue forth as the secret of their source is revealed." The preacher was tall and spare, the very image of ascetic holiness and intelligence, a little beyond middle age and more salt than pepper in his long brown hair and beard. The eyes were by far the most impressive feature of his appearance: not unkind exactly, but blazing with a constant comprehension that looked beyond the first thing before them. He held a walking staff in his left hand, nearby was belted an impressive mace, and his blue robes looked path-worn but fine and strong.

For several years, travelers on the Great Road had spoken of Alaetar of Shilar, the charismatic cleric preaching the dawn of a new age. It did not require belief to want him here, and the citizens of Trainertown had hoped for his coming a long while. A good speaker who, it was whispered, used his holy power openly and saw the future; he might be as loony as a bird flying upside-down but he would be good for business. So they had come to see him, this first day, in droves, and Alaetar was responding with a voice long practiced in rhetoric to match the spirit burning in his heart.

"How many long years has the once-proud kingdom south of this city lain in thrall? Since the last descendant of Areghel sat the throne in Reghalion and held straight the ways, which the demon bent in the days before Hope's coming. Men thought an empty throne to be of no consequence. They murmured that they needed no kings. For we lived in peace: and what needs a king, except to defend his subjects, aye, and to collect his taxes! That was surely not missed, not at first. But now we see the harvest of our indolence, and you fine folks have seen it firsthand, have you not?"

A few rumbles of agreement rose to this, for indeed the emergence of strange creatures to harass the outlying fields and cottages south of the Great Road had grown more frequent in recent years. Packs of wolves, for the most part, or at least things mainly wolfish.

"In Shilar, in Mendel, my children, they know nothing of this! Across their river-bounds they are insulated from your suffering, send no aid, perceive no danger." Now there were small waves of assent crossing the mall, as folks gave vent to an indignation no less sincere for being so recently discovered. "You good people, serving here as a waystation to those brave few who still dare to enter the Percentalion, are on the front lines of the struggle against Despair!"

Real applause and cheering greeted this remark, yet several in the crowd looked more frequently now to the clock-tower and began to back away from the preacher on the step. He raised his voice a bit higher in response, and the tall buildings on all sides of the mall rang with his tones as he played the space like a giant stonewood drum.

"Fewer and fewer now, they go, and even fewer return!" Cries of anguish, not disagreement, rose to meet his words. "Only this city, this one lighthouse still burns to greet the bravest and the best of us, who enter the jaws of hell on earth and live to tell the tale!" Cheers and raised arms, and a few more who moved farther away. The church's shadow now covered most of the mall; the preacher shifted a little closer to the step-corner to remain in the light. And his audience reacted with increased attention to his every move, some now pointing with evident excitement, and others seeming to ask their neighbors a question urgently and promptly being shushed with smiles and frantic gestures.

"Only *you* have stood ready, to recover them, heal their wounds, provide their needs, see them back on their way. Trainertown, most glorious city in Conar, the keen edge on the sword of Hope!" Thunderous cheers now, and those still pointing at the town clock were put down with pious glee. Alaetar took a pace towards his retreating flock, off the step and onto the tile-stone in his ecstasy. "But now, children of Hope, now the hour is near!"

A sudden ripple of laughter from his adherents stopped the preacher in his tracks for a moment. But cheers followed on its heels, and he persisted. "Soon the time will come" –more laughter intervening– "and those who have been unaware of the change of the hour will be caught and crushed by the wave of destiny! Mark my word, there are not years left to this land."

"No!" roared his crowd, and still there was laughter.

"There are not many months left!"

"No!" came the response, and Alaetar rose to his full height, raising his staff and booming his loudest.

"We may be only *days* from–"

"Preacher!" squeaked a slight young woman who worked free of her father's grip and stepped into the open space, now more than half the mall where Alaetar stood. "Preacher, get back! There's no time!"

"Indeed, mistress, precious little time for those–"

"No time!" shouted several laughing fellows across the way, and the clock struck the hour even as they spoke.

A deep wrinkle on his brow, Alaetar was drawing breath to rise above this mystery, retain the attention he had surely earned and expunge the hilarity, when he heard a rising patter, as if a sudden rain were falling. He turned to face it, and the crowd drew back until it was practically jammed against the opposite side of the mall, as around the corner came a lad all in white, two paces ahead of a pack of boys– with three or four girls– racing as if Kog himself were behind them. With not the slightest chance to defend himself, the preacher was tipped, turned, and half trampled by the tide of young humanity as the mall crowd simply howled with delight, spiced with various shouts intended to encourage favorites or distract rivals in the race.

"Hey there, Sipiwa, where are the seven bits you owe me, then?"

"Go, Anteris, you've got it again, boy!"

"Watch the old man, you lot. He's not to be harmed!"

"Areghel's Crown, Forge! The walls will still be standing even if you're the last one there."

"Sorry for that, preacher," said a grocer as he leaned in to help the cleric back to his feet. "Come Conar's Day, the masters let the apprentices out two hours early, and they love to sit by the south wall and watch until sunset." He brushed off the astonished preacher and handed him back his staff with an air of good will and even better humor.

A man in passing clapped the preacher on the back and handed the grocer a silver bit, saying, "You were right. Fully down, like the tree from an ax." They both laughed, and the grocer hastened to add, "Not any disrespect intended, sir, I hope you'll see. We agree with all that you were saying, lovely too. And don't worry;" with a smack on the shoulder that knocked him two steps on his way, "you'll soon learn what time it is here."

The city flew by Anteris on his run; familiar corners, the main south street where the left-hand boardwalk was best, a chance to skirt inside the rain barrel if no one was standing there, and that horse-rail in the entry plaza he could hurdle in stride as none of his rivals could. That, combined with his innate fleetness, always gave him the edge. But Anteris would run to the wall even if he were eating another's dust every time: the running itself was joy, a time when life was at last moving at the speed it should.

He was a half-block ahead today, but hurdled the rail for the sheer love of it. The grinning guards at the gate played "craven" as always, holding their spears crossed before his neck until the very last moment. They pulled them back with a ring of iron, and he blazed through underneath the barbican to the cheers of the few old men atop the parapets, who waited and watched most of the day.

"Anteris, again! And as always," announced old Calper solemnly, sitting with legs hanging over the outside of the wall and banging his wooden stump against the stone like a gavel. His pronouncements were always the final word in cases where the race was close. There was for example a day, last of the Swan, when Anteris fell ill with the fever. He'd been confined to his bed the entire day, and placed only third after the bell had rung.

The others came roaring through now, tumbling in a rush beyond the walls, vying for the lesser places. As the elders above exchanged silver bits and coins, the youths ran after the winner to the traditional finish-line, a small red flag on a pole fifty rods from the walls, set there as the line of utter forbiddance by the city council. Crossing the boundary was cause for imprisonment and fines for any citizen, so naturally no one could claim to have run the race without defying it. None of them were winded; all had plenty of energy left for wrestling, play-fighting, shouted insults. The son of the blacksmith, Forgisson, came over as always to insist on shaking hands with the winner. Anteris winced slightly from the grip, and more from the grime, acknowledging these as the price he must pay.

"I couldn't catch you with a stone's throw, Teri. Kog's bare tail, what in the Lands are you running from?" It was an old line, never answered; the strapping young man turned away and squatted near the ground of the southern expanse, rummaging in the turf and stone as if it would clean his hands to do so, which was nearly true.

Others called out to Anteris in greeting as he returned to the gate and headed up the inner stairs to the wall-walk where the old men sat by custom. Apprentices to the wheelwrights, masons, tailors, thatchers, carpenters and even the boy who assisted the town's one remaining alchemist all gathered below by now. Mingled with the formal guild-students were other children, those who worked for their parents at the inn, or in the merchant stalls, and a few who were still too young to do more than help at home. In all, at least three score human beings muddled around the south postern gate, much smaller than the east and west entrances to Trainertown along the Great Road. They stood or sat or played tag and some few on the walls or the grounds outside set up chairs, to watch the sun go down and chat and to take turns scanning the southern horizon.

"What do you think, Teri? Today the day?" Calper called out as the sage's acolyte reached the battlements. More ritual, something else the student loved about life in this city. Trainertown's size was perfect for an active boy, and its decline left lots of empty places to explore, along with the other apprentices (who were curiously interested in dodging chores) or on his own (late at night, when Anteris enjoyed feeling spooked). Everyone knew everyone, he had his place, and of all the wondrous round of fascinating work and splendid leisure, there was no single joy that compared with this. Sitting on the wall, near the old but within easy earshot of the new, waiting and watching for the merest chance that a hero might return from the benighted kingdom lying to the south. It was the only hour Anteris could bear to keep still, because now his mind raced to make up for it.

Forgisson paused from the free-form wrestling matches that pervaded the group below and called up to the wall, "See anything?" Knowing he would not, Anteris dutifully scanned the horizon. A trading road of rammed earth headed south from the gate, petering out within five furlongs of the walls, swallowed up by one of the least interesting views in all the Lands.

The histories told of rolling farmlands, small forests, streams and valleys arrayed south of the city just as to the north; now, the southern view was flat, grey, gradually sinking. Even the scrub-grass gave out into small patches, a few blades, and then nothing; hardened yet choppy earth, not soil. Anteris thought it looked like a blank page of nation where nothing had ever been writ. The Percentalion was a wasteland now, and to hear the tales it roiled with pockets of humanity, slices of terrain separated in an ocean of negation.

Yet this was not what the heroes saw, he knew from those tales. Those who dared to explore the chaos-land came through trees, ravines, experienced wild weather and of course the endless monsters. They sometimes saw them right up to the edge of town; that is, those who returned. But hardly any had ventured forth in months past, and none of those that did had yet returned. Anteris shook his head down to the apprentice smith, and finally turned to answer Calper's question. "Sure, this day's as good as any."

Chuckles from the veterans and pensioners greeted this remark, as well as a few exchanged coins behind his back.

"Oh and sure, but which is it likely to be then?" another old man casually asked; used to be a guard for the town but now his grandson held the post. To this Anteris only shrugged, and the men clucked their tongues in disappointment.

"Probably Pelian, yes Teri?" one of them prompted, and Calper cut him off with a scolding,

"No coaching, Hangert, now the bets are all off!"

Anteris grinned at the argument– another old feature–and returned to scan the horizon again. The sun was coming down to the western Marble Swords in the distance, beyond the reach of the chaos that blanketed the central kingdom. Indeed, men said one could look farther west than in earlier years, and the young sage was struck with loneliness to think of seeing so far away.

"Well, and it must be Pelian, anyway, I'll wager on that myself," grumbled Hangert, and men eagerly leaned in to cover this overt declaration; much better than betting on another person's word for what would happen. Nodding vigorously, pushed by his mistake to risk real money, Hangert repeated the argument all of them knew. "Who else then? He's been gone since last Raccoon, sure, but he's the one who's always returned. Fifteen armed men, four wagons, and that fox always manages to make it back. By Areghel's Crown, it will be him, sure, within the month–"

"Today!" roared four voices at once, and now another argument over odds began. Anteris looked out standing next to where Calper sat athwart the crenelments. "Who else indeed?" he wondered aloud to the old adventurer. "The party of Tixel, with the dwarf, has been gone over a year."

"Aye," Calper returned, "and the Conarian patrol, dispatched by the Mark of Conar's Helm after Pelian's last trip, almost as long. That wily merchant brought back news, of Maladon under siege by the dragon, and rumors of an enormous clutch of eggs hatching. 'Wings across the sky' were the very words he used." The ex-adventurer rubbed his grizzled chin in thought. "That dragon of Maladon. Same wurm as took my leg, you know."

"Thirty-six mounted retainers, in chain and with lance," Anteris breathed. He recalled the flawless day last winter they had all set out along the southern road, waving from almost a league before they disappeared. "How could they– I mean, all of them, lost, is it possible?"

"You know the answer, lad," Calper said kindly. "Yonder benighted kingdom has swallowed hundreds of would-be saviors, and worse and worse over the years. They went with no mage, no guide, no plan except their orders. Even Pelian has never been gone this long."

"Yet others have set out later than that. The short mage with his assistant, seeking the city of Stathos. And that group from the inner kingdom, led by the red-bearded warrior, they left only in Swan, not two months ago."

"Yes, and that merchant band, much poorer than Pelian's, they were headed out to search for Reghalion itself, only a little after. I give them slight odds, though. Too much confidence, not enough weaponry, too far to go. And what was that other group? I'm forgetting–"

"You mean the five, one a tall plate-armored knight, the halfling, and the lady as mage. They had a woodsman too. A bit earlier, mid-Dolphin they left," Anteris replied without hesitation, and Calper smiled.

"You never miss a trick. So then, just between you and me," he said dropping his voice a little, "who do you truly think has any chance? No bets on this, by the uncrowned king, you have my word."

The acolyte looked towards the western sun as he thought, and then sighed. "Sure and it must be Pelian, if anyone. He always returns, and he's been gone the longest." Calper nodded at this.

The noise from below became distracting then, and everyone peered down to see Forgisson winning a clod-fight against three challengers. Each combatant scrambled to pick up fist-sized clumps of the broken, barren earth near the boundary stake, and hurl them at a foe while dodging the return fire. The smith's boy used whiplash reflexes to twist or tumble away from most shots taken by others, and managed to aim his own clods with devastating success, hitting four and five times in a row, and usually in the face of his opponents, causing them to splutter and shake while he rearmed from the ground. Incredibly, he actually drove the trio back and finally won their submission with a shout, as he looked over the group on the ground with earth in both hands, daring another to step in. With no takers, Forge roared in triumph like a beast, crushing his earth-clods to silt and laughing. A few more coins changed hands on the wall.

"That boy's aim is unearthly," Calper remarked, turning to look pointedly at Hangert. "I could swear he's had training." Anteris looked at the retired guardsman, who rumor held had been a Stealthic and member of an adventuring party long ago.

The accused looked levelly back but said only, "That would be against the law; the boy's not yet sixteen." Anteris knew Forge, too, had only grinned when others asked if he were studying the Stealthic's art. He was the oldest of the group and would no doubt be the first to defy his parents' wishes and take off for the adventure they all dreamed of in the wide chaos-lands to the south. To come back as a conquering hero to the town of their birth, and watch familiar jaws gape at tales of monsters defeated, towns succored, lore recovered, wonders seen; this was the Hope the children of Trainertown lived on, and seeking its flavor Anteris had devoured the books his master reluctantly showed him. He saw Forge look up at the walls and wave as he returned to the main group, where someone had lit the firepit against the westering sun. Others brought out a few meats and vegetables, spiked on skewers to roast for their usual evening meal under the warm sky of late spring. Anteris felt rumblings in his stomach, but he refused to leave the walls while the horizon was still visible.

The old tales came out as the sky darkened to twilight, and all of them Anteris knew; once heard, he always remembered. They told of the bard Lirran and his magic harp — made, he let it be said, by Rallantan himself ages before — who could sing his way past the most murderous creatures until he disappeared a century ago. They recounted the fight of Palan Broadscar, disgraced knight of Conar, against monstrous Crulgor in 1877. He slew the garruk thane though mortally wounded, and won freedom for his captive companions; that story was known in part because the grateful men he freed with his death had commissioned Lirran to immortalize it in a paean. The elders urged Anteris to recite the King-List of Reghalion, from Areghel Demonsbane through his sons Kronwe and Konreghel and their various descendants, down to Palleghel, whose marriage was the last celebrated in Reghalion back in 1572. The young couple disappeared–according to common legend, for a love-tryst on Skysword's forbidden upper slopes– the very day before the groom's father, King Polonwe, died of a mysterious fever. The couple never returned, and the kingship fell vacant since.

Someone told of the sad end of Hypon, one of the stranded villages that lay in the eastern kingdom by the old maps; once trading in lumber and wheat, it had suffered from quakes in the earth and tearing storms throughout the 1970s. Against all odds, the town organized a migration, loading women and children into anything that could roll or ride in an attempt to reach the outside world. It was one of Pelian's earliest trips. He returned with a description of the abandoned town, and then the gory remains of the caravan, savaged without regard for the innocent by a tribe of garruk, and, it was whispered, by some other monster in their keeping.

But just when Anteris thought he'd heard them all, someone would surprise him. Today it was Calper himself, who first gave his favorite yarn about the manner in which he lost his leg, complete with the dragon of Maladon chomping his calf and his party in flight with him in train. He told it at least once a week, and spiced it with enough variations that most likely even he didn't know the full truth anymore: it was, after all, back in the 1950s, before anyone's time barring just a few of the oldest veterans. He finished at last and received the usual grunts of acknowledgement and doubt from his peers. But of course, once a man had spoken of dragons, it was put up or shut up with stories and so it was quiet for a time. Then Calper chuckled to himself and Anteris was prompted to ask, "What?"

"Say, Galwen," Calper said, twisting around to face back towards the wall-sitters, "do you remember that great pack of charlatans, from way back in 1955? The Hidden, we called 'em?"

"Aye!" Galwen returned with a sour laugh, "though I wish I could forget that lot."

"Who were The Hidden?" Anteris asked. "An adventuring party from long ago?"

"The last men ever hanged by this city," Calper intoned with a face like a funeral urn, and now the group was hooked. In the early evening, voices carried without an echo, and half the children below could hear that a new story-treasure was being unearthed.

They shushed the other half, and without need to come closer, they listened in from the ground.

"Hanged? What had they done?" Anteris asked again, his face filled with mystery and a bit of fear. Calper looked around as if he needed assistance to answer this bit of trivia.

"I believe it was treason, the charge we thought up, wasn't it men?"

"Aye, fraud would have meant only prison," came Galwen's answer with a wink.

Now Calper looked around his circle sternly, as if to say there should be no further interruptions. "There were four in the party, all men and pretending to be quite the experienced crew. Gave out some story of having adventured up north in Novar, against the Beserkers and their tusk-beasts, finding a Despairing castle in the ice. All foolery, most likely. But they came sweeping in here with a flourish and putting on airs about the method they had devised, to crack the chaos-code and sally into the Percentalion and back at will. So it was a week of free drinks all around for them."

He stopped to rub his chin and consider. "And all that week, what were they doing? Oh, they had this mysterious system, see, a way to calculate the angles and get to where the ancient towns were located without error, surely." He waved a hand to the southern horizon. "They spent their time pacing off distances outside town, with a man back by the gate there and another one up on the walls, right about where we are now. One had a scope on a stick and they tied every rope in Trainertown to it. Every last one. They measured out a *league* of rope, all tied together, and one of them way out there where you couldn't see him, standing at various angles while the others all would look at him and measure and scribble on their sheets and mutter together like a cabal of wizards. All in preparation for the day they set out."

"I remember," broke in Galwen, to Calper's frustration. "We gave them a trumpet-salute when they marched off. Trumpets! Scepter in slop, the cowards… I was not yet twenty that year, still in town; watched them go."

Anteris looked wonderingly back and forth at this normally-congenial pair, now so worked up with spite and grim humor. "What happened?" he shouted without meaning to. Calper pointed out south, and just a tick west, for emphasis.

"They *lay down*! Spent all that time figuring out how far a person could see from the walls over here, and timed leaving for sunset — so romantic — and then walked out to a spot they'd marked where folks couldn't see 'em, and then just lay down. Must have figured they'd wait there with supplies for four, five days or so, come back with a story of where they'd been. Some town in distress — they'd picked up plenty of gossip from folks here while getting free drinks, you can bet — and they'd give a 'status report,' call for supplies, weapons, and of course money, to stake out a rescue mission. And then they'd be off to Shilar and spend it. No doubt that was the plan." Calper spit over the walls, stared south a while, and then chuckled again.

"Did they get away with it?" Anteris breathed, rapt with shock and forgetting he already knew the ending.

Galwen gestured to Calper's back. "*He* caught 'em."

"How?"

Now Calper was shaking with mirth, hardly able to keep his tongue together. "What would you think, the odds? Eh, Hangert, what odds would you have given me? That my party would be returning, with me in tow like a Bordbeyond baby on a travois. This was the trip the dragon took my leg, did you know?" And everyone impatiently agreed that they did indeed know that one.

"Well, we're just coming in sight of the walls, and there I see this dun-colored sheet, or whatever, like a sail on a ship, with… with luh-luh-*lumps* under it." The old veteran could not continue for a time, and most around him began to chuckle as well picturing the scene. "And, an' they was just– j-just layin' in there, and I said, I say 'hey, what's *that*?'"

Everyone was enjoying the humor now. Anteris laughed briefly too, but recalled their fate, and became quiet.

"So," Calper resumed, "that was enough for the town, when my boss Otull marched those villains in at swordpoint. The council and the mayor met — we still had a mayor back then — and we decided right away, we couldn't stand for any more of that. It *was* treason, you ask me, and they got no less than they deserved." He pointed ominously below at the gate, for the benefit of the children in the ground-crowd. "They swung down there, maybe four feet off the ground, with their heads facing south so the Percentalion was the last thing they saw. Left the bodies up for days."

There was not a sound from the gang near the gate now, as everyone contemplated this near-ghost story in the waning sunset. Anteris, still looking out to the south as was his custom in the last-light, asked one more question.

"Calper? When you remembered that story just now, was it because you saw something to remind you?"

"Aye, lad. For a minute there I could have sworn I saw a little brown bump, just there where I saw them Hidden all these years ago. Why?"

"Because I see the bump too," Anteris replied in a whisper. "And it's moving."

Every man on the wall-walk was on his feet, and all the children spun around to face south as if they were being attacked. Most couldn't see anything this close to evening, but first one and then another shouted they could see it too.

"Crown of Areghel," Calper breathed.

"I see five of them," Anteris said. "One is tall, with the glint of metal armor, and there's another no larger than a child. It's the group that left in Dolphin."

The party was still a half-hour's march away. The children below stood in rows near the boundary stake; the elders crammed the walls above and behind, a week's worth of petty bets forgotten. No one spoke or moved. Finally, Calper nudged Anteris gently, saying "You were the first, lad."

The youth turned to look at him incredulously. "No Calper, you did."

"I saw a bump! Without you, we'd have told the story and packed it in. And those heroes yonder would have had to sneak into Trainertown like common beggars, with no welcome. The honor is yours, Teri. Hail them."

Anteris looked at the approaching figures, then down at the children below. Some of them were looking back expectantly. He cupped both hands around his mouth and shouted the traditional greeting.

"Where do you *think* you are?"

The leader of the distant group raised an arm in salutation, and the celebration began.

Entrances

The way to the royal castle at Cil-Cilurion is broad and public, and those approaching even the outer gates must prepare to be seen. Perched on a hill looking down to the Shilarian capital, the keep can be reached only by a wide, gently winding road up from the second bailey, so that any visitor describes a course like the slow sashay of a courtesan to the crowds below. The barbican gate, once the grill is raised, spans wider than two wagons laid front to back, and the broad paved courtyard within is visible from every battlement. The palace built against the far wall of this fortress gives access via two enormous double-doors. The passages within — thickly strewn with carpet and rushes — are well lit by high-set windows and rife with courtiers, guards, scribes, bureaucrats, astrologers, preachers, servants and nobility of every stripe from across the kingdom. By the time any visitor takes a single step over the portal to the main throne room and feasting hall — whether on an embassy, in duty to the king, or as the least fortunate prisoner dragged before the high court — he will have passed in plain sight of a thousand-score persons. Within that room, even at the latest hour of the night, there would be scores or even hundreds more.

Thus it was quite the notable event, on the first day of the midsummer's feast, when a savage Bordbeyond not only came among the king's court unannounced, but riding a horse.

The glittering court, in the midst of celebrating the year's longest day and its feast of love, fell quite to pieces at the dreadful aspect of the nomad from beyond the Great River. Armed at all points in piecework-plate, and with the traditional full visor obscuring his face, he rode his stallion a few paces across the hall and reined in, sitting for all the world as if carved there while on every side of him ladies fainted and knights clawed out their court-swords. The Chancellor moved before the throne with only the staff of office to defend his liege; the king himself was empty-handed, yet kept his seat with commendable poise. Dropped trays, mingled shouts and curses from the panicking press cluttered the floor and the ear: not since the days of legend had the uncouth, accursed folk who roamed the outermost borders of the East come to distress and threaten the children of Hope. The barbarian made no further move, but sat with the stout two-stick flail holstered over his shoulder and the tattered shield on his arm, bearing the device of the watchful eye.

Two knights of the king's Star-circle were the first to step forward; Sir Ridevan with sword in hand, and Sir Pors (who fancied himself the second coming of the revered Sir Percis of old, and could hardly have brought his rhomphaia into the court) clenching his fists in defiance. Shouting at the Bordbeyond to surrender, they came on eagerly, each wishing to outdo the other in courage. The intruder made no move toward his weapon, but only held his gauntlet up to plain view, opening the fingers to reveal a three-stemmed branch in his palm. Tinder-weed, a scrub that could survive even on the dry plains near the Swords of Stone, was a poor substitute for the olive, traditional sign of peaceful intent. But the imagery of the three Hopelords in its branches was unmistakable: the two knights halted in their tracks, and almost spat on the marble floor in disappointment.

Odric the Chancellor spoke for the king. “How be it, sirrah, that ye shouldst come in guile before this court? State thy purpose, afore the king my liege shall pass judgment on thee for this effrontery.”

For a long moment, the warrior neither spoke nor moved; then the words came in harsh, uneven shards as if his speech had been shaken and broken up inside his armor suit. “Come… I the people of the Shepherds, all… to make… to give, offer… demand of king Shilar one… knight-son, for… hostage.”

Gasps, shouts of outrage, half-steps in the invader’s direction from a dozen feet. Truce or no truce, such an insult, to dare utter a tribute-demand? The king, Genel Shilarion XXXI, held up one arm for silence even as he retained a grip on his temper.

“Warrior of the Bordbeyonds, we are certain not to have heard ye correctly,” he began in a frosty tone. The helmeted visage responded with a vigorous nod, which betokened a denial. “Verily, didst mean to say that one of our noble sons must accompany thee back to yon forbidding plains? What harm have ye imagined done to thy people?” There was a pause of a moment’s space after the monarch finished, and the warrior’s nod was now less certain; he held out his sprig as if for emphasis.

None could understand this pass, and few were minded to attempt it. “This sigil of truce saves thy life,” said the Chancellor, “but not thy person, in light of yon foul smirch to our kingdom and dignity. Guards, take this man in train and convey him to the donjon, to await the day he may see fit to speak more meetly to this assemblage.”

Pors stepped in and grasped the reins, a sign the intruder could not mistake, and cried, “What is thy name, miscreant, that the gaoler may record it properly against thy honor?”

That demand struck home, and the mounted warrior stiffened, then deliberately threw down his garland to rest on the stone at his horse’s hoof. His gesture was answered from a dozen places, as ballroom-gloves rained down from the crowd at every side, pattering off his armor like flowers and littering the floor with challenge. No knight here wanted to be the last to offer his body in defence of Shilar's throne.

But even as the Bordbeyond reached back to draw his flail, a young man in splendid garments stepped out of the crowd and held his hands up for quiet and peace. "Hold, good knights, I pray you, but a moment," he said gently, and grown men who had been in act of charging, or raising weapons, held fast at his voice. The noble youth faced the mounted man and bowed, saying clearly, "Eldest." Even as the crowd gasped to hear this honor, traditional greeting from Man to full Elf, conferred on an unknown stranger, the youth whirled to face the room, giving his unprotected back to the man now armed — another sign of trust.

"I know well, milords and ladies, that my experience of life has been confined to court and book, till today," the young man declared with an ease and humor that seemed to siphon off a third of the tension at once. "I have no experience at diplomacy, nor do I profess expertise in the customs of our neighbors from the utter East. But I know, as any child of Hope knows, that they are our brethren; living hard and truly on the borders of our kingdoms and protecting us — as they see it — from peril."

"Peril!" snorted Sir Ridevan. "These grimy savages scour the badlands imagining they protect us, *us*, the flower of Hope's knighthood, from threats beyond the impassable mountains?"

"Childish delusions, dreams of mad fools!" agreed Sir Pors.

The look the youth turned upon the knights was mild as melted soap, and yet each man checked himself at once. "I only hope," the younger said, "to understand more clearly his mission here, sir. No doubt I shall fail, and then there will be plenty of time for you to regale this court with your report, Sir Ridevan, of the scouting you have done of the distant Swords of Stone. The ride in which you gained this intelligence as to their impassability. I confess, I had not heard of until this moment."

"As to that, your hi– I only meant– what we know, of the histories, in books—"

"Aye, precisely," the youth congratulated him in a louder voice to all the court, "just as we know, from books, that these people, and not we, are the ones who took the charge to guard those mountains most closely. As I saw you, good knight, in your turn pacing these castle walls only two nights ago. Not much chance of an enemy scaling our keep in such peace as we enjoy. Yet an unlikely watch still contains honor, or so I am told."

Turning to Sir Pors, he added with the utmost gentility, "It no doubt slipped your mind, brave knight, that the Shepherds do not share their use-names with alien peoples, but take instead that of their oldest ancestor. I am certain you had no idea to give offence."

Wheeling back, the young man saw the intruder had laid his flail across his lap now, still in hand but not in threat. Stooping, the Shilarian took back up the sprig of truce and bowed once more as if to an honored guest. "I believe, Eldest, that we here have the advantage of you. The language we most often use at court is perhaps somewhat flowery for your ear." The Bordbeyond sat back at the sound of plainspoken Common; though none of the court could see his face, he seemed uncertain, as if unwilling to admit any inadequacy. "But I have read in books that the Shepherd People are all well versed in Elvish, the tongue of your mother Elosira." Here the armored warrior reflexively touched his left hand to his heart. The youth continued, to whispers of astonishment, in the Elvish tongue that few in the court could understand.

"I am poor, very, in this tongue and have little use in years at it speaking."

"This so quite is," responded the warrior, still in the Common Tongue, with a small chuckle.

"Then more equal in speaking we may be?" the youth pursued with a smile of his own. *"To me I know you must speak in the tongue of humans, as people of your father's race we are."* Together with the mounted warrior, the youth touched his right hand to his head, which earned him a nod of approval from the closed helm. *"But trust I do that you can hear me well, and the confusion, I do Hope, will be less than before. I serve you, perhaps, this way."*

The court listened rapt, hearing but half a conversation, and not the half to their liking.

"Did you perhaps mean, when you used the word 'hostage' *to indicate the exchange of noble sons from the Elvish 'hostia'?"*

"Yes, of course, a hostage."

"Well, the word other meanings has here. Please forgive, we have not… engaged, used this practice for centuries."

"You do well. It should be you." This brought shouts of outrage, again quelled by the youth's raised arm. The rider did not evidently note the lad's blue cloak was bordered in purple, but the effect he had on the court was obvious.

"If understanding I have, the Shepherds would send also someone to us? A sign of friendship and trust."

The warrior nodded. "Ancient councils dictate this."

The young man thought awhile. *"Once again, I am guessing only; do you mean, of your people a custom to exchange guests, to solidify alliance in trouble-times?"*

The warrior nodded again.

"Star-signs are clear; must be done." The court bubbled up in disagreement at this. Chancellor Odric leaned in to his liege, "Majesty, enough; your son has acquitted himself with courage, but we cannot bear up with this insult, to have the savages tell us our business in interpreting the stars!"

"Doubtless correct," the king nodded, "and yet let us give the young man his rope. Gareth stepped forward to ask for this; he may yet knit for us a bridge, instead of himself a noose."

"A rope-bridge, sire? The game is not worth the candle."

"Yet we have let him join, so he must finish the game."

"Tell more to me, Eldest, of these signs you see," said the youth, gesturing to the ceiling overhead. Looking up the warrior cried out, at the deep blue dome studded with brilliant points of light, mirroring the night-sky. The ceiling of the royal court shone with rare azure marble, built at the foundation of the kingdom more than thirty centuries ago. Set into the rock were precious stones, ensorcelled to move in imitation of the real heavens above. The constellations and major bodies were all depicted, invisibly shifting in exact alignment with the time of year.

The Bordbeyond's amazement showed in no outward way, after the first outcry, yet the silent helmet turned this way and that taking in the miniature zodiac. At last he pointed to the eastern ecliptic and the reddish planet there.

"The next year, the Sun of Life gives way, sign of Areghel, brings Convergence under Death. A crown is lost."

"We see these signs, but debate the meaning of here." The young man spoke with a gentle smile.

"You– doubt?"

"No, not very! Each man quite certain is, of his own view!"

The mounted man shook his head at this. "This the month of Ferret is. Too much action, no patience, thought ahead. All fire now," he said, then pointed at the constellation of Sword in Crown — barely visible on the northeastern ceiling edge and awaiting winter to fully rise — "but the Crown rests in water and lost is." He pointed almost directly east then, at nothing in the imitation sky. "And a death-omen comes, the sky dividing."

The noble youth looked thoughtful at this, though most of his outraged audience assumed it was just his imperturbable civility. "*We must think, consider with carefully the words you bring. Your guest is welcome here, and the matter of our… our person for hosting, we will consider.*"

"My message now delivered, to your patience thanks. The return to escort… person for hosting… soon, at best star-time."

The youth hesitated a moment, and almost turned to face the throne, but firmed his shoulders and nodded instead in agreement.

"But wait!" he added in Common. "I would send a gift with you, if it is allowed. For the person chosen among you, as a welcome… just a moment…" The noble youth patted himself down in haste, and impulsively seized upon the brooch of his cape. To the gasps of the audience, he unfastened it and as his velvet hanging joined the gloves on the floor, handed it up to the mounted warrior. "In token of friendship and a hoped-for meeting."

The Bordbeyond took the marvelous clasp, set with amethyst and beryl in a silver frame shaped like a castle, and after a moment bowed to the youth before him. Then there was a long pause, and some at court realized that the intruder was trying to think of a return gift. Yet the people of the plains were near-paupers; he carried only weapons and armor, no adornment of any kind on his stark outline.

The youth bit his lip and was trying to frame a polite assurance. But the rider's horse chose that moment to lift its tail, and the quiet ballroom echoed with four soggy slaps of *ploouf-ploup-plunp-poufp!* Two more women fainted, followed by cries of disgust from the servants in the back, who could not see but were told.

Gareth broke into a wide smile at this, and called out in a ringing tone that triumphed over the confabulation.

"Ah, sir, I thank you for your gift to us." Nervous laughter from the audience, but he continued, "For well I know that to the Shepherds this is the precious nightsoil of new life." That brought a moment of silence. "I shall endeavor to use this well in the season of planting now; and when our guest arrives, perhaps I shall have made something of this bond of earth between us."

The court was agog as the youth stepped back confidently with his right arm raised. "*Clear sight to the mountains,*" he invoked in Elvish again, a formal well-wishing among the guardians of the plains. The mounted man holstered his flail and answered the salute, saying "First to see the enemy." He turned his steed, neatly avoiding his gift, and rode through the doors. The young man held out an arm to restrain Sir Ridevan, indicating that the guest had his leave to go. And the leave of the prince of Shilar, in the absence of a denial from the throne, was quite adequate to the dictates of honor.

Yet as soon as the intruder was out of sight, the Chancellor Odric charged, "Follow him." The two foremost knights along with several guards shot like crossbow bolts, to be the first to do this duty to their liege, one much more to their liking than the command of the prince. Gareth motioned to a servant, handing him the sprig. "Modron, can you kindly collect this gift, and take it to the gardener? Ask him to mingle it with some earth and see if he can treat this sprig as a cutting in it, perhaps start it?" The servant nodded, but looked askance at the horse-pile. Gareth laughed, and without hesitation took up his cloak, neatly draping it over the offending article, and pulled it into a sack, as more folk of the court expressed dismay and shock. He handed it to the servant who hurried off triumphant and relieved.

The prince then turned once more to face the room, and again the hubbub quieted. Few courtiers had seen the prince do any more than stand near his father's throne in public, and all knew that Squire Hobsel was the young man's one good friend. What use, to approach or flatter an heir sixteen years old, in Shilar where the king surely knew the length of his own reign, as it lay written in the stars? The court, assured their prince studied in preparation for rule, had been content with that knowledge until today. They were amazed now at their prince's easy air and courtly manners, hanging on his next word as he surveyed the gloves on the floor. Here was a pretty problem indeed — thrown in a challenge unaccepted, for the foe had not picked one up. No man here wished to move first to retrieve his article, lest he be thought lacking in resolve.

"See the courage all about," Gareth remarked in an admiring tone, and these words brought a small patter of applause. "And yet," he added gaily, "if they stay here, how can there be any dancing tonight?" More laughter then; bending, he picked one up and turned to the eldest knight in view, saying, "Sir Stonemar, I believe yours was the first?" This happy resolution was to the general liking, and now the knights advanced gladly to congratulate each other and retrieve their articles.

"What a splendid acquittal, sire," Chancellor Odric said aside. "Your son is as polished in public as he is kind in private." King Genel nodded with obvious pride beneath his dignified face, and gestured that the prince should join him on the podium. Bowing, the youth came forward to stand in his accustomed place to the right of the throne.

The monarch rose and the summons-tone echoed throughout the hall. "Miladies," the king said, "we must apologize that ye were subjected to such uncouth treatment, an' sooth, e'en the prospect of violence. But we do give thanks as well, to the bravest knights in all of Hope, who stood ready to defend our throne and honor this day."

"We retire now to council, milords and ladies please attend me." He placed a hand on Gareth's shoulder then, and added with pride, "And my son, come also and give a report." Cheers and applause followed hard on this honor, and the son of the king for the first time retired with the land's highest nobles into the Council of the Talking Stick.

Squire Hobsel fell unobtrusively into line behind the prince as the lordly procession exited by the rear hall towards the council chambers. The two said nothing the entire way, nor even looked in the other's direction; yet when all filed into the hall the two guards of honor said nothing to separate them. The honor done to the prince, in allowing his attendance, might or might not extend to his squire, but no knight wished to be the first to test these waters, and so the two young men entered together.

The carnadine carpet was so thick underfoot it felt like walking on fleece. The vaulted roof was high and angled, set with chandeliers in a star-pattern. Everywhere the eye could see, there was rich, dark wood; side pillars cut from solid trunks lined the walls, the paneling between them polished to a dark sheen. All the windows set into the second story above, as well as the sole portal behind the king's seat, were heavily draped in dark red velvet, increasing the sense of quiet and somber reflection here at the heart of the kingdom. The council table itself was square-cut and hollow, with entrances at each corner to allow passage across the space inside. As the lords and ladies of the king's Council moved to their assigned chairs, the Chancellor took station in the center, and thumped his staff of office on the floor to formally open the proceedings.

King Genel sat in the throne on the west side, facing east. Gareth slowed a bit as the press of his elders took seats; sizing up the arrangement, he wove neatly between them to an open chair near the opposite end of his father's throne, sitting quietly among the lowest ranks of the twoscore invited nobility. Hobsel took up station against the wall behind him, with other guards and attendants, nearly in shadow. Genel smiled in recognition of his son's humility; if the presence of the prince's friend was noted, the monarch made no comment.

Odric exchanged his floor-length silver staff for the wooden scepter laying before the king's seat. This sacred Talking Stick had been used in Shilarian councils since the Dagnor Rokan; only the one holding the wood could speak in turn, except for the short question asked by another. Standing in the middle space of the tables all about, Odric held the staff to his liege, who merely touched it as he spoke.

"Milords and ladies, 'tis in my head that many important issues call us together this afternoon; sooth, 'tis meet that we should work before we dance tonight. Before work, dance and all, let us take prayer." Odric brought the scepter to the High Seer of Shilar, the elderly Lord Kalentire, who rose slowly and cradled it.

"Seer of the star-signs, lord of the nation, regard our counsels this day with approbation. Clear the skies above us, father Shilar, and show our course in the words spoken here." Though old and thin, the habit of speaking was strong in the High Seer, and his voice filled the room; many claimed to have seen visions when he prayed aloud, though this had been in his youth. Today, however, it seemed to some that a light radiated from where he was, slight yet pure. It winked across the room for one moment, to illuminate a chair whose occupant lacked a cloak. Kalentire's eyes were closed as he prayed, as were those of the king, and the prince; but not all, and after he stopped there was a profound silence.

Odric returned with the scepter to the king, who this time took it up in his hands. "Nobles of the Council, forthwith let us hear the matter of the harvest in Hirion. Baron Sterador, wilt thou favor us with thine assessment?"

The vassal of the eastern marches rose to take the wood and answer; and his words were followed by discussion of bridgework required for the city's west-gate district, some clarification of the lumber-tithes owed by northern villages, and an inconclusive disputation regarding the inheritance to a minor knight with twin sons. Some of the Council, particularly around the far eastern end of the table, could not completely suppress their nervous fidgets as the agenda proceeded without alteration for recent events. But these rules had been in place for twenty-eight centuries, more than five epochs of the zodiac; no man nor woman could speak unbidden without the Talking Stick, and even the ways to request a turn were generally considered ignoble.

Before the waiting grew quite unbearable, however, there came an urgent knock at the door — itself an exceptional occurrence. As Odric paused with the scepter in hand and bid entrance, some very unorthodox whispers and even exclamations followed as Sirs Ridevan and Pors appeared. They were abashed to be here, yet afire with news; motioned to approach the Chancellor, they murmured to him quietly at first, and when he expressed doubt with his eyes, repeated themselves, with the word "disappeared" quite audible.

Odric nodded to dismiss the knights, who practically fled the sacred chamber. With the doors closed, he turned to face the king and said simply, "Yon Bordbeyond hath escaped, milord." He wheeled to face the room, and his eyes caught those of the prince, apprising him that his choice of words was unfortunate. "The report of our knights and guards who didst attend him differ as to exactly when this transpired. But t'was well afore he reached the town below by the road. First Sir Pors… actually, my liege, it appears thy two distinguished knights stand somewhat at an impasse as to which of them… ah, sooth to say, 'twere become a point of honor between yon worthy lances." A murmur of appreciative laughter rippled the room at this. "But the guards be quite certain, the man wast riding his horse on a slow walk at least halfway down the access ramp beyond the main gate. And then suddenly, wast no longer there."

Odric held the scepter to the king, who touched it saying, "Tis in my heart that the Council now shouldst give its views on this sorcerous happenstance as the spirit may move the varied members." The Chancellor turned back to face the nobility, and for the first time that session the floor was truly open. Raised hands moved up like a wave from the bottom of the table, and as each higher-ranked arm ascended, all lower limbs deferred. The lord of Hirion spoke again, as indeed men whispered he did enjoy the sound of his voice in the ear of the king.

"Mine men at guard o'er the eastern fords have witnessed yon foul enchantment before, milord. Hailing to Bordbeyonds on the Plains past the river, we do mark them disappear from view though in plain sight. Tis clear the churls reject congress with our people as ever they have."

The Coroner Baron Kalney took the wood. "We hear much of the Shepherd People, milords, but little that we can prove. If one believes every story told, they live forever or die soon; they do not work metal, or write, or farm, yet they scry the stars, wield earthly magic, speak to animals. Our history tells us with surety, they descend from the children of Hope, yet they treat us more as enemies than friends. As for the magic used here, I would suspect some form of illusion. A mystic suggestion to a single mind, that one were no longer visible, could perhaps spread?" He held wide his hands in futility.

Lord Kalney held the Talking Stick out for another, and the staff worked its way down the tables, as court ladies, Barons, and Greatknights took their turns. Some, like Baron Sterador had been raised Knights of the Shield, and saw the Bordbeyonds as a threat. Other nobles administered the kingdom and its court; these Knights of the Quill tended more towards mystification at the unknown people across the river. Gradually, more and more eyes turned to gaze at the handsome youth among their aged circle, sitting all attention with a face that held not a shred of ill-will towards any living being. No prince of the realm had attended the Talking Stick in more than eighty years, yet the precedents were clear — after any Baron he could call for the scepter in all right. Yet Gareth sat with both hands flat on the table, content to wait the final turn. At long last, the room fell silent, and the king with a solemn smile gestured that Odric should bring the wood to his son.

Rising, Gareth took the scepter with reverence in both hands, and for a time he simply gazed at it, as the room stood still. The polished ash was so darkened by age and handling as to be a brown near black; the handle sloped gently along six planes from wrist-thick at the bottom to the width of a man's neck at the crown. Into each face near the top set a gem the size of a thumb-nail; smooth pink quartz to resonate with the practice of astrology, beryl which provides the king with vigor, fire-flecked white opal and transparent cats-eye to confer far-sightedness, the azure sapphire symbolizing wise kingship, and the silver hematite to confer grace and good judgement in speaking. With a golden ring at its top, a silver one at the neck and a silversteel band at the bottom, the scepter indicated Solar, Unal and Aral by their native metals. Legends vowed that this cubit-length of wood had originally been the base of Shilar's war-lance, recut to this use once Despair had been finally ejected from the Lands, and preserved these two-dozen centuries since.

Gareth looked upon the Talking Stick for a long time, seeming to take in its sanctity. Nodding once, he tucked it into the crook of his right arm and began to speak. Lady Blenia, the youngest councilor present that day, at the end of her long life could not recall that the future king ever looked directly at the staff again. "Milords and ladies, you are very kind to hear me today, and I hope you will be just as gracious when I have finished speaking." Nothing the prince said, it seemed, could possibly fall amiss: he aimed with his eyes at each listener. "I should relate what the emissary told me- merely so that the learned listeners here can correct my missteps in the use of the Elvish tongue." Briefly, Gareth reviewed the story of the offer to exchange guests. The council was amazed at this intelligence, and none of them, perhaps understandably, offered to amend the prince's grammar. Gareth would have retired the scepter then, but questions were asked.

"When will they invade again?"

"You have me at a loss, milord Baron, for I cannot recall the first such invasion."

"Will they come in force?"

"A force of one appeared sufficient today."

Sterador chewed his beard in anger, and many of the council reflected that the unseen sojourn of the Bordbeyond must have lain primarily through his lands, and therefore against his honor. He so forgot himself as to speak without the form of a question.

"I wouldst fain hear that plan my prince may suggest."

Gareth glanced at his father, then bowed low to the Baron of Hirion. "Perhaps the dancing has already begun?" he suggested to the disarming laughter of the room. "It is only on the third day of our midsummer festival, milord, that we encourage ourselves to turn our customs upside-down. Perhaps three sunsets from now, as common men declare their hearts for the daughters of knights, as the town clown lays a dunking trap for the mayor, when Gypsies are made welcome to eat dinner under the roofs of settled folk; then, perhaps, might a boy offer advice to the most senior guardians of the kingdom." Once again, the prince's formidable charm laid aside half the vassal's ire; pressing his advantage, Gareth sought earnestly to convert him and the rest with unexpected passion for the strange people of the nearer East.

"I ask only that the emissary of the Bordbeyonds be taken at his word, and that we treat less of his means and more of his motive. His people wish to exchange host-guests as a token of alliance with Shilar. Alone and unadvised, I would accept." This brought a susurration of alarm from the council, with many glances at the king. Gareth faced his father and continued undaunted, "Indeed if you willed it, I would go." Some rose to shout the negative to this, either from admiration for the prince or a sense of outraged honor: but none of it seemed to affect the speaker as he faced the king. "Refuse to comply if your heart and head wills it, milord, but do not refuse to understand." With that, the prince of Shilar firmly returned the scepter directly to his father and retreated to his lowly chair. Some who rapped the tables wished only to flatter him, or the king through him; others were in sincere agreement but the effect was the same.

King Genel considered in silence for some time. "Milords and ladies, it is in my head that you have given me much to think on. And mine son not least of all; we thank him for his service to the nation, in that a misperception has mayhap been averted." Gareth rose to bow to his father and this time the knuckling was universal. "Chancellor Odric, see to it that our good scribe, em, Bayneth?"

"Barnath, my liege."

"Barnath, that he is in attendance upon the court until further notice. I recall well that he speaks Elvish like a native. Have him housed near the court chambers, that we may be in perfect readiness for any return visit of our neighbors. Sooth, know we not when this 'best star time' may fall?"

The High Seer rose to take the scepter briefly. "Milord, who can decipher the ravings of savages who view the stars without glass or caliper? This month lays under Astor who knew many tongues and often carried the Hopelord Conar's messages through danger… If I were forced to guess, his return would be in Raccoon, five months from now. The father of Elves would govern the appropriate time to conclude a matter between the races; then too the end of a year is a natural time to conduct serious business, if indeed you believe this to be such a case," he finished doubtfully. The king drew breath to speak, but out of all expectation Prince Gareth rose to ask a question.

"Milord, what is the omen of death this man saw in the east, the sign that divides the sky?"

Kalentire looked long at Gareth on this, and some thought they saw anger, others fear, in his face before he said only, "Again, who can say? Your encounter was no doubt invigorating, milord prince, but the barbarian's claim cannot be credited simply because he could sneak among us to make it."

The scepter was brought back to the king, who contented himself with saying, "A matter for my head to consider, as I said. Today I can guarantee only that if any son of Shilar be sent to the plains, 'twill not be its prince." Vigorous knuckling greeted this remark; Gareth's face fell a bit, doubtless at the missed opportunity to distinguish his courage. "I thank you, milords and ladies for your service in speaking. Yet now, I must retire to change my garb, for the queen my beautiful wife has arranged to wear red this evening, and I would rather face Bordbeyonds in battle than fail to match her!" All rose and retired in his train with good spirits. Near the back, two young men were already thick as thieves in conversation too soft and fast for any other to follow.

Hardly anyone there, or who heard the news second-hand in the ballroom that evening, concluded that a new age of alliance had begun. But in later years, common folk in market stall and street corner would nod sagely and lean on third-and-fourth-hand knowledge saying, "Even then, our king knew how things would go. Aye, it were a glorious day when he swayed the Council."

⊕⊕⊕

A deep breath, a measured pause, another sip of tea. Cedrith faced the test now, and Conar's Board of Sages was waiting, but only an Elf knew the value of the right moment.

"I have shown you all the comparison of the calligraphy, the stylistic allusions and the very key — I would argue, even crucial — point of the differing marginalia, in the two tomes before you, masters. All three facets of evidence point in the same direction: the Aktarsull manuscript, long thought to be a copy of the Fanem, was in fact authored first, some ten centuries before its alleged predecessor. In all probability, the learned Sage Faltus Fanem, accomplished though he was in many fields, letter-copied the work of a man thought to be a successor to him in the post of Librarian of the Dark Archives. It is the work of Manlion Aktarsull which deserves to rest in the place of the original works, and the Fanem manuscript should take its former place among the copies."

Cedrith Fellareon bowed to the listening board, and took his seat before them as they silently seemed to deliberate. In all the seven faces, only one was well known to the Elf, and while the Healers Guildmistress Natasha Ioki held her outward mien as aloof as those of her colleagues, Cedrith could see the twinkle of amusement in her eye, even as she must have been communing with the others. Cedrith could not see over the high bench before him where the masters sat; his first thought, as he waited patiently, was that some magic enabled mental contact, but it could be that they quietly slid a ballot between themselves the while. Or perhaps some third way, a marvelous mechanism worked into the high bench by an architect of previous centuries. Truly, Conar was the City of Wonders and he could only hope to scratch a page or two in its massive catalogue of miracles before his posting from the Elven kingdom of Mendel expired.

By whatever means they deliberated, the masters left no doubt. Rising as a group, they split four and three to come around the board and approached with hands extended to congratulate the visiting Sage.

"My sincerest thanks, sir," said the Chief Archivist, "for correcting this error, so completely and, em, discreetly. I am doubly pleased that you had the sense to ask that this session be held in private. What Master Fanem could have thought these many years ago, I cannot imagine."

"I thank you warmly, sir," Cedrith replied, as the others pressed in to pump his hand as well. "I'm sure the learned man had good reason for his actions, and we needn't suspect, em, that is..."

"We needn't speak of it further, I'm sure you're correct. Still, a good thing to have matters in order. Why, I've not heard of a find as significant as this in my career. We'll be toasting your triumph for days, Guildsman. And have no doubt, we shall apprise your masters in Mendel of the dogged patience and exacting attention to detail you showed here."

As Cedrith murmured more thanks, his eye drifted back to the dais, where two young sages had gently closed both books and now took them from the chamber, to rest in opposite places to where they had been for over twelve hundred years. Cedrith fondly traced in his mind the divergent steps the two lads would take, a quarter-hour's walk through labyrinthine halls that had become quite dear to him this past year. The libraries of Conar were beyond measure for size, for the number of tomes, and for the scrupulous manner of their keeping.

"My friend, you've done it!" Natasha beamed as her large arms enfolded the elf in a bear hug devoid of all decorum. The round woman was impossible to resist, with a smile as wide as the room and a mother's attitude towards the Guild's visitor. Cedrith found himself wishing he could see more of this devoted, pleasant, humor-filled human.

Cedrith gladly accepted another cup of tea and a gracious toast from the Chief Archivist, to which everyone chorused their assent. He sighed, thinking that the letter to his beloved Kia tonight would have to be a work of art, to capture the happiness and contentment he felt at this, the zenith of his short career in the Guild.

The guards burst into the room so hard that the latch of the door cracked and splintered off the jamb.

"I need the Elf!" declared their leader with a tone as blunt as a hammer.

The Chief Archivist, who had jumped to his feet at the invasion, now sank heavily back to his chair at the sheer rudeness of this outburst.

"Why, you… Who do you think you are? This, our guest here–" he spluttered, but the guard was in no way cowed, and Cedrith could see in the man's eyes the dilation of a frightened cat. Only then did he note that the guards still held their spears.

"The Captain of the South Gate sent me and I'm to return with the Elf– your pardon, sir," he belatedly muttered to Cedrith. "To return with the Elvish Sage at once."

"This is an outrage, sir! You cannot believe this will go unremarked, such effrontery. What could possibly matter so much–?"

"There's been an arrest."

At this leaden word the Chief Archivist, who had just regained his footing, suddenly lost it again and sank down, only barely holding his knees off the floor by clutching at the side table. This furniture, as overburdened as the sage, tipped halfway, dropping the kettle of tea on the floor to shatter in a wet pool. Everyone tried to speak, but no one uttered more than half a gasp. As Cedrith felt the grip of doom descend on his mind, he noted the gentle double-tone of the alarm from the broken doorway, sounding with no urgency the need for attention: *fune-oon, fune-oon.* Just a quiet bell, perhaps to sound the dirge of a nation.

"An… arrest?" whispered Natasha, as shocked as the others but wise enough to keep her original seat. "That's not, it's… who?"

"I've seen the susp– the cri– the one they've taken into custody. And he's… unusual, and the Captain wants– he would like, sir, your assistance as an, um, foreigner, to identify him and check his story."

Cedrith licked his lips and managed to croak, "Surely the Mensor is present?"

"Aye, sir, the same who was there when this fellow first entered the city this morning. But they can make nothing of it, and you must come. Please."

"Of course, dekentar, I shall be happy to accompany you." Cedrith's words were as warm as he could make them, but his throat felt as if he had swallowed a decade's shelf-dust, and he could not at first make his legs work. Men were not taken under arrest in this city. Arrests were for those suspected of a crime. And Conar's Law had never been broken; that was an accepted fact all the children of Hope knew from birth. Cedrith finally rose with an attempt at composure, as he knew the mortals would look to him for grace regardless of their outer rank. He felt as if his stomach stayed back on his chair, and did not move all the steps he took to where the guards stood waiting.

"What is he, where, what did he… do?" stammered the Chief Archivist, in a lost murmur. Everyone wanted, and did not want, to know the details. The dekentar hesitated a moment before responding, and once again the alarm tone sang a solo, *fune-oon, fune-oon.* Finally the guard recalled the sound, and peremptorily slapped his badge of office; immediately the first half of the alarm tone ceased, signifying that the constabulary was on the scene, and leaving only the repair alarm sounding for the craftsman's arrival; *-oon, -oon.*

"I saw him at the first interview, milords Sages, but I did not see the, ehm, incident. From what I hear…"

"Yes?"

"He ran across the Grand Square an hour ago."

"*Ran*!" exclaimed Natasha. "It is not possible."

"There were a thousand witnesses, milady. A thousand and more. Sir, will you come now?" Clearly, the guard was as itchy to be gone as he was unwilling to have come.

Cedrith nodded, and took Natasha's hand, promising to return and tell her all the news. As he accompanied the guards down the outer hall and to the street, Cedrith noted the carpenter arriving from the opposite direction, looking askance between the guards and the shattered door-lock as they shouldered past him. Behind them, the remaining alarm tone ceased. Cedrith fervently wished to go back in time to the moment before he heard that pleasant bell, when his only thoughts were of his victory and his letter to Kia. Now, he was headed to witness the end of an era, the shattering of a city's peace; with news like that to tell, Cedrith thought, he might never take up the quill again.

⊕⊕⊕

Treaman saw the crowd ahead outside the walls waving, jumping, running back to alert the others, celebrating. All children, he realized, or nearly. For a moment, their rampant joy made him forget the weight and smell of the monster hide he was humping as he labored along behind Haltar. To one side, Mhoral was similarly loaded, and still complaining as if they hadn't yet escaped the chaos-land.

"Why must I carry these stenching hides? Let the woodsman take them all."

"What for?" Treaman retorted. "You've no rank to pull on me, unlike our fearless leader here."

"No," Mhoral admitted, "but they don't make you smell any worse than usual." This kind of bold-faced lie was the helmed Elf's usual fare, especially to the race of men; Treaman insisted on bathing daily and was always ribbed for that. But the remark coming anonymously from behind the closed helm had its usual effect, and everyone laughed. Linya grinned to Treaman in comradery, her sides flapping with sewn bags containing several of the creatures' organs he had guessed might be valuable. Haltar as leader and Bildon, as the smallest, carried the remaining provisions instead, but the smell was plenty powerful and clinging as well; even after three days of hiking with their questionable prizes, their noses hadn't become accustomed.

Haltar stopped, which was a bit unusual as he normally projected an air of perfect confidence. Raising one arm in greeting to the distant crowd, he turned his head, saying, "Treaman, you have a problem with your pack. Take it off to fix it."

"Sure thing, boss," Treaman replied, and thunked his entire arrangement on the hard turf with a thud.

"You too, Mhoral," the leader said, turning around and pretending to look over the rig.

"There's nothing wrong with my pack," the Elf protested, earning him one of Haltar's cheerful glares.

"If you prefer, I can cut some of the straps for you."

Grumbling, Mhoral went along with the charade. Haltar's broad caped back nearly blocked the town's view of the party by itself as they casually gathered around and fussed with nothing during the conversation.

"Those children there, like it or not, are going to be the news of us to this entire city," Haltar warned. "We impress them or no one cares beyond today that we found our way back."

"They'll be impressed," Mhoral assured him. "We're the first group to return from the Percentalion in almost a year."

"We found no humans and aren't carrying so much as a silver bit of treasure," Haltar ground on, ignoring the Elf as he did any interruption. "Here's where carrying that pack-leader's pelt is going to pay off." Everyone nodded at this. "I tell the story, you wait to talk until I bring you in. Linya, can you do that thing where you put your hands into your sleeves?"

The young mage smiled and produced the gesture; Treaman wondered how he could keep forgetting she was actually quite a lovely woman, so slight and quiet.

"Good, but stop smiling," Haltar advised; Bildon, perched on Mhoral's pack just to be annoying, pulled an exaggerated face of seriousness, and now Linya couldn't possibly do as she was asked. Haltar, without looking at the halfling, reached his gauntleted arm around to adjust his belt, giving Bildon a back-hand cuff as if by accident that knocked him off the pack.

Still looking at Linya, the strapping leader remarked, "We must get you a magical circlet for your hair."

Linya adjusted her cloth headband, face brightening with interest. "Perhaps one that could help me cast Light? Or a protective shield?"

"Whatever you like," the leader said grandly, "I'm just talking about the ornament for now. These hides," he gestured, "won't bring us any baron's ransom, even if we don't mess up the story." As everyone shouldered their burdens again and set off to meet the townsfolk, Haltar leaned in to murmur a moment to Treaman, "And these creatures need a name."

"What? I was thinking someone in the city–"

"These beasts are all unique," Haltar said with his usual confidence, "they are going to gape and stare and ask us what they are. No one pays a lot for 'monster' hides."

Treaman was stunned. "Well, I don't have a name for them!" he hissed.

"You will," Haltar rejoined, striding ahead with that maddening poise he always exuded. Treaman felt a wave of sickness, now that he knew he'd be called upon. Six-legged wolves? Savage dires? Invulner-dogs?

The crowd at the banner-stake pulled back into a semi-circle as the group came level, and Haltar stopped at the center-stage spot they created, with the light of the firepit illuminating his tall frame and the scar on his forehead. Haltar held his half-helm under one arm, resting the other on the pommel of his massive hand-and-a-half sword. He'd put his red cape back on as soon as Treaman had spotted the town in the distance; now he looked every inch the hero, and the party ranged behind him took places as well. Mhoral, impassive and still, the mysterious eternal Elf; Linya with arms in sleeves and her hood up for an extra touch; Bildon pacing the back quietly and making sure everyone could see the rare halfling among the big people; and then the skilled, experienced outdoorsman, standing with spear planted and trying to conceal the fact that he lacked a few months of nineteen years old.

An aged veteran with a wooden leg pushed forward from the crowd, together with a slender young lad in a white tunic, to grasp Haltar's hand. "Welcome back, sirrah," the elder said. "We've not had a party return from the Land of One Hundred Castles in many a week." He sounded envious.

"We are delighted to be the first," the warrior responded in a high good humor, and the children cheered.

"Did you reach one of the trapped towns?" the youth in white asked, and Treaman felt a stab of apprehension, that their journey might get short shrift as the leader had warned. Haltar said nothing, and the guesses came piling in.

"Did you reach Stathos? Or Maladon?"

"What about Reghalion?"

"Did you fight a dragon? Or meet one of the hellspawn?"

"Where was Skysword?" "Yes, Skysword, tell us!"

Haltar for answer turned to Treaman, and he stepped up a pace. The enormous peak in the center of the Percentalion was often visible even from eighty leagues or more, and rumors abounded how it could be used for orientation. Everyone in the party knew the answer, but the woodsman was the right speaker for this little scene.

"We didn't see it every day," he started, to gasps of recognition from his audience and a few whispers of "Worse and worse!"

"Most days the first two weeks, it was east or north-east of us–"

"Stathos, then." "Or Hollinsfen, more nearly."

"But suddenly, around the 25th Serpent, it was to the southwest."

"What!" "Too much too soon, worse and worse–" "Ruins of old Hypon." "No, the keep of Mad Hurfak!"

Here Haltar, having let their own enthusiasm stoke the fires that mere truth could not, held up a masterly hand, saying "Let us tell you the whole story."

They gladly did, without another word; and Haltar told it well. The hard days marching, the cold nights and storms, he mentioned with flattering economy; the group's perseverance with gullies and reaver-birds he wove into a tale of cooperation and courage. Treaman smiled a bit, back out of the firelight, at the inspiring tale of this other party that Haltar must have heard. Where, he wondered, were the pointless arguments about direction, the lonely, boring watches, the constant fast of rations never knowing how long the trip would take? Not one word about Bildon's pranks: the grease on Mhoral's packstraps or the added pepper in Haltar's food. And most importantly, Treaman realized, the narrative shied gracefully around the failure: no towns, no treasures, no triumphs. To hear the armored warrior tell it, this expedition had no other purpose than to meet these monstrous things, these… what in the name of all the heroes would he call them,

Treaman wondered again, even as the battle was well underway in story now and his cue coming.

"Back against the river they pushed us, and our efforts to cut them rang hard off their hairy proof," Haltar intoned, drawing his thick blade to show the nick from combat. A few children had raced back to town and now returned, with many of the elders, leading merchants and others; a constant crowd was emptying Trainertown and if the tale went on much longer they would all be here. "With the blow that caused this, I did no more damage than if I had hit a stone." Gasps and moans from the crowd, and now he sheathed the weapon and gestured for readiness.

Treaman grasped the largest hide in both hands, and as he listened to the tale of the fight, it came in full touch at last with what he recalled…

The spear-cast, aimed high, fell low and therefore struck the largest beast in the side, causing a flinch of pain as it bounced away. Against all expectation, Haltar suddenly rose from the water, shouting "MAGIC!" and clenching his favored fist-knife in place of the dropped sword. Sitting up now almost directly beneath the lead-beast, he had an excellent vantage for a short, powerful punch directly into the monster's underside. It ripped open like a canvas bag stuffed with eels; innards buried him again and blocked him from view. The leader's scream was deafening and Linya, in the midst of a spell, shrieked instead and covered her ears, stepping back into the water where she fell. Mhoral, intoning another magical chant, raised his glowing club and struck, first his own foe and then the leader behind him, leaving broad cuts in both that bled freely.

The three remaining pack-mates, wounded or otherwise, turned on the dying leader to nose under its torn belly and finish the job. Haltar floundered into deeper water still clutching his knife and deliberately dunked himself to clean his vision.

Treaman, staggering into shallower waters, drew his forester's blade, which he called Gutter. Coming unaware on his foe now turned upon its former leader, he was able to aim the short, one-edged blade carefully and strike hard parallel to its skull, slicing off its right eye. The creature howled and spun in his direction, slamming two legs into him and knocking him down. Scrambling up, Treaman was now forced to give ground away from the stream as the creature barreled in. He edged towards its blind-side, and eventually the lumbering monster had to spend more energy turning to keep him in sight than in pursuing him. Treaman finally achieved a full circling motion, giving no more ground and making it move to its utmost to keep him in sight.

"I've got a bead on him," he heard a high, light voice call from over by the trees. Risking a glance, he could see the halfling Bildon whirling his sling and in full aim at his foe.

Nodding, he shouted, "Now!" and the bullet whizzed in to strike and distract the beast. Treaman stopped circling, and the monster's momentum carried it thundering past before its six scrabbling legs could stop, its underside exposed. Treaman stepped up, reached in and disemboweled it with a strong slicing blow. Then the stench of its intestines hit him with its death-howl, and he fell like a toppled drunk at Bildon's feet.

"Aromatic!" the child-size Stealthic chirped. "What do you suppose it eats, to produce such a perfume?"

"Big-mouthed halflings," Treaman suggested with a gasp, as he struggled to his feet with small help from Bildon. Surveying the firelit field, Treaman saw Linya thrashing in the current, Haltar just getting back to shore, and Mhoral with two remaining beasts, both wounded, using his angled club to dramatic but no longer significant effect. He was bashing down hard on each skull in alternation, which apparently dazed his foes, but the glow was gone and they took no serious damage. Unable to mind his rear, Mhoral backed into a tree and was trapped. One creature bit down on his waist and he shouted with pain and outrage. But that attacker suddenly had a rider, six and a half-feet tall on his back, punching its head with a studded gauntlet and reaching down to hack at its groin with the broad-bladed dagger.

Linya, stepping ashore with the other creature close by, simply drew out a stick of wood the size of a quill and tapped the monster on its face. A sharp bright explosion of magical force snapped out, and the thing staggered back howling and waving three paws before its face in panic. Nothing bothered, Linya crab-stepped forward and struck again with the tiny stick, lightly on a foreleg, and another explosion this time dropped the creature completely, bleeding now from three places. Treaman arrived in time to help tackle and gut the one Halter had ridden; the fight in total had taken less than two minutes. Bildon tramped up to stand on the largest corpse and bowed to Linya, crowing, "And yet they keep insisting that size matters!"

"Only thus," Haltar's voice cut in rising to a triumphant ending, "with our blood and by the grace of the heroes, were we able to defeat these monstrous beasts."

He signaled and Treaman flipped hard with both hands clutching the hide. The largest of the monsters, once skinned, had a pelt the size of a skiff sail; Treaman held the back feet, and at the head-end he had retained, despite the weight and at Haltar's insistence, the top half of the creature's thick skull. Now it billowed to the ground much larger than its original size, its head moving towards the crowd as if attacking before settling with a heavy *cloump!* Squalling and screaming, the youngest in the ranks fled the ember-lit visage: even the city elders took a step back and some cried out in astonishment. Haltar had done his job and now put arms akimbo to let events take their course. Treaman uttered a silent prayer to Novar of his homeland, that the hero of the frontier would help him now. Many-Legged Terrors? Long-Toothed Devourers?

"What… what is this?" a smith demanded.

All eyes turned to Treaman and he swallowed with finality as if his mouth held poison. He drew breath and then said, "Hexavore."

A long moment's silence, and then men nodded to look again on the hide. Haltar's face held the same assurance it always did: the others looked happy as well, and Treaman let the relief wash over him. The creatures had a name at last: if they'd eaten him, they might never have been known to history.

The tanner strode forward, evidently of a mind to do business at once. Mhoral placed the other four hides next to the first and he took an edge in one hand, wrinkling his nose. "Take something extra to get the stink out," he ventured, and the haggling had begun.

"For which you'll have material nearly impervious to weapons that are not magical," Haltar responded cheerfully.

"How do I cut it, then!" the man exclaimed, and Haltar drew his punch-dagger.

"This enchanted edge been with me since my earliest fighting days, and I know you'll take good care of it. Or pay the four thousand silver pieces it is worth."

The tanner nodded, and signaled to the wiry girl to start gathering them up. Standing, he came a foot shorter than Haltar and had to crane his neck to face him. "Price, then."

"We have several tasks we need attended to while we restock," the leader said briskly. "Some supplies, board, repairs for our armor…"

The smith piped up, "I can fix your chain and plate, sir, and smooth that notch in the sword."

"This?" Haltar responded, drawing out the blade as if it had wronged him, "this is a trade-in; I'll need a new one." Mhoral sighed in disgust, as this was already an old story: Haltar had yet to depart for a second adventure with the same weapon. "Now, sir," he said back to the tanner, "you can pay us cash for the hides, or, if you would prefer to handle these needs in partial trade…" He let the offer hang there as the craftsman considered.

From behind the crowd — thousands now — came a disturbance, and men parted to let through a tall, spare man in blue robes with a walking staff. He strode right up to Haltar, and though he gave away several inches yet to the hulking warrior, still Treaman sensed an equal. This newcomer had not been in the city when they left, he knew; Haltar adopted a slightly more defensive posture, though confident as ever.

"You see!" the preacher cried, as if continuing an earlier discussion. "Against all odds, heroes have returned from the gaping jaws of chaos." The group relaxed a bit then, to hear an affirmation. "Those who can travel the Percentalion and back, who can defeat such hellish spawn," the cleric turned to nudge the giant head at his feet, "these are suitable vessels for the destiny that lies across this land."

Mhoral shifted nervously at this, and Haltar's face dropped a notch as he took in the after-taste of this fine speech. "Well met, holy sir," he said carefully. "We would be happy to hear more of this 'destiny,' if you would join us at the tavern–"

"Drinking?" the preacher returned in a dangerous tone. "When the people of one hundred castles lie in thrall?" It was a challenge no leader could ignore, and Haltar was not minded to try.

"Learned sir," he said in a low tone, "you see on the ground before you the last beings to challenge our courage. Our lives are in the service of this city, I assure you; we have every intention of returning to the Percentalion–"

"The way is south, sir." The preacher's eyes flared with a single purpose, and Treaman felt sure the evening was going to the blazes before his eyes. "If you lack the direction, I can lead you."

That was more than a step too far, and everyone in the party knew it. Haltar cocked his head wearing that crooked grin he always got before he slew something; without knowing what he was about.

Treaman lurched forward. "We need healing!" he blurted.

The eyes of the cleric turned to fix on him, and the woodsman stammered. "Linya and Mhoral, they've got bites and I could not find the right moss. Holy sir, can you heal them?"

The man in blue laid a hand on the woodsman reassuringly, and said, "Of course, young hero, if that is your need, I am ready." He moved to Linya, who shrank a bit, but let him see her clawed arm.

"I am Alaetar, dear lady, feel no alarm." He gestured slightly over her wound, saying "*Intacta volar.*" Mhoral, Treaman, and scores of people who could see all gasped and exclaimed aloud as the rips and scabs disappeared. Alaetar turned to tend to Mhoral's mid-section, and Treaman took the time to look meaningfully at Haltar. He had cooled from his initial murderous determination, and bit his lip in thought, which Treaman always took for a good sign.

"We are in your debt, holy sir, and now are much closer to readiness for our return." Alaetar straightened up and turned to face the leader again; the crowd made no sound, and even the fire had dimmed its crackling, leaving moonlight as a poor backdrop to read a man's face. "We need only some rest–"

"A bed, I beg you," Linya murmured, "and a bath."

"Food cooked over coals," Mhoral said with fervor.

Alaetar frowned, but Haltar inserted the winning stroke as easily as a needle into a sun-softened candle.

"And all this while waiting for the good tanner to give partial payment for this treasure… by making a suit of hexavore armor for our Stealthic here."

Bildon yelped in surprise, causing a rush of laughter around the crowd. The tanner, making measurements and test-cuts with Haltar's dagger, looked up, then over at the halfling in a calculating way. He nodded in agreement, saying, "Three days."

Haltar held his hands to the sides, and after a short pause Alaetar nodded, saying "Three days, then." Better than nothing, Treaman thought. The crisis averted, they entered the south gate with half the population of Trainertown around them. Folks began to clap their backs and wring their hands, vying to offer the first drinks. Yes, better than nothing by a long way.

The merchant vessel *Prism* slid upstream on the Glass River with all sheets furled and every oar in its rest. Without aid from the crew or the wind, against current and tide, the galleass approached the Crystal City of Hope's wizards as if pulled on a rope. Which, except for the existence of a rope, looked right. When the Harbormaster of Araluntir wanted a ship to dock there, it could; against his will, the pirate fleet of Bargon the Ruthful seven years ago had come to ruin, none of its corsairs getting as close to the enormous stone piers as the Mendelian trader already had.

Arrangements to land and trade with the Crystal City were as rare as silversteel spoons, and the captain of the *Prism* had no mind to waste the opportunity. Hands behind his back and absent the constant orders with which he generally henpecked his crew, he stood on the foredeck and let the magic of the Harbormaster guide his vessel. After it docked, he would meekly submit to the rigorous inspection of his holds, his crew and his person though it took the rest of the day. Not until late the next morning, after the Elvish sailors offloaded and reloaded the pre-arranged cargoes under the watchful stare of inspectors nearly as numerous, would he have any latitude to command anyone again.

But the security and wealth of trade with the mages made it easily worth jumping through a few hoops. Araluntir, city of wizards, guarded enormous lore, restricting passage across its walls since the founding. And of all the contraband outlawed by this sparkling city, the most forbidden was human. No outside person was ever allowed to remain in Araluntir, and of course none had ever wanted to leave the wondrous magical city where lore of the highest level was taught to the most deserving, the sons and daughters of wizards.

The Harbormaster personally boarded the *Prism* to sweep its cargo bays with the aid of his jeweled wand, that rumor had it could sense poison, magic, curses, life, and Despair. His acolytes followed in train — each of them, it was said, an accomplished mage capable of firing an unruly vessel in moments. Sailors with literally nothing to do for several hours submitted to personal searches, then walked where directed to a quiet place on the docks to eat, and stare up at the walls, and perhaps gamble, and certainly to wait. One staff-bearing guardian was considered sufficient to mind them, as the way to the dock-stairs was narrow and in the other direction was nothing but a few small warehouse sheds. A single crewman, walking aimlessly between those sheds, went unnoticed for a few minutes; his business looked to be of no consequence beyond, perhaps, its odor.

In the narrow alley, the Elf adjusted to the shaded darkness, then looked carefully on the walls until making out a faint smudge of the letter "P." The sailor rubbed it out as if from boredom, and then waited. A thin, lithe figure in plain black robes stepped from behind a pile of barrels and flashed a small signal, easy to miss. It was returned and the meeting that followed was accomplished in whispers and small gestures.

"You've come, my thanks," said the resident to the crewman.

"No," whispered the sailor, "my thanks to you, mage Pol; I can still scarcely believe you are affording me such a priceless gift. No person can enter Araluntir without the permission of The Five. And that has not been given to merchant or Mark in living memory."

"I have no gift to give," the mage insisted. "I simply wish to leave, and better that I go unremarked. My place is here to be taken, if you have what I need to take yours." Here the mage held up a small brooch-pin with a mundane stone, the sort of jewelry that could easily be mistaken for a button. "With this glamor, you will resemble me, at least until you trigger suspicion."

"Hopefully, I can avoid that for some time."

"But not forever."

"Certainly not. Your letter was most helpful and I have memorized the names, the routine. I shall certainly be ill for at least a week." A smile, and then a shrug. "But eventually… I will admit the ruse if needed, but first I will try to claim that the stone only masked my true appearance, not an exchange of identity."

The mage frowned. "It will not hold up. You say you have some magical skill, and I have learned by your letter of several in my own roster that you say you can cast. Still, if it comes to a close testing, you cannot master them all."

"Perhaps during my 'illness' I can learn them and extend the day of discovery."

"Aye, I had thought of that. Here is the list." The mage handed over a narrow, long sheet of parchment, and the sailor's mouth dropped in astonishment before looking back.

"One thing more," the mage Pol added, "under no circumstances should you spar with the fighting master. You could not fool her an instant."

"Say," the aspiring wizard said with pique, "I can handle myself. I too know the arts of open-handed combat." Dropping into a stance, the sailor demonstrated a few moves with notable fluidity. His partner merely stood unspeaking, and after a moment, the other dropped arms in defeat.

"Well, even if I am exposed, by then perhaps I will have proven my worth to the masters, and be allowed to stay in your place."

"And you are welcome to that place," the mage said, handing over the stone. "Now, how may I take yours?"

"Nothing simpler," the sailor said smiling, "for I have arranged the same magic upon my own appearance." The speaker removed a clip from his belt, a silver band with a set of small stones of unremarkable hue. As the mage reached to take it, the face and form of the sailor melted away, revealing a comely woman of medium height and blond, rather than black, hair. For the first time, the mage of Araluntir was startled, and she giggled quietly before donning his brooch-pin. Again, the visitor's features changed; now the woman disappeared, her clothing and effects as well as her hair, and there were twins of the robed wizard. The newer of the two grinned saucily as if daring the other to comment. With a slight shake of his head, the older of the twins donned the belt-clip, and within moments the dark-haired sailor was back in evidence.

"I only signed on two trips ago," the woman said, "and there's no one in particular I spoke with, as per your instructions." Her tones were now those of the robed mage she pretended to be, his the rough cant of the seaman as he replied, "Good. You know your quarters, your general routine, and all I can do is wish you good luck. Learn well."

"But where will you go? I've never heard why you wished to travel, nor any part of your mad venture. Who would ever wish to leave this place that every spell-caster in the Lands would trade a finger to see?"

Pol the Elvish merchant seaman shook his head once. "I was nearly born here, sent before I could remember. Your good fortune; you have no parents, no siblings here to remember you, no lineage to live up to. I have learned all I can from this city. I have been here too long and petitioned for permission to leave many times. I no longer accept the refusal of The Five."

"And where will you go?"

"To the heart of danger, where I may hone my understanding of myself."

The new Pol was dumbfounded. "What? You don't mean… the Percentalion? Alone?"

The false sailor was unmoved by the horror of his former self. "I have always been alone."

He turned to leave, and the robed one called out a last time, a bit too loud. "Don't you even want to know my name?"

Turning his head as he walked, he said, "Names are not important."

The woman in a man's form watched him silently rejoin the crew, and shook her head wonderingly. She hoped she wouldn't be blamed, once this ruse was exposed, for getting him killed. Then she examined the long, long list of spells mastered, and for a moment doubted whether he would die at once. Still, to enter the Percentalion alone and unarmed, that was a form of suicide hard to take a liking to.

Far above the docks, behind one of the many enormous pure glass windows for which the city was named, five robed figures looked down on the harbor. Their ornate vestments looked identical at first glance — the initiates spent months studying small variations in runes, reversal of symbols and color-schemes, and other matters which delineated the fields of study held by each of the masters. The tallest, a black human from the Southern Empire spoke first.

"So, it is done. He goes too soon for my taste. I fear great loss from his departure."

The slightly-built woman responded, "You have seen the signs in the sky. The approaching body is no planet or moon, and no record tells of such a phenomenon. By my reckoning, we have flirted with disaster waiting as long as we have."

The Elven master smiled, saying "Then the middle course, by displeasing all, is likely the best." No one bothered to affirm such a platitude, and he shook his head in recognition. "I can say this: Pol knows nothing of his past, his heritage, has not seen the sign in the sky, yet he goes at this moment into the heart of darkness. Truly, he has chosen. The rest lies with the heroes."

"Still, if we had consulted with the seers of Shilar–"

"They could have told us nothing, as their scopes do not have the power of ours. Yet they would have taken six months to tell us that nothing. The kingdoms have grown apart; we are ill-suited to respond to this call of destiny. No, the crowns of this world can do little–we, perhaps, even less than they–to answer the portents we see. It lies on the shoulders of the common folk, on those noble of character rather than birth, to save us if we can indeed be saved."

"I foresee fire and blood."

"As do I, fellow mages, as do I. But how else to forge a weapon, how else to win a victory?"

The guard detail escorting Cedrith left the wooden halls of the Sages Guild and moved down the broad paved thoroughfare towards the South Gate. The Elf felt stricken at the way his senses betrayed his conscience. By all rights, he should focus on the doom laying over the nation, and the awful personal consequences that would result from his unwilling participation. These thoughts were grim food, but his eyes and ears refused to cooperate by providing an appropriate backdrop. The crowd moving past looked as calm and normal as if nothing unusual had happened; of course, he reflected, the word has been kept quiet for now.

And the day; what a sky, such perfect alabaster puffs of cloud, the gentle breeze, the brilliant sunshine; it was a simply matchless day, Cedrith thought as he plodded along. Almost an insult, to have such weather at a time when dread and fear gripped his heart. Could these two opposite things exist on the same span of daylight? A broad swath of sun illuminated the perfect cobbling, the clean raised sidewalks, the whitewashed storefronts and living quarters and the crystal-clear windows of pure glass on all sides. The street itself, though not one of Conar's most traveled, was easily wide enough to let a pair of four-ox wagons turn around in parallel. The sun poured down in measureless loads of light, and the air was slightly cool without a hint of dampness. What a waste of a fine day, Cedrith thought. Or perhaps the ancient enemies of Hope are taunting us, that we have finally let slip our sacred trust.

The escort came to the Grand Square of Conar, bustling with traffic as it did at all hours. The scene of the crime, Cedrith thought before he could stop himself; a heart-pound of added fear struck him then, and he reflexively looked up at the giant wood-framed sign on the granite arch that overhung the street. The letters of the Mage Command were deep-cut and unmistakable — everyone who passed could not help glancing up to see "WALK" in the letters of the Common Tongue. Cedrith had never tried to disobey a Mage Command even for fun, as he was naturally a law-abiding sort. But he knew with certainty that its injunction, backed by the millennia-old magics of the city's founders, could only be resisted by someone of genius intellect, or the willpower of the Heroes themselves. You saw the sign, and thereafter you walked. Everyone on the Grand Square now, easily three thousand people at the ebb of the morning's traffic, was walking. As he stepped out into the open space, bordered by public buildings and under the full weight of that gorgeous day, Cedrith reflected that one man, at least, had run here, only an hour ago. But how?

Treading the square's huge marble slabs, Cedrith began to sense a difference in the behavior of the cityfolk around him: less bustle, fewer smiles or friendly greetings, more people "in the know," a few looking at him with the guards and nodding knowingly. The sage realized his behavior was more important than ever, and though he dreaded the attention, he paused by the central fountain to repeat the adopted ritual he'd learned when he first arrived. The leader of the guards was clearly eager to move on, but Cedrith murmured, "Just a moment, dekentar. This takes little time and is worth doing well."

With only a slight shake in his cupped hands, Cedrith reached from the top step to the stream pouring down from the hands of Conar's statue at the fountain's center. Though drawn directly from the salty Western Sea, the water from this fountain had a freshness he could smell clearly and was always wonderfully cool to the touch. As per the ritual, Cedrith let his first handful drop to the pool below, a libation in respect of the city's founder: gathering a second dose, Cedrith deliberately turned left and right, looking for anyone in greater need of water than himself, and when no one offered to accept (though many were looking), he emptied that as well. His third handful, Cedrith raised to his lips. As delicious as it always tasted, he drew no joy from the ritual today, but he did note a kind of dogged satisfaction that he had managed to act properly. No doubt, the disaster he was hastening to attend would result in his quiet dismissal from the city. Yet he could represent his home country and brother-race until then. Turning, he signaled to the guards his readiness to continue, and they moved across the rest of the enormous plaza without further conversation.

Down the street leading directly to the South Gate, a paved thoroughfare that bore on straight as an arrow and a spear-throw wide swallowed up Cedrith and the guard party along with hundreds of walking and riding citizens. Cedrith could see the South Gate itself in the narrow distance nearly half a league away. He marveled, as he always did, at the tremendous ancient architecture, a timeless and megalithic city that emanated security and order from every corner. The thought came sidling up to his mind, that the man who would bring all this to shame had himself come the opposite way up this street not two hours ago. With a start, Cedrith realized he knew nothing at all about the one he was going to see.

"Dekentar, this fellow who's been arrested, what is he like?"

The guard trudged on only half-turning his head to acknowledge the question. He said nothing for several paces, then shrugged almost angrily. Just as Cedrith was going to ask again, the guard suddenly said, "Strange."

"Strange?"

"He's– you will have to see for yourself, sir. The Captain feels– you being an Elf, and well-traveled, you might have… see for yourself."

With this, the man clamped his jaw dramatically to signal that he would say no more. Cedrith sighed and walked along, but now his mind tried to place some kind of frame around the subject of his impending interrogation. A male, and likely not a fellow-Elf or they would have said so. But, *strange*. Was he a massive bruiser of a warrior? Some sly mage? Perhaps the man was black, Cedrith thought. They were not unknown in Conar but rare and always assumed to be from the fiery Southlands. Dwarves and Halflings also lived here, little colonies of them in neighborhoods around the city. The more he turned his mind to it, the less and less Cedrith found he liked the one word the guard had used to describe the accused. For who could be truly strange in this grand cosmopolitan center of the Hopeful world?

They approached the massive, looming South Gate at last, with its portals wide to the traffic and an arched opening thirty feet over their heads as they neared. Cedrith had often been called to the Harbor Gate, and once to the largest of them all, the Eastern Door, by the guards, as a courtesy to Conar's Elvish visitors, and recognized the architecture.

As he turned to use the back entrance reserved for city officials, however, the dekentar held out an arm. "I'm afraid we're on alert, sir. We must use the front," he said apologetically. Cedrith riled for only a moment at this slight indignity, his reason firmly asserting to his pride that the circumstances more than warranted a little extra trouble. Still, as he put his hand on the latch of the outer door, set directly into the gateway arch and leading to the inspection chambers, Cedrith felt a guilty thrill, to think that now he was treading directly in the same path as the lawbreaker whose deed brought him here.

Past the magnificently liveried guards and through the twelve-foot double oak doors, Cedrith and his escort came into the Welcome Chamber. The man seated behind the large paneled desk on the right intoned the customary greeting, "Enter Conar in peace, deal in equity, remain in Hope." As the guards showed their badges to bypass the inspection, Cedrith smiled and bowed to the speaker, then advanced to the central dais to stand inside an engraved symbol of Hope set into the floor. An attendant brought him a goblet and Cedrith was invited cordially but firmly to drink in praise of the city's founder. Cedrith did so with a ready will, and kept his eye on the man behind the desk as the clear fluid, tasting thin and slightly sweet like tree-sap, flowed down his throat. After a moment, he saw a faint blue glow illumine the man's face, from some unseen crystal set into the desk's surface.

"I am a child of Hope then," he said with a smile. "What a relief."

The beauracrat looked up with a face devoid of humor and said only, "The man in custody now showed the same."

The guard dekentar had passed his patience by this point: taking Cedrith firmly by one arm he led him around the survey-station, waving off the man who would have asked the standard questions of a visitor, and headed for the inner door. Several feet before the portal, they passed through a shimmering purple curtain of aura suspended in the air, and as they did, a violet flicker clung to the sage as if it were material. The beauracrat rose from his desk and the chamber guards moved to block the doorway.

"By the Hopelord, what now!" bellowed the dekentar. "This man is a guest, and the Captain–"

“Never mind,” said the official implacably. “He has a magical item on his person and we must investigate it.”

Cedrith looked without comprehension at the man, then clapped his head with a laugh, “Oh, of course! My Diligent Quill! Apologies all, I came in such haste, I forgot to leave it at the Guild.” Reaching into his tunic, Cedrith produced a flat wooden box, and withdrew an elegant bronzed swan’s quill. He passed it through the curtain and demonstrated that it had been the offending item. “It can take dictation, write by itself; very useful when my hand is tired.”

“There, satisfied? Now we’re leaving,” the dekentar added, with a muttered oath for emphasis. As he steered Cedrith towards the inner chamber, he paused only long enough to lean in towards the man from the desk, and say, “Remind me to come back in an hour and slam your fool head into the wall.” The customs official looked back at the guard as if he had a summons to give him, but made no objection as the escort left the chamber.

With heightening emotions, Cedrith realized he was very close now to meeting the stranger in person. In the next chamber, he saw the massive desk of the captain of the south guards, manned by a strapping knight who rose to greet the summoned sage. Captain Bentine radiated command and surety, but as he reached for Cedrith’s hand, the sage could hear the relief in his voice.

“Sage Fellareon, thank you for coming.”

Cedrith meant to answer as he usually did, “I am delighted to be here,” but his throat caught and all that came out was “I am– here.”

Bentine sensed the sage’s discomfort and shook his hand all the more warmly, saying again, “Thank you.” He gestured to the door opposite. “The suspect– the man in question, is in there. I have the warrant signed and ready, merely lacking the charge to be filled in.” The knight reached to the parchment on his desk, but only lifted one corner, as if the thing were too heavy for his hand. “We need the facts, sir, and he has shut his mouth almost since we brought him back here. We can get nothing from him anymore; he's clearly hostile and I've nearly lost my temper. I'll come clean with you, Sage Fellareon: you're the only Mendelian I know, from your previous visits here, and before I can bring this to higher attention, I would have to file a report. I hoped perhaps you, with your manners and understanding… I would be grateful, that is, for anything you can do."

"Of course, Captain. The Mensor has been present, I understand? And was here at his first entrance as well?"

"Yes, but the learned cleric can give us no indications. As far as he can discern, the man was telling the truth, whenever he chose to speak. But he is mocking us, the tale is pure myth — and for this morning's crime, I have scores of sworn witnesses!" Sir Bentine gestured impatiently at a stack of parchments next to the warrant, and then ran his hand through his hair. "He must be a wizard, despite– it's a glamor on him, or some sorcery. Surely he's an agent of our ancient enemies, sent to test us, to break our will this way."

"Have Hope, Captain," Cedrith tried to assure him. "Let me meet this person and see what can be done."

Captain Bentine opened the farther door and ushered the sage through. The prisoner stood from his low bench, and Cedrith tried to take him in.

His first impression was that of a thin, elderly mage, with long, thick grey hair and a staff in the corner behind him. Then he noted the buttons and epaulets on his surcoat and cape, the broad-brimmed hat, the uniform color up and down him, and took him for a soldier, perhaps of rank. His eyes fell to the dark charcoal leather boots, with thick cuffs rolled down now but of the sort that could pull up over the thigh, and he noted the clean, sunwashed skin that sailors have.

Suddenly, as he took in the stranger's silver eyes, Cedrith realized with a jolt of fear that his face was unspeakably young — he lacked of twenty for certain, whatever shade his hair. He wondered if, despite the absence of other signs, the man was indeed an immortal. Surely he carried an age higher than his body, the sage thought. Strange indeed; Cedrith realized that some time had passed and he was staring. The prisoner was looking back quite frankly at him, as if he too were seeing something new. Then, with a smoothness that did not even raise a clink from the manacles around his wrists and ankles, the stranger bowed to Cedrith in a formal but unfamiliar way, saying only, "Eldest."

If the Elf had been stymied before, now he was knocked out of breath; the dignity and formality of this greeting from a man to an Elf was seldom used in modern times, outside of chapel or a great ceremony. The prisoner rose from his bow and regarded Cedrith again with those steely points, expecting nothing but trying to see all. Torn nearly in half, Cedrith's habits of courtesy at last decided him, and he bowed in return, giving the proper antique response, "Sibling. I am Cedrith Fellareon, a Sage of the guild on posting here to Conar from my home kingdom."

"Mendel, the land of the Elven race," returned the prisoner, as if reciting a lesson, and Cedrith nodded while gesturing him back to his seat. Bentine and the other guards stood apart and watched the proceedings with unmasked enmity, while the interrogation-cleric of Conar, the Mensor who checked statements for truth, stood somewhat closer and turned his head from side to side in the manner of a spectator.

"Where are you from, sir?"

"I came from the south this morning."

"And before that? Where were you born?"

"From the west," said the stranger, gesturing in the correct direction though he was far inside. "My father brought me here across the sea, a journey of two years."

Cedrith looked to the Mensor with alarm, but the cleric only shrugged to indicate that the statement appeared truthful. Cedrith felt again a thrill of fear, to imagine the power of the prisoner that he could so casually fool the detection of a holy man, here at the center of Conar's influence in the world.

"Where is your father now?"

"He is dead. I am an orphan." Again, Cedrith noted the youth in his face, and could not help admiring the steadiness and correctness of his conduct, under such strain. Then he recalled, a bit guiltily, that it must all be a part of the lie. His mind assured him this was the proper conclusion, but his heart sank on the thought.

"Why did you come here, sir? And what is your name?"

"I am called Solemn Judgement, sir; I have come to Conar to learn."

"A use-name, you are called after a thing to do. And now, I'm afraid sir, we must sit in solemn judgment on you this day."

The young stranger only gave a tiny shrug to this, as if to say, "fine, take your turn."

"You understand you are to be charged with breaking the law of Conar."

"This is as the guards have told me."

"Can you tell me why you would do so, sir?"

"Eldest, canst thou tell me what 'tis I have done?"

This set Cedrith back a moment, as the boy's face held no sense of guile or insult, but perhaps the start of a slow, boiling anger, which seemed to him out of place, but still righteous.

"You are charged with running across the Grand Square of Conar."

"In sooth, this is a crime." The statement was flat and matter-of-fact.

"Well of course it is, you spy!" Captain Bentine cried, "Do you deny the existence of the Mage Command, then?" Cedrith noted that this young prisoner in irons faced each speaker directly, and looked them squarely in the eye, despite his condition. His gaze never shirked or shied away, and his composure seemed unbreakable.

"Captain, if I may?" Cedrith interjected, and then turned back to Judgement. "Sir, as you entered the Grand Square this morning, did you note the word 'Walk' on the arch as you entered?"

"Don't let him take you in!" cried the dekentar, stepping forward in his passion. "He'll wrap some spell of words around you–"

"Dekentar, please. Sir?"

The Man in Grey considered the question a moment. "I saw a sign with writing on it, yea, engraved on yon arch, in troth."

"Aye," put in the Mensor seeing his opportunity, "and when I questioned you on entering the city this morning, you claimed you were able to read and write in our Common tongue."

Judgement turned to look at the cleric, who stepped back a pace, and answered him, "Aye, as I can, certes."

"Then you see," Cedrith explained patiently, as if to a student, "you have broken our laws. Either you resisted the Mage's Command at the arch, when you ran — which would be disturbing the peace of Conar — or you must have lied to the Mensor when you claimed to be literate, which would be a form of sabotage, entering the city on false pretences."

As Cedrith finished, he saw the gaze of the Man in Grey slew around completely to him, and a look crossed that straight young face he never expected to see: one of disbelief. The prisoner seemed to wrestle with himself for a time, and then sat back with a sigh that might have carried resignation, or guilt. Yet the fire behind the eyes was growing. A space of silence passed.

"So, sir," Cedrith continued carefully, "you see our position."

"Aye," returned the stranger, and again he spoke as if reciting a lesson, "for the law of Conar has never been broken."

"Just so. And your answer?"

"The law of Conar remains unbroken."

"How can you claim this?"

"Because I am no mage, and I do not lie."

"You lie now!" broke in Captain Bentine.

"And as you have already made clear," the stranger rejoined evenly, "I may not challenge you to an honor-duel for your insults."

"Outrage!" shouted the Mensor. "Sir Bentine is Captain of the South Gate, discharging a position held by his family for four centuries. He has no obligation to answer a duel-challenge from–"

"From an orphan. Aye." Cedrith thought the prisoner might assail someone, or curse, or in some way show his anger outwardly. Instead, he looked to the floor between his feet, seeming to sag beneath a nameless weight. Cedrith signaled for quiet and waited patiently, taking another seat next to the prisoner.

At last, the stranger said, "Eldest? What am I doing here?"

"We have explained our position to you. You have broken the law–"

The Man in Grey shook his head at this, like a dog hit by water. "No, Eldest, I mean- why am I here? Why am I left still alive, whilst my father should die?"

Cedrith was struck dumb with surprise at this question.

"He protected me from harm through my childhood, he was a warrior, a righteous man, advisor to a king… and there was persecution, my brothers slain. He brought me across a strange sea, two years over an endless ocean, and he taught me, Eldest. Every day he taught me, but he never said to what end. He spent his last breath to bring me to this land, where I am friend to no one and have no guide for what days remain to me."

Solemn Judgement looked up then, and Cedrith saw at last the cracks of pure despair in the walls of the prisoner's face. "Should I wish my days to be brief, then?" he asked.

The boy did not cry, even so, but Cedrith felt wet tracks spring into being on his cheeks without his volition. And something was decided inside him: if this young man was an agent of Despair, his power was far beyond human, and this sage was helpless to unmask him. But in his soul, Cedrith realized, he had already judged the youth to be an innocent; though there was no solution to the problem, he knew he would ruin his career in an attempt to assist him.

To cover his confusion, Cedrith stood and moved away, to a side table where the prisoner's personal effects were laid out. He touched lightly on them, and noticed a few camping tools, a coil of rope, a roll of parchments and a quill. On the last, his eye dwelt an extra moment, and Cedrith began to feel a teasing thought, something hiding from him in the back of his mind.

"Young Goodman Judgement, you say you are literate."

"I do, Eldest."

"Yet do you know what the sign on the arch reads?"

"Nay, sir, that language I cannot read and I know not what it is."

"Why," cried the dekentar, stepping forward again, "it's the common speech we're using now, as plain as the day! It says 'Walk,' and yet you ran!"

At this outburst, the Man in Grey stood again, but only looked at the dekentar as if he thought the man were crazy. Cedrith held the prisoner's quill and watched him carefully. At last, the stranger said, "Thou liest."

The dekentar would have gone for him then, but Cedrith and Bentine between them held him back. This time the stranger's gaze fell from the dekentar's eye to his surcoat, and now Cedrith thought he saw suspicion flare on the prisoner's face. Bentine threw the dekentar back to the wall with force, and kept a grip on the man's front while he hissed in his ear.

"One more word from you, dekentar, and you'll pace the basement cells for a month. We may be witness to the end of an era, but we shall remain men, and soldiers, do you hear me?"

The dekentar curled his lip in a sneer at the prisoner, but nodded his head once to show he had regained his temper. Cedrith heard but kept his eye on the stranger, as the teasing thought came ever closer to the surface of his mind. Still half-unsure of what he was about, he scrabbled a sheet of paper from the prisoner's effects, and brought it along with the quill to him.

"Please, Goodman Judgement, write the word 'walk' for us."

The young man looked askance at the Elf but dutifully took the quill and jotted down four characters; their lines were so neat as to look nearly printed by a press, yet none of the four suggested any letter of the alphabet to Cedrith.

Taking back the quill, Cedrith quickly wrote "walk" in Common, and showed it to the Man in Grey. "And this? What does this say?"

"I do not know. This script is strange to me."

Cedrith looked to the Mensor, who was straining to see Solemn Judgement as if he hoped to look through his skin. In a loss of composure, the cleric gestured and muttered as he cast this time, but there was no discernible aura near the prisoner, and at last, he stepped back, sighing with the effort and shaking his head in frustration. Cedrith sensed a moment coming, as if through a heavy fog.

"What is this nonsense, Cedrith?" cried Captain Bentine. "He's just jotting down babble to confuse us, or some evil code. Surely you don't mean, he can speak our own Common tongue as we do, but he cannot write it?"

"What I'm suggesting, Captain, is that if the youth insists he's telling the truth, we must examine the possibility. We know the Mage Command will affect anyone who can read it. All inhabitants of Conar can read, or very nearly, and those who only read other tongues are sorted out by the officials at the gate. This lad has told us an unusual story, there is no doubt. I don't think he's mistaken about something so elaborate, so if he is not lying, then… but how to prove it?"

Cedrith paced a bit while the guards and Mensor muttered among themselves, and Solemn Judgement watched him in pain. He was just realizing, this orphaned student, that he was illiterate after all, and Cedrith felt a wave of sympathy reinforcing his conviction that he must be innocent. He tapped his sides absently as he paced, and when his hand bumped something in his pocket made of wood, he jumped off the ground with a surge of hope.

"By the Moment! Your pardon, Captain, but I may have the answer to our dilemma here."

Pulling out his golden quill, Cedrith approached the paper and set it down flat on a line below the writing already made there. Stepping back, he said clearly the trigger-word "diktat" and then added, "walk." The quill jumped erect and scratched out the word in Common on the parchment and then stood at attention, waiting for his next utterance.

Solemn Judgement had not moved back at this display, though he regarded the animated writing instrument with his undivided attention. "Now then, sir," said Cedrith, "if you will trust me I assure you no harm will come, though it may well be that no good does either. Will you take the quill in your hand there? Ah but wait!" For the quill had begun to write as soon as Cedrith spoke, inscribing the words "Now then sir, if you will trust me…" Laughing, Cedrith said "desen" and the quill dropped to the paper at once.

"My apologies, Goodman Judgement, I am so nervous. Now then, will you take up the quill? It will do nothing, trust me. There, now please say the word 'diktat'." The prisoner did so.

"Now it is attuned to your voice instead of mine. If you would set it down on the paper as I did before." Judgement laid down the quill and stepped back.

"If you would, say the word 'walk'."

Judgement hesitated only a moment, then said "walk" and the quill at once came to attention and inscribed four characters on the paper. Judgement immediately said, "desen" without being asked, and it fell down once more.

Everyone crowded closer to the paper then, and Cedrith announced in a joyous voice, "You see, Captain? The exact characters he wrote before! The quill understands the native tongue of the speaker and it copied the letters this man had in his mind. I had hoped it would be so, but of course I could not be sure; this is such an extraordinary case."

"Gentlemen," he continued in a tone of unconcealed triumph, "I am delighted to affirm that the Law of Conar remains unbroken. This young man told the truth when he said he could read and write his native tongue, and he did not defy a Mage Command when he ran in the Grand Square today."

Captain Bentine looked at Cedrith with a face of utter shock, which then dissolved into a soldier's grin as he took the Elf's hand and pumped it hard enough to nearly break it off. "We have had a very close call! My deepest thanks to you, Sage Fellareon. I don't know what I—we might have… I can't say I understand it, even now. And we owe everything to you, sir! Our city is saved — it's not too much to say it."

Cedrith took the warmly proffered hands and stood in the midst of another celebration, feeling almost lost to his own honesty. Not an hour ago, he was receiving such credit for a months-long project concerning minutiae, a matter of the filing of books that were centuries old and which had likely never been read until he came along. Now, with no preparation and guided more by luck than anything, he was being credited with averting disaster to the reputation of the capital of Hope. It was almost as if all the imputed guilt of this young stranger, finding no home there, had transferred the weight of its feeling to his breast instead.

The stranger stood, chained and straight, as the conversation bubbled on the room's other side from him. Finally, Captain Bentine, looking around, saw the prisoner and gave a small start of recollection. "Now then, you young rascal, you will have to be more careful. You've had a narrow escape. And you must learn to read and write properly, right away."

The stranger just looked at the Captain, still as a stone. After a moment's pause, Bentine stepped towards him, bringing out a ring of keys.

"We'll just have those off now…" With a slight movement, Judgement drew his hands away, and the Captain stopped, confused.

"Here now, what's the matter with you? I'll have those off and you can go, as long as you behave from now on."

The Man in Grey said nothing, but stared the Captain in the eye with an air that spoke of threat. Bentine saw what he took for arrogance, but Cedrith saw the righteous fires returning. There was a long pause now, as Bentine's face showed surprise, anger, and then, slowly, recognition. He spoke in a lowered tone.

"I understand. And you are correct, young man. I was wrong, before, to call you a liar so loudly and so often. I apologize for my words and offer you my hand: would you prefer it now or when your own is no longer chained?"

Cedrith thought he caught the flicker of movement from the stranger's lip, immediately suppressed, and he marveled at his self-possession. Smoothly, the prisoner held out his arms for the keys: when the heavy irons clanked to the floor and Bentine had straightened up from his ankle-cuffs, Solemn Judgement did not extend his hand. But he did give a careful and formal bow, which the Captain returned in the Conarian style.

Judgement began to collect his personal effects, and some of the guards left, trying to conceal their haste to be the first to the taverns.

"Captain, will there be any formalities here?" asked Cedrith, and the knight nodded. "Yes, as soon as I can find a way to describe all this, the king himself will have to see the report. I'll send it over for you to sign. Until then, sir."

"Certainly, Captain," returned the sage, shaking his hand once again. Turning back, he saw the stranger already fully equipped with his goods in his tight belt-pouch and his cape and staff returned He was just settling the broad-brimmed hat back in place, and looked as if he could hike another eight hours today. And needed to.

"Young Judgement," Cedrith blurted, not knowing why, "may I ask where you are bound, after such an adventure?"

The Man in Grey regarded him calmly, "I must return to the Square."

Everyone in the room stopped then, and the dekentar was first to ask, "Why?"

Judgement seemed unwilling to answer the man, and said only, "I must."

"I was thinking," Cedrith put in, to cover the silence, "that you might wish to come to the Sages Guild. I realize you've had a shock, and I thought, if you wished to learn the written language here—"

Judgement nodded briskly at this. "Indeed, and soon, Eldest, my thanks. But first…" and again he looked to the dekentar and did not continue.

"If I may be so bold, Judgement," Cedrith pressed, with a sense of rising danger, "why for love or money did you run in the Square today?"

Judgement returned Cedrith's gaze and said, "I saw a man, followed by… other men. He was on the far edge of the Square, towards the western side, whereas I was by the fountain. And I moved to follow him, because… it was in my thought that he would need assistance. For he was unarmed, and these others wished him harm."

"What?" exclaimed Bentine. "Do you wish to charge that you saw a man under assault! In broad daylight in the center of Hope?"

Judgement only looked back with fire.

"Or do you claim to know the hearts of men," the Captain persisted, "when you say they wished him harm?"

To this Judgement snapped back with unusual vigor, "Aye. They wished him harm, Captain. I have come to know the look."

"Oh certainly, in the capital of Hope where no man has been assaulted in forty centuries. Who were these men? You have no authority to make arrests, sir, even if your fantasy were real. How would you describe them? Come, tell me."

"I saw only one closely," Judgement returned, and now Cedrith could hear the reluctance in his voice. He studiously avoided looking at the dekentar. When his silence did not suffice, the youth had to speak, and he seemed incapable of lying. "He bore a patch on his cloak."

"What patch?"

"That one," Judgement said, gesturing to the crossed green blades on a golden field that graced the surcoat of the dekentar.

The dekentar dropped back a full pace as if parrying a blow, and the Captain threw his gauntlets against the floor so hard it sounded like the crack of a whip.

"By the Hopelord's private parts, you rogue, are you bound and determined to land in jail? We no sooner work you out of the noose you were in than you accuse a house-man of attempted assault!"

"Captain," breathed the dekentar, "he has no immunity from me. Let me duel him to wipe away this insult."

Judgement seemed to get calmer as the storm around him grew. Facing the dekentar at last, he said simply, "Or we could allow the Mensor here to assess whether I tell the truth."

That was a blow, and everyone stopped in the midst of what he meant to say next. The cleric backed away in utter horror, waving his hands as if a snake was set on him. But the point had been made, though it did nothing to sweeten the temper of the two guardsmen. Cedrith, again without knowing why, spoke up.

"Captain, if you will permit me one moment, sir. I will undertake to accompany this man, take him to the Guild, see about getting him some instruction in literacy. He's clearly new to us, whatever you believe about his story. Let us not make a hasty miscalculation twice?"

Bentine looked daggers at Judgement, while the dekentar was literally out of breath with fury. The cleric, under cover of their inattention, actually fled the room, without his dignity. Cedrith would have been happy to follow him, but his mouth had run on, and now he must await the consequences.

And Solemn Judgement, the focus of all this ire and anticipation, stood wordless as if his hosts were discussing where to have dinner without him.

Finally, the Captain ran his hand through his hair, stooped and retrieved his gauntlets with deliberation, and donned them as he stepped closer to the stranger. Reaching back to his belt, he thumbed up a different key than the one for the manacles, a strong silvered bar chased with the symbol of a tower.

"Do you see this? This, young stranger, is the key that opens the cells in my prison here. It is used once a year… *when the Baron inspects the jail!*" He thundered so loud that Judgement's hair actually stirred. "I want you to go with this learned Sage here, and I want you to, to never cross my sight again. For by my family's crest, if I have to use this key because of you, I will never open that cell door again, do you hear me?"

In response, the Man in Grey bowed to the Captain again, this time unanswered. The stranger turned to leave, and Cedrith had to step lively to make it look like he was the leader.

As they reached the door, the dekentar was there and spoke in a growl, "And I will see you again, I promise you."

Judgement regarded him a moment, then nodded once. Before the guard could say any more, he was out and back on the street beneath the gate.

Cedrith scrambled after him, wondering how long he could suspend the doom that seemed to hang over the stranger's head. He felt certain some calamity would strike them with each instant, and yet he could not lie to say he was unwilling to be here. Cedrith was a Sage to the heart, and this youth was not one step short of fascinating to him; he followed him as a dog comes to its master, though knowing he holds a leash. For the moment, the path to the Guild and Square lay in the same direction up the main street, so the sage had a chance to think. His companion seemed perfectly content without conversation and for a time the city simply flowed past them. Cedrith began to wonder why he was feeling increasingly winded, and realized that Solemn Judgement was setting a hard pace, a gait for a soldier or traveler, not a librarian. He was loath to admit this, but it left him with less breath for talk, until they reached the Grand Square.

They arrived before the massive arch; Judgement came to a halt and looked up at the inscription overhead, identical to those on all sides of the grand concourse before them. As Cedrith came up and followed his gaze, the Man in Grey lowered his eyes and turned to his host. With a face set in stone, he remarked simply, "It says 'walk'." After a moment, the Elf burst into hearty laughter, which his companion did not share aloud, and the two men strode into the square together.

Lost in a sea of mid-day humanity, they ambled towards the central fountain, with Judgement looking up and about him in all directions at the huge buildings. Cedrith eyed him while repeating his water-ritual, and began to realize how fully alone the fellow was among humans. The square was as crowded as any noontime, yet people naturally gave track to the Man in Grey, as they had all the way up the street. Folks changed course to avoid intersecting his path, and many stared at his uniform color, large walking staff, and outlandish hat and boots. He never seemed to wander in his course, but stopped at a precise point, one step up on the west side of the fountain. Cedrith fancied he was standing in the exact spot he had been before starting to run. Judgement ignored everyone nearby, scouring the north and west quarters of the square with his gaze, searching without much chance for something or someone. So focused on this purpose, he made the square seem empty. Cedrith sidled up to him on the step, and noted that some few now stared at him as well.

"Why do you think, sir, that running in this Square is forbidden?"

"Surely," replied Judgement at once, "it is in the interest of the common weal."

"Ah, you understand," Cedrith replied with pleasure. "I had not imagined you would be exposed to the principles of law. Indeed, it is a ruling in favor of the greatest good for the greatest number."

Judgement nodded grimly. "For by running, I intercepted several score folk who were about their business, and caused them harm in that they were delayed."

"And moreso," Cedrith added, "you caused no small amount of fear, I do not doubt. For the people of the city know the strength of the Mage Command, and they did wonder at your apparent power to defy it."

Judgement looked directly at the sage then, and measured the weight of this. He nodded again, but the sage could see there was more, of course. An objection, which needed to testify.

"But you thought you saw a crime about to be committed, did you not?"

Silence from the Man in Grey.

"And surely, you wonder if justice were truly being served in this."

Still the youth said nothing, and only regarded Cedrith with a slightly narrowed brow.

"By the moment, man! You wished to save a life, did you not?"

"Certes, Eldest, you are laying a trap for me."

"Cedrith, young Judgement, I pray you. Well and here," the sage had to chuckle, "I was, in truth, thinking I have the better of this argument. Shall we dispute the point?"

The look Judgement gave him showed no hint of humor except in his eyes. "Aye, sir. But in order that I shall not be so easily outmaneuvered, let us switch positions."

"But you are new among us, young Judgement, and know nothing of Conar's traditions. That, in fact, is what I hoped to show you."

"Let us see what I can gather from my father's wit, if you will."

Cedrith could only shake his head in disbelief at the determination of the young man. "As you wish, sir. Hem. I put it to you then, that by intervening to save this man's life, you — that is, I — would do far more good than harm caused by some delay, or even a bit of fear."

Judgement nodded, and considered a moment. "But that is only to consider each act separately, as if they could be thrown in a scale and weighed against each other." Cedrith nodded encouragingly and the stranger continued. "If I cause two hundred people to delay, or change their plans, this alters their future, and affects two thousand. And the changes today effect more changes tomorrow. In such a vast and crowded city, the consequences of each act are magnified.

Who is to say a death or more might not be the result of a missed meeting, or a failed delivery, or a false step before a wagon?"

"That is well put, sir, and I see the force of your argument," said Cedrith with formal pleasure. "Our lives affect each other like ripples in a pond, long after the stone has sunk beneath the surface. But think you — all this about the plans altered and the hundreds and the thousands — this is mere speculation. You speak of the chance for greater ill, but I... saw with my own eyes... the man in danger, not someday but today." Cedrith felt the force of Judgement's position as he played advocate for it, and again when he looked upon the stranger felt the weighty, almost painful alone-ness of the youth.

"But urgency, even in sincerity, is no substitute for authority," Judgement said heavily. "The city not only has laws, but a tradition of laws it has maintained for–"

"Nearly forty centuries," Cedrith supplied.

"And to install one's own perception for the common weal is but sheer pride. Even were I a citizen, it were not my place to arrogate the law. We have, after all, men assigned to keep the peace. Men of noble houses," and here the Man in Grey let the point rest between them.

Cedrith recalled the dekentar of the guard, the matter of the crests, and that feeling of dread came stealing back to him. He smiled weakly and said, "Congratulations, young sir. You have won the argument."

"It was the stronger position," Judgement returned without a hint of humor. Then he returned his gaze to the western side of the square, still searching. And Cedrith knew who had really won. He stepped closer and dropped his voice a notch.

"Tell me what you saw."

Judgement regarded him briefly. "He came, I think from there," pointing to the enormous cathedral of Conar on the south side of the Grand Square, "a man all in white, walking along the edge of this open space. One man followed him directly, starting there, and another from that street, a third from the opposite side of that larger one on the west," he said, pointing to other locations far away and far apart. "I noted them because they all seemed to converge on the man; but he turned into the wide street there and I could not see them as they followed."

He turned back to face Cedrith again, and said simply, "So I ran."

"Because you thought they wished him harm."

"Aye. They would kill him if they could."

"Before all these people? And at least one of them a nobleman?"

Judgement heard these points without response or reaction, and Cedrith felt his heart sink again towards that promised calamity. He thought about urging the young man to desist from this madness, but could see the determination on his face. The sage sighed, and muttered a prayer to Conar, that the city's reputation was in his hands now and the Hopelord should start to help if he wanted it saved.

"You say he went down the Harbor Avenue. And came from the cathedral."

"That large marble building over there."

"Have you ever been in a chapel to Conar, or any of the heroes?" His guest shook his head. "Let us go there, then, I pray you. Perhaps there you can learn a little more about your adopted city, what guides us, and how such a thing as you imagine could never be, here." The Man in Grey seemed unimpressed by such blandishments; in desperation, Cedrith added, "And if the man you saw came from the chapel, perhaps someone there will know him." This brought a curt nod, and together they approached the massive portals.

Cedrith did not often attend the enormous cathedral to the Hopelord of Men, nor could he confess to being particularly religious at all. The city of Conar had holy houses to all the heroes, and Cedrith at times took a moment to meditate in a lovely chapel to Ma-Eldar located in the southeastern quarter of the city. He might remark to an Elvish friend in some quiet corner, how the huge, open and declarative nature of the worship of Men was most amusing for its simplicity. "The shallower the dive, the larger the splash," one of them would say and the other chuckle in clever appreciation. However, Cedrith would be lying if he claimed he was never impressed by a visit to the largest church to Conar in the world.

An acolyte within the doors greeted him with the traditional blessing, "May the law protect you," to which Cedrith responded, "And its peace reward you," as he moved up the marble stair to the entrance nave. Within, one connected open space lay before him, shaped in plan like the cross of Hope, with thirty-foot ceilings in each arm and an immense dome rising out of sight at the center to more than twice that height. Cedrith let the clean, lightly scented air fill his lungs and listened to the soft, ever-present music that reached his ears wherever he went: long, solid chords of brass that made him feel capable of anything, notes of triumph already earned, passages that spoke of walls protecting the innocent and evil long ago defeated. He marveled that such notes, seeming as natural and easy as a children's tune while he was here, could never be recalled once he left. He drifted ahead down the aisle and towards the altar, hoping to find a cleric who could assist him with the catechism of his guest. Suddenly, Cedrith noticed he was walking alone.

Looking back, he saw Judgement standing not ten steps in from the door, with his eyes staring past him and towards the ceiling of the central dome straight ahead. Cedrith returned with an apology, but his guest remained still as one struck dumb. Following his gaze, Cedrith could see that Judgement looked towards the central statue of Conar, rising massively behind the altar and extending out of their view above. Fully fifty feet it rose, and only the boots, lower legs, and long cape could be seen from here, plus the sheath of Conar's drawn sword hanging below. No doubt, he has never seen such a colossal carving, Cedrith thought, and gently taking an arm he led him forward.

Judgement went slowly at first, and ever more slowly as their steps advanced, until once again he stopped with the armored chest and shoulders in sight. Judgement's face craned up, and now Cedrith saw something like fear in his mien; he broke their silence to ask, "What is wrong, my friend?"

"Friend?" Judgement whispered without moving his face or eyes. "Who is this? He looks– I–"

"This is the statue of Conar, the Hopelord of Men, founder of the city, and father of us all, Goodman. Surely–"

"But it is not–" Judgement broke in, before interrupting his own unquiet. He abruptly took three steps forward, bringing Cedrith with him now as they entered the central space bringing the head of the statue completely in view. Cedrith looked up with his guest, to see the noble face, the far-seeing eyes and the brave, kindly, powerful radiance of the hero cast in stone. Cedrith knew well that sculptors of Conar had agreed for centuries: no statue of the Hopelord of Men wearing a crown could truly look like him. The massive face conveyed majesty, his eyes saw the shape of order itself and the mouth, composed and quiet, appeared to have just finished speaking The Law, the text of which was inscribed on the podium below him in letters of chiseled gold. Next to Cedrith, Judgement sighed, and looking back the sage could see undisguised relief, and a tint of shame, there on that normally impassive face. Without preamble, Judgement sank to the floor and sat, as if tired.

"Goodman, are you well?" Cedrith cried.

"Not… my father," was the only response. To this mad assertion, the Elvish sage could think of no answer. He stared at his acquaintance, and saw only the final moments of a complete recovery of composure. Once again, the face of the Man in Grey held no emotion, as if he regarded the statue's face to be a role model indeed. There were no seats in the massive chapel, and while some knelt along padded rails set to the sides of the aisles, most stood; the sight of the grey stranger sitting on the floor drew attention. A cleric from the side approached, and though Cedrith gave him a subtle hand-signal to assure that all was well, he continued until he reached the pair as the sage assisted Judgement to his feet.

"May the law protect you both, citizens," the cleric said. "I hope all is well with your friend."

"He is well, learned brother, he's just, ah, new to us, very new, and for a moment–" Cedrith said, mentally flapping about for an excuse.

"Learned brother," said Judgement, evidently recovered. "I am seeking a man who left this chapel perhaps two hours ago."

"Now, friend Judgement," put in Cedrith, "let us not be hasty–"

"He was being followed and I believe his life is in danger."

"What?" cried the cleric, loud enough to gain attention again. "Are you claiming an assault, emanating from this holy place? Who is this man, sir?" he hissed more quietly to Cedrith with an accusing glare.

Cedrith's mortification rose yet another notch, and he inwardly cursed himself for getting entangled in this ongoing avalanche of embarrassment. "He, he's new among us," he explained weakly.

"Sir," asked Judgement, "why are you so moved by my question? Does no man hate another in this entire city?"

"Why, for that, there are a million souls in Conar, young man, and I'm sure they feel every emotion that living beings can imagine. But the law, you must understand, the law is never broken. And of all places, here in the chapel of the Law-Giver himself!"

"It is not to be thought of," Cedrith assured his companion.

"It's out of the question, of course," the cleric agreed. "Any man who harbored the intent to do evil here could be easily discovered by the resources we have."

At this Judgement looked with renewed interest. "You mean, spells such as the Mensor used this morning?" The cleric nodded severely but with pride. "Of course, and better. Instead of waiting for a statement that can be tested for truth, we can also detect the presence of Despair itself, regardless of action or word."

At Judgement's level gaze, the cleric felt the need to prove his claim; he made motions with his hand, forming the shape of a symbol of Hope in the air, and said, "I call upon Conar to Detect Despair." He aimed his spell neutrally before him, but looked keenly on the stranger, as if to be certain of his intent. The air glowed briefly with the symbol he had drawn in blue fire, and a matching aura appeared over Cedrith. Around Judgement, however, the aura was not only blue, but crisp and sharp, so that the cleric's eyes went wide with surprise.

"There," he said, a little shaken, "you are a child of Hope, just, em, new to us surely, and a bit confused." To Cedrith, he whispered, "He actually shows some promise, with an aura like that he might one day–"

"He is here," Judgement interrupted, and pointed back at the entrance to the chapel. There, a tall and handsome youth dressed all in white but soaked to the skin was advancing back down the aisle. His face was carved not unlike that of the statue, full of meaning and a kind of unconscious courage: he merely walked down the aisle, yet his step was that of a soldier carrying out orders. To both sides of him, folks looked on approvingly, and some even rose from kneeling to bow: the noble youth (surely, he was a noble born) ignored all signs and set his focus directly ahead, in seeming at the three men before the altar but in fact at the statue behind them.

"Ah, now it becomes clear," the cleric sighed. "Your friend saw our young devotee Pron Dedicar, who has been demonstrating his piety to Conar for weeks now. The young knight has attracted quite a bit of attention — here, let us stand out of his way — and no doubt your friend — see here!"

Judgement had stepped into the young man's path and spoke quietly to him as he passed. He said only, "I see them," and Cedrith now gave up all hope of avoiding fiasco. If this nobleman was distracted in any way from his devotions by Judgement's mad fancy, all was truly lost for both of them.

The youth, who had ignored everything else, stopped short a moment at Judgement's words, and looked him directly in the eye for perhaps two counts of the music. Then he shook his head meaningfully and passed on, to kneel next to the altar and reach with one hand to touch the foot of Conar himself. An acolyte moved forward with a bowl of water and a plate of bread, but the young noble waved him back with his free hand, and bent his head in prayer.

The cleric now stepped forward and grabbed Judgement with a reproving hand, trying to pull him aside, but without success. Judgement ignored him and scanned instead the back and sides of the entry-hall, and Cedrith knew with a sinking heart what he sought. He hastened to join his companion, remove him from the chapel, try to get him back to the Guild and relative safety; but the grey man saw, and in the same moment moved.

He strode back up the aisle, out of the cleric's grasp and beyond Cedrith's reach unless he chose to run, which he could not bear to do though Judgement had already attracted attention. Reaching the back, Judgement turned to his right and walked directly up to a man standing quietly against the wall, who noted but tried to ignore his approach. As Cedrith caught up, he had only a flash of time for several disjointed images: the height and bearing of the man, the broadsword at his waist, the patch on his cloak — this time with three diagonal swords, still green on a field of gold — and Judgement's fearless stare, his staff at the ready.

"You were there? You've been watching?" Judgement demanded quietly.

At this, the noble could no longer forbear to return his gaze, and with that perfect mixture of confidence and scorn, he said only, "Do I know you, sir?"

Cedrith opened his mouth to speak, to excuse, to introduce, but again Judgement was the faster. To his utter terror, Cedrith heard him say, quietly and steadily, "I call upon Conar to Detect Despair."

There was no air; Cedrith knew he would shortly pass out as his lungs refused to work. Judgement drew the symbol before him with a single finger, and beyond all reason, a flickering image in blue fire remained behind; it shimmered and seemed likely to go out at once, yet its hue was bright and sharp.

"You dare!" the noble spat, his sword-hand quaking in indecision. But to Cedrith's heightened horror, there appeared an aura about the noble's frame: at first it was blue like the symbol, and then it began to shade more to purple, and as the symbol finally disappeared Cedrith could see just the slightest tinct of red.

Less than half an hour later, Cedrith had delivered the finest oratory of his life; at times he felt as if the speech had indeed been for his life. Excuses had been couched, sympathies implored, the king's name invoked more than once; in the end, Conar's tradition of law was responsible, as much as anything, for saving the stranger — and his guide, this time — from arrest. Much was said about Solemn Judgement's lack of discretion, his impolitude, his ignorance of the customs here. Not nearly as much was mentioned about his apparent ability to cast the miracles of preachers without any known tutelage. And as to the result of his investigation, Cedrith knew well enough not to say a single word, whereas his guest was quite accustomed to saying nothing as a matter of course. He and Judgement emerged from the temple free to go, though unwelcome to return.

Cedrith looked up at the brilliant early afternoon sky, the mocking weather, and upon all the people still going about the happy business of living normal lives, and felt as fatigued as if he'd stayed up past midnight. A bit shaky, he sat on the temple steps and took several deep breaths. When he looked up, there was Solemn Judgement, silhouetted by the sun and looking down on his host as if he had been carved in place for shade.

"Where to now?" was all he asked, and Cedrith, lacking the strength to stave off his worst fears any longer, began to giggle in hysteria.

"Perhaps we could visit the king? Is there some deadly insult or challenge you would like to level at him, then?"

Judgement looked on as if he hadn't heard.

"Yes, let us go and seek an audience with Conantis the Twenty-First. He's one hundred and fourth in line since the days of Conar himself to sit the Throne of Man, but I'm sure it should prove no trouble to you to find him conspiring to plunder the poor, or fire the harbor, or the Hopelords know what else!"

As before, the Man in Grey showed no response. Cedrith felt a great deal like weeping. No one else in all this capital was the stranger's host, or likely ever would be. What perverse fate had selected him, and why had he embraced it? The sage recalled his fascination with the youth, and saw him again, standing there with the Grand Square, all the bustling thousands, the whole city, the entire world as a backdrop in opposition to his single will. He was indeed entirely alone. This sobering thought righted his heart somewhat, and standing with effort, he stepped up next to the stranger.

"Goodman Judgement, why did you cast a miracle on that knight in there? Did you really seek to prove your idea to yourself?"

Judgement looked back at Cedrith with a gaze steady and strong but without malice. "To you," he said.

Cedrith gaped at this, without comprehending. "To me?"

"You said you were my friend," said the Man in Grey. "I wanted you to be able to trust me." When Cedrith could think of no response to this, Judgement nodded as if accepting defeat, and turned to leave in no particular direction across the square.

Cedrith called and ran after him at once. "Goodman Judgement! Stay– a moment, Solemn Judgement, I pray you." As the stranger stopped and turned back to face the elf, Cedrith searched his soul for a course to steer by.

"Goodman, I– I apologize. Your methods are, they are very direct, and I have not thought how my actions reflected… I want to help you, sir. I cannot in all honesty claim that I credit your tale– you understand, I hope? I believe, I presently hope that you are simply mistaken– as the guards were about you this morning. It is a possibility, yes? At any rate, there is no immediate harm to the young man you saw, we have established that. He kneels before the statue of Conar, and no man can threaten him now, as surely as I know my name, he is safer than the king himself. And if you insist on continuing to investigate, may I ask you a favor then?"

Judgement nodded, and Cedrith drew breath to continue.

"Will you come with me now, to the Sages Guild? Will you come along, and stay for at least a time with us?"

"Eldest–"

"My name is Cedrith, Solemn Judgement, please call me Cedrith."

"–I have told you, I sincerely believe this man to be in danger. That no one else apprehends this merely increases the responsibility lying on me, to my mind. Why should I abandon this place and go with you now?"

Once again, Cedrith realized he would have to argue a brilliant thesis, as he had already done three times this day. If only he had been given the chance to prepare for any except the first! He took a deep breath and plunged in.

"There are three chief reasons. First, my colleagues will be very interested in meeting and speaking with you, sir. You will receive food, shelter and I guarantee a friendlier welcome than any you have had so far."

He could see that Judgement was as moved by this argument as the cliff is by a breeze, and congratulated himself that he had decided to argue in ascending order of importance.

"Second, I intend to introduce you to the highest ranking person I know. She is Guildmistress of all the Healers of Conar, very highly respected among both the Sages and the clerical orders of the city. She is also," he put in quietly, "a true friend and a warm soul, a former Gypsy, in fact."

This point scored, he could tell. Judgement retained his face of stone, but looked tempted all the same. "Can she teach me," he asked, "about the forces of magic?"

"Assuredly, she would be the best of tutors, and I miss my guess or she would be most interested in your progress."

"What about the youth in white?" Judgement asked. "Can she tell me about this ritual he observes, the piety and its meaning?"

"Well, as to that, I'm sure it is personal–"

"He was wet, why is that?"

"I don't know."

"Can you tell me about the badge the man in the temple wore? Is he related to the dekentar? Does the gold background signify a similar rank, or perhaps a noble family? Do the swords always mean the same thing, or does the position–"

"Peace, Goodman, I beg you!" Cedrith chuckled. "There is no single person, most likely, who can satisfy the depth and breadth of your curiosity. Though I think it more likely that you will escape arrest if you spend some time among books rather than people." Cedrith followed Judgement's face, which could not hide his disappointment at this reminder. "And that brings me to the third reason." Judgement looked up and Cedrith knew he had set the hook now, and had only to reel him in.

"As you recall, I promised that in the Guild they would teach you to read once again."

Judgement nodded, and gestured that his host should precede him to the Guild. As they walked, Cedrith saw again how people quietly parted, glared, drew back, and how little his companion seemed to notice or care. He could hear him quietly humming an inspiring tune, something familiar, stirring, encouraging. Judgement was paying no heed to his own voice, just humming in a distracted way. With a shock, the sage realized it was the music from the chapel.

Late that night, his candle burning low, Cedrith slogged back to his cell with slow steps and aches all over his body. He had introduced Judgement to members of the Guild, and told over all his news several times while his guest had stood there like a pet ape, saying nothing and watching everyone as if he expected another arrest. Cedrith entered his quarters, putting his books and quill-box down on the side-table. He had set up a study desk in the common room off the library stacks for Judgement to use: with some rummaging and a lot of help from Guild members here, they had located a half-dozen primers on the common tongue and a few books on simple subjects, such as stories of the heroes for Judgement to practice on. No doubt his progress would be slow, but the lad was clearly very intelligent, and had a willpower that was indomitable. Plus he already knew the rules of written speech; once he mastered the pronunciation of the alphabet, Cedrith thought he might pass the first year's learning in a month, or perhaps a little more. The greatest difficulty was that no one knew his lettering at all, and so could not assist him with those vital first steps. A fascinating study; Cedrith already flirted with the idea of writing up the young man's progress for his Guild.

Cedrith sat heavily on his bed to undress. He was tempted to just lie down in his clothing, and for a time he tried it out. Bone-tired as he was, he chuckled to recall how he had shown Judgement to another such room, for his use as a guest while he stayed at the Guild. The young man had assumed the quarters were to be shared, and laid his cloak out on the floor for a mattress. Cedrith needed to repeat himself to make him understand that all the vast space, some six paces on a side, was his to use. He had left the young man there, and resolved to meet him at breakfast to lead him to the refectory and study area; he would need a little help getting around in the early days, and Cedrith felt true sympathy for him. He was nothing if not interesting, this Judgement fellow. Cedrith tried to imagine what he would be like in a year or two, and utterly failed to come up with a place for someone so inflexible, so intelligent and yet hard-edged. More likely, he would end up arrested in less than a week — Cedrith made the sign to avert Despair at the unworthy thought, but he tingled with it and all the day's events nonetheless.

After a few more moments of lying back, Cedrith felt sleep coming on indeed. He richly desired to fall into that quiet world where at last no more ingenious mental feats would be required of him, but this Elf was in love, and the greatest power of all must be served. Rising with a groan, Cedrith returned to his desk and took out his quill, rubbing his face with both hands and trying to think of how to begin.

Dearest Kia, he wrote at last, *You would be quite surprised at the things that have happened to me today, my love…*

Strength of Conviction

The weather had been foul in the vale of Maladon for nearly a fortnight, sticky and hot even in darkness, the dispiriting summer season where air hangs heavy and even lovers argue. More precisely, lovers in Maladon would have argued, had there been any. The planted fields around town, and the clear-cut copses beyond, lay still. By day the humans took cover behind walls of stone and fire; most of the animal life had been hunted out by the vale's scaly ruler. Only five beings moved across the ground, far from the town and near the heart of peril.

The scree up the valley's southern side offered scarce cover, a litter of sharp-edged, broken rocks that slipped underfoot and shaved skin off the hands. The drifting eldritch smoke, dark and choking, carried a stench of smelted bugs enough to make a strong man gag, much less an Elf with instinctive racial fear of any giant insectoid. But for once Mhoral held his peace, for no one is well advised to make much noise within fifty paces of a dragon's cave.

Treaman took a shallow breath and stood slowly to reconnoiter. The muggy weather made a haze of the far distance, but he could see back north across the vale nearly a league, to the central stream that meandered past the walled town where some two hundred women still survived. Only women; the stream fed a lake in the haze beyond the town, and on the main island there, less than eighty men desperately scraped for survival in a tiny wooden stockade. The valley sides were clear to the end of his vision — what the monster had not destroyed, the humans had cut for fuel, for walls, for weapons and for smoke-defense. The young woodsman saw the stump-meadows and felt a pang at the wasteful consumption: a generation would pass before there could be trees here again.

Turning back south, he wiped the sweat away and scanned the few remaining trunks and bushy copses nearby, mostly scraped of leaves, some twisted, broken and blackened by great force. From the cave ahead — a rip in the steepest section of the valley wall just higher than a man — smoke issued forth thickly but at intervals. Perhaps the winds inside the cave turned contrary, or perhaps it snored. The skies were clear, for now, but Treaman scanned them an extra moment to be sure. When he nodded to Haltar, the leader pointed the crouching party back along the trail to a rocky cut where they could confer.

"Alive or dead?" he interrogated the woodsman.

"Yes," Treaman grinned back, "absolutely one or the other."

The strapping warrior smirked in uncharacteristic frustration and hitched at his plate hauberk. Everyone sensed the difference in mood since the last few fights against the giant insects when the wood and fire ran low.

"He's still alive, of course," snapped Mhoral. "Nothing can kill a dragon."

"Except brave adventurers," Bildon chimed in brightly from a small rock he had converted to a chair.

"We're truly going in there?" Linya asked with real concern.

"These people need that dragon dead," Haltar said with his usual poker-face; and, as usual, Mhoral laughed in it.

"Those people needed the bugs killed," he hissed with a shiver. "We need the dragon, or its treasure, that's why you're leading us up there to get burned."

For a moment, it looked as if Haltar would rise to the bait of the helmeted Elf as he never had before. He shook his head sharply with drops of sweat spinning off his shoulder-length hair, and hitched his armor again, stiffly, powerfully flexing his arms. Treaman thought he'd never seen him so… impressive. He was concerned for Mhoral; perhaps today the back-talk would go too far. Something was definitely different, the woodsman thought even as his mind fled the idea of fighting a dragon. Their leader controlled himself and continued to plan an assault; Treaman looked him over closely, and… yes, he did seem larger than ever. His armor suit was tight, his shoulders even broader, his legs more defined. Wishful thinking, with a dragon-fight in the offing? The woodsman looked away before Bildon caught him staring; there'd be no end of the comments then.

"The dragon will be bad enough," Haltar admitted, "but the last thing we ask is to encounter more warnets while we're about it. Treaman, I need you to scout around above the cave mouth and see; the people of the town have never tried to clear this area."

"For obvious reasons," Bildon observed.

"Do you want any help?" Haltar asked, and Treaman shook his head, putting down his small tight pack and hefting his spear before setting out.

Behind him Bildon quietly called, "Less than a day this time, eh?" Treaman grinned; in truth, he loved the solitude and a chance to explore new places.

Toe-stepping half-bent in a wide circle around the cave-mouth, he split his attention between the cleft and the skies overhead; the grinding buzz of the warnets usually came too late to avoid a skyborne attack. All around he could see the vague outlines of a good land, but the scarring was everywhere. Trees snapped off and charred, rock-slides broken and partially melted, the earth churned up and even the grass thinned by burning. Not all of it was fire, he realized —

the smell and the character of the destruction told the woodsman there was something strongly acidic about the scaled monster who ruled the vale. None of the spoor indicated that it had passed here recently, however.

As he climbed beyond the level of the cave towards the valley-top, Treaman did see fresh animal signs, of a kind he had come to know since the party stumbled into this vale over a week ago. Quill-thin jabs in the earth, small piles of scentless fewmets, and another sort of odor wafted his way; he crouched behind some brush to scan more carefully. The warnets, whose sudden depredations had temporarily displaced the dragon in the fears of the vale's inhabitants, had always been present according to the tales they had heard in Maladon. Speaking to the women there — now undertaking all the tasks of guarding and fighting without their men — Linya had learned that the warnets always had a season, late fall, when they flew in greater frequency and attacked with less provocation. Winter killed off nearly all of them, it seemed, as well as another giant insect of the vale, a ground-crawling ant-like thing with thick hair and a powerful sting, that chewed crops and wood if not burned out.

Most years, the vale's people had set up a few traps or fire-lines to keep out the bug threats. But in the last three summers, things had gotten steadily worse, despite the lack of an appearance from the dragon. More warnets, more frequent attacks, and ever-more-angry arguments among the survivors — for now, the eagle-sized insects swooped down to attack and kill in all seasons.

These were the "wings across the sky" that Trainertown had heard rumor of from the merchant last year. The group had been relieved to learn it, until Haltar offered to help hunt for the bug-swarms in return for shelter and aid; they'd all known hard shifts since then. His master plan, of course, was to clear the plague away, then get a crack at this cave, and the wurm at least three hundred years old who still might live there. The warnets were quick fliers with steely skin and a vicious bite, venomed for extra pain that numbed arms and legs for hours. By comparison, the hairy stinging ants were not terribly fast and often found in small numbers or even alone; keep your wits about you and two good blows usually did for one, excepting Bildon. But their sting was disorienting, paralyzing, and deathly; Haltar, Linya and Mhoral had each felt it and the pain took the better part of a day to fade.

Treaman came out on the level hilltop, with the cliff of stone to his left. Perhaps forty feet beneath his boots the dragon coiled, and Treaman's legs and vitals tingled with every slow, soundless step he took across the outcrop. Looking down into the vale, he saw the town walls and the haze beyond; closer to the base of the cliff jutted the rock his party sheltered behind. South of him, the hilly terrain rose a little further and then leveled out into rocky wildland that he knew would soon bring him into the Percentalion's waste. Dragon to one side, alone and lost on the other; the young woodsman wondered which was worse. He would vote for scurrying back to the town with nothing but women in it and waiting to die of old age, but duty called.

He noticed a thin plume of smoke up here, seeping from the level plain above the cave several rods back from the cliff. A small hole in the rock, probably connecting to the cave, let out drifts of heavy black smoke like a chimney. Working his way from rock to trunk as cover, the scout positioned himself within a dozen steps to watch and listen. At first there was no sound, and he took this for an unnatural sign. Normally a wooded hillside such as this would be replete with small game, birds, normal insects. But today, there was not even a breath of wind, though there was… something, just beyond the edge of his senses. Treaman took a deep breath to relax, another to focus, and then held his third while putting his sleeve over his eyes.

He let the sound of his own pulse quiet, and made his senses pour through his ears alone.

There — a distant buzz, far and muted. Low and not urgent, not yet; and definitely more than one creature. So the warnets were here, as the ant-things made no sound. There was no cover nearby to conceal them; as contrary as it seemed they had to be in the hole. Maybe if he could approach quietly there would be a chance to plug the crack against them and then the fumes could kill or at least daze the inhabitants, as the women of Maladon had learned to do with their clever smoke cones and pipes. Even as he approached, however, Treaman realized it was a bad idea to hope for much smoke, given its likely source.

And the bad idea became even worse, when at only eight feet away something began to emerge from the hole. Treaman froze with his hands tight on the spear, as an insect large and furry as a cat nosed its way up into the air. It labored and groped, seemingly not under its own power, and the young woodsman felt the same disgust he had all this past week, as its antennae curled in different directions, tasting the air. Treaman had had the sense to approach from downwind, and now he prepared to step and strike, but the buzzing got louder and on reflex he searched the air above for a warnet. Nothing — the sound was below him, and as the hairy ant emerged completely from the smoke-hole, the young woodsman retreated a pace in fear when the warnet came out behind it. The two insects began to circle and nip at each other, but Treaman could hear more buzzing from below. Risking the movement, he continued to step back; he reached a small rock and huddled there as a half-dozen more insects emerged. For a time, they seemed to make war each upon the other; three of the bright orange-and-black striped ants tangling with another four or five sleek glossy warnets; but it was more.

The ebony fliers, while apparently attacking the ants, seemed in no mood to cooperate, and even took bites at each other whenever in range. Treaman remembered the time several days earlier, down near the lake, when they'd come upon a scene like this, warnets in battle with the furry ants. Haltar had hailed that — correctly, Treaman thought — as an opportunity to team up on the hated flying bugs, and the group had taken them out rather quickly. The only price paid was a couple of stings from the ants.

As one warnet went down under a rival's bite, Treaman began to understand. A warnet, having herded one of the striped ants away from the others, pushed it around and then, with a short flying hop, came down on its victim's back where its stinger was of no use. Seizing it with its legs, the warnet soared up into the air. Treaman was dumbfounded. He had won; why not bite its head off, why fly up to drop it to its death? Suddenly the warnet was stinging, hard and strong — but Treaman had never seen the flying bugs use a stinger before: he hadn't noticed any when checking the corpses. Now the other surviving warnets also took to the sky in pairings, and the puzzle unearthed itself.

The woodsman stood up, rapt and watching the macabre mating flight of the warnets. Without mercy or pleasure the fliers penetrated their partners, over and over well beyond need as their buzzing deepened, intensified, then faded and dropped. It was over in less than a minute, and the pairs cycled a bit wobbly back to the outcrop as if their mates were suddenly too heavy for them. They tumbled on landing, with a dozen legs scrambling for purchase in the air before the hairy females managed to get upright. Without a moment's hesitation or a backward glance, all three of them made for the hole, to clamber back in with each abdomen showing a spot of white beneath the stinger; a fertilized egg ready to be laid at once. The males sprawled where they landed, spent and slowing. Treaman figured they would not last an hour based on what he knew. But then, no sense taking chances; he strode forward with his spear hefted high and thrust a half-dozen times at the joints between body-segments. Chopping and slicing, he left the stench of dead warnet behind him as he moved on across the outcrop and down the other side. At his back, legs still slowly writhed and antennae quivered. Treaman was not without a tremble or two himself.

Nothing remarkable presented itself on the western side of the cliff. Treaman took a chance and trotted, kicking loose some gravel without making much noise. He slowed and resumed toe-stepping as he came nearer the jut, part of his game with Bildon who was also very sharp in his senses. Just once, he'd like to surprise him. From a dozen rods, he could make out the long, scritching rasp of the whetstone on steel. That would be Haltar endlessly honing his bastard sword; razor-sharp, and of course all the more likely to notch in hard combat. It was an old habit and an old argument, which Treaman knew well. He heard it as he came closer, certain that Bildon couldn't sense him over the noise.

"How much sharper can one blade get?" Mhoral whined.

"No sense being unprepared." The scritching continued under the sighs and tired chuckles.

"One blow, maybe two, and then you'll have a notch, or maybe it will snap altogether. Remember that garruk with the iron-banded club."

"That's the price of victory. I will get another."

"Hmph, if we live. If one blow, or maybe two, is enough."

"If it isn't, my sword's condition won't be your biggest worry."

Treaman crawled on all fours to a spot slightly above the group; peering over the rocky jut, he could see the foursome in a circle, and the picture matched his anticipation. Haltar sat with his splendid new bastard sword across his knees, rubbing the whetstone down its edge in long relentless strokes; Mhoral perched with his foot bouncing nervously, Bildon lay back against the rock as if sleeping, and Linya was gazing down like one too shy to speak.

"Linya, do we have enough torches, or any more of those fire-nets?" the foot-knight asked. Treaman realized the mage was looking down, not in modesty, but actually at herself. Realizing she had been spoken to, Linya straightened up and Treaman felt a shock as he saw the curves of her body against the tunic. Novar's manhood, was she really that shapely? And how could he have missed it? A thought walked up to Treaman's mind and knocked, but he couldn't find the door to let it in.

"We have one net and four torches," she said with a soft confidence she'd never shown before. "If there are a lot of those bugs left, we'll run out; and my fire-spells are limited, as you know." That sounded more like the mage Treaman had fought alongside — always pointing to her limits, willing but unsure of herself.

"Ideas?" Haltar asked, looking around. Bildon chuckled, but gestured for others to speak first.

"I know an enchantment for sleep, more powerful than the one I've used before," Linya said. "The study-tomes say it could work on a giant — if there were still any — but I doubt it would suffice for a dragon. I don't know how it might work if there were a number of smaller creatures…"

"Wondrous fine," Mhoral cut in acidly. "Her spell puts the bugs to sleep but wakes the dragon. All's well, though; Haltar here will thump him soundly upon his invulnerable mask and he'll surrender immediately."

Haltar stood to re-sheath his weapon and towered over the Elf. "I'm open to suggestions."

"You think so!" Mhoral spat back with unexpected heat, standing too in an effort to erase his leader's size advantage. "You walk in there with an adult dragon, you'll discover how suggestible you are. One glance into those orbs and you'll stroll willingly into its open mouth."

"Say it with me!" Bildon chimed in, and Linya played along, chanting, "Never look a dragon in the eye!"

"The whole venture is insane," Mhoral raved, as if trying to annoy Haltar on the point of his unchallenged leadership. "Wurm lairs are carved narrow and deep, we'll be lucky to come at him two abreast. One shot — one — is what we'll get. And a five-count after it wakes up, when you're standing there with that oversized strap-razor snapped in two pieces, we'll need to know what to do next."

"Proposal?" Haltar said quietly with his muscular arms akimbo and that crooked, dangerous grin creeping onto his face.

Mhoral tried to laugh, failed, and said, "Tunnel in from the side, give us another avenue to attack."

"Twenty years!" Haltar cried.

"I can wait," Mhoral rejoined, another time-honored tactic; suggesting the decades-long plan to mortal Men.

"You can hang by your privates, if anyone can find them," Haltar spat back, with more than his usual volume. "We are going to assail that cave and face a dragon, Elf. The first to do so since Sir Provental of Shilar, and we will succeed where he failed. Follow the plan—"

"Your plan! The one that uses comrades like swords. And when we're nicked in there, you'll throw us away and get—urchk!"

Like a cobra, Haltar's left arm snapped out and grasped Mhoral by the neck; the foot-knight lifted him bodily off the ground without seeming effort, and the helmed immortal, unable to speak, could summon no miracle to his defense. Bildon leaped from his seat and took one jump up at Haltar's arm but couldn't get a clean grip on the armored plates. Linya sat back unbreathing, aghast or perhaps enthralled.

"Treaman," Bildon said calmly but urgently, "come out, we need you."

Treaman's vitals felt watery, but that thought he'd wanted to have kicked in the door at last. He gathered his breath and jumped down from the rock, landing next to Haltar's shoulder. Struggling for calm, he said, "I'd like to point out something you may have missed."

Haltar held Mhoral like a wriggling fox and turned his head to regard Treaman. The woodsman knew he'd have little chance against the party leader in a fight; he needed to reach the man's mind, now that his legendary temper was aroused.

"You've grabbed Mhoral by the neck before," Treaman said conversationally, as Haltar continued to regard him, "but you've always had to use two arms to lift him off the ground."

The massive warrior flicked a glance at the Elf in his grasp, still choking and working with both arms to loosen the steel grip of just one of Haltar's hands. Smoothly and unhurriedly, he lowered him back to earth and let him go, whereupon Mhoral sat down with a human level of clumsiness. He raised his visor and took deep breaths but Treaman pushed his gambit with the leader.

"You," Treaman accused with a stabbed finger into Haltar's chest, "you weren't stung once by those ground-ants the other day. I pulled one stinger, in your foot. But you had others."

Haltar, surprised, gave a shrug, his hauberk still not fitting him. "There may have been three or four, I'm fine—"

"Where? NOW!" Treaman shouted, without making a move to look. No one in the party could force Haltar to do something he didn't want; he sometimes wrestled Treaman, Mhoral and Bildon at once for amusement, and did not always lose. The slender young woodsman felt fully afraid, but kept his eyes locked into his leader's for a long moment. With a lip-gesture that said "who cares," Haltar turned and hiked up his chain mail above the waist. Treaman cleared back the tunic, and there, just above the bottom rib, something black the width of a nail jutted a half-inch from his spine.

"Idiot," Treaman commented in a low voice. "Brave, manly, moron. This warnet stinger has been poisoning you for nearly three days."

"Warnets have no stingers, this was when I fell—"

"Male warnets have no stingers. Hold still, you colossal waste of food and air." Treaman had the upper hand now, as the closest thing to a surgeon in the party, and he used his pent-up fear to lambaste his leader back to a more rational state.

He rummaged in his pack for the root-knife he used to collect plants, and carefully dug a circle around the outside of the stinger. Haltar had no bigger reaction than if someone were combing his hair, but demanded an explanation, which Treaman recounted. The others were amazed to learn the ant-things were females, but Treaman was ahead of them.

"The venom must emphasize gender; men more manly, women more feminine. I don't know how, but it's a recent change, and it's probably what drove the people here apart."

"Makes sense," Bildon put in. "They said they were disagreeing about the tactic to fight the warnets. Women wanted to keep pumping smoke but the men were working on some kind of engine to throw lots of darts."

"Both good ideas," Haltar remarked over his shoulder. "Not much wood left around, but these people just can't seem to, I don't know, to argue properly."

"Those men on the island," Linya said with feeling, "I could tell all they wanted was to have me. I couldn't talk to any of them, not like the women of Maladon, they were reasonable."

No word rose to answer this from the four men, who exchanged glances while Treaman continued to work on Haltar. Finally, Bildon offered lukewarm agreement. "Well, yes, the men were quite interested in you. I mean, who wouldn't be, Linya? You're a fine-looking female. For a human, of course. You may not have noticed, when you were talking to the women, but, em, Haltar here got quite a few, um, glances too. But it was more as if… those men couldn't talk to you. I don't know, you big people are strange, but they definitely preferred to talk to us fellows."

"Yes, bad news for you, Linya," Treaman said, "I'm afraid you may have a stinger too. Though I'm not sure how I, uh, I mean, the right way to—"

"No," she said firmly, "I know I don't have a stinger in me. I was stung that one time, that's it." But she arranged her tunic a bit self consciously.

"Well," Bildon said, "you are smaller, maybe it affected you more. Astor's privates, we had better keep them away from me then!"

"One sting," Mhoral quietly offered, "and you might grow to reach my chin."

"I can reach your chin just fine from here," the halfling promised, patting his sling. The group humor was coming slowly back.

"And you?" Treaman asked Mhoral while still focusing on his surgery. "Just the one time?"

Mhoral nodded. "I threw up the whole night, though. I don't know how many of those I could take." And he gazed on Haltar's bleeding back with a look between awe and illness.

"Alright, boss, I'm ready," Treaman said, putting away the knife and taking a firm grip on the bloody stinger with three fingers. The leader put his hands on the rock and tilted his head side to side as if loosening for a bout he expected to win. Treaman set his jaw and said, "I want you to start counting and go up as high as you can."

Obediently, the knight said, "One…" and just waited until everyone started laughing. In the midst of it, Treaman pulled as hard as he could, and five inches of stinger came free with a meaty ripping sound.

Clapping one hand over the wound and pressing hard, Treaman waited as Linya brought bandages from his pack. Haltar, after a tight gasp, distinctly pronounced the word, "ouch" and then quietly waited for the dressing. When he straightened up, he looked around at the group, and nodded once to Mhoral, his version of an apology. The matter was settled and they were a party again.

"Now then, let's get into that cave," he said, adding, "while I'm still big." The group took seats in the lee of the jut and there was silence for a time. Haltar passed one hand over his chin, pulling his face into that serious mask that usually preceded an understatement.

"There may be certain difficulties with a frontal assault."

Everyone grinned like wolves at this, and Bildon made a rolling motion with one hand, meaning "go on."

"Treaman's report, in addition, means there are warnets in the cave as well. Dealing with both at the same time is surely… a problem."

Again Bildon rolled his hand, and Haltar turned to regard him. Smiling lightly, the halfling stood so that his head was nearly next to Haltar while sitting. He waved his hand from Haltar's mouth towards his ear, and said, "So, what do you need?"

Now Haltar broke into a grin as well. "I need… someone very brave."

More gestures from Bildon, and a wider smile.

"Someone to scout the interior of that cave, alone; skilled, and quiet, and reckless of danger."

Bildon's mouth almost divided his head in half, and his eyes were shining like one insane.

"Someone with a fireproof suit of armor—"

"Hey! That doesn't matter, my hands and feet are still exposed, to say nothing of my head."

"Yes," Mhoral put in, "by all means, let's not say anything about his head."

Bildon spun on the Elf with a warning finger. "Don't make me take this armor off."

"No!" Linya cried with concern, "Haltar, don't let him go in there! Stealthics are danger-drunk, you know that. We should go together."

"My dear, I assure you I was born for this."

"Don't die for it! Not without your armor! Don't—"

"It's fine, it's fine, Bildon," Haltar reassured him. "Without question, you are undertaking something perilous beyond measure. The suit makes no difference, we agree. Yes. Astor will be proud of you."

"Won't he though?" Bildon breathed with satisfaction, and hitched his belt before stepping out.

He got several feet off, when Treaman said, "Of course, if you die quietly, we'll never get word." The halfling stopped and turned back on this, staring down on the woodsman with annoyance.

"I never knew you cared about me," Bildon said with a wry face.

"Well," Treaman responded roughly, "about your hands and feet anyway". He took his spear and stepped behind the Stealthic with a grin on his face. "I'll just tag along in case the rest of the world needs to hear how brave you were. I'll stay back a few paces, you'll never know I was there."

"That would be the first time," Bildon quipped.

"You lie, you were just guessing I was nearby a minute ago." Bildon smiled broadly then and the two friends turned up the trail to approach the cave.

No more words; the Stealthic and the Woodsman glided up the rocky scree without a sound. Sticky with more than the heat, Treaman felt fear crowding in on his mind as the insane, hopeless prospect of facing the dragon came ever closer by his own footsteps. If the dragon of Maladon were truly three hundred years old, then perhaps there were some Elves in Mendel its equal in years. Mhoral put on a great show of mystery, but Treaman felt sure he was less than seventy. Man was lucky to live that long, yet this wurm would be considered a young adult among its rare peers in the world. Legends said Calliisse, in her lair near the top of Skysword, still lived, and that she had deigned to speak with Areghel two-score centuries ago.

The scouts reached the side of the cave. Bildon flashed some of the simpler hand-signs he had taught Treaman for situations like this.

'there- I- alone- you stay/ wait'

Treaman showed numbers with his fingers: *'five- I walk'*

Bildon nodded and stepped to the cave-mouth. Treaman could see that the lower third, almost the lower half, of the cleft was filled in with gravel. The men of the island, questioned at length by Haltar, had claimed the beast was wide as a wagon, and longer than three laid end-to-end when last seen in 1992. There was no way a creature that large could enter and leave the cave without scraping these stones away, so how did they come to be here? Incredibly, Bildon moved lightly up that barrier without dislodging a single rock; he stepped over and disappeared into the soundless dark. Truly, Treaman marveled in his fear, the halfling was an extraordinary athlete, round cheeks and stubby legs or no. He tried to hear the warnets but even with his senses calmed he could not make out the buzzing. Maybe it was too far back, or perhaps the males were all dead.

The time dripped by, an eternity. Treaman thought about dragon-fights of legend, like the tale told in his childhood days in Novar. The great mage Senetear came from the Crystal City to deal with the wurm of Shimmer Lake in the fifteenth century. Sailing alone to the island where the dragon laired with his mate, the mage had refused all assistance, claimed the deed as his alone, sent by the Circle of Five and determined to bring back enough fame to earn a place among them. Hundreds watched from the shores of the lake a league away as unearthly lights flashed inside the abandoned fortress, once used by the thane of Despair Trekarg. Cacophonous explosions rocked and collapsed its upper towers. All that night, the longest of the year in the dead of winter, the battle raged; and when it was done, one of the mighty dragons was dead, the other sore pierced and could fly no more. But Senetear, pushed adrift in his boat and found by the watching crowd the next day, came ashore a child in a man's body. The dragon had fought him with mind as well as fire and claw, and in that battle it was the victor. Stripped of all his lore, the mage had mundane memory intact but lacked the skill to read and write; he could not even speak in the Common Tongue. Weeping like a babe as he stuttered to express himself, he thrashed about for two days like a lunatic, and finally threw himself into the water clasping a great stone, preferring to meet his end at the bottom of the lake rather than start again at the bottom of life.

The fear kept mounting; Treaman suddenly realized he would have to void. With trembling hands he adjusted his drawers and faced the stone wall, letting the urine pulse soundlessly down between his feet. Finished, he still felt the same tension and weakness in his gut, and decided the time was up. It was enter now or never be able. Shaking badly, he stepped four quiet paces to the ebon cleft, took a deep, gulping breath and lifted his leg over the gravel, before bringing the rest of his body through and into the black.

Within six steps, the cave took a sharp turn and even reflected daylight from outside failed to reach. Treaman knew, contrary to the tales of city-folk, that pitch black is simply that. The Dwarves could see somewhat in the utter darkness of the underground, and Elves beneath the night sky saw as well as at dusk. But Men need light; his eyes were never going to get accustomed to this inky air. The stench of acid, warnet, smoke and other unknown things distracted him somewhat from the need to be terrified. Leading with his toes, he slowly stepped once, twice, and felt a wall under one outstretched hand. It was surprisingly smooth, as if worked though not by tools, and trailing along he felt no sharp edge or crevice. The floor too was no worse than bumpy under his feet. Without sight, he kept straining to hear, and while no noise stepped out for recognition he did… feel a sound, a nameless deep susurration or tone. Treaman's mind began a wild imagining, that this was the first drawn-out syllable of the dragon saying its own name, and that to hear it entire would mean the end of his sanity.

As if to prove his madness, those false-star bursts before the eyes that men see in the utter dark began to give way. Treaman fancied, against reason, he could dimly see. He stopped to give time for the illusion to clear, but it showed stubbornness, faintly but consistently suggesting the upper walls of the cavern. Not enough to distinguish Linya from Mhoral, probably, but enough to pick his way. Unless his mind was lost to him, there was a gentle corner ahead; he assigned trust to this image and let it guide his feet forward. One step before the turn, his foot lightly scraped something flat on the floor that moved under his foot. Leaning down, his fingers closed on a coin; his touch could not detect the cross of Hope that had been struck on all silver currency since the turn of the millennium. This, then, was the start of the lure that had brought Haltar here. The dragon of Maladon was said to be resting on a lair-treasure of substantial size. While the roads had been somewhat clear, the tribute it received from the humans of the vale had kept it peaceful. But as trade dried up and beggared the town, the wurm broke its truce and plundered. Worth his life and those of his companions? Treaman staggered with the shock, and wanted nothing else than to reel back out of this cave. Loyalty to Haltar could not have impelled him a step further. But a gasp from Bildon nearby pulled him onward.

Around the corner, Treaman saw another long stretch of cave — farther than he had supposed and still with the surfaces smooth. The nearer left side where he stood formed a kind of lower level or gentle well, whereas to the right and deeper in, the rock rose steeply several feet to block further view. Here was more light, not from any source down the cavern but gently emanating from all the ceiling. Moss or magic, the woodsman neither knew nor cared, for a few feet away he made out a bundly, misshapen form on the ground in silent struggle.

The woodsman dimly saw the severed bodies of two ground-ants; the legs were barely moving and he smelled their ichor oozing onto the cavern floor. At the base of the lower level, Bildon was engaged with a third. Spear in one hand, Treaman stepped closer and a few more coins pressed into the sole of his boot; another step and Treaman kicked something that could only be a dagger, which clattered away with a thunderclap. Incredibly, Bildon was actually riding the back of the repellent thing. Almost as wondrous, the bug was holding up a halfling three times her size and at least eight times her weight. But the stinger could not reach him now, as Bildon threaded his sling beneath its head-joint like a garrote and pulled back hard.

Too late, Treaman saw another female warnet crawling over the edge of the upper level, heading at first to one side of the struggle but then dropping something from its mouth and turning to attack. Still encumbered with fear, Treaman could neither run nor throw; he stepped closer and raised his spear to thrust. Bildon's hardest effort succeeded in severing the neck joint of his foe again, and he rolled back off its abdomen, directly beneath the new attacker. Treaman's blow penetrated its midsection, the thorax, with a splutch of spilling fluid, just after it sunk its stinger directly into Bildon's thigh. The halfling choked his scream as best he could, but again the echoes seemed cacophonous. Treaman fell down next to his friend and wrenched the stinger free; but the venom was in, and even as he worked to press as much as he could back out, Bildon started to shiver and choke. Treaman dragged him back across the lowest part of the rock well, as far as possible from the raised edge and the lord of the lair beyond.

Glancing back to check for more warnets, Treaman labored silently to push out any more venom if there, but the toxin was delivered by now. Bildon hugged himself as if cold, and quietly spat a little froth onto the floor. His eyes blazed with intellect, however, and whether he could not speak or wanted to maintain the silence, he began to signal with his hand.

'alone-I-alone [emphatic]'

Treaman nearly lost his temper at this and flashed back: *'you-alone-dead'*

Bildon may have shrugged, though he shivered hard; definitely he grinned tightly. He raised a shaky hand again to signal.

'there- monster- with- animals/monsters.'

'alive?'

'asleep. dead. uncertain/maybe.' Bildon shook his hand in an erasing gesture, meaning "new subject."

' more-important-there.' Bildon hesitated, then flashed signals Treaman did not know. He signaled misunderstanding, and Bildon scowled, biting his lip. Finally he started to trace what looked like a circle in the air with his quaking forefinger. Treaman thought about that, then pressed the coin into Bildon's hand. *'treasure'* he signaled.

Bildon threw the coin on the floor and it rang as it bounced. Treaman gasped a year of his life away, and almost cuffed his recumbent friend in panic. But seeing his incapacity flushed all emotions save pity and fear; he bundled his arms around the halfling and tried to keep him still and warm. Bildon's breath was slowing, his eyes rolled a little, yet he tried to communicate, though his hand was little better than a club from the shakes.

'small. small—' followed by the circle motion.

'small-circle [question?]' Treaman signaled back, and Bildon shook while his eyes danced with frustration. Reaching up suddenly, he grabbed Treaman's open hand, wedging his useless fingers between the thumb and forefinger. Dragging it over to his other hand, folded into a fist, he rammed the oval end of Treaman's hand-shape against the circle of his own, then turned to look at the woodsman with burning eyes.

Treaman looked at the whole shape, and knew. Leaning close to Bildon's ear, he gently whispered, "Egg."

The Stealthic nodded vigorously, then flashed his fingers as if counting.

'many. more than one.' Treaman signaled; another nod. Bildon's breath was very slow now, his lungs were icing up and even his shaking was subsiding. Treaman knew the halfling would fall asleep, but did not know if he could wake up. He started to lift him, to carry him back out, but the Stealthic squirmed and gestured onward down the cave.

'in/on. scout/look.'

'you-die-maybe/uncertain'

'look.'

Bildon's eyes were fluttering, and Treaman had to make a decision. Lowering the little man, he covered him with his cloak and wrapped him tight. Standing and taking back up his spear, Treaman looked down and could see in the dimness that the halfling was giving one more signal, with a hand half-under his blanket. It was one of the last he had taught him, just a favorite saying, and he didn't have the strength to complete it.

'fight—'

'Fighting is failure.' The Stealthic's creed; true courage cannot be shown, nor real glory won, purely through combat. Evading, outmaneuvering and anticipating violence, here was Astor's teaching. Treaman thought about it another moment, and then gently lay his

spear back on the cavern floor next to his sleeping friend. It cost him half his reason to do so, but there seemed no course in front of him that carried a whiff of logic or sense. With infinite caution, he toe-stepped to the rise, went forward onto his hands, and edged up the incline to peek over the top.

Just as his vision cleared the rise, a female warnet came into view not four feet from his head. Treaman ducked back and fumbled for his dagger, but the giant ant-like bug, headed more directly down the corridor, ignored him and continued on its way. At this close range, he could see it held a piece of gravel in its mouth; so that explained the barricade at the entrance, and also did not.

Sliding further to his left and away from the ant-path, Treaman again inched up to view the cave beyond the rise. There was only one stretch left, a large rounded chamber with higher ceilings and enough light to make out colors, and contours, and life. Treaman took in the view, and the last supports of his eroded reason crumbled away.

Along the opposite wall perhaps twenty feet off, the dragon sprawled with eyes closed. His enormous body stretched across Treaman's entire field of vision, more than ten yards of dark scaled torso, tapering and turning back for another five yards of sinuous pointed tail. Biting his hand, Treaman fought to control his breath and watched for a sign of respiration from the wurm. Long moments passed without a rise in its chest, or stomach or any spot that could have been its lungs. But there was still a trail of dark smoke issuing from its nostrils, seeking the crevices above and coiling along the ceiling to drift down the cavern over his head.

And there was more movement in the cavern. At the top of the monster's sheening mask, above the eye-ridges where its spine-spikes began, it seemed the hair on its head was waving in a wind. Except there was no draft in the cavern, and dragons have no hair. Treaman risked crawling forward until only his feet were hanging down the slope, and with a shock he recognized the shape and texture of female warnets on the dragon's crown. There were more than a dozen in plain sight, a mass of thick fur, grasping legs, plunging stingers. Silently they swarmed over the head and scruff of the dragon, constantly stinging into its skull, its neck, its spine. Treaman understood: over the years, by sheer numbers they must have gained the upper hand, and slowly subdued the massive lord with their venom, now dead and serving as the planting-ground for their new generations.

With his gorge rising, Treaman noted the dragon's back and upper limbs were pocked with small holes; some scabbed over, probably with eggs still inside, others open and suppurating with thin, reeking blood dripping down and hissing gently on its scales. The warnet larvae had feasted on dragon-meal for years, and the insects had become more aggressive, murderous, possessed of more potent venom since then. With horror, the woodsman noted the dragon's hind leg was completely gone, burned away with flesh fused to a stump of bone. Ragged holes in its wings, long shanks of scorched scale with indefinable alloys of other substances melted onto its frame; the wurm had sacrificed extremities in an effort to stave off defeat, tried to armor itself against further encroachment. It had probably slain thousands of its foes with fire and claw; but Treaman guessed that some females had at last roosted where so many clustered now, and struck enough venom into its frame at that vulnerable spot behind the mask to start the wurm on its downward spiral. Now, there were scores of scabs on its body, marking future generations of misery for this vale.

Treaman, feeling increasingly sure the smoke was just the long-banked remnant of the dragon's mysterious ability to breathe flame, risked getting to his hands and knees. He crawled just two paces closer, to get a better census of the party's foes and especially whether any males survived. One more female crawled off the body, picked up a small bit of gravel from a pile near the dragon's mouth, and headed towards the entrance. It paid him no heed; but Treaman felt something rougher than cavern floor under his hands and knees, and looked down.

He crouched on a plate of treasure.

Coins were the new floor beneath him, nearly all fused together by heat and acid. Gems studded several spots, and part of a case or box thrust from the mass. The light wasn't good enough to make out much, and his mind was already supplying details he could not confirm: a hilt, a book, statuette? And something round, larger than a melon, with marble-like markings… Treaman crawled one more pace, reached out and laid his hand on it, felt it move slightly, free of the coin block. And warm.

The dragon opened his eyes.

Completely surprised, Treaman looked full into those orbs not ten feet away, and was lost. Frozen with his hand on the egg, Treaman crouched unable to connect a thought to his body. The warnets could have laid eggs in him, if they liked and he was helpless to do anything. Nothing in his mind worked, not even his thoughts were his to control as a massive Presence swept across the entrance and seized him with a small corner of its attention. In an instant, his entire life and lore was sifted by a being who found nothing of the least interest to it. Treaman cringed in mortal terror, unbreathing; there was a pause, as the creature considered something beyond his ken. Then a flood of images ensued, a series of pictures each with a kind of thought-attachment conveying a feeling. Treaman was never sure what the order had been or which were real and which imagined later. They just came, like gallons of lightning-tinged water down the throat of his mind; drowning him, cutting and dicing his sanity.

Flame, endless washes of fire, filling the cavern, the rest of the cave, the entire world without; satisfaction, fierce desire

Its mate dying in combat with an enormous three-legged creature; horror, aloneness, distance in time

Treaman, stabbing at a huge shaggy wolf-like creature with one foot in a stream; weak, still brave- a judgment; hexavore, a good name

The dragon in flight over Maladon, sweeping down to douse the houses in fire while spears and arrows bounce from its hide; hilarity, innocent fun

The egg, rocking and turning to reveal a hole in the shell, a male warnet emerging; revulsion, insult, death better

Several warnets on a dragon's leg crisping as a gout of fire incinerates them; pain, loss, fey

Treaman again, leading the party through a murderous storm, something lashed to his arm that lashes on its own; separation, loss, an insult but preferable

A view of three massive legs, dark and unearthly, of giant size, then a wave of thick smoke; dread, something more powerful, awe

Three dragons flying, one much smaller, on a flawless summer day; sorrow, loss, a better path closed

Flame, an ocean of fire; release and duty done

A group of human-mortal-flies, Treaman among them, in heated debate; disgust, impatience, resignation

A pathway through light crossing a matchless crown; surprise, wonder, disbelief, destiny

Flame, everywhere fire and roasting of enemies; impatience, agony still restrained, a moment arrives

A dragon crouching by a riverbank, roaring for food, then a human hand larger than its head bringing a fish the size of a shark to its maw for greedy, grateful eating; concern, insufficient knowledge, an error repaired

Mountainous piles of insects swept together by a wind or some sorcerous magic, followed by a thunderous orange waterfall of flame hosing them into a fused mass; fondness, hatred, delight

Treaman taking the egg in his arms; now, agony, moment arrives

The dragon-eyes blinked once silently, and Treaman felt chains fall from his being. Unsure whether he willed it, the woodsman gathered up the egg, still slowly as if sound were the enemy. To his horror, the dragon gaped its massive jaws as the warnets above renewed their vigilance and belatedly redoubled their stinging. Its tongue, the size of a hall carpet, licked out and pulled in shovelsfull of the small gravel near its head. The enormous merciless eyes regarded him a final time, and Treaman was at last galvanized to act. Standing up, he turned to take three running steps and leaped off the edge of the rise clasping the egg like a great stone, sinking below the surface and into the well as the cavern behind him exploded in a ball of white-hot flame.

Treaman was sure he was on fire; his hair was scorched and the metal of his buckles felt like hot nails burning through his clothes to his skin. Freed from silence, he cried out as loud as he could, but heard nothing except the blast of fire, the wash of the flame-wave. He shielded the egg with his elbows as he landed hard on the stony floor and skidded into something soft wrapped in his cloak. The wave passed within the time it took his body to come to rest, skinned and hot and bleeding. Looking up by the flickering light of things on fire back in the treasure-room, he noted that Bildon was still asleep, his eyebrows singed and the cloak crackling crisply, but his armor no more than sparking a bit as it protected the rest of him. Even his hands and feet, it seemed, would make it.

More movement beneath his stomach made Treaman jerk up to a sitting position. The egg in his hands, weighing almost ten pounds, had a crack along one edge. As the wonder overwhelmed him, first one, then two holes punched out of the shell, and an exquisitely formed head emerged. By the dying light of its parent, the creature looked Treaman directly in the eye. And again, he was lost, this time with interest, and respect bordering on reverence, even love.

The thought came into his mind as if the voice had always been there.

{"Hungry!"}

The woodsman sat back against the stone and just looked on his treasure for a long, long time.

The day after Solemn Judgement entered Conar, Cedrith — contrary to his sincere intentions — did not see the youth all day. A messenger from Captain Bentine woke him while it was still dark, to inform that reports had already reached the castle, and he was summoned to attend the king. Dressing, venting and eating quickly and nearly in the wrong order, Cedrith accompanied the young man to the northwestern corner, the highest part of the city, where the enormous fortress seemed to grow organically from the outer walls and look down on the capital like a sentry. He met the Captain in an antechamber, and they hurriedly conferred, countersigned papers and then, after what seemed an eternity, were ushered to the inner council chambers.

Technically, Cedrith was in the presence of the king, and bowed as all did on entering to Conantis the Twenty-First; in truth, the young man sat his throne at the opposite end of the cavernous room where the Captain and the Sage made their report to the Lord Constable. Once more, the learned scribe turned makeshift ambassador repeated his tale, alongside the Captain's and in rehearsed agreement. They danced over some of the finer points in their story of a regrettable oversight, some momentary commotion, and the fine, patient work of the city guards in uncovering the mystery. Cedrith mentioned no whit of what had transpired since Judgement had left the gatehouse; the Constable showed interest only in the event, and did not so much as ask the stranger's name. It was agreed that the wording of the interrogation should be adjusted, the written test applied more freely in cases of doubt, and there an end.

Hardly five minutes' work, to men who are about their business, but add in the round trip, two searches, ceremonial greetings, waiting rooms, and a good bit of staring at the unparalleled architecture of the fortress, and Cedrith found he did not part company with the Captain until the mid-afternoon. For the second day in a row, he had missed lunch; thinking of the first day's reason brought Judgement back to his memory with a lurch, and Cedrith hastened to the Guild. With luck, his charge had slept in a bit and was only now getting down to a serious look at his primer. Cedrith wanted to help him as much as he could.

But Judgement was not in the study room. Cedrith noted his desk had none of the chosen books on it, and there were others in its place now. Puzzled, he checked the refectory and Judgement's cell: he had not eaten breakfast, the cook said, and his cell still held his staff, cloak and hat, but there was no sign of the youth. Now Cedrith began to feel vaguely ill.

Returning to the study room, he put his hand on the arm of a passing student and gestured to Judgement's old desk. "Have you seen the new student, sitting here?" The boy shook his head and would have continued, but Cedrith stopped him. "I need the one who was sitting here before him, dressed all in grey?"

"Him!" the youth returned. "He's still here — I mean, he was this morning when I got up."

"Where did he move to?"

The boy shrugged. "He was bringing books to this desk, last I saw." As Cedrith turned to look again at the desk, the acolyte took his advantage and moved on. The Elf saw, on second examination, that indeed one of the books from the previous day was still there, the dictionary of the Common Tongue. Yet there was also one for Elvish, and a small introductory lexicon of sorceror's tongue, the language of magic spells. Cedrith also saw two books on the history of Conar, written for children but nevertheless over threescore pages each, one on sailing, a tome of the hero-tales (for an older audience than the children's book Cedrith had selected), and an atlas of the Lands of Hope. As he rummaged the titles, Cedrith saw with a leap of his heart that there were note-pages inserted in various tomes, and the script was unmistakably neat and clear.

When Natasha greeted him, the Elvish Sage nearly jumped out of his skin.

"Mark of the horse, my friend, how nervous you are! I was going to scold you for not giving me the news — where have you—"

"Natasha, thank the moment!" Cedrith cried, grabbing her by the arm, "Have you seen Solemn Judgement?"

"How does one see a judgment?"

"The young man, the… the accused I was sent to meet yesterday. I left him here last night…"

"My dear friend!" Natasha exclaimed, laughing and hugging him close, long enough to overcome his nerves a bit until he chuckled with her. "You never came back to the chamber yesterday. I waited for you. And now, I hear you have been to see the king! Such an honor, so certainly you have no time for your former friends," she teased with that twinkle practically dancing in her eye. "But to ask me where the man I have never met is, that is too much to expect."

"I do apologize, Mistress. You don't understand, this fellow is — he's rather unpredictable, and I couldn't tell you all if we had the rest of the day. Suffice to say, it's very important we locate him at once; there's no telling what he might be up to now."

"No telling, is there? We are in a library, yes? Perhaps he is reading."

"But he cannot read! That is, I — I know nothing, I'm sure, but he could not read yesterday, to that I can attest."

"My friend, I can make nothing of what you are telling me."

"Never mind, Natasha; only please, come with me if you will. I must find him, and I assure you the effort it would take to discover this fellow will be richly rewarded."

"Oh, you could not rid yourself of me now with a crossbow, dear Cedrith!" Natasha rejoined, as the two of them moved towards the reference desk.

"Please, sirrah. Have you seen a young student, the one all in grey?"

The acolyte there looked almost half as interested in helping as the first student Cedrith had spoken to.

"He was here."

"When?"

"When not?" the man replied resentfully. "You showed him that desk yesterday before dinner, and he came back before I closed the room after sundown. He was slaving away over those children's books, making letters over and over."

"Yes, yes, he is, ah, quite diligent. But today, have you seen—"

"He was here when I got in," the student bore on as if Cedrith had not spoken. "He sits there with his books and writing, but he was really waiting for me. Up he jumps with a pile of questions reaching up to your head. What a nuisance! Talks like a magister, but doesn't know the first thing about how it's all laid out here. I had to show him the filing system, the indices, the stacks—"

"You showed him the stacks!" Cedrith cried with glances to the various hallways leading off into the endless library collections housed in the building.

"It was that or nurse him all day! He wanted this book, that tome, the maps over in the other wing. Creepy fellow; how old is he, anyway? I have to stay at this desk, damn your — em, I mean, begging your pardon, Guildmistress," the student covered, noting Natasha's presence and her badge of office for the first time.

"How long has he been gone?" Cedrith returned, still with urgency in his voice that the student completely failed to absorb.

"I told you, sir, I haven't been watching him."

"Lost in the stacks, and he hasn't eaten since… Natasha, come with me, please; we must search."

"Of course, my friend, I am with you. But where could we look first?"

Cedrith thought a moment, and his spirits sank to think of the endless volumes out there in the Conarian Guild. He probably knew certain parts of them better than anyone in the city, but Judgement could just as easily be in a hall, or on a floor, he had never visited once. And knowing his luck with the boy… Cedrith found himself back at the desk, staring at its contents while hardly daring to believe his eyes. He resolved, first, not to read Judgement's notes; it was an unwritten rule of the Guild that each member should be allowed his privacy, and notwithstanding his guest's ignorance, the Sage was determined to treat him with an equal's dignity. The titles, then; these were the only map to his guest's whereabouts. Cedrith sat, and steepled his hands while he thought. Natasha beamed at him proudly, and bustled off to return with two cups of tea. He sipped, was soothed, and then sought after Judgement with his mind.

The passing time seemed endless to Cedrith, beset with fears about the fate of his new — friend, he recognized strangely. This thought, and Natasha's calming presence, helped him clear his mind a bit as his eyes darted back and forth across the desk. Smiling, he cleared his throat and began to declaim as if arguing before the sage's board.

"He began with the primers we gave him yesterday, and this dictionary in the center is still with him. He moved from there to the hero tales and the general history of the Lands," he said, gesturing to a stack of four books on the left side of the desk.

"My dear Cedrith," exclaimed Natasha, "how could you know this?"

"My very dear Natasha," he returned, "I assure you I know nothing for certain, and likely a good deal less than that where this remarkable person is concerned. All is guesswork. Still… I know that when I am working through a stack of books, I place them on the left side of the desk and move them right as I read. I am right-handed, but this youth uses his left to write."

"I thought you said he could not write."

"No, I said he could not read. At least, not in the Common Tongue. It is the most incredible story, I must admit." Here Cedrith briefly recounted the interrogation at the guardhouse of the day before.

"Do you mean to say, he has learned to read in a single night!"

"Not precisely," Cedrith returned with a grin. "I told you that he speaks the Common Tongue exactly as we do, with a few, ah, older idioms, the occasional word we would find rather formal. But the sound of the language is exactly the same. I conjecture, mind you, that the rules of grammar for the written tongue must also be the same, or so close as to make no difference. So what we have here," he concluded slowly, "is not truly learning a new language, but rather a kind of letter-substitution. I suppose it could be like the secret codes you would make up with your friends, as children."

"Perhaps when you were children!" Natasha giggled. "But I see your point, yes. Still, the effort involved… how could he possibly learn well enough to read since last night?"

"Well I don't know that he understands everything, certainly. He may have begun with only the most commonly used letters — ah, look here!" Cedrith exclaimed, pointing to a piece of paper in plain sight atop the dictionary. "He has written out six of our most-used letters, and the alien symbols beneath each one must be those of his home country. Really, what an extraordinary student we have here! And it may be that he is simply skimming, looking for certain subjects or concepts."

Cedrith returned to contemplate the left-hand books more closely. "Two books of hero-tales, with marking ribbons in the places for 'Conar' —well, of course — and also 'Restol.' Hmmm, one of the more obscure Heroes, wouldn't you say, Natasha?"

"The West-Seeker, yes," she remarked, "patron of the sailor. Of all the Heroes, the only one to board ship and sail back across the Western Sea."

"But of course!" Cedrith exclaimed. "He is seeking to know more about the waters his father brought him across. And here, beneath the books, is a map." The sage brought out the old vellum scroll laid flat beneath the stack, and smoothed it down. "By the moment, Natasha, see this. I've never known a map that displays so much of the fabled Western Sea. Why, it shows no more of the Lands than some of Mendel and the western borders of the Percentalion. This must be very old, how could he have found it?"

Natasha gazed over the scroll with him, and then shrugged. "You said he was very persistent."

"I did indeed," chuckled the Elf, but then he grew more worried. "I suppose he was seeking to know whether he could return. But his world, I suspect, is removed by more than mere leagues of distance from our own. His manner and clothes, of course, are clues, and he seems completely unused to so many things we would take for granted here. Like a lad raised and trained but then stricken with amnesia. In any event, the Western Sea is known to be endless. Neither Restol nor any voyager since has ever returned from seeking the fabled origin lands of our people."

"So then. Where did his studies take him next?" asked Natasha.

"Where, indeed?" Cedrith said with a shrug, but after a moment, he reached for the largest book on the table, brass-bound and riven with a half-dozen marking ribbons. Its title, large enough to be easily read from across the room, was *'The Law of Conar.'*

"Ugh! He is not squeamish in his studies, I dare say," Natasha said. "Why did he move to this book… ever, not to say next?"

"There are two reasons, I think," Cedrith said. "Once he had dwelt on his arrival, and perhaps reflected on the impossibility of return, Solemn Judgement set about acclimating to his new land. And since he ran so close afoul of the Law of Conar on his first day, he tried to learn more about it. A good sign."

Passing his hand lovingly over the symbol of Hope in bronze on the front cover, Cedrith solemnly recited the inscription beneath the title, in the Ancient tongue, saying, *"Ar Aralte."* The symbol of Hope glimmered slightly as he spoke, and the side-clasp popped up. Only then did he reach to open the book, commenting to Natasha, "It's marvelous, isn't it? The power of the Ancient tongue binds us all to speak the truth. Hence, this tome can be locked against all evildoers simply by requiring them to say 'Hope Forever' before it can be opened."

"And mark of the horse! He must have done so," Natasha replied.

"Indeed, for he has set several marker ribbons within, you are right. This young man surpasses my understanding, I must tell you." After turning past the cover page, Cedrith let his eyes rest once more on the gilt Ancient letters of the fabled Law of Conar. Such was their power that once he began to read them, his eye naturally could not stop until he had seen it all. Just a single page, only a few score words, and yet therein was contained the entirety of the Law itself: Cedrith never ceased to wonder at the elegance and concision of the statement.

"Why are you chuckling, friend?" Natasha asked.

"Just imagine, my dear," the sage returned. "Our young friend goes in search of the Law of Conar and retrieves this enormous tome. Then he opens it — by whatever means, I must no longer be surprised at his abilities — and discovers, what? That the whole document is writ on a single page! And that all these hundreds of following pages in the Common Tongue, the real meat of legal discourse—"

"Ugh!"

" — it is all merely corollary, suggestion and amplification to the original Law. I wonder if he was disappointed, or surprised…" Here Cedrith spent some time checking the bookmarks his friend had made, with his brow contracting only further and further. "I can make very little of this. Here's one regarding the punishments for murder in various degrees, and another about elevation to noble status… the protections gained in court… and one on crimes against the church of Conar. It's a mare's nest, a very mortal coil of consequences. I cannot believe our friend is taking in much of this tangled legal writing. He must have given up."

"As we all should!" said Natasha with feeling. "Where did he look next, then?"

Cedrith turned his attention to the pile of books on the right-hand side of the desk. "Now our task becomes more difficult, and we draw hopefully closer to our prize." He examined the titles, and steepled his hands once more. "I can say with certainty only that this book was his last choice before leaving this room."

"How so?"

"Because, my dear Natasha," said Cedrith with a smile, "this book is the only one that does not have grey ribbons for bookmarks." Cedrith gestured to the wooden box on the librarian's table that had ribbons of all colors spilling from the sides. "After that, Goodman Judgement turned to other colors as the box had run out."

"Why Cedrith, whatever can you mean? Grey ribbons!"

Cedrith burst out laughing at this and patted his friend's shoulder. "Never mind, my dear, you will understand more after you meet him, but in this I am fairly certain. So he looked at last to… burial customs."

On this note, all humor drained from the room and the two sat in silence for some time. The black leather book holding the colored ribbons leered from the top of the right-hand pile, and disquieted them both without effort. "This tome is quite old," Cedrith said at last, reaching reluctantly to open it and examine the bookmarks. "The Children of Hope have always given their dead to the fire and sky, a funeral custom with small variations we have kept since history began."

"Why would this youth be so interested in death?" Natasha asked cautiously, her face showing something Cedrith could not immediately read.

"I'm sure I don't know… One moment; he did say that his father died in bringing him to our shores. Perhaps he wondered whether he had done it, em, properly?"

"Do you suppose the people of his land actually bury their dead?"

"As Despair does? May Ma-Eldar grant otherwise," Cedrith said with feeling. "And yet, he does seem to have marked places where the practice of cremation arose, and certain, ah, exceptions harbored by the native peoples. These are the very early times…"

"Yes," said Natasha, her face growing ever stranger, "the rustics, children of the Land who lived here before even the invasion of Despair. Some of them immolated the dead; others entombed them in rock, or deep water, or under the earth. Plus the legions of slain and earth-buried under Despair's rule… so that we can never be certain where they lie."

It had grown very quiet in the study room, it seemed. No citizen of the Lands could easily contemplate the idea of burial beneath the earth, sundered from the sky and heaven, and subject to the foul energies of necromancy. Cedrith's hand on the open book slipped a bit, and the pages fell back to the frontispiece. Drawn to look, he exclaimed again, "Moment in time! What…? Natasha, look, the author—"

The healer leaned over, then started back up with a gasp of surprise. "It is written by Faltus Fanem! The plagiarist?"

"As to that—" Cedrith started to temporize, but cut himself off. "Wait, there's news of more import here. There is reference here to The Nameless Tome, Fanem's restricted work. Judgement might have found his way to the Dark Archives, led by this title. He has no permission to view those books! It requires, well, membership, for one, and not as an acolyte either. Plus, great moment, Natasha, those stacks are often locked. The poor boy is likely lost and trapped."

"Show the way, my friend. We must see to him at once."

The open stack areas of the Guild covered four stories in height: a space filled with shelves, stairs, reading lobbies, discussion rooms and an amphitheatre for debates and dissertations. On its southern side the halls connected directly to the Healers Guild with which the Sages were so closely associated; across the western street lay an entrance to the Mages Guild, and the three franchises together created a bastion of learning that covered nearly a tenth of the city. On balance, the Sages library could have comfortably housed a population of five thousand, without need to remove the books.

The basement stairs descended to two smaller, narrower levels, brightly lit at all hours by glow-stones that it was the job of the much put-upon acolytes to recharge. Yet here were only the mundane storage rooms, classification catalogues, printing press and bindery. The closed stacks were above the fourth floor, and the way to the Dark Archives led up the narrowest of the three stairways accessing the upper levels. With so little traffic, there were neither torches nor glow-stones to light the way, and Cedrith and Natasha proceeded by means of a single candle the gypsy healer had taken from the study room. There were no windows on the stairs or on the upper level, to discourage unwanted intrusion into such somber subjects. Although they were climbing six-score paces above the street where another sunny day shone outside, Cedrith could not shake the sense that he was going down, deeper into the darkness and a step closer to hell, where the demons roamed for real far beneath the earth.

He was thus more unnerved than usual by the time they reached the landing and the solid oak door that led to the closed archives. Not until rattling the locked latch did he recall that the guest-key was back in his room.

"What an idiot I am! The door — Judgement!" he cried out with his face to the wood, "Solemn Judgement, are you in there? I shall have to go back, what a woolen head, it may already be too late. Judgement! Are you there?"

He didn't feel the calming hand on his arm at first, but when Natasha stepped past him and muttered a few words, gesturing with her free digits, Cedrith cut off abruptly, with his mouth open. There was a short pause, and then the metal workings of the lock clicked, with a noise that seemed loud as a hammer in that quiet corridor. Natasha turned the handle and pushed the portal open before stepping back. Cedrith stared at his friend agape. At last she giggled, much more like a mischievous girl than the respected healer he had known.

"If you are looking for a place to store your boots, my friend, I think I see one," she said, and when he finally closed his jaw, she added, "I am older than I appear, sir, and my previous career was not quite as dignified as this one." With that, the matronly Guildmistress breezed by Cedrith with the candle in hand, and shaking his head slowly, the Elvish Sage followed her into the Dark Archives.

There was no main aisle on this level; the shelves of books loomed from either side in uneven sizes and heights, forcing the pair to take a winding route as paths jutted, split and disappeared. Since patrons came among the tomes so seldom, there were neither glow-stones nor lanterns within. The Dark Archives gave an uncomfortable impression of disorder, as if each Sage through the years had come here just long enough to stuff the borrowed book onto a shelf and then fled.

Cedrith knew his way, but not his destination, and was only guessing Judgement's location from the Fanem tome. "The acolytes whisper of a ghost in this chamber," he said quietly, "a spirit angered by one or another of the secrets held here. They say it waits to murder the next one to read it."

He walked on several steps, then looked at Natasha when she did not say anything. The healer wore a serious expression on her face, as if expecting him to continue. "This is the point," he prompted gently, "where you exclaim in doubt or derision, my dear."

"Oh," she responded in surprise, "it was that sort of ghost-tale." On this, Cedrith stopped again and faced his friend.

"Do you — are you saying that you have seen a ghost?"

"Only once," she replied matter-of-factly, "but that one was in a mood to talk, so we did not need the protections my — well, it was not an issue."

Cedrith stared, and there was not a breath of movement beyond the slight flicker of Natasha's candle and the echoes it made in blank on the shelves behind them. He finally licked his lips and drew a breath to say, "My dear friend, you give me much to think about. I don't know whether to be reassured that you can face the terrors I tried to joke of, or worried that you may draw more adventures along with you."

"You disappoint me, good sage. Are you one of those hostile to adventurers?"

"Goodness, no," protested the Elf, though the thought of using that term for the respected Healer of Conar sent a wave of apprehension through him. He swallowed and took a deep breath, wary of what bad reputations adventurers had in most civilized lands, and tried for a diplomatic response. "You have always been to me a good friend, Natasha. I admire you for… for those qualities you have shown, your kindness and liberal tutelage and your great friendship. Your previous life is of no concern to me — that is," he added hastily at the slight, "I am certain that you have held these same qualities in your early years as you do now."

That brought back the twinkle and smile he hungered to see. "I assure you, my qualities have remained very much the same, dear Cedrith. It's simply that you do not yet know all of them."

"Deep waters, indeed," he rallied, "but if I may put off such joys of the intellect, we are on a search." He gestured around the next row of shelves, and they proceeded.

Turning the corner, they nearly tripped over the body of the Man in Grey.

He lay slumped aside and halfway across a six-pile of tomes, with his head hanging four inches off the floor and nearly upside-down; his left hand was still wedged between the pages of an enormous folio resting over his lap and several more books touched his legs and feet as they sprawled athwart the aisle.

"Great Hope, he's been attacked!" Cedrith cried, and flopped to the floor near Judgement's head and directly in Natasha's way. "Judgement, my friend, am I too late?" He felt the healer's gentle but insistent nudge and edged a bit to one side, cradling the head and looking for signs of a wound.

Natasha cleared back his long grey hair and placed two fingers above his temple for the count of three; then again aside his neck and finally reached down to clasp his wrist. "He's asleep," she pronounced, "deeply, but well."

"He's alive, thank the lords of Hope," Cedrith exclaimed, even as he felt the boy's breath on his hands.

"Let us move him down," Natasha said. They gently laid him flat to the floor, still in a half-bent position but more comfortably on his side. Judgement showed no reaction, but they could see his slow steady breaths continued. On the floor next to him lay a candleholder with just a smat of melted wax left in the bottom. "Poor dear, he must have passed right out, and all alone in this awful place. He is… so pale," she murmured, starting now to take in his unusual appearance. Cedrith looked on him asleep and realized it was the most relaxed he had ever seen this aquiline, noble face. Judgement looked like the fifteen years he truly was.

"Why, oh why did his researches lead him here?" moaned the sage, and reaching over the boy he took ahold of the folio and gently pulled it free of his left hand.

With a shudder through his entire body, Judgement cried out "Father! I am remiss—" and only then began to see his surroundings.

"It's alright, Judgement, it's me, Cedrith!" the sage cried, even as he fell back to the floor in a heap.

The youth tried at once to sit up, and stopped halfway as the line of his mouth suddenly stitched back — the only sign of the pain he must have felt from his cramped and book-bruised ribs. Continuing to right himself more slowly, Judgement looked to Cedrith and then the healer, his eyes alert and breathing heavily but without any other loss of composure. Now awake, his face took on the mask of an extra decade or more, and he looked somewhat as he had during the interrogation.

"Eldest," he said, still somewhat out of breath, "I do apologize for startling you; I must have fallen asleep, in my weakness." Then, looking to Natasha, he said carefully, "Madam, I have not the pleasure…"

"Young Judgement, this is the Healers Guildmistress Natasha Ioki of whom I told you—" Cedrith broke off as his friend immediately scrambled to his feet to execute a formal bow. He had to chuckle at the earnestness of his charge, and Natasha for her part was enchanted, laughing aloud and curtseying in return before grasping the surprised youth in a characteristic bear-hug.

"You gave my friend Cedrith quite a turn, young man," she scolded without heat. "He has been seeking more than an hour, quite concerned that some evil had befallen you."

For a moment, they could have been standing in any library hall. But Judgement said nothing, and after the echoes died the Dark Archives seemed to exert their power once more. Cedrith fidgeted in his haste to be gone, but he could not well bring his friend back before the other Sages without an explanation, or a story.

"My friend, Goodman Judgement, I am delighted and relieved to have found you well. I told you, yesterday — ahah! It seems so long ago to me — I told you then that I would extend my support to you, and I affirm that." Cedrith took a breath and laid his hand on the youth's shoulder. "Solemn Judgement, you must tell me nowwhat were you doing here? Have you knowingly broken the rules of our Guild by accessing these restricted archives?"

Judgement was alarmed but did not hesitate. "Eldest, I swear to you, I was simply carried by my research into… certain avenues of thought. I was, I admit, delighted" — and here he paused as if the word was cause for embarrassment — "I was able to somewhat read the language and was learning more with every page. You must know how it feels" — and here his face began to shine, his speech became enthusiastic — "I was conversing with the past, with new countries and men and an entire world unknown to me. The way you calculate tides — I do not understand it all — the classification of animals, I can see much for me to learn there; and the heroic tales, such great and wondrous men and women who fought so hard and so well; I cannot fathom how to live long enough to take this all in."

"You are right," Natasha commented, smiling, "this one will fit in well here, for a time. But I sense young Judgement is a man for doing, not only reading and writing." She paused a moment, as if assessing him. "And I am quite curious, young man, as to how you accessed these halls. The door is locked; you stole nothing, moved nothing?"

"No, Mistress."

"Then how came you here?"

A space of silence, and Cedrith could bear it no longer.

"This is very serious, Goodman Judgement, I must ask that you put yourself in my hands. If you came here knowing these were restricted tomes, there will be trouble, but I can—"

"I knew nothing. No one would speak to me. No one was here."

"Well then, what book were you seeking?"

"There were certain tomes… a man named Fanem, he wrote of their existence, books captured from authors who… who were from Despair. And they seemed to know — that is, Fanem hinted that they could tell of… but the language is parsed and complex, I could make little progress towards—"

"Avert!" Cedrith cried, tracing a symbol of Hope with a brow already sweating. "Judgement, you have gone too far, to look into necromantic tomes; the handiwork of Despair are not for the young nor the rash to read. What were you seeking?"

"To know… to discover if death is indeed the end."

A moment in time, where you could hear a pin drop. Cedrith realized he had not breathed, and drew a ragged one loud enough to frighten himself. "You sought… to raise the dead?"

"Nay!" cried the youth, making a symbol as Cedrith did, but this time tracing blue fire in his wake.

Natasha stared with her mouth agape at this display. "His intentions were pure, else we would never have seen this," she said slowly. "But young man, if not necromancy, then what — ?"

"I… should not say, Mistress. My thought is still too tangled. There are two things, or perhaps more, that I seek to know." Here he stopped short, but Cedrith would have none of it. Danger or no, he kept tapping like a hammer on the rock who was his friend.

"You must let us help you, Solemn—" but here he broke off, as the look the youth returned at the sound of his name was sharp and almost hostile. "Goodman Judgement," he reverted, "tell me plainly this at least: how did you come to this place?"

The gaze of the Man in Grey became calm again, though still reluctant. "I used—"

"What? How!"

"There is… a book server," the youth said meekly, and pointed back across the floor.

Natasha started to giggle almost hysterically, and Cedrith found he could not resist this infection. "You used… the book server? From the sehh-second floor repository?" Judgement nodded, but Cedrith persisted. "You were here late, and none were around. You returned to consult the catalog, and it showed the book up here, so you marched all the way up, and you found… the d-dd-door was locked… and so, sohahhso you came back d-down…"

"And you got—" Natasha supplied but also losing her control, "you, ah, bb-boarded the ssserverrrr," here she stopped for a prolonged period of chuckling, and Cedrith found he had to lean an arm on her for support as he joined in. Judgement stood at attention as if he was being interrogated and the laughter broke over him like wind on wood.

"And then," Cedrith mimed the motions, "you *inched* and *heaved* your way up, up, up. Did it take you an hour?"

The two looked at the statue-man and continued grinning until he was forced to respond. Finally, he lifted his shoulders a fraction of an inch, and this brought a burst of renewed laughter from them both. When they could finally control themselves again, they stood no closer to Judgement than previously, and yet the three of them were together now as not before.

"Well, I imagine we can make this right," Cedrith announced, clapping Judgement on the shoulder with one hand and rubbing his face with the other. "As long as we don't admit you actually understood anything — which sounds nearly true — and we get everything back the way it was. What did you have, eight books with you here?"

Judgement nodded and wordlessly gathered them back up, neatly inserting them in spaces far apart without hesitation or error. Natasha checked a couple and found the assignation codes were correct. "A mind like an executioner's blade, this one. We shall have to help him, as you say Cedrith, as he'll know more than we do soon."

"I think you do not exaggerate, my dear, or if you jest you may be proven wrong," Cedrith came again. "And now, my friend, if we return to the lands of the living, may I convince you by any means to eat, or perhaps even sleep?"

Judgement just looked at Cedrith and the sage raised a hand to cut him off. "I know, you are neither fatigued nor hungry, my friend. But still, amuse me and show you know how, alright?"

With a tilt of his head to one side, Judgement gave reluctant assent and together the three escaped from the Dark Archives with no losses from fearsome spirit or spited friendship.

In the months to come, acolytes of the Sages Guild became unwilling to enter the Dark Archives anymore, especially at night. It was whispered by some that a grim grey spirit could at times be spotted there, searching by candle-light for its lost tome and any evidence that one of the living had transgressed its will by reading forbidden words.

The Kingdom Chronicle 1454 ADR

Thus the final battle against the giants comprised the utter destruction of that foul and barbarous race, but at great cost to the kingdom of Shilar. For on the field south of Ranebruh there fell most of the flower of chivalry in that generation, including most grievously the king Gareth, formerly the Baron Moire who had rescued the kingdom by ascending to the throne after the tyrant Meleager. In full battle gear Gareth fell and beneath him the corpse of the dread giant Kur, with the king's battle-lance broken off deep in his chest. With the king fell several of the knights of his Star Circle; prominent among these were Sir Canlon and Moremein, and also Sir Pinthus (who, though only a knight of the quill did arm himself and seek to serve his king in the hour of need).

Most famous and chilling news of the day, however, was the report of the death of young Sir Counsel Broders, the knight who in earlier years had served as squire to the famous Sir Percis Ranelan, the Giantsbane. Percis of legendary reknown had slain half a dozen giants in single combat ere this war. In battle that day with Sir Broders by his side, Percis had outdone himself, slaying Guris and Greenar, the kin of Gorian and Garlan with whom the knight had previously feuded and slain, as well as Toggur and Tront, brothers who had cut down several knights in the battle. But Broders was thrown from horseback and crushed in the press at the thickest point of the melee.

And thus was it revealed that this brave knight, for years one of the best known and most well-liked nobles of the realm, was forsooth a woman. Rents in the armor revealed this fact beyond doubt to those who surveyed the field. All were shocked and dismayed to know the truth; and some did recall a'times the unvarying habit that Broders had of always taking rest alone, and of never bathing with the company whatever the occasion. By all report Sir Percis, when he did see his friend slain, was struck dumb and could not for his life make response to any who bespoke him. Percis withdrew from the sight of men after that day and many say he was never seen again- though the peasantry of the villages thereabout did claim to see a wild man living as a hermit in the woods nearby Ranebruh for decades thereafter. And some will claim the spirit of mad Sir Percis still haunts those woods to this day, wandering alone and listening to the blasted cold winds off the plains, searching for some sign of the life-friend he once thought he knew.

And the new King Pelessar after his coronation did order the fire-funeral with all honors of the tragic maiden who became a shield-knight, known to the world as Counsel Broders.

10th Ferret, 1995 ADR

My Dearest Kia,

I see from your last message — like fine wine to a man who has been drinking seawater — that you have numerous questions about my young charge Solemn Judgement. Yes, I am doing quite well, thank you! But I have no one else to blame for your interest and confusion, wondrous woman, as it was only my first letter that could have led you so far astray. And I do apologize, for I was too hasty in its composition. Let me remedy that, now that things are at last slowing to something like a normal pace. Yet before I address this labor — and a great one, I assure you it is — may I inquire not too eagerly about your progress in finding an empty house? I know this is an unfair burden to you, my dearest, but I am beset with impatience; most unseemly for a child of Ma-Eldar! I know that homes falling empty in Mendel are rarer than a dragon's kindness, but we cannot begin our married life without a roof over our heads. It would be a poor sign of my regard for you if I allowed the shame of building you a new home! I do not know how much longer my posting to Conar will last, but I assure you I will bend every waking moment to this task, and have no sleeping ones, once I return. As long as we both may live, dear Kia, I want my days to be spent with you.

Now then, to the matter of the Man in Grey.

You ask very plainly, "is he old or young?" and I answer just as plainly, "he certainly is." The youth claims to be fifteen years of age, though the calendars of our two worlds do not match, and it could be that he has turned sixteen by now. His hair is completely grey, eyebrows and eyelashes included, and this misleads a great many people. I have peeked when overseeing his studies, and it remains grey to the roots! Why this is, I cannot say; the lad states his hair was black until the voyage. But I believe that his sufferings have somehow changed him deeply. His father was persecuted, to hear him tell it (he speaks of this very little and very reluctantly), and fled with his youngest son across a vast ocean. He seems truly to have come from another world, and perhaps the inhuman strain of two years at sea, followed hard by the death of his father at the moment of landfall, wrought this visible sign of shock on his person. Some folks who meet him take Judgement for an Elf, where our people do sometimes have grey hair. And by the bye, he rarely sleeps, seeming to need very little for such an active day as he keeps; this only reinforces the notion among some of our fellow sages.

But the great thing about this youth, which I cannot convey in words, my dear, is the enormous composure he displays. I could say, "he is mature beyond his years" but it would pale in description of the iron grip he keeps on himself at all times. His peers, those in the Guild about his age, call him the Jolly One in tribute to the fact that he never smiles. Soon or late, it affects everyone around him. For the first fortnight, I trotted him off to a primer-class to cement his knowledge of our letters. I saw him once in the room, cramming his long frame into the tiny desk and surrounded by boys of six and seven. The room was as quiet as the night, and the teacher was too pleased to contain herself, as this giant mute sat erect and scratched out letters in his perfect penmanship, and all the rest stole terrified glances in his direction as if they expected to be eaten momentarily. If I were not so much his friend, I would remark that he casts a pall wherever he goes. The fact is, this young man projects such an air of dedication, such a studious nature, that even the most determined efforts at levity erode in his presence. His civility is perfect, and he treats each person with great formality, unleavened by the slightest smile (all this time, he still calls me "Eldest"!). He is driven, the very word, driven, and at the moment he knows not what he is driven to, so he studies everything to leave no fact unlearned.

And so now, I can easily answer your second question, "What is his subject?" for he has none, or perhaps he has them all. Many of the students here do not know of young Judgement (much less that he has already qualified to become a Guildsman before turning twenty). But every one of the teachers recognizes the name. He has consulted them — some would say harassed — for every subject in the lexicon, and he cannot be put off by a load of work, as usually suffices for the too-ambitious acolyte. He reads every book he's given in less than three days' time, and returns for more until he's summarily forbidden. Whether by poor instinct or malicious coincidence, he seems to gravitate to the most serious, even dangerous, channels of lore; he has been forbidden books on several occasions because they are assigned to the Dark Archives.

I told you the story of that first trip there! I thought we had lost the fellow then. The library-scribes, too, know this relentless researcher; he has been with us less than two months, and already they send the simpler catalogue inquiries to him. He's always there, like them; then too, just the sight of him tends to sift out the less serious. The scribes chuckle to see that, but I feel for him, my dear, I truly do. He sits alone.

I've taught him somewhat of language and Elvish practices, and I can tell you, it's exhausting work. I tried once to explain a little about our marriage customs — shows you where my mind has been — and no sooner do I finish than he barrages me with trivia. He wanted to know about the Conarian marriage customs, the noble versus the common practice, whether Gypsies get formally married (by the Moment, I did not know, I must remember to ask Natasha), how long the engagement, exchange of vows and presents. My head was dizzy, and I excused myself to take a walk. Nothing insulted, the lad follows me! More questions as we walked, then, and I could only be rid of him when, by happy circumstance, we passed the main temple to Conar. Yes, my dear, it's all too true, the tale I told of his first day in the city involved no exaggeration. The cathedral is barred to him, and I've pointed Judgement to a smaller chapel near the harbor where he can make his devotions. Still, he hangs about in the Grand Plaza many times, late at night, to await the procession of the noble youth, this Pron Dedicar, as he goes down to the water's edge. I had not noted the lateness of the hour on this occasion, so it served me well that the young knight emerged as we were passing. I let my friend's fascination with him do what my protestations could not: he followed him to the harbor with no further questions — for now!- and I went along, because whatever interests this incredible young man is of interest to me as well.

The more I look on that noble Conarian, the more convinced I become of his piety and the remarkable devotion he shows. He strays not one step to the left or right nor tarries a moment, but stares straight ahead as he walks directly into the bay. I had seen him once before, when an acquaintance alerted me to the oddity, and thought it some kind of purification ritual. The preachers I've met assure me it is an ancient and honored form of devotion to Conar the Hopelord. It evidently involves a near-complete fast, and I have never seen the knight accept food or water from any hand. Still, he has been on this rite for more than two months, so he must be eating in some way. And he never lays down to sleep, but I suppose he nods off while kneeling before the statue. Those endless hundreds of hours, he has shown devotion in this way... it would strain the patience of an Elf.

I try to bring these facts before my friend Judgement, as a way of illuminating the very best in the character of his adopted country. He nods, and then points wordlessly to two or three others among the crowd who are always there to watch Dedicar on his walk. Nobles, he watches for them, marked with family crests using swords on a field of gold. In vain, I try to argue that this particular family — the clan Altrindur — is among the largest and most honored in all the city; it is only natural that if a crowd were present anywhere for any reason, this group's members would be among them. My words fall on ears of iron, I can tell: young Judgement is set on believing that they mean harm to the knight Dedicar. But I have at least made clear to him the impropriety of such methods of investigation as he used on that first day! Like the rest of us, he watches and makes no overt move. With that, I must be content.

"What does he do for leisure?" you ask, and here I must tell you in all honesty, "absolutely nothing". He barely sleeps, as I

said; he eats only the minimum of all the food the Guild provides for free to its members — never wine or mead, only water — and when he can find no master to teach him, he is out in the City, learning trades. He has already apprenticed for two weeks to the bindery in our own cellars, learning the mundane methods of assembling manuscripts and preserving older copies. He has also spoken of taking work in a stable, at an inn, with a tanner; in each case he works a few weeks, and moves on. Just yesterday he asked me where he could buy a boat. "New ships are commissioned by the Shipbuilders Guild," I told him, "and I don't know how one gains a place on their rolls." He shook his head and said he most wanted a small boat, perhaps used, one he could work on and apply his skills from the carpentry he was cleaning up for! I marvel at the level of his industry, dear Kia, he shames us all. It is as if he has set himself to learn every single thing this land contains, as a way of keeping the course his father set. What a man he must have been, to have sired this prodigy of determination and thirst for erudition. He makes war on his ignorance, dear heart, and it is a massacre.

There are already subjects where no one I can find has anything left to show him. He is learning Elvish quite quickly from me, and a bit of Sorceror's Tongue; he shows an interest in Dwarvish, Halfling and the cant of the Southern Empire, but can find no tutors. My good friend Natasha, who instructs him in the study of miracles, says he is even reading some rather imposing volumes in Ancient at a steady pace, and seems quite at ease.

I grow jealous of this young fellow's place in your mind, though it is my own fault for planting the seed. Like the Ferret that watches over the zodiac this month, we are both made curious of this shiny discovery. Perhaps one day you will meet him, and can draw your own conclusions. But one more item on young Judgement: did I tell you that he swims! Like a fish, I assure you, I would not have credited it had I not seen it with my own eyes. We were at the harbor, of a late evening, as he was again awaiting the appearance of the young knight to wade into the lowering tide, and I remarked that without full strength the poor lad might be pulled into the sea. Young Judgement asked how well a knight could swim, and I laughed to say "as well as the rest of us." But I soon saw the lad was not joking — when does he ever! — and thus I learned of his talent. He could tell I doubted him, and so stripped down before my eyes and dove into the harbor without hesitation. I scanned for him in the dark waters, but kept mistaking a patch of floating seaweed for his head. I thought him drowned, it was so long before he came up, but then he emerged dozens of yards away, near a larger craft moored across the quay. He hailed it and climbed the rope hand over hand, spoke to the crew a short while, then to their great amusement he dove back in, head-first off the rail with his arms before him like a spear being thrown. He moved his arms over-head as he surfaced, and came across the water faster than I could walk on the dock. Truly, he seemed at home in the waves as he does on land, and was quite surprised that I should call this a talent in him.

But now I must insist we return to the subject of me, my dear! Do write as soon as you can with any news, and please convey my loving respect to your mother (who I know favors my suit for your precious hand). May I know no greater happiness than centuries by your side, and be home with you as soon as my duties here are completed. With all my love.

Yours,

Cedrith

⊕⊕⊕

The evenings by the walls were better than ever that summer, a few days after they nearly stopped altogether.

The fourth sunset since the party of the foot-knight Haltar returned to the Percentalion, the children were alarmed to see the preacher Alaetar join them by the fire. Conversations on the edge of the groundling party came to a sudden stop; three children fighting with earth-clods halted as if frozen, dropping them guiltily though he paid them no mind. All eyes fell on the itinerant holy man as he strode a few paces south of the rest, planted his walking stick, and simply watched. Anteris on the wall with the veterans felt that the Shilarian cast a spell of mordant maturity over anything of lightness, of hilarity or childhood. For Alaetar, there were no games, no distractions; the watch was a sacred duty he expressed in his every fiber. Aside from a few whispered words and some half-hearted quarrels, no one said or did anything until sunset came. The children went promptly home as if returning from a funeral, and any of them looking back could see the tall man still standing there against the dying fire, looking into the flat dark chaos beyond the boundary post.

To Anteris' disappointment, Alaetar returned the following night, and while the games and chat leaked back into the group, they were fitful, and farther from the fire where he stood. Even those who ate did so furtively, as if afraid he would notice them daring not to look south. Once he did turn back at a shout, glancing over those who had set chairs around the firepit; one child launched out of his seat as if poked from beneath, and the others all followed suit. Alaetar had looked a bit startled, noticing the children for the first time, and raised one hand in a fending gesture to say there was no need. But when he turned back to look south again, still the children did not sit for several minutes, to be sure. He said not a word to anyone, but only stared at them from time to time as if suspecting they did not speak his language; Anteris wondered, to look at him, whether

Alaetar even had a childhood of his own to draw on. The crowd the following nights became ever smaller.

Three afternoons later in mid-Salamander, Anteris walked to the walls instead of running. His work had gone late, and so he was not in the race, just passing the main plaza in the street towards the south gate when, to his dismay, the holy man emerged from a side lane and joined him. Staring distractedly ahead as though at some other city, Alaetar's pace matched the boy's unconsciously, and Anteris was unwilling to stop or run to break away. Neither could he turn aside, as he wanted, to climb the gate-stairs and join the other old men; he was "last" in the race today, for just the third time in his life (always from work) and he had to touch the flag post beyond the pit and acknowledge the shame. It was a rule. So he trudged on alongside the unspeaking preacher.

It was the kind of midsummer evening that Anteris loved, with a deep passion not even his present state could cloud. The sky was crystal-clear and stars were visible even before the sun was fully set. He spotted Elosira near the western horizon, and Areghel rising higher along with Conar in the east. He touched the post, turning his head to look for the moons, and came instead under the gaze of the preacher. He was caught in the noose of that powerful stare, as the holy man appeared to notice only now someone had been next to him.

Anteris looked up for a long moment, then gave the short bow he was taught but unable to duck his head and break his eyes away. Alaetar loomed over him with a serious face, and at last spoke; not in his sermon-voice, pitched to reach hundreds, but in an almost reasonable tone, sounding much more lonely. "You are the scribe's assistant, the apprentice to Valenthur."

"Anteris, holy sir."

Alaetar pondered this as if learning the sum of four plus five for the first time. "How long, young Anteris, before the heroes return?"

The boy gawked to hear this question, and the face of the preacher, while intense as always, did not seem angry or hostile. The man truly wished to know the unknowable. "Who can say, holy sir?" the boy stammered. "It is Pelian who has been gone the longest—"

"Not the merchants, lad. We take no notice of the pursuit of lucre here. The heroes, the five of destiny, how long will they be gone?"

"Most… most holy sir, there has been no rhyme to it. Perhaps, in this past year, the times have become longer than before—"

"The way's closed, you ask me," came a voice from the semi-dark behind the fire. Alaetar slewed around to face the new speaker, but could not find him among the crowd. His gaze carried such stern purpose that some of the children flinched back, though he stood twenty feet away. The Shilarian seer addressed them all, and now he used his crowd-voice.

"The way is not closed, children of Hope. Not closed, to those whom destiny has chosen. A mighty purpose has been vested in mortal bodies, and all this chaos," he said, waving grandly at the entire horizon to the south, "all this will again be set right."

Now Alaetar had spoken by the fire, for the first time since his coming there. And silence followed his words, for children have no part to play in the great movement of nations and destiny but to listen. Alaetar registered the fact that there would be no response — with vague surprise and disappointment — and turned back to look south once more.

Two more nights like this, and he would have been standing there alone. But that is when little Nayhan saved the summer. Too small to understand how fearsome the preacher was, the grocer's youngest trotted up from the fire and tugged on his blue robe. Alaetar looked down on him from an enormous height and Anteris held his breath, fearing the worst.

Nothing daunted, Nayhan simply asked, "How do *you* know?"

Alaetar stared at the four-year-old without moving, and then said a bit stiffly, "I have seen it, child. It is writ in the stars."

Nayhan furrowed his brow and looked away to the darkening sky, then back. "Which one?"

Time stood still an extra moment, and then the last thing any of them expected happened. Alaetar's face grew a smile; jerky and crooked, even embarrassed, but as certain as melting ice he melted. Kneeling down, he put one enormous hand on Nayhan's shoulder and gently turned him about so they could sight the sky together.

"All of them, little one, each is like… like an instrument in a very large band, with a time and a part to play. So then, which one is that?"

Nayhan rolled his eyes and explained with great disdain, "Conar, of course!"

"I see," Alaetar returned, impressed, "then where is his fellow Hopelord, Ma-Eldar?"

Nayhan turned to look south, but after a moment turned back. "He's not there. Wait, you cannot see Ma-Eldar in the summer."

"Indeed you can, but not yet, one must wait until… hah, until well past your bedtime," Alaetar said with a mischievous grin. "But no matter, we will listen to the Lord of Men now. What does he say?" And despite Nayhan's utter confusion, Alaetar gently turned the child around and pointed back up to the bright, tiny argent disk that marked Conar to the east.

"He doesn't say anything!" Nayhan insisted. "That is a star, not a person."

On this Alaetar arose with a serious face, as if he were being insulted. "Indeed? Then Conar is not the Hopelord of Men, and never spoke?" Now Nayhan was confused, and began to apprehend a bit of fear. But the other children, who had listened rapt to all this, were taken in.

"No, you're confusing him," Forge said rudely, and standing to show he was not afraid. "Conar the man lived and walked our lands centuries ago, sure; but that's just a star."

"In point of fact," Alaetar returned, "it is a *planatalis*. But that's of less importance at the moment. I tell you, Conar speaks." And for emphasis, he pointed again to the bright light above their heads. None of the children could have any notion what to say now.

"You there," Alaetar said briskly but still not angrily to Forge, "stand up there, stand straight. Drop that earth, now, and answer me. Do you read of Conar in the histories?"

Forge was too honest to be polite. "No."

"No?"

"I don't read. Sir."

The preacher took a deep breath and blew it out. Children from further in the back of the group were pressing up closer now.

"Well, but you have heard that Conar is spoken of in books."

"Sure I have! I can read, I just don't like to." General laughter on this, and Alaetar was visibly relieved.

"So then, does Conar speak in books? He is not a book, you would say, but can you hear what he says there?"

Now there was a slow, general chorus of *"aaAAaah"* around the fire. Alaetar pointed once again to the lights of heaven, saying, "Just so. Except the books speak of their past deeds. Up here, men can scan the future."

"Astrology!" Anteris breathed, and the gaze of the seer came around to him. "Of course, you can read the stars. But — I thought it was, well, just a skill, holy sir. I mean, of course you put the learnings to goodly ends, but — to speak to the Heroes? Truly?"

"And who else, young scribe, would tell us these things, would guide us to a goodly end? Conar and the Heroes no more constructed all heaven's bodies than they did write all the world's books. Still, they speak to us."

"How?" Nayhan asked. "Show me." And from the group of children there came echoes of this request.

Alaetar was taken aback once again, and Anteris could sense he was unused to this, young persons engaging him in conversation, questions coming thick and fast and answers half-understood and forgotten. Yet to his growing wonder — and Anteris never joined the veterans on the wall that night — Alaetar seemed to become only more patient, more willing to teach, the more the need of his wisdom became evident.

"So, we see that each of the Heroes makes a journey across the sky each night, and as the seasons turn, the trace of their steps changes. The place of a sky-hero speaks to us of their character, and this is the beginning of the message we should receive. In the last month, for example, which of the Heroes reached highest in the night sky?"

"Is it… Astor?" Forge asked.

"Aye, it is indeed. So Astor the Perilsgroom, the Stealthic of Hope who undertook whatever was most difficult and needful, was ascendant. And the seventh month is a time of dangerous deeds begun, such as kings marching to war in the days of legend, once the crops were planted. Perhaps if a man were thinking whether to undertake a long journey, to move alone and into a dangerous place…"

"You came here last month!" a child shouted from the back, and Alaetar waved her up to the front, where he bowed to her before the others and shook her hand.

"Now of course," he said looking at the girl and speaking gently, "there are many other factors to consider; I suggest only one now. On the night I first thought of coming, and for the day when I proposed to travel, I should have to account for the position of Astor, as well as his overlord Conar on both those days. How close were they and in what relation? Would the dangerous escapade have the benefit of lawful orders, or would it — ahm, be undertaken on individual initiative only?" Forge chuckled at this, and the preacher exchanged a look with the young man.

"But let us consider further, what of the constellations on such a night, or for such a question?"

"Constellations?" the girl said, and Anteris stepped up, pointing to the south-eastern sky.

"Pictures in the distant stars, like the Arbalest."

"You mean the Hunter?" Nayhan asked.

"That is what the rustic peoples would call him," Alaetar said with a tone of disapproval. "But look you: his legs are close together and his bow is very short. No, that is an Arbalest." When he could see that Nayhan and the others had no idea what he meant, Alaetar tried to explain. "You have seen them; bows that are short and thick, with a kind of crank…" and here he mimicked the motion so stiffly that the children all laughed.

"So, what does he say?" Nayhan asked and now Alaetar looked puzzled.

"Who? The Arbalest? Ah, but I see, you believe — hem, now, I must consider before I lead you further astray." He took a few strides back towards the fire as he thought, and again one of the children rose to give him a chair; again, Alaetar tried to refuse, but the child tugged his robe and was insistent, so he thanked him and took it. Nayhan, a little jealous, bumped the newcomer away from the preacher's shoulder and waited with the others.

"You must understand, the Arbalest is in the shape of a man, yes, but" — and here Alaetar groped for the right words — "but he is no hero. He has learned a deadly skill, and so he hires out to another lord or country or race to use it on their behalf, without love or commitment but for pay. In the lawless South, where the Elves of the Empire live, there are many such warriors. The Arbalest needs no courage, since he fights from afar, and he often kills without knowing whose life he has ended." The holy man's face showed his righteous anger now, and the children were hanging on his every word, glancing into the sky where the constellation had taken on a more sinister tone than they previously imagined.

"So we note him, up there in the sky, we mark his position and take heed lest his bolt fall upon us. In this year, he seems to have fired his weapon, justly called a quarrel, in the month of the Hawk. It flies yet overhead, and will land before the middle of Fire Ant. So we heed the danger of the Arbalest, yes. But we do not listen to him. Do you understand?"

Nods all about, followed by questions in packs. The Shilarian seer answered them all as best he could. Once, Nayhan coyly queried, "So, preacher, now you must tell us: when are the heroes coming back?"

"Ehm?"

"You can read the stars, so you tell us."

"Ah," he replied with a small smile, "there is where the stars cannot help us, little one. I assure you, I feel it from fourscore points of light in the heavens, that those vessels of destiny will return to us. You ask the heavens 'when' and the stars will say only 'soon.' And soon to a star or moon is not a short time, maybe, to a human being." He looked up a moment, and then with a wry face added, "Not every clock in the world tells the time as closely as the one your parents built." All the children remembered how they first met him then, and laughed.

Three hours later, in the middle of the night with both moons coming down to the south, the fire pit was barely a flicker of its former self. Alaetar and more than twoscore children were lying back on the grass, staring up at the night sky; questions had been sated for a moment, and Anteris was thinking deeply, as he knew most of the others were. Only the littlest, like Nayhan resting against the shoulder of the Shilarian elder, were asleep. The town guards came within five steps of the embers before they saw anyone was there.

"Crown of Areghel! We've had the parents come round to ask us where the children were," one of them exclaimed. The crowd of them roused to their feet. Realizing with terror how late it had become, the children fled screaming, but the guards began to chuckle, relieved that no harm had befallen.

So it went each night following, and near the end of Salamander Alaetar spoke to over a hundred young persons each night, teaching the fundaments of astrology and retelling the lore of ancient Heroes. The children laughed and played as before, the talk revived and became even more vigorous. And the very stern, unsmiling sermonizer from a foreign land was greeted among them with joy, a seat, food, and rapt attention for as long as he chose to speak. He never laughed on purpose, but now and again would smile, especially when the youngest asked questions. He brooked no nonsense or disrespect, and some of the older children found their gossip about the parents had to cease within Alaetar's hearing.

Once, and once only, did one of the older boys think to bring a heated dispute before the seer for adjudication. Alaetar, hearing both sides, stood and called upon his miraculous powers to detect lies in the speech; the villain was exposed with an aura of bright red, and arguments from that night forward practically ceased. Forge was told to stand straight a thousand times, and perhaps began to on his own. The children followed Alaetar's every word, and went about after him during the day in droves.

One night a delegation from the town council came to the firepit and, before everyone, announced that in appreciation of his efforts to instruct the young, Alaetar was to be publicly thanked and rewarded with a modest stipend. Only then did some of the children start to suspect they had been educated. And Anteris began to believe, a little, that a kind of destiny indeed was approaching this town after all.

"Please, Sage Fellareon, you must help me." The castellan spoke with repressed desperation, and seemed unable to utter more than three words in a string without plucking at Cedrith's sleeve. The sage's arm was already starting to twitch in anticipation of the next little tug, and the Elf murmured a rhyme of patience in his native tongue as he composed his answer.

"Sir, as I have said, there's no question of my willingness to assist any querent to the Sage's Guild. It is only an issue of my capacity. I know nothing—"

"Nothing of human customs, I know," the man interrupted, making rather more of Cedrith's inability than he was going to on his own. "But this is what suits you, sir, I assure you. I cannot — that is, my master cannot have any word of this inquiry emerge from the common crier's mouth. I need someone who can absolutely be relied upon for discretion" — here an emphatic pluck — "to breathe not a word of the opinion rendered."

"I see, yes, well—" Cedrith began.

"And also someone whose scholarship," the castellan continued, with another pluck, "whose research can gain for us the most accurate answer, come what may. My master believes the literature on this, ah, this matter…" Again a confidential pluck, as he came even closer to Cedrith's ear and absurdly dropped his voice though they were all alone in the chamber. "He believes it will be quite vast."

The only thing keeping Cedrith's heart from sinking into his breeches was the temptation to actually hit this maddening fellow. He was mildly shocked at such a violent impulse, however just it might appear; to cover his confusion he gestured to a sideboard in the chamber where a tea-set awaited. Taking due deliberation as he prepared two cups, Cedrith composed his mind towards the question. After a soothing sip, the matter began to clear before him and his spirits rose. Perhaps a martial spirit, in part, was needed here: the Sages made a kind of war upon ignorance, after all. Resolved, the Elf revealed his strategy.

"I believe I see the problem well, sir," he began, "and if you would kindly permit me—" He headed off an interruption with a raised finger, deftly moving his arm beyond the reach of another tug. "Your master of a well-respected house inquires to know the precise details of noble marriage customs. He is particularly interested in, ah, the settlement of any disputes that may arise in the process of an engagement. The specifics need not concern us, you have made that amply clear."

Moving to add honey that he did not require parried another attempted pinch on his sleeve and Cedrith walked back to the middle of the chamber, which forced his guest to follow for the moment. "The inquiry requires discretion of the highest order, a scrupulous and honest researcher who will show all needed diligence despite the rather thick and tangled nature of the work. The answer given must be able to withstand the most careful scrutiny, even in, ah, the eyes of a judge, which is not to say a case in court, Heroes forefend. A Sage who is interested enough to look for all the answers, and unlikely to share those with any inappropriate persons. You came to me, frankly sir, because as a stranger and someone likely to leave Conar soon, you felt this last object would be most easily achieved." And here Cedrith allowed himself the liberty of a stern gaze upon his querent, who wilted beneath it. Cedrith was far from insulted to have exposed this truth; his homesickness increased weekly and he pined for the letters he received from Kia.

"So you see, then, that you must be—" the castellan began, and again Cedrith indulged himself in the human custom of interruption.

"Not at all, sir, but I have in mind someone better. He is an excellent student, deeply interested in the early history of our country, and as determined as the Fire Ants who felled the proud oak in fable."

"And he won't talk to others?"

"That, sir, I can guarantee; he hardly speaks to anyone. Leave the matter with me and either he or I will be in touch as soon as we have a report. May we call at your master's estate in the city?"

"Well, yes, yes, but how will I know this fellow if he comes alone?"

"His name is Judgement, and I assure you he will be unmistakable. I shall seek him now to render your commission. Good day."

Bowing, Cedrith rang for an acolyte to guide the visitor out, and finished his tea with an air of triumph. He had found a solution to the tactical challenge of this visitor, and in his protégé Judgement had excellent hopes of final victory — not only that the answers would be found but that the issue would cease to trouble him. Marriage customs, to Cedrith, seemed a chilling prospect at best: he knew all the betrothal rituals he wanted, from his Elvish heritage, and exactly where and with whom he wished to practice them. The customs of humans, much less of their nobles, held no interest for him. If anything truly notable surfaced, he was sure young Solemn would provide an abstract. He went in search of the youth at once.

He was nearly to the chambers Natasha used for tutoring when the world shifted.

At first, Cedrith simply felt a sense of elation, which he credited to his clever solution to the research inquiry he intended passing off on his student. But it quickly grew to much more. Cedrith felt as if his every ache and worry had been dissolved in a warm mineral bath. Rested, happy, confident, full of energy, he practically sprang down the hallway; but then his step slowed, as the sage felt an imposing sense of something huge, and perilous and sacred. Still filled with joy and confidence, he became paralyzed with something very much like dread. Cedrith stopped in the corridor, not ten feet from the antechamber door, and convinced that beyond the simple wooden portal lay something too vast for the city to contain. Thoughts of courage and sacrifice ran across his mind; he regarded Judgement and Natasha now as more than friends, as shield-brothers he could lay down his life for. Only a tiny voice within the sage quietly observed that he had never picked up a weapon in anger his entire life. He heard a sharp though distant cry, female, from beyond two doors ahead. Despite the violation, Cedrith moved forward with clenched fists, determined to do his part.

It seemed that more than five minutes had passed, not only a moment. The joyous dreadful feeling ebbed away before he reached the first portal, and when he opened it, Solemn Judgement was just closing the opposite door on leaving Natasha's chamber. His face was as ever composed like iron, but the skin was waxy and there were beads of sweat on his brow. Cedrith felt himself rapidly returning to a mere mortal state, no longer heroic, his confidence draining away and the normal fatigues of his frame returning.

"Judgement, my friend," the sage exclaimed, moving to put a hand on the youth's shoulder, "are you well? You look… that is, what has happened?"

"I am well, Eldest," returned the Man in Grey with his usual impassive air, pausing only to brush some sweat from his brow. The formal manner of address in addition to the locked-down gaze of his eyes hinted something was amiss.

"I heard a cry; is Natasha alright? What has happened?"

"Guildmistress Ioki is within," the youth returned tightly. "She has… she has dismissed me."

"For the day? It's early yet—"

"For good, I trow." For all Judgement's face told, he was discussing the menu in the refectory, but Cedrith felt an icy grip on his spine.

"Dismissed, from the study of miracles? But you… you have always wanted—" Cedrith could not finish his thought aloud at the sight of the young man's stare, so clenched and showing now a fierce disappointment.

"Wait here, my friend, I beg you. I'll go in and see, I'll ask her, and I promise I shall come back soon. This must be a misunderstanding, I'm sure. I shall return in just a moment. Please, wait here."

With a small shrug, the youth adopted a waiting pose, and Cedrith turned the handle on the inner door, looking back at his friend before closing it behind him.

In the tutoring chamber, Natasha half-lay across a table, panting heavily and staring at no place in particular, as if dazed or terrified. Crying out himself, Cedrith ran to help her up.

"Natasha! My dear friend, whatever has happened? I saw young Judgement—"

Her wandering eyes focused better at the name, and Natasha turned to look Cedrith closely in the face as she gripped his tunic front and leaned her bulky frame heavily on her slender friend.

"Cedrith! By the heroes, you must help me!" She was still gasping with urgency and speaking in a sharp whisper as he half-led, half-hauled her to a nearby chair. Sinking into it, Natasha retained her grip and dragged Cedrith down to one knee at her side.

"Where is the boy? How long have I—"

"Solemn is just outside, I asked him to wait. I heard you cry out less than a minute ago."

"He's here?" she hissed, glancing at the door in fear. "He must… he must never know." Cedrith stared into the face of a woman driven to the very edge, a foreign face, no kin to the beaming motherly healer he thought he knew. He recalled their time in the Dark Archives, and began to feel the worm of doubt inside him. But in the end, he was true to himself. After only a moment, he threw his slender arms about the round woman and hugged her as if their roles were reversed. He had seldom felt so inadequate to the task, and missed Kia more than ever. But gradually the healer's breathing became a bit more regular.

"Now my dear," he said, "you must tell me what happened here. I felt… I mean, I heard you cry out. Is anything wrong? Please, Natasha, Judgement tells me he has been dismissed."

Natasha settled back in the chair but still did not speak.

"Has he done something wrong? Is he truly not to study with you anymore?"

Natasha only shook her head a little, but what she denied was unclear.

"He is normally so studious, and I thought you said he showed talent—"

"Talent!" she suddenly cried, followed by a strangled laugh. "Talent, yes."

"Natasha, please, tell me what happened!"

The Guildmistress turned such a terrible look upon the Sage, with eyes so determined and fiery, that Cedrith slipped to his other knee and shrank back a bit before them. "You must never breathe a word of what I tell you, to anyone. Swear."

Cedrith was startled, and again the thrill of doubt grew inside. "Why? What is so terrible that it must be kept from public knowledge, Natasha?"

But the healer was obdurate. "Swear, Cedrith. For your good and for his, you will tell no person what you hear me say in here today. Swear in the ancient tongue."

Cedrith swallowed, resolved, and spoke the word *"Promissar."* With that single word, he bound himself for all time, for no mortal can lie in the ancient tongue. Then he stood, and stiffly crossed the chamber to retrieve a second chair, which he deliberately drew up farther away from his friend than he had been.

"Now then, the truth from you, madam. Has Judgement been dismissed for failure to progress in the understanding of miracles?" Natasha shook her head. "Has he insulted you in any way? Shown a lack of promise?" At this, the healer again burst into a choked laugh, edged with panic. Cedrith leaned in closer and dropped his voice.

"Natasha, what happened here in this chamber today?"

"A few minutes ago," she responded carefully, holding her sides with both arms as if chilled, "he nearly summoned Areghel."

Cedrith was struck dumb. No mortal in recorded history had summoned one of the Heroes. Tales and legends of doubtful origin told of great knights and mages who conversed with Minions, the assistants and vassals of the Age of Hope. But Areghel, the first ruler of the Percentalion? The thought of it stopped his mind.

"I was instructing him in the basic themes of prayer, and today we began to use the Ancient tongue conversantly for the first time. You had told me his claim to be able to understand it, and I assumed... what did you think it meant, my friend, when Judgement told you that?"

"What it meant? I hardly know... but, well, that he was knowledgeable of the basic vocabulary—"

"The basics! Hah! Cedrith," she hissed, "I tell you, he speaks Ancient as well as you speak our Common tongue."

"As well as—"

"I asked him to give me a short sample of how to ask for something, and he responded with... with poetry, Cedrith! He spoke of his longing to be known to the Heroes, he asked... I don't know all he asked, it was too quick, too eloquent for me to follow."

"For you? You speak Ancient fluently, my dear! I have heard you during the ceremonies to Telhol the Healer."

"I speak as a student," Natasha said with a small smile that reminded Cedrith, a little, of the woman he had known. "I have spoken the words in church a thousand times, and I can get by reading elder texts, if they are not too long or on subjects unknown. But this youth, that boy out there… he could converse all day in the speech that Conar used. He began to pray, then, to Areghel — why him, I know not — asked him to 'look down upon me in my hour of need.' And then, then I felt — the room seemed like a closet, like a hat box. I could not breathe, and there was… a Presence."

"I felt it too," Cedrith breathed.

"Did you see Him?" Natasha asked with the wild look back in her eye. Cedrith shook his head, and she continued. "I began to see a… a shape behind the boy, enormous, just the waist and the surcoat of him looming up through the room. As if he stood on the ground of this building and his head above the roof. He was forty feet tall if he was an inch! And I saw the sigil of the Demon-Breaker, the martial fist with the sunburst, it is his device. Almost I could see through the walls and floors, as if the Guildhall here were dissolving, as if only He were real. He was coming, this boy called and Areghel was… he was—" and here the woman sank forward on her arms and wept again.

"And you cried out, anyone would," Cedrith supplied. "And this alarmed young Judgement, who rushed to your side, and so the… the sending was terminated."

"Praise the Heroes," she murmured through her sobs.

"Natasha," Cedrith said gently, "that young man out there, waiting for me, he thinks he has failed you."

"And he must continue to think so."

"Are you serious? Do you know how hard he takes his studies, how he would grate and chafe at such a failing? I cannot face him, to think, his suffering."

"You have given your word," Natasha returned, her face clearing now and showing a hard resolve Cedrith had never suspected.

"Release me!" he urged, voice rising with his body. "I demand it, you cannot hold me; think of the boy!"

"Think of the city!" she returned, also rising. "Solemn Judgement is young, as you have said, and he wants to do right, he wants to achieve great things. Can you imagine the peril to everyone in Conar, should he use this power in ignorance? 'In my hour of need,' he said. Cedrith, a man utters that prayer when he is surrounded by enemies, when his life and those of his companions are in danger."

Cedrith faced Natasha and took in her thought. "But Judgement... he wishes to know everything; he is so driven. His need was just to learn, from you..."

"Aye, to learn from me, today. Tomorrow, he might need to know something else, anything else! The entire city out there, Cedrith! And his belief, it is so... pure. I sense no barriers in him, no doubt, no hesitation. He is only one boy, and the many must be protected."

Cedrith thought of the conversation by the fountain. "He understands that, Natasha, I assure you. And that is why he deserves our trust. You must release me."

She shook her head again. "I will... I will find a way if I can, to channel his talent. But not now; he is too... he is too much for me, Cedrith. You must let me handle this in my own way. May the Heroes grant me wisdom, I must search... I need him, Cedrith. Judgement is the key, to—" and she broke off, biting her lip. More secrets, Cedrith thought, and he powerfully wished he had not come.

"I am bound by my word," he admitted stiffly, with an unfriendly glare at Natasha. She took it in and was hurt by it, as he in his anger intended. "I look to you to keep your promise as well, Guildmistress."

Natasha was bleak and her apple-cheeks were tracked with tears as she responded quietly *"Promissar."* So now they had each bound the other through the Ancient tongue, though hers was the far looser vow. Cedrith turned and left the chamber, not sure when he would willingly return to see Natasha again. The very thought tore at him, and his inner voice cried out that here was a kind, loving and hopeful woman who wanted what was right. But his anger still ruled, shouting that she had tricked him into the vow, and that she held secrets.

Judgement turned to him as he exited the chamber, now completely composed and as calm as milk in a glass. Cedrith thought he might break his vow, despite all. But the power of the Ancient tongue was complete; his jaw worked and he stuttered nonsense when he tried to just begin. As he swallowed to try again, the grey youth said, "So," as if accepting a verdict spoken by Cedrith's silence.

"She, ah, that is, Natasha, is well," Cedrith began. "She says… she says that she cares for your welfare, Judgement. And that f-for n-now you… are excused from your miracle studies."

The words fell on the student like blows from a whip, and he withstood them stoically, almost succeeding in showing his indifference. The cost of telling the lie was in no way lessened by the force of the promise, and Cedrith's spirits sank to know he was the perpetrator. Then too, he felt a chill of fear again, as he had when the youth summoned holy power in the Temple to Conar; this young man was indeed a perilous foe, and someday this lie would be exposed, Cedrith was sure.

"I have a daily hour without occupation, then," Judgement remarked as if noting that his room was dirty.

"Indeed not," Cedrith rallied to say, "for I have found your first commission, if you are willing to do some hard research." He felt worse for deliberately stoking the boy's studious nature in this way, but was desperate for a change of course. Taking his arm, Cedrith led him down the corridor, away from the scene of such a miracle and closer to the lie that was the rest of his life.

"A querent from a respected family has come, to ask about the customs of marriage in noble houses here in Conar. In specific, to know what customs, if any, govern the settlement of disputes over engagements. I know very little about any of the practices of Man, of course, and it's likely there will be certain fine nuances deep in the histories to be unearthed. Can you research the basic material, then provide me with an abstract and also make a report in person when you are completed?"

To Cedrith's delight, he could see the fire of interest taking hold of his student's mien as they walked. "Certes, Eldest," he said, reverting to courtly speech in his excitement, "for I trow this has been a subject much to my liking since… in recent days. I shall indeed endeavor to discern—"

"Excellent news, my lad! And I shall be here if you should have any questions."

"You may repose your trust in me," Judgement said seriously, extending his hand as if the two of them were making a bargain. Cedrith took it with only a slight reluctance for the misdirection the task was serving. As if he were truly worthy of the lad's trust! "I shall return my best answer to the House Enceris within two weeks."

Judgement turned and left at once in the direction of the stacks, obviously intending to begin his work without delay. Only hours later did Cedrith recall he had never mentioned the name of the noble house.

The Nameless Tome of Faltus Fanem - Prologue

It is indeed strange, to write the beginning at the end. I have composed this work of my lifetime, with my lifetime; and I know these will be the last words I ever write, for my death is surely as near to me now as the bottom of this page.

Herein lies the tale of my researches to this day, to uncover the work of the noble Exeter Palanquan, his struggle against the man-liche Wolga Vrule, and the secret of necromancy which that Child of Hope did undo. I shall hide this work as deeply as I may, that the enemy may never find it, nor the unworthy be harmed with more knowledge than their minds can bear. I keep this secret from all the world, my own Guild both ally and enemy to me; may Rallantan forgive me.

Let me tell you something about yourself, you who read this. You are intelligent, since you have followed the scattered clues and tried all the doors that this key unlocks. You are dedicated, burning with desire to know and do good; you have likely broken the rules to reach this page and serve Hope, and thus you have the beginnings of wisdom, to know the difference. And you are human, most likely young, for the elves do not care enough about today to drive themselves as needed, and the old have become too distracted to stay the course.

For those qualities, you will now learn how necromancy was born here in these lands, and how goodly mages who came long before us were able to undo their curse. You will risk your sanity to learn these things, and then your life to unearth the remaining clues that will make them real. I would have done these things myself, but soon now I will die and must content myself with pointing you.

But remember this, eager young human reader.

Once, Wolga Vrule was young and human too. Farewell.

Riddy didn't mind his life — at four years old, happiness was easy to come by — but the one thing he truly loved was his fortress on the sand. Father and three grown brothers too busy fishing, and a mother who only wanted him to sit still and not get hurt, left the youngest son literally between them, on the beach flanked by the cottage and the bay. In the sand, near the quay where the family boat moored, sat a tidal rock with an old hull turned upside-down on one side of it. The abandoned dory was his father's first craft, before sons and good luck brought him enough wealth for a four-man ship. The dory had lain unused on the beach for the decade and more from the new purchase to the surprise birth of another boy. Between the rock and the hull lay plenty of space for Riddy to sit or stand, the beat of the waves and the gull-cries dulled by the stone and wood. A hole in the boat had doomed it for further service, but let in just enough light to make simply sitting in the fortress a romantic adventure. Riddy had salvaged a piece of driftwood to serve as a door, tied to an oarlock with hemp and opening from the bottom: his portcullis, the entrance to his impregnable castle, which when lowered signaled that the lord of the beach wished to be left alone. And solitude he had in plenty; the men left for the day shortly after dawn, and once he had attended to minor chores getting their craft stocked or casting off, Riddy had until sunset to prowl the shore in search of tidal treasure. Whenever the sun was too hot, or the pickings too thin, Riddy retired to his fortress, imagining his next foray or counting through his plunder.

It was raining when Riddy's father returned from another day's fishing, and the boy kept waiting for his call, to come and clean the catch, to string them out and help stow the gear. At first, Riddy thought the stringing might wait; nothing would dry until tomorrow at any rate. But that was never his father's way, to let a chore go by when someone else was going to do it. So Riddy carefully peeked from behind the gate of his castle. His father was standing on the shore and talking to a Man of Ash, something about buying a boat. Riddy thought he had never seen anyone so old, and with his staff and hat he looked like a court mage from his fortress-imaginings. Several times, his father gestured out over Riddy's head, but since they were discussing a boat and not a castle, Riddy was not concerned.

Then the stranger took out some silver coins and handed them to his father, and they both turned to walk in his direction. Suddenly, Riddy knew, his keep was being attacked.

And he sallied out to defend it. Rushing towards the Ash Man, Riddy screamed his defiance; no one could have his fortress, not fair. He lurched into the Ash Man's thighs and pounded at him, without effect, until he felt his father jerk him back by the hair. He was crying even before the thrashing began, whipped with hemp across his backside even harder than the time he broke the good crock, and he continued to cry for what seemed an hour after he was thrown on the wet sand and left there.

When he recovered his senses, Riddy lurched painfully to his feet and turned around. His father was gone, though he could still hear him bellowing indistinctly at his mother inside the cottage. The Ash Man stood next to the rock, behind the wooden wall that was now just a boat again, but he had not touched it. He looked at Riddy, steadily and without smiling, seeming to wait for something. Several more minutes of crying did not make Riddy's lacerations heal, or the rain stop, or the robber go away. He tired and snuffled to a halt. The stranger made a small ushering gesture with one hand, inviting the boy over to the rock and wood between them. Riddy came, and after a few moments of silence, leaned down to open the door and crawl in. The knight of the beach sat for awhile inside his keep, peering up at the stranger through the hole in his ceiling and occasionally weeping quietly again in his hall of sorrow. The Ash Man looked at him like a giant through his roof, and also glanced at the cottage more than once. Riddy saw the man's face settle into a determined mask; it seemed to say "guilty," but Riddy did not feel accused. A short time later, the rain stopped, and Riddy realized he had slept. The Ash Man was gone.

He dared to feel better for that night, which he spent in the keep for fear of his father. But before dawn the next morning, the stranger returned. Riddy jumped when he heard the sound of heavy things hitting the sand behind the boat, and peered through the roof-hole, to see the Ash Man with a few tools and what looked like leftover planks of wood. Riddy felt a shadow of his anger return and, ignoring the pain of his breeks tearing free from the scabs on his legs, he emerged and stood with his arms akimbo, every inch the aggrieved property owner confronting the burglar.

To his surprise, the Ash Man neither retreated, nor stopped, nor spoke, nor yet completely ignored him. Working quietly in the predawn dimness, he examined his boards, measured them against the hull — still without touching it — and returned them to the sand. Each one seemed not quite correct for his needs, and it was a pile of trash, in Riddy's opinion. At last the stranger stood with two pieces, one in either hand, and looking at a rotted plank along the boat's port rail. He turned to Riddy, and gesturing with the two, silently asked his opinion. Startled, the boy quite forgot that the man was a thief and wrecker of his happiness, and stepped forward to take them, one at a time in his much smaller arms, to compare for himself. After a few moments, it was clear that the oak piece was much better suited than the pine; it needed to be trimmed down, but there was no missing it. He confidently held out the winner, and the Ash Man took it gravely, nodding in acceptance of his lord's orders.

Over an hour later, they were hard at work planing a replacement for the centerboard-rim, when Riddy's father emerged and bellowed for him to get the nets unfolded. Riddy jumped up and ran to do as he was bid, by habit, and only a few steps later stopped to look back. The Ash Man continued working, but paused a moment to lower the driftwood door to its closed position. He had never yet moved the boat as he worked. An hour later, as the fishing-craft set sail, the mage-thief was gone, and Riddy once again had the fortress to himself. But there was a sad sense of violation all around the place; another had been here, and his keep would one day be gone.

Treaman felt as if he hadn't stopped grinning in three days.

He stood with his party now, holding the mule by its lead and rummaging once again in his pocket for a bit of fish to feed Hallah. Haltar, back to his normally strapping size, and Linya, now slender and still pretty, were bidding farewell to the leading women of Maladon as a crowd from the town stood nearby. Further off, a delegation of four men from the island sulked, having already said their piece and looking a bit dourly towards the group. Bildon, still too weak to march, rode the mule nestled among tightly-packed bags holding as much of the dragon's hoard as they could carry. After purchasing one of the valley's only pack animals, Haltar had graciously assigned the remaining treasure to the people of the vale. By weight, Maladon owned two pounds in three, but since the party had worked it over before telling the news, none were the wiser that so little gold, so much silver was among their share. For the larger items, Haltar openly declared them and they had haggled for possession, allowing him to recover more coin and gem in return for whatever the villagers chose to buy out. Of the dragon itself, regrettably, nothing recognizable remained; the fire-blast by which it bartered its life for that of its enemies, together with its caustic blood, had obliterated its skeleton and most of its scaly skin. But Treaman's new companion was all the proof anyone would need.

The heat had broken and it was hard to think poorly of the last few days with an entire valley toasting them as heroes. Treaman's joy, however, was unconnected to his fame, his impending wealth, or the fact that as a man he had received plenty of attention from the women of the vale. Finding another piece of fish, he held it up to the tiny dragon coiling on his arm, snatching his fingers back with learned skill as it merrily gulped down the morsel.

{"Hungry!"} came the happy chirping thought.

"Sure, hungry. I see through you, you're always hungry," he murmured to his companion. The creature nosed at the pocket and Treaman stroked her neck, which brought it around to look him again in the eye and croon. Mhoral stared in fascination, still not coming too close after all this time.

"You talk to it? You can hear it, really?"

"In my mind. I can't explain it. Mostly she just says she's hungry."

"Are you feeding it right?" Mhoral had his visor up and his eyes were large with tension; he normally projected as much composure as he could in public, but Hallah had clearly unnerved him. "I mean, it's going to get too big soon enough…"

"No," Treaman cut in, feeling another of those strange moments of certainty that came to him around the subject. "She's not going to grow any more, or at least not much. This is it."

"As long as she doesn't get bigger than me," Bildon quipped from mule-back. He'd been much less afraid than the Elf, and had fed Hallah several times. Linya, too, had stroked the miniature dragon and admired its elegant beauty, whereas Haltar was more distant. Now, Treaman could sense the conversations around him were once again breaking down as everyone stared at his companion. Treaman held up his arm, and the thin reptile spread its light wings a moment for balance.

"Everyone is staring at you, do you know why?" he asked. Hallah looked back at him for a moment with those unblinking gemstones.

{"Hallah beautiful!"}

The woodsman laughed aloud, saying, "Yes, that is exactly right."

Haltar had again found just the words to describe the foray. Treaman's discoveries, the halfling's valor, and a dragon who "died by fire;" the tale was practically weaving itself under his deft and modestly-honest tutelage. Who wouldn't believe the party had assailed a dragon and won? He could reassure the people of Maladon that no dragon's issue remained to threaten their peace; with his perfect instinct about when not to speak, he never referred to Hallah at all, and simply let the sight of her do the talking. Much was said about the warnets, and Haltar assured both sides that the effect of their venom, if there were any survivors at all, would fade with time. Treaman's grin only widened a bit when his leader warned them with serious tone and pointed finger to beware the female's stingers and have them removed at once. Keeping his straight face, Haltar declared, "We have left no warnet egg behind to threaten the vale." That made him no liar, if another clutch were found, and it also stepped around the issue of those oblong shapes in Linya's waist-pouches.

The women begged the party not to leave. No overt threat remained to require protection, and the woodsman wondered, as he watched the male delegation from the island fort, how much of this importunity was for show. He shook his head as he watched Haltar demur, and wondered if the two sides could ever reconcile. The warnet venom, it seemed, affected nearly all the adult survivors on both sides, and not only increased their desire for sex, but almost destroyed each gender's ability to negotiate for it. The separation, while hardly happy, had been mutual in the interest of containing violence. Treaman and Linya had carried messages between the two groups, and by decorating the words with some sugar had hopefully managed to push things back together a little. But the venom pumped in over the course of several seasons would not fade at once. Haltar, with just a small dose, had been irresistible, and possessed of enough wit to control himself, though barely, had definitely had a busy week. No question, the whole party knew, their leader had taken advantage of the willing advances made on him by several of Maladon's women.

And now, with his helm and cape and shining half-plate, his thick black hair hanging about his shoulders and the bottom part of that scar just peeking out above one eye, he was the image of manliness still. Treaman could not suppress a chuckle, to think of the hearts the knight was breaking with his departure.

The thought came sudden and surprising: *{"Treeeman make a human baby too?"}*

He coughed and looked Hallah in the eye before whispering, "No… I, um, I left that to him." The thought of his virginity flitted past, and he wondered with fear if Hallah could read his mind. "Will you — ah, will Hallah ever make a baby?" The gorgeous miniature dragon looked steadily back, as if waiting for him to answer his own question. "Well, never mind, you're still a little baby yourself."

{"Hallah big! Big!"} The creature stood up a bit on his shoulders and extended her wings to almost two feet span; drawing breath, the creature held it and then puffed it out with a small "*pwhagh!*" Once again, everyone went still and looked; Haltar, who had been interrupted, was less than pleased. Hallah looked around at the group and then shouted in a voice only Treaman could hear.

{"Big!"}

"Yes," he assured her while stroking her chin, "very big." Satisfied, she settled back behind his head in the hood of his cloak and fell asleep.

The people of the vale became more and more excited as the time for leaving approached. Promises were wrung from Haltar on behalf of the party, to return, to give the news, to appeal for wood and livestock. Each member had been approached by individuals as well, with letters, inquiries, requests beyond number. Treaman felt a pang of worry, as he often did when he promised like the others to do his best, about the hopes they would be carrying away with their treasure. What chance, really, did they have even of escaping the kingdom's border, much less to find a return path? But, like Haltar, they all knew when not to say something. Catching the eye of the island-men, Treaman gestured to the two wrapped saplings he'd dug up and brought back from the southern vale near the dragon lair. They acknowledged him with raised arms in respect of his gift. He realized he'd like very much to return to Maladon. Then again, he would dearly like to survive the trip back to the civilized lands.

The woodsman felt his stomach sink as the party turned away at last and began their trek up and out of the vale. Twice they had ventured into the Percentalion, and once returned so far. Every trip had been nothing shy of sheer luck. The woodsman was the one the party depended on to guide them, but Treaman had seen no clues, unraveled no riddles on his trips so far. The chaos-land had lost him as surely as the others, and he knew that they knew.

Haltar took the lead, followed by Mhoral, Linya then Treaman guiding the mule with Bildon aboard. They were easily visible for the entire walk to the top of the valley, more than a league; each time Treaman looked back, the women and men were still standing exactly as they had been. At the ridge, the party paused and looked down, waved, and heard a distant cheer from the tiny crowd below. Haltar stood aside to let the party pass, Linya took the halter and Treaman stepped up to lead. Leave them with the proper image, he thought, try to look like you know what you're doing.

Now began the strange journey into the border-realm. The flatland in three directions seemed passively plain, marked by occasional copses, rocky shelves, or shallow draws. Only behind them could they see the declivity into the Vale of Maladon; even the hint of it, though mostly out of sight, carried more vitality than the rest of the horizon combined. The Percentalion near the edges showed nothing spectacular, much less threatening; it lacked color, ground cover, and nearly all animal life. If the party camped here, with the vale still in sight, the next morning it would still lie in the same direction and they could return to it. Treaman scanned in all directions, trying to wring some clue from the terrain, the barrier of no return he knew was near. They were headed on, Trainertown or bust, regardless; on the old maps, north and one point west by the compass from here, but now was the crucial time, before the rules vanished. The stories told of those who were skilled enough, only decades ago, to guide parties through. There must be a way…

On instinct, he sought altitude, leading the party up one side of a draw which elevated his view by perhaps fifty feet. Stopping at the top, Treaman took a slow, deliberate circle of the position, looking in all directions as no one spoke. Far to the south and west, a looming pile of clouds marked the massive peak of Skysword: as the legends told, it was in its proper place, with Maladon to the northeast of the kingdom. But it would not stay put; this unthinkably massive pile of stone some forty leagues away would disappear, then come back on any side, or any distance. The breeze was fitful and weak, perhaps the start of chaos there. Back along their path, the vale, seeming as if the sun shone brighter, the edges much more green. All other directions were nearly grassless, fully lifeless. Treaman tried to discern how high a mounded hill in the distance might be, but lacking other markers of known size made it impossible.

Up in the sky to one side he saw the folding lines indicating a small flight of birds. He watched them for direction, and for any indication they might give. Again the thought came surprising and unbidden.

{"More dragons."}

"No," he said to Hallah, "those are birds."

{"Birds? How look?"}

"They have feathers, and they lay eggs—"

{"From eggs like Hallah!"}

"Well yes, yes a little like you," he admitted with a smile. In his mind he imagined a songbird, and then a duck, an eagle.

{"Hungry!"}

"Oho, you want to eat a bird? Can you fly?"

The miniature wurm extended its head from Treaman's hood and stared up into the sky after the flock. *{"Hallah fly soon."}*

"I will miss you then."

{"Hallah not leave Treeemann. Hallah fly back."}

The woodsman felt a surge of joy to hear this, momentarily pushing back his gloom at the burden over him. Signaling to the group to remain behind, he drifted on in the general direction of the disappearing birds, getting a hundred yards away as he tried to think.

{"Treeeman sad."}

He scratched her head. "Just a little depressed."

{"Treeeman like the valley?"}

He laughed out loud, then checked himself: Hallah must be able to read his mind, like a lexicon, to have made a mistake like that. Trying to choose his words carefully, he said, "Treaman needs to lead his friends to… another town. Do you remember the town?" He brought an image of Maladon to his mind, then the sight of Trainertown the day they last left it.

{"Town. Stone-pile with humans."}

"Yes, fine. I must get there with my friends, but it is easy to get lost here. Sometimes we get lost for many days."

{"Treeeman not get lost. Treeeman find town."}

The woodsman sighed, drawing what comfort he could from his friend, and returned to the party. "Let's make for that hill," he said, not trying to conceal his indecision. "We can reach it before nightfall, and there will probably be wood nearby.

Haltar nodded. "Mhoral, keep a watch aft, let us know." Everyone understood what the leader meant, and the group set off without further word.

Several hundred paces on, Treaman looked around to the rear and announced, "Gone."

"Blast!" Mhoral exploded. "Moment in time, it happened again!"

"As it happened before," Bildon put in unhelpfully with a grin on his face. Behind them, the slim line of the Vale of Maladon had simply disappeared. Walking back a hundred steps, no one could see any indication that the valley had ever been there. In place of the gap was more featureless terrain, a few bushes, a few rocks. Treaman looked to the south, and the pile of cloud was also gone. East, it was east of them now, but no; as he took a few steps in that direction, the clouds there resolved into something more normal, closer, not the upper fringe of the mountain. His last orientation marker was gone; Treaman thought the sun had slewed around two points south as well. The party stopped to discuss.

"We know perfectly well what to watch for," Haltar said calmly, "but we still cannot see it."

"I did not so much as blink—" Mhoral started, but Haltar cut him off.

"We know, Mhoral," he said in a tone almost conciliatory. "It happened when we lost sight of Trainertown. Your sight has to be best for this job of any of us. I'm convinced, the point of no return cannot be sensed, at least not this way."

Treaman nodded. "I've kept watch with you, and it's the same. You don't even realize you're not seeing it." He looked around the group and said simply, "Welcome back to the Percentalion, everyone."

"Wake me up," Bildon said, "when you can say 'welcome back to Trainertown'." He nestled a little lower in the saddle and leaned back against a pack full of welded coins as if it were comfortable.

Treaman gazed over the party, the loot-packs on the mule, the scabbard of the lovely ax Haltar had claimed, the jewelry, book and chalice in the side-bag, the precious warnet eggs in Linya's pouches, Mhoral's elegantly decorated greaves. All the loot of the dragon's hoard, and fame, news, the treasure of hope for a pocket of surviving humanity: Treaman felt the impact of all that responsibility fall heavily on his shoulders. Looking back at where the vale should have been one last time, he shrugged and turned once again to face the hill, now showing a shadow in the afternoon light. If those rules still held, it was not very tall and not very far. The woodsman added that to the inventory of what he might know for sure about the cursed land.

Again he strode ahead of the group, and again he heard a friendly voice.

{"Treeeman not lost. Treeeman find town."}

"Oh, you think so?" He looked into the eyes of his extraordinary companion and felt again the nameless wonder of its existence.

Hallah stared adoringly at him, and he heard *{"Treeeman can do anything."}*. His heart lurched in his chest, and the young man began to believe. He brought forth another piece of fish, and then set out for the hill with a more confident stride.

⊕⊕⊕

Riddy never stopped being a little resentful of the Ash Man. But at some point in the first few days, he did start talking to him. He had taken to sleeping in his fortress every night, and after his mother had checked on him there a couple of times, she accepted his absence with a grace tinged by relief. Riddy still did his chores, but stopped speaking to his father at all: the anger and shame he had felt when the boat was sold left him, but the habit of his embargo grew like a weed in the hole it left behind. Whenever the intruder came by to work, he always knocked to let Riddy know he was there; a gentle *boum-doum* on the roof of his hall, and no more. If the knight of the manor was in, he would generally emerge to oversee the mage-thief at his work.

The Ash Man worked steadily and well, but seemed remarkably forgetful, almost foolish for a grown man. Starting with leftover pieces and hardware, he took an enormous time selecting which ones to use, to cut down or trim. Everything went into two piles, and the Ash Man was of two minds, it seemed, about both of them. Time and again, Riddy had to show him which way to set the saw, or which piece of thrown-away wood to use as a patch. Each time, the old man with the young-looking face would nod and accept the instruction, returning to work without speaking.

Riddy was not used to having his way in conversation with others. But the Ash Man was no competition and soon he found he was talking non-stop as they worked; about his treasures from the beach (he showed some to him; the Ash Man stopped everything to gravely examine each relic), or sometimes about fishing, or what little he knew of tides and weather. And Riddy repeated the hero-tales his mother had told him when he was just a baby. He would say, "Have you heard about Areghel and his battle with Kog?" or "Did you know that Conar turned the hulls of the White Fleet into the walls of the city overnight?" or "What about the marriage of Aballe and Ekhonon, do you know how they spoke their vows?" The Ash Man would give that chin-flick that said not yes, not no, but only "tell me." And Riddy would begin. The robber listened carefully as he worked, always nodding at the end as though well satisfied with the telling. But he never spoke unbidden.

"Have you ever sailed a ship before?" Nod.

"Did you live in your boat?" Another nod.

"Where is it?"

That brought a pause in the work, before an answer.

"I burned it."

"What? Why? Was it too small to live in?"

The Ash Man looked at Riddy for a long moment then, a slow thoughtful nod, and back to work. Today the thief was trying to carve an oak-knot into a pulley for the sail-rope, with little success. Riddy watched the work, then went off beach-plundering, and came back an hour later to see him still at it. There were three failed attempts lying on the sand where the mage-thief sat. Riddy tried to watch patiently, sitting on the roof of his keep and letting his feet drum against the wood just to hear a sound. The Ash Man never needed to say anything.

"Have you heard about The Man Who Went into the Sea?" he asked, in a bit of desperation because he didn't know the story well but he could think of no others. Again the mage-thief beckoned him, but he also stopped working.

"Once there lived a knight who didn't belong in the city, because his hands were cut. So he walked into the sea at night when the moons were full. He walked out until the water was right to the tip of his nose," here Riddy gestured for emphasis and jumped down to stand on tiptoe in the sand. "But Conar spoke to Restol and they made the sea go away from him until he walked all the way out to the bottom where it doesn't get any deeper. So he came back to shore, but the next night he did it again. Each time Conar and Restol saved him. This went on thirty nights, every day of the month, and finally Restol taught the moons how to do the job, so he could sleep. Then at the end of the month Conar told the knight it was better now, and he healed his hands, and the man walked onto a magic white ship, that carried him away for ten years. Then he came back and lived alone the rest of his days."

When Riddy finished, the Ash Man still did not work, and he did not nod as he usually did. Riddy thought perhaps he had never heard this story before, and it made him feel wise like a knight should around his mage.

What's more, he asked questions.

"Why were the knight's hands cut?"

Riddy didn't know, but that wasn't what story-tellers said. "He cut them in a great battle, or trying to defeat a dragon… but he must have cut his hands because they had blood on them," he added for proof. The Ash Man thought about this awhile.

"And this happened a long time ago?"

"Oh yes, very long ago; so long it was 'once'," the lord assured his mage. There was another period of quiet then as again the Ash Man thought things over.

"Do the stories say the knight's name?"

Riddy shook his head, and decided to turn the tables. "Why?"

The Ash Man looked out to sea, and said, "Names are important."

"My name is Riddy. Do you know what that means?"

The Ash Man looked to his host for a time with amusement in his eyes. "The riddy is a kind of fish, too small to be caught in a net."

"But sometimes it gets caught, because it is being chased by a larger fish," the boy exclaimed with some excitement and gestures, "and the net comes in and the larger fish gets jammed on the net and holds the riddy against it while it is caught. And then we eat the hunter, and throw the little one back in. To catch more, my father says."

"Is that why your father named you Riddy?" the mage-thief asked. "Because you help him catch bigger fish?"

"No," the boy replied honestly, "he says it is because we catch riddy only by accident, but I don't know what that means."

The Ash Man looked upon his lord with a face that seemed sad.

"Do you have a name?" Riddy demanded.

The Ash Man nodded, but only returned to work, and this time his effort with the whittling knife split the oak knot at once. Together they surveyed the wreckage of his efforts, pondering the problem with only the waves for conversation.

The answer came to Riddy in a flash. "I have it! Wait here."

He darted inside the fort and dug in the secret place, the sand by the rock for his plunder. A few layers down, under the driftwood piece shaped like a fork, was a smooth shell-stone, smaller than his palm and with an inside-curve all round. Riddy emerged from the gate and without a second thought held it out to the Ash Man. He stared at it without moving for a long moment, then looked Riddy in the eye, level with him as the man sat.

"It's a shell-stone. My father says if you leave a shell or a bone in the sand long enough, it turns to rock. Take it. It's perfect," Riddy urged, feeling somewhat a stranger to his young self to be so generous with the robber of his home. The Ash Man nodded soberly, and reached to take the shell, sliding a nail through its center and spinning it once to confirm his success. Delving into his pouch, he produced an entire silver coin and held it out to Riddy; the beach-lord just gawked at this treasure, and then took it with some gravity for the transaction.

But as soon as he had, Riddy began to feel angry again, tricked into agreeing: the shell, the coin, the boat — he had just sold his fortress. Just as his father had done.

Riddy scowled and shook his fist at the Ash Man. "I wish I had never met you!" he yelled, and then threw his bribe into the sea with all his tiny might. "You don't know, it isn't fair!" Riddy was starting to blubber again, and a part of him didn't want to cry, not before this courtier, not in front of his own manor. But he was only four and the tears came. "You are taking my house! My house!" The Ash Man looked steadily at him as he always did, and Riddy at last stormed back inside.

The next day, the Ash Man did not come. But the following dawn, he brought an armload of nails, rope and pitch and dragged behind him a pole, to be used as the mast. The work was nearly done, and Riddy knew his boat would return to the sea now. The Ash Man stepped to his usual spot and laid everything down, straightening up to look at Riddy and ignoring the fisherman's attempt at a friendly hail as he cast off. Under the thief's steady, almost gentle gaze, Riddy felt his anger and fear ripen, and he ran off crying, further down the beach than ever, and without breakfast to boot.

The burning sense of injustice gave strength to his legs and his tears blurred the distance. Before he knew it, Riddy had walked farther down the beach than he had ever done before. But he kept going, past other houses, docks, around rocky promontories where he had to step sharp or fall into the bay, and past grand sweeps of the shore showing him enormous stretches of water dotted with ships. Some were much larger than his father's boat, others as small as his keep; any reminder drove him further down the sands, his anger seemingly an endless fire. Riddy didn't slow his step until the thought came to him that perhaps he was running away from home. By then he was approaching the end of Landfall Bay, where the two largest promontories pinched in and nearly touched Guardian Isle. In the brilliant light of late morning, Riddy saw for the first time the cliff—carved island towers watching the ocean channels — and through the southern end closer to him, a glimpse of the Western Sea.

At this point the shore was rocky, and his legs were starting to shout, so Riddy curled up beneath a large stone jut and contemplated his situation. Or, he tried hard to do so, but he was only four and nothing mattered except that his home was being taken from him. And that he was hungry and his feet were cut and it seemed he had never been happy in his life. He cried some more, and was angry at his father until he grew tired of that. Without realizing it, Riddy fell asleep under the rock.

The cold waves splashed over his feet and Riddy awoke with a cry. The tide was coming in and already the land on both sides of his outcrop was underwater. He knew the way back would be over his waist, and Riddy could not swim, but he did not dare try the way on. So he backed up a half-step in the outcrop area and closed his eyes and jumped as far as he could back along the shore.

His head went underwater, but he held his breath and when his feet hit the bottom Riddy pushed up with them as hard as he could. The waves were coming in at the same time, and his body shot up like the wingfish, depositing him hard on the rocks before the outcrop. Riddy cried out and gasped and hung on as water washed over his back, and when it retreated he was safe on land. Crawling further up he rolled over and inspected his arms and chest, which were a mass of seeping cuts. Riddy lay there drenched, shivering and miserable; when his father had beaten him he hadn't done anything wrong either. Riddy sat up and watched the waves coming in, the wide bay and the small slice of the endless ocean he could see. He wondered how far he would have to walk out to reach the very bottom of the ocean, and whether Conar would ask the moons to hold the tide out to save him. When you are only four, it is not just happiness, but all the emotions that come easily; for now, Riddy was as deeply miserable as he'd ever been.

Then he saw the magic ship.

Beyond the island in the north bay's entrance, he saw a pair of white masts crowded with sails and looming above the land. For a moment, it was as if the island itself was a boat- but as the masts moved on into the bay, Riddy could see the rest of the marvelous craft. It was an enormous ship, longer than Riddy's house, with more than a score of men on board working her lines and sails, and from stem to stern it was white, the hull as bright as the sheets. Majestically it hove into the bay and headed for the quays before the city proper. Riddy realized he'd been breathing only shallowly, but now he jumped to his feet, his cuts forgotten and driven by a need to keep the wondrous vessel in sight. At first, by running he could stay abreast of her. But he tired very soon, and slowly it began to pull ahead. Within a half-hour he could see its stern and it had shrunk to half the size of his first view. Riddy slowed to a walk but kept going. By dusk, he was back in territory he knew, and he could see his father's craft already tied up. But Riddy did not think about what trouble he might be in for missing a chance at chores. He could think of nothing except the white ship, which was now a small bright patch across the bay and approaching a deep mooring. Boats were rowing out to unload cargo and passengers, and it might be here for some time before returning to the mysterious sea.

Riddy thought the magic ship was the most wonderful thing he'd ever seen; late fishing boats were returning to docks, and inside the cottage he could hear the sounds of dinner, but it was all like a dim echo to him. The magic ship held him fast, as the sun sank and the city lights grew. Riddy's thoughts stayed on the ship as tightly as his eyes; but then another, smaller boat came between them. It sailed smartly across the bay towards a quay in the inner harbor; and at the helm sat the Ash Man.

The spell was broken, and Riddy at once looked down, much closer to his feet and the rock on the beach. The pile of trash, every speck of flotsam and drek the Ash Man had brought with him at dawn had disappeared, and beyond the jutting rock, where his boat hull had been, was Riddy's fort.

On two sides adjoining the rock was set a small shed with a slanting roof, made of wood pieces bound with netting and wooden nails. On the final side, the driftwood piece that had been the portcullis was still there, still lashed properly at the top to open the way it should. But it fit neatly into the wall and stone on either side, without enough room to let a cat get by, and near the lintel there was a small hole in the door. Riddy approached the little house, and saw hanging on a hook before the door was a wooden stick on a loop of string. When Riddy pulled on his door, it did not open; he noticed the stick had three notches on the end, and a sense of wonder began to steal over him. He inserted the key in the lock and turned; he heard a bar of wood drop inside, and the castle gate was open. Riddy stole inside and set the bar behind him. Safe.

On the far side of his keep was a small roof-hole, covered by a flap for the rain but that otherwise let in just enough light to make the interior seem adventurous. Over by the rock wall, a small rug of sailcloth lay on the ground. Lifting it and digging with his hand, Riddy found the piece of driftwood shaped like a fork, but it was attached now by a rope hinge to a buried box. An entire wooden box lay under the floor of his keep and inside it was every single treasure he had buried there before.

Rushing back outside, Riddy saw a short ladder of slats set into the side of his keep. Ascending to the battlements, he stood and waved at the Ash Man as hard as he could. But it was drawing dark, and the mage-thief-sailor-builder, the hero who had created walls from a ship, never returned to that part of the beach to pay respects to his little lord.

⊕⊕⊕

"Ho there, boy! Where are you, are you here yet?"

"Aye, sir; I'm down here on the stable level."

"Hah! Act like you're a stable-boy, then, not a hand on board a ship! 'Aye, sir' indeed! Lad, where's Quester then, Sir Renan's charger?"

"Out, sir. The lord has taken him a half-hour since, rode out the front gate."

"Gone, then? I wonder what has happened…" The groom Till rubbed his grizzled neck and pondered a bit, before resolving to seek further. "I'll be out by the paddock entrance, lad, join me there when you're finished."

"Aye — yes, sir."

Chuckling at the earnest address of the new stable boy, Till headed around the corner of the stone enclosure that quartered the horses of House Altrindur. He crossed the plaza towards the manor at the center of a fortress set into the heart of Conar. The high walls of the urban precinct were taller than any other city building for blocks around; from the plaza within, Till could see only sky. It was easy to imagine beyond these walls lay a moat and a hill, not streets and the homes of city-vassals. He spotted one of the manor's domestics, the maid Sessa who carried in the meals, and called out to her. Get the best news of the house and eye the comeliest woman in it; a double bargain.

The maid, when called, turned back and waited for him. It was not that she had much eye for any man a decade her senior, and the way she carried herself declared she knew what a prize she was, but Sessa was no more in love with work than with the groom, and the chance to spend a little time outside the manor was fine with her. Till knew, and banked his hopes for the time being.

"So mistress, what's all the news of the house, then?" He knew she liked to be called 'mistress,' no harm in showing some respect. Sessa sat and smoothed her dress before answering, as if considering what portion of her vast gossip-treasure to share with a yardman.

"They hold up as well as they can, under the circumstances." Till nodded to this; the last two months had been under a blur, with the loss of the Altrindur heir.

"I reckon the father was waiting on young Renan to arrive, what with Banwen gone now. He came in last night, didn't he?"

"For the night. Yes," Sessa said, and there was more to her reluctance than the savor of a secret; she was worried. Till switched his hands to his pockets and thought of how to ask.

"So only the night then? My new stable-boy says he took out the charger this morning. I've not seen him. Where's he gone, then?"

"To the countryside, or the lower moon or the utter east for all I know!" Sessa threw her hands up in frustration. "I see him come in, all on fire to comfort his mother; such a noble, sensitive soul he always was. And I bring in a late supper to the dining hall; there he is with his parents, him sitting, them standing. And everyone stops talking, except to thank me, until I'm back out again. There was something wrong, I tell you. He was getting the news, and he didn't like what he heard, I say."

"Well," Till said carefully, "it was in no wise good news. His elder brother killed in a fencing accident, the same morning as he left last time. And Banwen soon to be married—"

"Sure, and it must have been a shock." Sessa waved off the idea impatiently, and Till felt even more attracted to her. She thought for herself, this one. "We all know how that was, here," she continued, more to herself than to the groom. "The parents were frantic to know where Renan was, but he was always one to go off on his own — looking for challenges, he's a dreamer — but I had this feeling about the lord and lady, as well as the son. There was… news, last night, I know it. And they none of them liked it much, either to hear or to give."

"None of them?"

"Till, there was shouting."

"The son, shouting! He's a quiet soul."

"Him, and his father too! I could only hear a word here and there. The father said 'inherit' once or twice, and also something about responsibility. And the young lord didn't take well to it, and I thought I heard him say 'wander'."

"So," Till concluded, "his father made it clear to him that he's the heir to the House Altrindur now, and told him he must settle down. Lord Renan doesn't care to lose his questing life, and rode out, maybe to think about it awhile." Till stood back a half-step to see how his version sat with the pretty maid. In one glance, he could see, not well. Sessa shook her head and the brown curls practically danced around each other beneath the headscarf she wore.

"No, it's more than that. Something else. I think—" Sessa stopped, and looked around at Till as if suddenly sensing she was saying too much.

"My girl, I want to know so I can set up the stables proper, I swear. I'm not trading any confidences you share. I hope you can trust me." And Till was quite earnest about that; no lie in letting his sincerity show. The lovely girl bit her lower lip, still thinking.

"Here it is then, Till," she said, and he thrilled to hear his own name from her lips. "Surely, Renan knew before he came to the room that his brother was dead. He met the guards at the gate; someone would sure have told him when he came into the city. So he's the heir, everyone can see that. Why raise your voice to it? No, there was something else, I just know it."

Till cocked his head and leaned in, as taken with the mystery as with his admiration for the detective. "So, what is it, then?"

"It's this, my dull-witted stable-hand. What else does he inherit, along with House Altrindur?" Sessa let that set a moment, nodding in grim triumph. "He also inherits… a new bride."

Till whoofed his air, honestly caught out. "Of course, then! Banwen was set to marry that diamond of a tiny girl, the house, em, House Enceris. Brilliant match. He was on his way to set the ring on her finger that morning, and then—"

"And then the accident, aye." Sessa was holding court now, her back arched like a Marchess and her eyebrow raised to match. "And what did those gutter-gossips say in the taverns for a month after Banwen died?"

"That it was his brother who had fenced him. They said he was the one, killed him accidentally and then ran. Those scum. I had nearly forgotten. A filthy lie. But now he's back—"

"And he hears his brother died, not an hour after they had parted company that month ago nearly, and that he was murmured responsible, and now that he is in line to inherit. And I bet my savings, he was told he must marry the girl now too."

"Sessa, you wondrous child, you have the right of it, I'll be bound." Till did not need to fake his admiration for the maid, and was never happier about that. "Surely that's it; poor Renan couldn't think for shock, and maybe he balks at being wed now, when he still has so much errantry to do. Political match or no, he doesn't care for the girl, that, em… what is her name, then?"

"Gemma Enceris, sir." The voice of the stable-boy coming from behind Till made him jump, and he would have been shamed but Sessa squealed a bit too. Till noticed that she had lost her queenly posture now, and was staring with wide eyes at the visitor.

"Eh, and how do you know this then, boy?"

The stable-hand spoke without answering. "He packed several things on his saddle-bags when I brought the mount to him, this morning."

"So, he's gone again, then," Till concluded, "maybe for good this time."

"You're right," whispered the maid, "for he said to me, not 'farewell' as he usually does, but 'goodbye.' He said 'Goodbye, dear Sessa, and thanks for all you have done for my mother. I've chosen to wander,' he said."

"'Chosen to wander'?" Till mused. "That doesn't sound worthy of him. Renan Altrindur is a model knight, fearless and honest. He's gone questing until now, but to just run away—"

"Chosen Wanderers," said the stable-boy quietly, and the other servants looked agape at him. "He goes in search of the Chosen Wanderers."

"Nonsense, boy, an Altrindur does not chase myths. Here, then, I suppose I have bad news for you; two lords without horses to ride, I don't need an extra hand any longer. Fetch your things and I'll pay you back here."

Nodding, the youth moved off to the barn, and Sessa leaned in to reprove Till under her breath. "Why do you speak down so to that old man, Till? And why hire an elder in the first place?"

Till had a chance now to pick up some airs with the maid, and he chuckled at her confusion. "He's fooled you too, has he then Sessa? Take a close look at his face, not his hair, when he comes back. He's lacking four years of you or I miss my guess, though he's studied enough, I can say that. Knows all kinds of strange things, like that old scrap-tale about the Castle of the Chosen Wanderers. The legendary order, watching on their high walls to save the worthy and helpless children of Hope… He works hard, like I'm riding his shoulders with a whip in my hand, no complaints there."

Till looked at Sessa, who was watching down the stable-way. For a time neither said anything. Then Till spoke for both. "Yes. Good riddance."

They said no more until the stable-boy returned, putting the rake by the door and draping his cloak around his shoulders while walking across the courtyard.

"Sorry again, lad," Till said, drawing silver bits from his purse, "but we won't have enough work unless the young lord returns."

The youth counted back two of the coins he was given and held them out to Till. "It is not Conar's Day yet, sir. I'm short on a full week."

"A tip, then!" Till growled, put in darker humor to have his generosity questioned in this blunt manner. But the former stable-boy was unmoved. Turning to Sessa and doffing his broad-brimmed hat, he said, "Mistress, would you consent to place these in the collection-bowl the next time you attend the chapel of Conar?"

Sessa nodded a little meekly and took the coins without allowing their hands to touch. Till called after the youth no longer in his employ, "Why not do that yourself, then?"

Without stopping the young man turned his head and said, "They will not let me back in there."

A few steps later, he was gone. Sessa said only, "I can well believe that," and rose to go back into the house.

Reunion of Souls

Most men's nightmares are the stuff of gross exaggeration. For Judgement, it is a matter of remembering, precisely and exactly, what happened when his father died.

Every time he dreams, it is the same. From the stern of the skiff, he pulls the fish line from the water, empty of all but its bait. Turning, he sees his father's silhouette, blocking the morning sun as he rows in the dead calm's fifth day. The son's eyes meet the father's, and the fisher sees that the rower knows — about hunger, about pride, about saying nothing and continuing to fish. As the son turns to cast the line back in, the teacher's voice begins again, reciting the litany of water-signs in the zodiac, their place in the calendar and sky, their meaning in isolation, their relation to the others discussed. The teacher pauses more often today, it seems, his throat dry from the constant pull of the oars and the memory of fresh water, now two days gone. The son notes the evident effort, but fails to question why. Judgement glances up, sees a haze gathering in the sky, perhaps enough for some shade, perhaps enough, later, to rain. He feels again the low crackle of something gathering. He hears about the Turtle, the Swan, the Dolphin, and tries to remember through his fatigue. Long journeys, transitions to new states of being, water brings these when signified by the stars. And exactly then, as he lays in the stern listening to the lecture, letting his father's knowledge fill him as rain would fill his mouth, Judgement sees beyond the broad shoulders, to either side of the noble head and the relentless pulling arms, the line that is too thick on the eastern horizon.

He is already sleepy, in his dream, and fading towards a nap. He knows he mustn't, knows his father would disapprove, and he knows too that the lecture will simply begin again at the point he fell asleep. Just a small part of him tries to protest, though, about the line. If it were land — which it is not, his father has already shown him about mirages — but if it were, why would it be so long and flat? One should imagine things that could be real, not … Judgement drowses in his own dream, and on the last flutter of his blinking eyes he sees the line has not only refused to vanish, it has grown just ever-so-more substantial, with seeming bumps on it. But still too long, too flat, as if the land were titanically heavy, crushing the world from circle to oval. Or as if the world itself were a colossal sphere …

And in his dream, Judgement is now asleep, a moment of utter darkness where his mind is held prisoner. He knows what comes, he knows even, a little, that he is dreaming, and can do nothing. He starts to pant and sweat, and lies helpless.

Until he awakes in his dream.

The scrape of wood on sand, the tang of something with leaves on it, the damp scoosh of surf, the screech of a hawk circling above. The lack of motion, except a tiny waggle at his end of the skiff. Judgement sits up, and two feet from him his father sprawls back, oars in hand, duty done, dead. The land is huge. He is alone.

Until he awakes from his dream.

The acolyte knocking on Judgement's door stands back a full pace and nearly drops the requested tomes. The wraith before him is stark and staring, with beads of sweat on his brow the size of chickpeas somehow holding shape like a horrid, liquid pox on him. The eyes, though burning, see little at first; he is breathing deeply and the acolyte is struck dumb. At last, the vision clears and the Man in Grey spies the books; he reaches wordlessly for them, and his sweat breaks, flowing down his skin as if he had dumped a tankard over his head. Mindless of all, the awoken man closes his door while the acolyte retreats as if from a hostile beast.

The sun had stayed where it should too long. The breeze died. No birds in sight. Treaman became aware of these things slowly, as if in a dream, and something inside tingled with alarm.

"Stop, everyone, stop right here." Mhoral and Bildon cut off their bickering, and Linya said, "What is it?" But the woodsman could not tell her, so he simply held a hand for silence and tried to focus.

Eight days out from Maladon, and when Mhoral grumbled that they were walking in circles, Treaman was tempted to agree with him. The same blasted, grassless, waterless, peak-less terrain on all sides, bursts of disorienting storms, sudden nightfalls, and too many times the sun had reappeared a third-way across the heavens. Skysword loomed from sixty leagues away most hours, but sometimes to the south (where it belonged), at others northwest, and once directly east. As often as the party changed course to match north again, the sky and horizon would suddenly alter around them. It happened several times a day, sometimes more than once an hour; the young man guiding the party burned from the sidelong glances everyone put in his direction.

In desperation, Haltar had called a night-march two days ago, and Treaman went along with it from lack of an alternative. Four hours in, the twin moons vanished behind a burst of clouds, and when they cleared the party could see from their polar track that the northward march had slewed around to the west, though no one took the slightest turn. They camped in low spirits on lower rations, and Treaman had not slept a wink.

But this quiet, this sudden stillness now, was itching in the woodsman's mind, just vaguely, far from where he could reach. And one voice in particular, could not be easily shushed.

{*"Hungry!"*}

Treaman frantically rummaged his pockets for any scrap he could give to sate his tiny dragon, though supplies were desperately low and he knew Mhoral would complain to see Hallah fed another crumb. Empty; he stroked the creature instead, hoping to soothe her and still focus some energy on the world around him. He had asked the group to wait on him a hundred times already, yet there had been no advance, no sense of progress whatever his efforts. Treaman would gladly have portrayed a guess as certainty, if he had any more guesses to make.

"Can we go now?" Mhoral whined from behind.

"You in a hurry?" the woodsman spat back, losing patience; he almost hoped for a monster to come along. When Haltar was in command, the Elf's complaints transferred to the foot-knight, who was better able to ignore them.

"Would Hallah like to go visit the pretty lady?" he asked quietly, and threw in an image of Linya finding a bit of food in her pocket though it was unfair to her. Hallah crooned and flapped off his arm to circle once and come stooping down on the mage's shoulder; the impact rocked her body a little and she laughed. Mhoral and the mule both cringed whenever the dragon took flight, and Treaman reflected there was justice in that. Stepping away from the group a few paces, he took some deep breaths and tried to bring his sense of nature to bear on this torn, unnatural place.

There had been no whisper yet of breeze, and Treaman felt it was the quiet before a storm. He tried to recall: yes, the sudden storms usually presaged disorientation, especially those with great force or odd effects, such as the hail with sharp stones in the center before they had encountered the hexavores. How long ago that seemed to him. Treaman spotted a small gulch within sixty rods, a tiny one-sided canyon or declivity of sorts that could offer some cover. At first the thought of shelter was just another fact to be logged, but as he tried to look elsewhere the woodsman found the idea preying on his mind. His nerves took an extra jangle, and when he brought the suggestion of the stillness, the storms and the cover together, something stabbed the center of his ribs so hard that he flinched.

He flogged his mind for other clues, the bits and drabs of lore he had heard from the men of Trainertown. Marking Skysword; everyone stubbornly agreed that could tell you where you were. "Ah," they would joke "but how to keep the little hill nailed down. There's your trouble!" Following water-courses, several others had averred, for surely water always led somewhere. The young woodsman had taken a liking to that lore, but it died a hard death on this trip. Coming upon a nice-sized stream, he led the group down-water for half a day. But it petered out without reaching a pond or confluence, and when they turned back it was only a shadow of its former self, ending sooner with no source. Two marches, one meal and what remained of the party's goodwill, for a wasted effort, unless one counted Mhoral's backbites and insults, in which case it was a trove of great value.

The lack of animals; this thought was a new one. The Percentalion had creatures in it, some of them hideous caricatures of the game and wildlife they knew, others normal at least in seeming, and a few monstrous beasts, the breed of chaos. All told they were thin and few, like the flora they had to feed on, so not seeing anything for hours wasn't rare. But no birds, no insects or bugs — did some natural instinct lead them to avoid the chaos-holes? Still feeling with his mind for any clue, and ignoring the restless sounds of the party behind him, Treaman strained and on instinct closed his eyes this time. Heard the drum. Very distant, like the first beat of thunder, but frighteningly real and famous, from the southern quarter. Garruk marched by drum when at war; and the garruk were always at war with the Children of Hope. Stepping quickly but quietly as if he didn't wish to trigger a change by himself, Treaman returned to the party and reported to Haltar.

"There's weather coming."

"We waited for that!" Mhoral spat, "There's *always* weather coming here. Right now, praise the Ageless, it's quiet enough. Let's make time."

"We need to take cover," Treaman said to Haltar, pointing to the small covert at the side of the gully. Hallah went to his arm and landed with dexterity, barely making it move despite her weight. She climbed up and curled at his neck as the humans conversed.

Haltar looked down on the young woodsman; as usual, his weathered handsome face was untouched by fatigue or fear, as if the past week in these wildlands was something only the rest of them had experienced and he had joined the group just an hour ago. Under that gaze Treaman felt like wilting. His instinct for staying put and taking cover, he knew, made little sense now and would make even less in a moment. But the party would do as Haltar decided.

"We need to remain still as we can until the weather passes," he managed.

"We need to make the best time we can before the weather comes," Mhoral countered immediately. "We finally have a clear break, we see the mountain, we see the sun, north it is."

"We'll walk straight into the chaos then," Treaman said weakly, but still facing Haltar as if the two of them were talking. "That's always happened before. We come out of the rain, or wind storm, whatever it is, and we've turned five compass points without trying."

"We make what progress we can," Mhoral argued relentlessly. "We're getting closer all the time."

"It took us five days to get to Maladon!" Treaman shouted, turning to look at the Elf for the first time. "That was three days ago, Mhoral. Three days! We're lost," he dared to lay the forbidden word before the group. "We're not getting back that way."

"And so standing still takes us home?" the pious warrior cried in derision. Hallah, sensing his mood, stood up on Treaman's neck and hissed at Mhoral, making the Elf step back a pace, and Bildon laughed. Haltar was in doubt, looking to both members and chewing his lip. Thinking; at least that was a good sign.

Treaman hated to give the news but there could be no trust without honesty. "It gets better. Garruk war-band coming."

"Where?" Haltar asked. "How many?"

"I don't know how big," Treaman said, pointing south. "They have a drum."

"That settles it," Mhoral rejoined. "We make time before the weather and we pull away from the enemy. If the chaos comes, it could split us away from them. North and now," he finished in a confident tone.

"We need to stay, get out of the weather, and wait," Treaman pleaded to Haltar.

"They'll catch us," Haltar said neutrally and the woodsman nodded. The warrior pulled on his face a moment, and looked Treaman directly in the eye. No one in the party knew whether Haltar had ever been a leader of men, when they severally joined with him over the past year and slightly more. Bildon speculated he was Shilarian or Novarian, a knight's son disgraced by some past misdeed; Mhoral repeated a rumor he had heard of a scarred gladiator from the Southern Empire, ringleader of an arena revolt who escaped to freedom, leaving his comrades to their fate. Once, Linya had whispered to Treaman, he mentioned a brother, still alive, but nothing more. Treaman knew his leader liked to drink, not to gamble, and was much more experienced with women. But the party all agreed: Haltar had mastered that art of making folks follow his lead; even now, hoping the foot-knight would take his advice, Treaman had the ridiculous thought that he would like his own course better if Haltar approved of it. The gaze of the party leader bore down on Treaman, silently saying "we commit to this on your head," and the woodsman nodded again in understanding.

"Head for cover," Haltar said briefly in a tone that brooked no refusal. Bildon twitched the mule's reins to tug him into motion, and they set off at a quick clip to reach the canyon-side. Even as they marched, Treaman saw clouds forming with uncanny speed to the northwest. The breeze at last sprang back into being, chasing them from the south carrying the sound of the drum to everyone, yet the clouds darkened and came on, against all nature. Treaman could smell something sharp and rank in the air, and felt more than ever that cover was urgent now.

"A little wet, a little cold, what could it matter?" Mhoral crabbed as if hearing him.

They reached the one-sided grade, and Treaman urged them a ways down it, to a rocky overhang that would shield them from one direction but hide the party from no one. The mule sniffed the air and shied, tugging Bildon a foot or so along before he could brace and redirect her; but the halfling always refused offers of assistance, regarding the animal as his province. They arrayed themselves in a four-and-two, with Bildon and the mule standing closest to the rock and Treaman, Haltar, Mhoral, and Linya in an arc before them. The stealthic scrambled up the side of the overhang and found a narrow ledge that gave him some field of vision. They settled in and listened to the rising wind and the pulse of the drum.

As he watched the sky and the boiling front of clouds coming in low against the wind, Treaman felt a wash of fear. Before, when they had been marching north, trying to get home, the hail or mudslides or quakes had still hit them. But that seemed less purposeful than stopping to let it catch up to you. The drumbeat from the south faded from hearing because the wind of the storm was closer, contrary, and picking up hard. Small items blew off the mule, who began to bray in panic until Bildon hopped down to quiet her. The sky was three-quarters obscured and the clouds seemed very low to the ground, moving quickly over the canyon. The rain, when it came, was sudden and full-force with no natural preamble. The shower caught on the overhang but everyone in the front row got wet. The drops were large, cold and tinged with browns and greens, stinking like the drain-water of a cesspool; everyone shrank back against the rock, but the clothing stained to drab shades at once.

It was several moments before anyone noticed the pain. Something in the fluid carried a sting; Treaman tried to pool some on his palm to study it, then shook it off with a cry, wiping his hand on his pant. The cup of his hand felt slightly sunburned; looking down the row he could see Haltar wrenching his helm forward and Mhoral throwing his cape over his head. The clothes, weapons, reins, ropes, and other substances seemed to take no harm; some kind of spent acid, perhaps. The mule flinched whenever spattered, but her hair seemed to give some protection and Bildon was there to calm her. The downpour continued and Treaman noticed streams of the green-brown vitriol running down the canyon, near to their position. Trying to keep his cloak above him, he stepped out and gouged a quick trench with his spear butt, slanting the water to the outside of the overhang. His hands were pocked with stings in just a few seconds, but the trench held and deepened enough to hold most of the "rain." He jumped back into cover and waited.

Within a half-minute of the hardest downpour easing, there was not a drop coming down. Treaman scanned the sky and thought he saw a slight darkening in one part of the cloud-cover, still venting its bile onto the earth. It was moving off in the direction he would have called southeast moments ago, faster than a man could run. He felt another jangle as he defined that vortex, and thought he could make out small terrain features disappearing in the "rain." The outcrop of stone seemed unaffected, but the runoff had clawed the ground, changing much of the previous orientation the woodsman relied on. Still no sun to gauge his position, and Skysword for the moment was obscured in the distance. The sounds of the drum veered in again, and from the south to one side of the outcrop the woodsman spotted the advancing garruk.

"Now we're carked," Mhoral muttered.

"No doubt you'd have been delighted to stroll under that gentle shower out there instead," Bildon quipped, climbing to the shelf again and taking out his sling. Mhoral ignored the barb as the size of the enemy band became clear.

"Light of stars," Mhoral breathed, "so many."

The party had heard of the evil garruk in the taverns of Trainertown, and Haltar spent several evenings with the veterans, getting stories for liquid cheer. Mhoral claimed to know much from his Elven heritage, and Linya had consulted the town sage — scribe, really — for a look at the kingdom chronicle. There were no garruk in Novar, Treaman knew, nor would any other Hopeful kingdom suffer the presence of the ranks of Despair. Only in the midst of chaos could their tribes exist on this side of the Swords of Stone; where they had hidden for the first ten centuries after the Battle of the Razor, no one could say. Pitted against the land the same as the kingdom's true inhabitants, they seemed somehow better used to the flux cursing the badlands between those pockets of calm like Maladon that still survived. Garruk were not as tall as humans but heavy and thick with overlong arms and thrusting under-jaws that could drop open like a gate. Tusks to rend your throat in close-combat, which they seemed to prefer; but the males were trained to use all the weapons of the original races as well. On their first foray, the party had encountered a small band of five warriors, and defeated their reckless charge by Haltar's prowess and Linya's bolts. In more ancient times, stories claimed war-bands as large as sixscore or more, but recent tales only told of roving, disorganized packs between four and ten.

But now, seventeen stocky, gnarled humanoids marched into view, led by an example of masculine horror taller than Treaman and moving, like his warriors, to the wounding hammer-beat of the Thralltap.

Treaman stared and winced as the leering drummer brought his ball-ended club down on the four-foot wide skin of the evil drum strapped before him; his jaw set on edge in anticipation of the next beat. *B-gurrr, ba-gurrr*...the wooden cylinder was deeply etched with fantastic symbols and crude depictions of war and slaughter; brass rivets the width of a thumb held the crimson sounding-skin tightly in place over the aperture. Legends told of how Kun, Despair Liege of the evil Elven race, created the garruk to destroy and pillage without thought for their lives. Together with Pelundrag, the Liege of magic, he devised sorcerous drums to control the bands who otherwise could not assemble without in-fighting. Authorities agreed there were only a few score Thralltaps ever created in those days, and none since; the sounding skin was said to be that of dragons, or demons, or of captured warriors of Hope. Without the drum, the garruk were little more than wolves with weapons, and rarely could three or more males gather in the same place for long.

To its unvarying beat the squadron marched in perfect unison, the sole exception that could be imposed on their frenzied abandon whenever it stopped. Only the leader could exercise the slightest initiative while the Thralltap played, looking to both sides and scanning the party for weakness, and once or twice coughing out orders. The garruk marched to altered formation as they approached, with slow, measured steps and blank faces; shields in a front rank and spears behind, set close but with plenty of room to outflank and overwhelm the party under the outcrop.

"They'll set over there," Haltar said, pointing casually, "and once their ranks are ordered they'll charge."

"That damned drum!" Mhoral cried. "If we could break it—"

"Not from this far," Haltar said, "but Linya, if you see a shot, take it."

The sound of the whistling sling behind them on the outcrop was broken by curses from the halfling, as the strap's length kept hitting the rock face behind him. But a stone whizzed out over their heads and flew to the group, skimming off a shield-rim and embedding in the side of a neck. The warrior did not so much as flinch, but continued marching as if made of stone himself, though the blood trickled down his shoulder as he strode.

"Balls of Astor," Bildon breathed.

"He'll feel it," Haltar assured him. "Keep loading. Try again."

Stepping away from the group and putting his sword-point down, Haltar raised a fist and called out to the enemy crossing the party's front, "Haltar Eltrinstar." The garruk leader, looking over, nodded once and answered the salute, calling only, "Kech." Now the leaders had announced their presence and thereby claimed the responsibility; the soul-guilt of their troops' deeds lay on their heads. Also, the code of garruk warfare required leaders to seek each other on the field. The brute hefted his spiked mace and barked out another order; the group turned by precise degrees and came into the double-line. The drum's dirge was working on the party now, all of them feeling the call that held their foes tighter than puppets, arrows on the string. It continued to pound from behind the rows, as the leader turned to shout out adjustments, moving one or two slightly up or down the line. Treaman could see that the feet of the front row lay directly in a pool of the fallen vitriol, deep enough to wash over the strapped wooden slats they wore. To his horror, he saw a slight burning steam rising from the pool, as the acid there worked on the flesh. Not so much as a twitch of pain from any mouth, no movement aside from their orders. Another sling stone struck home, buried in a breastplate and close to the heart. The mace-wielding brute showed no reaction, and Bildon swore again.

The drum pounded on; Treaman knew if it continued indefinitely they would all break and flee, as in the stories of garruk wars from centuries ago. The magic of the Thralltap affected the garruk first, but every thinking being soon or late; it shouted triumph for Despair, death for the order it temporarily imposed, and sang of tooth and strength overwhelming courage and steel.

Bagarrr, bu-guuurr …

{*"Loud!"*}

"Yes," Treaman managed over the din, "very loud. Hallah go on the rock-top and wait."

{*"Hallah help Treaman, bite dark-men."*}

"Hallah stay on the rock, safe. Go now." The woodsman felt relief tinged with loneliness as the weight of his friend left his shoulders.

"Mhoral," Haltar said through clenched teeth, "sing the battle song."

Mhoral gasped his pent air and breathed twice, then started to chant in Elvish, a tune of Ma-Eldar's day telling of victory over the darkness, encouraging the few to resist the many, and to Hope against all odds. Though the party understood not a word, the power of the miracle he manifested in the battle song was such that their spirits rose and steadied at once. The drumbeat was once again just a drumbeat. The garruk leader, hearing the unexpected counter, dropped his mace-arm in a signal and the Thralltap suddenly, blessedly ceased. Mhoral's fine baritone continued the song, while the garruk line literally rippled with emotion, pent-up hatred, and pain. The one whose chest Bildon's bullet struck fell silently forward on his face, allowed at last to be stone-dead. The others roared and charged across the intervening space.

Another sling stone, missing the leader's head; Treaman braced his spear and waited for the one directly opposite him to crash on it. Without any warning beyond the syllables Linya shouted, a large black bear appeared between the two groups, facing the garruk and wading into them with a roar. Impaled by two spears, it grasped one of the front-rank warriors and tore him to rags as they went down in a death-embrace. Haltar stepped up for room, and swung his bastard-sword in a deadly arc to split a skull, as a second-rank spear glanced off his plated shoulder. Treaman's foe came barreling in with a bark of rage, taking the spear-point in his side and driving on until it came out behind him. The impact slammed Treaman against the rock and he felt the air leave him in a rush. His foe gave a huge, reek-filled champ of those tusks, just missing his face, and then reeled away as the shock of the pole weapon turned to pain. The woodsman dragged out his frontier blade and thrust low, beneath the shield and into his guts. Using the saw-teeth on the back-side, he pulled up as he withdrew, hacking a trench to the sternum; his enemy fell away with a shriek and specks of his brownish-red blood arced everywhere.

An enormous mace crashed in from the shield-side, knocking Treaman to one knee with its force; a spear thrust that would have killed him passed over his head instead. Bodies everywhere, naked to the loin-clout and stinking of evil. The woodsman hacked at a thigh and was rewarded with another bellow. But as he rose, his foe was already aiming his mace for a swing, too close to be blocked. With a hammering whir, a flurry of scale and wing briefly covered the garruk's face, as Hallah stooped on him and bit down hard, coming away with the better part of an eye. All this din could not drown the dragon's voice in Treaman's head.

{*"Taste awful!"*}

"Get out of here!"

Even the crazed garruk at war had not seen this creature before; for a moment they drew back while it flew away. Haltar, who had downed three enemies in a brief span, cleared a space to Kech; the two of them saluted each other again, and engaged. All the garruk remaining on Treaman's side of the line paused, to await the outcome. Assisting their leader would be dishonorable; by the same token, if Treaman attacked any of them, he would fall prey to their combined ire, so he waited as well. Glancing down the line, he realized Mhoral, though engaging a garruk with his flail, was still singing, something he had never managed to do before. Linya alternated between simply stepping back as her slower opponents tried to take aim at her, and creating a patch of mystic fire on the ground nearby, which they naturally avoided. Whenever she had the chance, a light tap with her wand produced a blast of force and enough damage to slay at least one of her foes. But the mage was clearly tiring and Mhoral bled from the skull and left arm. Across the plain the garruk drummer waited, grinning.

Haltar brought his bastard sword around with a flourish, changing the angle at the last moment but failing to penetrate his opponent's parry. The force of their blows was tangible, and for a time the garruk thane actually drove the foot-knight back. The spiked mace and enormous blade crashed and clanged, and as expected, the latter drew not one but three notches on its honed length. One of them caught in the mace's wooden haft, and with a titanic wrench Haltar pulled it from Kech's grasp. Nothing dismayed, the garruk leader stepped in and seized the knight's middle, bringing his teeth in for a bite on the shoulder that penetrated the chain. Gasping but not crying out, Haltar dropped his fouled weapon and drew the punch-dagger from his back-belt without looking. Striking short with a powerful uppercut, he put the wide blade into the gullet so hard that the six-foot garruk lifted from the ground, his jaws torn away from Haltar and pinned together with the tip protruding from the bridge of his nose. Spurting blood from his shoulder, Haltar held his dead foe up an extra moment, then shook him off to the ground where he fell like a tree trunk.

With a leader slain, the code of the garruk was clear: retreat and await orders. Nine warriors scrambled away from the field of gore, three limping or holding an arm. But the Thralltap sounded once more; *B-gurrr, ba-garrr* … and at once the ranks began to reform in calm, iron discipline. Treaman's heart sank as he realized the group could never be dispelled by rout; the law of bodies boded very ill for the humans.

"Linya," Haltar said, returning to the group dragging his blade and clutching his bitten shoulder, "try." Sweating and winded, the mage nodded and sighted across the open ground, bringing in her lower lip and raising her arm with care. There was no shout, for this spell was well-known and easy to cast, though hard of success as with any distance-attack. A blaze of crimson fire sprang from Linya's hand and shot across the ground, missing the drum but striking a warrior nearby, who staggered but held his place in the trance of the beat.

"Missed," she murmured, and then sank back against the outcrop, sliding to the ground like a drunkard, having spent too much of her mystic energy.

Treaman's dismay was mirrored by Bildon and Mhoral, who both shouted her name and stooped to check on her. "She won't wake for at least a half-hour!" the Elven warrior cried, his song forgotten. Half an hour would be more than enough time for the Thralltap to do its work.

Bu-garrr, b-grrrrr …

Haltar stepped out and raised his wounded arm, spraying new blood on his face, calling "Haltar Eltrinstar;" but the drummer only leered back, refusing the mantle of leadership and the obligation of attack that came with it.

B-gguurr, ba-gurrr …

Treaman felt again the rising hackle of panic, and his inner voice argued it was not cowardice to run now, not simply yielding to the drum's spell but also to that of discretion.

{*"So loud! Hallah eat banger!"*}

"No!" Treaman shouted in his fear. "Hallah stay, stay up there." Looking up, the woodsman saw beyond his friend a dark vortex in the distance, still pouring down pain, but turned now from its former path.

"Oh, Novar's loins," he cried. "It's coming back."

The party all looked up to see the incoming storm, and moaned in recognition.

Bu-guuuurr, ba-garrrrr, b-gggurrrr …

Bildon pulled a blanket off the mule and threw it completely over Linya as the rest of them crowded back against the outcrop. Haltar's face, showing no panic and only a tinct of his pain, still registered indecision; he gripped his punch-dagger in lieu of the weight of his bastard-sword, too notched and heavy to be effective in his wounded arm. The bile-rain swept in, drenching the nearly-naked garruk who held their ranks as the drummer held his beat. The steam of their acid-burns roiled off their heads, necks, arms and legs as if they were taking an Argensian bath. Some were bleeding in a dozen places, but they held their ranks and the drummer, also smoking and bleeding, seemed insanely happy.

B-guurrr, ba-gurrrr …

“We’ll … have to … charge them,” Haltar announced. “Try to wreck the drum, before…” Mhoral and Bildon nodded, clenched jaws and weapons to wait for the word. No one looked up at the downpour; Bildon stroked the mule a last time, told her what a good girl she had been, loosened her cinch and wished her luck.

Bu-gurrr, b-grRHECKKTH!

Everyone, man and garruk, snapped around to see the astonished face of the drummer, whose mace had gone clean through the sounding skin.

“Made of flesh!” Haltar shouted.

The garruk began to moan with agony at last, and one speared the drummer as the others began to break in the party’s direction.

“Brace for it!” Mhoral cried, and Bildon clambered again to the outcrop, drawing two daggers. Treaman clutched his blade and saw in the eyes of his foes no hatred, only pain and panic. They weren’t attacking, just making for cover. Two fell from the vitriol before they were halfway; three others stumbled over flaps of their own flesh, easily put down by the first strike. Another four slammed bleeding and screaming into the party, and all was tumult and death for a time. Treaman had felt a moment of pity before, but now the lack of space dictated his actions. He stabbed and cut, but mostly just pushed to stave the garruk away from the cover. Behind him a wayward blow thwacked flesh, and the bray of the mule preceded a storm of hooves pushing everyone aside as it bolted directly into the storm. Bildon shouted in fury and leaped on the back of the offending garruk, burying two blades in the top of his spine and riding him dead to the earth. Mhoral stood with his feet astride Linya’s body and manfully swung his flail to keep the foes back. Haltar grunted with pain but slew with both edge and point.

It did not take long; two moaning prostrate foes lay in the rain and gasped out their lives, their voices drowned by the braying of the mule as it foundered and fell several yards away. Haltar caught Bildon trying to get out to it, bringing the armored elbow down hard on his head and using one foot to keep the halfling cursing but covered. Hallah, evidently unhurt by the rain, flew out to taste another garruk corpse, and then settled happily on the dead pack animal while voicing its satisfaction in tones that thankfully only the woodsman could hear. The storm passed on and the little rivers created by its sewage-wash began to drain down to trickles or sink into the rocky soil.

An hour later the clouds had cleared for good, and Linya was awake and binding Haltar's shoulder. Bildon, refusing all help, was grimly cutting strips of edible meat from the mule's body. The sun had stayed in the same orientation, and Skysword still loomed to the south, no larger than before. Mhoral recovered enough of his old spirits to start complaining again, and this time Treaman shared his grief.

"A dragon's hoard! Enough for us to live like kings for a year."

"Well," Treaman put in, "like barons for a month, at least."

"And it's all lost, this cursed country. We'll have to scavenge what we can carry."

Treaman gazed on the bulging saddlebags under the outcrop, the bricks of fused coins and gems within, the underblanket of a mature dragon. He glanced around the broken field, coming to rest on the spear he'd left thrust through his first foe. Something within him hardened; damned if they had come this far, maybe learned the trick of getting back, and just left it behind.

"I'll take first watch," he said. "I don't sense any new weather; maybe we're on the fringe already, judging by the mountain's size." No one in the party could raise the energy to argue or agree, but they broke out their blankets and bunked down under the outcrop. Even Hallah slept after gorging herself — she was delighted with the intestines Bildon suggested — and nestled happily next to Linya.

The night was fine and clear, and Treaman walked with his silent step around the camp watching the stars and collecting what he needed. At times it seemed the world was speaking to him now, slowly and carefully as if he had just begun to learn the language. He spotted some night-birds and heard the twitch of a lizard-like creature scrabbling away from its food as he walked past. Plenty of time tomorrow, he murmured to the scavenger, and plenty to eat. Towards morning after moonset, he sat atop the outcrop as he knotted ropes and belts. At times it seemed he could make out a reddish star to the far east, oddly unmoving. At first he suspected a trick of the horizon-air, or another chaos change; but it held as well as any other heavenly body. Something new perhaps; maybe an omen for getting out of this place by design. Treaman didn't dare to hope for that, yet. But something in him believed that they had truly made progress by staying still at the right time.

The party awoke in the morning to stares, astonished curses and quite a bit of laughter. Treaman, having stood the entire night watch on his own, now leaned jauntily against the most unorthodox cobbled contraption they had ever seen. The cylinder of the Thralltap lay on its side, and Treaman's spear, thrust through two garruk arm-rings belayed by scraps and bits of rope and belt, served as an axle. Reins from the mule now formed traces, and the saddlebags lay in a kind of hammock over the entire affair. Hallah topped the view, crouching like a queen smugly awaiting her porters.

"You clever dog!" Mhoral cried in unwilling admiration. "And you stayed up the whole night?"

"You were wounded," Treaman answered simply. "You needed rest like us mortals."

"I bet it's heavy to move, though."

"There's our Mhoral!" Bildon cried happily. "I thought we had lost you until just now."

"Well done," Haltar said, and Treaman felt the force of the compliment. Coming over, the leader slung his bastard-sword on top of the pile.

"Great! Heavier now," Mhoral griped.

"Such a sunny disposition," Bildon quipped. "Maybe I should ride as well?"

"You may as well, for all the pulling you're going to do," Mhoral returned, moving towards the traces. But Haltar didn't get out of his way, instead stooping under them himself.

Mhoral and the others looked to Haltar in surprise as he shouldered the leads.

"My arm's no good for man's work right now," he said matter-of-factly. "Let's go."

"Which way?" Linya asked.

"For that," Haltar said with a head nod towards Treaman, "we ask the woodsman."

Hit by this, Treaman snapped to his full height and did his best not to grin, though the others all were. He turned away to face the north — still there, more than sixteen hours later — and took a measure of the wind as he considered. He motioned them forward, and Haltar, with a single small groan, lurched the wheeled rope-cart onward. Hallah flew to Treaman's shoulder as they went, and in his mind he heard a voice he had come to cherish.

{*"Treeeman can do anything."*}

"You know, I believe you may be right."

{*"Hallah always right!"*}

"Why, there you go!" he chuckled.

Late that evening, after two more called stops for a wind-blast and a minor earthquake, they came into land that looked a bit less wrecked and pointless. To the unspoken astonishment of everyone else, Haltar had hauled the treasure-cart the entire way. It was well past the sunset that had marked their first return, but Mhoral reported with his Elven sight that there were children laying out by the embers of a dying firepit, looking up at the stars. A few minutes later, all of Trainertown was awake and a celebration not seen in years began.

⊕ ⊕ ⊕

His life has become little more than holding a line, enduring pain and staying awake, staying alive. The aching need for sleep washes upon him at all hours. He ignores the hand-span of tightness at the base of his back, reminding him how easily he could drop off any time he wishes to relax, and die. Hunger, too, has become an old friend; in keeping with the dictates he takes as little as he can, turns away more than half of anything offered (and every morsel from anyone he does not know). Plain water, earthy bread, no wine: that brings one too close to the arms of sleep, and what lies beyond that portal is worse. He feels the pit of hunger seeking to sink lower and lower in his body, until it bids to bore a hole through the bottom of him.

But easily the largest ache the young man suffers is the constant, drumming sense that he is alone in this world. Raised to noble standards, then cut off from all family while still a youth, brought here by the most astonishing of circumstances, and physically apart from everyone. His father is dead, the line at an end with him. He has no friends, not truly, and spends his days an alien in the largest city of Hope. He is alone, but worse, he is watched. He knows, even now, there are eyes on him, as he struggles to focus and to maintain himself against the hunger and the need for rest. Whether he stays here in silence, or whenever he walks abroad, they watch him, making him feel set aside, different, driven, and dedicated to a purpose apart. He is forever marked a stranger, as clearly by his one-color raiment that everyone sees as by his purpose, which no one knows. And several among those watchers, he knows, look on with hatred. He endures it; he remains awake and focused, and himself. This, he is sure, is how his father would have wanted it. It is all his heart's desire. That, and of course the lady for whom he had done the deed, though he will never see her again.

His instincts told him the time had come, and he stood even as the acolyte approached to say the even-tide was ebbing once again. From his daily routine these past months in the cathedral to Conar, Pron Dedicar had come to feel the rhythm of the tides deep in his muscles and bones. Even when his clothing dried he felt soaked in his core, becoming a creature of the sea. The aching cold, the briny wetness and the exhaustion that came of standing against the tide, these were still more pains that he had learned to bear, thrashing back and forth from church to harbor like the fly in a web. The knight did not mind — aside from the slight variation, the chance to stand and walk, he had become accustomed, perhaps addicted, to his twice-daily drenching. It was the call of the sea, and the closeness he achieved with drowning brought him an odd comfort, as the accident no doubt would satisfy his foes. Pron believed in the Heroes; should he slip or finally prove too weak, he knew he would see his noble father again at last, able to hold his head up when he faced him with the record of his deeds. And in a short span of years there would be Gemma, too, free now from a hateful bond, she could be with him again in the world hereafter.

But in these thoughts too was the gnawing of Despair. Pron felt fear's thrill as he began his walk to the water, and none of his dread was connected to the watching few he saw among the crowd, the ones who did not bless him, or kneel and call his name as he passed. These few others watched and waited for his slightest misstep, for any variation in the code he had invoked, but the loss of his life in this way, quietly executed at their hands, held no terror for the white-robed knight. It was instead the imminent danger that he might be too tempted, too desirous of seeing his father, of shedding this mantle of blame or simply impatient to break the cycle of gloom and hopelessness. A single step too few into the water, and the watchers would have the failure of effort they needed. Only one extra step into the waiting tide, and Pron would be free; but suicide was a crime against Hope, and he knew there would be no release that way except for his enemies. He must come close to arms of death, one step only away from drowning, and there stop.

It was quiet as ever in the still of the night, with a cloudy curtain overhead showing hints of the moons glowing through. Less than fifteen persons followed him tonight, and only two enemies that he could note. Pron praised Conar for waking the other dozen, his witnesses against the chance of a broken cord loosing heavy barrels or an unbraked wagon rolling death over his path. In the cold, tugging ocean ahead he would be strangely safe for a time, excepting the tide's pull and his own temptations: into the water, those who hated him would not follow. He clung to the dictates and the customs of Hope; he knew every step and neither varied nor tarried on his way.

At the harbor, Pron trod a path between the central docks, to the sand where no boats moored; he kicked off his sandals and stepped into the cold ocean. His ivory tunic dimmed to the color of the night-sea in the water as he walked, past the end of the docks in the shallowing tide and up over his waist. He was shivering before the water reached his chest, four rods and more from the shore-line. Extending both arms to the west he stood and felt the immeasurable tug of the sea, here at the farthest point a man could stand from the Law of Conar and not be drowned. He was alone, truly away from the watchers who saw only a stripe of white from his shoulders out among the waves.

Here is where Pron usually prayed. He smiled as he thought of it; spending his entire day kneeling at Conar's foot, when all the world thought him to be in constant prayer, he was really only fighting sleep, to stay alert for his enemies, and resist the starvation of growing despair. The grinding labor of remaining awake and alive consumed his day. Only now, a few precious moments where the tide was his only threat, could he spare his mind for Hope. He saw across the harbor the larger ships, the trade vessels of the kingdom that could carry a man out of the city, if he had a father still, or a relative or one friend to arrange the passage. Ships moored just a few rods away, perhaps three feet deeper into the ocean, and thus as well a hundred leagues from him. Pron prayed to Conar for some sign that he could go on. He had taken this walk many more than the thirty days required for cleansing; that portion of his penance complete, he earned the right to redeem his name with exile. But nowhere else; if not to the ship, where else could he go? He prayed for direction, for Hope beyond all hope and a key to unlock the chains that lay across him.

At first, he did not notice the seaweed patch.

Clots of tangled growth floated in and out around the bay tides, and no one paid them the slightest mind even when they could be easily seen. Here, on a cloudy night, the patch might well have been invisible; even when it was within a body's length it merited no notice except for one detail. It was moving slowly but clearly against the retreating tide. And coming closer to him. As it drew Pron's attention, he noted also that the patch was thick; he could now discern a solid trunk that extended down into the water, the size of a man. Pron felt his vitals chill beyond the numbing cold; his knee wobbled and almost he retreated a step, too soon, outside the dictates. Choking on his fear of the unknown, his spirit rallied, and the young knight reasoned this was the best of times to stand his ground. If the Heroes had sent a mer-beast to consume him, then his day had come and it would be no suicide. He would see his father again and be free of the burden.

But the dark patch with its solid under-growth stopped two feet away, blocked to view from the shore by Pron's own body. And now he heard a small sound, of breathing, and saw a slender rod of reed in the midst of the tangle, wedged there by chance, it seemed. Slowly, the patch grew a mound in its midst and a head emerged from the ocean, a magical creature with eyes that bore into him and hair the color of pewter beneath the weeds. The lower body, as well as Pron could see, was human, yet it floated at ease in water over its head. The ends of his own hair were soaked, but Pron felt them stand up near his scalp.

The creature spoke, and with three simple words brought a rush of emotions so strong that the Conarian knight nearly fainted.

"I see them."

The man from the temple! Pron had forgotten him after that initial buzzing disturbance in the back and had only a curate's word that the intruder, not a citizen of Conar, had been ejected.

"Who … who are you?" he hissed, as if he could be overheard.

"One who wishes you well."

"Get away from me, you must never — you will be slain and get me killed along with you."

"Then the Law would be broken."

At this rejoinder, the knight found himself checked. The gaze of the swimmer was steady and sharp, and Pron began to respect this fellow despite the absurdity and the peril. The hair had fooled him on their first momentary meeting, and now the tangle of weeds and darkness obscured him somewhat, but he began to see a youth no older than he, perhaps even younger. Still, what an extraordinary view to take!

"And what care you, stranger, for the Law of Conar?"

"I care for all the law, and for faith and Hope," was the steady reply. "*Ar Aralte.*"

The ancient tongue forbade the lie. 'Hope Forever' undoubtedly placed the grey youth on the side of right; perhaps a dupe of his enemies, but not a conspirator. Pron responded "*Ar Aralte*" and then added, "but anyone who truly meant to help me would need—"

"Three things," the youth interrupted and the young knight, so unused to this effrontery, was slack-jawed until the seawater lolled into his mouth. "I have a tongue, to bespeak a ship's captain for passage," said the swimmer, "and a pocket to hold your ring, and an audience with the House Enceris."

It was too much. This stranger, this boy, somehow he knew all. Pron felt his legs buckle and for a moment only the stranger's body held him back from the deeper waters. He clung to Judgement for a moment in a paroxysm of emotion before straightening back against the tide.

"Why," he panted still quietly, "why would you do this?"

"It will uphold the Law," the stranger said, "and … you are one against many." His gaze looked aside, scanning for the watchers back on the invisible shore. Then he returned his eyes to the knight, adding simply, "All in the kingdom should be free, or no one. I remember the face of my father."

As Pron recalled his own dear father, passed less than a half-year ago, he felt a sudden comradery for the unknown youth. Until this hour, he thought himself the last of House Dedicar. Now, merely ten years away, the prospect of marriage and noble issue, all because of this magical messenger, at home in the sea and empowered to break the bonds that held him. With a few hurried words more, Pron outlined the details of his need and the stranger listened without speaking further, before sinking beneath the waves again.

Turning, Pron waded out of the bay and started back uphill towards the cathedral. Heavy with seawater, chilled and struggling to ascend the long grade, in the absolute dead of night and usually watched by two or three of his noble foes, this was the time he doubted his strength the most. He could not tarry, nor divert his path, but must reach the statue again or his life would be forfeit: breaking the dictates would make his unwitnessed death no longer a murder but an execution. Many nights he had nearly stopped or fallen from sheer exhaustion. If he could only make it there, he knew his enemies would generally give up until morning; in the empty chapel space he might even lean his head and shoulder down on Conar's foot and sleep for two hours. Before full light, the curate would bring a roll and some water, just enough to meet the dictates. But getting there, that was usually the trick.

Except this night. Pron Dedicar returned to the chapel scattering streams of seawater in his wake with a powerful stride that spoke of an unquenchable strength, of vigor renewed, in short, of Hope itself. The handful of watchers had to step lively to keep up, and his noble foes could see no reason why this particular tide-walk would so reinforce his energies. None of them noted that his load was a bit lighter, by the weight of his House-ring.

⊕⊕⊕

"Tomorrow, my faithful, we face the enemy. Now, Children of Hope, comes the hour of battle and only victory will suffice."

The voice of Conar rang over the serried ranks like a deep silver bell. Cedrith swallowed his excitement and, tearing his eyes away from the magnificent face and form, the heroic figure looming larger than life before him, risked a glance to his left in line, as Solemn Judgement listened to the exhortation. The youth's lips were pressed into a thin edge, and his eyes were practically flaming with that righteous fury his host had sensed on their first day together. He was struggling mightily, Cedrith knew, to keep control of his emotions. Perhaps this test had come too soon, he thought; Judgement was mature of mind, certainly, but still just a boy.

"Our enemy still outnumbers us today as the drops of water in the Western Sea did outnumber us. Yet we shall cross these lands as quickly as we did that sea, borne by the winds of Hope which have ever sustained us."

That voice! There was such an intonation to it, of confidence and boundless courage: if it said he could fly, Cedrith knew, he could hardly doubt it. And as Conar gestured to the setting sun, his lordly reach and mighty hands literally framed the ball of light above him. His cradling grip captured much of its fading fire and seemingly made more powerful beams of the rest between his fingers, some striking the closest of his followers as they stood armed for war, and others glancing past them, off the end of the stage and falling on Natasha to Cedrith's right, as well as others in the audience. The assembled sighed with the beauty of the moment. Then came the speech of The Promise, which ended the first act.

"From the third sunset following this one, you shall stand with me on the heights of yonder mountain range. And all the kingdom between here and there shall be free of Despair for ever. The Law shall rule you, and this nation shall be a leader to the kingdoms of Hope unto all generations."

Applause, the footlights gradually shuttering and in the darkness the threescore actors began to exit. Cedrith leaned back in his seat and again glanced to Judgement on his left. Natasha looked onstage somewhat longer but also bent closer to gauge the initial effect of their experiment with bringing the culture of Hope before their friend's mind.

Judgement sat erect and his hands clenched the arms of his chair, in the section reserved for paid attendance, his feet firmly planted as if he were listening for a call to flee. His breath was shallow, and his eyes darted left and right in his stony face; already aware of his friends' attention, he was clearly trying to frame a polite remark.

Cedrith forestalled him, saying, "My dear friend, if this sort of entertainment upsets you, I apologize and of course we can leave."

Judgement turned to his hosts with a mask of civility. "Not at all, Eldest," he said, ignoring Cedrith's sigh of resignation. "I find this form of … education … most, most novel." After a short pause, he added, "And I will say, it brings to light a certain … tangible dimension to what I have read."

"Yes," Cedrith agreed, hoping to draw him further. "The situation before the first War of Liberation was strategically quite grim, as all our sages concur. Our ancestors had landed here, and Conar with his magic caused the walls of the City to spring into being in but a single week, using the hulls of the White Fleet as material for its ramparts."

"But still," Natasha added, "Despair owned all the lands hereabouts and held the kingdom in thrall for ten centuries before Hope arrived. They were masters of the beasts here, and had created foul races to aid them. As well as the Makine, of course- that was worst of all," she finished in a low tone.

"Makine," Judgement repeated. "It is a word for some kind of metal construct … like a crossbow?"

"Not a bit of it." Natasha tutted. "Makine are evil, but the soldiers of many Hopeful kingdoms use the crossbow."

"The precise definition is somewhat parsed," Cedrith admitted quietly, as Judgement turned his attention to him. "Makine is the term defining complex constructs of a certain kind; they have metallic workings and are certainly much larger than a crossbow. Makine require so much metal in their construction that to make even a single one would damage the earth from which the ores were drawn. That is one of the three criteria we apply."

"So then," Judgement said immediately, "a catapult, though large and containing works, would not agree with the definition, as it is principally made of wood."

"Just so, as wood grows and can be replaced."

"And the other two things that make a Makine?"

"Sshh, if you please," Natasha whispered. "The very word is not considered polite in public, young Judgement."

"Apologies, Mistress," he said gamely, and his sincerity was so clear she had to chuckle.

"Besides their size and use of metal," Cedrith continued, "these, em, devices, are also universally quite destructive. So, say, a gigantic door made of steel would be, perhaps, excessive, but it is not a, ah, it does not answer the definition. So engines of war made of metal and quite large, yes," he finished quietly, "these would be Makine."

"Metallic workings and destructive, I see. And the third?"

Judgement's friends both hesitated in distaste. At last Natasha said, "The third sign of a Makine … is that it is *always working*," dropping her voice to a kind of hiss. Then she sat back, shook her head and shivered.

Judgement either missed the point or was playing his sarcasm. "You mean, it is never broken?"

"No, friend," said Cedrith, "though they were legendarily sturdy and difficult to destroy. What Natasha meant is that once they are, em, begun in operation, they can continue their actions indefinitely."

He paused a moment to let that thought sink in. Judgement's face changed with comprehension. "It would continue to … to destroy … without further guidance?"

"Just so, my friend. Whether designed to batter walls, or throw flame, or crush rock, it would never need reference to human intervention, never need to be guided, or corrected. It would slay the maker's foe and friend indifferently, unless the magic of its operation were invoked. It would destroy until the end of time."

The three sat in silence awhile as the newcomer contemplated this. Finally, Judgement said, "And Despair, the forces of evil, had this Makine in the days we are seeing re-enacted here."

"If the ancient sources are to be trusted, my friend, they had scores of them."

Judgement gulped involuntarily, and Cedrith was impressed, for the youth had shown no sign of outward fear in the two months since he had met him.

Natasha amplified, "Yes, that was one of the darkest horrors these great Heroes faced," she said grandly, gesturing to the stage where the lights were slowly coming back up.

At this, Judgement's face darkened and he said, "Not these. The Heroes were … not these." And Cedrith began to sense where he had gone wrong, in demanding that the youth attend the theater with them.

The second act, to Cedrith, was the least exciting of the three; at previous productions, he had even dozed off as Conar delivered a few businesslike speeches about the coming battle and received several visitors. Most of it, to his taste, was more than a touch political: this noble family and that had an ancestor with a line or two, and to establish once more that their forefathers were camerate of the Hopelord probably was the driving force that paid for the play. Cedrith looked to the noble boxes and saw them in their spanking finest. Only one small but prominently placed balcony stood empty, its draped banner bearing the single green sword on a field of gold. Still in mourning, the family Altrindur; that was a loss, the sage admitted to himself.

Judgement, as always, seemed immune to boredom though the act stretched on over an hour. He sat erect and attended carefully to all that happened. This of course only increased Cedrith's restiveness, and he leaned in to his friend to whisper, "Watch, as the sun goes down, a little hitch." The glowing ball of the setting sun, shedding light across the theater and turning slowly redder as it approached the far side of the stage, moved through a field of blue, the shimmering curtain of the sky that artfully concealed the backstage area and created a wonderful image of the daytime heavens. The clouds that dotted its field were artfully executed, picking up the hues of the setting sun and seeming to blend into the true sky above the open roof, creating a sense of endless world focusing down on the stage. Judgement attended carefully to where Cedrith gestured, and just as the sun moved behind the stage-right column, the glowing ball seemed to stop, as if stuck, then describe a tiny circle in mid-air, and finally exit a bit wobbly. A few chuckles broke out of the audience, marking those who were in the know, as was Conar the Manfather himself, who skillfully paused as if in thought before continuing the dialogue with his war-captain Areghel.

Natasha, who seemed at first as fidgety as Cedrith, leaned in now as the warrior-woman Aballe announced the Gypsy visitor, and Conar agreed to see her.

"Father of Men, she is indeed no threat to us, for the woman is aged and hardly walks. Yet you are tired and the morning's battle beckons. Should you rather rest than take her in?"

The armored frame of the heroine was taller than most men, and her silver crest and long spear would have made her loom. Yet Conar's head rose a half-foot above hers, and the colossal impression of his body diminished her, even before his gentle rebuke.

"Jewel of House Verinten, beloved of my son Ekhonon and defender of the city, I love you well for your concern. But whom should I see, if not a refugee of this land, fleeing the grip of Despair who comes to me without arms and in need? I am not fit to lead Hope's army if I have none in my heart. Send her to me, I bid: I shall await the woman within."

Natasha sat back with a sigh, murmuring, "They will not show it, then."

"Show what?" Cedrith wondered; he knew the act was ending and this was traditionally the final scene.

"I had heard," Natasha whispered as the footlights faded, "that the company was working on a new scene, where the conversation between Conar and the Mother is shown. It was to have been the Prophecy, in counterpoint to the Promise of the first act."

"Ah, so we would know more around the matter of the choice he made!" Cedrith exclaimed. "That would have been interesting. Yet we know the result: Conar chose to receive the Gypsy gift of friendship with the thinking animals, especially the horse."

"Yes, but it would have been an honor to see it onstage!" Natasha exclaimed with a little pique.

"Mistress," Judgement said, "the stories say that on the night before this battle the Gypsy woman also visited the tent of Mauglir, Despair-Liege of Men."

"The stories do not lie," she agreed.

"And she offered him the same gift?"

"Not the same, but the same choice of gifts. And Despair chose the other, the power to curse one's enemies in exchange for death."

"Aye," said the youth, "but the stories do not tell one important thing."

"And what is that, young sage?"

"Which general did the Gypsy visit first?"

Cedrith said, "Ours, certainly" and Natasha said "Theirs, of course," at the same time, and then they looked to each other in surprise. Normally, a laugh from the third companion would break such embarrassment, but Solemn Judgement merely sat and awaited a definite answer.

"Well, Natasha," Cedrith said weakly, "perhaps we can visit your friend backstage…"

"Alendic," she supplied.

"…and he may tell us about that."

"Which is he?" Judgement asked, polite yet terse.

"Alendic? Why, he is the *cardinus* of the company, dear Judgement," Natasha responded with pride. "He plays Conar."

Judgement did not apprehend the intended compliment, murmuring only, "He plays him, indeed."

Cedrith, ever the peacemaker, tried to distract from this thorny point, saying, "You should come with us backstage, my friend. You could perhaps meet the cast, and, ahm, I am sure they would give you a tour of the theater which is one of the very oldest buildings in this city."

"Sooth?" Judgement asked with a questioning brow.

"Certainly, all the set pieces, such as the sun and sky, the pillars, many of the costumes, all were created in the very beginning. At Conar's express command," Cedrith added, hoping to bolster the case. And it was evident he had given Judgement something to think about, for the lad sat back and gazed to the stage with a renewed sense of interest. Cedrith leaned in as this brief intermission ended, to whisper, "I should perhaps warn you, my friend. There is even a Makine in the theater; long disabled, I assure you, but real and used as a set piece in this act."

That settled the matter, he could tell, even before the footlights came up and the rotating stage brought into view the scene of the ruined battlefield at the site of the mountain pass where Conar would establish the fortress known as the Helm. Ruined trees smoked in the foreground, and the artisans of the theater had carved deep gouges in the earth, littered with the stage-made bodies of horrific creatures slain as they climbed up from forbidden depths. The brilliant beams of the sun, now recycled back to the stage-left side, were bright and strong, though they did little except magnify the sense of wrack with the long shadows they cast. But at first, every eye in the house was drawn to the back, near the upstage edge where loomed the metallic monstrosity, three stories tall with limbs clearly bent askew from their initial design and now canting over, as still as death. Yet the audience gasped to see it, even the regular attendees unable to suppress their horror of the device.

The action of the play, by traditional formula, had moved from living connected moments in the first two acts through a future day, to show the workings of Hope over time. But the audience was transported rather to the distant past, and again felt as if they beheld a vision, rather than a mere play, about the days of yore.

Conar entered, his gigantic frame carrying the cradled form of a wounded comrade as a father would his child.

"The victory is ours. From the sea to the height of this mountain pass, the land is free of Despair."

Conar laid the warrior gently against the trunk of a tree and continued to address his gathering followers coming onstage.

"And as quickly as we have won this kingdom, just as quickly shall we liberate the remaining lands in thrall."

Cedrith clucked quietly to see the wounded warrior's costume, nothing less than the modern-day wear of the minor nobleman playing this bit part. Another necessary nod to patronage, now this fellow could say he was an important part of the action to his fellows in future years and pontificate as if he were one of the great actors of the day.

"Not even a wound or a rip in his outfit," he tsked to Judgement, who had been attending to Conar's speech and now glanced where Cedrith pointed. He nodded once, and said, "Four swords; an older branch of the clan." Completely at a loss, Cedrith looked again at the noble, and finally located the device, four crossed swords on a field of gold. A chill ran through his spine that felt nothing at all like the thrill of victory.

"This secure place would be happily chosen for a fortress of great strength. Whom can I entrust with the building of the keep and its guard until we move again to free the eastern lands?"

As Aballe stepped forward to volunteer, Cedrith saw Shilar and Areghel behind her waiting for their charges, and the three City Brothers who would speak after them.Each character loomed well over seven feet, and he marveled as always at the easy way they moved and the natural gestures they made, holding weapons and even picking up items as if they were not in costume. The youth next to him was straining with interest, carried away with the gravity of the events unfolding before him, and biting his lower lip with tension. Cedrith placed a calming hand on his arm and felt the muscles like steel plates beneath his shirt.

"Have you guessed the secret of the Heroes' miens?" he asked gently, and the young guest almost bitterly shook his head.

"Verily," he admitted, "'tis a marvel to mine eyes, Eldest. And 'twere not Makine, sooth?"

Cedrith hastened to assure him as the dialogue continued.

The triumphant tone of the final act sustained itself marvelously in Cedrith's view; it was a virtual parade of the great Heroes and Heroines, driven by concise dialogue outlining the great deeds already done or gently presaging those still in the future. Conar handed out rewards to his closest vassals: to Shilar, the promise of lordship over the easternmost kingdom closest to the perils of the enemy, to Dunedin the affirmation that some mountain fastness nearby would serve as the center of a dedicated order of knights with a special purpose. The audience buzzed with renewed excitement at the colossal figures, the flashing armor, the ringing tones from so many Heroes onstage at once. Finally, the main body retired and the three City Brothers approached. The first, brightest and tallest of the three, Conar's eldest son Ekotelh spoke.

"Father, Law-Giver, does this region also contain the site wherein we may found the city promised us in vision? It shall be as no other before it or since, and it is in my heart that the sooner such a Hopeful deed is begun, the longer it will spread Hope by its existence."

"Beloved son, my prescience does not extend so far as you would wish. This City of Heroes — for so it shall be known — will arise, but whether these tall mountains of marble cliffs and canyons, or the blasted and ruined lands beyond it still in the demon's thrall, can contain your seat, remains yet to be proven by deeds and time."

Then Areghel stepped forward and begged a word, as the three sons of Conar stepped back.

"My liege-lord and Hope of all Men, I too can see the misery of those folk trapped in yonder wastelands. A vast stretch of earth between these mountains and the great river, ruled by that hateful monster, vassal of Mauglir and demon of the earth who is already my sworn foe. I would give my life to save even some of those mortals from his grip, and I feel in my heart a yearning to fight for them, yea even with mine two fists I would fight against the demon Kog if I could free that land for one day."

"Great warrior and mage, this shall be as you say and more. I hereby accord you lordship over yon kingdom, to be ruled by you and your line for all time, in preference to the demon Kog. Already you have defeated him in combat since our landing, and I foresee a second conflict in which his defeat shall be uttermost; at least, to human power as we know it. You shall rule this kingdom well and straightly, with justice and establishing peace for uncounted

thousands who will bless your name, for as long as your line does last."

As Areghel knelt to receive the kingship from the Hopelord, everyone's eye was drawn to the opposite side of the stage, where the third son of Conar, Khoirah the traitor, stepped quietly off while his brothers listened. The theatre murmured in confusion. Cedrith felt a light touch from Judgement, and turned to see an inquiring glance.

"It's unheard of," he whispered. "Khoirah delivers the play's final speech, except for the triumphal chorus. This is where he turns from hero to betrayer. He hatches his scheme to use forbidden magics and see the future that he might know the site of the City of Heroes."

"The speech is the Profanity," Natasha put in, "to match the Promise and Prophecy of the first two acts. It is a charge to us in the audience, to be ever-mindful that Despair still exists. But where is he?"

The cast followed Conar from the field off to the left. Then from the stage-right side where Khoirah had exited, a single actor came onto the empty battlefield, of normal human size, wearing a costume identical in hue to the one on the son of Conar moments ago but now reduced to a mere mortal in every aspect, except for a mask over his face. The audience gasped at the idea. In his arms the actor cradled something wrapped in cloth, which moved slightly as he spoke. Cedrith realized with horror that an actual infant was playing the role of the baby Telhol, Conar's youngest son, another first for this production.

"Hush, littlest brother; all is well and the battle's won, your prowess was not needed! My liege and brothers retire now to celebrate the victory, and the quest for our wondrous city is put off again. I shall not tolerate any further delay, and I can gain the knowledge with mine own courage, and the right rituals, on a night just as this one. It requires only one drop of innocent blood..."

The actor gently lifted just the edge of the cloth bundle as he spoke these words, revealing the head and hair of the child, and his meaning was unmistakable. Women in the audience screamed and fainted at the mere thought, and strong men jumped to their feet as if to fight or flee. The house grew in uproar and some of what the actor said to finish his speech was lost. The mask was unmoving throughout, showing only the clever and scheming features of a traitor. Regardless of the alarum on all sides, his face spoke of a plan that would remain undetected. Cedrith sweated and gasped aloud, as the enormity of Khoirah's crime channeled through a human-sized vessel seemed to increase the force of the violation. The actor suddenly raised his free arm, and almost as one, those who were standing sank back in their seats. The audience quieted against its will, and his final words rang out above the hall:

"For every man must do what he can to advance the cause he holds dearest, and all means are worthy to that end. Thus shall it ever be, and though of less account than my elder brothers I shall be the one to accomplish more than any man here today. By my name I swear, no risk is too great to achieve my proper place."

Thunderous boos accompanied his exit, and the returning chorus was greeted with cheers carrying the palpable relief of a grateful audience. Everyone took to their feet to sing the anthem with the players, and the theater rang with the well-known words that spoke to Hope Forever. Judgement stood at attention with his hands clasped behind him, nodding occasionally at phrases he could catch. The actors began to take their bows, and Cedrith cheered especially hard for the woman playing Aballe, whom he thought did splendidly. Natasha hooted and whistled like a commoner for her friend Alendic. Judgement kept his hands clasped as if waiting to be dismissed. But when the actor who played Khoirah stepped almost shyly onstage, still in his mask as if for shame, the usual good-hearted boos or polite cheers nearly died out. The memory of the astonishing interpretation the company had put on his performance was too fresh, too painful. A mere smattering of applause, and no cheers, accompanied him to the front of the stage, yet here Cedrith could see Judgement deliberately bring his hands together to join the few.

Cedrith felt exhausted by the performance as the stage-lights went down and the audience filed out; he said as much to Natasha, who responded, "Imagine how the company must feel!"

"Indeed, let us go and meet this marvelous friend of yours. Judgement, I beg you, do come with us, this will be a great education." The youth nodded grimly and the trio of friends swam against the exiting tide to reach the stage. Soon, the theater was empty, with only one stage-lantern lit for the occasional member of the troupe who moved about near the curtain on clean-up business. Cedrith noted it was eerily quiet, and the base of his neck could always feel the presence of the enormous Makine still forty paces away in the darkness at the back of the stage.

The time was probably not as long as it seemed before they were greeted by a resonant and cheery baritone voice, calling "Natasha, my dear one, you've come as you promised, and with friends!" Stepping onstage was a tall blonde man of excellent form and as handsome as the day was long, the very image of an actor in every nuance of his posture, gesture and composure.

The bulky matron was only half-way up the steps before Alendic seized her under the arms and swept her entirely onto the stage in an enormous embrace. Cedrith and Judgement filed up behind as the two friends hugged and chattered in easy counterpoint.

"Why do you make me wait so long to see you? Say you'll be mine!"

"Away the flatterer, you have another three girls waiting on you tonight, and their weight is not mine put together."

"You wrong me deeply. Who could look at a pale slip of girlhood once he'd had a glimpse—"

"—of what I can do, yes, I've heard it before; heal your shattered leg, on the Coldon Ridge—"

"Truth."

"—and that scar on the plains of the Percentalion, from those cougarrants—"

"I have it still, look here."

"Stop, you, and keep your shirt on, there's no woman here to be impressed with your muscles, you renegade. Now act the gentleman for once and pretend you're glad to meet my friends."

Alendic pivoted smartly to face the two men and reached to take Cedrith's hand first. "Sage Fellareon, my dear friend has told me much about you, and all good things."

"Then she has certainly not told you all," Cedrith parried, getting a warmer laugh than he expected in return. An actor, he reminded himself.

"And here," Alendic said, "is the young man I have heard of; Solemn Judgement, I presume?"

The grey-clad youth stood straight, ignoring Alendic's proffered hand; only after it was withdrawn did he offer a stiff bow. Nothing put off, Alendic chuckled and returned it, copying the style on the first try. "Welcome then, sir. Natasha has warned me you would be a stern customer, but I hope you will not object to the hospitality I have prepared. This way, all, to my room back-stage where we may refresh ourselves and talk."

The area behind the stage was nearly as vast as the playing space, and with several dozen people still moving back and forth it seemed they had walked into a scene. Natasha and Alendic were chattering so steadily as not to notice, but Cedrith had learned to be mindful of the young man and called out to them. Judgement, intercepted by a quartet of men carrying a long set piece, now stood impassively behind a low wall painted with sea-waves.

"Oho! Sorry, my friend," called Alendic amiably as they waited for the men to lumber past. "Natasha tells me you sailed across the sea, but can you swim, sir?" The two of them chuckled at this, but Judgement only raised a brow.

"Yes," he responded matter-of-factly, and as if to prove the point, leaped up to grab a fly-rope and kip over the ocean, landing neatly next to them again. Cedrith felt he was still standing between two sides, and the sense of dislike from Judgement was palpable. The evening was not getting off on a promising foot.

Entering the room Alendic led them to, Cedrith was stunned at the luxury on all sides. Rich red walls with gold piping, delicately sculpted ornate marble serving-tables, and chairs the size of thrones arranged at comfortable intervals greeted his eye.

"Do you often entertain royalty, sir?"

"Not unless you count ourselves," Alendic rejoined gaily. "That chair you are sitting in now is the one we use for Conar in*Founding of the City*. I shall be very happy with Shilar's throne here, which we insert to some scenes in various plays, as it matches his Mien; and the love of my life," gesturing to Natasha, who tsked him, "graces the Seat of the Sun, which we use during *Days of Argens* to chronicle his establishment of the southern empire. The walls and other appointments here are from that set: they come apart at the seams with just a few wooden pins. And young Judgement sits the chair of Areghel, king of the Percentalion and the bane of the undead, which seems fitting."

Cedrith looked at Alendic in alarm; it was as if the smiling, smooth gentleman was trying to unnerve his guest. And it might be working, for Judgement appeared as if only pride were making him stay in his seat, now that he knew its purpose.

Natasha, evidently oblivious to any problem, had poured wine into four chased goblets and passed them around before sitting. In mere moments, she had finished hers and was starting a second, laughing all the time with various light jokes between her and the actor.

"A wonderful vintage," Cedrith said, "clearly from Mendel. I am honored."

"Nothing but the best for my guests," Alendic returned, "though perhaps I should say, second-best, for I have never tasted nor been able to procure any of the famous Kira-Ashton that I've heard tell of."

"Ah, that would be most difficult," Cedrith admitted. "I've only had the pleasure myself twice; and I'm related to the vintner! Distantly. Not made from grapes, but a special kind of apple."

"Then it is perhaps like a cider?"

"No," said Cedrith smiling, "not at all like a cider, I'm afraid. But still, this is more than sufficient, and I thank you."

"But not good enough for us all, I gather," Alendic said, still smiling. "Young Judgement, you take no cheer with us?"

The goblet next to the grey man's seat was left untouched, and he seemed content to make no answer. Cedrith tried to maintain a semblance of civility. "My good friend takes no wine, at least to my acquaintance, Alendic. Would it be too much trouble to ask for a pitcher of water?"

"Water?" Alendic asked. "Seriously? Just water." Shrugging, he knocked on the thin wall and called out, "Hey, Bartaeus, if you're still back there, could you bring me a jug of our finest water, thanks."

It grew quiet in the room and Cedrith felt more uncomfortable than ever. "May I compliment you, citizen Alendic, on a splendid performance and produ—"

"Thanks, sage," broke in the actor with some force, "but I am most eager to hear our young friend's opinion." Cedrith, still unused to the human habit of interruption, was too jolted to gather himself immediately and could protect Judgement no longer. Alendic sat forward with a kind of intensity the Elf did not like to see, and Natasha, whom Cedrith had begun to think was getting tipsy, had said nothing for some time but only looked at them both.

Judgement returned the actor's gaze levelly and without response.

"What say you, sir? Did you like my performance at all?"

At last the youth was forced to speak. "I did not see you."

"Hah! Well played. What of Conar, then; did you think him any good?"

At this jocular riposte, the Man in Grey suddenly stood as if being assailed; Alendic rose in answer and Cedrith felt pulled to his feet between them. Quietly, Judgement hissed, "I did not see him either."

"Sir," Cedrith pleaded, "I beg you to take no offense."

"Of course not," Alendic returned. "I cannot yet make out that your friend has said anything. What did you see, then, young man? Tell us in your own words."

"I saw … apery. A band of children playing, with toys that a roomful of silver could not buy, but child's play. I heard trumpets and saw flashes, and dazzling frames of figures like shadows on a wall, when the young ones tell ghost tales behind a candle to amuse and affright each other. I saw all that was to be revered and respected in life, being made the mock of, as miscreants will in class when their teacher is late. And I wondered," Judgement said in a low tone with his gaze fixed on Alendic, "when the door would close and the teacher arrive to fix the punishment."

A silence then, to hear a pin drop. Cedrith felt sick, and could not muster even the energy to sit back down, nor did he dare. The two men stood and faced each other from just out of arm's reach, the younger breathing visibly, the other just assessing, it seemed. Natasha remained seated and took a slow, deliberate drink. Out of all reckoning, Alendic suddenly turned back to Natasha and broke into a boyish grin.

"Oh, I really like him," he exclaimed to the healer. "Do you know, I've just been insulted? He's so eloquent, I had to think to be sure!

And he's straight as a rod, doesn't back down. You were right, my dear, as you always are."

"Righter than you know," she murmured back with a quiet smile.

"Good in a fight too, I suppose?" Alendic pursued, turning back to the youth almost aggressively but still with that persistent grin. "Do you have the sword?"

Cedrith started to sputter incoherently, completely unsure what was happening. Judgement shook his head and replied, "I have no training to the blade. My father said it was a weapon for grown men only. I bear a staff at need."

"Indeed? Let us spar a bit, then," Alendic said, turning quickly and rooting among the drek of the room's corner.

"Hold, hold, just a moment, sir," Cedrith managed, and then ducked back onto his throne as a stage-pole came shuttling past on its way towards Judgement, who caught it one-handed. With a cry of triumph, Alendic straightened up and turned around with a thin table-leg in one hand, serving as a rapier. Alendic advanced towards the grey youth and adopted a fencer's stance, saluted with elaborate decorum and then crab-stepped in to slash twice from different quarters. Cedrith cried out, but Judgement ducked the first and parried the second, still one-handed. Alendic pressed in harder and faster, with nothing staged about his attacks as he slashed at the youth's head and feet. Judgement dropped back three steps at speed, gripping the pole two-handed now and blocking everything. Finally the wall forced him to stop, and a sweeping blow from the tip of Alendic's weapon slapped his cheek, raising a welt instantly. At once Judgement's face hardened; the next attempted attack was met by an aggressive block followed by a riposte that thumped Alendic's exposed ribs and knocked him nearly down. Stepping in, Judgement whirled the staff overhead with a flourish and brought it down hard at Alendic's head; the block was sufficient but staggered the actor again, and his riposte was weak. Judgement merely moved his head to evade it, then grabbed the wood with one hand, as he could never have done with a steel blade, and pulled his opponent to him chest to chest. Both men were breathing hard now, but the actor was still smiling as if he were wearing a mask of joy.

"My good sir, were I not such a manly fellow I could kiss you." This, spoken from a few inches' distance, seemed to bring Judgement back to himself, and he thrust his admirer away with a rough hand. Not knowing where he was or what he was doing, Cedrith stepped into the created space with his arms flung wide.

"Enough, gentlemen, I beg of you. You, sir," to Alendic, "what is the meaning of this rough treatment? We come to you as guests—"

"My dear sage, not to worry," replied the smiling actor smoothly. "I assure you I hold you both in the highest regard and am absolutely delighted that you would choose to visit. I had heard Natasha here speak of your young friend in glowing tones, and I was eager, as it were, to see the truth of her claims."

"But what can you—"

"He is testing me." The statement from Judgement was calm and matter-of-fact, as he sat again and drank from the water glass.

"Testing!" Cedrith cried, looking both ways now and not knowing whom to believe less.

Alendic looked at Judgement for a moment, then back to Natasha, who quietly shook her head. "Testing, a harsh word," he began, "but it is true that I hunger to know you better, sir. As to our little spar, I am satisfied as to your evident skill. Perhaps we could train together in the arena, if you have an hour to spare each week?"

"The arena," Cedrith asserted forcefully with some anger, "is for the settlement of rivalries and disputes. Soldiers who argue over dice, or young buckos over women, will resort to the arena, not gentlemen of honor. I ask again, what grudge do you hold over my friend here?"

"A grudge!" Alendic seemed genuinely surprised, though not yet put off enough to cease smiling. "I can see I've bungled things, by your reaction, good sage, and I humbly beg your pardon. You've found me out," he said, in a tone of contrition but with another sidelong glance at Natasha. "The fact of the matter is, I've been trying to … to audition your young man here."

Now Cedrith could feel a smile stealing over his face, though he still felt at sea. Turning to Natasha, he said, "I could have sworn I heard your friend say 'audition'."

Natasha for answer beamed back at him in her motherly way, with just a hint of mischief. Alendic, who had returned to his seat and taken a drink, gestured with his cup. "Ah yes, audition, nearly as bad as test. Suffice to say, dear sage, that this youth interests me with regards to a … certain performance I have in mind. A small company, one show only, sort of a return engagement. Hardly any audience, truly, but I must admit they are very … unforgiving, if you take—"

"Stop, Alendic, I won't hear even you speak that way about—" Natasha seemed upset and even hurt, and Cedrith's confusion was nearly complete. Alendic bowed from his chair to his friend, took another drink, and thought awhile. Judgement sat as if he had turned to stone in his chair, with his gaze fixed on Alendic.

"I know, let us change the subject for a bit, and speak of history," Alendic continued. "Our production tonight concerned the events of the First War of Liberation. And speaking only to the text," he said especially for Judgement's benefit, "I would say it was accurate?"

Judgement nodded curtly. "Certes, as I have read in the histories."

"And I hear you have read them, indeed. But now then, what happened next, eh, after the curtain fell?"

"It is said that Conar launched the second invasion, freeing the Percentalion and the kingdom of Shilar."

"Indeed. But between the two wars, good Judgement; what happened between them?"

Judgement seemed puzzled. "Between the wars? The accounts speak of seven days."

"Yes they do!" retorted Alendic with joy. "But it was seven years."

"Nonsense," cried Cedrith. "The ancient texts all agree."

"Indeed?" cut in Natasha. "I was not aware that you were used to reading the texts in Ancient, my dear."

"Well, that is … you know I fumble at the fine meanings of the tongue of power, dear Natasha. Nearly everyone, even at the Guild, when they speak of 'the ancient texts' really means—"

"A translation, precisely," finished Alendic. "As do I, sir, I assure you. But Natasha here, she is quite the scholar, and we've been poring over the scripts kept here in the theater."

"I don't understand," Cedrith said, as Judgement leaned in closer to listen.

"These sacred plays," said Alendic, "are the true source for most of the history contained in your books, my dear sage. There is every evidence that they were composed by close camerate of Conar himself, perhaps even … well, I have seen the texts, and Natasha has assisted with our translation. I tell you in all seriousness, these are the originals from which our history and knowledge of the Heroes has been drawn. Conar clearly wished the deeds of all the people — not himself, merely— to be kept intact and presented to descendants for all generations. The building too, and many of its features, such as the Miens, are very,*very* old."

Alendic sat back then, and the room had grown suddenly quiet. "Some of these writings," he said slowly, "are in correspondence script. Not block-print. Not the hand of a scribe, if you take my meaning." And they all did.

"I see we have at last caught the interest of our young friend," Alendic said while reaching for his goblet. "What say you, good Judgement, would you like to study the little 'play' I have in mind?" With narrowed eyes and clenched fists, the Man in Grey nodded slowly.

"But mind you," said Natasha, "read only what you are shown and say nothing out loud in the ancient tongue. Is that clear? If you can translate what you see into the common speech, say that or write it down. But no more." Cedrith could feel how her words hurt the youth, though he did not show it. He was reminded of that fateful day, and looked at the throne on which Judgement sat; the thought of Areghel brought a chill down his spine.

"When should we begin?" Judgement asked, and Alendic, his smile painted back in place, rejoined, "When is convenient for you, good sir?"

For answer the grey youth stood, which caught his host by surprise. "Such industry! To the scriptorium, then." With an elaborate grimace he rose and gestured the way with one hand while retrieving his goblet with the other. Natasha followed closely in a mothering posture and Cedrith brought up the rear.

"Ho, Bartaeus, still with us? Do you have a light, please?" They proceeded through turning, cramped corridors behind the massive stage-wall, and the way became gradually darker until a lamp emerged from a side-door and a young man in light-hued clothes stepped before them.

"Here, Alendic, the oil is full with this one."

"Thanks, lad, and well done tonight."

Cedrith looked at the fellow carefully without recognition, but Judgement turned at the first sound of his voice. He held out his hand, which the actor grasped, and shook it gravely.

"You took the role of Khoirah," he said, stating a fact. The young man nodded and hung his head. Cedrith and Natasha murmured their praise, and Alendic cocked his head at Judgement as he took the lantern.

"You are an astute judge of the human frame, young Judgement. That costume and mask—"

"He has an honest way," Judgement replied quietly, and Alendic's face showed surprise, then hardened back into a determined smile.

"He's right, lad; and you're the first to play the role naked in centuries. We brought back an ancient custom, and I for one think it was a brilliant idea."

"Yours, sir," said Bartaeus, and the lead actor laughed in a loud and good-natured way.

"Why, so you're right! Get some rest, friend. We'll see you tomorrow."

"A few clean-up chores left, sir, thanks."

The party moved down the corridor without him, and Alendic continued, "He's an earnest fellow and a good talent; too shy still, but we'll cure him. One day he could be *cardinus* … when I've retired, may Conar grant!" The actor opened an over-sized doorway and swept to one side, ushering the others in.

The scriptorium was a true room, not cobbled together from slats but with stone floor and wooden walls; they were near the center of the building now and there were no windows, making it seem more like the Guild to Cedrith. On a large, high table was a reading podiate and an enormous tome, one of many from the shelves behind, was open. Hanging the lantern nearby, Alendic shoved a large stepstool in place with his foot, saying, "We leave the scripts up high so we can check them during our performance, while wearing our Miens." Kicking over a second stool, he and Natasha slid a plank on top so that a viewing platform stood before the book. From the floor, Cedrith could see that it was truly giant-sized, with pages nearly like bedsheets and a cover as thick as his thumb. The four stepped up and out onto the plank, and bent in to peruse the writing, which was normal-sized but seemed tiny by comparison.

"Let us see, here's the script of tonight's play; we don't need to check it much, except the fellow who played Ekhonon. Lazy fellow, really, not that many lines … so, we want the notes, following the script, a few pages on, just a moment." He carefully reached his arm fully under each page and lifted them to turn with delicacy and a practiced hand. Cedrith could see the remarkable age of the parchment, and thrilled to note the script-writing, which changed hands several times over the course of the excerpts he saw.

"They treat the parchment with a kind of thin veneer," Natasha whispered, "to preserve it against time."

"Yes, I can see these are originals, impossibly old," Cedrith responded, and then turned to Alendic. "You did not think to have copies made?"

For answer Alendic looked back at the Elf a moment with an incredulous face. Judgement, however, nodded in appreciation.

"Here's the spot," Alendic said. "Look you there, this passage right after the first combat of Areghel and Kog." Cedrith was the closest to the page indicated, and with a gulp leaned over to take a look. The characters of the ancient tongue were at once labyrinthine and irresistible.

"Thus the Helm … was begun, and Conar did … ask, em, order a halt of … of seven circuits of the sun," he read, without much confidence.

"Excellent, Sage Fellareon, quite right," encouraged Alendic. "You have translated just as your colleagues who wrote the histories have done."

"But the proper word," Natasha put in, "is not 'circuits,' but 'cycles'."

Judgement leaned in, actually brushing against Cedrith in his eagerness, who gladly gave way. He read the passage and nodded, saying, "Cycles, perhaps ages or even … no, *generatios* would be used if it were an entire zodiac of years." Natasha protectively put a hand on his shoulder at the mention of even a single word, and after a moment the grey youth tore his eyes off the page and straightened up. He faced Alendic and concurred, saying simply, "Seven years."

"But how?" Cedrith protested. "What could have happened between the two enemies for seven years?" Once again, Alendic looked past the sage to the healer, who this time gave a small shrug.

"Judging by what is written here … a truce."

"A truce! With Despair!"

"Indeed, a pause in the fighting, and more than that, a chance to—"

"No, Alendic," said Natasha quietly, and Alendic stopped in mid-word. Cedrith's suspicions blossomed again and he turned to face Natasha squarely.

"And by what right, madam, do you instruct your friend to withhold knowledge from the Sages Guild?"

"Why," rejoined Alendic gaily, "she is the *cardinus* of our company, the one whose production I was just describing. We are desperately trying to get back into a theater that people have literally died—"

"Enough. The evening is over, my thanks to you Alendic. We are leaving."

Natasha climbed down, and Alendic with a resigned air signaled for the others to follow her. He was biting his lip as they walked through the halls on the way back, and Cedrith could see that this exit was not to his liking. As they passed another large archway, he paused and said, "Just one more stop on our little tour. I would like our young friend to see something."

Passing into the side-room, Cedrith could see that it let out on the other wall through a similar large arch, and beyond was a wing of the stage itself. Near the center of this room, a row of magnificent helmets hung as if suspended in mid-air, each gorgeously decorated and colossal.

"Behold, the Miens," said Alendic with a gesture and a quiet voice. "Here we don the appearance of our Heroes before taking the stage, and here we leave our best efforts behind when we are through." He turned to Judgement then and spoke for once in a voice without bombast or wit.

"You said you saw mockery tonight, and I believe I understand. But think you this. A few steps in that direction, you may stand directly beneath the helm of one of the characters from our play tonight. Conar," he said, pointing to each in turn, "Shilar there, Dunedin, Ekhotelh, and there on the far right, Khoirah, whom we elected to retire early. There is no way to fully describe in words what happens, young man; only watch."

Alendic handed his lantern to Cedrith, lined himself up behind the helm of Conar, and came closer with deliberate steps. As they watched, the helm itself began to seem the center of something more. The misty outline of a cloak, greaves, a shield, a mane of long straight hair … the very image of the heroic figure they saw became more visible. Alendic's feet rose from the floor as he walked, until he was standing nearly a foot above the wood. Cedrith felt a growing charge inside him, between elation and panic, and Alendic's body faded from view as he entered the coalescing frame of the Man-father. For a moment, it was a statue, seen from behind, and then it turned to face them, Conar at close range looking down on the three with his regal face and lordly eye.

"I am not fit to lead Hope's army if I have none in my heart."

The words were the same, the tone, the intent, but now the Hopelord looked down on Judgement, and the youth was transfixed. The huge figure of Conar turned back into line then, lifted his arms to his head and pulled up his great helm. As he did, the form of Alendic became visible almost at once, and sank gently to the ground, where he momentarily put his hands to his knees to catch his breath. Soon, he looked up with his usual smile back in place. "After an evening's performance, I need to lie down for a few minutes."

"The Mien is more than a costume, not even a glamour of magic. It bears … the spirit, I vow, some small dose of the essence of the figure it mimics. When I act as Conar, I am unable to speak freely, only to quote those lines I have learned in character. And I may only act as Conar would act in each scene."

He came to Judgement and faced him at close range. "I want you to know, when I spoke of 'testing, ' that you were not the only subject, my friend. Members of a … company, those who will work and train together, they must have more than separate talent. They must trust and respect each other."

Judgement stiffened, and Alendic raised a hand to forestall him. "I wanted you to know, this work here, which has been my life for the past five years, is work I have taken seriously. For my first year, I studied the scripts, and before I learned them thoroughly I was struck dumb when I put on a Mien. On my first day I couldn't even move. Ask the people where Conar is, and many will take you to a stone statue in a church; but the image they see, the voice they hear? It is for me to bring them that. Someone else? Perhaps, if a better man comes, I will not stand in his way. But failure, that we cannot think of here.

"What you call a mockery I call a high vow and a deep purpose, one to which I have given my all. Would you care to don a Mien, sir?" And here returned a shade of Alendic's natural wit and taunt.

Judgement considered the words, then turned to face the row of helmets. He took two slow steps towards one of them — Cedrith could not recall which one — and the Elf saw his stride shrink, as if he were wading into water. Just barely could the outlines of some magnificent shape be seen; then Judgement stopped, and after a moment, stepped back. He shook his head, then turned and bowed once more to Alendic, who smiled and turned to leave.

But behind them, Judgement spoke. "May I see the Makine?"

Everyone froze, and Cedrith felt suddenly cold.

"The Makine?" responded Alendic, with a meaningful look to the healer. "I am your servant, sir, and it does indeed complete the tour, I admit, to see the other side as it were."

Back into the hallway and by larger corridors they came onto the stage, and everyone reflexively looked upstage where the metallic thing lurked in darkness beyond the range of Alendic's lantern. Without need, he said, "'Tis back there," and a moment later moved in that direction. Cedrith was already as close as he wanted to be, but it wouldn't do to stand in the dark, so he came along.

As they picked their way past stage-holes meant to look like rents in the earth, and around the blasted, torn trees, their footfalls on the ramped platforms rang hollowly and increased the sense of loneliness. Without noticing, the foursome huddled closer together as the radius of the lantern uncovered the lower edges of the misshapen iron pile.

"Our scripts were never very specific," murmured the actor, stopping about twenty feet away and holding up the light, "and we do not know if there were any kinds or classes of these things. We believe that arm there, and perhaps that one as well, had blades of some sort on them — maybe the length of two men each — and that large black case near the middle, we only guess, may have held another arm of some kind, or it may have provided protection for an, em, human rider."

It was impossible to believe the thing was dead, towering there in the uneven lantern-light; its gargantuan shadow made it seem both threatening and perilously unsteady at the same time. Whether it animated or fell over, Cedrith's imagination ran wild and he felt sure he would have to withdraw in moments if he wished not to faint. Natasha, too, was holding her ground but breathing quickly; the horror of the Makine was deeply rooted in the Children of Hope.

Judgement, after looking both left and right at its length and features, stepped smoothly closer, right past Alendic and directly beneath one of the murder-arms. "Yes! By all means," said the actor in a rising, slightly forced tone, "take a good look, sir. It is quite inanimate, of course, and, and there should be no … that is…" He trailed off, for once at a loss, and the Man in Grey, quite absorbed in the sights, seemed not to notice anyone else was there. He stepped right up to the edge of the thing, at a point where most of its arms came together with a kind of box; made entirely of metal, it had various apertures and lay near the ground. It was canted over on its side, bringing one of these rectangular holes within easy reach. Without preamble Judgement thrust his head into this to look around.

"Judgement!" Natasha hissed in terror, and Cedrith gripped her arm for support. The lantern in Alendic's hand quavered, and it seemed more than ever that the monstrosity was moving, preparing to swallow the young man whole. He pulled his head back out, turning to Alendic to say, "What is the function of these small staves?"

"Staves," Alendic croaked, holding the lantern to one side as if trying to see, but still rooted to the spot halfway between Judgement and Natasha. The youth, with a calm face, raised an eyebrow and said, "Can you not see them from there?"

There was nothing for it now, and Alendic gulped, taking three steps closer to his guest. Shining the light into the hole, he brought to view a set of small metal sticks, resting in slots on one side of the space within. "Ah, those," the actor said, "I have never seen … that is, we, we have read nothing to say what, in the texts, what might be…"

Judgement held Alendic's gaze an extra second. Then he turned back to the aperture, casually reached his hand through, grasped one of the metal rods and pulled it down to the bottom of its slot. A rasping screech of metal resulted, followed closely by Natasha's shriek as she fainted dead away. Not expecting her bulk, Cedrith could only half-catch her and fell to the stage with her atop him; only that added shock kept him conscious through the terror that pulsed his being. A tiny rain of rusty flakes came down from beneath the box, and it seemed each one could be heard in the silence that chased the echoes from the stage. Judgement examined his handiwork, shrugged, and turned back to his host, who looked on him with a waxy face sheathed in sudden sweat. They both nodded then, as if they understood each other.

"Yes," Alendic said quietly, "I think you will do just well, young man."

Cedrith felt a light behind him and smelled something acrid. Looking up from the ground where he struggled beneath his girthsome friend, he saw Bartaeus standing in shock, with a patch of dark wetness spreading across his midsection. Cedrith was not sure how he had avoided the poor young man's fate himself, but for now, there was Natasha to attend to. Alendic led Judgement back to where she lay, and told Bartaeus to fetch water "and a new set of clothes, of course. Poor fellow, probably the last we'll see of him in this theater." Soon they had revived her, and the Healers Guildmistress was simply furious with Judgement for his misdeed.

"What in the name of the Hopeful Kingdoms did you think you were doing?" she thundered.

Judgement made no attempt to reply, but Alendic, his smirk stealing back to its accustomed place, said, "He was passing the audition, dear heart. And we both know it."

"Now, then, do not be cross, my love," he soothed as she gathered breath to scold him as well. "The lad is inspired by his youthful desire and obvious enthusiasm," this with a wink, "to outdo himself, and we should be lenient with him."

"Aye? And what, pray, is your excuse, great actor and respected gentleman of the city?" Natasha seethed at the *cardinus*. But as they stepped down from the stage and through the house, Alendic was back in his imperturbable form, able to quip on immediate notice.

"For me, madam, I claim only the fire of my love for you, which has ever burned—"

"Like the blaze of a funeral pyre, I have heard it all before. If either of you attempts these manly pranks again, I shall oversee a funeral pyre indeed."

"This, from a peaceful healer! A follower of Telhol, and sworn against violence."

"Your company is enough to make me forget my vows."

"Hah! Exactly my hope, dear heart, but alas, the wrong vows!"

Natasha thumped him then as hard as she could with her open hand, but Alendic only laughed the louder, and Cedrith had to chuckle as well.

"I must thank you once again, sir," he said to Alendic at the entrance, "for a truly unique evening. I feel as if I have seen two shows this night, and I can hardly say which one I find more memorable."

"You honor me, good sage, and I hope to have the pleasure of your company again. As to your difficulty, I cannot say I share it: give me the second show, for the first is one I have done before."

"And if you ever try the second again," growled Natasha, "your production will abruptly close."

Alendic bowed low and kissed Natasha's hand, then shook with Cedrith. Turning to Judgement, he said only, "I shall see you again," and received a terse nod in return.

As they walked back to the Guilds, it was quite easy to slow to a normal pace and allow Judgement to move ahead through the wide, dark streets.

"I don't suppose," Cedrith said quietly to Natasha, "that you will tell me a single thing about what happened back there."

She was still quite moved by her recent experience, but his curiosity restored some of Natasha's playful nature. "It depends," she returned, "on your good behavior."

"Mine! Did I start a fight, enter a Mien, try to reanimate a Makine?"

"No," she said, as if admitting a fault, "but I have hope for you yet, sir."

⊕⊕⊕

The Kingdom Chronicle 1995 ADR

In Salamander of the Sun year denoted 1995 Ante Dagnor Rokan, the attention of all the Hopeful kingdoms was gained by the extraordinary second embassy of the Bordbeyond people unto the king of Shilar. As detailed in this chronicle under the previous month of Ferret, a lone warrior had alarmed the court and delivered a message to the prince, Gareth son of Genel XXXI, begging that guests be exchanged between the nations as before times of impending war. Beyond all expectation, the second embassy — much larger this time, fully a score of armored warriors with strange banners and extra mounts — was met at the crossing of the River Sweeping by an honor guard from the Baron of Hirion. Fully five dozen knights, with their squires, attendants, wagons and some families, kept the passage secure around all sides of these guests of the kingdom as they made a slow progress towards the capital. Crowds of common folk emerged at every village, with some reports of ill-talk and discontent at the strange habits of the Shepherds. But order was maintained on the Baron's honor, and the caravan did arrive at Cil-Cilurion in safety.

There the king, in attendance with the court and availed of interpretation suited to the occasion, did hear the matter of the embassy. Though this early visit took the court somewhat unawares (and risked the king's honor therefore, as Shilar is the lord of foresight), preparations had been taken in sufficient part, and the good knight Sir Tustic, son of the Baron of Prestering, was introduced as the one chosen for the exchange. The young man was an excellent horseman and jouster though only twenty-three, and excelled in hunting and outdoor life, and thus was considered a splendid choice.

But young Tustic and the court were shocked to hear the embassy's business, and here the fine efforts of Prince Gareth, through no fault of his own, came to ruin. The head of the embassy, a helmed warrior who as usual gave no name, announced that the prince's gift had been accepted, and that in accordance with Shepherd custom the daughter of their highest chief was now waiting on the plains beyond the River Sweeping, to join the young man in marriage. Much confusion and disarray were the sad fate of the Shilarian court upon this announcement; reports agree that at least three warlike men were injured and it was two full days before negotiations could resume. The wise King, through iron exertion of will, was able to house and sequester the foreign delegation the while. A quarter adjoining the gardens with ample courtyards for the visitors' taste (as they sleep under no roof unless imprisoned) was evacuated with haste; the high walls of the precinct served to keep them safe from any further opportunity to visit chaos upon the court. Meanwhile the crown and his sages conferred without ceasing.

So little is recorded, even throughout the breadth of this chronicle, of the ways of the half-elven people that nothing could be made clear immediately. But the indications King Genel was able to glean from his advisors were a sad confirmation of the embassy's announcement. Prince Gareth, by sending such a splendid gift to a person unseen and unknown to him, was by that token offering his hand, in the view of these folk (perhaps a custom they had absorbed through their long exposure to the remnants of rustic cultures said to inhabit the Swords of Stone). It was protested in council that this was surely not the young prince's intent; but all knew the honor of the giver lay in his open-handedness, not his first thought but in the conception of the recipient which the giver must fulfill. Even in Shilar, this is the practice among those of noble blood and commoners alike.

As the court, on reconvening, tried to digest this dreadful news, the Bordbeyonds became increasingly agitated apprehending a refusal. Their leader again made clear, through repeated interpretations, that failure to consummate the "proffered union" was sufficient cause to take up arms. The unworthy suggestion of some councilors that the embassy be at once detained was refused, in part because its failure to return would have brought the same result.

All witnesses agree that in this crisis, the prince behaved with flawless decorum, and indeed won himself even nearer to the hearts of the kingdom. Visibly stunned as were all witnesses to hear the news unfold, yet he faced the threat with great courage and composure. Before all the court, he stepped forward in lieu of formal permission to speak and offered to accept the responsibility he had unwittingly triggered.

No effort of the king's officers could suffice to restrain the Shilarian court at this; shouting down the prince as he endeavored to elaborate, a crowd of knights surged forward, seizing him with cheers and alarums and took him off, parading him to the court, the castle and even the city without as an exemplar of nobility and patriotism. The king, it was said, bore no part in the demonstration, nor did he raise his hand to arrest it. For three further days after the embassy broke up in such chaos, the prince's exact whereabouts were a matter of some dispute. Certain sources indicate he had been taken to a foef outside the city for safety, while others averred he was back in the royal chambers by the first nightfall, and there did argue in private with his royal sire, that against all decency and civilized custom, he should be compelled to take up the awful duty.

The immediate result of the embassy was that the Bordbeyonds were forced to return, bearing suitable gifts but lacking an answer, as King Genel refused for the moment to speak yea or nay. Even the question of when the answer might be delivered, or how, was not taken up; yet he thanked them with formal dignity for their visit, making no mention of the offer or the threat. The half-elven leader declared only that the ceremony must take place by the end of the following year, 1996 ADR, before withdrawing. Under the vigilant eye of Baron Hirion the Shepherds returned to their land. The king meanwhile withdrew with the seers, it is said for a deep and intimate study of the heavenly signs which can be seen nowhere better than from Cil-Cilurion.

The precise record of those deliberations have not been made available to this chronicle. But it seems evident that the bulk of those astrological determinations were naturally not favorable to a match. A Sun year presaging centeredness seemed hardly suited to the act of sending Shilar's next crown to the easternmost hinterlands of Hope. The following year, when the proposed marriage would have been consummated, lies under the sign of Areghel, the grim captain of war and Demonsbane, whose descended issue came to ruin and whose very kingdom now lay under the chains of increasing chaos. And yet if war were to be avoided, a blunt negative could hardly be politic. The prospect of fighting may have seemed welcome to some among the Shield Knights, those who had been foremost in the kidnapping of the prince. But wiser heads noted that the half-elven were indeed Children of Hope, if sadly primitive and estranged by their cursed fate. The horror of internecine warfare deeply impressed all but the most avid.

After much deliberation, the great king announced to the court that he would seek the counsel of the crown of Mendel in the matter. Messengers were dispatched, and met with great courtesy by the Ageless Lord Tithalis, direct in line from Ma-Eldar's son Mendel. An invitation for a royal visit was returned and accepted, and the king of Shilar, not feeling any pressing sense of urgency, set the date for the ides of the Lion 1996, a full year away. Some at court murmured that such timing was as good as knowing the answer already, but others held out hope that war could be averted through the wisdom of the immortals.

⊕⊕⊕

The deep forestlands north of Cil-Cilurion are quite unlike the gorgeous and orderly Halfwoods to their east. Men, not content to dwell in wood before it has been cut, treat the trees as a crop to harvest at need, and to shelter game during other seasons. The edge of Sir Ganelake's foef is largely free of the touch of Man, for wood is plentiful throughout his holdings. This forest, aside from its great beauty and suitability for hunting, is widely understood to be lonely beyond measure, and perhaps even haunted.

This precludes the common folk from entering, but not Shield Knights of Shilar, who take no note of danger. The knight and his squire riding through the cushioned copses and across bracken-bridged streams have the world to themselves; hunting is their purpose to judge by the leather gear, but hardly the point as shown in their leisurely and careless pace. The knight in the lead seems content to take in every ancient bole the horses pass and each bright-colored wing they flush. There are deer and quail in plenty, staring in wonder as they ride by, but neither young noble reaches for a bow.

"Gareth, it was not your fault." Far from the court, the use of titles often lapsed among the chivalric orders, though naturally none would speak this way in public. "You told them. You volunteered. Your father decided otherwise, there is no shame to you in this."

The prince of Shilar nodded absently, then pointed to a red-tailed songbird jumping from log to branch in a patch of slanting sun ahead. He let his horse peter to a complete stop, abandoning all pretence of heading anywhere for now, and allowed it to graze as his squire came abreast of them.

"What do you suppose lies ahead of us?" he asked, and Hobsel sighed.

"East? We probably left Sir Ganelake's land an hour ago. We'd need to turn back soon if you want to shelter with him tonight." Hobsel glanced over to see if the prince cared about this, and saw no sign. "So it's royal domain for two days more, at least. You could command anyone you saw, but there won't be a soul, until you reach the Halfwood." Gareth gazed towards the climbing sun and said nothing; Hobsel grinned and went further.

"There of course you would be accorded every courtesy by the little folk, no doubt feasted and regaled with stories of your fabled namesake. And whenever you were ready to ride on, an honor guard, never dreaming, of course, that you had come to visit, without your royal sire's knowledge … or permission." Hobsel began to sense their mind-journey moving in an unpleasant direction now. Swallowing, the squire continued, "And after perhaps four more days of not-too-leisurely riding — and jogging for our hosts, of course — why, we would reach the Sweeping. And there an end."

"An end at the Sweeping?" Gareth mused quietly, as if neither rivers nor directions were known to him before.

"Well of course!" Hobsel cried with some heat. "Where else? Back west to your host, so that he does not become affrighted at his lost honor and summons his levy to search for you. No, not interested, I see; south then, back to your father's house. Or north, perhaps, we could cross the hills and enter the Plains of Ranebruh, to search the wind-blasted flatlands for the ghost of Percis." Now Gareth did turn to look on his squire with patient affection, and it softened the mood a little. "So then. East to the river, perhaps a week more away from men, until you must return or face the fact that you are not returning."

Gareth nodded and rubbed his face as he gestured back east. "I understand," he said conversationally, "that north of Hirion there is a ford."

"Across the Sweeping. Into the Bordbeyond lands." Hobsel's tone betokened shock as at a criminal undertaking. "By the star of day, Gareth, you mean to go."

The prince did not move or speak, and his face looked down at the grass his horse was cropping.

"You would give yourself to the Shepherds. Disobey your king's command, and leave your father. Great Sign, Gareth, you mean to marry her."

"Or," Gareth responded as if choosing between two hats in a market, "I can return, and obey, and allow a war that my nation would otherwise have avoided."

"This war lies not on your honor! Silly man, everyone knows it is not your fault."

"By doing one thing, I can prevent it; then by doing otherwise, I cause it."

"I won't let you. I have an oath to the King, I will bring you back. Gareth," Hobsel pleaded, "you know this duty lays on me."

"And then," Gareth rejoined with a small smile, "when you defeat me, and bring me back strapped over the saddle like a rustler, the burden of duty will transfer to you. For I surely will not murder you to lose my bachelorhood, though both the kingdoms were consumed in flame."

The prince leaned forward slightly extending his right arm to his companion, who grasped it briefly but fiercely even as the tears sprang up. Hobsel rode a few paces on, then turned to face the king's son.

"It would be a magnificent adventure," the squire muttered through a grin.

"Not for you, dear Hobsel. I won't involve your name in ruin and disgrace. If I do go, it will be alone."

"Oh, so just like you!" cried the squire, the fit of pique returning. "Always seeking to take the risk, the injury on yourself, and void it from all others."

"Not so. I am but indifferent brave," the prince protested, whereupon the squire spurred forward until they were even again. Reaching down Hobsel pulled up the leg of Gareth's pant, exposing a thick, faded diagonal scar running halfway around the calf.

"Proven liar!"

Gareth looked bemused down on the old wound, and murmured, "Yes. I suppose that wagon had you in mind for this."

"And the panicked oxen, sixteen hooves as well as two wheels. Who drives a haywagon past a torch procession, anyway?"

Straightening up, the squire stopped the false-rage and became fully serious. "You saved my life that day. I've waited seven years to pay you back. If you decide to face death today, I'm going with you."

"This was no loss to me. Do you recall? I met the Healer of all the Lands the day I got this."

Hobsel looked down as if ashamed and said, "I remember everything about that day. We met."

"I had seen you at court, the year before when you were fostered."

"But we never spoke, until you pushed me out of death's way."

"Oh, not death, surely," Gareth said as was his habit. "And not well enough to get my own clumsy leg from the path. Stars of tomorrow, that was painful."

"Truly?" Hobsel said, amazed. "You never said a word, but I was certain you would not walk again."

Gareth's mouth split the distance between grin and grimace. "I said nothing, trusty squire, because I shared your view at the time." His laughter won, and he added, "I actually worried, they would not let me see you again."

Hobsel's laugh rose toward a shriek. "Milord prince, the king your father would have had this foolish squire slain, as surely as we are here today."

"So, she saved us both, the healer Natasha. What a magnificent woman," Gareth breathed. "Not the Guildmistress then, by two years yet; do you not think it strange, that I saw her before all that?"

"Truly incredible," Hobsel mused. "I had not thought, but she was merely a Gypsy then."

Gareth nodded. "No longer of her clan, but traveling with some group of adventurers." Noting his squire's surprise, he added, "I have made inquiries, in the years since. A prerogative of rank. She is alone now, risen to power and honor in Conar, but in those days, one of that adventuring class all us right-thinking folk despise. You recall, the tall wizard, their leader? What an impressive face, I thought certainly he was a lord. And the handsome fencer with the ready tongue, and one or two others I think. But she, plainly dressed, honest face of no immediate remark … she could have walked right by. I was in disguise from the court and she owed no deference."

"Not the first time you sneaked away to mingle with the common crowd!"

"Nor the last, thanks to your assistance! But she knew me not from a peasant, that's the point. I was just a boy of ten who'd gotten his leg twisted and shattered beneath a wagon-wheel."

"I … never thought of that," the squire responded softly. "I knew you at once, I couldn't think, I was so afraid. Are you saying … do you mean it was your fate that she healed you?"

"The others didn't wish to stop, but they seemed to know. Once she laid eyes on me, there would be nothing for it. So the leader just put his hands in his sleeves and waited there, while she came over. I'll never forget it, Hob; she laid her hands on me and murmured the words of power."

"And hey, bingo!" Hobsel said. "There was just that scar left, a little redder than it is today. I know. She was a great healer, even then."

"She had the heart of the land in her," Gareth returned sincerely. "She would have become the Healers Guildmistress if half the stars had fallen from the sky. I consulted old Kalentire, that very night about her, after you sneaked me back into the castle."

"Old Star-Eyes? You didn't dare!"

Gareth chuckled, putting his right hand over his heart to indicate an oath. "He was furious; here I was demanding to know about someone not present and whom I could hardly describe, much less name. The poor High Seer, kept thinking I was trying to win a lover! But even then, there were signs … the old Guildmaster in Conar passed away less than two years later, and we heard the news: one Natasha Ioki had been elevated. So quickly to the City of Wonders, already working in the Guild, to have risen so far and so fast. Everyone was amazed, but not me."

They sat their horses awhile then, as above them a jay called out his disgust at the intrusion.

"Hob, wasn't that the same day, or nearly, as your sister Hillel went away?"

The squire coughed and said, "The same. I … was out looking for her, when you … when we met."

"Do you ever think about her?" Gareth asked.

"Every day." Another pause, long enough for the horses to shift and saddle-leather to creak.

"I had heard the talk," the prince confirmed, "that your father wanted a marriage for her, but she was looking for adventure." The prince hesitated at the sign of his squire's disquiet. "Is it true, as some whispered? She wanted to be a knight, like the Lady Alayne from the days of legend. Or Tarly the Miller's daughter, who bested the Ebon Baron—"

"Or Aballe," Hobsel said quietly, "she … she always used to talk about Aballe, who fought in the Battle of the Razor."

"I hope she is happy and well," Gareth replied. "I'll tell you honestly, Hob. I thought back then, whatever her troubles, she was taking the easy path by running from them. I never said it, but I thought it, and I crave your pardon for it now. I know from her twin what a noble character she has." Hobsel flushed and could not look the prince in the eye. "Perhaps when I am king we can look for her; as long as you still wish to know."

The squire nodded quietly, then spurred horse around to face the sun like the prince's. "East, then?"

Gareth looked towards the deeper forest for some time, and then turned back, with Hobsel somewhat relieved behind him.

"It would incur dishonor to our host," Gareth remarked, "to leave without word."

They rode awhile in silence.

"And then too," the prince added, "I may not be done arguing this matter with my lord the king."

The Enceris urban precinct was small, though elegantly designed. It functioned on a quarter the staff of the city's elder houses, such as Altrindur. Speculation had run rife that after the marriage, Sir Banwen's parents would use it for a kind of retirement estate. Now, it appeared the match would be delayed with his death, despite another heir, and some whispered that it might even be off.

But none whispered that within the walls of Enceris; in fact, those few who lived behind the enclosure and few streets of the precinct hardly spoke at all. The lord was over sixty, a widower content to pray and read; his butler took care of all his needs and had for a generation. The daughter, his only child, seemingly absorbed her father's reticent ways, learning all that was needful to fill the station of a noble lady and quite self-sufficient in the prime of her womanhood. An hour or two in the back-court garden was Gemma Enceris' only pleasure, which she had shared but once before. The house castellan saw her there now, by a window on the stair leading up from the entrance hall. Down in the garden and out of earshot, she was sitting on a marble bench and pouring her heart out to a statue standing before her.

Damn the man! The devoted servant shook his head and gripped the sill, as if straining to hear through the glass, over the five rods, down the storey, through the light fog to where his mistress spoke. How did he know, this gaunt specter now intruding to the garden, who greeted him a half-hour ago in the entryway? The castellan still felt the shock at this visitor, when he opened the door expecting to confront some unwanted peddler or a commoner looking for work. Instead, he drew back from the rigid stern cast of face, the severely plain clothes and foreign manner. He had not managed a word, when the grey-haired youth said, "I am Judgement." A verdict, passed on him? The castellan took a long moment to remember, this was the name of the man the Elvish Sage had said would come. But what manner of scribe was this? Still unspeaking, he stood there agape like a peasant until the intruder said simply, "I have the lady's answer."

How did he *know*? There had been no hint, no clue in his charge to the Elf. The castellan had only implied it was his lord's request, to cover that he himself was the only querent. And indeed, he had asked on the desperate chance that it offered some hope to his mistress; so it was truly the lady's answer he sought. But this grim, uncouth working man; how could he have divined that? With shame, he recalled how he stepped back, and wordlessly gestured the man in. Better to have barred the door, rung the bell for city guards. He tried to make some excuse, to demand to know the answer personally, anything to keep this rough and determined character out of her sight. But the man only repeated his will, to see the lady.

"Out of the question," was his response, quite proper. "No common man may take an audience with a maiden of noble house."

"Even on her business?" was the reply, stolid and astute. The grey man paused a moment then, and finished, "To the lord then, if you wish it."

And there was checkmate; he could not reveal that the lord had requested no such answer. The churl remained silent, and only stood waiting, deaf to all threats and commands. Finally, the castellan had said, "The lady of a noble house sees none of common rank in public," which was true enough. To this, the stranger said only, "Perhaps she has a quiet hour in some private place, such as the garden." Again!

As if he knew her most intimate schedule, could see through the stone to where she sat among the flowers at that moment.

Hardly knowing where he was and with the greatest anxiety, he had surrendered and waved the man through. "You will speak when you are spoken to," he hissed, "and you will never touch her, or I shall have you beaten forth." At that, the grey man stopped just a moment, and turned his head to look him in the eye. No more words; since then the castellan had watched like a hawk from the stairway window.

She spoke and spoke, a steady stream without interruption from her stoney visitor. The castellan had never seen her so animated, except … and then, as she stopped with an elegant hands-up gesture that said "what is the use?" the stranger merely said a word or two and pointed briefly at the back wall, the one nearest the outside streets where the ivy hung. The very spot! She stared, and her tears began to flow though her smile never dimmed. How could this be? How did this common sage's acolyte know of the secret meetings between her and her lover?

As if to complete his confusion, the man drew forth a small ring. In answer, the maiden put her hands to her mouth in shock, and then with a cry and a bright smile that pushed back the mist, she threw herself around the stranger's neck. He did not move a muscle, to his credit, and after a moment Gemma recovered herself and sat again. But this time her eyes held hope, tinged still with fear but alight with life. With wonder and awe, Gemma held out her delicate hand and, without touching it, the grey man dropped the ring in her palm. She donned it, and the castellan knew the matter was now settled. Betrothed, and soon widowed, most likely; she would have been with either match. But his lady's will be done.

The stranger bowed with simple propriety and turned to go, but she held his hand, importuning him with repeated words and great anxiety. He nodded his head without looking back, and as soon as he was released continued to make his exit from the garden. The castellan hastened down to meet this mysterious intruder; still he had no idea what to say to him.

At the door, the stranger offered no assistance, evidently intending to leave without another word.

"But stay," the castellan offered. "I must fetch your commission."

"Knowledge is reward enough," he responded, donning his broad, flat hat and reaching for the latch. Something in this dismissal irked the castellan, and he grasped the man's sleeve with more force than he wanted.

"What insult do you offer? As if I could let you go unrewarded, having made milady so happy," and turning on his heel he strode back to the study to retrieve the coins. Returning with a pouch, he laid it solidly upon the grey man's hand with a jingling thump; he could see from his face that this fellow had never held so much at one time before.

After a moment in thought, the grey man held it back out, and before the castellan could upbraid him, asked, "Can ye arrange a passage?"

"Passage? What, I'm to run an errand for you, now!"

"The white ship, in yon harbor, 'tis said to be bound for the Novar colony."

"So, it's to be a long trip for you then? And what joy could you have in the frozen north." The sage returned no answer to the castellan's jibe, and when he met the man's gaze, he suddenly knew all. His knees turned quite wobbly beneath him, when he thought of the outrage, the secret within the secret he already bore. But then he thought of how his lady had laughed through her tears; she wore the ring now. Damn the man! How did he *know*?

He reached for the bag, and then the guest was gone.

⊕ ⊕ ⊕

The knight urged his mount over the outcrop and onto the small rocky niche, reined in and sat back straight a moment. He had crouched, chest parallel to his horse's neck, scanning the stony mountain path for so long that his spine shouted its protest, but he was eager to look around. To his left and below, the mountainside with its nail-thin scratch of a path dropped away; further out, the eastern ridge of the Marble Swords loomed high beneath his position, and beyond that the knight could see the westernmost lands of the dread Percentalion. Cloud-ships moved by at a level with his eyes, and eagles soared only a little higher on the horizon. To his right, the stony path continued up and into the vast peak, and a few paces further on it disappeared into a solid wall of cloud, rising higher than he could see before him. The knight sat his mount and contemplated the measureless mass of white, looking as solid as down. He thought of a clean canvas before an artist paints, and mused for a time whether he was starting a new work, on himself. Or perhaps it would be his shroud.

The knight had worked his stallion slowly up this path since finding it four days ago. The food and any grazing plants had given out yesterday; the temperature steadily fell with each hour's progress. More than once, the mounted man passed through clouds, and couldn't recall the last time he had felt dry. Now, outside this looming portal of solid mist, he was soaked through his cape; drops fell from his helm, onto his breastplate, and seeped between the links of his mail to drench the tunic beneath. By rights, the man should have been shivering hard enough to lose his seat, but Renan Altrindur felt only a kind of searing elation within, a thumping certainty of nearness to his goal that burned from his center and warmed him. The Castle was said to be far above the earth, behind a wall of fog that always misled the unworthy, winding them around for days until they came out elsewhere. He did not know if he would succeed or be one of those so lost, but he did know that his human strength would not hold out against the cold, the wet and the hunger for another night. He would come to the fortress of the Chosen Wanderers today, or give his life in the attempt.

Urging Quester forward, he steadily and fearlessly entered the wall of cloud. Expecting the path to be just as thin, twisting and treacherous as before, Renan was surprised and then thrilled as it began to widen ever so little, and level off just so much. All around him the world was white, and the air seemed thicker than water, yet curiously refreshing. He thought that he was drinking and breathing at once, but could not muster a chuckle. The quiet of the mountain enfolded him: he heard not even the hoofbeats of his horse. It seemed an hour, but finally he saw not a thinning of the mist but the emergence of something so real, so marvelously substantial, that even the mist could not obscure the sight of it. A massive wall, blocks the size of a man, without mortar but tighter than would allow a knife's blade between them. And in the center of the wall, an enormous portcullis of solid steel bars already rose, a foot-thick bridge of petrified wood lowering before him. Renan had to remind himself to breathe; then he urged Quester forward. On the middle of the drawbridge, the knight was bathed in a pool of radiance and a voice from above arrested his progress.

"Who seeks entrance?"

"I am Renan Altrindur, knight of Conar," replied the rider. "I seek to join the holy order of the Wanderers."

"There are no families, no kingdoms, no allegiances within these walls, young knight. Do you accept the rule of the Chosen Wanderers, forsaking all other bonds to clan and country?"

"I do," the knight replied, and without a moment's hesitation he reached to his left breast and tore loose his family patch. A single green sword on a field of gold fell to the wood beneath his charger's feet.

There was a long pause before the voice resumed.

"Your sincerity shines clearly, Sir Renan. And yet … you are bound to marry."

"I reject this claim!" the knight cried with heat. "I have sought to join this holy order all my life, it is my destiny as I know in my heart. I shall have no part of the unworthy pact struck by my family, which was without my will and against justice."

"Aye, so we see, you speak the truth. And yet the view of the Wanderer cannot lie, young knight. It is troubling … but enter and take the path you have chosen."

With a thankful prayer to Conar on his lips, Renan spurred on, and entered the Castle of the Chosen Wanderers.

⊕ ⊕ ⊕

Diary of Valenthur the Sage

28th Gryphon, Sun Year 1995 A.D.R.

I have never before hosted a tea like the one today, and do not hope to again.

Nine days since those bravos returned from Maladon, and the clock has been turned back a century or more. Trainertown has once again sunk into a pit of riotous licence and shock, differing only in scale from the "glory days" of my youth. No market time, no noon services, even the apprentices' sunset ritual (which I had reservations about) — all gone, replaced with one running celebration. The grocer hasn't enough vegetables; I send Anteris for a new flint and the drigoodman is out; an hour before noon, and the center of town is yet deserted, but mid-night sees the carouse still underway. One flint, for the love of Hope!

We are all become like the moths in fall, flitting towards a candle-flame that fascinates even as it consumes us. An entire city, fourteen thousand souls by our last census; overthrown by five freebooters who dragged through our gates a mass of treasure greater than a year's haul from adventurers of the elder day, when the city was twice as large. Who would have thought the old wurm had so much treasure with him? Though of course it was not just him — C'nussik, if I do not miss my guess — but his mate Ssil as well, and their united hoard of nearly four centuries. I see the piece-parts of it wherever I go; some loose jewels and a very fine necklace, as Councilwoman Trebetha pointed out to me just yesterday; an axe, no doubt enchanted, sitting in a place of honor on the smith's work-table as he puzzles over it with their leader, Haltar. And of course the happiest man in town, Sikeltsor the silversmith, earning commission on every pound of this mingled metal, to refine and separate the melted blocks of coins and gems, and create more ingots in the past week than he had in his lifetime. The greatest wonder: his hottest forge at peak temperature, so that silver and gold ran like milk, but every so often in the middle of a block, there would be an ancient coin of precious silversteel, barely glowing and still perfect when cool. I sold several books and bought one, just for the chance to examine its history. Thus even I fall into the flame.

In truth, it is a staggering cache, I cannot deny it. With it, these rootless wanderers have bought a city. All has been catalogued, taxed and banked; if even one of them wished to take his share and leave, we would not have two silver bits to rub together across the town. Ingots of solid metal come forth from Sikeltsor's shop and are placed on reserve, papers of credit issued, accounts kept. I hear the council has already written urgently to Conar and Shilar, to ask for coins in exchange. Praise Conar, only the kings may by right strike currency, or else the last shred of order in this city would have blown away like leaves in the storm. But in the meantime, barter must do, and no service or meal, favor or finery, is too good to be offered to the conquering heroes. Of course, they are liberal with their wealth; why not? They have no plan to settle, or work, or advance the world around them.

Someday (may it be soon) they will leave us just as they left before, with no more to their name than what they carry on their backs. In the meantime, they will see what they can buy. And the answer so far has been: all. I must correct the record, surely the innkeeper Fairnum is even happier than the silversmith, as he will be the recipient of so much minted largesse when accounts are settled. Their leader Haltar has toasted as many newfound friends as can fit within the tavern's walls, each night and well into the morning. Ale flows like rain in the gutters, and to as much useful purpose. I shudder to think the price poor Marindya has paid, leaving her family to take up with him. She has moved directly to the room he keeps over the inn, and is on his arm everywhere. Willingly! He dresses her in Argensian silk and bedecks her with dragon's gems, parades her like the new Marchess of the city; if we had nobility, and provided they were in the habit of drinking to excess and surrendering their bodies. The halfling takes rides on anyone's shoulders, laughing and exchanging barbs with all and sundry; the crowds love to see him target their tankards with his sling while up aboard a drunken reveler, and bet on his aim.

The maiden sorcerer is nearly forgotten in all this din, off to seek further lore with the city mage by the east gate, but I doubt there is much Obis can show her; he confessed nearly as much to me before she left the last time. She pores over his books and practices in his casting study, sleeping on the floor and paying him rent. I heard there was a tome of some kind in the hoard, perhaps old enough to be of historic value, and was resolved to ask Obis if he had seen it. No need now.

But the rest … I saw the elf Mhoral on the second day and greeted him courteously in his tongue, but he appeared put off and ended our conversation abruptly. The last seems young but clean and well-enough mannered, drinking with the rest but at least not boisterous.

So: complete disruption of the daily routine, constant shortage of needed items at market, absolute bedlam in the streets at night. Men who last month were hard at work now fall down drunk in the alleys. The guards arrest their own kin, break up fights; the forge and the kiln and the carpentry open their shops at all hours, as a new idea is hatched, another rumor prepared against; whims spread like fire, and everyone burns. I have made no progress on the Chronicle since their return. We all veer and float nearer the flame. Anteris follows them in the afternoons, until the strict curfew I have set for him to return. I have lost two years of progress with that boy, I can see it in his eyes. Adventure and heroism, it is all he can think of now.

But the tea. That was the broken string that ruined the music.

Once a week, whatever the weather-or-whether, I have held my tea with a single invited guest. We adhere to civilized custom even so far from the City of Wonders, and I have always found it relaxing and stimulating to take two hours on the final week-day to focus conversation on one other person. Most of my fellow citizens, bless them, are quite put off by the formality (and the need to wash their hands), so I try to spare them. But variety is the essence of this pleasant habit, and the council are regular invitees. I had determined to extend the courtesy this time to the itinerant preacher, Alaetar. I was eager to plumb his mind about astrological matters, as Anteris had told me of the man's fearsome erudition in that scientia. *I thought perhaps I might share some of my views on the history of our country, and get his opinions in return. It was likely I should need to mention his visit to Trainertown as a part of the Chronicle for 1995, so it would be good to have some of his personal information. And I was certain we would get on well, though I had never spoken to him before. I recalled him lobbying vigorously for the party to leave at once, after their first foray. Perhaps I could inveigh upon him to use his influence toward that end again. Anteris carried my note and brought back his polite acceptance verbally.*

That afternoon, we closed the shop early and Anteris buzzed about helping me to clean and set. I thought he seemed even more animated and happy than usual; it is clear he reveres the preacher and I pondered that awhile. But his happiness is so open and pure, it renews me, and I am certainly willing to indulge him in this. My varieties of leaf were running a bit low, but I calculated that by having the most common stock for myself, I could save a fair selection for my guest, including one from southernmost Shilar that I had never cared for. I sent the lad to market, for a nice variety of fruits and to pick up the pastries that my dear friend Cellesi the baker creates for me each week by our arrangement. The clock striking the tenth hour past dawn was the last happy moment I knew.

Anteris returned with apples — only apples — and plain rolls. He explained the grocer had not been able to stock anything else, and as for Cellesi … foolish me, I had never reckoned that she would be not only frantic over the fate of her dear Marindya, but bereft of her assistance as well. I felt dread as the barrenness of my board stared back at me for the long half-hour. And then my guest arrived, completing my misery.

⊕⊕⊕

Valenthur's quarters occupied the south-western side of the second and third floors in the Sage's Guild in Trainertown. It was by all accounts the finest space in the building, and if there were any better he could have had it, for the rest was empty. The library downstairs, small and immaculately kept, was his sole province, and the stipend Valenthur earned for composing and copying the Kingdom Chronicle was quite adequate to his needs, including the upkeep and training of an apprentice.

Most hours of the week it was so quiet throughout the enormous manor that even a skittish cat would have no cause for alarm; no sound louder than the scritch of quill on parchment and the calm, measured tones of question and answer. Once a week, the clink of fine porcelain and crystal, a few moments of earnest conversation with one unfamiliar voice, and perhaps a genial laugh or two. Most tea-afternoons, Folio just rested atop a pile of tomes, and some of the sage's guests did not even note he had a pet.

Anteris, of course, knew Folio well, and she even let him stroke her briefly, especially when, as now, he carried a dish of salted riddy for her to eat during tea-time. "A treat for everyone today," the boy told the cat, straightening up to catch his master's glum look at the table where such poor fare stood to greet the expected guest.

"Should I polish the silver, sir?" he asked a bit plaintively.

"All is perfect, lad, thanks for your help today as always," Valenthur rallied, but Anteris could see his disappointment writ large already.

The visit-bell over the doorway sounded once, indicating someone at the foot of the stairs was ascending. Valenthur had engaged the carpenter to construct the outer stair and doorway so that guests could come and go without disturbing the library, and he was inordinately proud of it. Gesturing for Anteris to get the door, he took his seat and looked in every way the master of the manor as the scene was set. Anteris opened and stood back, revealing the landing outside.

Two persons stood there, a man and a woman, neither one nearly as tall as the Shilarian guest the sage expected.

Valenthur, farther back into the shaded room, could not make out their faces, but Anteris brightly said, "Welcome masters, most welcome!" As they stepped across the lintel, the scribe noted with alarm two of the adventurers from the party recently returned, the mage and the woodsman, and he scrambled to recall their names.

"Ah, good day, ahm, goodman, that is, I am just—"

"Scribe Valenthur," the female cut in, "I am Linya and this is Treaman, we seek your assistance on scholarly matters, if you can spare the time."

"Mage Linya, your reputation precedes you, I assure. In point of fact, I am engaged this afternoon." He looked them up and down, as if seeking any excuse to eject them. But both were quite clean enough for members of the working class. Linya wore a simple but elegant robe of red weave and carried in her hand a bronze head-piece of some kind, thin and set with a large blue stone. Her companion, looking extremely fit and toned as he stood silently, was dressed much more drably, in brown and dark green, but with a most interesting silver-grey ruff of some sort around his neckline; not fur, likely a kind of treated leather, very unevenly shaped, perhaps worn. He held in his arm a large, thin tome of burnt leather binding. Both were stone sober, despite their reputation, and to Valenthur's disappointment. Then again, his eyes strayed to the book in the woodsman's hand and he seemed a bit torn.

"We were hoping," the woodsman said, "you could help us with the languages in here. It's the antique Common Tongue, and we want to be sure of some things."

"Of course, sirrah," Valenthur replied loftily, "I would be happy to assist, when I am not engaged. Perhaps tomorrow in the evening—"

"Can you do it now?" the young man broke in; when only stony silence came back, he added abruptly, "We can pay you."

Anteris watched a frost descend over his master's entire body; before he could think of something conciliatory to say, the visit-bell sounded again.

Suddenly, the room seemed terribly small. Valenthur looked frantically about as if for another exit to usher his unwanted guests through. But there was only the inner door and stair, through his own bedroom and leading to the library. Making frantic gestures, he herded the pair to one side, while Anteris again served the door. There stood Alaetar, looming almost to the lintel and looking as serious as if the morning's sermon was still before him. Valenthur drew breath to give his formal greeting, but Linya got in first.

"Alaetar! I'm so happy we caught you. I need your help, holy sir." At once, the preacher's head swiveled from his host to the young sorceress, all his attention given to her request for aid.

"Naturally, child, how may I assist you?"

Valenthur opened and closed his mouth twice without managing a word as their conversation continued heedless of him.

"I am attempting to enchant this head-piece," she continued. "I was just able to take a brief break between casting. The ritual instructions call for a blessing to be invoked in order for the final spells to take hold. The curate of the church is not able to do it, I'm afraid. Are you familiar with the procedure?"

"Only from history, I fear, not from practice," the preacher replied with some excitement. "I recall well the story of how the Tridium was created for Areghel to hold the kingdom. The blessings there—"

"Indeed, history!" Valenthur managed in some desperation. "I was hoping we could … that is, that I could benefit from your opinion as to—"

"Did you say the Tridium?" Treaman interrupted, as Valenthur hissed in exasperation. "That's mentioned in part of this book. What is it?"

"What is the Tridium! Young man," Alaetar bent his gaze to the slender woodsman, who leaned a bit away, "you are in no condition to serve as one finger on the hand of destiny if you are ignorant of your place in it."

"Yes, holy sir," Treaman replied gamely, "would you like to see the passage?"

"At once, if you please."

The three moved to the tea-table then, trailed by their fluttering host. Delicate rose-figured porcelain and faultless place settings bumped aside, along with part of the linen cloth, to make room for the large folio. "See here!" Valenthur cried out, just saving the steeping kettle from tipping off one edge. Linya opened the volume to an early page, while Treaman, looking on, casually took an apple from the plate and munched.

Linya pointed to the script, and Alaetar nodded, saying, "Ah yes, the famous prophecy of the Percentalion. This was uttered by Rallantan after the First War of Liberation, nearly four thousand years ago. I had not thought of it for some time, with all that has happened recently." He composed his face, and read out the text:

As Areghel's line sits the Kingdom's throne
Ways keep straight, Kog's day is done.
But failing the seat, hell's place repeat,
And no child of Hope alone
No branch of Conar's bone
May demon cheat, his eye align,

Or Tridium seat, till the heir assign
The fivescore castles his own.

"And here," Linya continued, pointing to the map on the opposite page. "We think this is Reghalion, the capital city, with some of its surroundings shown. These lines, we think they are meant to show the lower slopes of the mountain."

"Indeed," Alaetar nodded with vigor, "that is doubtless the capital, abandoned these long centuries. Accounts told of the main street running the entire central length of the city, like this. See the palace here, with the towers up against the rear side? Lo, this faint line between them…" he bent down to examine the map at close range, moving the table-lantern closer for better light.

"So. What does it mean?" the woodsman asked. "What is this Tridium?"

"The Tridium," Valenthur asserted forcefully, "refers to the three holy items of power which Areghel received from the Hopelords. Now if you will excuse—"

"By the power of the Tridium," Alaetar continued despite his host's preferences, "combined with the force of Law in his spirit, the rightful king Areghel was able to re-establish the peace and straight ways of the Percentalion. This is lore you must learn, young heroes, if—"

"No, by your leave, holy father, I will have none of this here." Valenthur was desperately trying to re-arrange the tea set around the enormous open tome, reluctant to touch the thing adventurers had brought into his house. He looked nervously at Anteris and continued, "I will attend to this request tomorrow, but for now, you must go."

"I thought you were a sage," Linya said.

"I am a civilized man! Here there is order, and moderation and civility between persons, not this … this rude invasion to speak of wild rumors and treasure-maps!" The scribe was truly enraged now, looking to Anteris with guilt and to Alaetar with shame, but both these humiliations only stoked his anger at the adventurers in his presence. He shouted, and Anteris shrank back in real fear, not used to seeing his master this way. Alaetar stood with a face carved in surprise, one hand on the tome; he had not so much as noticed the ruin of the tea settings.

The woodsman tried to mediate, saying, "Wise sir, we only wish to learn the value of what we have found in the dragon's lair. If it is a question of payment, I can assure—"

"It is a question of honor! We teach our youth that an unstained soul is beyond price, sir. Get out of my house, now!"

It seemed to Anteris that Folio had chosen an ill moment to stroll into the room and over to her plate of salted fish.

To Valenthur, it appeared that the woodsman had the ability to shrug his shoulders in an odd, rippling fashion, as if the leather ruff were actually alive.

The sage and the cat realized their error at approximately the same time.

The miniature dragon uncoiled from her master's shoulder and hissed at the shouting stranger. Valenthur staggered back with a cry, slamming into the table and knocking the best tea-kettle to the floor after all. Alaetar exclaimed, Anteris shouted and Folio, hit with hot shards of broken kettle, screamed as if her tail had been kicked. The dragon, noting the creature on the floor, pipped eagerly and launched down in its direction.

"Hallah, no!" Treaman shouted. "Do not eat the cat!"

Valenthur, witnessing an attack on his pet, screamed in horror and threw the first thing to hand at the flying monster. Thus the second tea-kettle followed its mate into oblivion against a wall, but not before knocking a pile of books off a side-shelf and into the dusty fireplace.

The dragon landed next to the cat, frozen in place with its back forming a peak like Skysword and every hair standing separate from all others. The intruder gave a friendly sniff and clack of the jaw, and in response the frozen feline broke into an unearthly wail as if giving over its spirit. Then Folio fled, seemingly in three directions at once, looking fruitlessly for a hiding place. After a quick circumnavigation of the room, which caused Linya to careen into Alaetar and made Anteris sit suddenly, the cat decided the table was the best of a bad lot, and tore up the cloth climbing its side. Any item not already overturned was naturally in the path the cat chose, and the lantern was the most unfortunate of these. In the ensuing douse and relative darkness, Alaetar had no chance to repel boarders, as Folio climbed his tunic and beard with merciless efficiency until crowning the summit of his hair and clinging there with all twenty nails.

"Monsters! I am assailed!" the preacher cried, tugging without success at the claws and fur on his scalp. The tiny dragon, its nose caught by the smell of the cat's bowl, had sauntered to the spot and was devouring each fish whole with audible relish.

"Churl!" Valenthur shouted at Treaman. "I shall have you arrested for this assault."

"Good," the woodsman replied in encouragement, looking past his accuser, "that's good."

"What? Are you daring me to call the guards?"

"Yes," the woodsman said soothingly, "you can have all you like, that's fine."

Linya had managed to coax the cat half-off Alaetar's head, but one rear claw was still twisted through his hair and the other clinging tenaciously to his shoulder. Anteris was up and trying to sweep shards, blot spilled tea, save the tomes and ask what else he might do, all at once and without much success at anything.

"Anteris, a light!" Valenthur called from the floor where he sat hugging two books to his chest. There was some fumbling, more moans from the cat, soothing sounds from Linya, gasps of pain from Alaetar, smacking and chewing from the corner by the cat bowl, and the sound of a small, inoffensive chuckle. A few moments passed while Anteris' shadowed form fumbled and worked. "The light, lad?"

"I'm sorry, master," said the apprentice. "The flint, it's very worn."

"Ah the flint, yes. Of course," was all the scribe's reply.

With a quick gesture Linya created a point of white light on top of the lantern, which shone steadily without flame or heat. Everyone straightened up something, except Alaetar who still struggled to disengage his reluctant tenant. Valenthur went from mess to disaster, exclaiming in undisguised woe and shock. The small dragon, having emptied the bowl and banging it against the floor in its beak two or three times to be sure, smacked its lips, cawed sweetly and took off with a heavy set of flapping from the floor, climbing up to the ceiling and circling once in victory before landing on the woodsman's shoulder. An exit now open, Folio at once abandoned any human assistance and shot from the scene as if fired from a crossbow. It would be two days before she put her head out into the main room again, for love or food.

Valenthur looked up from the ash-grate to see Linya assisting him, wiping a book on her bright red dress and asking "Are you alright, wise sir?" He was too astonished to say anything, and she carried the conversation for him. "Please forgive us, we get very interested in matters of our own and did not, well … and I am very sorry about your cat, I hope it will be alright."

"Say, Linya, come see this!" Treaman exclaimed from up at the table. Rising, they came over to the preacher and woodsman, who were poring over the map, lightly soaked in tea-water, by the sharp light of the spell. In this contrast, additional lines were appearing all over the page and the commentary came too thick and fast to note the speaker or the message.

"A path! Up the mountain,"

"Yes, and the mark of a fist in a sun."

"Areghel's line! Something up there, certainly—"

"More writing here. Under the palace wall, see, very tiny…"

"Sword in the mud, it's not Common, what is—"

"That is the Ancient tongue, I'll be bound." This last from Valenthur, whose excitement was evident even to his acolyte.

"These trees, they were not shown before!"

"A cave, very high up—"

"Fading! Write it down!"

"More tea!"

"The water isn't working."

"Perhaps it needs to be hot; can you heat this?"

"At once, mistress." There was a pause as Anteris went to fetch hotter liquid.

"Can you read Ancient?" Linya asked Alaetar.

"In all honesty, mistress, my ear and tongue do better than my eye. If I hear the words, as in church, I can of course tell you what was said. On paper…"

All eyes turned to the sage, who looked as if he were just accused of a crime.

"You expect me?"

"Sage Valenthur," Linya began, "could you do us the great favor—"

"You invade my home," the sage replied with dripping scorn, "suborn my guest, wreck my things, petrify my poor pet, corrupt my acolyte; have I left anything out?"

"Well, Hallah hasn't eaten you yet," Treaman replied calmly. As Valenthur's jaw fell open, the woodsman continued smoothly, "Never mind, Linya. It looked like a very complicated passage, maybe even verse." With a sidelong glance at his host, Treaman leaned down to pick up the tome. "Very small print, too, too tough for an older gentleman. We'll find someone else."

"There is no one else," Valenthur replied with force, and as Treaman turned a blandly surprised face back to him, the sage realized he had been trapped. He held out an angry arm for the tome and snatched it away, taking it to a seat and thumbing open the wet pages.

He read a while in silence, squinting down at the letters on the map-page. Time passed slowly, with only the rhythmic, tenor drip of tea off the cloth to the floor to mark the moments. Valenthur turned pages, taking care not to tear the soggy parchment, and exclaimed wordlessly several times. It was clear he became lost in the text, and suddenly started with surprise, shouting, "No! Cannot be!" looking up to recall he was not alone.

"What is it?" Treaman asked.

"I, I'm afraid you've been taken in," Valenthur said with a mask for a face. "This work is old, perhaps, but a forgery assuredly." This statement met with stares, and the sage ascertained the explanation would have to go further. He approached the table and opened to a later page.

"See here, where the author details the Tridium; this is in the Common Tongue, but a bit antique, as you said. The standard description of the Sword of Air, the Crown and Scepter, it is all here as I have seen it many times in volumes of the Kingdom Chronicle, those penned by my predecessors." He stood back a moment to let them lean over and take it in.

"The Sword of Air, most wondrous blade, wrought from a slice of the noonday sun…"

"—set with sapphires of true kingship, the Crown banded with sard to ward the mind of the king from demonic influence."

"With the Scepter, the lord of one hundred castles may single out the despairing heart, and strike down the evil one with lightning."

"So?" Treaman said, looking back to Valenthur, "if these descriptions are familiar, why doubt them?"

"Because the author has overstepped his bounds, and attempted to imitate the royal seal of the house of Areghel. Do you see it at the bottom of the page? All these, these instructions" — and here Valenthur briefly turned back to the page with the map and ancient verse before flipping away— "are supposedly set down by a high official in the king's court. This book, you are to believe, is from the hand of a chamberlain, or at least a close scribe, of the king himself! One of Areghel's descendants. And the seal was to be the proof. But it is a fake, of course. Another lure, set to pull in the gullible." His tone and face were smug.

Treaman took back the book and flipped to the last page where the seal was imprinted. "What's wrong with it?" he demanded to know.

"Oh, the sigils and marks are all right, there's no trick to that. I've seen others like them. But only a mark of the true seal would pass the test of his name."

"His name?"

"Yes, you must call upon the name of the king Areghel, founder of the line, and then the seal will glow. In the Ancient tongue of course."

"So why not do so!"

"There is no need. The royal seal was lost with the dissolution of the court in 1572 ADR; there has not been a document brought to light with the true royal seal of the Percentalion in—"

"But you have only to say the words!" Treaman shouted, his distrust fully aroused now. Behind Valenthur, Anteris entered the room unseen.

"It is not needful," the sage said with finality.

"What? Merely say 'in the name of Areghel the king' in Ancient, tell me why not."

The sage did not reply, and things were quiet. Then a small, steady voice behind the sage said, "*Ac nomin Regente Areghel.*" At once, the seal on the page began to glow with a blue tint, cresting and fading within moments. Valenthur's face was red and hard as rock. Treaman whooped and swung Linya around, making the small dragon hop in the air for a turn before landing again.

"It's real! Real! The map, the notes, it's four centuries old if it's a day. Once we get it translated, we'll take the notes to Haltar."

Outside the clock struck the hour of dusk, and Linya broke away.

"Goodness, the time! I must return to resume my casting or the whole process will be lost." She grabbed up her head-piece and turned to Alaetar. "Holy sir, would you come and attempt the needed blessing on my head-piece?"

Alaetar looked down with favor on the little mage, catching nothing of the expression on his host's face. "Of course, dear child, I shall be happy to do my best. Lead the way." Without a word he left; without a word, Treaman and Valenthur faced each other for what seemed to Anteris an hour. Anteris saw the pain and anger in his master's normally kind and pleasant face, and shivered.

At last the woodsman moved to the lantern; taking out his own flint, he expertly lit the wick in a single try. "The spell will give out in just a while longer," he said, closing the book and tucking it under his arm. Bowing, he said, "We appreciate your assistance, wise sir."

Valenthur drew himself up in his chair to his full height and declared, "Not one silver bit will I accept from you, sir." Nodding, Treaman turned to go, but at the exit stopped and said to the door, "What? Oh, yes, alright." Turning back he asked, "What was the food in the cat's dish?"

"Salted fish," Anteris said, astonished. "A small catch called riddy."

"Riddy, thanks very much!" the young man said brightly. His dragon crooned and they left.

Anteris diligently and quietly cleaned the entire apartment, forgoing the free time he normally used to follow the adventurers, as if in penance. Valenthur sat quietly and alternated between weeping and frozen anger. None of the three felt any great hunger, and went to bed with the sun.

The next morning, Valenthur was determined not to set foot outside the door, for fear of the ridicule the tale had brung to the city. But Anteris returned from the grocer with an excited face, full of the good news.

"It is Alaetar, master. He has been up early and of course everyone wants to hear what he has to say." The scribe shrank back to think of the coming blow, but Anteris hastened to change his mind. "He speaks of the great discovery that has been made. The key to ancient lore, and the hand of destiny and a great many other things. And he has made clear that it all began here, in the study of the sage Valenthur."

"What? He credits me?"

"I've heard the story a half-dozen times already, master. The book open on your table, studying by magic light, the puzzles opened, the knowledge gained. He says it happened here, and by you, sir!"

It was better news than the sage could have hoped, as he was sure the tale would be of the wreck of his fine tea. His face hung divided to think his name would now be associated with these five and whatever hare-brained scheme they set in motion next. When the visit-bell sounded, he and Anteris looked to each other in surprise; as they heard a loud bumping noise coming closer and higher, their feelings turned to apprehension. Tearing open the door, they saw the grocer, manhandling a knee-high barrel into the room and the drigoodsman behind him.

"I have a fine linen cloth and a few tea-things for you here, Valenthur," the latter said as he elbowed his way past. "Having more guests this week for tea?"

"And this barrel represents the remaining stock of salted riddy in my shop," the grocer added. "That woodsman bought the other one for himself. Horrid taste, I say, but it is cheap food and it lasts forever."

"What is the meaning of this?" Valenthur demanded. The grocer handed him a note as if to explain. Inside, in ragged letters it read, "I am happy to say that I have not a single silver bit to give, as you requested."

⊕ ⊕ ⊕

Cedrith was enjoying a meal with several local sages in the refectory. The wit flowed freely, and the Elf was just beginning to get the Man-based humor of double-meanings around words such as "lay," when the conversation died down, and he knew his friend stood behind him.

"Solemn! Join us, you must be famished, eh? Tell me if you've heard this one—"

"Eldest, may I seek your counsel on a matter of my studies?"

Cedrith stood, and did not quite mark where the quiet clucks of disgust originated.

"Sure, he doesn't need to swap spit with us," jeered a fellow five years older than Judgement. "He already knows all the jokes ever told, the Jolly One, that's why he doesn't laugh."

"Is it true?" yelped another, only half in jest. "Tell us the one, then, about the sailor and his three wives."

Judgement looked levelly at the others, and said, "I know the one about the fire ant and the mandolin beetle, as the winter came on."

"That's no joke!" the first one scoffed.

"Meaning," Judgement replied, "that you see no humor in it."

"Right."

"Just so." And turning on his heel, the Man in Grey withdrew, Cedrith shaking his head in train.

"Guildsman," Cedrith said as he caught up to him in the hall, "I have not yet saluted you on your formal enrollment. You are the youngest in living memory to have qualified for membership. I congratulate you."

"I have had excellent teachers, Eldest: it is a testament to them, not to my poor efforts."

"I would never have taught you such modesty," Cedrith jested, and the look he received in return showed how little progress he had made in some areas.

They arrived in the study room and Judgement's desk was as always covered with books, notes, folded papers, and more. "So," Cedrith said as they arrived, "what can I do for you? Sort out some matter of precedence in the awarding of bridal gifts?" The thick book atop the right-hand pile looked familiar; picking it up, Cedrith saw it was a tome on gardening by Faltus Fanem. "What is this? I thought, your commission for the House Enceris…"

Judgement returned a blank stare for a moment, and then started. "Ah that; my apologies Eldest, I had been … absorbed. The matter is resolved; here is the abstract."

"Resolved!" Cedrith took the folded parchment, sealed in wax with the scales of justice that his protégé had adopted on elevation to Guildsman status. "But you never mentioned … do you mean to say you have found the answer?"

"Aye, the salient issue is summarized within, and I have included my references. I asked you here—"

"Wait, wait a moment, I pray you. Let me take this in awhile." Cedrith sat and broke the seal on the parchment, scanning the initial paragraphs of the neat and incisive review without really comprehending what was there. "I told you … I said I would be ready to assist you whenever you needed it."

"It was not needful. In fact, I had already made some initial … enquiries in the course of my other studies."

"Other studies. Judgement, everything that has ever been written is one of your studies, and half the things that have ever been done!"

The Man in Grey returned a look that seemed to ask, "What is your point?" He said only, "The essential matter, once all the variations of custom have been classified, is fairly simple. A woman of noble rank can make a choice of intended, or she may bow to her parent's wishes in the matter, or in rare cases the family's overlord may appoint a husband where a noble maiden is orphaned or a ward of the crown. Whichever means are chosen, they do not, in themselves have the weight of law. The actual betrothal, by any method, is achieved when the maiden dons the bond-ring of the groom, showing the signet of his house."

"I see. And your scholarship here, to judge from this entire sheet of reference tomes, has been as ironclad as I would expect. Well done again, Guildsman. I am, I suppose, only mildly surprised that you would have accomplished this without aid. Truly, I wonder what matter remains wherein I could supply your need." Cedrith smiled in genuine friendship with this, but knew he would not raise a response from Judgement: whatever the kindness or insult, his lips remained as straight as if chained onto his face. The eyes, that was where to see …

"I have found," Judgement said, "six of the seven unrestricted tomes authored by Faltus Fanem."

"By Fanem?"

"Aye, including the three that he wrote … on his own. I have three of his four … copied works here. And I seek the fourth."

"The fourth," Cedrith repeated stupidly. "The fourth … book on gardening?"

"Nay, the fourth book he copied, whatever the subject."

Cedrith felt as if his mind would not work right; the request was nonsensical. "Judgement, we classify books by their subject. You know that. It is how the library is organized. We distinguish between the original and later copies, and otherwise the author of a given work is of no importance."

"It is vital!" Judgement replied with heat. "Please, Eldest, can you recall the title and its location?"

"Why, of course, *Guildsman*, if you really wish it. But—" Cedrith could see further protest would fall on deaf ears, and decided he must simply trust his former pupil. The whole idea, of noting books by their authors, still dazed him. How would it profit, to know the personal list of each author? What Judgement asked, if carried to its end, would entail a second catalogue of the entire library. Scanning the titles on the desk, he realized the original works of Fanem were in one pile, and the infamous plagiarized works in another. He wondered how Judgement could have replicated most of the work that had absorbed Cedrith's mission here. Then he saw on the desk his own report to the board, soft-bound in leather, from just a few weeks earlier. Of course; as a member, Judgement now had access.

"Ah yes, well, the missing tome is ... it is the *Tools of the Vinyard*."

To his shock, Judgement actually pounded the desk with his fist. "But I have been through the section on Horticulture myself, three times."

"Oh, no, well you see, the archivists tend to classify based on the first term in the title. A quirk, I grant you; that book was housed under Manufacture."

"Of course! Dull of brain, that is it." Judgement snapped around and began walking with his rolling stride towards the stacks. Cedrith, who could not for worlds understand the speed or the urgency, hastened to catch up to the distance-devouring gait of his fellow.

"My friend, why is the location of this tome so important to you? What matters it whether a tract about farming tools is written, or copied, by this man or another? We seek to preserve knowledge here, not reputation."

"Yes, a worthy goal, Eldest. But how have we 'preserved' it? Is all knowledge available to any querent?"

"Certainly not: you know about the Dark Archives."

"Certes," said the grey man, and he stopped momentarily to give Cedrith a look somehow laden with humor though lacking a smile. He continued up a set of stairs, saying, "but you do not perhaps know where they are."

"What?" Cedrith lost several steps in the chase, while he once again stood in a stupor. Jerking back to himself, he ran up the flight and just saw his friend turning around the corner of a stack. Hastening to the aisle, he saw Judgement looking carefully over the rows of books, scrutinizing the titles until with a small cry of triumph he reached out to seize a fat tome. Cedrith recognized the characteristic binding and saw the letters, *Tools of the Vineyard* on the spine.

"Now, for the original," Judgement said.

"Just three aisles over but the other end," Cedrith replied with surety, and his friend nodded while already in motion.

"I would be lying if I said I understood a single thing that is happening here, my friend." At this offhand remark, Judgement pulled up short and faced Cedrith.

"I have been rude, in my haste, and I should apologize, Eldest."

"No, not at all Judgement, you must not be so—"

"Ask what you will."

"Very well then. What are you after?"

The grey man took a breath. "Do you recall, I spoke of my interest, that day in the Archives, in the question of the nature of death?"

Cedrith felt dry and just nodded.

"Do you know, Eldest, what Faltus Fanem wrote about in his own right? When he was not copying the works of other men?"

"Yes, Guildsman," Cedrith replied, happy to have found an appropriate counter-title. "You may recall, I made him an especial study."

"Your report to the committee was an excellent redaction of his style, most helpful to me. Faltus Fanem authored several important works about the nature of magical energy."

"'Thaumaturgy,' to use the word worth a gold piece," Cedrith supplied and Judgement nodded.

"He was quite an authority, and I might venture one of the most advanced in his field."

"Well, as to that," Cedrith replied, "I must say I could hardly follow some of his ideas, he seemed quite disjointed and illogical in places."

"He wrote guardedly, I would say. Like a man who is keeping secrets."

"Secrets? Of what sort?"

"Did it not occur to you to wonder, Eldest, why a man who wrote several books on the origins and possible uses of magical power would choose to copy the works of others about gardening? Or plants and tools?"

Cedrith was honestly surprised to shake his head. The training of the Guild was strong; sages did not often consider the authors they read as men in themselves. "So," he managed, "you obviously have considered it. And the answer is?"

Judgement held up the tome in his arm and thumped it with his free hand. "He needed to write something."

"But he had already written something!"

"And he needed to take up space on the shelf."

Cedrith leaned in with a searching glance, and then broke into a chuckle. "I know you are not trying to be obtuse, my dear friend, but I remain as ignorant as before."

"Come. See." Judgement drew Cedrith with him to the end of the aisle.

There, he located the book with the identical title to the one he held. Holding the Fanem tome over the spot, he turned to look at Cedrith. An acolyte with a double-armload of books came around the corner, saw Judgement standing there, and wordlessly turned back around without stopping.

"What was the same about every single forgery Sage Fanem committed?"

Looking directly at the scene of the crime, Cedrith still had no idea what his friend meant. Judgement waited a decent interval, and then prompted with a single word, "Bigger."

"I beg your pardon?"

"The copy in my hand is bigger than the original, do you see?"

"Ah of course, yes, Fanem did write some pretty fat books, I see what you mean. One of them had extra pages, blank for no reason, and the margins were usually huge—"

"With lots of decorative marginalia, yes; your point about that was extremely useful to me, Eldest."

"So? He made his books big, what is the point?"

"When this forgery rested improperly here, what happened?"

"Happened?"

"The other books had to move down," Judgement said, and taking a rough measurement with his fingers, he moved to the end of the shelf and matched the width to the next-to-final tome, which he withdrew with an air of accomplishment.

"Every time he copied out a book written by another, the size of his replacement forced books down to a lower shelf. See."

Cedrith could read the spine as Judgement held out the book; *Implements of the Mage*. "This is a work about the forging and use of instruments in magical experiments," Cedrith said slowly.

Judgement nodded. "As the other three have concerned special plants, used as reagents for potions, and the astrological considerations for casting divination rituals. Each forgery pointed to a book which held clues, disparate indications that are otherwise found together only in the restricted stacks."

"And Faltus Fanem," Cedrith said, "is also the author of an eighth book, a work in those Dark Archives."

"Aye."

"One that no one in the Guild has ever mentioned, but that you have learned to look for."

"Aye."

"And led by these clues, you have been able to learn … what, exactly?"

"Nothing, exactly, Eldest. It is still only hints and themes," Judgement admitted, as they walked more slowly back to the study room. "But there is a picture emerging; and knowing now about the truce—"

Cedrith noticed a knot of sages in animated discussion ahead of them. As Judgement entered earshot he ceased speaking; the group also fell silent and parted to either side as they passed through. Cedrith looked back at them, wondering.

"Guildsman, do you ever … do you speak to the other sages?"

"I have many questions, Eldest."

"No, not the tutors; your peers, the ones your own age."

Judgement arrived at his study table, set down his finds, and, sitting, began to read the copy first. Cedrith tried again.

"Did you have any … friends, when you were little? In your home country?"

Judgement was still thumbing through the Fanem copy-book, and said only, "My elder brothers, Render and Germane."

"None else?"

"We lived apart, a secluded high mountain-valley. My father oversaw our studies and training. When he was home."

"And your mother?"

"Died as I was born."

"Your brothers?"

"Died as we fled the persecution."

"And your father perished bringing you here. So you are alone."

This was not a question, and received no response. Judgement slowed in turning pages, and then with a small "aha" focused on the decorative margin drawings of the copy-book and reached for his quill. Cedrith bent in to look. Judgement had stopped at a point where the tome discussed the proper implements for pruning, and Fanem had decided to decorate the top-left passage with some of his characteristic marginalia, this time shaped in the style of grape-leaves twining down the side of the page.

"Note the leaves which point at certain starting letters," he said, and Cedrith followed his finger as Judgement took them down. "The 't' in 'twine,' a 'w' from 'whose,' an 'o' in 'of' … 's,' 'i,' and then 'x,' from a poorly hyphenated 'extra,' rather a stretch there."

"Two-six? Are you serious? Surely that's just a coincidence," Cedrith said.

But Judgement had already turned to the second book, and wordlessly opened to the twenty-sixth page. After a moment, he stabbed with his finger and read aloud.

The circle, designed with the lines of Hope as well as the symbols shown, can be inscribed on a surface of pure and unbroken stone to serve as an amplifier to the mage's natural energy when creating the healing elixirs referred to in Tarmal's Flows of Life. *The stone-awl is to be used in the drawing, and the same instrument should be employed throughout, making every mark at a uniform depth. The barrier thus created will also shield the caster and any Hopeful beings from the advance of undead creatures, and has further properties in the preparation of certain components that are useful to other protective rituals, as described hereafter.*

Cedrith reached down and covered the page with his hand, stopping the recitation. Judgement looked up at him with his usual calm, hawk-like gaze, waiting.

"This, this is extraordinary. You mean to tell me that Faltus Fanem has left clues to … necromantic practices hidden all about our library. For what purpose?"

"Not necromancy, but its opposite; the methods and rituals to defeat the curse of raising the undead. And he wrote to preserve the record of his achievements for posterity."

"But he could simply have compiled it openly in a single tome."

"Which he did, Eldest. 'Tis *The Nameless Tome*, the eighth book of Faltus Fanem, and it lies in the Dark Archives. Where even the record of titles is hidden, and very few men have read a word in centuries."

"Very few," repeated Cedrith with meaning, "but not quite none. You have been to the Dark Archives, have you not, Guildsman? And more recently than the first time, unless I miss my guess."

To Cedrith's surprise, the Man in Grey actually dropped his gaze, and said, "He has the answer, Eldest. I can sense that he knew, he could tell me … the nature of the end of life and of its true sequel." He looked back up at Cedrith with a light in his eyes. "Have you never wondered, Eldest, what becomes of the soul when the body expires? The Heroes still affect the world, the stories tell, and sometimes have appeared to us. Thus, is it possible that we, as children of Hope, also live on?"

Cedrith pulled up a chair and sat next to his colleague. "Have you spoken to anyone about this research?" Judgement shook his head, but Cedrith pursued it. "Have you spoken to Natasha?" He saw the young face harden, with anger or perhaps hurt, and another shake. "My friend, I know you are disappointed in … in your studies with her, but she is the Healer of the Lands, and likely knows more about the d-da-dangers here than anyone, certainly than I. I am not adequate to this task, of judging what you have done here."

"I do not request your approval," said Judgement with a low tone hard as flint. Cedrith sat back, a little offended but still sympathetic to the young man's earnest desire.

"You misunderstand me, my friend," he said soothingly and placed his hand on Judgement's shoulder, which brought his gaze back around. "I think you, Solemn Judgement, Guildsman of Conar's Sages, are one of the finest, most upstanding and Hopeful men I have ever met. And really, for a human, you are not a bad sort at all," he added in an attempt at levity. "I wish you to be safe, and I know that any mortal who delves into these mysteries is like a child playing with straw and torches. Will you at least consider my request?"

"I shall, of course, Eldest. Soon — when my researches are in more coherent form — I will seek the Guildmistress, I promise."

"No, please- don't promise me," Cedrith said at once, "nothing good can come of that, I fear." It was Judgement's turn to be puzzled, and Cedrith felt his stomach turning sour. "But tell me more, if you can; what have you sought in this arcane lore?"

"I believe that Faltus Fanem may have discovered a way to somehow protect those who had died. To make their spirits immune to the forces of necromancy and their bodies safe from reanimation."

Cedrith whistled low at this. "What a blow that would be. But it did not happen; we have no such ritual in our history."

"I believe his researches became known to the enemy, and Despair may have taken steps to stop him or destroy what he found. I cannot be certain how far along his researches were, since he has been so … obtuse in these writings."

"I should say! Honestly, he wrote that he was insane and I took him at his word. Yet I wonder." Cedrith rubbed his chin for a moment. "I seem to recall … in the back of the Fanem Archive book, there was a kind of appendix … some other researcher whose life he had a few remarks on."

"Verily?" Judgement was clearly tense with excitement.

"You must forgive me, my friend! I was not seeking to learn specifically about the man, merely his dates so I could place the sequence. You bring me a whole new way of thinking about the world, sir."

He considered awhile as Judgement waited.

"I think," Cedrith said carefully, rising, "that I should perhaps request permission, as a Senior Guildsman and distinguished guest from Mendel, to look once again at that text in the Archives. Just to be thorough, you understand; we would not want to leave any other book in the wrong place. It could be — just for interest, I mention this — that I could have the tome in my cell, perhaps by around sundown. That is, in case you would wish to know my whereabouts, for any reason."

Cedrith turned to go, his mind brimming with thoughts and still half-torn about what he was doing.

Behind him, Judgement quietly said, "Eldest."

He turned back, countering, "Guildsman?"

"You asked earlier, I believe, if I had made any friends here in this world."

"I did, in truth."

"I am not sure I can judge such matters, sir. But I believe the answer is yes."

Cedrith smiled fully, and bowed to the Man in Grey before leaving the room to seek the Chief Archivist.

Back at his desk, Judgement sat awhile in thought. Taking a ribbon-wrapped sheaf from near the bottom of a pile of papers, the Man in Grey scanned its title, penned in his own hand: "A Man Who Walked Into the Sea: The Conarian Noble Custom of Sanctuary". Looking in the direction Cedrith had left, he started to put the papers back, then hesitated as his eye fell across a sheet of scrap-vellum, already written on. Between some now-unfamiliar characters the word "walk" was written three times. And also among those lines was inscribed:

Now then sir, if you will trust me

Moving decisively, the Man in Grey used the scrap-sheet as an envelope, folding the tract inside and addressing it as follows:

To the Distinguished Sage of Mendel, Senior Guildsman Cedrith Fellareon

To be delivered in the case of death

Beneath the address, he sealed the package with the mark of the scales of justice.

⊕ ⊕ ⊕

Excerpt from The Nameless Tome of Faltus Fanem

The power of necromancy is bound up with the force that hatred and fear can exert on the inherent magic of this world. I have written extensively on the nature of magic itself in other titles, but for those unversed it is sufficient to note the following.

FIRST: Magic is literally everywhere: not bound within the mage, nor drawn from other realms, but tapped out of the air, water, earth and flame. There is enough magical energy in the pages of this book to set the room you sit in on fire.

SECOND: Your body, in itself and so long as you live, is the most powerful magical instrument you will ever come in contact with, barring only the body of someone else. Life energy, about which I know too little, is to magical energy as oil is to a flame. Or it is like the influence of a magnet upon iron.

THIRD: The sum and total of casting magical spells consists in only this: the caster learns how to align his body to the energy of the world, which naturally faces aside from him but can be turned. The body of lore learned by wizards is a series of words, gestures, mental concentration images, and (for larger and more permanent magics) the use of materials and items in concert which accomplish this end.

By what means do water and earth, wood and stone turn from good to evil? No change in physical substance, but instead of the alignment of each smallest portion of its tangible matter, is responsible. In the state of nature, this condition is known as neutrasm. *When aligned towards the hopeful mage (or when the caster brings himself into proper alignment, which is the more nearly accurate description) then this same object should be seen as achieving a state of* pronasm. *From this alignment, magic can be cast, causing flame to appear in the midst of rain, light to dispel the darkness, and all manner of super-neutrasmic effects. The mage's life-energy, as stated, catalyzes this process and limits its effect, for by conjuring too greatly or rapidly the caster becomes exhausted and risks losing consciousness or even life. But when the mage has become dominated by fear and hatred, he seeks to turn this alignment in its opposite direction, away from* pronasm *and beyond* neutrasm *to its nether pole. Then matter aligns to the caster in a relationship of* miasm. *Sorcerous plagues, blackfire, abominable creations, contact with the planes of hell, and other catastrophic effects are the result.*

When a mage reaches the end of his earthly span, this well-practiced habit of alignment has potential to spread. The vessel of energy contained by a human life, as formerly asserted, is the fuel for tremendous magical affect. The condition or alignment in which the mage passes from the earth, then, has a much-increased consequence for the balance of miasm *and* pronasm *in the land.*

But here is the awful truth, which Wolga Vrule discerned; on the approach of death, the minds of all men turn to FEAR.

Some few, in all history, may have escaped this curse. Telhol, for certain, was one, blessed be his name and the example he set for all. But for the rest of us, yes and me, and you as well dear reader, the choice is to fight. And with the fight, driving it onward and even fuelling its success, behind all struggle is fear. And with fear comes miasm, *and the potential to poison the world around us. Vrule, the first necromancer, mastered the foul art of accessing the* miasma *in every corpse, calling it back to animation through the fear of death that contaminated its soul when last alive.*

The plague he unleashed did not simply bring death. It was a plague of fear, aimed to make all men his servitors after death.

The fear-plague takes many forms but for our purposes there are chiefly two.

FIRST, *the tendency for anyone who has died to leave behind a corpse susceptible to raising. Even the most virtuous normal child of Hope, upon death, feels enough fear to contaminate his physical shell. The good deeds and intent, the long habits of civility and caring, these are released in a shower of* pronasm *upon death, and all the world immediately near is the better for this. But the fear, even a moment or two of it, is enough to cause a thin cloud of* miasm *to cling to the body, and this abides even when the corpse has crumbled with the years. Though the child of Hope is burned, as is only proper, some small residue of* miasma *remains behind, connected to the frame that once was. By this connection the necromancer can summon back the body to mindless motion, unwilled obedience, and lifeless servitude. The tales speak of gaunts, and skeletal forms which the Lieges did raise against Conar and his vassals in the early wars. When we as children of Hope contemplate the horror of seeing even a single dead body, something we instinctively sense as children, one can better understand the staggering terror of the practices of Despair, who did inter their dead in the earth, together in massive* kemetaria. *Rumors of vast fields of such bodies, awaiting the day of summoning, remain among us even centuries after the Battle of the Razor. Largest and most fearsome of these was the Tombs Thanazun, a lost space somewhere in our Lands that holds the bodies of thousands to this day. Masters of power designed tombs for themselves, surrounded by the corpses of their faithful workers and guarded by unspeakable creations, the horrid ghouls. To this day the burial field remains unfound, yet those necromancers who wished to access them are thankfully sundered from that lost* kemetaria *by the Swords of Stone.*

Our mages and clerics learned various arts to destroy these bodies, or to quell the connection between them and Vrule. But there were always more dead, including thousands slain by Despair behind their lines, slaves and captives, and the unfortunate weak, who could supply them endlessly. Bad enough, but …

SECOND, Vrule also discerned for some of the dead, enough fear, hatred, or other negative emotion ruled their late life that not just the mindless shell, but the being itself could be recalled. The amount and purity of miasma *could be used, in rare cases, to pull back the being's soul, if you will, and bind it to its former body, or to a place, and cause it to act again in the world (if not truly to live). These dread beings, driven by the need for revenge or some other base emotion, would stalk and speak, possessed of great strength, or the lore of their former lives, and with conscious intent wrought still more evil on the Lands. Revenants, ghosts, and others haunted certain parts of the world, with the power to drain life from new victims, a monstrous and foul act which not only weakened Hope but spread yet more* miasma *through the world. 'Twas this path that Vrule practiced upon himself; he transformed without transition through death, which is natural, to an un-life which defies and desecrates nature itself, as a liche.*

In both these forms was the death-plague released upon us, and among Despair as well and even the rustic peoples. These events happened during the First War of Liberation, and continued through the Age of Balance until the Battle of the Razor, which brought our knowledge of Despair's forces to a close (praise the Heroes for that wondrous deed). And for centuries after it first appeared in the Lands, the plague of necromancy tormented us, and sages, priests and wizards bent their efforts to sever this connection, and find a cure for the effects of miasm. *The one who succeeded, beyond all doubt and unknown to Hope, was Exeter Polanquan. The story contained in this tome is his biography — a word I use to describe a text dedicated to the life of a single person not yet counted among the Heroes — and his successful but mortal quest to destroy necromantic power.*

Nothing that Exeter Polanquan wrote survives. His notes were all destroyed by his enemy, who thought his work done with the man's death. The tale turns now to my wondrous mirror, the discovery that made my career, rescued this knowledge, and ended my life.

The Second War of Liberation

Excerpt from the Conar Scriptorium Tome

In those days following close upon the full liberation of the central kingdoms, the Hopelords didst establish in power those vassals to whom Conar had promised foefdoms from the earliest days. To Areghel was given the lands formerly ruled by the Earth Demon, thrall to Mauglir the Despair-Liege of Men, the one-eyed leviathan whom he had met again in combat and slain. Thereupon Areghel founded his seat of power in the new city of Reghalion. The Sword of Air, Order-Brow and Scepter of Law were vested to him on his throne, and thereupon the ways became straight and nature restored. Thus were many peoples freed from terror and others did move therein to settle and work the land and divers endeavors.

Areghel, seeing the vastness of his domain and the scattered nature yet of its settlement, undertook to ride its length and breadth with his chosen followers. His purpose was twain: to hunt down such remnants of Despair as remained within his bounds, and to take census of the kingdom's places as they existed now that order had been restored. Where there were inhabitants, or the land was meet to support them, Areghel did choose to found and locate fivescore keeps, or fortresses or in some cases walled towns already existing. This great census was established for the first time by the king in person with his army, and in later years came to be recorded through the crown's representatives, who didst separately hold each foef in the name of Areghel. Thus did the kingdom come to be called the Percentalion.

But in one distant corner of his domain, the host came nigh a dark place, entangled from woods and vales, in which the creatures of Despair still didst dwell; hell-dogs and earth demons and a large tribe of garruk. In the fighting the Reghalion host was victorious, but the enemy didst withdraw to the deepest coverts and gullies and the mounted host were hard pressed to follow them with advantage. They convened then at the center of that land to encamp and consult.

The captain of the mounted host, the good knight Hollin, did come to the king and spake, "Milord, with thy permission I wouldst fain take my men and hunt yon foul creatures within their haunts until they be utterly destroyed."

"Nay," quoth Areghel, "for therein are you placed beyond advantage, and our losses would be too dear. Rather then we shall build here in the midst of them our fortress, and yon enemy will thereby be pricked in pride to attack. And following the battle and our victory, if I am not wrong, then shall the fort serve as the center of our foef for the greater protection of the innocent who shall come to settle herein." To this the men agreed with ready will, and in their depth of lore and energy they did erect the fortress in but three days, according to the plan their king had devised for common use.

Then indeed the enemy did come, as Areghel had foreseen. The garruk didst throw themselves at the walls, and were repelled with heavy loss. Then the captain with his cavalry did ride out against them with dreadful execution. The garruk fled, those that survived, and the captain in his zeal did pursue them. But in the thickets of the tangled draws further from the walls, the captain and his men did encounter there the hell-dogs, lying in wait and now leaping from ambush upon the mailed knights. The crimson-glowing eyes of the beasts, the black skin and three monstrous taloned legs were most fearsome, and the keening deathly howl of the hell-dogs did strike many of the knight's horses to terror-death. The knights stood to in a group afoot and were sore pressed.

Then did Areghel envision their plight (wearing as he did the Order-Brow) and the king rode out to do battle and succor his men. In his right arm he bore the Sword of Air, for it pleased the Demonsbane to smite insentient beasts with the blade, and reserve the proof of his body for those with language and thought among his enemies. The light of the Sword brought illumination to the deep vales and thickets wherein the fight took place, and the hell-dogs, though not taking flight, did fall back somewhat from its approach. Then the king Areghel did marvelous execution among the foe, smiting down the dogs so that they burned and died, and nothing grew in the heart of this vale forever where their corpses had fallen. The king thus drew nigh the knights of his host, who being greatly cheered by his coming, redoubled their strokes on the enemy and drove them back.

Yet even the lord Areghel fell prey to that same battle-wonder as had beset Hollin his captain, and he did pursue the enemy to the deepest portion of the tangled ground. And therein did the last of the hell-dogs, master of the pack near the size of a stallion, lay its ambush and sprang from the side upon him. Struck by the weight of the beast of deep earth, the lord of law was borne to the ground and did swoon. The shining blade fell from his grasp and lodged in a tree bole.

But the captain, following hard upon his lord, came upon them and grasping the mystic blade, pulled it forth and did assay an attack. He fought with doughty skill, yet the blade worked not as well in his hands- for he was not of the line of Areghel though he were indeed a noble soul. The hell-dog was wounded, but in turn did bite and maim the captain, taking his left arm so that he fell and would have been lost. But enow Areghel recovered his senses, and springing up did engage the creature with his hands, and in a mighty set of blows did slay it. Then the king and captain recovered the Sword of Air and returned to the victorious host.

But reports continued that fell creatures survived in the dells and draws, and after the honored dead were interred in flame, Areghel met with his retinue in council. The king wast fain to complete the census, so near to its ending for he had in sooth established all the one hundred castles and this was the last.

"Verily," quoth he, "It is in my heart to return now to Reghalion, *and come with the host before the planting time, that we may complete the work so well begun here"*

The captain of his host stood forth then and said, "Yet it were not well done should we abandon this sturdy fortress in the face of evil. Prithee make me thy vassal in foef and I shall hold this keep against thy coming whatever may betide. And the enemy shall not take it whether I live or die before thy return, I so swear."

And the heart of Areghel did misgive him somewhat that his vassal in such zeal should swear so dread an oath. But he did extend his hands to clasp over the remaining right hand of the kneeling captain, and accepted his fealty and made him thereof the vassal in foef of the hundredth keep, and charged him to hold it against the enemies of Hope until his return. This the captain swore to do, and thus did Areghel ride out with the remainder of his host, leaving a strong garrison well supplied to enforce the law.

And in this tragedy did strike, for as Areghel returned to his capital he did learn there of his lord Conar's command that the host of Hope shouldst again assemble to do battle with the legions of Despair across the River Sweeping. The forces of Areghel in the main didst ride off to fulfill their part of the levy; the detachment detailed by the king to supply and relieve the fortress of the hundredth keep didst lose its way in yon tangled land, and was set upon by garruk with fell beasts in their train, and forced to retreat.

Not until the following autumn was Areghel returned from war beyond the distant Great Forest, and he was wroth and distressed to hear the tidings. "I am remiss," quoth the king, "for in taking my good knight Hollin upon his word I have bound him to it, and now methinks shall woe betide." Riding in all speed to that most distant portion of his realm, he came not upon the hundredth keep though he used all the might of Scepter and Brow to discern it. Men tell of a single scout who did see a dark and empty castle at the dead of night, surrounded by siege-posts and the dried track of garruk of whom many corpses were on the field without. But the gate and barbican were locked full tight and no living being did answer when hailed. And the scout making this report to the king, yet still could not lead him to the place the following day. Then the king was greatly grieved and did foretell that the keep would remain accursed, by the great zeal of his captain and the machination of the enemy, for all time. Thereafter he ordered that no man should further search for the hundredth keep, and all men gave it up for lost. That dark vale was then emptied of all evil, and many wicked trees hewn and crevices filled, and another settlement made there of goodly aspect. And the king named it after his valiant captain, and there an end.

⊕ ⊕ ⊕

Natasha met Cedrith at the Street of Forges and together they ferreted out the shop of Nador the silversmith. A deep voice within answered their knock with a gruff "Come in!" as if they should have known, and they took two steps down into the hollow house, where firepits in the center of the lower room sent smoke skyward by an interior airwell built through the upper stories. The thin but sternly-muscled man in the grimy apron barely looked up from a goblet he was chasing with filigree. He pointed with his fire-awl towards the back, behind a half-wall where the sounds of infrequent, short taps could be heard. "He's back there, slaving away. It'll be ready soon, or it should," Nador finished with a slight rise in his voice to make it carry. He listened a moment, until he heard one more soft tap, and shook his head with a humorless bark. "He'll be at it all day, if you let him."

Natasha beamed at the smith as if she wanted to set lunch before him, and Cedrith thanked him before moving with her towards the back. Around the half-wall, the Man in Grey sat erect at a bench, bending a flat strip of silver into a circular shape by hammering it, slowly and precisely, around a molding bar. To one side on the bench lay his father's silver cross, cleaned and detached from its chain in preparation for the forging.

"Good day, my friend," Cedrith said, while Natasha waited until the space between taps to seize him in a motherly hug from behind. Judgement nodded in answer but remained focused on the task before him, gently pushing the silver band around the bar until it was nearly closed. Putting down his hammer, he slid the piece free and set it on the edge of the table with the open space toward him. Picking up a file with his left hand, Judgement carefully lined the edge and began to carve a slot into either side, just large enough to accommodate the cross's lower end. Nador, finished for the moment, drifted around the corner and spoke. "I can trim that cross-piece for you, son: won't do any harm to the rest and it will look more symmetrical." But the Man in Grey only shook his head briefly before continuing. The smith shook his as well, muttering, "Nice work, that, but weird; the bottom bar is too long."

"He says all the holy symbols in his home country were shaped that way, and none had the circle around the ends," Cedrith replied. "So many things I always want to ask him," he said quietly to Natasha, "but he seems very reluctant."

"Let him be," advised the Guildmistress. "He is finding his way and it must be terribly hard."

"It won't be a proper holy symbol—" Nador began, but Natasha shushed him with a gesture that seemed almost angry.

"He is sincere, my good smith: I have instructed him and I know his purpose is worthy. The symbol will work, I feel sure of it, so long as we do our part," and here she patted the flask of holy water at her side. "He crafts the symbol to be representative of both his lands; perhaps it won't work for anyone else, but that's nothing. He believes, and that is the most important thing."

"Yet he is following a set procedure, surely," said Cedrith, becoming really interested. "I know little of miraculous lore, but I had always thought the process was very similar to the magical. The wizards take an item, cast spells upon it within their circles, repeat the process to fix the enchantment, and then another set of spells to make it permanent. Surely this is the same?"

"Not at all, Cedrith. The theory Judgement follows here is sound: he plans to enhance a master-wrought item of fine quality. And he will use silversteel, which is innately magical. But holy items cannot be manufactured regardless of the maker's will; they must be brought about by true belief, which is why they are so rare. I have tutored him about the devotion of Hope, and he affirms every tenet; indeed, he seemed to know all of them already. He is a believer, and his piety is strong. He could be a preacher himself, if he chose. But it is the quality of that belief, not the mere knowledge of lore, which matters here."

Judgement had finished filing the notch, and placing the ring around his cross slotted the long bottom arm into the space. Once again he picked up the hammer in his right hand, and tapped it gently towards fully closed, all the while watching the other three arms to be sure they were flush.

"I notice," Cedrith said to Judgement, "that you use the hammer in one hand, and the file in the other." This remark did not absolutely require a response, and thus received none from the intent apprentice. "And I note from previous visits," he persisted, "you use a quill with your left, and lift the bellows with the right again. One for precision, it seems, and another for strength?"

"My father thought it best that no part of the body be left inactive," Judgement said almost unwillingly. "He would say there are different crafts in the kingdom, yet all men should work together and not be idle while the sun is up."

"And so you have trained to different tasks with either hand?" Cedrith asked. Judgement nodded and the sage chuckled quietly. "What a man he must have been," he said to Natasha aside.

"Do you notice," she whispered back "he never speaks directly of having honor, or being just or noble? He says only, 'I remember my father's face.' It is very, very important that this forging succeed, I think. He needs to wield the power, but he must bring his sire with him."

"It is all so new to me," Cedrith murmured. "I am used to simply studying things; the words about a craft, or a war, or a spell, are the same as the thing itself to me. Maybe better, because they are so easily understood. But young Judgement is always up and doing. He has already become a full member of the Sages Guild, the youngest in a century, and I don't doubt but he will surpass me soon."

“Oh, surely—” the lady clucked in deprecation, but Cedrith held up a hand to forestall her.

“I have no illusions, Natasha; he is truly a talented student with a voracious appetite for all subjects. I shall be very glad to say that I started him on language, in later days when he is justly famous. I mean that, he will be one of the best among us. But beyond this … he works! He trains with the mason, the smith, the shipwright, the bookbinder. It never ends! I always hear that he has finished a few weeks’ course of learning with some craftsman and then is on to another, often two at a time, and while studying!”

“He’s a smith-born, I will tell you that,” said Nador quietly coming up and hearing some of their talk. Judgement was still fitting and placing the piece prior to the heat, and the three of them stood back a few paces, probably out of his hearing. “I’ve had him here two months, next week, and already he’s learned more than any apprentice I’ve had in my career. He listens as if he’s forgotten how to speak, and watches as if his eyes just opened last night. Last week I let him try a bit of jewel-craft, setting a stone to a ring for a noble customer. It’s journeyman work, most boys would not have been ready in less than two years, but he did it so well the customer never doubted it was mine. And the lad still wouldn’t take commission on it, just his prentice-wage as agreed. He sweeps, he stokes the forge, he handles the grease, and all this time, he’s never left enough flagging or scraps of metal over to sweep up in your hand. If he asked, I’d take him on before the echo died.” And nodding his head for emphasis, Nador turned back to watch his student in the final stage of the forging.

Having set the cross into the silver ring, the Man in Grey carefully opened a small wooden jar filled with dark-grey filings. Taking out a pinch of precious silversteel, he sprinkled a few grains at each juncture between the two pieces, front and back, carefully wiping the excess back into the container. Then he set a glaze of warmed wax over the joints and waited a few moments for it to harden. Meanwhile, he opened a small forge-door to one side of the open area, and the three watchers felt a blast of heat from within as the coals glowed nearly white-hot. Sliding the piece onto a long handled stone plate, Judgement said a silent prayer and then nodded to Natasha and towards a low flat tray near the forge. She uncapped her flask and poured the holy water three inches deep. Then Judgement flipped open the forge-door again, knelt, and thrust in the piece.

Cedrith drew breath only shallowly. He knew the timing was crucial here. Too long and the piece would melt and lose its fine edges and décor; too soon and the joints would not set, the piece would snap loose at the first stress. The wax coating by now was vapor. Silversteel had a much higher melting point than silver, of course, but these were only filings, a mere salting of the magical metal to amplify the intent of the forger. Cedrith was sure Judgement had already waited too long; he uttered a short prayer to Mickhel, progenitor of the skillful Dwarves, that this work might hold true.

Judgement withdrew the plate and the silver piece was slightly glowing with the heat. Smoothly, he tipped the stone towards the flat pan and his piece slid down into the holy water. Natasha spoke the standard invocation of blessing on the symbol as the steam roiled up and hissing filled the air. Judgement stood a mere spectator now, and his stone face seemed to Cedrith rather resigned.

The steam cleared away, and there the piece sat just beneath the water's surface. Nador put a finger in the pan, and nodded that it was sufficiently cool. Judgement reached in and withdrew the holy symbol, looking large and unusual with its extra-long bottom arm, gleaming with water and perhaps, Cedrith fancied, with something else. They all gathered around and praised the workmanship: truly it looked as if it were formed of a single piece of silver now.

There was a long moment where no one moved or spoke. Judgement lowered the item and continued to look at it carefully. At last, Cedrith cautiously said, "So. What happens now? Should you … do we test it?"

For answer, Judgement merely reached for the chain and refastened the item around his neck. Natasha said, "No, my friend. We do not question or test the piece. The time will come. We simply believe."

"But … I mean, what—"

"This is not the work of mages, dear Cedrith. The ability to call upon magic power is a kind of craft; the ancients would say a*scientus*. You succeed because you know, you have learned and remember and proceed in the proper order. The most vile and ignoble creature in the Lands could cast a spell, if he only knew the words and the lore, and had the strength remaining. But the miracles of Hope do not regard knowledge, only the worth of the self." Natasha beamed at Judgement, and moved toward him for another inevitable hug. "And this youth — this man, here — he is most worthy, I feel it!"

She wrapped her arms about him, which as usual brought no response from the Man in Grey. Nador snorted and cried, "What, boy, have you never been hugged by a wild Gypsy woman before?"

Natasha giggled at this, but Judgement looked to the smith seriously, and said only, "Yes."

"Well it doesn't show," the smith returned. "It's a fine piece of work, lad, whatever happens. You are still determined, then, to leave me at week's end?" Judgement nodded, and the smith sighed. "Ah well, nothing for it. Good work, lad." And he turned back to chase his goblet, saying only, "Nothing else for the day."

Judgement retrieved his cloak, hat and staff, and donned them before leaving with his friends.

"You always go about prepared for a long journey, it seems, friend Judgement," Cedrith remarked. The Man in Grey nodded to this, and the trio walked awhile in silence.

"Actually," Natasha began a little coyly, "I may have a journey in mind for you, young man. And perhaps a first test of your symbol, if we succeed."

Everyone stopped walking there in the midst of the street and looked at the Guildmistress. "Your quest," Judgement said with certainty, and the Gypsy nodded.

"Do you have a clue, then," Cedrith asked, "how to get back to … where you were?"

"I have … Hope," said Natasha. "Come, let us discuss it further in comfort."

"Where to, then?" Cedrith asked. "If I may be permitted to listen, that is."

Natasha smiled at him like the rising sun, and took him by the arm for emphasis. Judgement said only, "To the theater," and the Healer nodded.

The trio knocked at a side door, avoiding the stage and whatever apparatus might have lurked there to affright them. Cedrith was pleased to see Bartaeus open, and Judgement once again respectfully shook the young man's hand, which made him blush. He gestured them back through a maze of passages, already changed by the new play being prepared, to a side-room that was simply a large wedge between two hinged walls and open on the third side. There Alendic was waiting, decked out once again in brilliant blue, and pouring glasses already for all. "Welcome, good Sage Fellareon, I'm so glad you could return to this chat. And well met, Sage Judgement," he quipped, saluting the Man in Grey who ignored him. "We have been sparring every other day," he confided to Cedrith, "and I'm pleased to say the number of bruises on my ribs is steadily dropping."

Cedrith looked to Judgement for confirmation; the youth shrugged and said, "He always calls out before he attacks."

This drew a peal of laughter from the actor, and a confession. "I admit it, I have become uselessly dramatic, I'm afraid. But you'll be pleased to know I have your favorite drinks waiting." Gesturing the company to seats, he motioned the goblet containing water to Judgement's attention.

There was a silence, and Cedrith sensed that Natasha was framing a way to begin. He tried to supply her, saying, "So if I understand correctly, you two wish to suborn my young friend here into a life of adventure."

"Suborn!" Alendic cried. "I like that, almost better than 'kidnap'."

"Cedrith is right," Natasha said. "Young Judgement is still learning the ways of our land, and he cannot choose properly without knowing what lies ahead of him in terms of his reputation."

Alendic, for once, made a grimace and an ugly sound. "Reputation: a word to describe how good you look standing around in clean clothes, getting older."

Natasha laughed and turned back to Cedrith with a twinkle in her eye. "Very well then, my good *reputable* Elvish Sage, you shall describe for the lad the place of the adventurer, and then we will tell him our tale."

His mind racing, Cedrith temporized with a drink and tried to settle his thoughts. "Adventurers, hem, a difficult thesis madam. There can be little question that opinions differ widely on this: adventurer means everything from hero to thief, depending largely on whether the last ones you met were successful. And they have generally been very, very few. Nearly all folk you meet in the Lands are … content with the life their parents led, the village they were born to, the craft they were shown as a child. In this we follow traditions as old as any we know: from the first landing of Hope, some were farmers, some tradesmen, some of the warrior class."

"Was the voyage long?" Judgement asked.

"You mean, did they have a settled life in some western land? No record I know of will say; perhaps the leaders upon landing ordered it so. Conar and the Hopelords established the honorable trades and children were proud to do their part by upholding those of their parents. For the knights and mages, this meant constant warfare, since the entire Lands, to begin with, were occupied by Despair. Many heroic deeds and feats were accomplished then. In recent centuries, it must be admitted, we have lived in settled ways without the advent of any invasion from the East. The nobility, the high mages and clerical classes, still exist in accordance with tradition. But their occupation has been, ah, more customary than, em, adventurous. We read or hear the stories of our ancient Heroes, and they thrill us, to be sure, but we take the meaning of our devotion to them less … less literally."

"Surely, this is so in the lands you came from?" Alendic asked Judgement quickly, another thrust.

The youth returned his gaze and shook his head slowly. "Nay, the nobles of my former home were always much occupied."

"Were there kingdoms of Despair near to yours?" Natasha asked, and again Judgement shook his head. To Cedrith's surprise, this confident and straightforward young man actually bit his lip.

After a pause, he said, "The nations … made war upon each other."

"For Hope?" Alendic asked.

"For gain, usually," Judgement returned matter-of-factly. "To expand this border against another, or to capture wealth in a port city or a mine." His guests were shocked to silence, and Cedrith could see the youth struggling to maintain his composure, embarrassed to make such alien admissions in present company. "I had heard tell of battles fought to avenge a previous defeat, or in fulfillment of a debt. In some wise, the nobles fought … to keep in practice."

Cedrith drew a deep breath and tried to continue. "Well, as you have studied in our histories, it is not so here, praise the Heroes. Our lands have dwelt in peace for twenty centuries, thanks to the Lords of Hope and their followers."

"Ever since the *Dagnor Rokan*," Judgement replied, "the ten-day Battle of the Razor that broke the ranks of Despair forever and ejected their armies from the Lands."

"Well, nearly all," Alendic responded. "In the far corners of the kingdoms, on this side of the Swords of Stone, there have been undiscovered places, deep delves or thickets, caves and abandoned castles, where danger lurked."

"This is undoubtedly true," Cedrith agreed, "though most would say that none have ever emerged to bother us. Thus over those centuries there have been, on occasion, a few who went in search of them. It is a different path, Judgement, a life apart; and I would be remiss if I did not say that many, very many folk regard such adventurers as unwelcome" — at this choice of word Alendic barked into his goblet, spitting a little wine over the side — "indeed, as a menace."

"What this civilized and polite fellow is taking so long to say," Alendic continued, "is that if you joined us for any length of time, you would be rejected by most right-thinking folks. You'll be thought of as a scavenger, treasure-hunter, a pirate on land … that is, when you have money to show. Otherwise it's a beggar's welcome, a strong kick or a call for the guard. Hard days of marching, nights on watch, fighting for your life and risking your skin to pull a comrade out of the fire. And that great privilege will only follow another score of months that we will take in hard training, to prepare for this first sortie. Frankly, you'd be a fool to accept," the actor finished with a confident flourish. "But it's all a leaf in the wind, because you'll come."

Cedrith protested, "Now, that's hardly—"

"I can read you like a first-time chorus boy," Alendic sailed on, "and you'll do anything she asks. Won't you, lad?" He leaned in, and stared the Man in Grey straight in the eye. Judgement nodded once and slowly, and the actor sat back with an air of accomplishment. "Me too, lad. Me too." And here he looked at Natasha so earnestly she could not forebear to smile at them both.

"Judgement," Cedrith asked, "are you certain? Is this what you want? Have you considered the risks involved?"

The Man in Grey looked levelly back at his tutor. "You mean," he said, "that if I join them, people will reject me?" And Cedrith felt the bite of his laughless wit.

"But surely it will be dangerous … Alendic speaks of great peril."

"And I may die from it. Aye." The youth's eyes flared a little at this, and Cedrith could see his pride was stirred, no doubt as the others had hoped. Still, there was more; Cedrith sensed Judgement had not yet learned to care very much, whether he lived or died. This adventure was a mystery to the youth's agile mind, and it promised the kind of furious activity he always sought. He had to admit, it seemed a perfect fit.

The healer sighed, and started at the beginning.

"Eddoran was our leader, a mage and a scholar; he and Alendic were friends from childhood."

"From the southern headlands," Alendic supplied. "I fought him past the guards and he talked me out of jail."

"I had left my band, I was restless I suppose. The Rom are daring compared to settled folk, but they look after their clan and avoid anything that smacks of real … well, I left them. I knew something about healing already; by the Heroes, I was so young then!"

"And like wine, you have only improved with age, my dear," Alendic offered, and she waved him off, dropping into reverie as he continued.

"Eddoran and I found we could get into twice as much trouble in the same time with a healer aboard. And we had Baythan, a big bruiser of a warrior bored with his lord's service, plus Semel, a quiet, sour fellow who knew his way outdoors and gambled off whatever he earned. Over the years there was sometimes one, or sometimes two others we would bring along. Some died, some cashed out; say, remember when we had enough, back in eighty-seven, for an attendant with a pack mule? What was the little fellow's name, spoke with a stutter. We had plenty of food and treasure in those days."

Natasha snapped back to the present, and smiled again. "No. I remember those dreadful days on the Colton Heights, in the winter of eighty-three, when we all nearly starved."

"Surely, because you always felt so responsible for us, Mother dear! Take my word for it," he quipped to Judgement, "cougarrant is horrible eating. Even if you manage to kill one, which we nearly did not."

"Can you imagine, me, starving?" Natasha said to Cedrith good-naturedly, and the Elf felt pressed for how to respond. "But enough of this maundering. We were a band of adventurers, and we little cared what decent folks thought of us. Whether we did more good than harm, I won't say. But we managed to get skilled at our trade, and we eventually decided to try our hand at exploring the Percentalion."

Cedrith lowered his goblet and sat back in his chair. "It's not possible. No one can enter the Percentalion and return to tell the tale."

"My friend," Alendic retorted, "no insult intended, but among my former *disreputable* peers, the saying went that if you still had a pulse you were bound for the land of one hundred castles soon or late. And it isn't true at all that you cannot return from there; we are the living proof. Although our route was even more roundabout than usual."

In the space of silence that followed, Alendic rose and refilled the wine goblets. He turned to Judgement and said, "Let us have the history, then, lad, just to prove you know what you're about."

Judgement did not hesitate. "In the earliest days, the land between what is now the Great Road and the River Sweeping lay under the rule of the Earth-Demon, Kog."

"Oho! Not so loud, if you please, sir," Alendic broke in. "We don't like to say the names of Demons and Dragons without good reason. Call it an ignorant superstition, but it can attract their attention."

"I thought Kog, em, I mean, that he was destroyed by Areghel in the Second War of Liberation," Cedrith said.

"As the legends say, yes," Alendic returned. "Defeated in single combat during the First War — where Areghel put out his eye — and then slain at last, when the Demonsbane took over his kingdom."

"And so," Judgement continued, "as long as Areghel or his line sat the throne in Reghalion, the ways of the kingdom were made straight. But when the last of the heirs in direct descent from Areghel Demonsbane died, the curse of Despair overtook the land again."

"Aye, though not all at once," Alendic said, sitting forward in his chair. "I wasn't alive then, of course; this was three hundred years ago."

"Four hundred twenty three years, in 1572 ADR," Judgement corrected.

"Aye, good young sage," Alendic said with a tight grin and rising to make a saucy bow, "but for the first hundred years or nearly folks could not see a difference. Only gradually did people have more trouble traveling about the kingdom. By around 1700, you needed a learned guide to be sure of crossing out to the Road or River, but there were hardly any strange creatures or weather to be seen. Things became worse and worse, though, and the trade dried up completely. By the time our fathers were born, a man who marched a day into the Percentalion might as well close eyes and point to get back to where he started. Many of the hundred castles have fallen empty, though some few towns and forts remain, by some whim preserved against the ravages of chaos."

"All those people," Cedrith mused. "I never thought before, what they must have suffered. And still suffer … I supposed they must all have left. Isn't Reghalion a ghost-city?"

"Yes," Natasha agreed, "the stories do say that there is no living soul in the capital. But the Land of One Hundred Castles is not entirely empty, though whether that is good news or bad, I cannot tell."

"We sought to reach one of those islands of humanity, as some had done before us. And instead we found…" Natasha could not continue, and seemed close to tears. Alendic rose with a gallant bow to her, and said, "Let us have the histories continue the tale. We have taken the liberty of transcribing a relevant portion of the notes from the scriptorium."

He drew out a leather-bound journal book in which the first third of the pages were thickly inscribed. Flipping through, Alendic read from the middle of a page. "'It was in the time of quiet following the war' — meaning the First War of Liberation — 'that many hurts were healed and building began, and the freed peoples were raised up in a certain measure. The Lords of Hope thought of the great harm that was done, notwithstanding their efforts, and took counsel how to limit them. Thus was a plan undertaken, on a narrow path between bloodshed and surrender, to reduce in some wise the potential for renewed conflict to do damage unto the land and its peoples. The Enemy, when approached via herald and under truce, were of mind to agree in part. Thereafter was the Hopeward created'."

Cedrith stirred, "But … what has this to do with your, ahm, adventure in the Percentalion? That land was under Despair's control in the time you are reading."

"Quite correct," Alendic responded, his face growing serious. "What seems to have happened, as best we can tell, is that the two sides agreed to … create a place, neither here nor there if you will, and to stock some of their most powerful weapons within it. These were to be held under heavy guard, and nearly cut off from the world. Nearly. We, by the blindest chance, stumbled across an entrance, one within the lands held by Despair at that time, now lost in the

Percentalion, and we entered the Hopeward. We may have been the first to do so in centuries, I cannot tell."

"And?" Cedrith was fired with curiosity. "What happened?"

"We were destroyed," Natasha said in a voice of sorrow, and Cedrith looked to her in alarm to see tears on her face. "Baythan and Semel were slain, Alendic and I badly wounded by a … a horrible *thing* that serves as the guardian of the place."

"We barely escaped with our lives," Alendic said with a small smile but looking pointedly at Natasha as if arguing.

"And your leader, Eddoran?" Judgement asked quietly.

Natasha looked to him with a face of agony, and said in a tiny voice, "He … is still there."

"Do you mean he died?" Cedrith asked.

Alendic spoke for Natasha. "We are not certain. His wounds were very bad and Natasha had expended all her healing energies. She used, something we found there—"

"A Mortal Coil," the healer supplied, finding her voice again. "Eddoran had sensed its powers with a spell, and I had to do something. He said … he said it would preserve his condition, stop the passage of time for him, or nearly. And we knew we had to leave, and we … we didn't know the rules!"

Natasha broke into sobs, unable to contain her grief any longer; Alendic rose and went to her with a most respectful air, while Cedrith exchanged a glance with Judgement.

"There, my dear," Alendic said gently, "we know the rules now."

He turned back to the others. "This Hopeward is surrounded by magical protections, aside from its inaccessible location. The locks and guards put over these relics are formidable, and in addition, there are strictures around entrance, exit and … upon the choices you can make while there. It was part of the agreement between the two sides."

"I still cannot take this all in," Cedrith said, "that Hope would actually deal with Despair, under any circumstances."

"You've read of the weapons in there," Natasha said to Alendic. "You can just imagine what they could do in the wrong hands."

"And theirs, at least," Alendic shrugged, "were surely in the wrong hands. But there are magnificent items as well, from our side."

"Why have you waited so long to return? Pardon me, I do not question your courage; but have you been recruiting others?"

Natasha shook her head. "It is one of the rules: the gate to the Hopeward opens only one night in years. Not always the same interval—"

"I've learned more about the stars of the zodiac than I ever wanted, these past few years," Alendic added. "Makes my head hurt, but we've finally unlocked the pattern. Here, lad, this part is in Ancient; see if you can repeat it." He handed the notebook to Judgement who took it eagerly and began to render aloud into Common.

"With any two who enter, another must attend, for none shall enter the gate in pairs. Those who have come before may enter, and the pairs also may follow the thread. Visit alone and one must remain behind."

"We think," Alendic interjected, "they may have had some idea that one person from each side would enter simultaneously, with a third as a kind of arbiter."

"Those who enter and pass the guards," Judgement continued, "may choose to either exchange a worthy piece for one residing there, or to release an item of their choosing from the Ward. The remaining one will then also choose, and the sides will change thereafter."

"So then," Cedrith said carefully, "when do you foresee your next opportunity? When will you return to that Hopeward, with Judgement this time?"

"In five years, 2000 ADR," Natasha responded confidently.

"'The doors shall open,'" Judgement continued translating, "each declining ten cycles of Aral, from one hundred until ten be reached; this begins from the day of the opening, namely this third year since the Liberation. Then shall the doors return to closed for a … century, a century of cycles, unless it be that the Ward is empty, for without one remaining the doors cannot admit another.'"

"As we have divined from the texts," Alendic supplied, "that first year, the year the Hopeward was created, corresponds to the thirteen-hundredth year before the Battle of the Razor. Every rotation of one hundred years plus ninety plus eighty and so on adds up to five hundred and fifty years. We entered in the year 1990, the tenth of the Fire Ant, and here we are in seventh of the Fire Ant nearly halfway between times. We happen to be on the shortest end of the rotation, the one with only ten years on it" — here the actor glanced at Natasha again with concern — "and so we have remained here, in the city where the Hope-ful gate lies, preparing and awaiting our next chance."

"Our only chance," Natasha said bleakly.

"In the meantime," Alendic rallied, "we intend to continue studying, and training our skills, to be ready for the day. No mistakes this time, we will be much better prepared, and with this marvelous fellow at our side, making just three as the strictures require—"

"I cannot go with you," Judgement cut in, and his leaden voice mirrored the disappointment on his face.

Natasha was shocked. "Cannot?"

"I will be either gone from this city, or dead, within a week."

"What?" Cedrith cried, leaping to his feet. "My friend, what can you mean? Are you not well? Why would you leave us- that is, where would you go?"

Judgement made no answer, just sitting there with the notebook across his lap. At last, Natasha gathered herself to say, "When?"

"By the night of yon ebb tide, which I make to be four nights hence." Cedrith heard the clue of excitement in the youth's choice of words. It tore at his heart, to think this remarkable fellow would be leaving him. As much difficulty as knowing Solemn Judgement had engendered, the sage hardly knew how he had lived before meeting him. Even now, wrapped as usual in stubborn mystery, the presence of his friend made life more interesting. Nevertheless, he knew it would do no good to pry.

Alendic turned back to Natasha with a sigh, and the Man in Grey resumed looking at the notebook. "Ah well," said the actor, "it cannot be helped. We shall find another, my dear, or it may be that good fortune will bring this one back to us, before the time. I know you had high hopes for him, but he is determined on another course. We must trust the Heroes will provide us an answer."

Cedrith could see the tears welling up in Natasha's eyes again, and realized her connection to Eddoran was deep; she must love him, he realized with a shock. And to have waited helplessly these long five years already ...

"Mistress," Judgement said, his head still bowed towards the book, "I am sorry but there has been a mistake."

"Aye, and we hold no ill to you for it, lad," Alendic said with some spirit. "We won't bind anyone against his will, your life is your own. And my ribs will be thankful—"

"There has been a mistake," Judgement interrupted, "in the calculation of the gates."

Silence then, for a long space. Natasha stared at Judgement, who returned her look with his usual stoney mask. "What do you mean?" she asked at last, with a quiet but dangerous edge in her voice.

"You have calculated the rotation as one hundred years, then ninety years, and so on."

"Indeed, as the ancient text clearly states."

"The ancient texts state the word is 'cycles'."

"And just as you said yourself," Alendic returned, "the word 'cycles' is properly translated as 'year,' not 'day'."

Judgement slowly shook his head. "The term is quite specific when used in reference to astrological bodies. It means 'a complete transmigration of all movements or phases.' A new cycle begins when one may first observe the body in the same place as it had been."

"Of course," Alendic said with ill patience and some of his usual taunt, "and the full cycle before repeating is one calendar year. We have gone over this carefully, young sage."

"But this text does not refer to cycles of Solar, the sun. It says 'cycles of Aral,' the lower moon."

"And the importance of this?" Alendic snapped.

"Cycles of the moon are but six months long."

Natasha dropped her goblet, and Alendic swore in a gasp. Judgement closed his eyes a moment, then returned to meet the healer's gaze. "Your door opened on the tenth of this month in 1990, and will open again in three days."

Her mouth was open but no air passed in either direction, even when Alendic gripped her shoulder seeming to need support. Judgement, as if they were discussing the date for a carriage trip to the country, said, "And the next gate will open in the year 2045."

"Fifty years," whispered Natasha. "Ah Eddoran, forgive me. Forgive me." She lapsed into sobs that shook her rounded frame, and Alendic looked on her with a face of great sorrow, patting her shoulder until they subsided.

"My dear," he said. "My dear, I am so sorry."

"We are going," she said calmly.

"Of course we are. We'll take what the Heroes send us, and perhaps, in the end, we'll all be together." And he stood over her quietly for a time.

"And," Judgement interjected calmly, "I will be with you."

Everyone snapped around to look at him then. "Three nights from tonight, is the night before I … do what I must."

Cedrith rose from his chair to speak, driven by a sense of common decency. "No," he said, hardly able to credit the sound of his own voice in his ears, "no, Judgement, I forbid it. When this project was mooted for several years from now, filled with training and … and time to prepare, to become an adult, I had grave reservations. But now, you are — it is not to be thought of. Natasha, you will agree with me in this."

From the silence that followed, Cedrith foreboded great ill. He turned to look at Natasha and saw again that unfamiliar face, the one that served her desperate need and not her kindness. She ignored Cedrith and looked only at Judgement.

Cedrith hissed in horror, "Natasha!" but received no response.

Alendic carried on the interrogator's role. "You realize," he said, "that a very likely death awaits you with us."

"I am beholden to the Guildmistress for my education, which is to say, my life. I will go."

"And your other charge? This mysterious deed of the ebb tide?"

"For that," Judgement responded, "if I do not return, I will entrust instructions to another. If the Heroes are willing, the needed work will still be done." He looked at Cedrith, who felt himself practically shaking with emotion.

"You mean me," Cedrith said, still feeling as if someone else were speaking.

"Eldest, I will entrust you with the task, in writing. The letter is prepared, addressed to you and among my effects."

"That is as you wish, Guildsman. But don't bother with your pen and paper. I'm coming with you."

Alendic laughed with a condescension he did not bother to conceal.

"Certainly, sir, right this way! We are taking the children from the orphanage as well; stay to the left there, you without any weapons."

"I did not propose that I would be of any use to you in a fight," Cedrith said rather stiffly.

"Your usefulness, my good *reputable* sage," Alendic spat with verve, "will not be an issue. This is a rescue mission, not a parade. You presume on your friendship with Natasha too far."

"I have few illusions, sir, as to what may remain of my friendship. With anyone," Cedrith said; with rising temper that would have shamed him at any other time, he held his ground and looked to Judgement as well as Natasha. "Friends, after all, build their relations on trust, not on" — and here he glared at Natasha even as he felt his voice crash against the power of his promise, and began to stammer — "-on see-se-secrets!"

He saw Judgement looking to him with a puzzled brow, and knew he could go no farther there; but now the gentle scholar was feeling truly angry, and let his concern show in heat.

"And she's not the only one, is she, young Judgement? Your 'deed' to be done; this has to do with that knight in the cathedral, does it not? From your first day here, you have carried this … this obsession beneath your hat, risking the Law of Conar for your own stiff-backed pride. And now you will no doubt lay some portion of this madness on me, to complete my ruin. As you wish. As you all wish.

"But I too, will have my way. I refuse to let this young lad run off with you to his death, and bear on my soul the thought that I let it happen and did nothing. I shall be there; screaming for help and cringing in fear, no doubt, but there, when it happens."

Alendic slapped a hand against his face as if he were trying to hide in his own sleeve. Natasha, truly stunned by the force of Cedrith's speech, sat back heavily in her chair and said nothing. Cedrith could hear himself panting, and saw his hand shake as he reached for his goblet and drained it.

The actor looked up, and said, "Be reasonable, Sage Fellareon. In three days time, we leave through the gate. Do you think you can get past my guard if I should bar you?"

"I have no training whatsoever to weapons, sir, if that's what you mean. I quite agree you will be able to put me down like a child should it come to a fight between us. I have not had much time to consider, but perhaps if you would be kind enough I could borrow a weapon from you, for this duel."

"Borrow!"

"And furthermore, I would consider it a great courtesy, before that time, if you could lend me a few hours to instruct in the more basic points of fencing." Cedrith sounded remarkably calm, and Alendic's smile began to steal back to its place. "Then, when you had to kill me, I could at least give a good accounting—"

"Enough," Alendic chuckled. "I yield, sir; your courage far outpaces your skill, and that will have to count for something. If you come here tomorrow, we will spar a bit, though I hardly think it will be enough to keep you alive."

"I am in your debt sir," Cedrith said, bowing.

"Not to worry," Alendic returned, "far more than likely, neither of us shall live to see the debt paid."

Natasha sat forward and said, "Cedrith, you cannot come."

"My mind is quite made up, Guildmistress," Cedrith said, being purposefully quite formal.

"I mean it. You may not come through."

"I acknowledge your leadership, but I am coming. I shall follow you every moment if need be, to ascertain your whereabouts. I shall summon the city guard to keep watch—"

"Silly men!" Natasha cried, with a small smile that looked familiar. "Would you stop posing for a moment and just listen to me! Cedrith, you would be the fourth."

Judgement quoted again from the notebook, without looking. "'None shall enter the gate in pairs.' Only three may go."

"Or one," said Natasha.

"No," Alendic said firmly. "I go with you."

Judgement stood. "Five, then."

"Who?" Natasha asked in wonder.

"I shall provide him, if I am able."

"You!" Cedrith cried. "From where, may I ask?"

For answer, Judgement gave only that small shrug he had learned, but his eyes spoke of a plan.

"No end to his talents," Alendic quipped, "and so young. Extra food, I can see, for the Rucksack."

"Ah, yes," Natasha said with a smile, "your infamous Rucksack of Resource. We shall need tricks we have never seen before, on this trip."

"And how fortunate, dear lady," Alendic responded with a bow, "that in my recent tenure here, I have learned some."

Alendic poured more wine into the three goblets, and raised his. "We meet here then, three sunsets from this moment. May the Heroes bless our venture." They all toasted and drank to this, and there was nothing more to say.

⊕ ⊕ ⊕

The Castle of the Wanderers was filled with sight and wrapped in silence. Dismounting in the courtyard, Renan met an old man who came to meet him; the hale elder already bore towards the Conarian knight an attitude somewhere between that of a squire and a peer. He showed Renan the stable for his horse, and after they both tended to Quester, took him to the chapel and refectory, the back-gardens and field, the scribe-house and simple quarters he would call his own. Less than ten words passed between them, none of them a name.

Renan changed to the white and silver garb of a Wanderer and felt deep wonder as he donned the tabard graced with an image of the tower. No ceremony, no initiation or chant or group affirmation; he was treated from the first as if he knew his duties. And in his heart he did.

Set into a cleft of the highest peak in that area of the Marble Swords, the castle was more of a palisade, walling off a small valley from its eastern end, being completely unapproachable from any other quarter. The mists so prevalent before the castle gate were only seen near dawn behind the walls.

The upper tower and ramparts were the only areas not shown to Renan immediately. He ate heartily in the refectory on the simple fare the order raised and grew; he spent time weeding and herding like a commoner in the glorious sunlit fields.

There was time for study of the ancient history of the Lands, and Renan found himself drawn particularly to the chronicles of the Percentalion itself. The tomes here, though not gilt or decorated, were large and very old. He read of the early days of the Wars of Liberation and was amazed at the level of detail displayed by the various scribes of the Order. Each account was penned in person by a knight, witness to the events described, and little effort was spent to draw it all together or make sense of it. The message was simple: history was to be found in the deeds of those who lived it, not in the wisdom of librarians who spent their lives in contemplation. Even the rough hands and childlike grammar of certain authors, on reflection, made sense to the Conarian knight, and he smiled as he pictured these brave men of long ago, probably more fearful to record their own deeds than they had been to face the dangers. Over the first few weeks, he was stunned at the annals of courage, the sheer number of rescues and heroic duels fought by his predecessors long since deceased. And he felt a strong sadness to realize the slow deterioration of the kingdom to the east, as later entries described a capital city abandoned, travelers increasingly rare and imperiled, and chaotic forces abounding.

Renan also noted the small size of the present Order, to his alarm, though he kept his thoughts to himself. Each knight he saw with the tower-tabard greeted him formally and warmly, often without words, as they moved about the grounds to labor, or practice arms, eat or rest. By his own count there were no more than twoscore full members, among which he did not include himself, another ten or twelve of squire-rank, mainly those too old or injured to bear the armor, and occasionally a few refugees brought here by the strange magic of the tower he had not yet entered. In his heart he knew there were questions that must be answered, yet he did not ask them, sensing the time would be right later. Nothing could change his devotion to the Order, for which he had searched all his adult life. If needed, Renan would willingly be the last one here and close the gates forever at a hero's request. What matter, then, to count heads and guess about the future?

He ate meals with the others, in silence and full contentment. The food was good, the taste perhaps improved by the clean high air. Every time Renan caught another man's eye, he saw the clear calm gaze of a fellow in arms, who knew the morrow might bring his death and had no regrets. What call for casual conversation, for witticisms or badinage that impressed the ladies? Each member knew his worth with no need to boast of it. Renan's only regret was that he was not shown his work, and for that he sensed the time was coming.

Nearly everything in the quiet fortress was made of stone. Simple woolen pallets on the beds, vellum books and the wooden hafts of weapons, were among the only exceptions. Furniture, dishes, spoons, farming and crafting tools and other implements were often carved of solid marble. Mystic globes of crystal provided light, and others of granite emanated heat. Many tables, beds, and even some buildings had been carved straight down into the rock itself. Renan wondered at the enormous planning it must have required to envision the castle entire, instead of the patchwork of additions and improvements most modern baileys featured. The giant bucket to draw water from the deep well was carved of slate, and the thick chain links that held it had been ingeniously hewn from a long vein of black marble. It took three men just to turn the wheel to raise it.

In quiet afternoons when labors were done, Renan enjoyed walking to the edge of the cliffs behind the castle, beyond the fields in small meadows where the herds grazed. Copses of miniature trees grew no higher than his chest at this altitude, and were carefully minded by the Order as the only source of living wood. Walking among them, Renan felt gigantic and tiny at the same time; though he looked over their topmost branches, he knew some of these boles were centuries old. Standing among them, he could feel a deep sense of quiet and wisdom, just beyond the reach of his hearing.

He prayed often in the chapel to Conar, feeling now for the first time that his devotions had purpose, his requests were urgent and meaningful, and he carried with him the haunting sense that now, his inmost thoughts were heard as never before. The statue here was only life-sized, but wondrously carved from white marble; here was a leader and king of course, but also a companion in arms, armored as the Order were and ready to ride with them. In the tilting field and arena, Renan strove with a ready will to hone and improve his skills, and found himself by no means the worst of the company. His partners, though far more experienced in real combat from their incursions to the cursed land below, bore no pretence and earnestly asked for his tutelage for this move or feint, as they readily showed him their own. No one here was the true enemy.

In the midst of one such tilt, with the lance at which Renan particularly excelled, the bell from the tower rang once, gently but with resonance and a tone that lasted for minutes. Before it had died away altogether every member of the Order was standing in the courtyard, gazing up at the light emanating from its highest window. Even now, no one spoke, and Renan at last felt a bit left out; evidently a knight was returning but he had not known the details since this member had left during that first evening while he slept. But some looked to him with smiles so sincere and affirming he could not doubt the wisdom of holding his tongue just a while longer.

From the lower entrance where a circular stair was visible rising towards the upper levels, a knight emerged, tired and stained, proud and victorious. Others stepped in to clap his back or grasp his arm; another knight, fully armed and visored, stepped into the tower to ascend the stair. The returning hero looked about and spotted Renan, advancing to grasp him by both arms. From the look in his eye, Renan could tell this was the same man whose voice he heard the night of his entry to the Order. The two embraced heartily then stood back and gazed on each other in friendship while the others formed a silent audience.

"I am Niles," said the knight. "By our custom, the training of the neophyte lays with the man who admits him. But I was called the hour after you arrived and have only just returned."

"I am most pleased, then, to make your acquaintance sir," Renan returned with an honest grin. "What if you had been slain on your mission?"

"The annals do not say. But I knew that I must come back, this time of all times. Most welcome, brave knight, most welcome."

Renan's joy soared to its proper place, as the two men turned back towards the tower and he moved with his guide to complete the mysteries of the Chosen Wanderers.

⊕ ⊕ ⊕

Early evening on the Ninth of the Fire Ant, and a rare autumn thunderstorm pounded down on Conar. The orison windows in the Healer's Guild were high and clear, meant to let in the light of day, so the lightning-flashes looked as if each stroke landed inside. In the comfortable, modest quarters of the Healers Guildmistress, a round, pleasant woman knelt before a small statue of Telhol, earnestly making her devotions. The kindly, serene face of the youngest son of Conar belies the career of a man who taught that the way of peace cannot be spread in places of safety, but only in the face of great peril and near the edge of violence. Whatever comfort he offered to the woman in her silent prayers, she eventually moved away to her desk, there to peruse a book on loan from the Dark Archives of the Sages Guild. It lay open to a page showing a spiral-shaped ring, with the head of a snake. She read its description, for the fortieth time, and let her head sink onto her arms in sobs. A brilliant flash of lightning made the chamber brighter than day, and she sat up with a shout; wiping her eyes, she returned once again to prayer.

Backstage at the theater, the company held an impromptu celebration, drifting in small groups past the dressing room of the handsome *cardinus*, who alternated between unending toasts, unconvincing excuses, unwavering reassurance, and unseen packing. Beneath the actor's bench, a strongly sewn rucksack nearly the height of his shoulder lay festooned with small pockets, coils of cord, tool-holsters and inner chambers. When the thunder boomed overhead, everyone shouted a greeting and hastens to down another libation. Between every few visitors, an item or two was secreted, after some judgment, in an accessible place. His laughter came easily, his smile never faded, and none of the females of the company found him willing to accept their offers this night.

In his cell, Cedrith had squared away his belongings and now alternated between pacing the walls and sitting before a blank sheet of paper addressed to his fiancée in Mendel. He directed himself to write, stopped, laughed aloud without joy, and threw down his pen with unaccustomed distaste. In the corner stood a simple mace and a small round shield, and looking at them, the sage shook his head for a long while. The lightning boomed, making him jump, and brought him somewhat back to himself. He shrugged, and with a grimace sat at the desk to write the only words that occurred to his mind, however overdone and hackneyed they may have been:

My Dearest Kia,

Should you be reading this letter, it will mean that I have died …

⊕ ⊕ ⊕

Osar the blacksmith was angry enough to be called from his supper to the forge, in the midst of such a downpour. But shouting curses from his window at whomever it was to go away only brought renewed pounding. So he stormed down the inner steps from his home into the shop and over to its door in a foul mood. Throwing it open, he staggered back at the sight of a Man in Grey, bearing a tall staff, with streams of dark water sluicing off his cape and the brim of his broad hat. The lightning cracked behind him, and for just a moment, the smith believed that his time had come. But the stranger replied to his stammered demands only by holding out a letter, bearing the mark of his colleague Nador the silversmith. Reading it, Osar grunted reluctantly, shuffling aside to admit him, and pointed wordlessly to the pile of cold-forged ingots in one corner.

The stranger doffed hat and cape, and took his staff to the anvil where he began to measure out several iron plates against it. Osar lingered awhile, to be sure the stripling knew how to use the tools, and was reassured on that score at once. With skill, the youth started to pound a band of finger-thick iron around the end of the anvil, at the right spot on its cone to fit the end of his wooden cudgel. After only a few blows, he stopped and moved to another while giving the first strip, barely bent, a chance to cool. Osar read the note again. "Cold-forged iron," he said, "that's a rare bit of business these days. You'll be at this all night." The grey-haired lad made no verbal response, but took a moment to lay out a strip of silver coins on the side-bench.

Shaking his head, Osar rumbled back into his house, muttering, "Wants to fight with demons, eh, putting cold-forged iron on his stick. Well, he looks the type, by Conar." He lay awake half the night, between the crashing peals of thunder above and the much dimmer, but more disturbing sound of another man pounding below in his own shop. But sleep he finally did, and by morning the grey man was gone.

⊕⊕⊕

In the second floor above Fairnum's Tavern, Treaman set about packing in the room he shared with Linya and Bildon. He paused a while, seeking some place to put a wooden tube with the map-copy inside, and then stuffed it into the bulging central chamber with most everything else.

"Take me an hour to find anything I really need," he muttered.

Bildon hefted his much smaller pack for weight, then put it back down. "Someone really should design one, with more pockets, and perhaps some holders for tools, a real custom job."

Linya nodded in agreement, but as she seemed to carry so much less than the others, they failed to feel her empathy. She was already done and the evening barely dark outside.

"So we're going back," she said simply, sitting on the edge of her bed.

"And why, this time?" Treaman mused with a grin. "We have wealth still, though our leader's way of winning over the town has made a dent in it. What's his reason for going back in, I wonder?"

"Because Mhoral says we shouldn't?" Bildon suggested.

"Because he's onto an even greater treasure," Linya countered, "and though of course he won't tell us, we all know what it is."

"Reghalion?" Treaman asked, and Linya nodded.

"Reghalion. The long-lost, likely haunted, ridiculously perilous capital of the Percentalion. What he specifically hopes us to find there — aside from the usual wagonload of trouble — I don't know. But that's his reason." She mused for a moment, and then added, "Annoying Mhoral is simply an added benefit."

Bildon laughed aloud at that as, on cue, a knock at the door preceded the Elf. He preferred a separate room, and Haltar naturally had needed his privacy, so the group had rented the entire second floor from Fairnum and he was delighted to oblige.

Ignoring the chuckles on his entrance, Mhoral looked around and asked, "Are you coming?"

"What, another carouse!" Bildon cried, but popped up and grabbed his boots.

"We leave in the morning, what better time then?" Mhoral had the same strange look he always did when drinking or celebrating, as if he knew there was something better to do. But he was second only to Haltar in the group when it came to holding down ale, or at gambling; and no matter how stinking drunk he got, Mhoral rose to the defense of any party member in a fight as if he were stone sober.

"Come on, Linya," Bildon pleaded. "You spent every day these past three weeks studying and casting, you deserve to enjoy yourself." It was clear the mage didn't need too much cajoling, and she went for a cape against the night air. "What about you, Treaman?" she asked. "Coming along?"

The woodsman considered for a moment, but then shook his head. "I want to finish packing, get prepared. Have a good time, but remember we go before sun-up." Linya stopped a moment to put on her new head-piece, and Treaman thought to himself it was the perfect complement to the appearance of the sorceress. "You look more the part than ever," he said to her as she adjusted it.

"Wait until you see what it can do," she replied with a wink. They left to the sound of Bildon begging her to give a hint about its magical powers.

"Just promise you didn't give it the power to charm Halflings, I know you've always secretly desired me."

"Sure, desired you to lose your voice," Mhoral said behind the closed door.

Treaman drank the silence for a long moment after they left, looking over at Hallah sleeping atop his bed. Alone with his thoughts, he realized he wasn't going to sleep tonight. The group had assumed he could guide them now, that all difficulties with navigating the chaos-land were resolved. He knew better; some ideas, a little confidence, but still it was mostly luck. He began to run through the list of observations again as he rose and paced the room, and he opened a window to let in outdoor air and better place himself in nature. The night sky was clear and the weather crisp, the ninth of the Fire Ant. Could be excellent hiking weather. Treaman wondered if they would be back in time to see the leaves turn, and then remembered the significant chance they would not be back at all. His heartbeat turned to ash inside him as he felt the responsibility weigh down.

Another knock on the door, and the enormous frame of Haltar shouldered inside. "I thought you were leading the party," Treaman said.

"I came back to fetch you," Haltar replied. "The people want to see the whole group that's saving their way of life, before we leave."

"The hand of destiny is missing a finger, eh?" Treaman retorted. "I bet I can guess which one."

Haltar, to Treaman's surprise, grinned big and friendly. "Let us see," he said, taking a seat on Treaman's bed without noting Hallah and holding up one hand with fingers spread. "I believe we can all guess which of us is the pinky." So saying, he folded it down into the palm.

"Oh but you would never tell him to his face," Treaman shot back, enjoying the game.

"For myself, perhaps the bow-finger," Haltar said carefully.

"Because it's the tallest?"

"Because it mans the weapon," the foot-knight insisted. "Linya, we shall assign the ring-finger place, yes I think folks would like that."

"Leaving myself and Mhoral."

"The Elf is the thumb," Haltar averred decisively; Treaman raised an inquiring brow. "Because he comes first on the hand, we'll tell them, measuring down from the wrist. Between us, because he sticks out and is usually sore." Treaman laughed so loud at this that Hallah awoke; Haltar, noticing, stood up at once and moved away, still not trusting the creature.

"I hope you're bringing something to keep that scaly stomach fed."

Treaman re-opened his pack, revealing most of the center compartment filled with a small wooden cask of riddy. "She loves it and it keeps forever; there's one problem solved, unless we're out there a year."

In response to this, Haltar dramatically pointed to Treaman with the remaining finger of the hand. "That, my dear woodsman, is up to you."

"Haltar, I … I need to know where we're going."

"You will," Haltar responded from the door with that same maddening confidence. "Will you join us?"

Treaman nodded half in surrender. "Yes, soon, but not for long."

Haltar grinned now in a more predatory fashion. "Just a few drinks." And then he was gone through the door.

The young woodsman looked back out the window and felt the leading edge of colder weather on the night air. He recalled to his mind the bitter winters of his Novarian homeland with a fierce glee: a competitor beaten several times, and now beyond reach.

{*"Bbbrrrrrr!"*}The dragon had sampled the images in Treaman's mind; for amusement, he thought about the enormous montori bulls he had seen as a child, plodding past on the snowbound plains with a hostile Northmen tribe in attendance. Tales told of hairless beasts in the Argensian Empire that were as large, with the same trunks and able to carry several men; he wondered if he would ever see them to compare.

{*"Big! Like Hallah!"*}

"Yes," Treaman agreed, chuckling. "Perhaps a little bigger."

{*"Hungry!"*}

"Awake!" he shot back, going to the large barrel in the corner and removing the lid. Fairnum had been paid two months' rent in advance, and would probably hold the rooms until spring unless he was in desperate need. The group was using the room to store many items, extra weapons, clothing bought for fun; letters of credit which mysteriously established the group's wealth were on file with the banker. It was not a subject that interested Treaman much, but he was happy to have a place to store the rest of his friend's food. Feeding her two of the smelly fish, he stroked her head as he thought about the morrow.

"People going back to the messy-land tomorrow," he said, using the term his dragon had adopted. Hallah looked up at him with those jewel eyes. "Maybe Hallah would like to stay in the town, safe."

{*"Hallah go with Treaman. Help save him from messy-place monsters."*}

"Lots of food here for Hallah," Treaman persisted, pointing to the barrel. "The nice man here could feed Hallah," he said, though not at all sure that Fairnum would agree.

{*"Hallah go with Treaman. Save him."*}

"Yes," Treaman admitted with a stroke under her chin, "more than likely you will have to."

A third time came a knock on the door; the apple-cheeked blonde who peered fearfully in had clearly been crying. "There's … someone to see you," she said quietly.

"Thanks Marindya; but Haltar is out—"

"I know where he is!" the girl wailed, pulling her head back and retreating down the corridor with a yowl of pain. Through the small opening she left behind, the slender lad in white entered.

"You! The scribe's apprentice—"

"Anteris, sir."

"Yes, but as I said, Haltar is away."

"I came to speak with you, sir; that is, if you don't mind. And if … if you still have the book."

Treaman stared at the boy, uncomprehending. Anteris looked to the doorway as if expecting pursuit, then back.

"I thought — if you don't mind … perhaps I might look at it, and be of some … assistance. With the translation."

"Oh! Oh, I see, yes … yes, by all means. Come in."

Waving the boy to a seat, Treaman rifled a chest by the wall and pulled forth the tome wrapped in hide. Mhoral had fair-copied all the Common speech and they spent over one hundred silver pieces for a single sheet of onionskin parchment from the local mage to trace the map. Tricky work, for as it turned out the added lines were only visible when wet with hot fluid and under magical light. It had been only the sheerest chance that they discovered this in Valenthur's study a few days ago. Tracing through wet paper was an ordeal, but the thin vellum was remarkably strong and light, resting now in the scroll-case for their use in the wild.

Treaman unwrapped and opened the original tome on top of the chest so they could both see. He flipped open to the map page and pointed directly to the tiny scrawl beneath the drawing of the palace wall. Whereas the other lines and markings had faded without the heated water, the words in Ancient remained intact.

Anteris bent down to examine them, and slowly worked out the words.

"*Supir … mentum … ar … loctu.*" He sat back and considered. "The mind is where the highest hope? No, that is in the wrong voice. The place of hope is in the high mind." He shrugged helplessly. "I am sorry, sir, I am only a student."

Treaman patted his shoulder in a companionable way, though he was indeed bitterly disappointed. "Not to worry, I'm sure we'll make sense of it somehow. Let me just jot down those translations." Even with his back turned, he could tell the youth was watching his every move, and when he faced him again, Treaman could see the fire in his eyes, though his face was saddened by failure.

"So, you work for the scribe?"

"The sage Valenthur, yes sir. He is the author of the Kingdom Chronicle."

"I see," Treaman said to be polite. "So this work has kept the events of every year since…"

"Since the founding of the kingdom of Conar," the boy stated proudly. "It takes half a floor of the library just to house the volumes."

"Have you read about the Tridium, then?" the woodsman asked deferentially. His good intentions to ask either Valenthur or Alaetar had been effectively wrecked by that first, and probably only, visit.

Anteris nodded and Treaman gestured for him to continue.

"The Scepter of Law, the Order-Brow and the Sword of Air were all created for Areghel after the Second War of Liberation. The first was of gold set with the gems of kingship, to tame the earth and set the ways straight. The second, a matchless crown also of gold, helped the king to see across his kingdom and locate Despairing forces within it. And the Sword, forged it is said from a slice of the noon sun, allowed him to call upon the power of Hope to assist him in war.

"All of Areghel's rightful issue, when invested on the throne in Reghalion with Sword, Scepter and Crown, could hold the ways straight and keep back the tide of chaos which had engulfed the kingdom before. And which does so again, now that the line has ended."

"Clearly," Treaman said, "these were mighty artifacts, if the legends are true, ensorcelled with incredible power."

"And very valuable," the boy replied with some suspicion.

"And much better found than lost," the woodsman riposted. The youth took this in, torn between his teaching and his longing. "Listen here, I do not advise that our path is best for all, nor even very many. I can do it, and I do it rather well" — Treaman realized he was talking to himself now — "and it is work that needs doing."

"I know," Anteris said quietly. "I wish I could help you."

"You have, you have," Treaman assured him, as it cost him nothing to be kind. "The translation, it gives me something to think about."

"The difficulty, sir, is that the Ancient tongue has many synonyms, more even than the common one. Place, location, and mind, thought, opinion, then high, highest, top, summit, crown, peak, above—"

"Peak? Hold, hold on there," Treaman said, reaching for the note paper again. "So this word here, 'supir,' could mean any of those things? How about 'peak-hope-locate-mind' or something?" Maybe you can find your hope on the mountain, the peak, Skysword."

Anteris looked again on the passage. "The place … of hope, at the peak of the mind. It doesn't seem quite—"

"Crown!" Treaman shouted, and Hallah whooped and rustled on the bed in response. Anteris looked to her, smiling if a bit nervous. "Oh she's fine, we just have a — she gets excited when I do, never mind."

"What do you mean by 'crown'?" Anteris asked.

"I'm not sure; how about 'find the crown with a hopeful mind,' does that work?"

"No, sir," the student said with a broad smile, "but perhaps 'the crown of mind.' The Order-Brow!"

"Wonderful! But where?" Treaman asked eagerly.

Anteris bent once again to the paper, and slowly said, "The mind crown, hope in place. The crown in the highest place. I am sorry, sir, there seems to be no verb. It is a riddle."

{*"Hungry!"*}

"Do not trouble about it further, Anteris. I appreciate the help. Excuse me, my dragon is hungry."

"How do you know?"

"Oh, she can make herself understood." Treaman smiled as he lifted the lid from the barrel. He saw the young man looking at her with more interest than trepidation, and wanted to reward him for his help. "Would you like to feed her?"

With shining eyes, the boy looked to the woodsman, who handed him some riddy. He held them out gingerly to the dragon on the bed, who craned forward and snatched them with gusto. Once she nipped his finger and he cried out but laughed as well.

{*"Boy Good!"*}

"Yes, he's very good," Treaman said, stroking her.

"She is happy?" Anteris asked.

"She says you are good. Though of course it isn't always perfectly clear what she means. A bit like Ancient, I suppose. It depends how much of your finger she got ahold of."

They both laughed then, and rose to leave. "I hope you will return triumphant, sir," Anteris said sincerely.

"I thank you, Anteris; for my own part, any condition in which I see you again will be good enough for me." At the bottom of the inn stairs, Treaman looked both ways to be sure Valenthur wasn't in sight, and they said goodbye. Then the woodsman went to join the farewell party; it did not require his tracking skills to locate, he simply followed the noise to its center.

⊕ ⊕ ⊕

The Wall's Walk was a guards' tavern, frequented by the men of Conar's watch when between duty shifts, and half-full when the stranger entered. He stood by the door in his unfamiliar uniform, looking for someone. The talk never died out completely, but it did leach down to a simmer, and everyone was aware of the grey man by the time he spotted the dekentar of the south gate. The guardsman finally saw him as well, drawn by the fading noise, and as the two locked gazes, the latter's face hardened towards hatred. The elder man stood and stormed over to the door, stopping within arm's reach of where the young stranger stood silently with his iron-shod staff in one hand.

"What are you doing here?" the guardsman challenged.

"Keeping your word for you," the grey man replied. "You said we would meet again."

By now, it was quiet enough for all to hear. There could be no mistaking such intent among men of war, and the dekentar threw back his cape with a motion that cleared room. Smoothly, the Man in Grey stepped in a half-pace, just enough to make drawing a weapon difficult.

"You think I'm afraid of you!" the guard bellowed.

"Quite the opposite, I'm counting on your courage."

"The arena then! You name the time."

"The time is tonight, before sunset."

"And I'll be there."

"Then you will miss me, for the place is the theater."

Chuckles bubbled from the surrounding tables. "Oho, I get it; he only wants to *rehearse* for a fight!" "Dear me, what can you wear that goes with grey?" "I love those wooden swords they use!"

The dekentar boiled over at this easy, neutral jeering. "You think I'll stand to be mocked? You'll eat arena dust for this!"

His opponent did not retreat an inch, and kept his voice low and calm. "You mean, a fight to the blood? Is that the extent of the insult, all you wish from my body?"

This offer shut the dekentar's jaw a moment, and some among the closest listeners caught the gist as well. "—fight to the death, he said." "Conar's balls, look, it's just a lad." "Hair is grey, but—"

"After all," the stranger pursued, "if you don't feel I insulted the honor of your clan sufficiently, I can always add to my story. Would you prefer here or in private?"

"I will kill you!" the dekentar cried, clenching his fists.

"Aye," returned the grey youth, "if you can. But on my terms." Wheeling to give the dekentar his unprotected back, he returned to the street. His adversary could not forbear to follow, and behind him the tavern returned to normal.

"Terms!" he shouted as the grey man turned back on the curb. "Are you offering a death-duel or not?"

"Just these: you accompany me tonight, into the theater, and together we take whatever adventure may pass. The following morning, if we both survive, I will go to the arena with you and fight barehanded against your sword, if that is your wish."

"What crazy talk is this, an adventure in the theater. What game are you playing with me, you Gypsy thief?"

"The details … would do nothing to convince you. But take my word if you ever did, there will be the risk of death inside that hall this evening, for both of us. If you have no stomach to fight for your life, then do not come."

"I'm not afraid of you."

"Aye, of me you should be the least afraid, I agree."

"No," the dekentar said, growing wary. "Men cannot fight in the theater or anywhere else in Conar except the arena. I'll not be tricked into breaking the Law."

"We will not be inside the theater, but…" and here the stranger broke off, confirming the guard's suspicions.

"You coward! No tricks, no evasions, you meet me in the arena or else I'll let everyone know how you wormed about when faced by an honest man."

"You think my honor will—" and the stranger cut himself off, seeming for once uncertain of his course. He took a moment, then leaned in uncomfortably close to speak in an ear despite their privacy.

"You perhaps asked members of your clan, about the man in the cathedral."

"Aye," hissed the dekentar, "the baron's son you insulted is a cousin, he told me how you tried to demean his honor with your spell."

"And he assured you, did he not, that the knight at the statue was worth watching."

"Oh aye, it's vital that we not let him from our sight, not one moment." The dekentar drew his chin up proudly. "I have been asked to help keep the watch myself. Never fear on that score."

"Certes, he must never escape."

"Never," the dekentar affirmed.

"Then you will meet me at the theater this evening," the stranger countered evenly. "Unless you are with me, whatever you believe, then

I promise you this: within the week, that man will indeed be gone from the city, and your clan will fail in its efforts to keep him here."

The dekentar started to deny it, but the Man in Grey overrode him. "And you will be the only one to know that I told you this. Thus the blame for the knight's escape will lie on you."

The guard pushed back from his enemy then, and glared at him with undiluted hatred. "I'll have you arrested."

"Indeed, on what charge?" the Man in Grey riposted. "Conspiring to help the most admired man in the city? On my honor, Conar's Law will be shattered, just to hear my tale. And we shall be sure to have a Mensor present, when I tell it."

The dekentar was startled to remember that day, and now his scowl looked as if it would tear his face in half.

"You spit dung all over the name of the clan Altrindur, and for what?"

"I expect you to believe none of what I say, but I bear the clan no ill will. There has been … a terrible error, and I seek to uphold the Law."

"Banwen Altrindur is dead!" the dekentar hissed.

"A man defended his betrothed from an unwanted advance. No more."

"Fantasy! You're mad, and a coward, and you are here to destroy this city. I'll see you dead on the arena floor."

"Aye. Tomorrow. But tonight you will accompany us. When the deed is done, it will be too late for your honor."

The dekentar, breathing hard, suddenly burst into a string of curses; some guardsmen about to enter the tavern came to a halt and stared. To judge by the reaction of the Man in Grey, they were arguing about the weather for the morrow. The dekentar turned back to the door, and punched it as hard as he could with his gauntleted fist.

"You will be there," the grey man offered to his back. After a few moments, the dekentar nodded.

"One thing more. Say goodbye to your family." The dekentar laughed at this, and turned around to insult his foe again. But the stranger was gone.

⊕ ⊕ ⊕

Excerpt from the Nameless Tome of Faltus Fanem

When I discovered Polanquan's Plane, the glassy surface of his mirror showed me the end of his story first. Yet it was only after long research that I saw anything there besides my own reflection. Today, I see only my reflection again, and I know my race is soon run. Even were my enemies not coming, my mind cannot much longer hold what it knows. I am prepared; be you the same, reader.

In the midst of my magical researches some months ago — I write this in the sixteenth century since the Dagnor Rokan, though I have taken pains to make it appear I lived four hundred years earlier — a friend wrote to beg my assistance. He was heir to the fabled Hall of Mirrors, which had been established in the early days of the city and unfortunately fallen on harder times recently. Artisans have recovered the lore of fashioning reflective surfaces in glass and so the curiosity of seeing mirrors in his family hall was no longer a novelty. In clearing the house for other purposes, my friend uncovered a mirror lying in a forgotten upper chamber of the manor that emanated magical aura. Its surface was perfectly smooth showing a magnificent reflection, and the dark wooden frame was carved in the style of the more recent period, yet of a tree quite rare since much earlier times, first or second century ADR, I thought certainly. Who had saved ancient wood for so long? I became intrigued, as the mirror appeared to be a scrying tool, but heavily limited in some way. I knew it would take substantial attention and study before I could master the process of aligning its pronasm *to me, and unlocking its secrets. Something about that quiet, perfect plane of glass spoke to me, and I became determined to know its message. Thanking my friend sincerely for his gift, I packed the mirror away to my country estate, taking leave from the Guild so that I could concentrate on the task. I was several months there in seclusion, and never heard that my friend had died of a rare disease within two weeks of my departure, one that had struck him within a day of his discovery. The arm of the Enemy, hidden somewhere beyond this world, is long.*

The sorcerous energies bound into this scrying tool were of a powerful yet limited nature, a kind I discuss at length in my work "Thaumaturgy Practicum." A mage who worries, perhaps, that a mystic tool such as an enchanted sword will do too much damage in the wrong hands, can place wards upon the item so that it only expresses its function at the fulfillment of some condition. These limitations became very popular in ancient times, shortly after the Wars of Liberation, though some complained they made artifacts too difficult to use well. In recent centuries, wards and limitations have become rare, but so too have items of great power or the need to create them.

Such limitations can require a password, or function only in the presence of the threat the item is designed to counter, or nearly any such condition the creator can imagine (provided he has the time and strength to create them). In the case of the Plane, the limits were severe, and my efforts to learn about the item triggered more such guards, until my chance to discern anything had nearly vanished before I could see the danger. The key came on an inspired day — evening, actually, for I had worked beyond the sunset without realizing it — as I sensed from my casting that I could, if I desired, unlock the mirror's scrying capabilities now at will. Yet I learned also that if I were to do so, and use it to view, say, the city of Argens or Conar even once, the mirror would forever become "only" that; as if the ability to see across any distance were a trivial matter! I had in my possession a tool with which I could view any location, even ones I had only read about, and more, it seemed to have the chance to look back into time. The possibilities for learning beggared my ability to describe them. But I sensed with certainty that this tool could serve its created purpose, if allowed now and for all time to do less. Knowing as I write, what was meant by this intelligence, I deliberately describe it in such a way to you, dear reader, that you may understand the choice I made. I later realized that the Plane's creator, Polanquan, knew his enemies could never choose less power, thus forming the item's most effective ward.

I took several hours for contemplation on this, and I prayed to Rallantan that he would reveal to me the proper course. The wisest of the Heroes, advisor to warlords and mages, he who unlocked the secrets of the early world, is now the inspiration for bards and sages everywhere. I confess I have been an indifferent devotee until recent days, but I always guided my life by the precepts he laid down, and in this fateful hour, when my inner voice whispered I was choosing the path of my remaining days, I came back in the end to his most famous dictum: "Knowledge is power." Reflecting on that I realized that the strength of the item could never be separated from its truest purpose. Turning aside from its free use under my control, and accepting what its limits would show to me, I activated the Plane. My reflection vanished and I saw instead visions of the ancient age: the Plane of Polanquan could scry across time, and it showed me what its creator intended should be known.

When next I came to myself, my servants informed me that two days had passed. They had thrown a rug over the Plane after I became agitated, screaming and thrashing. I was weak with hunger and thirst, terrorized from lack of sleep and unable to move to my bed without assistance. Every scrap of blank vellum in my study was covered with notes, taken by a stranger using my hand. As I lay abed sipping watered wine and reading them over, the memories came back to me, from the ending first moving towards the start. The story in full, dear reader, is lost to us, I am responsible, and by that I mean you may thank me for your life. What I dare to reveal hereafter, some part of that story, I tell in the proper order for your convenience. But take warning from what I saw first, and which I describe now, lest you follow in Exeter's path, and in mine.

My first vision in the Plane was of a man, in the act of creating the mirror itself. The pouring and casting had been completed and now he set the beveled glass into the dark wood frame he had prepared. All about him in his workroom were the materials he had evidently used in its creation; I saw melting fires still smoldering and raw ores in heaps. I saw later, but already sensed, the work had taken him months. And more: a second mirror, identical to the one being made, stood in a corner. At last he had completed his mystery, exhausted as he was, yet he moved with great urgency to carefully wrap the new mirror unused, its glass still warm; summoning servants he marked down an address I could clearly see. The very Hall of Mirrors in the city of Conar! The man left no indication of who was the sender, and the men who carried the mirror did not wear the livery of his house. It was sure to be treated as an anonymous gift, and put in a remote place, hidden from the Enemy.

I could see clearly through the mirror but I could not hear; the vision was soundless. Moving rapidly about the room and around the manor, the man gathered papers and books by the armload; to my horror, he brought them back to his workroom and burned them. He was in frantic haste now, constantly starting at every noise and looking about in mounting fear. One remaining servant, clearly offering to help, was dismissed with a gift of a golden candlestick, obviously a permanent parting. The man shouted at the butler, ordering him forth with hysteria, and the servant reluctantly took his leave.

He seemed to have completed the destruction of those of his own writings which had somehow offended him, and now sat at his desk in a state of high agitation. He knelt for a brief prayer, and then rose to pen a final document. It was a last will and testament, in the Ancient script, and I could clearly see the date, to my shock; it was the fifth year by the old calendar, the very earliest days of Conar! I was scrying a man who lived during the lifetime of the Hopelord, and Shilar and all the Heroes. It was blasphemy to even think it, yet the man who writes in Ancient cannot lie any more than if he speaks it. How had he managed to disguise the style of his mirror after that of a far future day? Of course, his creation itself was proof that he could scry across time. So his mirror sent away would one day appear to have been the creation of a later age; still more disguise. I saw his name, Exeter Polanquan, and vowed to research him.

He had not gotten very far in his writing when he suddenly turned as if at a sound. His eyes went wide at an intruder I could not see, and he stood for combat, composed or even resigned. The mirror carried no sound, and he did not speak to his unseen assailant; but just before the death-fight erupted, the mirror-maker looked for an instant directly into my eyes. In a flash that shocked me to my core,

I knew: he had foreseen the moment of his death, knew even that I would one day be watching him die, and desperately hoped that not all would be lost. I have been haunted by his need since that moment.

The duel was furious, destructive, powerful and brief. Exeter Polanquan cast bolts of mystic force, erected spell defenses, summoned creatures to his aid; his face though etched with dread showed no sign of panic. From his foe came every counter-force required and more; the room they were in dissolved in a shambles yet the defender remained untouched, as if by wicked design until his energies were spent. He fell to one knee and at last his foe came into my view: tall and impossibly spare, cloaked in black and with skeletal hands, neck and jaw. It came to me that in these early days Despair roamed free, indeed over most of the Lands; this powerful mage must have transported himself to Exeter's home by spell, and could well escape with no guards in call. Yet the creator of the mirror must have known that no force could stop this foe; indeed, he had foreseen it. Now, as the home burned and fell around him, this wraith stepped forward and dragged Exeter to his feet. The enemy placed one hand across the mage's face and I saw scars spring into being like tracks of rain as he soundlessly howled. Energy moved from the man to the monster, and I knew I was watching his very life drained away into his foe. The skin of his hands and neck darkened and shriveled, his wounds ceased bleeding, and shortly thereafter a gently-smoking corpse fell to the floor. A small trickle of miasma *arose — surprisingly little, I thought, and then again reflected on his foreknowledge — and the creature seemed to inhale that as well. Leaning down, it incanted a spell with dry lips and carved with its naked hand a rent in Exeter's chest, ripping forth his heart. Another incantation and the heart was cased in crystal, tucked away in the creature's robe. Calling out, the enemy commanded Exeter's corpse to rise, and it did; I knew the horror of seeing the undead, a soulless gaunt now enslaved to the sorcery of Despair. Powerless yet aware, the shell that had once held a child of Hope turned to do his master's bidding, to uncover the secret place, bring him his notes, and later to destroy the dopple-glass. I realized with a thrill that both paper and plane were fakes, set to confuse the foe. The monster ordered its thrall to destroy his own manor house by fire, and it did so without hesitation. Well satisfied, the enemy turned away, and it was then that my servants, hearing my wracking screams, had run to intercept my view and carry me off.*

For I had looked upon the face of the liche Wolga Vrule.

⊕ ⊕ ⊕

The rain hung on past noon on the Tenth of the Fire Ant, and by the time the sun broke brilliantly through the clearing clouds the City of Wonders had been scrubbed clean to its last corner and crevice. Architecture two millennia older than the Battle of the Razor shone as if new, and everywhere folks went about last business with a spring in their step as if the day were only starting. Outside the theater, Cedrith Fellareon stood with his traveling cape and gloves on; a large sack leaned against the doorpost, keeping his weapons from public view. He paced uselessly, drawing no comfort from the unseasonable warmth of the westering sun. At this hour, hardly anyone passed and he was alone with his thoughts. Finally, a city guardsman approached down the lonely lane, evidently in no hurry but fully equipped as if for duty; he hesitated at the theater door, bowed briefly to the Elf, and then stood looking carefully past him in both directions on the street.

Facing opposite ways, the two men started and whirled at the same moment to each other.

"The dekentar from the south gate!" Cedrith cried.

"You! The Sage, his friend," the guardsman said, and then spat to one side. "He's roped you into this as well?"

Both men swallowed what they were going to say next, and just stood for a time in embarrassment. Cedrith extended his hand and the dekentar took it briefly. "So you are the fifth?" the sage asked, and in response the soldier looked askance at him.

The ring of iron on stone brought them both around, as the Man in Grey came down the street. He stopped before them, nodding to Cedrith and saying to the dekentar only, "You have come."

"Aye, but I'll not stay," the dekentar ground back with hatred. "You tricked me into this meeting, but I'll not follow you anywhere, as a fifth or a fiftieth!"

"You will have no complaints of the leader," the youth assured him.

"Who?" the soldier demanded, as the theater door opened on cue to reveal Natasha Ioki standing within.

"Guildmistress!" he exclaimed in shock and bowed to her. Cedrith noted the woman's stern look and was surprised to see her accept, for once, the privileges of her station. The guardsman's immediate deference reminded Cedrith that he had come to know one of the most famous persons in the city. Indeed, the Healers Guildmistress was revered throughout the kingdom, and this one, so recently ascended to her station, combined marvelous skill with a commoner's touch and popularity. He had introduced young Judgement to her; all that lay ahead weighed on his heart.

She gestured for the others to enter, and behind her stood Alendic with an overlength pack on his back. No one hesitated, and no one spoke as the four men accepted her leadership without further comment. Natasha and Alendic guided the others through the theater's side halls and out onto the edge of the stage, where the proscenium lay open above to the sunset sky. Here was a heat-brazier, a lantern-pole for light and a table with food. Alendic dropped his rucksack to the stage floor with a heavy thud, and Cedrith followed suit.

"This is a rescue mission," Natasha said crisply with arms akimbo on her wide hips. "We seek to enter a place of great danger to retrieve a fallen comrade, or his remains." She looked hard at the dekentar next. "You will see things you had not thought possible, and some will appear very threatening. But we are not seeking a contest of strength."

The dekentar nodded, yet Alendic carried on.

"As you know, the Guildmistress is a follower of Telhol and will take no direct part in a violent act. We all must be prepared to defend her person—"

"I can handle myself," the lady protested, but Alendic ground on.

"To defend her with our lives. For I assure you, without our leader none of us will ever return, alive or otherwise."

The dekentar swallowed, but nodded and said, "I pledge my sword to the Guildmistress of Conar."

Alendic said, "Ah fine, and let us take a look at how good that sword is, shall we, sir?" Drawing him over to the center of the stage, the actor unsheathed his broadsword and a long bullwhip. The dekentar drew his blade and unlimbered his shield, but the actor said, "I see a main-gauche there, can you fight two-handed? Good, then leave the shield and let us spar this way."

Cedrith and Judgement watched the fight with interest, and it was evident that, while the dekentar had skill and decision, Alendic was a master-swordsman. Time and again, as he circled and danced, he drew the dekentar on, not giving him pause and forcing his best moves and steps. Frequently, he licked the whip in his partner's direction, never a strong blow and always from different angles; his strikes were unpredictable and the guardsman was cursing with frustration long before he started to sweat.

"He did the same with me, that whip," Cedrith murmured to Judgement, and the Man in Grey nodded in agreement.

Natasha ignored the fight, instead praying to one side and checking again her belt and small pack. With a shout Alendic signaled the fight was over and congratulated the dekentar with good spirits. They approached the board and poured large tankards for themselves.

"Nothing but ale tonight, dear sage," Alendic quipped, "but you'll be happy of its warmth before we're through. I recommend it to you." Cedrith accepted a tankard and sipped the unfamiliar brew; Judgement neither ate nor drank.

"This place, to which we go," Alendic said, "will be frightening and alien to your senses. We stay together, and in a fight follow my instructions; with luck, we shall make it at least to the halls of glass. After that…"

"What are the halls of glass? What of this place?" Cedrith asked, but Alendic only shook his head, remarking, "Better not to say too much."

Natasha came to eat a barley-cake, and said, "It could be several hours before the gate appears; the sources do not make that plain. We must remain ready."

"Where did it appear, when you came here?" Judgement asked.

Alendic walked near center stage and pointed to a chalk outline he had made. Judgement looked over the space with great attention but evidently made out nothing. For the first few minutes, everyone stared at the spot. The remainder of the half-hour, it was difficult not to glance in the direction constantly. But by the time night had fallen, all curiosity was exhausted and Cedrith found himself wandering the upstage area examining the backdrop, with its overhead ropes and catwalks.

He took in the ancient but vigorous colors of the scenery, not daring to touch the thick supple curtain drawn tight and painted with great detail. Cedrith could smell that unmistakable scent of the theater, a world in paint and sawed wood, and realized that a strong sense of unreality had hold of him here. Surely, all this talk was another play; Alendic and Natasha would burst into laughter at the prank and fall on each other until the tears came. Only a small and quite unreasonable voice deep inside him insisted that at any moment, a mystic gate to doom would open, and then he would be called upon either to die or forswear himself. Neither option seemed in the least bit possible to him. Was this what adventurers truly did, he wondered. Did they constantly vow to face death, and then keep their word?

Musing so grimly, he nearly collided with a ladder set against the stage; looking up he saw Solemn Judgement balanced on the topmost rung. With only the bright stars overhead for light, the youth was peering at something high up on the metal track that held the sun to its course. Framed by the night-heavens, the youth's face seemed younger, in its eagerness, but that changed as soon as Cedrith spoke.

"My friend, what is the matter there?"

"The track of the sun, perhaps you recall, during the play it seemed amiss?" Cedrith had to think a moment, and then the scene came back to him, the day they had met Alendic.

"Is it broken then? A bad repair, possibly?"

"I had thought so, but it is intact. A bit dirty perhaps, just a moment—" and here Judgement reached with his gauntleted finger into a part of the track that Cedrith could not see. "There, it is cleaner now. There is no sign of repair, or breakage. The sun is meant to describe a small circle before it sets."

Cedrith tried to address his mind to this mystery, but everything about the setting foiled him. The mundane fact, the pointless conclusion, and the background of death that awaited them — he could not bring himself to think about stagecraft at a time like this.

As ever, his companion did not need outside guidance; turning atop the ladder, he called out, "Alendic." Cedrith realized it was the first time he ever heard Judgement address the actor by name. The man came over, and Judgement repeated his observations to him.

"A circle at sunset? You are joking, surely — no wait, I take that back," Alendic quipped, and then mounted lightly up the ladder to stand next to the Man in Grey; Cedrith reached out impulsively to steady the wood. It creaked under so much weight, but neither man paid the slightest heed as they both craned in to see the track.

"Getting too dark, and the moon's not up yet," Alendic muttered. "Hey, Natasha, can you bring a light here?"

The Guildmistress walked in their direction but did not carry the lantern. Looking up at them with a quiet face, she said, "Judgement can do it."

The youth looked down on her and replied, "Mistress?"

"The miracle of light is elementary," Natasha said, and her face held a look of consequence. "In the Ancient tongue, you merely call for 'light,' and your belief will supply the rest." She stood with arms crossed, daring him from below.

Judgement looked back with a hard countenance, and then turned to face the track again. Raising one hand, he called in a steady voice, "*Luxar,*" and a blue sphere of light came into being in his palm, slicing the area with illumination and shadow. Alendic nodded down to Natasha, then clapped Judgement on the back as they both looked in again.

"No doubt about it: this track was designed to make the sun do that," Alendic chuckled as he slid down on the outer frame of the ladder. "And here I thought it was just the quirk of an old hall, put there by Conar to tease me and distract from my speech." Judgement came down more slowly, using one hand as he continued to cradle the light in his other.

Everyone was gathered now and looking on the still blue fire in their companion's grip; even the dekentar had a different temper to his gaze, for the moment. Cedrith reached out to touch Judgement's shoulder, saying, "This is very well done indeed, Guildsman."

Judgement looked to Natasha as if asking a question. Cedrith hoped the time for release had come, but she spoke carefully in return, "You have done this … properly."

Alendic quipped, "Yes, well done," and then aside to Natasha, "Tell him the one to destroy undead." She cautioned him with a finger and he held up both hands.

"The call for light is quite easy," she clarified, as if deliberately making a smaller thing of what had happened. "With practice, one can summon light that mimics one of the moons, or the sun, if the need arises, for various purposes." Cedrith thought she was giving the youth further reason to doubt his ability, and began to dislike her again as he had before.

The dekentar said simply, "It's a miracle," and as at a signal, Judgement clapped his palm shut, making the light disappear. He stood in thought as if the others were not there, but Alendic fidgeted at once, and moved back to the table. "A celebration, come," he said with a gesture meant to lead them. They followed, Judgement the slowest, still thinking as the tankards were poured.

"The sun governs the zodiac year we are in," the grey man said. "It speaks to the center, the heart of power and mystery."

"Indeed," Natasha replied. "As the month now is named for the Fire Ant, the good soldier, and the planetary influence," pointing to the brightest star overhead, "is Areghel, also reinforcing the notion of battle in a righteous cause."

Judgement nodded. "Yet also," pointing closer to the horizon-south, where the walls of the theater blocked their view, "it is the last month where the bolt of the Arbalest can fall before he retreats for the winter. Not a good omen, for sudden death to fall from above."

"Astrology, too?" Cedrith said half in jest. "Are you reading our doom in the stars tonight, Guildsman?"

The youth with a man's face returned his usual steady gaze, and said only, "It was part of my training, my father's teaching. He knew and named all the zodiac you have here, in this world. But their order is altered, and the calculus of the generation is different."

"The order is different, you say. Which month were you born to?"

"By sign, the Hawk. By number, the tenth. But the days of each month varied … there."

"Well then, this being the tenth month, why not declare that today is your birth-day?" Cedrith suggested. "And for lack of certainty, we shall call you sixteen years this day, old enough to inherit, were you a nobleman. Old enough to win your spurs," and here Cedrith paused, hoping he hadn't touched a sore spot with the orphaned lad. "If I recall correctly, this is the generation of the Hawk as well, so the symbol of your first world is still represented. I say we take this as a sign, and commemorate it accordingly."

"All signs can be interpreted, Eldest, but the Sun … this is surely most important. For it to be itself a mystery—"

"Sink the sun, and the raft of stars with it," Alendic scoffed as he pressed a tankard into Judgement's hand. "I've had enough of astrology for two lifetimes, and I won't even see all of this one. Teach me none of it."

"To Solemn Judgement, then," said Natasha, raising her mug. "On this day by custom we praise the honored one. I call him honest."

"Well-spoken! When he chooses to speak at all," Alendic put in, raising his goblet as well.

Cedrith joined in with his arm before his mouth.

"To the man, of all I have met, most noble," he managed, feeling a bit odd but wanting to compliment his friend.

They all looked to the dekentar then, who seemed startled. After a moment and a scowl, he slowly raised his arm, and said only, "Persistent."

A general laugh followed this, and Natasha concluded the toast, "On this the tenth of the tenth in 1995, then, a happy birth-day to Solemn Judgement." They all answered, "To Judgement," and drank.

Cedrith saw that the young man had not moved to drink, and was staring again as if through the group. This truly was a breach of manners; he murmured, "Judgement, the toast."

In reply, Judgement said, "Eldest, the door."

Whirling around, the party looked behind them in the direction he was facing. Unal the upper moon had risen over the proscenium to shed its pale blonde light across the hall. On the center of the stage there was a shimmering rectangle of golden radiance where nothing had been before.

In all the theater, across the stage and hall and as far as the brilliant stars overhead, there was not a sound. The group stood stock-still and stared; Cedrith felt a wave of fear so unmixed he became sick. Alendic put down his goblet with deliberation and moved to take up his rucksack. "The end of the party, everyone, or perhaps its beginning. It depends how fey you feel." Everyone shuffled closer to the portal now, and Cedrith took his mace and shield from his pack, clumsily limbering his hands as the others armed themselves and arrayed about Natasha at Alendic's direction from the front closest to the gate.

"We step through together, and then remove from each other a pace so we can work," he said tersely. "Keep Natasha defended from all sides, at all times, clear?"

"May the Heroes protect us," breathed the Guildmistress. Judgement, standing to the rear, held his staff in both hands across his body; his face was calm but his knuckles were bereft of blood. Cedrith, to one side of Natasha, caught the dekentar's eye as he looked around. The guard signaled with his eyebrow and shrugged up with one arm; Cedrith realized his intent, and obediently held his shield a little higher.

"And … now," Alendic said, as the party stepped through the portal together. An instant later, they stood on the other side of the shimmering curtain, still on the stage.

Natasha, Alendic and the dekentar began to exclaim and curse and demand all at once. Ten minutes later, the frustration level was peaking: the group had tried walking through both ways, using Natasha as leader, running instead of walking, every variation they could think of. Alendic threw his sword to the stage floor with a curse, and the others scattered a bit to get some distance on the mutual tension.

"How much longer will it stay open?" Alendic demanded.

"Not long," Natasha said. "Perhaps the night. Probably not past moonset."

"It's a fake," the dekentar swore, "all part of the trick this liar is playing."

"The notes," Judgement suggested. The leather-bound book was produced from a top pocket on Alendic's rucksack, and Natasha began to read, pacing slowly and keeping within the light of the stage-lantern.

"'With any two who enter, another must attend, for none shall enter the gate in pairs…'"

"It is as I thought," Alendic asserted. "There needs be only three of us. Sage Fellareon, you and the dekentar must remain behind."

Cedrith felt a rush of nameless emotion, but the dekentar ground in. "Not one chance of that. I'll not allow him to escape me."

"'Those who have come before may enter,'" Natasha read to herself, "'and the pairs also may follow the thread.' See, Alendic, there can be more than one pair, it clearly says so. 'Visit alone and one must— '"

"Mistress," Solemn Judgement interrupted, "do not move."

Natasha stopped, and looked at the Man in Grey.

"Back, one step," he asked, and she did. "There," he said, and slowly walked to come between her and the portal. The upper moon bathed the scene, and as he came to a stop Cedrith could see nothing whatever on the bare stage he stared at. Judgement stood looking down for a long moment, then stooped with deliberation as if he were afraid of scaring off a stray animal. Biting off one of his gauntlets, he reached down with his fingers and placed them on the stage, brought them closed, and raised off the floor a thin silver thread. Cedrith felt a jolt to see one end pointing directly towards the portal while the other ran now to join with Natasha's body. As Judgement stood, the line rose with him, not sagging or tight, coming to rest at the level of her heart.

The Guildmistress looked down at her bosom in wonderment: the others too watched in awe, until the dekentar muttered, "It figured he would see something grey."

"As good an explanation as any," Alendic rejoined. "All right everyone, in a line with Natasha to the rear. Touch the string as the lad has, lightly, and follow me through. We'll take formation on the other side."

The dekentar stood second to Alendic, and Cedrith took position behind Judgement. The Man in Grey looked back to him a moment, with a face that nearly spoke of pity, and the Elf found a part of him desperately hoped he would be released, even now. This youth, one quarter his own age, might offer, one last time, to let him remain behind, to free him from his foolhardy vow. But another part of Cedrith knew he would still refuse, and he wondered what had become of the sage he used to know. Better yet, what was about to become of him, headed to certain death in an unknown place?

Through another wave of illness, he smiled brokenly and said, "We must all do our best, I suppose."

"I shall remember the face of my father," was Judgement's response. Then they stepped through the portal and into the Hopeward.

⊕ ⊕ ⊕

Clash of Wills

The first day out had gone very well. The group left quietly in the early dawn, some exhausted from the revels and too little sleep, others elated from not sleeping at all, and Hallah still sleeping. Treaman wondered why Haltar had opted for this furtive exit, instead of a full-town send-off at high noon. But the intensity with which the tall, scarred warrior had led the carouse the previous evening made its point for him; no townsperson could have had a better image than the joyous, liberal heroes of the evening's light. Now, slipped away while the rest slept, they would seem beyond human, magical, mysterious. And as long as they managed to return, that should all come out just fine.

There had been the usual fall in spirits, as the tiny town suddenly disappeared behind them and the broken, formless, useless terrain filled the view on all sides. But here again, Treaman thought, was a cancelling of ills. Already tired from the previous night, any morale lost in their return to chaos went less noticed.

And it had been a good day, with open terrain, no monstrous beasts, and a clear sight of Skysword to the south. Treaman's instinct to stop, or divert paths kicked him on two occasions. In the first, the party took shelter on higher ground before a quake tore the valley path they had been on to chowder. For the other, a storm, there was no cover but no harm either from normal-seeming rain. And on both occasions, the sense of disorientation was less; the sun did not turn nor the mountain move, and everyone noted this unexampled success.

As the sunset approached, Treaman took a half-hour to forage the choppy scrub-woods to the east and succeeded in landing a hunting kill. Hearing a small grunt, he came upon a set of hairy ground-sniffing animals with flat heads, short legs, hornless. He brought down the largest with a single cast of his spear, ending its life without pain. The party was delighted at his return, even Mhoral the cook making a few eager remarks, of another night before turning to the dried rations. The woodsman also found some roots as a bonus, which his senses told him were not poisonous and tasted somewhat like turnip. The meat was not nearly so familiar but it went down well enough; Hallah announced it was very good raw. Bildon had foraged plenty of dry wood and bracken to stoke up the campfire for warmth later, which Haltar graciously allowed.

Treaman settled back that evening with an air of real accomplishment, tired and sore but with his hiking legs already coming back to him. A good mood pervaded the group; Bildon's prank, involving a dagger point and the place Mhoral had reserved for his seat, brought only a bark of pain and a mild cuff. Someone that day was due for one, so now all could relax; the stars were bright and a hint of the autumn season that the outside world was having could still be felt here in the borderland of chaos.

"So," Linya mused aloud meaningfully, "we are back and headed… where, exactly, I wonder?"

Haltar continued examining the edge of his sword, newly forged and wrapped in finest leather on the hilt, as if she was asking Bildon, or Hallah. Everyone grinned.

"Maybe back to Maladon," Mhoral said as if the idea did not interest him.

"Surely," Bildon countered in argument, "we'll need to visit the other ninety-nine before doing one again."

Haltar continued to behave as if no one was speaking, but he did find some unspoken jibe funny enough to gently smile. Treaman waited until the leader drew forth his accursed whetstone, and when the first stroke was just begun, he cried out, "Reghalion!"

The stone hesitated just the slightest fraction–breaking Haltar's oft-repeated rule about the smooth unbroken stroke–and he fell into a full smile, dropping it to the ground in surrender.

"Come on, Haltar," Bildon cried, "who are we going to tell now!"

"I just wonder if we are up to the challenge," the foot-knight replied gamely.

"No, you don't," Mhoral countered at once. "You have made up your mind, and if we die, we die."

Haltar gazed back at his nemesis for a moment, then shrugged and nodded. "Near enough, yes. I don't think finding that book could have been an accident."

"As was the case," Bildon piped in, "with nearly everything else we've done."

"I wonder," Linya said. "Is that how things happen, are we all just stones rolling around in a giant box we call the Lands, and sometimes we collide?"

"Or," Treaman added, "is something aiming the box, tilting us toward one side?"

There was a long silence then while they stared at the fire. Then Haltar added, "Or some one."

Everyone stared at their leader from the corners of their eyes, at this uncharacteristic expression of philosophy. Bildon broke the mood by waving his fingers dramatically, intoning, "The hand… of *destiny*!" Mhoral threw a bread-rind at his head, which the Stealthic ducked and caught with ease. "Not bad, for a pinky," the halfling said in praise of himself as he stuffed it in his mouth.

"And what will we find there?" Mhoral grumped, quickly adding, "Aside from our destiny, of course."

Haltar for answer slowly reached down and picked up the whetstone again, as if his part in the conversation were over. Linya sighed in annoyance and carried on.

"The legends say that Reghalion is a gho– that it has been abandoned since the last heir sat the throne. All the things you would expect in a tragic tale, I suppose – a sudden plague, hailing storms, unusual cold in winter. And of course the ways became less sure. No record in the Chronicle speaks of contact with the capital since shortly after the end of the ruling line, around the turn of 1500. I found that much out by consulting the library, before we, Treaman and I, that is–"

"Before his dragon almost ate the scribe's cat," Haltar drawled while sharpening.

"She just wanted the fish!"

"At all events," Mhoral added, "we likely will have no further recourse in the Sage's Guild of Trainertown. But the true question is, how quickly was the city abandoned?"

"And what might still be there, of both the breathing and breathless varieties?" Bildon finished. They all looked at the fire a moment in silence.

"And most especially," Treaman added, "the Tridium."

"The Sword of Air, Order-Brow the Crown and the Scepter of Law," Linya continued, "worn by the ruling line all the way back to the days of Areghel. If the legends are to be believed, three artefacts were powerful enough to keep the ways straight across the entire kingdom, to restore nature out of all… this," with a gesture to the world around them.

"And what of it?" Mhoral asked. "A sad, moving tale, of course. But what use to us? It's been four hundred years. The Tridium could be anywhere by now."

"Indeed?" Haltar inquired, and when Mhoral nodded, asked, "How, exactly?"

"What do you mean 'how'?"

"I mean, describe for me how it was done. The tragedy has struck, the king has died, his heir disappeared up the mountain with his lady-love. Search parties have not returned, and the plague has struck. You, the seneschal of the court, have charge of the Sword of Air–" and he tossed his bastard sword to the Elf, who caught it by the hilt. "So, do you stick this under your cloak?"

"Nonsense, it shines like the sun, but of course it has a sheath."

"Yes," Linya agreed merrily, "I believe the description mentions gold wiring in the shape of Skysword, with moonstones, sapphires, not to mention the silversteel hilt and pommel-gem of purest emerald–"

"Cover it!" Mhoral snapped.

"So then," Haltar pursued, "you're the seneschal, and you carry this sword-shaped hempen bag down the castle corridors. Whistling nonchalantly perhaps?"

"Oh don't be–"

"And," Haltar said with a raised hand, "when you got out–let us be merciful and assume a secret passage–you make it through the Tallwoods surrounding the capital and across the wild kingdom, to… where? And to do what, with the most famous blade in all the Lands?"

Mhoral gave no answer.

"To use it? By whose right? And how without word getting into the histories?" Still nothing from the Elf. "Or to prise the gems and goldwork for money."

Now Mhoral's face blanched with shock. "Don't be blasphemous, Haltar. Not even you have that right."

"No, Mhoral, I agree with you," Haltar said, sitting forward earnestly. "I think there is no way those treasures would ever be pawned or destroyed, nor could they have been moved from the city. Most likely not even from the palace. And the legend seems to say that this series of calamities befell in less than a year. The city was emptied of people more quickly than they knew. The Tridium hidden, kept safe at first–"

"And before long," Bildon cried eagerly, "all those who knew where, would have been dead or gone."

"But what would any of us do with the Tridium?" Treaman asked.

Haltar shrugged. "I cannot see everything, woodsman. We find them, we bring them back if we can, and then the powers of the world will decide what happens."

"No harm to the artefacts."

"Why on earth for?" Haltar asked with a serious face.

"But naturally," Bildon said, "there would be the question of a reward."

Haltar's smile crept quietly onto his face, and his shrug was small.

"Of course," Bildon breathed, "if we found even one of them and came back, we would be the most famous adventurers alive."

Whatever Haltar was going to say next was drowned by Linya's scream. Treaman saw her looking across the fire and up, and felt her horror even as his head was turning.

There on the plain, what had been eastward at sunset, was an enormous stone fortress, not three hundred paces away.

Everyone leaped to their feet, snatched up weapons, and fell back. On the open scrub-plain, this ensured they were perfectly lit by the blazing fire, but no one could think for some time. Finally, Mhoral muttered, "So, it would appear that staying still is not always safer." Treaman stared in drop-jawed fear at the impossible edifice before them; he had speared the ground-stag just on the other side of this fort. He might have been… the woodsman felt his knees go weak, to think he'd roved a half-league from the others. All his confidence leaked away into the starry night and drained towards the dark, lightless fortress before him.

The group waited the longest time; having given fate the first move they were willing to allow it a second. The manse stolidly refused any invitation to fade or crumble, nor did any sound or movement emanate from it. The fortress gate was facing directly towards the party, with its portcullis in place; the ramparts of the square outer bailey were made of stone, and each tower-top extended another storey overhead in wood. From the inner courtyard rose a central keep, a large tower three stories high, completely of stone. Some wood was rotted away in places, but the structure seemed sound though old; it fairly ached of emptiness.

Haltar said, "It appears permanent. Armor up everyone, we're going in."

"Are you crazy?" Mhoral demanded. "Is the liquor still working on your brain, Haltar? That thing appeared out of nowhere, and the instant we step inside it might disappear again, taking us with it."

"Then we'll be there," Haltar said imperturbably as he reached for his chain shirt.

"Are we sure it 'came' here?" Linya asked.

"I feel certain I would have noticed it," Treaman said in a tone dripping with sarcasm.

Bildon flashed a single finger rudely in the woodsman's direction. "Quick, how many fingers am I holding up?"

"Just Haltar," Treaman replied and everyone laughed at this.

"Very witty, but what about this place," Mhoral persisted, putting on his helm and keeping the visor up to argue. "Does it strike you as odd that it comes into being right on top of us, and with its door facing our direction?"

Treaman looked over thoughtfully, and said, "That was east… when the sun went down. Moons aren't up yet."

Haltar stopped in the middle of packing his kit, thinking. "The ancient forts would all have had west-facing entrances. The Castle of the Wanderers, now, that was a watch-tower so it faced east. But west was the tradition in the Percentalion. Mhoral, where are those notes? The sketch-maps near the back of the tome?"

"You mean the city map; Treaman has it."

"No, the other sketches. One of them was a border fortress, as I recall."

Mhoral shrugged and produced the sheaf of note-pages they had paid the mage Obis–or rather his two acolytes–to copy over. Rifling them in the light of the campfire, Haltar found what he was looking for.

"There. An outline like this place; and the text says that Areghel gave orders they should all be established along an identical plan. Law-givers," he muttered, shaking his head. "Order in everything… but it says here too that the army on patrol would always know the layout and how to immediately occupy or defend each one; that's a good point, admittedly."

"Come, let's go," Bildon urged, his foot already tapping.

"What's this, the stables to the left?"

"It's not marked. What about the central tower, how many floors?"

"Looks like four, and rooms within each. It seems to be pretty large, wouldn't have guessed from here."

"Come on!" Bildon cried. "It's there, let's go. Do you want to stand around throwing lots for rooms to sleep in?"

"This sketch is terrible," Haltar said with disgust. "Those scribes should be whipped."

"I told them to focus on the text," Mhoral said tensely.

"Well that's a splendid job, Mhoral. Centuries-old piece of history, let's just skip over the drawings."

"How was I to know? We traced the map of Reghalion ourselves, took Treaman and me a day–"

"Because you thought you knew where we were going already!" Haltar thundered, and the Elf flinched at the justice in this.

"So you're telling us you knew this fortress was going to appear?" he sulked.

"I'm telling you to make no stupid assumptions next time. If there is one."

"Tell you what, why don't you all wait here where it's safe," Bildon said, "and I'll just trot back to the town and get the book."

Linya quietly reached over and grabbed the halfling by his sleeve, though he had made no move to go. Looking at him so her headpiece was prominent, she warned, "Don't make me use this."

He grinned back at her and whined childlike, "But I want to go!"

"Yes, plenty of danger, my little Stealthic, don't worry your head about that." Haltar had finished his preparations, and gestured grandly to Bildon to take the front.

"But we're still outside," the halfling said, pointing to Treaman.

"I don't think we're going to encounter anything between here and the gate!" Treaman rejoined tartly.

"How would you know, you didn't even see the fortress!" Bildon cried in triumph. With that, the group left; except for the campfire there was no mark of their presence behind them.

But as the group approached there were other signs, and Treaman noted them. Calling out, he squatted down near a thin, rotted trunk that had broken off near the ground. Working it, he pulled up not roots, but a sharpened end, where the stake was driven into the earth. Sweeping about, Treaman saw the remains of others, in a line facing the fort and angled in. He looked up with a hard face.

"Definitely not here before." Haltar nodded in acceptance of the report.

"So we're already standing on the ground that wasn't here an hour ago," Mhoral noted glumly. Bildon quietly reached over and walked his fingers lightly up the Elf's spine until he flinched and batted the arm angrily away. "You antic midget! Leave me alone."

"No, wait, better," Bildon promised, "I'll go in alone first, then when you come I'll wear a blanket and come out from the side, moaning 'oooaaahhhh'!"

"Better use a pole," Haltar advised. "It would be embarrassing for a ghost to get stepped over."

"These stakes couldn't be here to defend the keep against horsemen," the leader continued.

"No, they face in," Treaman agreed. "They were set against the fort, by enemies, to hinder a sortie."

"Garruk?" Linya asked. No one answered, but Bildon pointed.

"The gate's still closed. No breaches in the walls."

"Well, there are no stories of garruk being entrusted with Makine," Haltar said, rubbing his face. "So they must have tried to starve them out."

"And the good news," Bildon put in, "would be that they succeeded."

They approached the front gate slowly, ever on the alert for a sign of movement from the battlements that steadily loomed higher above them, blocking out stars in the eastern sky. Behind the portcullis was a solid wooden gate-portal. Bildon hopped up the portcullis like a ladder to the top. "Parts of the gate are rotted away up here," he reported, then skipped back down lightly to the ground. Taking out a dagger, he chipped away at one section through the grate and started flaking back large pieces almost at once. Treaman helped out with his spear, and in a few moments they had cleared a square section behind one of the grates, a little more than a foot across. Without pausing, Bildon kipped up and put his body through feet-first. All his little frame radiated confidence and even joy, and being cut off from his companions seemed no hindrance to him.

"So we'll just wait out here, then," Mhoral remarked.

"Keep your visor on, I'll find the wheelhouse in a moment. First, perhaps the garderobe." Bildon stepped to a side door under the barbican and moved through without a sound, as usual. The time wore on and the metallic creak, when it came, sounded like a catapult stone against the wall. The portcullis shivered slightly, but did not rise.

"A bit rusty!" came the halfling's voice from within the gate-tower.

"There should be a crank-pole," Haltar called out. "Use it for leverage, if you can lift it." Bildon's return-curse made the leader smile, and the party heard the clunk of something heavy being dropped, and clattering around for a while with more curses. Linya mimicked the act of covering her ears. Came the creak again, and this time the iron grating began to rise. When it was five feet off the ground or so, Haltar called, "Good, lock it down," and a moment later it stopped. Everyone began to hack away at the first hole to enlarge it, and the entire side of the oak portal came sagging away as it fell into three or four rotted chunks.

Bildon emerged from the side-door, making an exaggerated show of retying his trousers. "Thanks, Haltar, good advice to use a pole," he said, patting his middle with a lascivious look. But nothing could quite dispel the sense the party got from looking out into the bailey of the abandoned fort.

The outbuildings marked on the map were fallen in with age and the elements, in some cases mere suggestions, like a floor plan. Fallen walls and crumbled barrels, wagons, lumber piles and other detritus were everywhere across the expanse of the bailey, but nothing rose higher than a man. All attention naturally moved to the massive black tower thrusting into the sky. Arrow-slits in the second storey seemed to watch the tiny humans crouching in the gate-way for a single false move. No door was in evidence on the ground this side; a small postern-sized door was set into the second storey level, but the stairs winding up to it had been of wood, and only rotted remnants were left on the ground below them.

"What happened to the people?" Linya whispered.

"Might have gone over the walls," Mhoral suggested, and Bildon countered, "Yes, so that hundreds of years later we'd be fooled."

Haltar moved like a stalking panther when danger threatened, completely at ease and ready to uncoil in violence at any moment. He paced carefully a few steps along the inner wall, returned, and entered the side door Bildon had used to check the wheel-room. "I need a light in here, Linya," he said from within. The sorceress smiled, closed her eyes a moment, and a strong white light grew from the gem on her headpiece, shining in front of her like a hooded lantern. She turned to join Haltar without noting what her light briefly showed, but Treaman caught sight of a disquietingly familiar shape against the wall. He said nothing until Linya was out of sight, and then nodded at Bildon, who nodded back knowingly. The two of them stepped quietly towards the spot, and behind them Mhoral repeated, "So I'll just wait here then."

It was indeed a corpse; human, mailed and skeletal. It slumped with its back against the inner wall. Its sword and rotted shield lay within inches of its arms, indicating war-readiness; but no signs of broken ribs or other damage.

"Did he die fighting something inside the courtyard?" Treaman asked, and Bildon shook his head.

"It's as if he was on duty and suddenly… starved to death?" They returned to Mhoral, and a moment later the light from the side-door grew greater as Linya and Haltar returned.

"I was looking for some kind of rig, a hole through the stone, to trip the grill from the outside," the leader said, shaking his head.

"Some of them died here," Treaman reported, pointing. Haltar listened, and did not get any happier as he did.

"So where to now?" Bildon asked, his foot starting to tap again.

"Aral will be up soon," Treaman said. "We'll be able to see better."

"No problem here," Mhoral put in glibly. "There's another body to the right of the tower, and one up on the battlements," he said, pointing.

"Only the tower matters," Haltar said. "We stick together. But I wonder what's behind it." He looked to Treaman, a little hesitant. "Can you get your beast to fly around and see?" It was rare for him to give heed to Hallah in any way.

"Would Hallah like to fly behind the stone-pile and see what's there?"

{*"What is there?"*} came the thought, as if expecting an answer.

"Treaman does not know. Perhaps there is food."

{*"Hungry!"*}

The dusty silver creature crouched, leaped and took wing with increasing ease, gaining height and circling the courtyard in front of the party.

"She is so beautiful," Linya breathed, and the woodsman felt that same surge of love and pride he always did when anyone noticed his friend.

{*"Nothing good. Broken and old"*}

"What about behind the tower? On the other side, can Hallah see?"

{*"Hallah go behind."*}

"Good girl." The dragon arced around and glided with speed and ease clockwise around the stone keep. In just moments, she reappeared again on the opposite side and flew back to the woodsman's arm.

"So? What did Hallah see?"

{*"Nothing good. Broken and old. Hungry!"*}

Fingering up a riddy from a side-pouch, Treaman reported all was quiet. The lower moon peered over the north wall as the party moved out across the courtyard. A few small clouds scudded by, but not enough to obscure the light, and Linya's radiance bathed a swath in front for several yards. Several other armored corpses could be seen, against the wall or on the stairs and battlements; the scene gave every impression of men who had all died in the midst of duty.

{*"Shadows move."*}

"What? Oh, yes Hallah, the moon makes the shadows move."

They reached the central tower and looked around the base by Linya's light. The holes in the stone spiraling up to the postern above them were filled with rotted wood, the remnants of the support-joists that had held the winding stair.

"There isn't going to be an entrance down here," Haltar said. "And if Linya tries to blast through, it could bring the whole thing down. Bildon, can you reach that?"

"Of course. It isn't even impossible, and I can do most impossible things," Bildon quipped.

"If we grapple the top," Mhoral suggested.

"Save your rope," Bildon muttered, and drew forth his daggers. Walking around to the north side of the tower, he gauged a spot where the joist-hole was slightly over his head. Leaping up, he drove his left fist with dagger-point into the hole, where it lodged in the wood. Swinging, he punched with his right into the next hole up, transferred his weight using his feet for leverage, and brought his left hand to join the right. Yanking the right dagger free, the halfling began to repeat the process, coming counter-clockwise and rising further from the ground with each iteration.

The party looked up in admiration, and Haltar shook his head slightly and slowly. "The nimble little scut," he muttered.

{*"Shadows moving."*}

"Yes, Hallah, is it pretty?" Treaman had not noted any aesthetic sense in his friend, but something in its tone sounded almost worried.

{*"People shadows move."*}

"Well, yes," he responded, looking down at his own vague outline on the tower wall from Aral rising. "It is slow, but–"

{*"DEAD people shadows move!"*}

Treaman stared at Hallah, then followed her gaze. By the inner bailey, above one of the skeletal corpses, a dark blotch of something was rising, as if the man were still alive, and standing, and his shadow was shifting on the wall. Flesh crawled on every part of the woodsman's body and he had to clear his throat twice before he could say, "Trouble."

But others had noticed it too; as all over the bailey dark forms were rising in the light of the lower moon. They worked and wove and one by one struggled free of the bodies beneath them; detached, they glided on towards the living with shadow-arms holding shadow-weapons, rippling in the moonlight. As they came they shivered, at times losing ground and shape, then forming up and coming closer. On the battlements, shadows rose against the crenelments, leaned to the edge of the inner wall and seemed unable to come further. But more than half a dozen on the ground level were approaching.

"Bildon," Haltar said cooly, "you may wish to see this."

The halfling, releasing his right-hand dagger so that he swung back and out dangling on his left, surveyed the scene with as little evident effort as if he hooked one leg over a stool. "An adequate portion of peril," he noted with envy. "Shall I come down?"

"No, get into that level and drop a rope, we may need it."

"At once, great leader," the Stealthic replied, and continued his upward progress at a faster, somewhat riskier clip.

Mhoral drew out a bent blade of wood, like a smaller version of his odd-shaped club, and hefted it. Aiming with care, he threw it with a sideways motion at an advancing shadow, and the v-shaped missile spun and flew with speed. Cutting directly through the shade, it traveled on, while the creature shivered once and continued. Mhoral limbered his flail and waited.

"Can you destroy them?" Haltar asked.

"With a miracle? No," Mhoral said, biting his lip. "No, I have not that lore. I can think of nothing."

"Linya, try fire."

The sorceress threw out an arm from her place behind the three warriors, and a blaze of flame shot forth at a different opponent. The bolt coruscated briefly on the thing's shadow-chest, tearing through and ripping some dark fragments with it, though not many. But the shadow for a moment seemed to flicker in all directions, rippling violently and almost splitting into several slices. It stopped and shivered vigorously, diminished but not destroyed. Others were coming closer.

"That seemed to hurt a little. Get ready to light the ground, as big as you can."

"How about that wagon?" Linya asked. "With enough force I could probably light it on fire."

"Oil would be better," Treaman said, fumbling in his pack over-shoulder for a flask. He drew it out and aimed at the wagon a few feet away, but Haltar said, "Wait!" Holding out his bastard-sword, he said, "Pour some on first."

Treaman grinned. "This will ruin the fine edge, you know."

"Don't remind me," Haltar ordered, and a few seconds later Treaman lobbed the other half of the oil at the broken-down cart.

There were seven or eight shadows on the ground and approaching the party, who backed up against the curving wall of the inner tower. Absurdly, Bildon continued to swing and stab his way up to the second storey and was close now to the narrow lintel of the door. Treaman took a stab with his spear at the flickering darkness before him, and was disheartened to feel no resistance to his blade nor evident effect. The thing shivered back a slight bit, but that seemed to happen all the time. It swung at him with the shadow of something blunt like a mace, and he dodged. Mhoral, intoning his chant, swung the glowing flail directly at another and blasted it to shreds in a single sweep. He looked around eagerly for other foes to hurt while the miracle lasted.

Treaman, unsure what to do, stepped back and sheltered behind his shield. "Hallah, fly away!" he shouted, and the creature took wing on the force of his emotion. His original opponent and another were sliding closer to him, when Haltar cried, "Now!" and Linya let another flaming bolt fly at the wagon. It erupted in flame on the scattered oil, crackling and sparking in the rot-dry timbers. Immediately every shadow in range splintered and shivered, slipping away toward their origin points and shrinking in size before battling to hold some semblance of shape.

"The light!" Linya cried. "They cannot hold shape against the light."

"It's uneven," Haltar shouted. "With just the moon they could align, but now…"

Treaman looked up to the battlements, and saw the shadows there turning down towards their bodies. Less affected by the wagon-fire at this range, they seemed to be holding together better, but unable to come down to the ground level. Now he saw one, then another turn back, with the shape of shadow-bows in their ragged hands. He drew breath to call out, but suddenly his throat felt an icy grip and he was unable to make a sound. Mhoral with his flail and Haltar with his flaming sword were out in the courtyard, pressing their advantage and following up the disoriented foes. Treaman put one hand to his throat to tear loose the hold, but felt nothing under his fingers besides the skin of his neck. He veered toward panic, and the thought in his mind grew distant.

{*"Shadow on wall! Treeeman see!"*}

His vision already starting to spark, Treaman whirled to face the wall; another shadow, flickering somewhat in the light of the fire but still holding shape, had reached out with both arms and was strangling Treaman's shadow by the neck. He felt a wave of fear at this irresistible attack; on instinct he hurled his spear, transfixing his foe harmlessly and embedding the point in the ancient mortar. Linya, seeing the throw, turned and the light of her headband slewing in that direction hit the attacker like an earthquake. It began to split and zig-zag against the stone, and released Treaman's shadow-neck. Linya cried in disgust and then called out a casting tone, firing another bolt of flame at the monster. It took the blast full on and spattered into blots of darkness.

Treaman drew a shuddering breath.

"Mhoral, Haltar, look out for–"

Mhoral's arm sprouted a black stick and he screamed, dropping his flail. Haltar, by sheerest chance, had his blade up still flickering with flame as a shadow arrow struck it, flensing into fragments harmlessly.

"That's enough, we're leaving," Haltar called. "Bildon!"

Up above, the halfling had reached the lintel and levered himself onto the narrow ledge before the door.

"Almost have it," he called, working the lock with a tiny tool in his hand.

"Out, now," Haltar commanded. But the Stealthic was in the midst of danger and fast becoming drunk; a shadow-bolt broke on the wall near him and he laughed in appreciation.

"That does it," he called in triumph, pushing in the portal. "I'll throw down a rope and you can–"

Looming from the darkness inside the second-storey doorway came a one-armed figure in knightly tabard and chain, bearing a sword and with a look of anger set in its face like stone. The guardian was less than a foot away from Bildon as he turned, but his reaction was that of an acrobat. Calling out "Catch!" he vaulted backwards and twisted his body flat to increase the chance of those below to save his life. Treaman was the closest and holding no weapon; lunging to one side he managed to grasp the little one by the knees and fall with him to the ground face-first in the dust of the courtyard.

"Elegant," the halfling said as he kipped to his feet.

"Next time," Treaman spat back with some dirt in it, "I'll have more notice and miss you completely."

Another arrow lodged in Linya's leg, and she screamed and fell. The knight moved to the lintel without treading, over the edge and down to the ground, more swiftly than jumping in a way that spread fear to see.

Mhoral, calling out the weapon-charm, swung his retrieved flail at him and missed; Haltar from the other side swung his bastard sword two-handed and the knight parried with a single-hand grip. Yet the party-leader reeled away as if he'd been pushed unawares. Treaman went to help Linya to her feet, covering her from more arrows with his shield. She put her hand to the arrow but pulled it away with a hiss. "So cold!"

Mhoral, still with a bolt in his arm, swung again, and again missed though he was in clear range. His weapon struck, and did not strike the foe. Bildon's thrown knife, too, went directly at the foe, but seemed to miss inexplicably.

"Treaman, get her out of here! Bildon, out, you can't do anything." Haltar never looked at them but waded back in with his sword weaving an arc like a swooping hawk. The knight, his face still set in determination and fury, responded with a parry and thrust, and shouted "Hold!" in a frozen, deep voice as he attacked. Treaman could see on the battlements the shadow-archers stop and rest their weapons, and with Bildon they aided Linya to the gate-tunnel. Mhoral, standing to one side, swung his flail in a circle as he chanted and waited an opportunity. The two fighters engaged with manly skill, their blades weaving together and apart in ringing counterpoint. Haltar, moving as fast as Treaman had ever seen him, put forth a sustained effort of thrust, feint, sweep and dodge. His blade, feeding on so much wind, whipped up the last remnants of oil on its edge, and for a moment he looked as if he were striking with a slice of fire. His best blows could not penetrate the knight's guard; yet the being slowed slightly, and when Haltar stumbled leaving an opening, the foe instead held his blade with a look on his face now tinted with wonder, and even doubt.

"Thou art, thy blade…" he spoke in his frosty tone.

But before he could finish, Mhoral saw an opening and stepped in with his flail to strike. The miracle-chant still had its glow on the weapon, and from the side he landed a shot with a hard crunch.

Crying out in rage, the knight dropped his blade. Spinning to the visored foe and shouting, "Garruk dog!" he reached with his hand directly through the helm as if it were raised. Within, his hand stopped on Mhoral's unseen face, and the metal-echo scream of the Elf was terrible to hear.

Haltar drove his bastard sword completely into the knight's ribs, leaving a foot of steel there when the blade broke against his armor. The force of the blow, followed hard on by the body of the big man, knocked the being aside and broke his contact with Mhoral. Dropping his hilt and grabbing the reeling Elf in one hand, Haltar fled; the knight's recovered blade sliced his back open through the plate and chain, but Haltar gritted his teeth and bore up, dragging and running with an enormous exertion of strength.

The group ran back into the tunnel together; Haltar stuffed Mhoral under the grate, and Treaman assisted Linya. Only after he was outside did Treaman notice Bildon was nowhere to be seen.

“Bildon!” he screamed, and immediately there sounded a response from the wheel-room. “Go! Go now!”

Haltar, wheezing and holding his back with one hand, took a half-step in the direction of the gateroom door, but the shadows and their captain were coming on now, the dying light of the wagon-fire causing them no further hindrance. With an oath he flung himself under the grate even as it lurched into motion, slamming into the ground so that its points bit into the earth.

Like a shot, Bildon ran from the side-door, with shadows not three feet away. He took two running steps and leaped with hands overhead, aimed like a spear at the portcullis, neatly fitting his body into one of the square holes and tumbling like an acrobat when he hit the ground.

The party scrambled and cried out and dragged themselves a few steps further away from the cursed keep. To Treaman’s horror, the shadows misted through the iron grate as if it was still up, and he gave himself up for lost. But a ghostly horn sounded from somewhere inside the bailey; the shadows stopped, slowly turned and answered the recall, disappearing under the gate-tunnel. The keep again stood silent and unmoving, unchanged except for the torn wooden gates from the first time the party had seen it.

Hobbling and crawling further away, the party at last made out the embers of their campfire, not yet burned down from when they had left. Everyone collapsed. Treaman looked around; Linya and Haltar bleeding, Bildon smiling tightly, dirty and smudged from head to toe. Hallah was nowhere in sight. Mhoral, gasping and sobbing, reached weakly up to his helm and tore it off, revealing to the moonlight a face webbed with white scars.

Perhaps, not such a good day after all.

⊕ ⊕ ⊕

Cedrith felt a blade of something icy cold cutting down through his entire body, by inches, as he traversed the gate. He shivered and heard the echo of his cry in the stony cavern where they emerged. Higher than the proscenium arch in the theater, but now enclosed on all sides, it was a spacious, rock-cut tunnel in something that was not quite rock; it bent down and out of view both left and right as he stood. Ahead of him was an arch cut into the opposite wall, and Alendic already stepped towards this, urging the rest to hurry. But Cedrith was still too stunned to move, his mind slow to realize that he could in fact see, though now neither moon nor lantern was present. Focusing through his fear, Cedrith looked towards the lights.

Spaced irregularly around the cavern walls, some near the ceilings, none standing on the floor, were arrayed a dozen enormous beautiful beings. Their faces were human, clothed in the style of ancient days, and they looked like costume-statues perhaps from a back room of the theater. But they lived. Each was armed with sword, mace or staff, and radiated light from their very selves. Cedrith could not bring his eyes to bear on any one of them long enough to remember; he thought he saw long blonde hair, a shield marked with a constellation, a spear, wings. At the opposite door, Alendic turned back and realized the party was still twenty steps behind him: Judgement and the dekentar had come a few paces, but Cedrith and Natasha trailed badly behind.

The closest of the floating beings raised a scepter to point at the actor by the door. Alendic, cursing something gone awry, quickly held up a halting hand and pointed back with two split fingers at Cedrith and Judgement while looking at the floating being of light. He, perhaps a leader, nodded sternly and gestured. Mystic energy flowed from the scepter's tip, and Cedrith saw its glow bathe him completely, even as the caster began to shrink and the Sage felt his stomach lurch with nausea. An attack? But they were so beautiful!

The caster and other beings around them were moving away, he realized, leaving the party behind in darkness as they glided down the tunnel and out of sight in the distance. The sensation of twisting and falling increased, and Cedrith fell on his knees to vomit. Looking straight down now, he screamed with the bile still in his throat, for there was no floor under his feet, but an endless, segmented shapeless drop, with an enormous glowing crack along one cliff wall. He emptied his hands and hugged both sides while vacating his guts, and began to realize what was happening around him.

His vomit splashed on something at the level of his knees; the floor was made of solid crystal. The sensation remained, nearly knocking him down and nearly lifting him off the floor at the same time. Cedrith felt the same way he had on the ship to Conar, heeling and rolling in a storm the sailors called gentle; the same sickness, because everything was moving. There was even a slight breeze. Looking ahead, he could see the cavern advancing and curving down before him; behind, the view retreated but also down. Below him… that he could not stand to do again. Cedrith's mind was too terrified to move another thought forward for him. He huddled sideways on the invisible floor and waited to die.

Natasha quietly spoke, saying, "*Luxar simil Aral*," and a soft light came into being just above her head.

"We've missed the Hopeful entrance," Alendic spat, cursing again. "I feared we would, but still."

"What by the fiery balls of Argens is this place?" the dekentar cried.

Natasha bent over Cedrith's form. "The sickness will cease when we arrive," she said. Cedrith tried to talk, but his throat was now dry and his stomach still threatened, though empty, to take over his breath. She nodded, understanding, and said only, "The other side, where the outer gate leads back, to where we first entered, five years ago. In the Percentalion."

Cedrith could not take in the shock, the violation that came with this news. Marooned in this alien place, with the only escape-hatch leading to the land of chaos-rule? He moaned without restraint. Judgement, legs spread wide and staff planted on the smooth glass floor for support, looked about him as he faced in the direction of their movement.

"It is like a wheel, around a pulley," he suggested uncertainly, but Alendic nodded.

"Yes. The floor where we stand circles the outside of the Hopeward, and whenever there is an entrant, the inner surface rotates to bring the intruder to the opposite pole. There, an archway like the one we missed lets into the center of the place… down there," he finished, gesturing to the open space beneath their feet.

"Impossible!" cried the dekentar. "We would drop to our deaths in the chasm below there."

"Do not ask me to explain it!" Alendic responded with heat. "I have been here before, guardsman, and do not require your belief, only my memory. Once in there, the ground will seem solid beneath us and we shan't fall. This floor beneath us now will look, from in there, like a wall. If we choose not to use the gate to the Percentalion–a course I highly recommend!–we must make for the opposite, inner arch, through the center of this place, to the other side again. But first things first. We'll be lucky even to gain the arch, once we arrive."

"What do you mean?"

"You saw the beings of light, awaiting us when we came through?"

"Aye, they cast some sort of spell, I think."

"A blessing, which should help a little, for a while. That was the Hopeful entrance, now on the opposite side of us. The entrance hall we approach now is… well, differently guarded, if you understand me."

No more words then, as the party, excepting Cedrith, shuffled and slipped into a trio around Natasha, and faced in the direction of their movement. Alendic placed the rucksack between his legs and rummaged in an outer pocket for something. The sensation of motion began to subside; Natasha's gentle light showed a widening in the cavern, a shimmering golden aperture on the left-hand, outer side, and another arch across from it. All around the walls and ceiling, bumpy, irregular portions of the surface were in motion, writhing, scuttering, turning to face the group.

"Protect the Guildmistress," Alendic ordered again tersely, "and make towards the arch as soon as you can."

Cedrith still lay half-crouched on the floor, staring at the moving things and trying to make out shapes. His eyes did not want to do their job; beaks, horribly long arms, and three evenly-spaced legs. There were more than a dozen of them, maybe more than a score. Some had eyes, others what looked like rocky feathers; none were taller than a young child, but they were squat and seemed full of vitality. With clawed feet they gripped the walls and strode heavily down to the smooth floor, calling like strangled birds. Shocked into action by their strident screams, Cedrith fumbled after his shield and mace and with the dekentar's help hauled up to his feet. Alendic threw something glassy on the floor in front of them; it exploded with a staccato *kra-pouff!* and an enormous flash of light etched the dim cavern like a lightning-strike. Most of the creatures waved their upper appendages before their heads and slowed their advance. Alendic charged in with his broadsword swinging and the melee was on.

After the first instant, Cedrith had no time to see more than flashes of the others; one of the creatures stalked in range of him on heavy, stubby legs and licked out a long tendril at his left side. Holding his shield too low and too far out, Cedrith let its ropy arm get around his guard; the end bit through his sleeve, leaving an acidic kiss on his arm. The sage cried out in pain and backed off, holding his shield even further away and poking weakly with his mace like a pole, to stave the advance of the creature.

Behind him he heard a growling cry of triumph–perhaps the dekentar–and a squeal of inhuman pain, smelled a revolting odor of something wet and hot, and another explosion with a brief flare of light. Cedrith's creature, facing close to Alendic's direction, craned its head back on its long neck and squirmed in momentary confusion.

"Cedrith! Shield up, damn you! Bash when they get too close!" Alendic bellowed and Cedrith obeyed, but kept backing away until he saw Natasha to one side, exposed by his retreat. He covered and came inside the reach of the creature's next strike, which again evaded his sagging shield to snag his forearm; more pain, and he jerked away while moaning in fear. He swung clumsily with his mace and felt it bounce off the tough spongy flesh of his foe, which cacked and skittered away momentarily, but then waddled back in unhurt. Cedrith's shield arm felt like it was on fire now, and he heard a faint bubble-pop from his naked skin where the tendril had touched. He saw another creature scuttle past in Natasha's direction, and involuntarily turned his head to see. It lashed out at the healer, who dodged and then laid her open palm on the monster's chest, calling out, "*Placidus, ar termontem.*" With an open path to rend the unarmed woman, the creature let both its arms fall and began to quietly walk away. Beyond her, Judgement swung his staff in a mighty sweep, bowling down a cawing foe and shattering its shoulder.

All in a flash; Cedrith snapped his head back around to see his foe attacking again. He held up his shield and swung, missing with the mace; the creature's claw-hand snapped near his own head, and the tendril once again evaded his shield, though the block was better, coming just far enough around to snag momentarily on his sleeve. Cedrith began to circle and give ground, already out of breath and feeling he could not continue much longer. Twice again they exchanged swings, his mace catching in the monster's claw-arm while his shield blocked most of the tendril in return. Cedrith found he could think of nothing else but that snaky acidic rope of demon-flesh, coiling in to get him; he tried to remember Alendic's whip and how to block, but he was too tired. It was maddening. His shield-arm sagged, and its arm writhed in to grab his tattered tunic; just a touch, a slight jerk in the fabric.

Like a constant pluck on his sleeve.

The sudden thought of the castellan's bad habit caused Cedrith's anger to crystallize into a fey humor. With a bark of laughter he pushed back his terror and found a focus for his ire. Tapping that, the once-gentle sage slammed his mace full at the monster's head; a glancing blow but enough to make its arms drop a moment. Stepping up, Cedrith bashed with his shield as hard as he could, just as Alendic had taught him. Indeed the creature staggered back and fell to the ground. Shouting in triumph and grim joy, the sage waded in; half-kneeling on his shield he pounded down repeatedly with his weapon arm, rebounding the monster's rising head back to the crystalline floor three times, four, missing once or twice with a glassy ring. The body lay still at last, though its limbs writhed, and the sound of shouting drew his attention back to the main fight.

Turning, the sage cried out in horror; somehow he had become separated from the group by twoscore paces, and the remaining demons were between him and the party fighting in the lee of the stone inner arch. Three monsters broke in his direction now, with arms and legs working inhumanly and beaks clacking a rending rhythm. All his recent bluster drained from Cedrith at once as he backed away. One of his adversaries trotted in and snapped with its beak at his waist. Crying out in fear, Cedrith took a wild, half-swing, half-poke with his mace; his strike bounded off a hard claw and the weapon leaped from his hand to land behind the monster as it collided with him and pushed him another step back. Cedrith's heart stopped as he shuffled away with both hands on the shield now; the floor reverberated with ringing tones as the mace rolled unseen. Distantly, he was aware his companions were screaming for him to stop, but it was just noise to him until Judgement, leading a desperate charge through the ranks and away from the arch, shouted, "Eldest, the portal!"

Cedrith felt a stab of fear at this; without fully understanding, he turned his head to glance behind him. So close to his eye that his lashes seemed to touch it, his vision was blocked by a golden, shimmering vista. He was an inch from the mystic gate, which led to the Percentalion. One more step; his feet froze in place of their own accord, and Cedrith was weeping with the hopeless effort to hold his ground against the incoming monsters. Several claws and ropy arms began to flail at him together; he took stings and jabs in four places at once. And he could feel them, pushing and shoving at him, trying to herd him now one more step back.

He heard Alendic bellow, "Shield *up*, damn you!" and the few hours he had spent under the man's tutelage took hold. Cedrith threw his shield so high it blocked his view; a moment later he felt something like a stone hit the wood, and another bright flash illuminated the cavern. Squeals of annoyance, the sound of metal on flesh, and squawks of pain followed; Cedrith did not dare look, even as two or three more bites and thrusts came at him. The next time he was clutched from around the shield, he howled and tried to bash; but this body was too tall, and had hair the hue of iron.

Solemn Judgement hauled Cedrith a vital step farther away from the gate; when he lowered his shield, the Elf could see two of his three foes were down. The dekentar and Alendic were teaming up on the last; a few steps farther away Natasha was weaving like a drunken woman, but managed to touch one more demon and gasp out her incantation. In a blurry haze, Cedrith staggered between Judgement and the dekentar towards the stone archway; Alendic gathered up the healer in his free arm and they made their way, a half-dozen monsters still in the area but wandering slowly with arms down for the moment.

Now through the stone arch, Cedrith heard a gentle sound as of something sliding; looking back he could still see, but hardly hear, the monsters in the cavern. A man-high wall of crystal had come down from the arch to block passage. It was too clear to judge its thickness, but Cedrith felt intuitively that it was quite strong; any sheet of mere glass that long and wide would have broken as it moved.

After the cavernous entry cave where they had fought for their lives, this chamber seemed claustrophobic and stuffy to Cedrith, who was gasping hard and moaning from his exertions and injuries. It was cold here, not bitterly but wet. Everyone was badly winded. The dekentar huffed with widened eyes as he leaned against the straight-cut, symmetrical wall. Judgement was watching the demons out the way they had come, his back to everyone, but his chest was visibly rising and falling with speed. Natasha, who seemed nearly out on her feet, still hobbled over on Alendic's arm to check Cedrith; looking down at himself, the Elf saw a horror of bloody cuts and burning welts on his torso and all his limbs. He caught his breath in fear; but she took it in swiftly, put a shaky hand on his worst wound, and murmured, "*Intacta volar.*" The gash closed almost at once into a wire-thin line, and even the bruising and burning in its vicinity ceased.

Natasha guided her own considerable bulk to the semistone floor and passed out with a manner that suggested a professional level of practice. Cedrith cried out, but Alendic looked her over, nodded once and said, "She will revive in time. Used more of her energies than we wanted, but it could not be helped." The actor took Cedrith's mace from his own belt and meaningfully tightened its cinch-loop over the sage's wrist. Then he stepped to check each of the nether exits from the chamber, darkened to view.

The dekentar came to sit beside the healer, and Judgement half-turned so that he could see Cedrith. "The last time… you came through," the dekentar said to Alendic, "what was the battle?"

"We moved faster," Alendic replied with an ironic grin, "with Eddoran's magic and leadership, we just came directly from the gate, through to this arch. Those little ones were not so great a challenge, then. He was, indeed, a great mage…" he trailed off a while in thought. "And to think, if we'd simply waited, the floor would have brought us to the other side!" He shook his head and chuckled bitterly at this.

"You have been here before?" the dekentar asked, and for several minutes Cedrith listened as if to an evil fairy tale while Alendic affirmed briefly their former foray. His breath calmed, but he never started to feel truly rested; in fact, a sense of oppression near panic edged over the sage and he realized he was beginning once again to feel ill. He hesitated to interrupt with still more humiliation; but the dekentar suddenly wiped a brow and announced, "Conar's balls, I've caught a fever from those demons."

"Most likely not," Alendic rejoined, "it's just this room. We cannot stay here once the Healer awakens." The actor had broken open a large side-pocket on his rucksack and withdrawn all manner of cloth strips, ointment, wooden splints and more, the paraphernalia of a surgeon. As the erstwhile actor bent over the others to examine and bind up their cuts and burns, Cedrith could see Alendic too was sweating despite the cold, and seeing him in distress only increased his own.

"What do you mean? Is the air in here poisoned?"

Alendic shook his head as he bandaged Judgement's thigh. "Better not to say too much." He pulled the binding tight, and Cedrith winced in empathy to see the blood seep around its edges, but Judgement only looked down as if surprised that he had been hit at all. Still, he shortly afterward swayed and then sat down next to the dekentar, who moved a bit further off even as Alendic tended him. Cedrith could see the sweat on all their faces now, and the sense of illness was quite strong.

Judgement forced himself back to his feet and moved to look through one of the arches: this brought Alendic around with a sharp warning.

"No! Better that you don't–"

But the youth had peeked through the middle archway, and now stood back a step, swaying again. He looked to the glass entry door, with its horrors prowling outside, then down at Natasha near his feet, then back to the arch. He sat again, and Cedrith saw on his face a rare look of discomposure.

"What is it?" the sage asked, but the Man in Grey just sat with his head down as if trying not to see more than needed. Cedrith and the dekentar now looked to Alendic, stuffing his supplies back into the pack, and he shrugged in answer, saying only, "We are… between."

Natasha stirred slightly, and Alendic shifted to be near her head as he knelt. He placed one hand on her forehead, and soon her eyelids fluttered open as her breathing deepened.

"Are you well enough, my dear?" the actor asked.

Natasha smiled a moment, then grimaced, saying, "Ugh, this horrid room. I am sorry I passed out here."

"Nonsense. Do you need water, perhaps a little ale? Are you hurt?" Alendic asked almost eagerly.

"I am fine, Mother dear," Natasha said, sitting up. "How are the others? All of you, any wounds?"

Cedrith looked down at the half-dozen places where Alendic had bound him, feeling the burn-pain even through the salves. But to his shock Alendic said, "A few scratches, we can move on; if you are ready, that is."

"I am, thanks. And thanks also, Alendic, for those marvelous gems of light. The demons of darkness were most alarmed."

"A trick, from one of the Argens plays. It likely won't help us again, though I have much more room in my pack, dearest." He helped her to her feet as the others also rose. Natasha glanced at the other arches but did not look through, instead turning to face the group as the sweat stood out on her brow.

"We should not tarry here. This room is… between, and we shall gain no rest but only a growing sickness that you all feel now. Through those arches are… well, it is difficult to describe accurately–"

"Like the arms of the celestarium," Judgement supplied quietly.

"Very good! If you have seen in the Sages Guild, the table which shows our land as the surface, but with various rings of metal surrounding it to hold the moons, sun and stars. Each of these arches is like one of those rings: we will be able to survey the entire center of the Hopeward, the surface of the table, if you will, and will be carried by it to… to our next destination."

"Like the outer hall," Cedrith suggested weakly, thinking of the illness of motion that had made him vomit.

"Yes, but our course was slow enough not to trigger the feeling… at least not for us," Natasha responded. "At any rate, there is no choice, and we cannot abide here."

"Between," Judgement said, forcing his face into the proper mask of stoicism, though it rippled at times. "We see the floor of the outer hall behind us, and think 'there is down.' But as the *cardinus* said, through there, ahead, the way 'down' is altered. The walls have become the floor. But here… it is both…" and he trailed off.

"Which way then?" the dekentar asked through tightened teeth.

"That is our decision, of course," said Alendic with a small grin. "Each ring is named for Aral and Unal, the moons, as well as Solar, the sun. Why this arrangement, we cannot determine. But their orbits are like those for which they are named: from our left, Aral's path is shortest and fastest, and we believe it leads deeper into the maze than the others. Last time, we took the path of Solar and the result was… less than desirable."

"Then, perhaps the course of Unal would be safest," Cedrith suggested, "as it would avoid all extremes."

"We had thought of that," Natasha admitted, "and we should all be of one mind in our choice."

"Aye, so long as we choose quickly," Alendic quipped, and then as if to punctuate he turned and threw up in a corner.

The dekentar was panting, and said only, "Choose any, but now!"

Cedrith looked at Solemn Judgement, who hesitated only a moment before saying "Aral. Let us move more quickly to embrace the adventure." Cedrith shrugged and the group moved to the left-hand archway with weapons drawn. Alendic said, "Once through, do not move, not a step," and added with a wry smile, "The Hopeward will provide our transportation again."

For one second, Cedrith thought his mind could not hold. As he stepped through the arch, he briefly experienced *down* in at least three directions. His foot felt square beneath his ankle, but his body reported a sensation of climbing, or twisting as a vast cavern opened before his eyes. He fell to his knees and tried to take it all in. Curving to either side behind him was an enormous crystalline wall, mostly darkened on the near side, but glowing with white light at the far end, over a league away it seemed. He tried to take in the fact that recently this wall had been beneath his feet, but after a few moments the sense of *down* organized itself in a new direction, towards the vast interior plane of this place instead. Yet not quite straight to the floor; even as his senses cleared and the illness fell away with relief, Cedrith could detect a small motion, and a slight tilt to his vision. The floor immediately beneath his feet was ascending, and he realized he stood on an immense ring of mingled material, perhaps ten feet wide and less than three thick, already turning well past the archway he came through and now rising slightly above the rest of the ground. Ahead of him stretched a small world whose floor was made of this same, neutral-colored, hard material just as the ring beneath his feet and the walls of the outer cavern had been. Bumpy like melted rock, but veined with harder, darker metals and softer, nameless textures that gave slightly under his boot, the ring seemed too thin to hold. Even as his mind swam, Cedrith realized they were already more than thirty feet above the cavern floor of the Hopeward's interior, describing a path like a moon in orbit. Overhead at varying angles, two other rings also circled beneath the colossal ceiling, the center of which was a vast, rocky field of milk-white crystal half a league across.

The ambient light that allowed him to see emanated from two sources: a dim but pure radiance from above, as if the sun shone outside the quartz ceiling, and a volcanic glow from the enormous crack in the floor beneath, out of which heat, steam and light rose, suggesting an endless depth. From their increasing altitude, Cedrith could see more and more of the cavern, though parts were obscured by the gouts of steam below. The chasm-crack ran the width of the entire world, and the sage could see that in a matter of minutes their ring would be passing high above it. With a thrill of terror, Cedrith noted that the ring easily tilted far enough to spill them to the ground, or into the magma crack. He felt no sense of tipping here: the *down* of the ring remained directly square with its surface. Yet he could not shake the fear that once they were above the molten doom, the rules would change and tumble him to a fiery death. His eyes and feet continued to argue and Cedrith felt himself shaking.

All across the cavern-floor, decorating the world below on both sides of the chasm, Cedrith saw planes and plates of glass. It resembled a maze, of the kind made by hedges in noble gardens, and instinctively the sage saw the hand of an Elvish intelligence in the design. Some of the door-like planes were etched with symbols, faintly sheening white but unintelligible at this distance. The alternation of enclosed halls, roofed-over sections, open areas and what seemed to be random single pieces standing free just begged the mind to decode them. It was like a map, or an enormous cipher set in glass and sprawling over scores of rods to either side. In scale, it was unmistakably human, and Cedrith thrilled to imagine the enormous effort, the magical or technical skill that must have been aroused to undertake it. Without much hope, Cedrith tried to trace a path from where the orbit of their ring landed ahead to any place, either an outer exit or the central space where a stone-ish bridge spanned the chasm and stood studded with pedestals.

But after a few moments of trying to work a mind-path through the maze, Cedrith heard a sound sonorously deep, not harsh but strong enough to make his jaw vibrate. Two long tones, then a third; the sage tried to imagine what enormous horn, what trunk-sized pipe could sound so low and steady, and failed. It was as if a titan's finger rubbed water along the edges of the glass walls themselves, a music made for larger, less mortal ears. Before his eyes, the Halls of Glass shifted. Walls rose through the air or sank into the cavern floor; some doors pivoted without hinges to become walls, or slowly swung up to make ceilings. Other planes appeared in the same way; in less time than he could tell, the entire layout had changed. His heart sank, and Cedrith took a step closer to the edge in his fascination and dread.

"Hold! Don't move!" Alendic hissed as he clamped a hard hand on Cedrith's arm directly over a burn-mark. Cedrith cried out, but not from pain; the moment he lifted his foot, the sage had begun to feel that the cavern floor was *down*; without the actor's hand he felt sure he would have come free of the orbit floor completely. With his second foot back down, Cedrith's body once again defied his eyes and insisted that the world was sideways. But the tingle running through his frame was acidic and he sagged against Alendic for a time. The actor, almost heedless of his rescue effort, continued to stare down at the glass world and tap his free hand against a leg in count. Nearby, the dekentar had fallen to his knees, and Judgement stood looking with rapt attention at the world below, especially towards its center. Natasha risked a quick shuffle-step to stand next to the youth, and nodded to the others that this was safe. They scooted slowly together and sat, except Alendic still tapping and counting.

The dekentar looked out over the cavern and swore softly. "The Heroes created all of this?"

"As far as we can tell from the records," Natasha said carefully, "they conjured it together. With the Lieges of Despair."

Cedrith felt his faith offended again. "Together? No, Natasha, you cannot be correct. The opposition of Conar to Mauglir, as Ma-Eldar to Kun, and so forth… it cannot be questioned."

He expected an argument, but Natasha's shrug was both confident and dismissive. "We only need to know how to navigate this maze, not where it came from. You have seen the walls shifting, but what is most important–"

She was interrupted by another series of four grand, deep tones, and everyone looked down to see the labyrinth of glass shift, turn and change again. Alendic stopped tapping and uttered a scorching oath, the kind Cedrith had only heard from sailors (and only when they did not know he was nearby).

"Forty-two again!" he cried, turning and shuffling to plunk down next to the group in a rare ill-humor. "We will never decipher this code."

"You believe the walls shift on a pattern of times?" Cedrith asked.

"It must be, the tones always come and the walls always change afterwards. But there is no sense to it. I can keep a fair beat–an actor must stay in meter to recite a long speech–but the intervals are anywhere from twenty-five to seventy-one counts." He took out his dagger and poked the ring-floor in his pique.

"We will accept the path that the walls give us," Natasha murmured; Alendic responded by levering up a clod of something earthy and flinging it over the side. Cedrith gasped and gripped the floor in panic, until a few moments proved that he was safe. "At any event, the spaces allowed by the Halls of Glass will vary in size; you must be prepared, we could be separated temporarily, but always seek to come back together."

"Why would anyone create such a maze?" the dekentar wondered.

"There's a quick way through, I know it!" Alendic cried, still digging with his knife. "Those who created this ward wanted it to be difficult, next to impossible for anyone to return. But they could not bear to lock it away completely. Each side had contributed some of their most prized weapons to the hoard, there on the bridge. You can cross the outer hall immediately, when among friends." Here Alendic started to draw the Hopeward in miniature with his knife on a soft space between the kneeling party. "So too it's possible to take one of these rings–and the Heroes grant it is ours–to then navigate the Halls of Glass quickly, reaching the bridge at the center, avoiding…" and there he trailed off, with a half-apologetic look at Natasha.

"Avoiding what?" the dekentar asked.

"Never mind, sir," Cedrith cut in, mimicking the wise actor. "Better not to say too much." He gazed absently at the diagram Alendic had cut in the ring, and noted with horror that it appeared to be oozing something brown, and thicker than water.

The ring was passing through a curtain of steam now, and emerged above the magma chasm. The bright russet heat pushed on their faces even from twenty-five rods over the cavern floor. Cedrith gripped uselessly at the flat ground near his knees, his mind arguing forcefully that he would spill off. Below, he saw a bright, mortal lake that roiled with thick bubbles of blast and once, he thought for a moment, a curve or current drawn across near the surface in a sinuous… something. The fear of falling was too great to think about much else, and the ring seemed to the Elf to be slowing, or even stopping. They coughed through the acrid steam and waited together; the low tones of another change muted by the hissing below.

From this angle, there was a direct line of sight to the massive central bridge spanning the chasm. As wide as a throne room, the space was lined with a double-row of pedestals in circular crystal cases; within each was an item still too far away for Cedrith to fathom: a blocky metal base, a sword, a glint. A raised area near the center overlooked the treasures and standing there, tiny but clear, was a human figure that noticed them and looked back. To Cedrith's view, the dark, spare outline revealed not a single feature; it seemed veiled in something darker than the steam, a nearly indigo cloud that stayed down, heavy in the hot air. He felt a spasm of pure terror in his spine.

He whispered, "Who?"

Natasha also looked down on the distant figure and for a long moment did not answer. Finally, she said, "The warder. A ghastly lord of Despair, commander of the forces bent against our coming. The one who shattered us, took my love from me… a necromancer."

At this last, Solemn Judgement snapped around to look keenly on Natasha. "What is his name?" he asked tensely.

Natasha only shook her head, and Cedrith said, "Why?"

Judgement had returned to stare at the figure on the bridge. "Names are important."

The distant man-figure gestured, with what looked like a scepter in one hand at the party: taunting, menacing, a salute. Natasha was energized and spoke with urgency. "Listen to me, all of you. Despair will work on us; whatever weakness we have, he can… we will start to argue, fear, doubt each other, but you must not give in! Become not like that which you hate."

"I'll never be like him," the dekentar snarled with a glare at Judgement.

"More of Telhol's tripe," Alendic cut in, combative. "We'll be forced to fight and there's no sense in looking away from that."

"True Hope rests only in Peace, in sacrifice," Natasha returned, but Alendic ignored her and addressed the others.

"Once we land, I shall attempt to speed our passage through the Halls. Stay together if you can." He turned to Judgement, leaning in towards him with intensity. "When the final test comes, before the bridge… you must be prepared to use the opening I give you."

"Why can we not wait, on landing, to plan more carefully?" Cedrith heard himself say. He was feeling detached, his previous fears returning fresh as the ring started down now toward its landing. Natasha seemed insistent, Alendic imperious. The dekentar said nothing but kept glancing towards Judgement with ever-more-hateful looks. The youth ignored the guard, but returned Alendic's gaze with distrust.

"He's already cast on us!" Natasha cried. "The workings of Despair have begun."

"Nonsense," Alendic argued. "We're facing the test now, nothing changes that."

For a time no one spoke, and Cedrith felt the worm of doubt growing now to a size that could swallow his innards whole. Protect the lad, he thought to himself, that's the only thing. Help Solemn all you can, and it will be over for you soon in any event. He gazed to his friend and erstwhile charge and felt a hint of his returning usual humor.

"You've been quiet," he remarked. But against the present mood, his innocent comment turned sour. The dekentar barked a laugh filled with contempt, and Judgement's look in return was snow on a glacier.

Alendic grinned with none of his usual good humor, saying only, "He'll be fine, just remember what I said, in case I am… cannot communicate when the time comes."

"And what is that supposed to mean?" Cedrith cried, feeling angry now. "Are you and Natasha competing to see who can keep more secrets?" They both glared back at him, but Cedrith sailed on as his usual composure dropped away. "You lead us into the jaws of hell and then pull back from any hint of how we can escape."

"No one demanded that you accompany us," Alendic spat.

"Peace, both of you!" Natasha commanded, but clearly feeling none herself. The dekentar half-rose and shuffled to sit next to her.

"Something… familiar," Judgement murmured, so quietly Cedrith almost failed to hear him. The youth was looking out over the cavern as they descended, at nothing in particular.

"Familiar? How– you can't mean you have been here before?" Cedrith asked, and did not get even a shake of the head in answer. "Something about the walls? The treasures, something you read? The chasm?"

At first Judgement shook his head, and then spoke a shade louder than usual. "The chasm. It is like the cleft."

"The Great Cleft?" Natasha asked and the Man in Grey nodded.

"It runs the width of the world. Perhaps this cavern is like a map…"

"But the Cleft was not created until centuries after the Ward," Natasha pointed out. "In the days before the Battle of the Razor." To this Judgement nodded in acknowledgement, but Cedrith could tell something still gnawed at the youth's memory.

The ring was now approaching the cavern floor. They were coming down into a large box-shaped room with no ceiling but five glass walls, more than fifteen feet high. Three walls screened corridors behind them and had mystic symbols etched on the glass. Everyone carefully stood and shuffled into formation around Natasha, though the landing room seemed empty. They stumbled stepping from the ring to the floor, and Cedrith, though fully warned, fell to the ground. No one seemed to notice, and that only increased his shame.

"Search for treasure," Alendic ordered, adding, "Call it a time-honored superstition." The group dutifully looked around the floor and clear walls, but the surface was smooth and hard everywhere. Soon everyone was gazing instead down the three corridors beyond the panes etched with symbols, across the Halls back towards the chasm and the central bridge. The effect of each clear wall was distorting, but Cedrith was certain he saw slight movement as of many things in a large chamber perhaps sixty-score steps away. The longest hallway, beyond the door pointing most directly at the bridge, seemed to come closest to that room, though he knew the rules would change within moments.

Natasha said, "The tones never change the doors from the landing rooms. At least that was our experience when we came by the ring of Solar. On the next change, one of these will open. We will take the one that chance sends us."

"Actually, we will not," Alendic responded, moving to the long-hall door and plunking down his rucksack. First he drew out a simple rope and grapnel, though his face did not hold out much hope for his prospects. Sure enough, in several tries, he easily caught its hooks over the top of one wall or another; but the sharp iron prongs could gain no purchase on the glass and the rope came back each time with the first tug. Alendic coiled and put it away, but held up a finger with a gentle smile as if to say, "wait for this."

Reaching carefully within he removed a long wrapping of soft cloth and uncovered an unusual device made all of glass. As the group gathered round, Cedrith could see it was two tubes, joined in a V and with a stoppered opening at the base, while on the nether ends rested two bulbs of glass, each about three-quarters full of liquid. Two turn-valves affixed between the bulbs and the tubes of the V were closed to prevent the liquid's escape. Alendic removed the stopper and held the V by its ends, then carefully turned each valve slightly open.

"Stand back, everyone, don't let a drop of this get on you."

He stood close to the chosen door and tipped the V slightly down. The twin liquids dripped like syrup, combining as they exited the tubes directly onto the star-pattern symbol in the center of the crystal door. Alendic passed the tube-end back and forth in a serpentine fashion until the symbol was spackled with it. Cedrith smelled a strong tangy scent and saw the glassine portal begin to smoke and gently crackle.

"Alendic," Natasha breathed, "what are you doing? This sacred place–"

"This death-trap," the actor cut in, "will not prove our undoing as it did last time. Like sheep down the slaughter-pen, thank you, no. Not this time." He stood back and stowed the tubing after carefully wiping the end with the thick cloth and returning the stopper. Cedrith saw holes in the cloth by the time it was back in the sack, and even Alendic's glove was seared as if by fire. He looked it over ruefully and muttered, "Never too careful. Alright, lad, try your hand with the staff, right in the center."

With a look to Natasha, Judgement hefted his iron-shod cudgel and swung it overhand at the center of the door. There was a resonant crash but no other effect. "Again!" Alendic called, and Judgement complied. In perfect time with his second blow, the tones of the cavern started again. On the fourth swing, Cedrith heard a loud crack, though the door showed no effect. Now the door to their right, across the room, opened into a shorter corridor.

"Enough, Alendic," Natasha shouted over the dying tones with urgency. "We must take the path the Lords have given."

"No, Natasha," he responded with heat, "this place will not dictate to us. The safest way is the most direct. Again, lad!" he bellowed at Judgement. "Don't swing like a child, we are doing man's work here. Pretend it's an actor!"

Judgement moved his hands together at one end and swung the full length of the staff against the center of the door. Another crack, and now a ragged stripe cut a diagonal across the portal. At that moment, the dekentar screamed in pain and panic, and when Cedrith looked he too cried out. A stony hand had grown from the floor near their feet, and gripped the soldier's ankle. On reflex, the dekentar swept down with his sword and cut halfway through the wrist of the monstrous appendage, ripping his foot away so hard he stumbled. Without pause, the arm continued to grow from the floor, reshaping itself and rising high enough to grasp at his calf, barely missing. From the corner of his eye, Cedrith saw movement, and turning his back to the door, he saw irregular corn-rows of claws rising all across the chamber.

"The Arms of the Earth!" Natasha shouted in fear. "My magics will not avail against creations without mind or spirit. Alendic, the open door, now!"

"Once again, lad, with me," Alendic said to Judgement and timed his broadsword to hit along with the staff. With a basso crackle, the entire door shattered into man-sized shards. Cedrith, next to the dekentar, poked with his mace at the arm now as tall as his chest, while the guardsman hacked closer to its base. But Cedrith's next blow was a bad miss, and as he stumbled forward another arm came down across his back, enfolding him. Now his fear rose through the top of his throat, as Cedrith felt the arm weighing heavily down on his body while his feet began to sink into the not-stone as through soft snow. The floor, once hard enough to hold a man's weight, was suddenly thinner than tar; it was over his knees. A second cloying arm draped itself over his head, its stony fingers over his eyes; he would be dragged below in only moments.

The horror of being trapped beneath the earth, having the world above him, no air, struck home. Cedrith screamed as he had not since childhood. He was aware of nothing around him, only the growing weight and, distantly, the sounds of men cursing and something hard being chipped away. He screamed again, and felt stone crumbling off his legs, his heels scraping on a flat surface, movement that he did not cause. The weight was gone, and hard grips under his shoulders felt warm and fleshy. Another earth-arm passed before his vision, and a lightning-quick sword sweep cut off its last two feet, to fall into the ground and reform. Cedrith huddled beneath his shield, dumped in the hallway beyond the chamber of hands.

For a few moments the party stood–Cedrith lay–within the corridor and stared breathlessly at the waving limbs a few feet off. Judgement, unsure how far the arms could advance, kept his weapon at the ready and feinted as the closest seemed to weave near the shattered portal. Cedrith scrambled to his feet, and felt a keen sense of wrongness all around him. The violation of the sorcerous arms, the priceless doorway broken, the other hallway back across the chamber, now unused: it all seemed an evil which could have been avoided.

"How could you?" Natasha fumed at Alendic. "To destroy a door, when there was another way."

"Natasha, my dear," he soothed too tersely, "we cannot handle this place like an egg, it can kill us. I did not know how long we had–"

"Those Arms could have killed Cedrith! And you knew–" she cut herself off, and Cedrith saw a knowing look pass between them.

"You knew there would be those stone-hands," he said, his voice sounding unusually close in the hallway after the open cavern. "The last time, in the chamber near the sun-ring, you already knew–"

"It... it happened there as well, yes," Alendic admitted, "but all the more reason not to be herded. I spent many months, dear heart, seeking out the alchemists who could attempt this reagent for me."

"A Universal Solvent," Cedrith breathed. "I thought it was only a legend, or surely that the secret was lost."

"Damn nearly," Alendic quipped with pride, "and not cheap. Can you believe, no one had given any thought as to how to hold the stuff! I worked that out too, at no small expense. But now–"

"Now," Natasha cut in, "you will swear not to use it again."

Alendic bowed immediately, and replied, "As you wish, my dear. Not until our lives are again in peril." Grinning at his escape, Alendic pivoted towards the end of the hallway and marched off, followed by the dekentar, Natasha, Cedrith and Judgement bringing up the rear.

"Stay within arm's reach," Alendic instructed, "and be ready to move where I say when the changes begin. We must try to stay together, but if separated, do not panic, seek to rejoin as soon as you can." The hallway turned left then right, offering no choices but wending steadily deeper into the maze. Sometimes the ground planed gently underfoot but large vistas were always visible through the crystal walls, though the distortions rendered the view nearly useless.

"Is that a space up ahead?" Cedrith asked Judgement, pausing a moment at a corner and looking in the general direction they were moving. Judgement stared as the Elf pointed but said nothing. "It looks like a tall... light of some kind on the right," the Elf said, "and a rift or a cave to the left of it."

The tones sounded again, the ground vibrating with their pulse, and Cedrith looked wildly to both sides with his heart pounding. But of the many changes happening smoothly and silently in all directions, none of the walls moved in their immediate vicinity. Alendic signaled for them to continue, but Cedrith noticed Judgement had remained in place, gazing down and lost in thought.

"Judgement– Solemn," he hissed, though Alendic overheard anyway, and finally "Guildsman!"

The grey youth came around at this and began to catch up, murmuring "Something… familiar."

Alendic walked back and snapped his fingers under Judgement's face. "Not a game, boy! We're not working on a puzzle-block back in your precious library."

The Man in Grey lifted his gaze and the actor saw those stony points. The older man flinched a bit, but drove on.

"You came to serve Natasha, as I– as we all did. Keep your wits about you." He stood to one side and gestured for Judgement to take the point, saying, "Where I can keep an eye on you." Judgement stalked off down the hall at more than his usual punishing clip, and Natasha, whose legs were shorter than anyone's, had to tip-toe jog to keep pace. She did so without complaint, and indeed began to giggle after a time. It spread to the others in the party, except their new leader who never looked back and missed the joke.

At an end with turnings left and right, Judgement stopped without looking back, waiting for an instruction. Alendic gauged the way ahead through the walls, then called out, "Right." But at that moment the tones sounded again, and a wall rose from the floor barring that direction. At the same time, part of the wall began to swing down like the hatch of a chest, on top of Cedrith and Alendic. "Back!" he cried, and dragged the sage with him to bump over the dekentar as the plane came fully down to form a floor, then folded up to seal the way back. Other changes in the near area went unmarked in the excitement; when everything stopped, the group stood in a hallway leading only in the left-hand direction. "Still together," Alendic quipped, "that's a favor. Onward then."

The way turned back and forth by odd angles, with only one or two side-paths that quickly dead-ended. At times, the view of the space ahead was relatively clear, and Cedrith began to think that the light and dark were very similar in shape somehow; but there was a constant rippling effect caused by the intervening walls, and things jumped and stretched with each step. Judgement set a lively pace, and there was not much call to talk at any rate. When he stopped, the dekentar nearly ran into him from behind, and cursed the need. Alendic hailed from the back, and the grey youth motioned to his left where a break in the wall led out into the open cavern. The way also kept on within the Halls before them.

"Should we leave the Halls of Glass?" Judgement asked as Alendic came to the front. The actor looked briefly out but shook his head vigorously. "Never. Under no circumstances leave the Halls before the bridge." He refused to elaborate, and when Cedrith looked at Natasha he saw nothing to enlighten him. The group continued, and soon came to a passage where the hallway narrowed to less than three feet across; it widened after perhaps ten steps, but this section was roofed in crystal and had a glass floor instead of stone. Again Judgement stopped, and the group gathered to deliberate.

"Have you ever seen something like this before?" Cedrith asked.

"Not on our previous trip," Natasha responded. "Yet it looks innocent enough." Alendic chuckled at this, and paced back and forth before the opening, passing his sword's blade into it, tapping the floor and trying to reach the glass ceiling above. Cedrith thought the chamber beyond was fairly close now, but the angle of the glass walls prevented his making out any details.

"You suspect a trap?" the dekentar asked.

"Every second we are here," Alendic responded, but then shrugged. "There's nothing for it, no way back and we will not leave the Halls."

"We could wait for a change," Cedrith suggested, but the actor shook his head.

"To my thinking, the more changes, the worse for us," he said. "Let's move on before the way ahead is so cramped we have to crawl."

Without preamble or permission, Judgement moved into the narrow space. He turned his shoulders slightly, but still the sides tugged at the edges of his cape, and bent down one side of his broad-brimmed hat. His iron-bound staff lightly touched the wall and rang it like a bell. Cedrith forgot to breathe, but before he could tell, the youth was through; he looked ahead and above, then turned back with his usual flat expression to wait for the others.

The dekentar pushed in, and after three steps Cedrith's heart jumped as the change-tones rang out. The dekentar stopped and tried to turn back, but got his shield and drawn sword jammed before his body. Judgement walked back into the hall, seized the guard by his collar, and yanked him forward several steps into the wider area: no surface in their vicinity had changed shape or position and now the tones were fading. The dekentar angrily slapped Judgement's hand away, bringing his sword quite close to him and taking up a fighting pose. Alendic barked at them to stop and charged through the gap at a trot. Cedrith, looking to Natasha, bowed and offered her the path in gentlemanly fashion. She nodded with a sparkling smile and stepped in, turning her body sideways with her head facing forward. The sides pressed against her ample flesh, and after a step, the healer adopted a kind of swishing sideways dance with her hips and torso, gently working her body forward. She even began to hum a naughty tavern-tune, and the men were chuckling by the time she was halfway through. She stepped out at last, and Alendic made a popping sound as of a cork from a wine-bottle. Natasha laughed and slapped him playfully. Cedrith trailed his shield and stepped through after her, emerging with a slight bow to the others as they re-ordered themselves.

Up ahead the hallway ended in a crosswise hall. The branches left and right were narrow and only three steps each, terminating in doors facing ahead, into the chamber they had distantly spied. Cedrith could see clearly now that the patches of light and darkness he had glimpsed before were actually statues, carvings of warriors at least ten feet tall, standing near each of the two doors. In the center of the chamber between them, the rippling distorting effect continued, almost like water running over the glass wall, but somehow standing free in the room's center. The left-hand door, nearer the black statue, had a set of three jagged marks, regular and parallel to one another but not suggesting any letter or rune Cedrith had seen before. On the other side, in the lee of the white statue, the door carried a symbol of a circle with a center-dot, like a simple target, whose meaning was equally obscure to the sage. As the party walked back and forth viewing these things and taking in the chamber beyond, Cedrith felt the rising fear overwhelm any previous good humor he had felt owing to Natasha's antics. Another arcane challenge lay ahead of them, and his terrors took position in the wings of his mind, ready to make their entrance.

"I'll bet my best cloak," Alendic announced, "the doors will both open at once, and this hall will close behind us, as it did before. There's not enough room for us all to stand in front of one. We'll have to be at both ends and ready."

There was a long moment's silence then; everyone looked surreptitiously at the black statue as if afraid it would notice them. The dekentar chewed his lip and said, "So where is the problem? We step through these doors, and we'll be together at once on the other side. You don't believe… the statue will attack us?"

Alendic for answer laughed rather long and hard. Natasha screwed up her face into a half-grin and said only, "That, in short, my good guardsman, is precisely what he believes. And I'm afraid I must agree with him."

"Then if you will allow me–" the actor began, reaching for his pack.

"No, Alendic," Natasha said, "do not use that foul reagent again. Our lives are not in danger."

"Yet," he responded cheerfully, but obeyed the healer.

"You saw this before," Cedrith accused, "on your previous–"

"No, no," Alendic cut back testily, "not the last time here, anyway, but in other places, yes it's just the sort of thing. Why else have the chamber?"

"You suspect more than you say," Cedrith persisted. "What about the water, the doors… what are you not telling us?"

"Peace, sirrah. I will divulge my thoughts when I deem you ready to hear them."

"And why not now? I am ill with the cloud of secrecy around you, Alendic. Is this the trust of an adventurer, the way you always treated your companions?"

"You go too far, sage. I have never claimed that you were one of my companions." Alendic retained his eternal grin, but the way he stepped in made it clear he was prepared to draw sword in anger.

"Peace, both of you, and as you said, Alendic," Natasha announced. "We are indeed in this together, and Cedrith is correct that we should share what we know. I will say this: standing before another such chamber five years ago, we had quite a long wait before we could enter. Let us divide ourselves as was suggested, and then while we hope for the best, we will be prepared for the chance that my *companion* predicts." Natasha placed the slightest emphasis on her choice of word while looking at the actor, and his grin grew into something much more wholesome.

"Alendic and I will stand by the left-hand door," Natasha offered, "and you three on the right."

"No chance of that, my dear," Alendic countered. "I won't risk you anywhere near this black statue."

"And certainly not both of you," Cedrith said, drawing the actor's gaze. "You are, em, the veterans of this sort of thing"–the Elf bowed to the actor–"and we should not risk you both in the same place if we can." Alendic nodded at this with some respect.

"Then I shall stay on the left," he said, "and you, Natasha, on the right. That will help me to keep my mind on my work," he quipped lasciviously, and the healer shook her head as she moved to take up station. "Who else, then? One more to stand with me."

After a moment's pause, both Judgement and the dekentar stepped to Alendic, and Cedrith was ashamed at how relieved he felt. The guardsman clenched his fist and said, "I won't let you that far from me while we are here, you gypsy mongrel."

"Mind your tongue, sir," Natasha called out and the dekentar snapped around. "Solemn Judgement is worthy of many titles of honor, but he hasn't spent enough time with the Rom to be called a Gypsy yet."

The dekentar's blank stare of incomprehension raised a laugh from Natasha. "Never mind, sirrah, I ask that you accompany me now; it may only be a moment, as you have said."

He reluctantly assented to this arrangement, and so Judgement stood in the left-hand hallway with Alendic, while the dekentar shouldered his way closest to the opposite door, followed by Natasha and Cedrith. They waited and watched the chamber beyond for a long moment, followed by several long minutes. The statues did not move, and the column of water seemed to flow down and up at the same time. There was no exit from the chamber in sight. The tones sounded, and after a long stretch sounded again, but nothing nearby changed shape or position. Each party member leaned against a wall as they waited. Alendic reached to a side-pouch of his rucksack and broke a piece of jerky to hand to Judgement, tossing another piece across the way to the others.

The time stretched on. The more Cedrith looked at the statues–plate-armored warriors with high helms and long swords–the less he liked the situation. But when his gaze fell on the water-column, his sidelined fear cleared its throat and prepared to barge onstage.

"Natasha," he said, mainly to distract himself, "you said that both the Hopelords and the Lieges of Despair created this place. Was it in a single, great enchantment, or was it- em, built in a more conventional way?"

The healer shrugged, and Alendic called, "What difference?"

"I hardly know. But as little as I like the whole idea… if Hope worked on, let us say, the rings overhead, and perhaps Despair wrought the chasm, and so on, we could better unravel their intent."

"Aye, I've thought on this much," Alendic said, "yet I cannot see the line, the neat partition of labor. This chamber is clearly sign of both powers at work. And the devilish walls themselves…"

"The walls themselves are all beautiful," Natasha averred. "Their design must have been Elven."

"Or Dwarvish," Cedrith countered, "with all the complexity of their movement."

"Only sorcery could cause what we have seen here," Natasha replied. "I think Hope built some of the walls, and Despair others."

"Then how can they all be beautiful?" Cedrith countered with a smile.

"Perhaps Hope built the maze and Despair the chambers," Natasha said. "Those Arms of the Earth are clearly spoken of in our records, sorcery of the Liege Pelundrag."

"Then why the white statue," Judgement said quietly. No one had an answer to this.

"Why should there be a mystery of any kind?" Cedrith asked with some pique. "All these centuries we've lived without knowing of this place. And how many others were ever created, secrets buried in our past?"

"I think," Natasha said carefully, "that the Lords passed on the traditions, but we did not keep them well. We grew lazy it seems, and only a few knew the full story."

"The nobles," Judgement said in a voice with some bite in it.

"What is that supposed to mean?" the dekentar demanded from across the way.

"Did you notice," Judgement said firmly, "that in the ancient records, there is no mention of 'nobles'? This man was a knight of Conar, that lady became a High Curate of Astor, and so forth. But they were never set apart with a name for themselves as a group. If Sir Percis slew a giant and saved a village, he was called noble for the mettle he had shown. But the sages of history did not assume a child had those qualities simply because of who their father had been."

"Are you saying we Altrindurs are cowards?" the dekentar snarled.

"And if a person of common birth performed a wonder," Judgement ground on, "such as Tarly the Miller's Daughter in the challenge of the Ebon Baron, her cleverness and courage were praised with the word 'noble' that is now reserved exclusively for the sons and daughters of a group, a sect of those who know."

"You landless orphan, jealous of your betters; how dare you cast insult even as you scheme to break the Law of Conar?" The dekentar had pushed his way back to the head of his side-hall, and his glare was mirrored by the Man in Grey. Cedrith stepped out into the central hall to put his body between them.

"Sir, you do my friend wrong to accuse him; he speaks only of the record of history. Stay your hand here, we must remain together while the danger threatens."

The dekentar spat contemptuously and said, "I will not release you from your vow, villain. Tomorrow at the Arena you will pay."

"But what of all this chatter?" Alendic asked. "There is now a noble class among us, what of it, lad?"

"What is it that they do?"

Silence then, and Cedrith felt the shock of all the rest as he turned and stared.

"Where the dragons? Does Despair threaten to return through the Swords of Stone, and if so, who guards against that? Are there giants on the earth still? Do the garruk war-drums sound on any frontier known to Hope? Are sorcerers in Araluntir's city striving to still the magics conjured by their enemies from unknown quarters? Bandits, a stampede of farm animals broken loose, anything! But there is no work for the noble class," he panted, "no work, no war, no wrongs to be righted, except a gaping hole of chaos three hundred leagues across, the kingdom of the Percentalion, a mortal wound upon the heart of the Lands of Hope that bleeds harder every year."

The dekentar pushed halfway through Cedrith's guard, throwing off his arms and crossing the hallway then. "Shut your mouth, you filthy peasant!"

Alendic interposed as well, and his drawn blade could not be ignored. Relentless, the Man in Grey continued behind him.

"Renan Altrindur, indeed, lives up to his charge, and seeks to bear the burden of his rank against the disbelief of all. He seeks a myth, say his peers, when he rides after the Castle of the Chosen Wanderers, but he pursues an *occupation* as a knight. He recalls that the word '*nobilitara*' denoted 'worthy of trust' and does better than his brother, who sought to marry a woman against her choice by speaking through their fathers instead of with his own words and heart. But for the rest..." Judgement made a dismissive gesture with his hands, "they wait and watch and keep their secrets."

The dekentar would have lunged for him then, but the tones suddenly sounded, and after such a long interval it made everyone jump. Natasha screamed. Cedrith and Alendic scrambled back for their places, followed by the dekentar, who retreated to Natasha as well. Some walls farther away slid and melded, but neither door opened before them. In the silence, Judgement dropped a final word.

"So it is that the Guildmistress and *cardinus* here have, through diligence and intelligence risen in the city to hold high positions. And like true nobles of the day, they judge what it is fair for the rest of us to know."

Cedrith gaped at the unmistakable offense and ill-will behind this statement; just as he did on their first day together, he doubted whether his friend was in his right mind. He looked at all the others and saw fear, distrust, repugnance; his spirits sank to their lowest point and he reflected that he was as far from all the things he loved as any voyage could have taken him. He looked back to where Judgement stood against a wall, his cape wrapped tightly around him and his head bent as if he were cold. All alone even here, with his life in peril and any chance of return resting on the actions of just a few others. Even us, he rejects.

Like a dim echo, Cedrith's earlier thoughts came back to him: protect Judgement, see to the orphan lad. But the idea carried no force; he was shocked too deeply by the young man's blasphemy. If only Natasha had continued the catechism of Hope… but now Cedrith realized he was starting to lie to himself. Some, at least, of what Judgement said was true: there were too many secrets in the present age.

And he had a duty. He could not choose to abandon the young man now, simply because he acted unpleasantly. He reflected that he could hardly have been less pleased with Solemn Judgement than he had been on the day they first met. Patience, now as then; patience and duty.

Natasha began to murmur under her breath in the tongue of power, and put her hand to the glass facing the chamber. Everyone looked on, no one spoke as the energy of her casting radiated into the next room, spreading like a pool of spilled light across the space. An edge of the light touched the nearer, white statue and a dim glow answered it. "There is life within," Alendic said. "I have seen her spell before." But the energy carried on, even as Natasha's breathing became more labored, and reached to the center of the chamber and the column of water there. Again the glow was reflected, though the hue was quite different, it rippled like the column itself. Natasha stopped chanting and leaned on her hand to catch her breath.

As they watched, the column's movement slowed, and it changed shape, reaching a branch of itself in the direction of the energy that had touched it. Moving closer, it increasingly took on the shape of a human hand, and by the time its fingers touched the glass, they were small and short, matching Natasha's as they occupied the same space. The healer stared unmoving at this wondrous image, her eyes widening with a kind of understanding. On the column of water there now appeared a face-like mask, vaguely female and gazing as if blind.

"It… lives," Natasha whispered. "It guards the chamber… we must speak in truth of our nature…beware the black!" she screamed and finally pulled her hand away.

The tones sounded impossibly deep and strong. A plane of glass sprang from the hallway floor, dividing the group from each other; Cedrith saw the rising wall also bisected the chamber cutting off the white statue side from the black. The two rune-scribed doors slid down into the cavern, revealing the chamber beyond. And Cedrith heard the sound that stone makes when it creaks, as the two statues rustled with movement turning to face the intruders.

⊕⊕⊕

The bells in the clock tower rang fast and strong, meaning a human hand on the rope. Either the city was on fire, or under attack. Everyone turned out to the streets, and then to the walls as the matter made itself known by word of mouth. Refugees from the Percentalion.

Anteris practically flew to the southern parapet, meeting Calper and the other old men on the way down, frantically putting on any piece of armor that still fit and arguing over which weapons to take. Out on the southern plain he saw two figures, smaller than toy soldiers in the distance, scrambling in the direction of the town with larger, bulkier blotches on their track. The humans were still too far off, even for the slow, deliberate pace of their harriers. As Anteris watched, two of the beasts circled ahead of the pair–a man and a woman, he could see now, both unarmed–and cut them off from the city and safety.

The town guard, accompanied by the veterans and trailing a stream of curious onlookers, issued from the southern gate and hastened to the limen of the boundary stakes as if they marked the seashore. Another twenty rods to the edge of the pack, and the humans were stopped now, surrounded by five shaggy beasts, helpless to go further. The man, somewhat older and clearly tiring fast, held a large ungainly stick of wood, which he swung wildly to all sides trying to cover the younger woman, who clutched a small parcel wrapped in a cloth to her shoulder. It was just the way a woman would hold… Anteris' heart sank to hear the thin, distant wail of an infant.

The soldiers seemed of two minds whether to advance further; most pointed with urgency at the monsters, but the captain was yelling of the need to wait for bows. Anteris heard an eye-watering curse from the middle of the group, and then shouted aloud to see Forge run towards the monsters alone. Screaming more ribald names at the beasts, the youth came within five paces of the one closest to the town. It finally turned ponderously on a half-dozen legs to face the intruder and its misshapen head was half a foot taller than the boy's. Hexavores! Anteris realized, and his spirits shivered to think of the tale the foot-knight Haltar had told them that night by the fire.

Nothing fazed, Forge yelled again at the beast, and when it roared in return, he neatly flung an earth-clod directly into its maw. Choking and shaking with rage, the creature spat out bits of hard dirt; Forge made a rude gesture with his finger and the monster lunged for him. The smith's boy danced back out of the way and turned to flee; not as fast as Anteris, but plenty speed enough to elude this massive carnivore. After several paces, the beast gave up and returned to the circle.

Seizing the chance, the man had dragged his partner several steps into the gap, but the hexavores moved to cut off the way, and he was again stopped and forced to swing with all his might in huge circles. The monsters radiated perfect confidence, and took their time, giving most of their attention to each other as they closed in, nipping and growling at rivals for pride of place, in a fight already won.

Enough was enough for those at the stakes. Surging forward in a rabble, thirty or more adults ran upon the spike-backed beasts, yelling to distract them along with Forge (whom they ordered home, receiving more gestures for their trouble). And turn them they did; three of the monsters on the side closest to the city ponderously swung around to face the crowd.

There was no order or plan, as various persons shouted "Aim for the head!" "No, the vitals!" "The eyes, that's what they said!" A hail of weapons rained down, including several objects not meant to be thrown, along with one crossbow bolt that a veteran had loaded. Everything missed or bounced away, and the creatures panted at the meat all around. But first things first; the two furthest from the crowd hedged in even closer, ignoring the man's branch and preparing to strike.

Some of the soldiers, seeing how little avail their weapons were, began to fall back. But up through their ranks strode a thin figure in blue robes. Anteris saw from the wall but could not fully believe; the middle-aged man nearly as thin as he was, standing to before these five monstrous beasts.

With his mace held to one side, the preacher looked on the nearest with a face of boiling fury and outrage. Alaetar reached to the sky with one open hand and called out, "*Heu, thybolda Aralun victoris!*" and brought the arm down to point at his foe. From the clear blue sky, a crackling bolt of silver-white lightning fell directly on the hexavore, with a cascade of fragments and a sharp report to hurt the ears. The hexavore, in the midst of a fearless snarl, simply incinerated in the blast, its protruded eyes glowing with pale light before exploding, and the hulk of its body falling like a tree and singed up and down its length, even to the pads of its feet. Hearing and smelling their pack-mate defeated, the remaining creatures now dropped their pursuit of food and faced the preacher.

Again he called out, and another bolt fell from the heights of nowhere to destroy a monster. Stepping between the corpses to stand next to the couple, Alaetar came within two feet of the largest. Though startled and confused, it instinctively bit at him, catching his arm in its massive jaws. Crying out and pulled off the ground by the tooth-vise, Alaetar brought his mace down on the horny skull; there was a small flash of force and the beast howled in unexpected hurt, dropping the preacher and pulling away, leaving numerous clots of its brain on his weapon as it staggered back. One of its mates, sensing the chance, fell on the wounded one immediately, and gained a clear shot at its vitals.

Alaetar scrambled to his feet hugging his wounded arm and stayed with the couple. Together the trio edged around the remaining hexavore, now harassed by a youth on one side who was coming very close and throwing clods at his eyes, to the front by a screaming mob of meat, and on the third side by a trio who moved between the smells of death. Seeing a chance, it lunged at the woman trailing a bit behind the others; but Alaetar called out in the tongue of power "*Innocens defendar!*" and a corona of blue force interposed. The hexavore's teeth caught, and did not catch, on her frame, and the threesome slipped by.

Snarling in annoyance, it turned to assist its mate in devouring the wounded one, still alive. And as all three beasts stood together, Alaetar–though staggering with exertion–pulled himself erect and again invoked the powers of heaven with a voice that cracked as he shouted. Anteris saw the bolt, larger than the two before it, lance down and envelop the three remaining hexavores completely. For an instant, they were lit in mid-struggle by a sheet of brightest light; then the monsters passed from view as the blast grew too great, and hurt the eyes. The report was so cacophonous that the man and woman fell to their knees; several moments later, Anteris heard the echo of it slap back and forth among the buildings of the town beyond him, and a nearby window broke. As the intense flash of ground-light cleared away, there was nothing to be seen where the three monsters had stood.

Alaetar could barely hold upright, but the people of the town rushed forward to raise him, and the other survivors, on their shoulders with a tremendous cheer as they paraded back to town. Everyone was eager to claim a piece of the glory, and it seemed there was plenty to spare. Anteris watched as they passed below through the gate, Alaetar quaintly puzzled as if he could not imagine why the fuss, and the two others just staring and shocked, holding hands as they were hoisted within the city. Anteris scrambled down then to be in the front at the central mall; he took a narrow alley for a short-cut and ran into Forge along the way.

"You hero! Those things had teeth as long as your hand!" The scribe's assistant was so enthused he even slapped the smith on his dusty tunic, which raised a small cloud.

Forge grinned and shrugged. "Not many as can do much with a mouthful of dirt."

"Well you should know, you spend your day chewing on it, seems like."

"I can do for you too, if you want," the apprentice replied with a mock-punch, but the two of them were too happy to bother pretending a fight today. Together they elbowed and ducked their way towards the front of the mall-crowd, still laughing.

"But how did you know? I mean, you came so close."

"I talked to the woodsman," Forge replied, "when I brought the knight Haltar's chain shirt back to him. Astor's balls! You should have seen when we took it off him, right there in the smithy. One of those garruk had bit him, and the links were driven through the jerkin, right into his flesh! He just tugs it free like a loose thread on his shirt, and hands it over all clotted with blood. But on the return, he wasn't there, so I handed the finished job to that woodsman."

"Yes, Treaman. What did you think of him?"

"Ooh, nothing like Haltar. He's near as young as us; well, as me anyway." Forge was always careful to emphasize the one-year difference in their age. "I got him to tell me the story about the hexavores again; he said they're slow, and jealous, and cocky-like. So then," and here the boy shrugged as if to say everything he had done in the fight made perfect sense.

Now they came to the mall itself, where the procession halted and cheering paused. The three were let down on the steps of the church to Conar that dominated the western side; they sat on the top step, and the crowd could see them easily. The woman nursed the child, and the two adults kept staring at the stone all around. Members of the town council, honestly overjoyed and only a bit put out to have to jostle with veterans and apprentices for the places of honor, came forward to welcome the couple.

As they spoke, goods were quietly passed from the merchant stalls to the front; water-pots for washing, clean cloths, tankards of ale, binding for Alaetar's arm, apples, bread, new sandals, a walking stick, children's clothes, milk, a toy. Anteris knew they were being welcomed by the speeches, but not a word stuck in his mind; he waited like everyone else for the questions.

And eventually, the council had finished their say, including a sincere toast of praise for Alaetar, which brought a massive cheer. He was standing now, and looking silently down on the couple as if he could see back to where they had come from. As the whispers of the power he had displayed circulated, those few who hadn't seen it took another look at the itinerant preacher, and no one was laughing anymore.

The questions at last began, and only the first one went well at all.

"Where have you come from?"

"From Hollinsfen," the man said.

"The southwestern side," "Sixty leagues," "Nearer eighty," the murmurs ran in response.

"Just you and your wife?" a councilor asked.

The man and woman looked to each other, and both broke into tears. After a time, they leaned together, with the greatest tenderness but in a way that did not suggest intimacy. The leading men and women of Trainertown inquired, apologized, solicited, and finally waited with the others.

At last, the man could manage to say, "This… is not my wife. I am Canith, and she is Piree. Shelia, my wife, died on the second day."

"How many set out with you, then? And how long ago?"

"How long? I cannot… certainly it was three weeks, we only measure the seasons anymore, not the days."

Now the young woman spoke through her tears. "There were twenty-nine of us, when we left."

A gasp ran around the mall, and Alaetar exclaimed in dismay. "Do you mean, of all those, only you two, and your child…?"

"This," the woman answered, dissolving again into tears, "is not my baby!"

Many in the crowd cried out in shock at this, and one councilor whispered, "But, you are nursing, madam!"

The woman simply looked up at her, with eyes that told of madness, and the need to think no more. Now the older man leaned in again, and simply placed his hand on her shoulder. All around them, the mall with eight thousand citizens fell completely silent.

Anteris felt as if he were looking on a noblewoman naked, standing there with hundreds of people gawking at the grief of these three. He was helpless but wanted to help. Looking around at the crowd, he saw men his father's age and older, standing there as if struck on their heads, and realized they had no more wit to turn this sorrow than he did. Anteris felt wrongly treated then, as he began to realize that adults, contrary to his life-long belief, did not have the power to make everything better. He waited quietly with them, as if in church, and listened to the woman's sobs. Acting just like a grown-up, the scribe's assistant knew that more than another day had passed for him.

"The child's mother," Canith managed, "died four days ago… I believe it was. Her name was Aurell. Fell into a scrabbly pit and we… we couldn't reach her, no way to get to her."

"She asked me to hold the baby, just a moment!" Piree cried out, mimicking the action with the child at last asleep in her arms. "I've missed the feeling, s-since…" and for a moment the young woman just gargled whatever words would have come next. She took a deep shuddering breath, "She wanted to adjust her sandal, and she slipped. She… she looked up, at… at me and said… she said, to take care of, t-t-t-to…"

"We stayed for an hour, calling down to her," Canith continued, "but then, the reaver-birds came–" and he stopped as Piree screamed in horror, waking the child who murmured urgently until she nursed it some more.

"I threw rocks at the accursed things, but there were so many. So many." Canith sat there completely spent.

"What do these reaver-birds look like?"

"You haven't seen them?" Canith asked, and roused his dull mind to the effort. "They are like large dirt-brown crows, with an extra joint in their wings. Beaks like a bent nail and their eyes… entirely white. One or two, we'd just hit them with something, drive them off; carrion eaters. But there were… so many. And Aurell, she couldn't– always two or three could get in before she– I kept the child from seeing, I didn't know what else to do… and her cries, stopped, then we left."

"That was after the flood," Canith remarked as if it were years ago, "when we were caught on the little hill. There were still seven of us then, I think."

"Wait, this is all backwards," Forge cried out, abrupt and loud. Everyone looked at the smith's son, and when he saw Alaetar among them he straightened up automatically.

"Quiet, boy, they have enough to task them now," a councilor said.

Anteris saw the shame stoking up on his friend's cheek, and his jaw simply started working on its own.

"Sometimes, that's how you must hear a story," he said, a bit too loud and fast, and sounding like a child indeed.

"Please, good people, continue," Alaetar said to the survivors of Hollinsfen. "Say what pleases you, in your own good time."

"Let them sleep, even better!" cried a voice from the crowd, and a general murmur of assent came up to greet the thought.

But Canith shook his head and cried, "Once and done! After today I shall never speak of this again until the day I die, and may it not be over-long in coming."

Gasps and signs against Despair rippled across the mall and Alaetar straightened up in shock as well.

"Nay, speak not such an unworthy thought, Goodman Canith. You are here, and others not; not for you nor I to question this happening, nor to dictate the future, but instead to read it, study upon it and obey."

"You saved our lives, holy father. I meant no–"

"Long may you and your– and this good woman survive, and keep what counsel you wish."

"We left," Piree continued, "at around midsummer. Are we still in Gryphon?"

"Fire Ant," several voices assured her.

"Harvest time, then," she murmured dreamily. "The wheat in Hollinsfen was just over your knee when we left."

"Why did you leave?" one of the councilors asked. For answer, the two just stared. "I mean," the man added, "with all the peril, did you realize? Is Hollinsfen in danger?"

"Danger, no." Canith replied. "We simply wanted to join the others."

No one responded to this.

"The others," Canith repeated somewhat stubbornly. "Can you take us to them soon?"

Folks in the crowd began to look on one another and whisper. Anteris, seeing their hesitation, felt a sharp point inside him start to drag down into his gut, and he nearly doubled over with the realization.

Piree stood now and looked out. "Where are they? My uncle, he came out three years ago. And two cousins, and Teltin, the very short man who used to be our carpenter. You could not have missed him?"

"People have left Hollinsfen every year," Canith said deliberately, like a dirge. "We want to be free, among the children of Hope, away from the loneliness and the sameness, the lack of news." He suddenly stood up next to Piree, desperate and almost angry. "Where are they? Take us to them!"

"Sir," a councilwoman said, "Madam. We have not received any refugees, nor heard of any, from any castle or town in the Percentalion since…" and here she shrugged with an expression of dismay. Canith and Piree stared, then slowly sank back to the steps.

"But there have been scores of us," Canith murmured. "I thought, our fate was particularly hard, but surely–"

"Had you seen Pelian?" Anteris blurted out.

"The merchant-in-arms," Canith replied, nodding. Piree said, "It was two years ago, year of Astor." She looked to the man who again nodded. "He brought goods and sold them quite dear, but stayed only one night." Several in the crowd nodded, remembering the man's history, but Anteris added, "Not this year, then?"

"No," Canith replied, "not since then, nor have we had any other visitor. Except a garruk raid the next spring, Elosira year. But this summer, one of the sons of our elders, lad named Brig, rallied us up to make our way out. Said he could see a sign in the sky, and it was an omen to lead us."

"A sign?" Alaetar inquired sharply. "What sort of sign? What did you see?"

"Not I, holy sir; only Brigarthelon could see it."

Alaetar made a dismissive gesture then. "So you followed this boy into peril, when you could not tell if he were true or no?"

"He saw a sign," Canith said deliberately, "in the night sky, and he led us toward it. North by east, he said, towards the red star."

"Red!" Alaetar cried in shock, and then quickly folded his arms with chin down and pressed lips. Watching him, Anteris felt afraid, and glanced east though the sky was blue. He wanted to ask, to beg, but could not make his mouth move for the world.

Canith had started to speak again. "And so we took to the hill, just before the flood, because that ruined fortress was so… it was haunted, I'll be bound and any man may laugh who wishes. There were five men left, and Piree and Aurell and one other woman, and we all agreed. This was four sunrises ago, I think. But before we could reach the hill, the keep behind us just disappeared."

"And," Piree put in softly, "the mountain moved again. From south, to the west." Small nods and whispers around the crowd to this.

"And after that," Canith finished heavily, "the garruk came."

Exclamations and moans; Piree sat quietly but shivered despite the cape someone had passed up to put around her and the baby. Canith, looking down, saw a solid pair of sandals next to his torn, battered feet. Reaching down, he held them up to look, and then gestured with them like a toast to the anonymous audience, with a smile of thanks before putting them on. He acted for all the world as if someone else, not he, had a story to tell.

"How many?" someone asked at last, and he looked up again.

"Eight, I think there were eight. No drum. But one had an arbalest, and there were hammers, spiked maces… we ran for the hill, not that it would help, but they came on howling in a pack."

"How did you–? What happened to–? Did you–?" No one dared finish their thought.

"We were almost to the top," Piree said, "when we saw the man in black."

Everyone leaned in then with astonished faces; Anteris forgot all his terror, his empathy, anything that could distract him from this new surprise.

"A man, alone?" "A human, out there on the blasted lands by himself!" "You must be joking–" "What did he do?"

"He sat," Piree said matter of factly, with a small grin. "Very still, his hands across his lap and his eyes closed. I thought he might be dead, or some kind of large manikin, or a scarecrow. And all of us ran right up to him shouting and screaming; we thought he'd be left there and killed at once, and I suddenly realized, looking at him, that he hadn't breathed. And then I thought he was surely a gaunt." Gasps and half-screams greeted this observation.

"But then he did breathe," Canith continued, "once, very slowly, and opened his eyes. He looked around at us, and then heard the garruk coming, and stood up to walk down to them."

"What!" someone shouted. "To surrender?"

"To fight."

"This black armor," the smith began, "was it chain or plate?"

"He wore black robes," Canith replied, "and his hands were empty."

Too many started shouting now for him to continue; but Anteris saw both Canith and Piree had a kind of light in their eyes as they thought of this person, something much more like life and hope than they had shown before. Eventually something calmer presided around the mall.

"I will enter this church," Canith said, "and swear before the altar of Conar. He fought the garruk with his bare hands."

"And sometimes his feet," Piree agreed.

"A martial wizard," Anteris whispered, loud enough to be overheard by many who nodded. "Like the royal guard of old. I thought there were no more."

"It is a rare mastery," one man commented, "since the days of the kingdom, there have been none known to teach it. Outside Araluntir's city… but no one goes there."

"Tell us," one of the councilors asked, still sounding dubious, "was he able to slow them, give you time to get away, with his death?"

"Did he manage to slay any of them before—?"

"He slew all of them," Canith returned evenly, and again the mall erupted with incredulity.

"It was as if his arms were invulnerable, or… no, no one could be so lucky so long. They attacked him two and three at a time, no room for more. But even from behind, they could not touch him. He blocked their weapons, and when he struck back it seemed their bodies were made of straw. The smallest of them lunged for his legs, to take him down; he simply leaped in the air, as you or I would hop. Yet it carried his knees past the level of their heads, and when he came down, his right foot smashed the garruk's spine so that he folded a little bit backwards."

"And towards the end," Piree said without smiling, "he held his fist aloft and it began to glow. He struck, and his foe, in his head, and…" she shivered again and could not continue.

"Three of the men and that other woman," Canith said, pausing to try to recall her name, "fell before the man in black could intercede. Finally there was only the one with the crossbow left, thirty yards away and more. He had taken careful aim at his back, and I cried out."

"So that was how he died," the councilor concluded, but Canith shook his head.

"He whirled about. He caught it."

"In the chest?"

"In his hand." And Canith pointed to the door of the church, to remind everyone of his promise.

"Then he flipped it about," Piree said, "and threw it back. Thirty paces, at least. Into the garruk's eye."

"Eight garruk males," Forge said wonderingly, "with his bare hands."

"But what happened to this remarkable warrior?" Alaetar inquired.

"I have never seen anything so strange," Canith said. "We tried to come down to him, to thank him for our rescue. But he held up one hand–still he had said no word to us–and motioned for all to wait. He stood still for what seemed a long time. Then he paced partway back up the hill, turned back down, and began to… to practice, I think."

"He was going over the fight, in his mind," Piree insisted. "We saw him stepping, turning, blocking thin air, striking. The entire fight! And two or three times, he froze in mid-step, as if he were thinking about something. Then he would nod and continue. And when he had finished throwing the bolt, he sat down and again stopped breathing."

"Well, we waited for him, there was nothing else to do," Canith said. "And perhaps an hour later, he starts to breathe again, and opens his eyes and speaks to us."

"We thanked him for our lives, and he just said 'any would have done the same.' We asked him to come with us, and he shook his head, said he must go where he was bound."

"We asked him where that was," Piree said, "and I'd have followed him anywhere. But he simply pointed to his own chest and said 'to the center'."

"We begged him, but that's all he would say," Canith continued. "So, with darkness coming on, we simply left him sitting there, and walked away." He looked to the crowd, and then cried out, "What else could I do? There were still four of us, and the baby too. He was clearly insane."

"A good man," Piree averred, "but you don't get anywhere by standing still."

Anteris looked all around the crowded city-center; behind him the bell rang the hour, for once completely ignored. Some had placed blankets down, others chairs; food was passed everywhere, and the pace of the city had come to a stop around him. A kind of somber holiday, he thought to himself. He broke a roll and handed half to Forge, quietly saying, "Better me to you than the other way around," and getting a punch for his trouble. Together they sat and munched and waited for the two to continue their tale. The sun was setting, and Anteris knew soon the lights of heaven would be visible. Looking again at Alaetar, he felt the chill tap of fear, to remember the red star. Until today, he thought he had merely been seeing things.

Cedrith, Natasha and the dekentar shuffled into the chamber of the white statue without a word, as if at a chapel where the hero was unknown. And still alive. The warrior-statue took one step on its booted feet to bar the way, and reached to draw its weapon with a grinding ring. The dekentar stood with shield slung to cover the healer, and Cedrith edged in from the other side with his, though his knees felt watery. Natasha, weaponless before the giant warrior, seemed used to the situation; she fearlessly stepped out from between her escorts and held up her palm in the Telholian gesture of friendship. "Hail, guardian, we are children of Hope and mean–" and then ducked quickly as the statue's blade cut the air overhead. Cedrith and the dekentar stepped aside to clear her retreat, and the sage realized he had seen this bulky pacifist dodge blows several times already. As large as she was, Natasha was quite adept in some way he could not fathom.

The pair of men backed away until they were within a body-length of the water column, and instinctively Cedrith turned his head to look behind him into the other half of the room.

The bisecting wall had split the chamber in half down its length as it had the outer hall, severing them from Alendic and Judgement. In the room's former center, the wall had a gap filled by the watery thing, looming nearly five feet wide and over eight feet tall. And on the other side…

Judgement had moved further into the chamber leaving Alendic closer to the door, weapons drawn and in full combat with the ebon stone-warrior. Its sword, long as a man, crackled with a painfully dark luminescence, hard to look at; as it slashed down at the Man in Grey, he swung his staff to block. The statue's blade sparked with blackfire, and the impact sent the young man reeling.

Alendic stepped in from behind and landed an expert, but seemingly useless, blow on the statue's calf. It took a further step after Judgement, then wheeled to face the new threat. Alendic skittered back towards the entrance, and the grey youth alertly stepped in to land two quick blows on the statue's unprotected back; his iron drew sparks but had no other obvious effect.

Again, the statue belatedly slowed, turned and pursued the younger foe. As Cedrith's view of the trio crossed from glass wall to the water-column, they suddenly shrank–a black warrior the size of a child chasing two magical moving toys–then ballooned in size to normal men and giant foe. The sounds of their combat and Alendic's shouts were muffled behind the crystal barrier, though the chamber held no roof.

"This way, boy! Hit him now. Good, again! Alright, he's for me next, back away, back! Take this, stone-pile, and that! Ho, then, lad! It's time to rescue your elder again!"

The two men fenced with skill, but Cedrith could see it was a dance of death. He knew, without knowing anything, that the ebon statue would never tire, or slow, or stop. The flesh had limits.

The white statue took another swing at Natasha, which she rolled to avoid, gasping and coming up awkwardly still in harm's way. The dekentar, though awed by the magic before him, took a stumbling step and a half-hearted swing, but did not distract the statue.

"Stay back!" Natasha shouted, still dodging and weaving her arms for balance, "I can take care of myself."

She alternated very deftly between giving ground, changing direction, feinting and avoiding the white-stone slashes when they came. The statue was not quick but relentless, and aside from the entrance there was no way out of the chamber.

"You cannot keep this up forever!" Cedrith shouted as he huddled near the water-column with the dekentar.

"You have… to help," she cried back in passing, and clearly running low on breath.

"What, me? I cannot fight that–"

"Cedrith, use your mind! The water-spirit… told us to declare our side… but… doesn't work. We are of Hope, stone-ears… Hope!" Natasha barely avoided the next blow but turned and ran to gain a little room, then waited for the statue's next advance.

Behind him, Cedrith heard a shout of pain, and whirled to see Alendic down on one knee, clutching his waist where the black blade had nicked him; the wound still crackled with sparks of blackfire, and Alendic groped for his dropped sword as if he could not see. Judgement, without hesitation, stepped in behind the statue and furiously swung his cudgel in a weaving motion, slapping the ends on the statue's torso and hip in alternation. Four blows like a quick hammer, and the statue turned away from the actor still grimacing and not looking to his sword. Now Judgement had no partner for distraction, and gave ground with his staff held high to block the colossal blows. Each one staggered him and threw off ebony sparks of flame, which hurt Cedrith's eyes even as he watched. Natasha shouted again, gasping for breath.

"I am… a *human*, damn you! I am of Hope! Cedrith!"

"Natasha, this is insane!" the Elf shouted back as she dodged heavily into a wall to avoid a sweep of stone. "We are here facing death because of some little trick, some forgotten word? We have no chance now to decipher this– you can't–"

"Cedrith, you must! I cannot think– ach!" she cried, ducking low and then staggering backwards. "Water-spirit… spoke of… must be something… haugh!" Finally losing her balance, the healer could only throw herself directly backwards into a reverse somersault–something she doubtless performed better five years ago–and could not regain her feet. The white statue pounded in and raised its sword again to strike down at the woman on her hands and knees.

The dekentar shouted, "We are Hope!" and then to Cedrith, "She said we had to speak the truth, and we are."

The sage put his hands to his head as if his brain might escape. Desperately trying to marshal his thoughts, he turned away to face the water-column, looking up into its face and hoping it would speak to him. It gazed blindly back–Judgement beat off another swing and circled to his left without much room–Cedrith saw the water-face and suddenly the memory came back to him.

"No," he exclaimed to the dekentar, "she said 'speak *in* truth'." He cupped his hands as he stepped towards the white statue's back, and shouted for all he was worth, "*AR ARALTE!*"

The dekentar hissed, "We've said that!" but Natasha, beneath the blade, understood at once and echoed, "*Ar Aralte! Ar Aralte!*"

In mid-sweep, the white statue halted its attack, then straightened and faced Cedrith. Whatever elation he might have felt at saving his friend evaporated as the sage saw the statue take slow steps in his direction with its sword still raised.

Then he realized what was needful. "Say it," he urged the dekentar.

"I have, plain as day," the guard replied, and Cedrith actually hit him with the flat of his shield. "In the Ancient tongue, fool, say it!"

"*Ar Aralte… Ar Aralte!*" the dekentar said at last. The statue stopped, turned, regained its post, sheathed the stone-sword; it came to attention and gestured with its free hand to the opposite end of the chamber. There a panel of glass became visible, with the target-rune etched on its face.

"You've done it!" Natasha breathed heavily, edging around the statue and then jogging over to embrace the sage as he had remembered her to do.

"I don't get the point," the dekentar said stubbornly.

"It's quite simple," Cedrith replied. "These statues were created long before the Common Tongue developed as we speak it today. To 'speak in truth' means to use the language in which a lie is not possible." A loud clang and gasp distracted the threesome, to the nether side of the chamber where Judgement was backed against an angle of the wall and desperately heaving his iron-bound staff to deflect the onslaught of the black statue. Alendic, still woozy, was beginning to focus his eyes a bit and had grasped his blade but was hardly able to stand, much less fight. He rummaged desperately in his rucksack but was in obvious pain. Natasha lurched to the edge of the wall, very close to the water-column, and called out to the others.

"*Ar Aralte!* Say it, friends, quickly!" Dutifully, both men cried out the words meaning 'Hope Forever.' But the statue did not desist.

"Moment in time!" Cedrith cried in horror.

"What is it?" Natasha asked. "Why did it not–"

"The black statue," Cedrith hissed in horror, "made by Despair, it would require the… other pass-word."

Natasha threw her hand into her mouth at the realization and Cedrith felt his knees go weak again. His mind could barely form the idea of the word of power; '*Drago,*' meaning 'I Despair.'

No man alive could call that word out loud.

⊕⊕⊕

The First War of Liberation

Excerpt from the Conar Scriptorium Tome

Thus the wave of Hope did sweep the land 'twixt the ocean and the western slopes of yon Marble Swords, and despite loss-grievous to Hope, the forward army of Despair was full shattered and many taken. Even unto the north-most pass through the mountains didst Hope strike, so bold and swift that Mauglir's thane Trekarg was taken unawares, and lost the heights with his fastness there to the assault of the sons of Conar, Ekotelh, Ekhonon and Khoirah. 'Tis thought that full fivescore thousand persons won free from Despair in the space of this war. Straight through the pass the foes didst rout, and as Hope rested a space 'twas Conar's chief vassal Areghel did carry the van with his retainers, raiding east and south unto the country beyond the Marble Swords.

In yon blighted kingdom the earth demon Kog held sway under Mauglir the Despair-Liege of Men, and had by his sorcerous might caused the land itself to resemble e'en that hell from whence he were summoned. Expecting no assault by the assurances of his overlord, Kog was now overwrought with rage at this insolent invasion of his domain, and moved with his hell-beasts and lesser demons and his newborn tribes of garruk to meet Areghel's van in battle.

The preachers among Areghel's host didst summon awesome miracles to their aid, and his knights visited great slaughter upon the myriad foe. Yet the mage-knight's force, having moved far enow too soon, was flanked and in danger of losing its withdrawal; nor wouldst Areghel fain take retreat for any cost, for he visioned the plight of this cursed land and burned to undo it, as all who heard him didst aver. Verily, he forged ahead and did break through the ranks of Despair coming to grips with Kog in personal combat.

Many in his honor-guard were there to witness the struggle, which lasted less than an hour yet altered the terrain thereabouts. The enormous were-shape of the demon made shift to its owner's will, and thus Areghel was harassed by tentacles, pincers, monstrous spines and arms like living poisonous serpents. So quick as yon hero didst strike them off with Tanagar, his two-handed blade, there grew more by the demon's will. By spell and strike, the man proceeded against his foe, and despite all changes did drive him back. Then with a puissant effort the demon seized the mage-knight's blade, wrenching it half-forth and breaking it in twain.

Throwing away his hilt, Areghel cried out, "Tanagar, no weapon made by man could have served me better; but now I call upon the force of Law itself, to enter me in Hope and serve me to strike this demon down." Then didst seem to the knights on yon field that a great light bore from the sky upon Areghel, such that Kog could not approach him and the enemy fell back in great dismay. Nor did the lord of chaos seem to know what transpired before him, but each of his divers faces showed fear.

Areghel emerged from the column of light with great strength renewed and lo! He did make shift to combat the demon with his bare hands. The shape-changer threw out new limbs, created earth-fires, and cast sorcerous bolts at his foe; yet for Areghel, his open hands were now swords, his fists like hammers, his forearms shields, and his feet like rams as he dealt swiftly with two and three assaults at once. Battering his foe with buffets, Areghel drove Kog back and ever back roaring in fear and disquiet until, with a tremendous sweep of his open right hand and a shout that split the rocks nearby, he did down Kog upon the earth and shatter his main, true face, severing his eye from his body and stretching him senseless.

The horde of Despair withdrew in fear and rout on this, mayhap taking the demon's form with them (else it were some sorcery unknown to Hope). Meanwhile, the horn of Conar himself, the Law-Giver and Hopelord, sounded the call to assemble to the rear, and thus Areghel was minded to obey without admitting retreat. Moving with due speed to the mountain pass, Areghel met with the other lords of Hope and with Conar, and there was round rejoicing when the news of the war was shared on all sides.

Then didst many of Areghel's retainers, who were witness to the great struggle, throw themselves at his feet as suppliants and beg to be shown the wisdom of this great mastery. "For well we know," they said, "that the demons of Despair are more fey than any other foe, and our weapons are of little use against them unless enhanced by great spells or forged in cold iron. And we would learn to destroy them with our bodies as you have."

Areghel, with light now shining from his very eyes, to this replied, "Know you that the learning is a hard one, and you must allow that Law itself will move into your body, and live inside you, and guide you ever more. Only in this wise will you be enabled to hammer the demonic, and the undead, and other forces of Despair with your own flesh."

And the retainers didst say with a ready voice, "Aye, let this be done to us as hast been to you, and we will be your true followers, and forswear the use of any weapon at your command."

But Areghel said, "Let you learn the use of weapons, and spells of magic also, for these too are good. Remember always, that even the greatest of them may fail, but the Law within yourself will be your truest support." And the retainers didst fain to do all that he said. And Conar, who wondered at what he had heard, yet took thought that it was most good.

Thus the Demonstrikers were begun, a royal guard for Areghel and his issue from that day forward as he ruled the kingdom Conar would assign him. Divers other lords were assigned their places as well; Dunedin a mountain fastness in an unknown place, for a special order that would serve and succor the most worthy of the helpless, and to Aballe, the task of building a keep in that very pass, to guard the way and the beginning of the great road that the Hopelord envisioned.

Thus the Helm was begun, and Conar did order a halt of seven cycles of the sun. It was in the time of quiet following the war that many hurts were healed and building began, and the freed peoples were raised up in a certain measure. The Lords of Hope thought of the great harm that was done, notwithstanding their efforts, and took counsel how to limit them. Thus was a plan undertaken, on a narrow path between war and surrender, to reduce in some wise the potential for renewed conflict to do damage unto the land and its peoples. The Enemy, when approached via herald and under truce, were of mind to agree in part. Thereafter was the Hopeward created, in the manner of an historic exchange.

First did the Hopelords send messengers under the symbol of the tripartite olive leaf, to signify that their peaceful intent was sworn and abuse to them would bring the ire of their overlords. The Heroes so dispatched were Mendel, son of the Hopelord of Elves, Khoriah, bright shining third son of Conar, and representing magical powers the mage-knight Areghel so recently returned from victory.

Despair did hear the embassy with much suspicion at the first, as such a treatment had never been proposed between these sides in their brief history here. When presented with the matter, the Despair Lieges took counsel in private and didst return with much smoother seeming to resume negotiations. Yet at first they didst dissemble much unwillingness, arguing that the most powerful weapons and lore were already in their possession, and that they should thus lose the more by such an exchange. Whereupon the messengers of Hope hastened to assure their enemies that the balance of power would be well struck with yon priceless items in their possession which they would commit likewise to the Ward.

"Yet how may we trust that thy power will be equal to that which we may nominate?" Despair demanded.

"Yea, but ye shall bring so much as ye think fit, and we shall do the same, and thus shall we both gauge the wealth of the other's measure, and each side shall speak, and be satisfied," the Hopeful messengers replied.

"But still," Despair responded, "the matter of the access, and the placement of the entrances, and the assignment of the guardian remain unknown."

"For that," Khoriah dared to answer for Hope without full leave, "we shall craft the entrance rules in concert. Let you devise such rules as seem safe to thee, and we shall hear them. The placement of the door known to ye shall be as close to the frontier between us as ye shall dare." And here Mendel and Areghel smiled, for they could see that the Lieges were in sooth pricked by this, and would place their gate very close. In such fashion the entire enterprise might come under Hope's control through the pride of their enemies.

"And the first guardian ye may choose," Khoirah continued, therein causing some unquiet with his fellow counselors. But the Lieges didst confer a moment and announce, "Yea, for our choice lies already in your keeping as a prisoner. The thane of Mauglir lord of powerful Men shall be the warder in the first instance."

"That one," quoth Areghel in some alarm, "be not a living Man, but the foulest necromancer who hath raised our own dead against us. It were in my heart to destroy him mine own self."

"This we well know," the Despair Lieges replied, "and for us we are content that he should have the honor."

After this the embassy didst strike with Despair the compact of the Hopeward, and withdrew without assault to report to the Hopelords thereof. And in three days' time, the embassy of Despair did arrive, with a symbol formed of two swords and a staff interlaced in tripartite fashion, as if a mockery of the peaceful olive, and didst claim whatever honor their enemies should choose for them, as if they cared not. But they didst deliver the message of their Lieges regarding the access and order of entrance to yon wondrous place yet to be created.

Thus spoke the embassy of Despair.

"With any two who enter, another must attend, for none shall enter the gate in pairs. Those who have come before may enter, and the pairs also may follow the thread. Visit alone and one must remain behind. Those who enter and pass the guards may choose to either exchange a worthy piece for one residing there, or to release an item of their choosing from the Ward. The remaining one will then also choose, and the sides will change thereafter. The doors shall open each declining ten cycles of Aral, from one hundred until ten be reached; this begins from the day of the opening, namely this third year since the Liberation. Then shall the doors return to closed for a century of cycles, unless it be that the Ward is empty, for without one remaining the doors cannot admit another."

The lords of Hope did list to the strange conditions, but upon conferring, they found them good and didst agree to them all. The embassy of Despair declared that it was well satisfied, and left without injury.

⊕ ⊕ ⊕

"Before the flood was the day without sun."

Dinner-time had come and gone and still the mall was filled with people, sitting on whatever they could and listening to Canith, formerly of Hollinsfen, recount his incredible tale. It was increasingly clear to Anteris, sitting with Forge behind the preacher Alaetar, that the three of them had no business surviving their ordeal, the only refugees in living memory to escape from the Land of One Hundred Castles. Piree and the baby slept next to the balding man on the top step of the church, with blankets and pillows piled around them passed in from the drigood store. Fairnum had sent his children around with platters of ale and everyone enjoyed the fare as the stars came out. There had been no work today, and if things went much later, tomorrow was not seeming a likely possibility either.

Canith slowly unclenched his body, bit by bit, as he told the story in no particular order. His movements were far less jerky, his look more composed, and it seemed to Anteris that in the last half-hour (by the town clock above) an element of weariness had begun to creep over his face.

"Do you mean, the entire day, without sun? Which day was it?"

The man shook his head, thought a while, then shook his head again. "It was before the flood. More than a week, less than two."

"Sunny throughout," murmurs from the crowd. "Was it cloudy, or a burning smoke?"

"There was no sun," Canith replied, quietly and firmly. "There was… light, though less than needed, and some clouds, yes, dark and filled with… but it was as if the sunshine was, dimmed or fogged, and Solar itself…" He shrugged. "We all became alert to it by the second hour, and everyone was watching out across the sky as we marched. Nothing. Light, but no sun."

"Shadows?" Forge asked and Cranith nodded. "Aye. Dim but enough to mark the time. And enough to show where the sun should be. But all day, nothing."

"Was it the weather did this?" "Or mayhap a vale you walked through."

"It was the Light-Drinker." Canith drew breath to continue.

"The land was rolling with patches of grass, I recall a small stream, and then ahead of us in the direction we had chosen there was a hill of some size. We thought at first, we had made it to another village. On the hill we spotted a cave, and we thought to take shelter there for a time." Canith smiled without mirth. "As if there could be any such thing as true shelter in hell. The dimness grew less, or I mean more, as we approached, and we should have taken our hint from that but we had no leader once Brig died… in the pit of tar." Canith shivered, murmured, "poor lad," and then stopped.

Another tale of horror, then, would have to stand its turn, Anteris sensed. After waiting for Canith to resume on his own, he gently prompted, "What happened at the cave?"

"The Light-Drinker, we called it later; when we were still fifty rods away it came forth from its lair. It ran upon us so swiftly, like a rush of wind. And started to eat people whole."

The mall was so quiet one could hear the tiny wheeze of the baby as it slept. No one drank, or shifted, or said a word.

"It was a horrendous beast, half the size of this church. It was furred, I think. Or perhaps… the dimness around it was greater, you could somewhat see it, but then– and all its movements seemed so, sudden. Four great legs, massive trunks and clawed, but with a man's grip in front. It shambled, or slithered from the cave down the hill and its voice was like a great gush of steam, with a crackle like fire. We tried to run… but the thing drank the light, and we became lost.

"One man, Tael I think it was, a farmer, he was right next to me as we fled. He kept yelling 'this way! this way!' and I ran with him, but suddenly he turned. He ran right around in an arc, until he was headed straight back into the darkness, to the creature. But still he yelled and pointed 'this way!' as if he were running straight. And I… I called to him, but my stomach felt all queasy and I fell down. I watched from the earth as the thing snatched him up… he was still looking back over his shoulder at me, he thought he was getting away. I saw his face, dimly though I was so close to it, he was so… so surprised."

Piree stirred in her sleep, and again Canith laid a hand gently on her shoulder. "Her husband died on that day as well," he said in lowered tones. "Best not to speak of it when she awakens. They were married in Gryphon last year."

"But how did you escape?" Forge hissed.

"We were saved."

"Again? By the man in black?"

Canith shook his head; then he stood, turned to the open doors of the church behind him and knelt in prayer. As they saw what he was doing, many others stood or knelt nearby, and Alaetar also took a knee. Canith drew a deep breath and spoke aloud.

"I thank you, Conar the Law-Giver, for creating the Chosen Wanderers. Thank you for the brave knight who rode out and saved our lives, though some of us died later, we would none of us have made it without him. I don't know what we will do now, but… well, I trust you will let us know. Keep that good knight safe. Keep him safe as he saved us. Thank you, Lord of Men."

Canith's style, like his prayer, was simple; as soon as he finished he slewed around to sit again on the top step. "As sure as I'm here now, it was a knight from the Order. I had heard the stories in my youth…" and as he looked around the mall, Canith could see the others all nodding. "And Pelian, the merchant, whenever he came to Hollinsfen, he always used to say he had never seen one, in all his wanderings, so naturally I wasn't… well, we weren't thinking there would be one coming. It's the kind of story you hear when you're young, yes? And then later, you don't hear it anymore."

"Where did he come from?" "How could he have been there in time?" "A knight of the Order, are you sure?"

"The monster was turning back and forth, grabbing and crushing and eating, and people were running around as if blind, and I thought the dimness was growing, wider and deeper. I just lay there where I fell, its jaws passing over me as it struck. I felt hot wet things coming down on me. I couldn't think any more, I just waited for it to step on me. But then I heard the bell, and saw the bridge."

A sigh passed around the crowd now, as the features of the well-known tale came from his mouth. "The Bridge… the bridge of light… how could it be?"

"I was right beneath the monster, and it was darker than dusk, but suddenly as I looked there was a bridge, made of light." He looked around helplessly. "It was just as in the tales. The monster stopped and turned to the side the bridge was on, as did I. I looked directly down it and it seemed I could see an endless way, to a magnificent stone tower on a high mountaintop. And down the path, a knight on a destrier. He was many leagues away, and yet he spurred his horse to charge. And suddenly he was there."

Canith stood in his excitement and as he spoke his voice rose.

"He charged straight in, and the monster, it was if it could not see him well. As if the light and darkness themselves were meeting, and neither… beat the other, but they… met. The bridge was just as bright, the monster still too hard to see. The Wanderer leveled his lance and called to his horse. 'Ho, Quester!' he cried, 'In, and at him!' He charged in; struck him full on in the body where I could not see.

But the lance stuck and it shivered to splinters. The monster's roar was huge, I covered my ears and I think I screamed. It seemed to bleed, perhaps, for near where the wound should be was darkness leaking into the air. And the dimness seemed to fade a bit.

"The knight–with the symbol of the tower on his shield and a visor over his face–drew his blade and moved in. The monster lashed and batted him from his horse like a pot off a shelf. But he came up swinging… what a manly fighter he was. We have no knights in our little village, even in the old days; we all just take up weapons at need. But this man… he was a warrior born, so brisk in his movements. He chopped and parried, and the monster now looked slow, and confused. Darkness leaked from it everywhere and the day began to brighten.

"Folks could find their way, and I got to my feet. We ran, in several directions but at least away from it, while the knight continued to give battle. The roars and calls were constant. I looked back, ashamed that I had run, and saw him, at the base of his bridge of light, I could see the glint of his polished armor. He had lost his shield now too, but wielded the sword in two hands, bringing it down again and again in mighty blows. He was chopping the beast in pieces, it seemed."

Canith sounded exhausted from the telling, and now Piree was awake. He kept speaking, but more subdued now in consideration of her.

"Nine of us gathered ourselves, to one side of the dimness. We kept walking away with whatever we had saved; that was the last of the handwagons, that day. But looking back we could see it was brighter again, just a small blot of something dark with the bridge of light slicing into it. We heard a final roar, and I think the knight must have destroyed the beast. The light won, and after a short time, the bridge began to… to withdraw to the west, like a fading rainbow. We never saw him again."

And Piree added simply, "Bless him."

There was quiet all around the mall then, a few folks murmuring the words, "Bless him," in an echo. Canith was clearly done, no more tales today, and he sat with a sad face staring down. The baby between them made a burping sound, to the general laughter.

Alaetar stood and addressed the people of Trainertown. "Children of Hope, we must not prove unworthy of the lighter burdens placed on us in these momentous times. Great heroes are at work, as you have clearly heard, and you stand ready to succor them should any come to you in need."

Murmurs of agreement met this, and he used it. "How much less, then, could you overlook your opportunity to assist these worthy people who come to you in such great want."

Now the agreement was quite loud, and he raised his hand for quiet. "Your kindness is not in question here; I see enough gifts and supplies near them to prove your good intentions."

It began to dawn on Piree and Canith that the things passed to them were theirs to keep, not just the food. Piree touched the fine blankets, saw a new dress; Canith peered down again at his new sandals. And the tears began to come for both of them.

"But we… we cannot pay you back," he said to no one and everyone, "and we cannot carry all this!"

"You shall need a house, surely, to keep this in," Alaetar said with meaning. Anteris leaped to his feet in an instant.

"There are many houses you could use! I can show you all the best ones. That is," he added, suddenly thinking of the question of property, and looking around for the council members, "that is, if they can be made available."

A hurried consultation at the foot of the steps concluded with nods on all sides. "The town can easily spare lodging in any vacant property to the west of the square. Subject to consensus, if you agree to shoulder your share of the taxes in, shall we say, three year's time?"

Canith flushed with shock. "I… I cannot imagine."

"What was your occupation, goodman?" Alaetar inquired.

"I was a hostler, for the plowing teams. Oxen and mules, mainly, some horses."

"The western gate stable has been unworked for nearly five years," someone shouted. "We need a good man with horses, saves one of us having to muck and feed every day, and meet the stage three times a week." Applause and cheers.

"Would you do this alone?" Alaetar asked Canith, and though standing the older man still needed to look up at the preacher with the implacable face.

"I don't understand. I am too old to marry. I should be no good at–"

"Only good enough to bring this woman forth from the most perilous place in the world!"

Canith and Piree looked around at the crowd as if Alaetar were discussing their most intimate secrets. And he was. The preacher turned to the young woman.

"Mistress, my sincere condolences on the loss of your husband and child. I cannot imagine what misery you have been subjected to. This city has an obligation to the destitute, and I must ask you: is it your intention to raise this child, whom you have brought from the jaws of hell, and keep it as your own?"

Piree's face held mute agony as she listened to the preacher; though his voice was neither raised nor hostile, Alaetar's face was carved as always in that intense expression of consequence, of right and wrong and urgency.

She looked to the baby, and took it up in her arms to hug it. Rising, she looked back to him and said, "I have cared for this child for four days, it has had my milk and my warmth when I had no thought but that we should soon die." She looked to Canith and held out a hand to him. "I did not die, because I was saved. By this kind gentleman, who did not perish against the dark-beast or the garruk, but who took my arm and found roots enough for one to eat, and who slept with no shirt that I might have something to cover myself and the baby." Here Canith's face was bathed in tears, but he smiled a little.

"We have said no word to each other, you and I, Canith. You knew my mother and father, you saw me marry. We all had such plans, just a year ago. But now, this preacher is being quite insistent, so it seems we all must have some answers."

She faced the crowd. "I am Piree, and I claim this child. With the town's approval I shall raise it as my own."

Canith said, "And if she will have me, I shall marry Piree, and do my best for her and her child."

Women everywhere were weeping, and Anteris saw quite a few men. He wasn't sure why, the whole thing made perfect sense to him. Hadn't anyone ever read a happy ending before?

"But the house," Canith said. "Where shall we live then?"

"I'll show you," Anteris volunteered. "The two-storey gable on Verdant is the best, the one with the blue shutters."

"Don't go there!" little Nayhan yelled in alarm, "That house is *haunted*!"

Laughter from the crowd did nothing to defuse the horror from the smallest children among them. One of the council took the steps and signaled for quiet. "What is the meaning of this? No house in Trainertown is haunted."

"It is! It *is*!" the children wailed.

"Enough!" Forge had stood up and was looking a bit sheepish but grinning still. "We wanted you to stop following us. So, we put a sheet over a scarecrow from the fields, and then…" The rest drowned in laughter, and the mystery was resolved.

"My good sir and madam, then," Alaetar said with a gesture towards the doors of the church.

Piree's face dropped in shock, and all the color drained from Canith's. "We… we are not ready yet."

"You could wait," Alaetar intoned mercilessly, "but why? The church is here, the guests are here, I am honored if you would allow me to officiate; and any other day would have to be later than this one."

"You go on, dears," said a woman from the crowd, "go and say the words in there and we'll have the celebration dinner ready by the time you're out." A thousand people cheered, and another thousand began to put planks over saw-horses to make tables; cloths, food and chairs appeared as if from nowhere, and the entire mall was quickly turning into an enormous feasting-hall under the night stars. Canith and Piree, looking abashed and shy but smiling at each other, took hands and followed Alaetar into the church.

⊕ ⊕ ⊕

Judgement made an error at last, in a room where any misstep could be fatal. After swinging up to block the ebon-sword, he countered with a strong staff-sweep at the ankle of his foe to knock it down. It was an attempt born of frustration; the statue weighed twenty times as much as a normal man. Judgement's weapon recoiled as if he'd struck a building, which was nearly true. He had his back to the far wall of the chamber from where Cedrith and the others watched helplessly; and with his weapon out of position, had no ground to give when the statue swung again, but could only drop to the floor in the lee of those massive feet.

The swing barely missed, but the corona of blackfire came too close to his eyes. Cedrith saw Judgement shake his head, and then cooly lurch in a random direction, hoping to escape for the moment past his foe. He did, and as the statue slowly turned the young warrior gained away. But now he was running directly towards the water-column between the two chambers.

"Judgement!" Cedrith called. "Ware the water!"

The young man, his eyes as glazed as those of the water-spirit, stopped at once and turned with staff outstretched before him, cocking his head to hear the statue.

"Alendic is ahead now and to your right," Cedrith cried, "the statue is coming on, perhaps twenty feet– no, ten."

Judgement ran to the left without hesitation, around the edge of the room and trailing his hand on the glass. The statue turned to follow, and for a time the grey man kept ahead by running around the outside. Alendic could see better now, tracking Judgement's flight with one hand still groping in the rucksack.

"Lead him to me, lad. Run past on my left here, and keep going!"

Judgement was coming in any event, moving counter-clockwise around the chamber with the statue in grim pursuit. Cedrith saw its face now, and felt a chill of something nameless; it was a handsome, aquiline mask, devoid of emotion or strain and with a blank gaze as if it had been struck with its own demonic blade. Was it modeled after some real person, a thane of Despairing kingdoms from millennia ago? Did the statue contain the spirit of that mortal being, bound to do the bidding of the Lieges for all time?

As Judgement passed along the wall within ten feet of Alendic, the actor brought a gem from his bag. "That's right, you bastard in basalt, just ignore the wounded, keep after the boy." Alendic's grin was fierce and he held his side tightly with his other hand. As the statue lumbered by, he lobbed the gem almost casually into the stoney face and leaped to one side, crying out in pain as he hit the ground. The gem struck the statue squarely, and instead of a flash of light there came a tremendous explosion. The trio on the other side of the glass wall jerked back by reflex as shards spattered within inches of their heads.

"There!" Alendic rejoiced from within the cloud of smoke and dust, "that will pretty you up, you mindless pile of stone! How do you like that, eh? A gift from an admirer!" At the far end, Judgement turned back to stare into the murk; his eyes were aflame with vision again and he breathed heavily, but still his face was as unmoved as a judge.

Smoke and cacophony obscured the view; then Cedrith saw the tall black body emerge from the gloom, still treading after Judgement now with half of its face destroyed. Raw, jagged stone was its countenance, as it stalked past the trio huddling beyond the water-column; the Elf could see just one of its eyes still staring out, painless, sightless, relentless. Judgement resumed the retreat, while Alendic hobbled closer to the water-column and his friends, dragging the rucksack behind him.

"Damn! I have no more– Natasha, can we do something?"

The healer still held her hands to her face in horror, and the look she exchanged with Cedrith told him she was empty of hope. The sage glanced back at the white statue, still gesturing to their escape, and unworthy thoughts clamored to be heard. He looked back to the mute mask of the water-guardian, and his mind raced. Through the water, a tiny grey man blocked and retreated from a mammoth assault.

"Speak to it."

"What?" Natasha said in wonder.

"You must try! It spoke through you once. Ask if there is any way-"

Natasha obediently turned to the standing pool and once again held out her hand. "Spirit of water, creature of ancient knowledge, we appeal to you for help."

The dekentar jerked back a step as once again a liquid arm reached out toward the healer's. Judgement ran past, dodging wide around

Alendic, who threw curses at the statue along with an extra dagger, to no effect. The water-face looked more and more human and female as the fingertips touched; suddenly, Cedrith saw a flow of water less than an inch thick rippling over Natasha's outstretched hand and arm. In a flicker, her upper body was coated, and before she could draw breath it covered her neck, mouth, nose.

The creature poured water forth without losing shape or volume. Natasha began to choke, but spouts of water from her lips did not clear the passage for air; reflexively, Cedrith reached out to seize her, but as he pulled her back the length of the spirit's arm simply extended as before. He felt the cavern-cold water flowing up his arms now, and as it climbed the sides of his neck he drew a deep breath and continued to back away. The water covered his ears, and Cedrith heard a roaring, the ocean echoing inside a shell the size of the chamber. He had a vague but powerful sense of life, eternal waiting, arbitration between opposite sides, a merciless balance. With an effort driven by his fear of drowning, the sage wrapped Natasha in a protective embrace and fell back, rolling violently in an effort to break contact.

Natasha's hand came away from the spirit's, and as they fell to the floor the layer of endless water sluiced from them to pool across half the floor. Cedrith was thoroughly soaked from head to toe, beyond a dunking on a rainy day: he was too heavy to stand for some time. Swearing, the dekentar stepped in and turned her on her side, but Natasha did not move except to dribble some last fluid from between her teeth. He tended her desperately, trying to get her to breathe.

"Natasha!" cried Alendic from the opposite side, frantic to see his companion down. Judgement turned to look, and Cedrith saw the statue reduced to his friend's size by the massive water-column between them. As it bore down on the youth again, the body loomed large into view past the water. Judgement was trapped again, and if he took a single blow he was finished.

"Natasha! What has happened to her?" Alendic screamed, losing concern for all else.

"She… took in water, she may have drowned."

"That's impossible! Her arm got wet–"

"And I tell you there's enough in there to fill this room!" Cedrith shouted. "That… thing, it is… is like the sea!" Staring back at Alendic, Cedrith saw Judgement beyond his shoulder, across the room and with the statue bearing down. A jolt of fear went completely through him as his eyes met the boy's, and a flicker of understanding passed between them.

"The sea!" the Elf cried.

"Eldest, mind your head," Judgement replied, and hefting his staff like a spear, he suddenly threw it with all his might past the statue's broken face. It did not flinch, and the missile flew over the crystal barrier and into Cedrith's side of the room. Without pause, Judgement barreled tight around the statue to one side, tucking into a ball and rolling under its attack, coming up again and charging to Alendic as the behemoth slowly turned.

"Conar's balls, lad, what did you–?"

"Put your arms around my neck," Judgement instructed. "Hang on."

"Are you insane? You can't run with me!"

"And hold your breath," Judgement added laconically. "It will be good practice for you."

Not checking to see while Alendic got the rucksack secure, Judgement took two dragging steps, and without pausing leaped arms-first into the water-column.

"Khoirah's pile, he'll kill the actor!" the dekentar cried. But Cedrith, seeing the two small men working desperately beneath the surface, shook his head. Judgement began to make clearing strokes with his arms and kicked steadily, strongly.

"He can swim, dekentar."

"He can what?" the guardsman demanded incredulously. At that moment, Natasha coughed hard and more water came from her mouth, followed by a ragged breath and the flutter of her eyes.

The black statue halted at the edge of the column. The water-spirit, mask facing towards it now, formed a second arm and wrapped them both protectively around its middle. The statue hesitated a long moment, then turned away. Inside the column, Judgement and Alendic were toy-sized again, and as the youth kept stroking, the actor hung on with eyes closed and cheeks full of air. Cedrith realized with dread that the effect of the water could not be explained away; the pair came closer but only slowly, as if each stroke gained inches instead of feet. The endless water inside the column defied its outer limits, where it appeared less than a man's length thick. Even now, the boy's strokes were slowing, and he still looked no larger than a child.

Cedrith stood and moved to the edge of the column, staring at the rippling vertical surface with his friends thrashing inside. "Please," he called up to the blind lady above him, "you have to help them. They belong here. *Ya'on Ara.*" The mask stared down on him without evident response, and he heard again the uncaring crash of ocean breakers, the immortal clock of tides in his mind.

Cedrith felt sad, to know that the moment had indeed come for him; not unexpected, but he would have preferred flame to drowning. Taking a deep breath, he thrust his arms into the water, soaking again in an instant as it broke over him, reaching for his friend several fathoms away. Judgement saw and thrashed harder once, twice, came only a few inches closer…

And grasped hands, suddenly huge as a stone statue, all in wet grey and nearly as cold. Cedrith let out his air in surprise, and the dekentar pulled him free with an enormous wrench and a release of loose water and a riot of falling flesh. Slowly, the men rolled over, choked, gasped, tried to curse, tried to laugh, managed to live. Natasha, still coughing, sat up as more water flooded past her knees. The water-column, unbroken and undiminished, slowly drew all loose fluid back into itself; its face regarded them without comprehension.

"I don't believe any of this," the dekentar said with finality.

"If you wake up first," Cedrith rejoined, "reach over and shake me, please."

"You," Alendic gasped to Judgement, "are without the slightest… doubt, the least sane person… I have ever met."

Judgement panted a few more times, then gathered the effort to say, "I told you I could swim."

"That you did." Alendic staggered to his feet and immediately began to check the rucksack. The dekentar helped Cedrith, then the healer; Judgement walked near the white statue and retrieved his staff. The party staggered together, gazing at the water-woman and the blasted black statue in the chamber beyond. The actor grinned, making a rude gesture to his foe.

"The next folks to come through here," Alendic remarked proudly, "will know they weren't the first."

"Enough boasting," Natasha chided, still winded. "That door won't last forever."

The white statue remained stone, Cedrith guessed, having heard the passwords from Alendic and Judgement already from the other side. The group shuffled to the far end of the chamber, and as they came close to the door with the same target symbol as the one whereby they had entered, it slid aside and let them further into the Halls of Glass.

⊕⊕⊕

Excerpt from the Nameless Tome of Faltus Fanem

I have gone mad, of this I can have no doubt. It is only when I drink the potion I devised that I can be sure of my sanity for even an hour, and I know that I have but one more dose I may use before the power of it kills me. So I must conclude the draft with no draft, so to say, then drink, and write the introduction to the story at my end. The introduction will be most important, I feel sure. I must give someone a warning.

This is not lunacy in the stage-antic sense. I am not subject to raving fits or violence, I make no public spectacle of my insanity. It may be that my servants detect no difference in my behavior (and this has been a feature of my days for at least a half a month; in some lives I lead, it has been years). Whether mad or sane, the bulk of my time is spent much the same: I study and write, mutter to myself and eat or sleep very little. Perhaps none of me are truly mad; perhaps it is only my many lives that forms the insanity. The very hard thing about my madness is that I can no longer be sure which is which.

I recall one life in which I knew nothing of Exeter Polanquan, and that existence was surely the most blessed. It connects in my mind to a childhood I feel certain I had, happy and calm, filled with progress for my studies, and a measure of praise and respect from men I see dimly in my memory, who were once my colleagues. But far more powerful and real to me is the life of a second sage named Faltus Fanem who lived in the twelfth century ADR, an expert on various mundane subjects (rare in this day and age to have many masteries, I wonder how I managed it). I wrote several full-length books about horticulture, viniculture and more; I had a great love of growing things once, or at least I believe it was me. And I lovingly installed these tomes in proper places all about my beloved Guild of Sages, back in the twelfth century. Each book to me had a special place, with passages more meaningful, more important than the others, and I marked them in loving detail. I recall writing these books, and dimly that other men would come along later and copy them. I felt quite sure of this last point, though I don't know why. But the complete roster of my works held a kind of wondrous shape, a puzzle, and I have devoted hours to consideration of the bright and dedicated soul who would one day reassemble it.

There are others as well, men who lived my life with memories and hopes, but I tend to forget them. I have the most curious impression, that one of those men was married, for a time, and until recently. Perhaps in my madness I have built some things from wishful thinking. Surely the saddest of all, and I fear at least one of the real lives, is the one where I do know of Exeter Polanquan. As great as he was, as much as I came to admire his craft and dedication to Hope, his tragic death and the ruin of his works fills my eyes with tears. Then too, the life in which I know of Exeter is the one where I see the Face that haunts my every hour of sleep. Perhaps I only dream of Exeter as well, and the mirror, and the ritual against the risen dead. But the Face of the one I shall not name, that I know is real and no depth of insanity can dim that knowledge or remove me from it fully. This potion here only makes the Face more real to me, and I think that is why I will die with the next drink. I hope so.

As I saw the great mage Exeter's life backwards I chronicled it in these pages, in the proper order for you dear reader. He scryed the evil one and observed his foul rituals to raise the dead; I saw that in the mirror he made. Praise the Heroes, I only saw Exeter, not he upon whom he looked. But I followed his researches in the ensuing visions of his Plane. The proper words, the gestures, the use and arrangement of stones of earth correctly purified: all these things Exeter did and so I have recorded them for you. He dared to watch as his foe stripped away the secrets of the cosmos and discovered the blasphemy of undeath, developed rituals to exploit it, and created his first minions to fight for Despair. He observed him closely; too closely, for he was found out at his craft, and the enemy destroyed him for his intrepidity.

Yet there remained one piece-part to the lore: I had tested the observed steps on the body of an elderly relative before cremation and it caused no change to the balance of pronasm *and* miasm. *Perhaps only one more essence, or word, or an attitude of casting, remains, and I know not what; but Exeter knew where. He scryed his nemesis, the necromancer, and saw his movements in his own time. He dared not reveal what that secret was, but he made clear in the notes he wrote out before the mirror's view the name of the dread place wherein that secret lay.*

He burned his papers on his final day of life, but I saw the instruction he had writ: "seek ye the Tombs Thanazun, by the planes."

Plunging into every book the Guild held on ancient lore and the works of Despair, I found only scattered reference to Thanazun. Hardly any history mentions the Tombs, as much from revulsion as ignorance. Suffice to say, Despair practiced interment of bodies in the earth, probably throughout all of time, but certainly once the nameless Face had made his dread discovery. For now the bones and flesh of those slain could be summoned back to serve a second time the will of the necromancer. And a few thin fragments suggested that the Lieges of Despair did construct somewhere within their bonded lands a vast burial ground, kemetaria *in the Ancient tongue, wherein were left the remains of tens of thousands of the dead. The reports of scouts and rustic peoples told of rows of numbered graves, as they are called, marked with the sign of Despair and placed under rock. Buried alive, in some cases! The inhumanity of our enemies was truly unlimited. And in the center of that* kemetaria, *in large tombs built far below the earth, thanes and mages of Despair had palaces and underground keeps constructed to house them and their slaves- by all evidence, for use during life as well as after death. Here the nameless master of the Tombs worked and promulgated evil from that nexus of Despair.*

But even Exeter Polanquan with his marvelous lore could not find the Tombs Thanazun on the maps of his day; he scryed his enemy "by the planes" as Exeter named his mirrors, yet knew not where the evil one stood. In the Wars of Liberation the ground on which it lay was surely conquered, and Despair has held no land in all the centuries since. Perhaps the entrances were destroyed, perhaps lost in the Great Cleft or drowned by some change in the course of the River Sweeping. No mention or clue to their location survives. Yet there, if they still exist, will be the final secret to protecting those who have died from the curse of necromancy. That warlock (I shall no longer name him, except at need) was captured in the first war, after he had ended Exeter's life (perhaps even in the foray in which he invaded our then-tiny kingdom). His fate beyond that day is unclear; the legends quote that Areghel, among others, wished him destroyed.

Telhol the blessed healer and then only a child, spoke to spare him in hopes that he might volunteer the cure for undeath. And the Lieges of Despair, it seems, bargained for his life (such as it was). But it is clear the evil one never appeared again in the wars or the annals of history.

But he lives. I have felt him in my dreams, and he has become aware of me. *At night I lay back abed and when my eyes close, I see a vision of all the lives I lead, circling above my head like the spokes of a great wheel. I view the zodiac of lives, slowly spinning and I feel more than ever confused and lonely to know which, if any of them are truly me. And at the center of the great wheel, instead of comfort or a sign of Hope, I see that Face, the dread of which has driven me ever further to madness. Last night, when I thought myself beyond any further shock, I lay staring up at that Face, when I realized I was not asleep and my eyes were not closed.*

So. He has found me as well, and scrys my life as he did to Exeter. I have seen the visage of our mutual enemy–the enemy of all Hope–standing amidst his palace of rock and crystal with the treasures of ages, bending the power of his malice towards me. This morning I recognized that the Plane, conduit for my visions, served also his needs to find me. I had it destroyed without comment to my servants, who thought it merely old. It is time now to finish the book, the means I have chosen whereby another may scry the past. I shall take it with the blank first page, and my potion, up to the Dark Archives and there drink and write, and be done. All of my lives will end, and we are content. Remember, you who read this, to seek the Tombs Thanazun; may this book be your plane. Ar Aralte! Even in our madness I claim our heritage.

⊕ ⊕ ⊕

The glass hallways were always narrow now, never allowing more than single file. There were many turns, often every dozen steps or less, yet real progress was minimal as the passages twisted on themselves and switched back from the changes. When the bass tone-chords came, some surface nearby always moved, and Cedrith felt completely on edge as the time wore on. The danger of separation that Alendic warned of was constant, and every moment he felt a threat as if in combat.

Through several glass walls, he could now make out a large open space, as the halls came to an end some two hundred straight paces further on. There was no abrupt terminus; most hallways ended within a few rods of where they were, but some seemed to extend and partially segment the cavern beyond, creating an uneven appearance that like everything else hinted at a pattern. The glow of the central chasm could always be seen, but not felt from this distance. Underfoot there was glass as well as overhead; the air was close and breathless. The open cavern in the distance was still distorted by the intervening panes, and looked littered with something. The cavern ceiling, near the central core over the bridge and cliff, was a rough milky-white crystal of stupendous dimensions, stretching scores of rods across and filtering in a small amount of ambient, white light to supplement the fiery glow of the chasm.

Nearby, the passages were close and layered tightly upon each other; many wall panels had runic markings etched on them, sometimes on endings or turnings and sometimes in the midst of halls. Some were even on parts of the floor or ceiling, though it made no difference to touch them. Cedrith could hear a deep, gnashing metallic hum at times, that made his skin prickle and stabbed the nerves between his legs. The air itself began to seem darker, not with twilight but with a kind of dank tint beyond the glass walls; whenever Cedrith thought he could actually see it he felt a charge of fear.

Every third turn, the dekentar complained that they were making no progress; Natasha looked increasingly drawn and haggard and Cedrith sensed she had no heart for whatever lay next on their path. What could have happened to Eddoran? Still here, she had said; but who could survive in this dreadful world? The soaking Cedrith had received in the guardian chamber was not drying; in fact, the corridors seemed to sink lower and get even colder.

All things considered, the skeletons came as something of a relief.

Waiting a few moments to be sure they did not move, Alendic and Natasha approached to inspect the corpses lying across their path. Three tall armored warriors, males to judge by the remnants of their clothing. Their bodies lay heaped nearly atop each other, as if carried here and carelessly dropped, yet two were in lighter-colored rags than the first and bore different markings on their helms. All was rust and rot about them; the first, largest and wearing dark armor, had two of his ribs shorn away beneath the severed shield.

"A stupendous blow," the dekentar remarked, and Alendic said only, "Aye," but seemed to know.

Cedrith spotted some disks near its disintegrated waist pouch; he picked one up and rubbed at the verdigris. Slowly, a kingly profile came into view; yet the coin was made of iron, heavy and dark. He fumbled with the inscription as he continued cleaning and finally muttered, "For—fortior, prama-tik. *Fortior pramatik*." He looked up at Judgement and asked, "Power in riches?"

The Man in Grey answered, "Wealth to the strong." Natasha nodded and Cedrith quickly dropped the currency of Despair to the floor.

The dekentar said, "But that would mean… this warrior here–"

"Is centuries old, yes," Alendic put in, "entered back when Despair still controlled the Percentalion, and slain by the same… obstacle."

"What obstacle?" Cedrith queried, his distrust of the leaders aroused again. Alendic just looked back at the sage with his jaw set.

Natasha interposed another question. "How did he get here, so far away–" and again stopped maddeningly short.

Cedrith felt overcome with suspicions and was about to take it up with them when seized by a sneeze.

"Cedrith, dear friend, you are shivering!" Natasha cried. Indeed the cold had become hard to bear in his wet clothes, but Cedrith was so taken by the corpses that he hadn't discerned the cause of his shaking. Everyone was wet, but the sage was suffering worse than the others.

Pulling the group a little farther down the hall and making them sit close, Natasha rummaged in her pouch, saying to Alendic, "My turn for a little trick." She withdrew a half-dozen flat plain stones with painted symbols on each side, and the actor grinned in recognition.

"That rustic shaman, from the Novarian hills near Snowdon, you traded him a small scrying mirror. Oh my dear woman, you've kept those all these years since that winter… was it '84? Or even '83!"

Smiling from her knees like a proud cook, Natasha simply murmured a single word, in no language Cedrith recognized, and set two of the flat stones on the floor. They began to glow and Cedrith was amazed to feel substantial heat, as if she had lit a small campfire. Almost at once, the walls nearby misted with the wetness leaving their clothing, cutting off the long, twisted, ominous views and hinting at normalcy.

"Incredible!" he remarked as he passed his hands near them.

"Yes," Alendic quipped with eyes of fire looking at the healer, "and those stones are nearly as warm." She waved him off with one hand while seeing to Cedrith at her side, an arm around him and once again the matron.

"I recall a woman just like you," Cedrith said dreamily as his shivers subsided.

Natasha smiled a bit though her face was still pale, and said, "Tell me about her."

"Kind and happy," Cedrith replied sincerely, "ready to do anything for a friend, and the whole world her friend."

"Be sure to tell them," Natasha said in a small voice, "tell them all about that nice woman, when you return."

Cedrith was shocked at the loneliness in her voice. "You will tell them, continue to show them, when you return yourself," he managed gallantly, but there was silence for a time.

"I am truly sorry, to all of you," the Guildmistress declared. "What lies ahead of us is almost impossible to describe. This guardian, the monster who controls the Hopeward, has made use of the bodies of those who failed, before us, as the undead." Cedrith looked at the skeletons behind them and felt cold again, though he was now dry. "Skeletal foes, like those bodies there, and gaunts, an undead with flesh and hearts removed by their maker who controls them. And more," she continued. "Worse."

"What will we do?" the dekentar asked directly.

"Stay together," Alendic said. "Protect the Guildmistress. Persevere. And triumph, of course," he added with his usual grin, "if we have time."

The glow of the heat-stones was fading. The warmth stopped altogether, and each one cracked into pieces with a small crisp snap. "An excellent trade, if I do say so," Alendic declared.

Natasha shook her head. "I could not understand him, when he tried to say that each one would 'die.' I was so worried that he thought the mirror, too, was permanent. It only had two scryings left in it."

"You both had your hearts in the right place," Alendic said, "and he no doubt learned from experience, as did we."

"How do these stones work?" Cedrith wondered.

Natasha shook her head. "The rustic peoples are very primitive and few; many city-dwellers refuse to believe they ever lived, much less that some survive. But their ancestors were here before the landing of Hope. Even before Despair; in the Age of Emptiness without a written history. They drew upon the elements of the world, used gems and stones. They had magical lore, but none of it focused on creating permanent items, as we do. They were adept with potions, and talismans like these stones, with one use each. Some say they communicated with spirits of the earth and sky."

"And of water, mayhap," Judgement said quietly and everyone snapped around to look at him.

"What are you saying?" Natasha asked sharply, "Do you think the Lords of Hope made a pact with the rustic powers to build this place?"

Judgement shrugged. "None have been created since. Whatever built this edifice, it has abided through many centuries." He leaned in, took up a shard of a warming stone, and pocketed it. "We must try to be more… permanent."

"Not all permanence is to be desired," said Natasha bleakly, and now the Man in Grey looked in turn at her.

"Tell him, now," Alendic urged.

"Alendic, no, he is not ready–"

"My lovely woman, were you thinking of bringing him back here later?" Taking her by both arms, Alendic spoke seriously for once. "We wanted five years but were not granted them. Natasha, I am charged with your protection."

"I can handle–"

"Dear woman," he cut her off firmly, "do you remember what Eddoran said?" She caught her breath in surprise. "He turned to me and said 'keep her safe, Alendic.' And I have endeavored to do exactly that. Do not strike this weapon from my hand. Please." Cedrith heard the sincerity in Alendic's tone; there was more here than practicality or strategy.

Natasha reluctantly faced the young man, still sitting.

"The undead," she began carefully, "are a terrible curse, and our forebears have learned certain methods to destroy them."

To her surprise, Judgement nodded at once, and Cedrith thought of the hours the youth had spent with the Nameless Tome, which even the Guildmistress of the Healers had not.

The youth carried on in reply. "The preacher uses miraculous power to sever the connection between the corpse and its controller. In effect, she turns the *miasma* and restores the natural condition of the victim, which is death."

Natasha looked at Judgement agape, and then to Cedrith. "Where did he learn such mysteries?"

The sage forced a sickly smile, and could only stutter, "S-See-secrets all around, I suppose."

"Well then," she said more briskly back to the student, "one incantation we have learned is this: I say it now in the common tongue, but the call is made in the Ancient one. 'Destroy undead, by Hope.' Do you know those words?"

The youth nodded and reflected. "Were it better to say, 'may Conar grant me the power to defeat this undead foe.' Or mayhap I could call for aid in my hour of need, upon Areghel, whom the histories–"

"Stop!" Natasha cried, and Judgement obeyed, looking on her steadily. Silence then, as Natasha was again set back. Alendic urged her with his elbow and she ignored him. "Not the phrasing I have been taught. You cannot, certainly, render that into Ancient?" Cedrith could see she was almost taunting him now, and Judgement rose to the bait. He hardened his jaw, closed his eyes a moment, and then steadily uttered, "*Areghel permam toxis calem bellatara victorum.*"

Instantly, the skeleton of the Despairing warrior behind the party exploded into fragments. As Cedrith cried out and huddled back, he saw a wisp of purple fog drifting up from where the body had lain. Everyone leaped to their feet and drew weapons now, carefully eyeing the remaining pair of bodies. Alendic capered for joy, and Cedrith saw that Judgement was breathing quickly, glancing down at himself as if for recognition.

"He can do it!" Alendic crowed. "Probably lying there in wait, set to rise on some condition, but you sniffed it out, lad!"

"You must husband this ability," Natasha said worriedly. "Each such effort can be exhausting and our foes are many."

"Who are you?" the dekentar demanded with a rising tone of fear and anger. "You come among us determined to cause trouble, and show the face of a child but the power of a great mage, or preacher, or what not." He faced him as if expecting the grey man to attack, though Judgement still rested the butt of his staff on the crystal floor. "Who are you, I demand to know!"

"I am Solemn Judgement," the youth returned evenly, "third son of Final Judgement, not 'come' among you but brought here. I seek knowledge, as I was taught–"

"Why? You 'seek knowledge,' the greatest of secrets from our highest-ranking healer… why?"

"To fulfill the charge left on me by my teacher. That I may remember my father's face."

The dekentar spat to portray his disbelief, and Judgement showed no interest in further convincing him. Alendic stepped between them and said, "Do you mean, your father taught you this miracle?"

Judgement returned a hard, long look, and then at last dropped his gaze. "No," he said simply, "he did not… speak to me of miracles. I must not have been worthy. But I believe he had the power."

"You say he taught you," Alendic pursued, only a little less aggressively than the dekentar had. "What sort of teaching did he give?"

"It is not important."

"What subject?"

"Languages."

"Aye. Aught else?"

"Mathematics, the science of living things, history, astrology, herbal lore."

"I see, but not–"

"…crops, hunting, navigation, woodwork, armed and unarmed combat, some rudiments of metals, the admixture of chemicals, rhetoric and logic, certain aspects–"

"It's a lie!" the dekentar shouted, and now Judgement did take up his staff. But Alendic placed his hand heavily on the young man's arm and kept himself between them.

"Shut up, you fool," he hissed at the dekentar. "I don't know the origin of your quarrel, and I agree it's easy enough to pick a fight with the boy. But he's never told a lie in his life, face that."

"He offers insult to the greatest house in Conar!"

"Then the greatest house in Conar deserves it," Alendic responded imperturbably. The dekentar cursed and stomped away to stand near Natasha, while the actor turned back to face the youth.

"So, then; a most impressive man, your sire. And you have said, I believe, a knight and advisor to a king?" Judgement nodded, but turned his face away and was careful not to look at Natasha. "You have told us nothing, young Judgement, of the heroes of your land. Take no offense, I pray you, but you spoke of your nations as if… they were nearly Despairing. Yet you came from the west. Do you mean to say your father taught you nothing of this?"

The grey man did not reply, and Cedrith could see he was in pain from some internal doubt. Stepping a little closer, he spoke gently. "My friend, you told me on the day we met, there was a persecution. And your father kept you and your brothers in a remote place during your childhood." Judgement nodded once and slowly. "Do you know why?"

Judgement drew a deep, slow breath. "I trow… he wot our–his–beliefs to be greatly despised in somewise. He never spake openly of it, though the study of any subject such as history doth naturally lead in that direction. He quoth only the stories of the ancient days of my land, when… our hero did walk the earth."

He paused again and looked down. "Here in the Lands, ye have a high tolerance for one another, I trow. This man may follow Conar, another Astor, or Helmon and it moots not between them." He took a step away from the rest, and then turned to face them. "In mine father's land, 'twas not so, of that certes. On the night–when mine father came and didst flee with me–wast a large crowd, an army of soldiers. I had been asleep, and I saw everything a'fire. Fire everywhere, and my brothers did lie still 'pon the ground without. As mine father carried me to his horse, and fought through yon ranks and away, I heard voices shouting. They yelled divers words I knew to be foul curses, among them 'heretic' and 'puritan.' Thy language hath no such words, nor do I trow their ken."

It was the longest speech Cedrith had ever heard the young man give, and the silence that followed it was complete. No one spoke until he looked up again.

"How many Heroes are revered in your country?" Alendic asked, and Judgement said, "One."

"I don't understand. How did one man change an entire nation? What army did he lead? What great magic did he wield? When did he come among you?"

Judgement shook his head. "I know very little of this, mine father saw fit not to instruct us. But 'twas a great book, writ in the Ancient tongue, which I didst see him read a'times. He was wont to carry it with his person when at court. Yet of late evenings, when I could a'time outlast him in resisting sleep, I did take it down and read therein. Paltry glances, in sooth, different passages indifferently chosen."

"Your father's hero, did he come from the west?"

"Nay, he was born in an eastern desert."

"Like Telhol…" "…or Novar." "To which throne?"

"None. He learned to work in wood."

"Then what heroic deeds did he do?"

A long pause then, while the change-tones rang almost unnoticed, and a longer pause thereafter.

"He revered his father. And he survived death."

"He was a necromancer," the dekentar said with venom. Now Judgement raised his staff and moved for the guardsman with murder in his eyes.

"Ye wish mine blood, wouldst fain wait not for tomorrow night."

Alendic moved to intercept the youth before he could raise his staff for a sweep. Natasha laid a hand on the dekentar's arm and began to remonstrate with him, who stayed his ground with a mocking smile. Cedrith felt again the group fraying at the seams, none of them truly partnered with another, distrust, hatred and fear on all sides.

Suddenly the change-tones rang again and this time the walls took them all by surprise. One side of the hallway pivoted from a center-point near where the healer and guardsman were standing, as other planes of crystal swung down from above to block the old ways, while a new break formed to the opposite side. Standing on solid glass slick with the dew of their wet clothing, no one could resist the pivoting wall; Natasha and the dekentar were swept around, with the two skeletons, until they stood on the other side from Alendic, Cedrith and Judgement.

Cursing with cheerful vigor and moving even before the walls had come fully set, Alendic put his rucksack down before a rune symbol set into the offending divider, and pulled out the covered cloth.

Natasha immediately shook her head and shouted, "No! Not again, Alendic!" Her voice though more muffled than one would expect, was clearly audible to Cedrith; yet Alendic grinned as he put one hand to an ear and shook his head with feigned incomprehension. Judgement stood guard facing the far turn as the actor uncovered the glass tubes and began to drizzle the fateful liquid over the rune, shaped like four crossing lines or perhaps two overlapping x's. Natasha pounded her fists in frustration, and for a moment Cedrith thought he was imagining things. But the skeletons rose behind the Guildmistress and the dekentar, called up to movement and armed with rusty swords.

Cedrith cried out, "Beware! Behind you!" pointing with frenzy, and they turned in time. As the dekentar whirled to present his sword and dagger, his skeleton slowly raised its larger blade, then suddenly swung with much faster speed. The dekentar parried on his main-gauche; Natasha dodged her foe, then pointed at the undead thing and called out in words Cedrith could not distinguish. The creature hitched violently from its waist, as if all the bones were held together on a long string that Natasha had just pulled, tumbling into a pile on the floor. The dekentar countered with his sword and hacked well into rib and spine. One more pass, nearly identical to the first, and the second creature was also reduced to bones.

Alendic had hastily rewrapped the glass tubes and without waiting for Judgement, he began to hammer away at the smoking, hissing symbol with his broadsword. Judgement brought over his cudgel at once and struck with him on the third blow, producing a cracking sound as before. But the change-tones rang out, and again a portion of the ceiling above Natasha and the dekentar folded down, putting them further away than before. The symbol-wall in front of Alendic sank into the floor, replaced by a new divider with no seam between them. There were now two new barriers between the party, and Alendic craned his neck towards the roof and howled in frustration.

Cedrith watched as the actor keened with all his voice, drew a deep breath and howled a second time; the hairs on the sage's nape rose up and he felt his hold on sanity slipping again. Judgement stood like a pillar, watching Natasha and the dekentar who were looking both ways in their hall and soundlessly conversing. Alendic, seeming to come back to himself, looked wildly in all directions around the halls and then back to Natasha; he pointed at her with force, and the two began to exchange signals with their hands and arms. It was clear they were deciding direction; to Cedrith's left, though the angle of the halls would bring them further apart initially. The distant two began to move off with the dekentar leading, and Alendic spun to regard his companions. His voice was brisk, but taut and toneless.

"Cursed place. It happened as I guessed; now we must step to it and seize the next chance to come together. Still, more likely we'll be set upon first; better us than her." He looked back and forth between his two companions, and Cedrith saw he was wrestling with poor choices. Intuitively, the Elf reached a hand towards the rucksack. Alendic pulled it back on reflex.

"Allow me," Cedrith said. "You know I'm no good in a fight, and you can be free to move."

Alendic's lip twitched toward a grin, and after securing the main hasp, he held it out to the sage with a bow. "Drop it at need, however, my good Elf; even you will need to fight as well as you can." He stepped off to their left, and Judgement followed with Cedrith in the rear, hoisting the bulk of the rucksack over one shoulder. It was tightly packed and he could feel something large and round in its main compartment.

The walls of their new chamber created a big irregular space, angled together ahead to form a narrow turning corridor. "Into the hallway, quickly!" Alendic barked, and the three of them gained the narrower passage where Alendic's blade and Judgement's staff were tightly packed for room. Between their shoulders, Cedrith saw the corridor ended after only a few feet in two angled doors, each with a rune; both led down straight halls through what looked like several more such doors, and out into the open space beside the chasm's glow. The stepped bridge in the distance led across the inferno to a central space resting on a massive mesa in its middle; overhead the mist-crystal ceiling loomed with its jagged bumpy edges glaring down and suffused with pale but pure light. It was impossible that such a dome could hold, it must come thundering down to crush every iota of life below. But closer, jostling together and shambling steadily down both of the corridors before them, over a dozen of the risen dead lumbered towards the three sparks of life in the hall of glass.

"Ma-Eldar, preserve us," the sage murmured in a choked whisper.

"We must gain one hallway now," Alendic rasped. "If we wait for the change-tones, we'll be caught here between both of them, I know it. Damn this place!" And he craned his neck to see that Natasha and the dekentar, though far off through many halls, were yet unthreatened.

Judgement reached a hand to the rune closest to him on the left-side passage, another sun-burst, and closed his eyes. Cedrith could not hear clearly, but thought he heard the youth humming beneath his breath.

"Judgement, what is it?"

"Something… familiar," he said. He opened his eyes, leaned down to put his mouth next to the sun-rune, and sang three tones in a strong clear voice.

"*Beee-daahh-toh!*"

Silently, the rune-door sank into the floor, admitting the threesome to the chamber beyond it. As they crossed the threshold, it rose again, sealing half their foes further behind them. Alendic was slack-jawed with joy, and crying out incoherently he seized the grey youth in his arms and lifted him off the floor.

"You wondrous lad! Who cares for a manly reputation!" and he kissed him wildly on the cheek as he set him down. As if nothing at all had happened, Judgement stepped to the next portal, incised with four wavy lines and a pair of spots, and repeated the tones. Nothing happened, but the youth immediately moved to a different set, and Cedrith could feel, even with his poor musical sense, that it was the continuation of a theme which now seemed vaguely familiar to him as well.

"*Booo-leee-da-teee*!"

The second door opened in the same way and now there was only a single door between the party and their advancing foes, still two rods away. Judgement looked back to Cedrith with a hard glint of amusement in his eyes, answering the unspoken question.

"'Tis the music from the Chapel of Conar."

Cedrith twitched with the shock, then laughed out loud. "That music! You were there one day, your first day, your only visit–"

Judgement shrugged, saying, "My father trained me in the theory of music, and it seemed… memorable."

"Wait, this music," Alendic said, "teach me the notes, quickly lad. This is our salvation; we can now maneuver our way back from these Halls at will. It's the secret of how the Hopelords could come here in safety. What is the tune?"

Judgement stood a moment eyeing the actor sardonically. "Aye, for you did your reverence to Conar on the stage, not the church." He repeated both tone-series for Alendic, who gave them back perfectly the first time, then repeated them for assurance. Cedrith, feeling he should also partake, tried his best, but his voice was never strong and he felt no more certain after the brief rehearsal than before. Two more tries on the third door, and Judgement came to the proper series to drop the portal with the rune shaped like a merger of an R and a backwards L. Then the way was clear, to the undead. The party crossed the threshold and abided their approach.

Alendic, noting that Cedrith was already shaking, gave him a grin and a quick clap on the shoulder. "This won't be as bad as it looks, dear Elf," he assured him.

"They are… the living dead." Cedrith whispered.

"And we shall defeat them," Alendic returned. After a moment, he added for explanation, "You see, with the undead, it is very simple: either you beat them, or you join them."

"You make the situation marvelous clear," Cedrith managed, and Alendic laughed, quite literally in the face of death.

The very slowness of the risen became their greatest horror to the Elf. Each step or drag seemed to take an eternity, giving Cedrith ample time to absorb every horrid facet of their appearance. The broken jaw of one, a missing foot of another stumping nervelessly on an ankle; armless, toothless, heedless, they came on. For centuries they had awaited the party, knowing neither patience nor its opposite, and now they came on to tear and chop and be destroyed in turn. As a learned Elf, Cedrith had spent more time than any human contemplating eternity: he knew his body would stop aging at some point, and instinctively he felt that moment had not yet arrived for him. He believed, as all Hopeful Elves, that a truly great Moment, one in which he chose the manner and proper time for his death, was ahead of him. But as he stared into sightless sockets, smelled charnel shreds and heard the scrape and step of the undead, Cedrith faced the horror of a moment removed, stolen, raped from sentient beings who once lived. As it could be stolen from him. Unwitting and unwilling, their bodies kept coming; his mind slid by the thought that their souls still watched and the sage nearly screamed.

The first blow of combat, struck by the Man in Grey, broke the tension. As his skeletal foe raised its axe to strike, he coolly stepped in and blasted down with the head-end of his iron-tipped staff, shattering shoulder, neck and the lower skull in a single blow. Alendic stepped up to cover his flank and engaged a fleshy gaunt with his longsword. Cedrith cowered and saw behind them rank upon rank crowding into the narrow hall, heedless of the hindrance they proved to each other and accepting the loss of their advantage in numbers without question or volition.

Alendic parried the gaunt's sword and then thrust his blade directly into the hole where its heart had been removed. He made a quick back and forth flexing motion, and the gaunt's upper torso slumped forward in its bag of rotting flesh, spine severed and tumbling down in a heap. Cedrith turned his head to throw up as Alendic side-stepped, letting the gaunt fall past him and half-into the sage.

"Finish him," he ordered, swinging to block a skeleton's attack.

Cedrith cringed away, barely holding onto his mace as he splashed vomit he didn't know he had onto the wall and partly back on his tunic. Judgement and Alendic were furiously at work now, with no room for back-swings or full sweeps, poking and stabbing frenziedly and calling to each other in barks and gasps. Several of the undead were down– suddenly Cedrith felt something cold clamp around his calf. With a cry, he saw the gaunt, one arm clutching his leg painfully hard, the other groping from the half-severed upper body while its legs twitched uselessly in their skin-sack on the floor. The sage was plunged into utter terror, trying to jerk his leg free and away, but dragging it closer to his fellows. Its other hand clamped around Judgement's cape, dragging him unexpectedly back; a skeleton's hatchet chopped past his altered guard and the Man in Grey cried out from a rusty wound in his side.

"The Heroes blast you! Cedrith, I said finish it!" Alendic bellowed in a voice of command. Still Cedrith could only see the gaunt, its mouth champing neutrally at both points of life before it. Finally, driven by revulsion, he raised his mace and smashed it down into the waist-high skull, crushing old bone into dried brain and nearly tearing the head free of the upper spine. The creature promptly let go and dropped soggily to the glass floor, folded backwards against itself like a book, finally unmoving. The sage only wanted to vomit again, but Alendic cleared a small space by kicking a skeleton back against its fellows and turned a moment to berate him.

"Come out of the audience, you worthless bookworm, or I'll let the next one bite your manhood off!" Facing back to his recovered foe, he struck hard and severed a bony thigh, shouting, "We must reach Natasha! When we down them, step up and as you love another second of life you *finish* them! *Damn* you!"

This last was unclear, perhaps a curse to his enemies, but Cedrith finally felt a layer of the tar around his heart retreating. He advanced on the fallen skeleton and smashed it, four and five times, until no three bones were connected. After that, the details blurred into a haze of shouts, wounds, blistering curses and the smell of the grave filling every pore.

"Areghel permam toxis calem bellatara victorum!" Judgement's voice was forced and high, but as Cedrith looked around, he again saw an undead foe explode and fall. Alendic beheaded his final opponent in the same moment, and the three of them panted for a time leaning on knees or weapons. Strewn in the passage around them the bones and flesh were nearly knee-deep, slain a second time in a battle beyond their will. Cedrith felt the violation deep within, pushing past his exhaustion and terror; he noted his knuckles were oozing blood from some unremembered scrape. Judgement bled from his side, covering the gash with one reddened glove as he leaned on his staff. Alendic, with slight cuts in several places, advanced to the edge of the corridor and looked out across the open space.

"There they are!" he cried, pointing to a long hallway that extended like a finger into the cavern: Natasha and the dekentar were walking down towards its end, where a box-shaped rune marked a probable door.

"Can you walk?" the actor asked the youth, and for answer Judgement set out a bit stiffly in that direction, jaw set and hand still clamped.

Cedrith had been thoroughly enervated while shut up in the Halls of Glass for so long. Yet now, as he stepped onto the open rough cavern floor–a low plain rising toward the bridge side under the looming crystal roof–he could feel the distant heat of the chasm, see the massive bridge, and felt a new kind of fear. Now he was an insect crawling exposed and far from safety. With undisturbed vision, he could see that the litter of the open cavern was bodies: bones and flesh and the tatters of ancient dress, scattered in random patterns across the entire area, nearly a hundred of them. The grinding chug sounded again, this time not muffled by glass; the sage cried out, dropping to his knees and needing Alendic to come back and haul him to his feet. Even Judgement stopped moving and stared. Closer to the bridge, the land rose slightly and hid something loud and large back near the edge of the chasm where the horrid sound originated.

"What–" Cedrith choked, "what is that?"

Alendic held him by one arm and leaned in to murmur, "I call it The Harvester." He said no more and for once, Cedrith did not press.

Stepping back by Judgement, Alendic put out a hand to urge the youth to his quickest pace, and the three of them stumbled forward to the end of the jutting hall where their companions stood. Daring to glance once more in the direction of that rise, Cedrith clearly saw an indigo mist roiling up and gently drifting in their general direction. When he'd only guessed it was there, the sage had felt a charge of fear; now, faced with unmistakable evidence of the deep purple fumes, Cedrith felt his knees go weak.

"What is that?" he gasped, and Alendic did not respond.

But Judgement quietly said, "It is *miasma*."

From the distant bridge a dry, deep voice called out in a language unknown, the unseen master declaiming an incantation of Despair. Wherever the mist rolled as it came down into the cavern vale, each corpse it passed began to rise up. Alendic and Natasha matched their hands on the glass door between them, and the dekentar stood gripping his weapons uselessly. The actor tried both the song-tones he had learned, but the door did not budge. Cedrith stared about him, seeing undead moving in their direction, more than a score now and in the open to approach from three sides. He entered a timeless state of shock, in which nothing happened except the inexorable onset of his doom.

Behind him he heard but did not see the dim echo of Natasha calling, "You must say, 'I wish for healing,' Judgement! Say it!" and then the quiet, gasped words, "*Intacta volar.*"

Cedrith cried out when Alendic grabbed him roughly by a shoulder and thrust him to the front, completely before the rune door while snagging the rucksack from his back. The sage tried to turn away but the actor pushed him back around to face the doom. "You must hold the line, sir! One more trick to pull from the sack–"

He heard Judgement say, "There is not time to use the solvent."

"Indeed," said Alendic with grim good humor, "but only hold them a few moments. Don't look back! And remember, boy, what I told you. Cedrith, I'm sorry, but there's nothing for it. Farewell."

There were four creatures lumbering closer now, and Judgement to Cedrith's left tried to cover as much of the front as possible, leaving the sage the space next to the door. The Elf, ashamed of himself but certain that Alendic had fled back into the Halls leaving them to die, still could not take his eyes from the undead before him. Shouting his family name, the grey youth lashed out with his staff and a gaunt went down before it could strike. As the youth turned to parry two more attacks, Cedrith huddled behind his shield and blocked some of a saber-thrust from a skeletal foe, screaming in fear the while. It was just as he had predicted, and the sage's spirits sank low. Dimly he heard the words "No! No!" muffled behind a glass wall, and then he was too absorbed to even register sounds as he tried desperately to evade the thrusts of several blades before him.

It came so suddenly Cedrith was unsure what really happened. A blade striking down between Judgement and himself, striking down from too high an angle to be held. A quick follow-on stroke, and then a third, as if the blade weighed less than a dagger. Three foes down in a moment; no creature pressed Cedrith for a space and he glanced back to his left, then shrank against the glass in shock. The colossal sight, the golden voice.

"Now, Children of Hope, comes the hour of battle and only victory will suffice."

Conar the Hopelord, more than eight feet tall, strode into the fray past him. The change-tones rang out and for once, the door at the end of the hallway simply opened, to admit the dekentar and healer to the company. The undead swarmed to Conar's massive frame like night-moths to the lantern; he swept his longsword to full impact, destroying two corpses in a blow and shrugging off the effect of their strikes against him. The dekentar, after a moment of staring, plowed in to one side and Judgement to the other; Cedrith huddled farther back and sheltered Natasha as best he could.

For her part, the Healers Guildmistress of Conar ignored the fight, uttering a string of curses against her seeming overlord, of a kind that Cedrith had never even seen written on paper.

The image of the Hopelord strode slowly forward, sweeping his longsword in one hand like a baton, describing double-loops back and forth and occasionally pounding down with his off-hand fist or catching a haft bare-handed. Nothing seemed to affect the Mien as the undead crashed around him; his countenance carried the same calm assurance of victory it did onstage, and even the gaunts and skeletons appeared to hesitate an extra moment before his awesome aspect. Cedrith heard the distant unseen voice cry out in surprise, though followed by laughter; this struggle with undeath was providing amusement. Judgement was clearly running on nervous energy, his face sheathed in sweat, and the dekentar was bleeding from two points on his arms. More than twenty of the foe had been cut down and lay still; Cedrith had encountered no real threat since Conar stepped in. He picked his way past unlife and limb alongside the healer, a length or so behind the melee. Natasha had finally subsided in her harangue though she still looked daggers at the giant moving steadily ahead towards the bridge. Three times, Cedrith saw her gaze at those rising stone steps in great fear, though nothing yet appeared there.

They were halfway up the rise when the corpses were at last defeated. Looking back the Elf could see where twoscore skeletons and gaunts lay strewn, marking their progress. The dekentar and Judgement leaned on their weapons, gasping. Conar simply turned to look down at the group, regal and secure.

Eventually the dekentar rasped, "By the balls of Conar, what is that?"

Judgement, addressing him with a stone face, said, "Mayhap you do not take in the theater?"

Natasha, still breathing heavily, stood with arms akimbo and faced off against the image of the Hopelord without a scrap of reverence.

"How… *could* you!" she screamed in a tone near tears. "The destruction of the walls, and now this blasphemy against the Hopelord himself. This ancient power, so far beyond our understanding, and you… you snatched it up like another healing potion! You have stolen– you risked– I can never forgive you this, Alendic."

Cedrith was shocked to hear such raw anger in Natasha's tone, though he shared her dismay at what her companion had done. Conar stared down at her a moment with what looked like admiration on his face, and finally said, *"From the third sunset following this one, you shall stand with me on the heights of yonder mountain range. And all the kingdom between here and there shall be free of Despair for ever."*

"And don't you quote meaningless scripture!" she raged at him. "Speak to me, explain yourself, and take that off at once."

The Lord of Men did not respond, but only stood looking down at the Healers Guildmistress with great attention. Cedrith started with recollection.

"He told us… he can only quote the lines of the play when he wears the Mien."

"Then take it off at once!"

"Nay," Judgement offered, "the effort might exhaust him too far." On this, the Mien held out a mighty arm towards the grey man in affirmation.

"So what does he mean by the third sunset?" Natasha demanded.

After a moment, Judgement responded, "'Tis the promise."

"What?"

"He quoth the Promise speech of the play. A clue. 'Tis the promise he made wouldst fain keep thee safe." Now Natasha simply stared up at Conar, and could not reply in words.

Everyone jumped in alarm when the unseen voice called out from behind the bridge, and large walls of crystal emerged from the cavern floor very close to where the party stood. Conar seized Natasha by the scruff of her dress and hauled her protesting through the air another four feet back, as an enormous box of glass formed around the area where the destroyed undead lay. Some panes of the four walls had rune-marks on them, most did not; it had a ceiling but no floor. The dekentar swore in wonder as the entire prism scraped into movement, plowing the riot of flesh, joints and organs within it towards the edge of the chasm. Natasha shrieked in revulsion as the enormous crystal box reached the crevice and thrust more than halfway over the lip. The crushed and torn bodies fell down from sight into the magma below.

As they watched, the box slid back from the edge, then stopped. A few moments passed, in which Cedrith had time to reflect on the horror of mass-interment and disposal afforded bodies already insulted by the chains of unlife. Weakened to his core, he leaned against the nearest person–the dekentar–for support. The large glass box, meanwhile, sank into the cavern floor and disappeared.

"At least," Natasha managed, "they are at last interred by fire."

"Good news," Judgement averred, "for the Hopeful among them. For the Children of Despair… perhaps more suffering."

Natasha looked in horror at Judgement and quietly moaned.

"Where to now?" the dekentar said, looking to Conar. Saying nothing, he pointed with his sword-arm at a spot to the right of the bridge, over the crest of the rise. Natasha shook her head desperately.

"We cannot, we mustn't– no, we must find Eddoran."

The visage of the Hopelord looked steadily at her and then gestured to the bridge.

"No," Natasha said, "he must not be there. Among the dead, surely, we should search. Or perhaps another way, back in the Halls…" though it was clear as she trailed off that the healer had no hope of this. This time, Conar shook his lordly uncrowned head and pointed again to the right of the bridge, where the purple clouds originated.

"You cannot mean to defeat that… that thing?" Natasha gasped in horror.

Conar smiled gently at her.

"I am not fit to lead Hope's army if I have none in my heart."

"It is the purple cloud," Cedrith offered, and Judgement nodded. "As long as that continues to come, undead will rise against us. We cannot defeat them all."

"But that– we cannot," Natasha started weakly.

"Jewel of House Verinten, beloved … I love you well."

"And never mind that saucy love-prattle! You bend the sacred script to innuendo again and I'll slap your face for you." Natasha seemed furious, her chest heaving with emotion; but she gestured brusquely that they should ascend the slope towards the source of the *miasma.*

The group did not march the path before them; it was a trudge from the first step, dispirited and slow. Conar matched pace to his earthly companions, taking a step for each three, and still was in the lead. Cedrith felt such unexcused horror of what lay ahead that he could hardly move; the broad shoulders of the fearless Mien made him hungry, to see again the courageous face, and that alone pulled him along in the wake of the Hopelord. But no mortal force could move his feet further when they reached the top, and his eyes beheld the Makine.

The rise flattened out suddenly, bringing the whole abomination into view in a moment. It was a metal box the size of a cottage, with one aperture facing the bowl and three enormous leg-shaped supports driven down into the cavern floor like nails, holding it in place. Two multi-jointed arms stretched five rods long, tipped with scythe-like blades and smaller, sharp pincer claws along their length. These swept horridly back and forth in an irregular criss-cross motion, slicing the air, making a killing field of the distance to its center. While Cedrith watched in moaning horror, the entire construct vibrated as if with joy, to the grinding clash of its inner workings. Metal on metal gnashed, ground and tore; a short swerving tube near the center spurted a wash of flame out across the field beneath the waving scythes, and from some unseen port behind the box came another cloud of purple fume, wafting directly at them on the currents of the Hopeward.

At first sight, the dekentar fell to one knee as if hit by a scythe-blade; Cedrith stood in the back and panted, unable to look on or to look away. Natasha beside him chanted verses from the Telholian practice, "Only in Peace is Hope protected; the sacrifice beyond Hope brings Peace, and requires it; love and violence cannot bear company…"

The cloud surrounded them, moving too fast even if they could have mustered the spirit for a retreat. As the wave of tangible *miasma* touched lightly on Cedrith's skin he held his breath; to his shock, a trail of purple mist emanated from his mouth and nose and joined the larger cloud, fueling it and sending a tendril above, twisting towards the bridge like a snake. The dekentar also emitted purple, with shocked gaze and shaking frame. Cedrith nearly fell, but as he leaned a hand towards Natasha, he noted that her chanting continued, and the trail of vapor from her–coming from the eyes–was tiny and dim. The sage summoned the will to look at Judgement and the Mien: they stood firm, on alert and with weapons drawn but evidently unaffected by the poisonous cloud of fear. As the mist rolled past them, the three strings remained, moving up and out of sight above the steps of the massive stone-like bridge. Down in the cavern vale, the original mist spread and hugged the ground, nearing places where the dead still lay.

Cedrith looked to Natasha, and managed to dredge up his voice. "They… they will rise and keep coming. And our fear– we will feed the evil of this place. Until we… are dead, like the valiant ones who came before us."

She nodded bleakly, looking to Conar ahead of them, and said only, "The Harvester."

A voice rang out from the crest of the bridge, dry and cracked and long unused aloud.

"Welcome, mortals, back to my lonely abode. I am pleased that you have made it so near to the blessed sight of me; with regret, I am constrained by the rules from coming to meet you. But I send as my ambassador another you have longed to see."

A pause then, while Cedrith caught from the corner of his eye dozens of the risen dead approaching up the rise. Everyone looked to the bridge, and there came into view a tall man in robes. He used his eyes to spot them from afar, turning his neck and looking below; he walked with a stride that was quicker and smoother than the undead, coming down the enormous tread and onto the rise less than a furlong away.

"Eddoran!" Natasha breathed, and Conar stiffened in recognition as well.

At first, Cedrith felt his spirits rise to see another living human, and glancing to Natasha saw a spark of hope there as well. His long hair streaked with white framed an aquiline face; his form was thin but seemed vital and strong even without armor or weapon. As he approached, the man in robes held himself like one used to leadership.

But there were other signs: an uneven hitch in his step, the colorless pallor of his flesh, no smile on his face. He overtook a skeleton advancing on the party, and a moment later, Cedrith realized with a pulse of dread that it had not altered its path to attack him. And his eyes… as the man came closer, Cedrith could see a gaze of mute anguish, bordering on agony. His pace slowed–barely–as he came closer, and now it was clear he was struggling physically not to approach. Suddenly, Cedrith realized the man had not taken a breath.

The next moment, as if his left hand escaped its master's control, the robed man reached up to tear back the side of his tunic, exposing the rent in his chest where his heart had been removed.

Natasha screamed and fell to her knees. Cedrith saw a ring on the man's left hand, shaped like a serpent winding around and biting its own tail.

The voice again snapped over the stairs with gleeful malice, "I suppose you've noted by now he is no longer quite himself. The effect of the Mortal Coil can be quite beneficial, so long as healing is not delayed beyond a few days. Of course, what with years passing… well, no one could have predicted the full effect of your little experiment. I did what I could for him, I promise you. As such, it must be admitted he is neither fish nor fowl at the moment. Still, I must insist that the lovers embrace after such a long parting."

The thing that had been Eddoran lumbered towards Natasha, still on her knees. She looked him full in the eye. Working his lips and drawing a ragged breath he managed to cry, "Natasha! He controls my body, but I– my mind, Heroes save me–"

"I bring you a sacrifice beyond Hope," she said quietly, looking up to the gaunt with complete repose and resignation. He reached a hand tenderly to her, fixing his fingers in a spread across her face as the scars sprang up and the energy of her life leaked forth like steam. It was over in a moment. Even as Natasha screamed in agony, her right hand calmly reached up to Eddoran's left, and gently, smoothly, removed the ring from his finger.

As if dropped from ten feet, Eddoran's body collapsed to the cavern floor and rolled against Natasha's kneeling lap; she threw down her scarred and broken face over him and wept with a release that had been years building. The dekentar and Judgement stood by silently as the new corpse was bathed in tears, and the slow shuffling step of the risen grew more audible.

Conar spoke, quoting the Hopelord's paean to the dead of the First War of Liberation. *"Let the memory of their courage abide with us, and the thought of them live on in the tales we tell, even as the momentary flame consumes the shell in which they lived such noble lives."*

With a start, Cedrith realized the expectation of flame was all too real.

"Natasha! Stand back!"

But it was too late: a small box of crystal panes formed from the floor on all sides, trapping the Healers Guildmistress, the dekentar and the body of Eddoran together. Cedrith could only watch as Natasha's horribly-scarred face pressed against the glass, her eyes showing full knowledge of what lay ahead.

Judgement stepped forward but the box was already moving, and Conar barred his way with an arm, the lordly face showing concern and tension as on the eve of battle. Spinning on one heel, the colossal Mien charged back onto the plain atop the rise, dropping his sword and striding directly into the ambit of the gyring blades. Suicide, Cedrith had time to think; then one metallic arm came slashing down and Conar caught it bare-handed above the man-high blade in both arms. Quickly turning to face behind him, he moved one arm away from the first and managed to grab the second blade, though it lashed into his invulnerable mid-section briefly. He struggled as the pair of serpents first squirmed for freedom, then subsided under the mastery of the strength he bore.

Conar turned his face to look at Judgement and Cedrith in turn, eyes alight with passion and saying only:

"Now comes the moment of the test, children of Hope."

Judgement saw, and his face drew itself into a terrible resolve as he looked towards the center of the Makine across the plain. Dropping his staff, he charged in past Conar and towards the aperture that beckoned beneath the swiveling tube of flame.

Cedrith, beyond the power of rational thought, felt a madness overtake him completely; gripping his mace, he screamed "Rallantan!"

at the top of his lungs, turned and ran around the top of the rise after Natasha and the dekentar.

Before he knew what was happening, Cedrith had bowled over a skeletal foe in his path, taking a cut on his shoulder, but past him before he could feel the pain. The rough line of the undead paid him no heed, drawn like a magnet to the Mien above and beyond; in a moment, the sage was through and stumbling on after the small box of death. Natasha and the dekentar were jogging desperately to remain uncrushed as the cavern floor moved constantly beneath their feet; the body of the mage Eddoran was bumped along casually, cruelly on its way to interment. Cedrith had no idea what he could do to help or stop the rush toward death, but his madness carried him onward. He knew he could not turn back, to approach the risen or that horrid Makine, with his life on it.

Yet the chugging grind of the massive engine snapped his head around like a whip, and he saw Judgement dodging under the struggling blades and their sharp-tipped side claws to come within a few feet of the aperture. Conar still held the two jerking scythe-arms in his mighty grip, and the strain showed in his face only as passion. Above Judgement, the swiveling tube slewed around to his direction, as if guided by some mechanical sense of smell; the grey youth dodged when the Makine's whine reached its peak, but Cedrith could see it would be too slow. The sage stopped and shouted in alarm uselessly, as the burst of flame billowed out and engulfed the Man in Grey.

For two long, agonizing counts the flame burst forth and Cedrith felt his hopes turn to ashes inside him. The flame fading, hope was quickly reborn, to see a man-shape roll to its feet and run on. He was further in than he appeared! Only the edge of his cloak was fired, and he ignored this now as he moved straight in towards the Makine's central box. Without hesitation, the Man in Grey mounted a step and threw himself within. Cedrith glanced back to see the crystal tomb approaching the edge of the chasm now and his madness swept back over him. He ran towards them, shouting incoherently.

The dekentar was yelling within the cube of glass; noting the small size of this space, he had pressed his arms and legs tight against the corners to lift his feet off the ground, and Natasha now did the same. Between them, and aided by her considerable girth, the two made a press of flesh in the last instant before the box overran the chasm's edge. Cedrith was many steps away but could already feel the great heat of the lava below, and close enough to see the enormous strain on the dekentar's face as he pushed with all his might to remain pressed into the corner and not fall. Eddoran's corpse dropped from the lip and out of sight, the thin, tearing scream of the healer his dirge. Another long moment, and the box began to retreat to the land and safety.

Glancing back, he saw Judgement looking down at something within the belly of the monster. Cedrith marveled at his utter composure, the unbroken trepidity of his movements; it chilled him to think that the youth seemed almost at home. Reaching, he began to pull with his right arm against a rod, harder and harder, taking all his concentration. As Cedrith watched, he forgot until too late that the fire-tube was still active. Swiveling into position, it suddenly bathed itself, the entire center of the Makine in an enormous burst of flame. Black smoke leaked from every corner and the entire device shuddered and jerked; one of its legs came free of the cavern floor, canting the thing dangerously towards the edge of the chasm. As the wave of fire passed, Cedrith saw Judgement still in the box with his left arm blazing. The youth cried out angrily, and kept pulling on something within. Another shudder, a rusty rasp that echoed across the cavern. The grinding chugging roar of the Makine cut off as if on cue, and Judgement cooly turned to wrap his left hand with his cloak, smothering the flames.

The second leg came ripping free and the entire mass of metal began to tilt towards doom. Conar, who had relaxed with the Makine's death, now strained to hold the scythe-arms back like belaying ropes, his booted feet churning the earth and stone as they dragged towards the cliff. Judgement gathered himself and hurled his body through the aperture and clear of the metal legs, just as Conar let go; thirty feet of towering, horrid metal bowed over the edge and fell into the chasm. Seconds later, a thunderous concussion of molten impact swept the entire world, nearly drowning out the shriek of rage from above the bridge. Everywhere, the undead lay down and were still.

His mind reeling, Cedrith turned back to face the pair trapped in the glass cube. He knew there were only seconds left before it crushed the living, and when he saw that one wall had a rune inscribed on it, his heart leaped with hope. Stepping to the edge, Cedrith cleared his throat, desperately tried to remember the notes, any sequence from the song. Only an inchoate choking sound came forth, like the huff of an angry fox. Within, the face of the dekentar was panicked as he desperately tried to wedge his sword between the crack of his wall and the ceiling. Natasha, her face horrendously scarred, was weeping but showing a kind of peace, deliberately not looking up as she awaited her end. Cedrith tried again to sing, and only coughed as tears started on his cheeks also. Calling his friend's name, he placed one hand frantically on the etched lines of the rune, praying to Ma-Eldar and Rallantan for deliverance.

Snatched his hand back, stinging with pain. Noticed at last, that this rune was shaped like a pair of overlapping x's, and slightly cracked.

Heaving his mace around into two hands, Cedrith screamed and smashed the head into the center of the rune. Shattering crystals blew into his face giving him a dozen cuts, and his forward stumble was met and overwhelmed by the dekentar's charge, tackling healer and Elf together and falling beyond the reach of the sinking cube.

Spent, trembling and crushed again under Natasha's frame, Cedrith passed out. There was a moment of blackness, and blissful silence, in his mind; then he came to on his back, not knowing at first how long he had been there. Natasha was standing up, a few feet away, looking down on him; the scars across her face made Cedrith wince, but she seemed at peace, calm now though still with tears in her eyes. Rolling his head, the sage winced from the cut on his shoulder, but got his eyes around to see across the rim of the rise to where his other companions were. There stood Conar, waiting the approach of Judgement, who limped over with his left arm still wrapped in his cloak, to pick up his dropped quarterstaff. The two stood there without conversing.

It was a moment before Cedrith could sense the heat rising nearby.

He felt a fog around his mind, as he belatedly noted that the light too had increased; not from the ceiling above, which if anything was further clouded by the purple mist, but with a red-orange radiance.

Natasha still looked at the sage, as if she might just take a nap while standing. Behind her now loomed an enormous sinuous column of molten fire, rising, tapering, finally showing a tip on the end of an arm extending fivescore fathoms down to the chasm-pool. The air was dry, becoming hot. Cedrith was struck dumb; Judgement was turned away, and only Conar could see.

With a reflexive violent tug, Conar ripped off his helm and Alendic's voice shouted, "Natasha! Look out!"

The Guildmistress seemed to come out of her daze, and half-turned to see the tentacle of lava moving to embrace her.

She was knocked violently to the ground, as the dekentar again slammed into her body; left standing with his sword and dagger against the molten onslaught, he raised his blades and began to call out.

He was swept completely away, flaming, to drop with the tentacle below the lip of the chasm and out of sight.

Natasha and now Cedrith scrambled to their feet and stared into the space left by the loss of their fifth man. It was only a moment, as the shout of the Man in Grey behind them brought them around, and then running in his direction.

Alendic, still half-seen through the larger frame of the Hopelord as it faded, was emerging from the Mien-state; as he and Natasha sprinted on stumbling legs to reach the others, Cedrith could see the wounds appearing on the actor's body. Each gash, burn and hole caused a new cry of pain as it came visible; all the damage taken by Conar in the fighting being visited on his mortal frame after the sudden removal of the helm. As they reached his side, he was lying against Judgement's lap, blood from his scalp nearly obscuring his eyes. Natasha, with a scream of anguish, flopped beside him and brushed off his face, crying, "*Intacta volar. Intacta volar!*" Cedrith could see that cuts and wounds closed as she spoke, but mainly smaller ones and some only partially. New ones kept appearing and his visage was already ghastly. In the midst of a call, Natasha's eyes rolled back and she slumped to the side, caught once again by Cedrith as he labored to remain upright. Judgement too bent down and called, "*Intacta volar!*" closing a huge rent on the actor's left arm; but Alendic used the newfound strength to slap his aid away.

"No! You will harm yourself, save… save your strength, boy. I am done for."

Natasha came to at the sound of his voice, and cried out though still exhausted. "No! Alendic, no, you must be well, we can heal you—"

"My dear, I fear this is where we part company."

"Don't leave me. I … I am so sorry, Alendic, but I am too weak. Eddoran took– I am no longer–"

"Your strength, wondrous woman–" Alendic stopped as a fit of coughing overtook him, thick with blood, "…your pure purpose, is what brought us here against all odds, as much as your beauty."

"Stop! Can you not for one moment stop that salacious chatter!" she cried in heat that trumped her exhaustion. With one hand she covered some of her scars, white and large as snakes under the skin. With a wavering arm, Alendic reached up to gently caress the other side of her face, and his eyes spoke of a vision from years ago.

"My dear love, would you ever suppose… in all these years, that I was lying?"

Natasha looked down on him then with horror.

"But I– Alendic, Eddoran and I– you must be joking–"

"Joking, of course!" he managed, nearly angry, still grinning with thin lips stretched over agony. "Joking, but never lying, not to you, my… my love. And I watched… your love for him these past five years," Alendic managed through a small burble of blood. "I watched and of course, my dear, I fell as he did."

Natasha sat back, shaking her head slowly and seeming to draw in breath endlessly. Alendic looked then on Cedrith with eyes that lost focus; more gashes were appearing around his neck and head, and speech was increasingly difficult.

"I apologize, good … good sage," he coughed, "you must… do your best now, for … for her and your young friend. Per… perhaps we shall meet soon, as it is." He nodded once and added, "Get … get them back."

Cedrith could say nothing but only took his hand and held it. Alendic glanced at Judgement above him, whose face was slipping as if it did not fit.

"You were right … boy. I was, in the end … only playing a role, was I not?" He was seized by a wracking cough, but Judgement leaned down to speak in his ear.

"Verily," he said, "thou hast played him well."

The actor went still at last, mimicking the end of breath so perfectly that Cedrith admired his craft; his small inner voice uncharitably insisted that this was real, and the adventurer was indeed dead. Natasha, bereft of two loves in as many moments, fell limply across his torn body, and Cedrith realized he had seen this act before. Frantically he began to pull her away from the corpse, and Judgement realized the point as well, joining in with his uninjured arm. The Guildmistress shrieked in dismay when her hands lost contact, and she wept and screamed his name as the crystal box appeared to take him to his companion's grave. Then Natasha subsided against Cedrith in wracking sobs and he sat with her, only a few steps from the very middle of truly nowhere, holding her up against the full weight of Despair.

⊕ ⊕ ⊕

Haltar wanted to march further away before the sun, but Treaman was frantic to find Hallah. The keep did not return, a blessing, and the woodsman with Bildon circled within easy sight of the banked campfire, calling out for the little dragon. Both moons were down below the southern horizon, and clouds scudding on the wind obscured most of the stars. The night was hugely cold, biting and numbing with wind driving it ceaselessly further into the body. Mhoral for once did not complain; he lay by the fire hugging himself and shivering despite its warmth, with Linya keeping watch over him and Haltar, trying to doze through the wounds on his back and ribs. Every few minutes, the two searchers would return to warm up, and Treaman's heart sank lower with each trip.

The moment came with its usual suddenness, startling yet becoming natural.

{ *"Treeeman!"*}

"Where have you been?" he cried, looking all about and unable to see any hint of his friend.

{ *"Hallah waits for Treeeman, top of stone-pile."*}

"What? We are not there, Hallah, can you come to us now?"

There was a longish pause, and then he heard { *"Hallah come."*}

A flutter of wings, and his companion stooped to his shoulder as if from a wall ten feet away, though there was no wall. Treaman stroked his friend with joy, but could make no sense of what had happened.

"Where were you? How did Hallah get here? Where is the castle, Hallah?"

The creature simply craned her neck around to stare him in the eyes with its twin jewels, and waited for her friend to answer these questions.

Shaking his head, he returned to the campfire and called to Bildon.

"I can't explain, she says she was at the keep, and then when I asked her to come she was suddenly right here."

Haltar had roused and was already rolling up his blanket. "So how far off is it? Does the keep move, can it still see the place?"

"She… doesn't understand distances very well, I can't get anything from her about that."

{*"Hallah smart! Understand all!"*}

"Yes," Treaman cooed at once, "very smart, and brave, and I am sure also very–"

{*"Hungry! Yes."*}

The group rose to leave and Treaman selected local terrain instead of guessing the direction of moonset. Some league or so away was a copse of scrub-trees, larger than normal. They covered ground for about half an hour, and Treaman in the front realized that Bildon was essentially talking to himself. No one, even Mhoral, was responding to his jibes and banter; the halfling didn't seem to have much stomach for it anyway. The woodsman reflected that they were in desperate shape; Haltar's main weapon broken again, his own spear left in the tower wall, Mhoral probably drained and certainly in poor spirits, wounds for all except the Stealthic and no clear sense of where to head for shelter.

He turned back to face the party and they halted, with the copse now just a few rods off.

"I believe," he said slowly, "that the keep, being able to appear, or move even when we do not, is an exception." He felt like his brain was plowing through hard soil as he talked. "Not that there are hard and fast rules, but it's… I don't think we'll see other places like that."

Everyone just stared back at him silently. Treaman doubted whether he should have had this conversation aloud, and changed the subject.

"Should we go on or back?"

Haltar returned the look steadily and said, "We should go where we can be sure of getting." Treaman threw out his arms at that, saying "Fine, the trees it is. At least there will be cover while we rest up."

Still halfway there, Treaman got a twinge that hinted of changing weather, impending chaos. Looking around, he saw clouds closing in from behind him. He pointed to the storm, and the group picked up the pace to reach the trees. A rustle of birds took flight as they came within a few steps, and Treaman could see it was a large flock of those horrid reavers. It puzzled him, since the party had only seen them during the day, he assumed they would not be nocturnal. Why would the party's approach flush the carrion-birds so soon, and why not take cover as the storm approached? The birds screamed and circled but stayed nearby, as if confused, or tempted.

Breaking into the copse the party stopped near the boles of the first trees. Treaman felt the softness of scrub-grass beneath his boots, noticeable compared to the usual stone-hard packed earth. He wondered how far the copse extended; perhaps it was even the outskirts of another pocket of humanity, though his instinct was to doubt it. The storm approached and everyone watched as it closed in. Judging by the acrid smell on the wind, it would be another toxic rain.

He checked the trees for cover. Short but thick, twisty and wrapped in heavy same-colored vines; the leaves of the trees and the vines entwined throughout the bole and branches, like two wrestlers locked in a mutual stranglehold. In the uncertain light, it seemed to Treaman that some of the vines were twining, shifting, getting a tighter grip. The storm, the birds, the ungainly grove all hummed on his nerves. Calling across the wind to Bildon, he shouted, "Can you see the moon yet?"

"Trees in the way, I'll just– hoop!" Bildon, normally so nimble, was turning to one side of his tree, but seemed to forget to inform his feet of the move. The Stealthic fell flat on his face, bending awkwardly forward from his waist. His feet and ankles appeared fully stuck in place, and twisting his head around to look, Bildon shouted, "Roots!"

Panic ensued: everyone tried to move, couldn't, and fell. "Daggers!" Haltar shouted, and Treaman was already ahead of him, hacking at his feet and ripping them free. His nerves were jangling now, and even as he moved away from the grass, he looked back to see as much as he could.

In a flash of lightning from the approaching storm, he saw it all:

Roots and grass blades flailing slowly beneath the feet of the retreating, stumbling, cursing party.

Reaver birds swooping in agitation lower to the trees, some few landing on the ground.

Vines on the trees shrinking around the boles out of sight, vines that were not plants but hardened limbs.

Something reptilian or insectivoid with vine-like limbs dropping from a low trunk onto a reaver-bird, crushing and biting it in half in a single move. The camouflage of the trees no longer sufficing, eight or ten of the panther-sized monsters came snaking down to do the hard way a job the clutching roots would have made much easier.

The copse was a death-trap, plants and monsters in concert to snare hapless animals; reaver-birds hovered in the area for carrion and occasionally paid the price. Now the rain started, stinging hard at once and pushing the fleeing party back towards cover and danger.

"Treaman!" Haltar shouted over the rising storm, "what do we do?"

The woodsman hitched his cloak over his head and surveyed the scene with a tight chuckle. "Boss," he called, "do you remember that whorehouse in Cryssigens you told me about? The one where the women are slaves, and tied down over the end of the bed so they can't move?"

Haltar looked at the woodsman as if he were crazy, but nodded. "So?"

"Like that."

The party held in a line for several seconds, weapons ready and cursing as their flesh got wet. Haltar spoke his commands with confidence despite their ridiculous nature. "Into the trees and across, at the trot. If you meet a creature, hit it but keep moving. Step high and don't stop! Now!"

With a yell of pain and fear they charged in. Treaman was well under the first several boles when he sensed, more than saw, something to his right and higher up. Leering out from the trunk head-down was a monster at his shoulder level, jaws gaping and one foreclaw reaching in his general direction. He swung wildly, felt his sword glance off the carapace, and kept on. The grass was sticky underfoot, reminding him to pull up hard with every step, and he saw the others do the same. The party seemed to be picking their way over broken glass, except Bildon, who slowed and began to hop instead. A grounded monster lay close to his path, and it swung its head around as if sniffing the halfling; Treaman could see it had no eyes, and perhaps no ears either. Haltar, between them, lashed down with his punch-blade and half severed its neck-joint; squalling, the beast upended with four legs writhing horribly. Bildon somersaulted over the pre-corpse and the group was beyond them, headed to the other side a dozen rods away.

The rain was pelting down now, the leaves unaffected but some drops getting through to the people beneath, even under the thickest branches. The five huddled close to three separate trees, Linya alone on one end. Bildon, on instinct, started to climb his, but Haltar grabbed him back roughly, hissing, "Idiot, they live up there."

"Keep your feet moving, everyone," he ordered as quietly as he could. Treaman looked across to the creatures, most of them down from their trunks now. They didn't immediately react; truly blind, they turned in all directions. But soon they began to swivel in the party's path, padding on four legs each, thick ridged tails dragging behind them. The sight of those blind, shiny-hard heads swaggering in low to the ground was unnerving at twenty paces; Treaman did not feel like seeing it any closer. Naturally, the rain seemed to have no effect on their carapaces.

"They see us," Mhoral warned.

"They have no eyes."

"They hear us," the Elf snapped a bit louder.

"Then shut up, by the balls of Areghel." Haltar was in no mood to be conversing. "Linya, fire when I say?"

"Yes, but–"

"Now!"

Linya barked out a word and the ground before the party erupted in flame. The stench of the crisping root-grass was disgusting, almost like flesh; the lizard-things came pounding in now, and the filtering rain dampened the effect of the blaze almost at once.

"I tried to tell you!" the sorceress shouted.

"Run, the other side again, now!"

Coming through the guttering flames, the party seemed to confuse the semi-reptiles, who were clearly blind. Treaman slashed at one in passing and it was very slow to react, missing his leg with claw and jaw. Mhoral, in a frenzy, screamed in his native tongue while taking four whacks at his closest opponent, and got a claw-rake across his leg for the trouble. Treaman nearly turned back to cover him before he broke away and went with the woodsman after the others. Near the center of the vale, Treaman spotted the body of the crushed reaver-bird and on an instinct scraped it up as he ran. It came free only in pieces as the grasses had closed around it.

{*"Hungry!"*}

"Soon!" he shouted, and panted up to the others.

The rain was now very heavy, and the shelter they stopped at was nowhere near as good as the first one. The sting of each drop on any naked skin was like a hornet, and though clothing held up, the soaking was starting to burn. The woodsman examined the top half of the avian corpse in his hand; it was absolutely bloodless, though alive less than two minutes ago. Grass-ends stuck out of it everywhere, like thinning hair, and the top half of each stem was stained brownish-crimson. It was beginning to make a horrid kind of sense.

Mhoral panted heavily without looking at his wound, and said, "Rep-reptilian... Not... bugs." So that was why he had hit the thing so often and gotten hurt for it; Treaman knew it was important for the Elf to have that squared away.

"What are these things?" Linya called.

Haltar pointed to Treaman, who shouted back in frustration, "Oh no! I have enough right now, thanks."

Bildon, taxed by two sprints and frustrated that he had no part to play, looked up at the tree-limbs with envy. So doing, he forgot to move his feet and got them stuck again; cursing, he tore them free and started stamping with vengeance as if he could kill the devil grass with his boots.

"Shut up," Haltar said. "They're coming back, and fast."

"I thought they couldn't hear us," Bildon protested.

Treaman watched the waving snouts and then it came to him.

"They can *feel* us," he cried. "The stamping, through the ground."

There was a moment's pause. "If we don't," Haltar said, "the roots will hold us down."

Everyone stood still for a second, then continued ripping their feet free and trying to put them down quietly. It was too much, and Treaman started chuckling. Haltar looked at him and cocked an eyebrow.

"Whorehouse?" he said.

"Like that," the woodsman returned cheerfully.

"The other side, again, now!"

Ten minutes later, the tactic had run itself out. The rain seemingly hovered directly over the cursed glade, and the party had run across it five more times. Three of the lizard-things were dead, as well as two or three reaver-birds seeking cover or an early taste of the dying. Mhoral's leg wound was stiffening up, slowing him to a gasping hobble; Bildon had a seeping wound on his neck when a frenzied reaver-bird flew straight into him, before he could strangle it; Linya had cast the fire twice more, to no real effect, and was heaving loudly even when standing still. If they tried to run again, Haltar would need to carry her. Inspired, Treaman had them stand on a burned patch once, and the lizards blundered straight past them with no vibrations to guide. But the rain came down too hard there, and they had to give it up, so the chase was on again. They huddled now on the side they had first entered and considered their options.

"We're going to have to leave this garden spot," Haltar said.

"The rain… has to end… sometime," Mhoral panted.

"Why doesn't it burn the bastards?" Treaman exclaimed, then cried out again as his wet clothes scraped his skin with pain.

"Not… Hallah either," Bildon said, pointing to the woodsman's rider. Hallah had flown several times through this melee; she had contributed the intelligence that reaver-bird did not taste good, and that she was still hungry. Now she huddled on Treaman's shoulder and watched the proceedings as a kitten would a bell-toy. Her master's impending demise seemed to make no impression on the dragon's mood.

"Yes," Treaman agreed, eyeing the wandering lizard-things. "Something about the scaly skin, I suppose. But this whole… thing. It's remarkable, in a way. How did the lizards and the trees, with these vines… I mean how does it–"

"Treaman," Haltar broke in, "concentrate."

The woodsman looked back angrily at the leader, but only for a moment. "You're right. Let's head out the way we came. The storm chased us, and maybe it will move on the same direction. We'll get out of it sooner that way."

Everyone knew the chances of this being right, and the consequences if it weren't. Treaman started thinking about the garruk and the scars on their naked flesh after just minutes in the toxic-rain.

"We'll wait until the lizards are as close as possible," Haltar said. "Until then, let's try to make as little vibration as we can."

They huddled miserably and moaned, stepping carefully with toes-first, which was very tiring. Linya was not getting rest, practically passing out on her feet; Haltar positioned her boots on top of his, and stepped for both of them. The lizards nosed generally closer, and everyone steeled themselves for the rush into the storm, and eventual oblivion. Treaman was wondering how much longer when he was distracted by a cracking sound from the tree next to him. Glancing up, he saw a hollow bole opening slowly, leaking wet fluid from the rain and something else. As he looked on in horror, the hole extruded bits of shell and then the noseless beak and eyeless head of a small lizard-creature. Born from the tree, existing in partnership with it and vines; a small world of chaos and death, a weapon made of flesh to harvest the unwary. Bildon saw it and cried out in disgust.

Haltar yelled, "Go! Now!" and they ran away into the storm.

The pelting was painful at once: their clothing, already soaked through, conducted the heavier rainfall straight to the skin all over them. Moans rose into ragged screams, and Treaman smelled something smoking. He had no ideas left, could see no other terrain or cover, just a few distant stars twinkling in a direction he could not place. The realization shot through him a moment later: stars overhead meant clearing, and the rain was indeed slacking off. Behind them the storm still squatted on the copse, drenching the death-lair. Within forty more agonizing paces the precipitation was barely noticeable and the cold night air was clear.

The men began immediately to strip off their clothes down to the naked skin. Haltar set down Linya, who he had half-carried the last length, and said, "You can do as you like," before starting to shrug out of his plate and chain. They hollered and cursed as they got the wet material away from further contact; incredibly, nothing made of cloth was burnt or dissolved in the least, but the skin was red all over where the rain had soaked through. Getting his boots and breeches off last, Treaman stood there without a stitch on, hugging his arms and fitfully trying to pull more liquid from his hair without touching it too long.

Turning before thinking, he saw Linya standing there also naked except for her diadem, and he became incapable of further thought for a long second. She noticed him and he nearly fell down from shock; turning away, he scrabbled for combustibles on the ground as if his life depended on it. That was in fact true, but he was grateful he had not been aroused in those fateful seconds. Time for that, no doubt, later; life with the female mage was never going to be the same.

Using his skill, ranging hard and fast in the chill night air, the woodsman returned to the party bearing a small armload of twigs and grasses. Hallah, sensing his need, flew off and returned with a branch in her teeth, which he gratefully accepted. Piling it carefully he pulled out his tinderbox and sprinkled in some shavings, from a stock he always kept dry for such occasions. Two strikes and a small flame sprang up, more for comfort than real heat, but with some potential.

As he stood, he saw the others clustered near, Linya next to him, all still naked with their clothes held in front to dry them. Only Treaman had nary a stitch, but now it would be unseemly to reach for cover. So he stood there, and the grins spread all around.

"Like that!" he shouted to the night sky and everyone laughed with relief.

"So," Linya said demurely and taking the tiniest peek towards Bildon, "it's true what they say."

"You bet your last silver bit it is," Bildon affirmed, and then asked Haltar in a stage-whisper, "What do they say?"

"Something about three legs all the same length," Haltar returned gamely.

"Told you he's a demon in disguise," Mhoral ground out but with a grin.

Shaking his head, the woodsman went off to find more fuel.

He had to range farther afield, and was just thinking about risking a quick trip into the grove, when he jumped to hear the snort of a mule. Looking up, he saw a lovely light grey animal not three rods away, haltered to its partner and two more pairs behind it. The team was hitched to an enormous wagon, and spaced behind it at two rod intervals were at least a half-dozen more. The animals looked Treaman in the eye without comment; but the man behind them was less indifferent. Treaman ran as the driver called out.

He arrived back at the tiny campfire and said, "You might want to get dressed."

"Still soaking wet–"

"Now." Then the others heard the horn, and saw the lead wagon. Above the front riding board was a pole and a small flag running up under the moonlit sky. The lead wagon pulled into a gentle arc that brought it sideways to the party, and the others followed in a neat curve. Now a brace of horsemen burst forth from between the line and trotted in the party's direction. They scrambled to cover at least their privates as the mounted men came closer.

"It's Pelian," Haltar said.

"The armed merchant?" Bildon asked. "I've heard tell of his wagons in Trainertown, like a moving fortress."

"But no one's ever seen them this close," Haltar responded. "He parks them out in the chaos and runs in his goods by handwagon. No one knows how he does that. I don't think most folks realize how… large his operation is."

Treaman could see even Haltar was taken by the scope of this caravan: the line of wagons stretched to twelve now, each pulled by six mules and manned by a crew of at least two. There were more horsemen and a dozen other persons walking next to the line. Another call of the trumpet, and the line stopped as the four horsemen arrived within speaking distance. Treaman glanced back, and saw with relief that Linya had gotten into her wet robe.

Haltar raised his arm and gave the traditional greeting, "Where do you think you are?" Two of the four horsemen dismounted and stepped a bit closer, while the others kept in easy reach of their sword and shield. One man on the ground was a simply enormous black-skinned giant, a head taller than Haltar and dressed in a striped hide that proclaimed his southern heritage. A Nubian, Treaman realized, a thousand leagues from the land of his birth. He stood a pace behind and to the right of the other, a much shorter man with a deep complexion, hard, staring eyes, above a small well-formed face with tight thin lips that always seemed compressed, never relaxed.

He scanned the party as if evaluating the price of their half-naked bodies on a southern slaver's block.

"Haltar Eltrinstar," the foot-knight continued, focusing his attention completely on the smaller man as if his bodyguard did not exist. "We are two days out from Trainertown, for whatever that's worth, and were just… camping for the evening." Treaman could sense the circumspection in his voice, and took his cue accordingly.

The small man heard this without responding at once. Haltar continued for him, as if a courtesy. "And you of course, are the famous Pelian Keranth, merchant of the Percentalion and most experienced explorer of unknown lands since Novar."

The flick of a smile at one edge of the merchant's mouth indicated the compliment had scored. He nodded in acknowledgement and returned, "And you? How are you known?"

"Mainly by our deeds," Haltar said after a moment's pause. "We are an adventuring party from various lands, as you can see, at work in the Percentalion since late Hawk. This would have been after your last departure, but perhaps you have visited Maladon since mid-summer, and heard tell the dragon is dead." The comment brought Pelian's eyes back to Haltar like a snapped bowstring, and his horsemen shifted in their seats in obvious surprise. "I believe they've declared a need for lumber, among other things, if you have any," Haltar continued carelessly, but watching the merchant like a hawk for any sign of reaction.

The merchant's face betrayed nothing, and he said only, "You?"

"We all were there," the foot-knight said, including the group and excluding a direct answer. "At present, we are headed elsewhere, and would value provisions and other items, if you have them."

Now the merchant smiled fully for the first time, and Treaman relaxed a bit but still wished Pelian had stayed serious. "What may I offer you from my poor, depleted stores?"

"Food, dressings, healing salves if you can spare them, and a new sword to replace–"

"And what, may I inquire, do you have of value for me?"

Haltar smiled broadly. "You will find our credit in Trainertown is of the very highest level."

Pelian's smile in return disappeared. "And out here, you will find it is greatly less than that."

"We travel light, without room for luxury goods."

"As do I. Perhaps this concludes our business."

Bildon jumped up in a rage. "We could buy your entire line of wagons, with everything in them!"

"Not mine, sirrah. They are entirely beyond your price."

Things were taking an ugly turn. Treaman knew the party desperately needed supplies, and protection. Looking back at the line of wagons, he could see men debouching, setting up camp. The wagons had turned into a tight circle, with only small spaces between them, and the mule-teams were inside the ring, somehow, in a manner he could not make out from this distance. But to one side he caught sight of a small group of men approaching the copse in the moonlight, one with an axe clearly visible.

"Perhaps, kind sir," Linya said as Haltar tried to maintain his composure, "you have magical items you wish to see identified?"

Pelian shook his head, barely polite and starting to show signs of impatience. "I have no need of intellective spellcasting."

Mhoral and Bildon could think of nothing to say, and stood there trying to look unworried. Treaman from the back said, "What are your men doing in that copse there?"

Pelian looked at him and said, "Foraging for wood."

"You need to call them back, now." When the merchant only arched an eyebrow in response, Treaman said, "Or you could wait, and hire us as replacements."

Still Pelian stared, though he shifted in some concern.

"Do you think we're standing out here in our skivvies for the fun of it?" Treaman cried. "I don't want anyone dying for my wit, or your poker-face."

Pelian turned, spoke in an unknown tongue to his Nubian and pointed to the foraging party. The giant black cupped his hands and called in musical tones, like a trumpet; the party stopped and after a moment turned around.

The merchant spun back to assess the party some more. "I shall speak frankly with you, as befits civilized persons. At first, I took you for refugees; the various towns always lose some poor souls to the hope that they can escape from this country with a rake in their hands and a prayer on their lips. Your state of dress–pardon me–did nothing to dispel this notion. Now I am to understand that you are indeed in need of supplies, probably of shelter, and yet you claim to be the mightiest band of adventurers to grace the Land of One Hundred Castles in at least thirty years. I am perhaps understandably somewhat dubious. Your letters of credit are no doubt authentic, but I must be forgiven if I forego examining them in the absence of some other evidence."

As the party stood aghast, Treaman suddenly laughed out loud. Haltar and Pelian turned to look, and he laughed again. "Would you excuse me, sir?" he said gaily to Pelian. "My dragon is asking to be fed."

"Your–?" the merchant gaped, at last letting his composure slip. Hallah uncurled and snapped up three riddy from Treaman's pouch as he stepped forward in clearer view next to Haltar. The horses shied and the black giant unfolded his arms. Everyone stared open-mouthed at this wonder.

"Last of the old wurm's eggs," Haltar said briefly, as usual letting pictures do what words could not.

Pelian had shut up his face again, but the eyes betrayed him; Hallah's every move gained his undivided attention, even as he kept speaking. "I will be delighted to offer you food and protection," he said carefully, "provided you obey the rules of my caravan to the letter. We may discuss barter for goods you require, once I have attended to the security of the campsite.

"Follow Braja and do explicitly as he instructs. You will not understand him, but he understands me and has full freedom to enforce the rule of the caravan. Well met, brave adventurers." And with a final, almost hungry look at Hallah, he returned to his horse, giving a few more foreign words to the Nubian before remounting.

The party packed up in haste, as the mounted horse-guards left with Pelian. Finished dressing, they hoisted packs and walked up to Braja standing by his horse. He held up one palm to stop them, pointed to Linya, and then to his saddle. With some hesitation, she came to the side of the horse, and Braja bent to offer his knee as a step.

"So," Bildon mused aloud, "a classy operation."

"Or perhaps just a classy servant," Mhoral offered.

"I don't know," Haltar drawled as he sauntered up next to Braja while looking elsewhere. "I've always heard these black-skins are cowards, with hearts like rabbits." Everyone stared agape, including Linya from horseback as Braja straightened. Haltar slowly turned to face him and kept talking, as if to someone else. "Probably has his tongue cut out, that's why he can't talk. And from what I hear, Bildon, his third leg is shorter than yours."

Braja showed not the slightest reaction, and pointed to the encampment as he took the reins. He walked ahead and the party ambled behind him in perfect silence.

"What on earth was that?" Treaman whispered.

"I think our friend here does not understand the Common Tongue," Haltar observed.

"Either that, or he has the discipline of a martial wizard," Mhoral muttered.

"Or maybe talking like an idiot is not against the rules of the caravan," Bildon put in cheerfully.

Haltar smiled, then deliberately called out, in a foreign tongue Treaman had never heard him use. Braja's step slowed and his head half-turned, but then he continued. Haltar nodded like the man who sees the best move in chess. "Clever bastard," he muttered to himself.

"What is it?" Treaman asked, and Haltar motioned all heads closer as he whispered.

"I spoke in the Southern tongue, used in the Empire," he breathed. "I don't speak it well, and it's not the language Pelian used. He might have known the Nubian's tribal language. I said 'no slaves in the north kingdoms.' I think our little friend here heard me. And I'm only guessing, but I think I gave him some news."

Now the party was passing between two wagons and into the encampment, and for some time no one could say a word in any language.

Inside the tight circle of wagons was a small village. Tents had already been constructed with clear avenues between them. A latrine-pit scratched in the earth just inside the circle had nothing near it. Cook fires burned and men stood watch atop each wagon on the cardinal compass points.

Treaman stared at the mules, still in their traces, now turned in from the wagon-yokes by means of a marvelous mechanism that, once released, allowed them to be walked to the side. They were brushed down and fed from bags; several smaller animals were kept in a pen set up from interlocking wooden fence-sections. Treaman estimated there were at least fifty persons in the caravan, and maybe eighty.

Braja led them to a small cookfire where five or six persons were eating, and indicated that the party should be fed; then he bowed to

Haltar and left. The drovers handed them stew and bread without comment, and the group sat to one side. Their clothes dried more quickly with the heat of a real fire nearby.

"What kind of man needs such a huge operation?" Mhoral said.

"One who is finding enormous wealth," Haltar replied. "Everyone, learn what you can."

"I do need to use the privy," Bildon said, standing and sauntering off. Linya politely asked if there were a mage in the caravan, and was answered with a point and the words, "Number four, with the green trim."

Treaman walked to the *keran* and asked if he could be of any help with the horses. The men there only stared at him, and belatedly he asked Hallah to look around the wagons for food, which she eagerly flew off to do. That loosened the tongues a bit, and Treaman returned satisfied that whatever else Pelian might be, he valued his animals.

"The question is," Haltar rejoined when he heard the news, "whether he values anyone higher than that."

"And what have you learned?" Treaman countered.

"That Pelian does not often take in boarders," Haltar said quietly, while pretending to hitch his plate pieces more tightly. "No one in sight can take their eyes off us, though they're busy as bees, and Braja there is only pretending to coil rope, as if that would ever be his job."

Linya returned with the bad news that wagon four, home of the caravan mage, was Pelian's own; she had not tried to gain an interview but only asked the driver. Several minutes later, Bildon was simply standing there, and only Treaman noticed him before he started chuckling.

"Yes, very clever little lad, what did you find?" Haltar said.

"Well, the latrine is very well laid out," Bildon said with a grin. "And also," he added with a rising tone as Haltar lifted him off the ground by his collar, "these wagons are nothing like what they appear to be."

"What do you mean? What's inside?"

"I couldn't get there, not a chance, they're watched constantly. But I'm telling you, every single edge along the outside, top, side and bottom, has some kind of hinge."

Everyone tried not to be obvious as they looked around; their cookfire was near the center of the encampment, so only Mhoral could nod with any confidence as Bildon kept speaking.

"The wood is thick and close-set, couldn't slip a dagger between the boards. The wheels are reinforced with steel around the rim and on the spokes; they must weigh three of me each. And there are springs underneath. Springs! Like coaches in Conar, first-class construction."

"And able to hold even more weight," Haltar added thoughtfully.

"And," Bildon added with meaning, "there are women in the last wagon, number twelve. At least six. Plus children."

"He's probably self-sufficient," Haltar mused, "even growing his own labor force. Clever bastard," he said again. He looked to Mhoral and said only, "You?"

As far as Treaman could tell, Mhoral had not left the cookfire, though Haltar's orders were never optional. Looking up with his bitter, crooked grin, Mhoral said only, "There are no Elves in this caravan."

"What?"

"Have you seen one?" he turned to Haltar, then Bildon, and received head-shakes all around. "I looked, from here," he continued, priding himself on his night-vision. "But it's more than that. This is not a group that an Elf would find himself with."

"More than that," Haltar said, nodding in agreement, "Pelian would never tolerate it. He needs short lives and short memories."

"And here comes our host now," Mhoral said casually. "Let's hear what else he needs."

Pelian approached with Braja and two other men carrying bundles that they laid down at the cookfire. "A tarp," the merchant said, waving his men to lay it out, "that persons of your ambition should find useful."

The Nubian wordlessly took the bundle of cloth, opened it at the bottom, and folded down the wooden pole in its center. Indicating to Treaman the metal reinforced holes around the edge and the door-flap, he demonstrated how it could be set up quickly and cover an area wide enough for six, as long as they did not mind close company.

"The fabric is treated and will repel rain," Pelian said with emphasis. "All manner of rain." Braja showed a small hole near the center, which Treaman understood could be used to vent smoke. He nodded in appreciation.

"We are in your debt, sir," Haltar said, "and we always pay our debts. Would you have me sign a remittance now?"

Pelian held up a forestalling hand, and indicated packets of food and other essential supplies, quite a generous variety, but small enough that they could be carried. Everything Haltar had mentioned, except a sword, was there, and several other items besides. Treaman felt interest, and then apprehension, as he surveyed the stores.

"Please, let us not rush into negotiations. Look over my poor wares, select what you wish as a group if that suits you, and then we may negotiate the price." His face was again as calm as well water, but his eyes kept flicking over to Treaman. "In the morning, we will set out just after dawn, and you may ride in wagon one, there with the red awning. It is the safest position, in case of trouble."

"We would hope to be of service in any such event, sir," Haltar replied. "No doubt we are unfamiliar with your plan of defense, but if you wish–"

"You are my guests. My plan of defense is more than adequate, I assure you." He hesitated, and a drover approached him deferentially to speak.

"Master, the lead beast–"

"Silence," Pelian ordered firmly and the man retreated. "And now, I must wish you a good evening, for even I require some hours of sleep." Here he bowed with stiff courtesy to Mhoral, and retired with Braja and the bearers, leaving all the stores behind in the party's care. The Nubian was donning thick gauntlets as they left.

"Look, but don't take anything," Haltar said, and his voice conveyed his displeasure.

Bildon sidled up to Treaman and whispered, "I think we both know how that merchant would like to be paid." Treaman nodded, and reached out to his friend, saying quietly, "Hallah, are you nearby?"

The response was immediate: {*"Hallah here! Hungry!"*}

"Hallah awake!" Treaman shot back, glad to have the confirmation and a little worried about her. "Come for food, where are you?"

{*"Treeeeman not see?"*}

"No, are you far away?"

{*"Hallah not far, on green wagon. Box smell bad."*}

"What?" Treaman snapped around to the direction of Pelian's wagon, where the leader and the drover huddled near an iron-banded wooden pen of some kind, completely solid to his view.

"What do you mean, the box smells bad?"

{*"Hallah see. Hallah smell. Box bad."*}

"What does Hallah see?" Treaman asked in some frustration.

{*"See. Hallah show. See."*}

On an impulse, Treaman threw himself into deep concentration, eyes closed, ignoring all else, and tried to do the reverse of what he did when he showed Hallah an image from his own mind. At once, he saw Pelian, Braja and several others near the pen, as if he were sitting atop the green-edged wagon. On this side, the box had small holes, clearly for air, and the men were speaking soundlessly while preparing to open it. Braja held a thick whip in one hand and a slab of meat in the other that could not have come from a deer, or even a horse. The other men held iron flat-ended poles, as if to push something from a distance. Even without sound or smell, Treaman could take from their body language a clear sense of danger, and his heart jumped.

"Hallah," he said quietly, "I want you to walk, not fly, but slowly walk to the other side of the wagon. Do you understand?"

{*"Hallah sneaky, like boy with Treeeeman."*}

"Yes, Hallah very sneaky, just like boy." Treaman smiled. The view in his mind moved with his friend to the back side of the box, and he did not believe the dragon had been seen. "Now," he said trying to keep his mind casual, "fly back for food."

The camp was growing quiet; except for the group hovering around that pen, most everyone was asleep. A woman came to lead the party to the first wagon, where she opened the back door and let them in. The interior was not made as a sleeper or coach but a storeroom for goods, yet it was not very full. Except for several long boxes along the inside wall facing camp-center, there was nothing on the floor, and only a lantern on a hook to provide light. But the place was very interesting nonetheless.

"Did you notice," Bildon said as the door closed behind them, "that the wagon hardly sank at all with us getting in it?"

"I bet that happens to you a lot," Mhoral said.

Haltar rapped the wall. "It would take five minutes to chop through this, must be four inches thick. Rivets, straps– ho, what's here?" He pulled back a bar and opened a viewport on the outside wall.

"Look," Linya said, "there are more, on both sides, and a hatch in the roof. Probably for smoke."

"We could hold off an army in here," Treaman said, and then to Haltar, "Think we'll have to?" Haltar shook his head, which did not exactly answer the question.

Treaman reported on what Hallah had seen, and Haltar shook his head again. "For defense, maybe; there's all kinds of monsters in this land."

With little further comment they settled in, lowered the lantern and went to sleep. Treaman appeased Hallah with a snack and some petting and she began to doze on his chest without a care in the world. Treaman lay back and listened to the distant, muffled sounds of the caravan mules outside the wagon, and the breathing of the sleepers within it. He was always last to fall asleep with the party on adventure, unless someone else was on watch, and it comforted him to hear them all resting, gave him a sense of wellness that nearly equaled sleep. Bildon snored as if he were big as Haltar, and Hallah wheezed at a remarkably slow pace for her size. Linya often turned and sometimes spoke in her sleep, nonsense syllables like the ones she used to concentrate for spellcasting; Treaman could only guess the substance of the mage's dreams, and the idle thought of her casting naked would not leave him. Mhoral hardly breathed at all, in seeming, so shallow and slow did his chest rise and fall. Haltar always slept with his arms at odd angles, muscles showing around the disordered blanket and sprawled as if someone had sapped him in an alleyway. Treaman surveyed the group and settled closer to contentment, relaxing for a time from the ordeal of the journey.

The baying monster cut through his entire being, freezing him in place. He forced his head to turn in the face of his fear as the unearthly howl cut off; the others lay undisturbed, and Treaman doubted whether he might be dreaming. Time passed and his body lay there enervated by the promise of utter ruin, the destruction and power and hatred for all the living that had emanated, he felt sure, from the box by wagon one. His heart pumping like a hammer, body bathed in sweat, the woodsman lay in dread of another call, quite certain he would not sleep any more that night.

But sleep he did at last, not noticing throughout the morning hours. He dreamed of an enormous pile of stone moving in his direction, manned by naked women and adorned with flying reptiles. He fled, but felt his feet turn into wheels that slowly rolled and bumped over the packed-earth terrain. He could neither gain away from the moving rock-pile, nor did it catch up to him. In front, Bildon and Mhoral pulled him along on ropes, arguing with each other about how heavy he was. Treaman dropped in and out of this dream, and others even more absurd, until the sound of the trumpet call awakened him and the rest of the party.

⊕ ⊕ ⊕

The hiss and steam of the chasm ceased to threaten after a time; it became the background upon which Cedrith felt his life would surely end. Time refused to move. Natasha soundlessly leaked tears on his tunic and leaned on him as if her muscles no longer worked. The stain of her grief stayed warm in the cavern this close to the magma cliff.

Judgement sat a pace away, his left hand and arm wrapped with the remains of his cloak and his quarterstaff trailing uselessly in his right. The youth's face was a mask, as ever, but the dark stains on his makeshift bandage and the smell of burnt flesh belied what must have been needling agony. Cedrith realized they could stay here until they starved, and the idea seemed almost attractive. No more decisions, the undead no longer a threat; some pain before the end, but the Hopeward guaranteed the intruder a burial by fire, which was preferable to the alternative.

The hiss continued; he might have dozed a while, certainly his vision was blurry and his senses slowed. Eventually the stony portions of the cavern floor beneath his knees became uncomfortable. Cedrith dared not shift with Natasha leaning on him so heavily in her grief. But the pain and the ebbing circulation prompted him towards some kind of decision, much as he dreaded it. Looking at Judgement he saw only the same alert emotionless gaze as usually occupied that horribly-mature face; just the slightest hint of gingerness in the way he held his left arm told of the pain. But he looked back at Cedrith with a face that asked, as ever, "What should be done next?"

Cedrith summoned his energy, and gently, slowly moved Natasha's head back from his shoulder. Shifting his legs from under him, he gasped a bit from the rush of returning blood and its pain, and focused on her face, downcast and broken and scarred, while he thought of what to say.

"Natasha, it is time to go home, if we can." There was no response from the Healers Guildmistress, no movement except the tear-tracks glistening by the light of the chasm, and weight against his arms as before.

"Natasha, we cannot stay here..." Again, he might have been talking to the wall. Cedrith began to wonder why not, and his original feelings rushed back, to despair, to stay and starve and be done with deciding. He looked again at Judgement, and a spark inside him rallied up toward an ember.

"Natasha. Judgement is hurt."

Now her body began to move by instinct, and she turned to the youth on the ground next to her. His stolid expression belied any injury, but his hand still smoked a little beneath the cloth and when she gently signaled for it, he complied. With infinite care she pulled back the burnt torn strips, easily from the top layer but more slowly as the skin became visible. Cedrith gagged to see the ruin of that hale young flesh, and how the cloth of the cloak, shirt and gauntlet had now become fused in places, so that pulling them free renewed the bleeding. Natasha's tears had never ceased, but now she began to snuffle and moan as she worked, in a way that sharpened the air of sadness, but also brought it a little closer to the earth.

Cedrith rummaged in the rucksack to produce clean water, salve, and bandages, which he laid at her knee. While she worked, he carefully and reverently replaced the helm of the Mien inside. It occurred to him that the artefact must be returned to the theater; this was a true reason for going back, one he had not thought on. Since before… he looked on the mute, vacant face suggested by the helm's nosepiece and cheek-plates, and felt a wave of grief at their loss. He covered the Mien and never looked in the pack again.

Natasha cleaned and teased free the fabric from the ravaged arm and hand, wailing involuntarily at the pain she knew she was causing. Judgement tightened his jaw and once or twice hissed free some air, but otherwise gave no sign, as if worried he might disturb her.

The fire had eaten into the blood and in places near the bone; Judgement's frame was spare as a rod in his youth and vigor, he had no fat to offer for such a burnt sacrifice. Cedrith's nerves danced in pain just to see the awful wounds. Judgement's gauntlet was a torn, fused ruin and came off in strips, laid on the ground where Cedrith fancied the earth seemed to soak up the clotted, cooked blood more eagerly than stone should.

Finally rebandaged in white dressing that immediately turned dirty burgundy with seepage, Natasha took several deep breaths and calmly pronounced, "*Intacta volar.*" Under the strips it was hard to tell if any improvement at all had occurred, but Solemn deliberately flexed his fingers with a rock-hard jaw, and said, "This be much improved, I thank thee."

"Perhaps," Cedrith ventured meekly, "you could invoke healing on it yourself." As soon as he marked the words he looked to Natasha's downcast, tear-streaked face and felt the bite of the implied insult.

Judgement, sitting back, caught Cedrith's look and shook his head. "Sooth, I trow can admit of no further restoration." Cedrith was sure that the pain was still very great, more than if all the youth's fingers were broken, but there was nothing more to be said.

They quietly passed the water-skin between them, and Cedrith drank sparingly because he could not be sure of his stomach. With wine, it would have been very different. They sat a while longer, and then he said, "Well, we should try to go then."

"Fare thee well," Natasha said formally, as if to her knees. "I stay here."

"Natasha, please," Cedrith said in shock, "you will die here."

She nodded and looked to the cleft where Alendic and Eddoran had been interred. "And soon."

"Thou may not," Judgement said with a voice like a hammer. "'Tis not given thee to end thy own life, for that way lies Despair."

He worked his way one-handed up from his knees and stood between her and the cleft as if she would make a run for it.

"And who has given?" Natasha asked with a dim echo of her former fire. "Was it Telhol? Did Conar make this rule?"

"Nay. But 'tis a rule, sooth. They did obey it and so shall ye."

"So then, you make the rules for me."

"I have not the wisdom. And yet I shall enforce this one."

"Young Judgement, I am staying, you need not concern–"

"I too, will stay then."

"No one is staying," Cedrith said, realizing his choice only as he made it. "Against all odds, we have survived the terrors of this dreadful place, and we will not dishonor the memory of those who lost their lives to secure our own." He stopped nearly breathless with the effort.

"I… lured a brave man to his death," Judgement murmured in wonder, "and I knew not even his name." He looked up at Cedrith. "But I will. And shall honor it."

"There, and the same for Alendic, Natasha. Come, we must honor him, and go."

The interruption from the voice on the bridge was so well-timed as to be conversational despite the volume and malice.

"On the contrary," it boomed, "I cannot let any of you leave just yet. There is still an important choice for you insects to make. Now, *COME!*"

Cedrith had never heard a living voice utter a Mage Command before, and to his knowledge no wizard had achieved the ability to speak such a spell, outside the Crystal City, in several centuries. But he knew the compulsion he felt when he read the signs in Conar. Instead of a paternal restriction, this was a positive imperative, demanding compliance against his will. With horror, Cedrith saw his feet take steps up the rise, and towards the bridge. Just a little to one side Natasha also paced in an exhausted, defeated shuffle. The sage shouted in fear, but no effort on his part could waylay his path or even slow it down.

With an effort, he wrenched his head back for a moment to look behind him. Solemn Judgement stood where the party had crouched, staring in puzzlement at his retreating companions. Cedrith realized that, as astounding as it appeared, the youth's spirit had actually resisted sorcerous power of a kind unseen in the lands for more than a thousand years. Judgement's face, composed and almost serene, was a beacon to Cedrith's spirits. But those spirits fell, when he saw the Man in Grey take his staff and trot to catch up to them. The boy should have saved himself, he thought, yet to his shame, the terrified sage did not cry out these words.

At the end of the rise, large steps of black stone rose out over the chasm towards a high mesa of something stone-like at its center. The arching steps blocked further view for now, and Cedrith split his fear between the incinerating magma below and the crushing crystal rock ceiling above. A cloud of thick deep purple mist boiled at the top of the stair, seemingly painted all atop the platform it led to. Cedrith knew his own fear was part of that *miasma*, and felt certain he would add to it soon. Compared to that, death from burning or crushing became remote and insignificant. Only the compulsion of the spell kept him moving to reach the top of the stair.

Judgement had caught up on the wide steps, passing slightly in front as if he could protect them. Natasha, who had gone completely calm as the spell took hold, whispered, "Judgement, go back, save yourself."

"I have said I will stay with you. Teacher."

Natasha smiled. "Then slow your step, with us, as if you are compelled."

He nodded and copied their gait, as she continued, "This will surely be our doom, we should have no illusions of resisting this mage. We must stay true to our vows, our selves, but as for our bodies, his will shall be done. I ask you both for your forgiveness, that my actions have brought this ruin upon you."

"Natasha, I…" Cedrith tried to speak. "I hold you innocent of my own choice, my lunacy. Though I doubt Kia will do the same."

"No other person dooms me," was all Judgement would say. After that, the exertion of the climb itself took too much breath to allow for further talk.

The treads were deep and wide, only larger men could have taken them a step at a time. The heat from the chasm below was alarming and made the air difficult to breathe. There were dozens of steps, each one bringing them closer to the rock-crystal ceiling overhead, massive and jagged and tinted by the haze clinging all around. Off to the sides, Cedrith could see the massive rings turning through the cavern-sky overhead. On one such he had rode to the Halls of Glass, and the doom he now approached.

At the top of the massive tier, two pillars framed the landing. On the left a massive black statue of a three-legged monstrous being topped the pillar, surely a demon of some kind. To the right, Cedrith saw only chunks of white stone; as he drew closer he recognized the two booted feet and sword-point of a statue, probably of some heroic being like one of the Hopeful Minions near the entrance. Between the two pillars, as they finally reached the top, Cedrith saw the Hopeward itself, now up close as he had seen it from afar on the ring of Aral.

The mesa-top was smooth and more than a hundred paces across, blocking out the heat from below. Through the darkness imposed by the indigo cloud into which his unwilling stride carried him, Cedrith beheld a dozen looming podiates in two rows, each made of stone below and bearing a clear crystal cylinder above, encasing an item of some kind. There seemed no order to them at first–each row contained some items of dark color, some of lighter, some weapons, some not, some empty–but Cedrith felt a deep foreboding about all the items in the row behind the demon statue. At the end of the pillared way, two stone arches stood on the left and right edges of the mesa, evidently leading to a drop and death in the chasm below. Between them, the rock floor rose several more steps to a dais twenty paces wide. There stood a tall robed being, only a little like Eddoran, in decayed dark robes bearing a scepter in his skeletal right hand.

His hood was back and the head was completely hairless. Not bald; the crown of his head looked as if it were no more a home for human hair than a marble bust. All his skin was dark and wizened beyond years, beyond parchment or wood; even the age-folds had flattened and died long ago. The eyes, as the three came closer, were strangely unremarkable, small and hard to see. In a moment, Cedrith realized they were only pupils, moving on stalks no longer covered with white vitreous jelly. Noseless, earless, lipless, the face was barely able to grin, which it did constantly. The teeth inside were small and horribly stained, but solid enough to clack with every movement of his jaw.

His frame was almost impossibly tall; standing on the dais he looked full seven feet high. The robes, richly decorated once with cloth-o-gold, seed pearls, silken swaths and hanging jewelry, had faded with the immense passage of time to look like soiled burlap. Under the bottom hem, the feet must still have been partially shod, but as he strode eagerly to the edge of the dais, the sound of his pace–a mixture of leather and bone and flesh–was horrible to hear. The scepter in his right hand was the only clean, undecayed facet of his entire appearance; black wood or iron with a flanged metal top, projecting wicked spikes to the outside while within an egg-sized gem reflected all the darkest hues of the rainbow.

He spoke, and both Cedrith and Natasha gasped at the shock of it; the sage fell to his knees and elbows, lashed with pain to hear a voice that should never speak. With desiccated lips, dried throat-chords, and just a nail-thin worm of a stump where his tongue should have been, the monstrous lord of evil yet spoke with perfect elocution, in powerful, dusty tones that reverberated as if they emanated from one side of him. It was all wrong, violently off, and Cedrith quietly murmured, begging him to stop with every word.

"You cannot imagine, I assure you, how very long I have awaited this moment. I am mortified–hah, yes! mortified indeed–not to have been able to come forward as would suit a proper host. But the rules, you see, are quite constraining. Still, you are here, at last, and destiny will be served. That is, indeed, the most important thing.

"My prison, as you see, while quite impressive, is not very hospitable. I have made certain modifications where able but all in all, I have… endured." Here his smile was quite intentional. Cedrith heard a male voice babbling quietly nearby. Looking up to Judgement, he saw his face pulled into a rictus of disgust, the eyes flaming and even his bad hand clenching unconsciously. But unspeaking, as usual. Cedrith clasped his shaking hands over his own mouth, and the noise stopped.

"My dear white queen, come forward insect, that I may reward you properly."

He gestured invitingly, and Cedrith sensed no application of sorcery; he seemed merely to ask. Natasha looked up to him with a face of resignation and moved to the steps. The purple mist was everywhere like a heavy fog, and Cedrith recoiled to think it was entering his lungs with each breath, but was helpless to halt it. The presence of so much *miasma* might have been starting to affect Judgement, breathing more heavily and quivering slightly as if he might flee. The poor lad, it was finally too much for even his brave spirit. Cedrith thought wildly that when the moment came, he might do something–stand or shout to distract the fiend–and give the youth more time to escape. Only then did he realize that he carried neither his mace nor shield anymore.

Natasha ascended the steps and stopped with her hands folded before her like a schoolgirl, head down, waiting. The monstrous man extended one claw-like hand to within inches of her face, mimicking a caress as he examined her.

"Ah, dear woman, you have been through trials, I can see. You've met your lover at last, five years a flicker of time but difficult, I understand, for insects. And did it bring you joy? I think sadly not. But to discover there and then, another lover so quickly, and to lose him as well. How dreadful, to become promiscuous and yet remain lonely."

Cedrith could see him nearly caper in glee, and recoiled to hear the voice when he spoke, the creak of tendons when he moved.

Natasha raised her head slightly, without hope or fear. "I came not to receive but to give. Eddoran is now at peace."

"Not to take? What kind of adventurer is this?" he said in a mocking tone. "But do not mistake me, I recognize your dedication to the creed of the Healer; in fact, I relied upon it. I have followed your career in the Guild with great interest, my white queen.

"How remarkable, that you should have ascended to leadership in such a short time after leaving this place. The freedom of access to ancient tomes it gave you, the respect and support your mission required. Such wondrous fortune, that the old man should die just then; a disease of some kind, I believe."

A moment passed, and then Natasha's head snapped up to look her captor in the eye. What followed was a peal of horrid insane laughter, dry and heartless. Cedrith quailed from his knees, begging out loud for it to stop.

Standing next to him, Judgement murmured, *"The arm of the Enemy, hidden somewhere beyond this world, is long."*

"Yes," the monster mocked, "I have guided your course the past five years since you came to my attention. I saw as you reached your position of leadership, used the influence it gave you to find a worthy spot in the theater for your associate. Such observations are an art, which I learned from one of my… earliest servants." Here he indulged himself in another gruesome chuckle.

"And that strutting popinjay you brought back with you, your second lover, what was his name? He ensured the rest, just clever enough to save your life and deliver you here to me. So here you are. Now, my dear, we both know what you wish from life: its ending. You, poor Hopeful insect, have not the power to grant yourself that sweetness, but I can. You only need to choose."

Here he gestured to the rows of crystal. "Choose you must. For now that you have ascended to my presence, the gates to home will not open for your companions until you do." Here the monster pointed with his scepter to the two arches; Cedrith fancied that his voice moved as he did so, as if the rod were the source of his speech though his jaw was clearly moving, his tongue spasming within.

Natasha stood frozen in shock, not comprehending his words. The skeletal creature prompted her with a hand lightly holding up her chin, which smoked as he continued. "You recall the words. I practically led you to them. *'Those who enter and pass the guards may choose to either exchange a worthy piece for one residing there, or to release an item of their choosing from the Ward.'* So then, take your choice, white queen."

He released her chin then, and Natasha staggered back in pain and weakness, barely conscious now. But she rallied enough to gainsay him.

"I shall make no choice against my vow of Peace. These are weapons of war, I choose none of them."

"An' shouldst thou dare to assail her again," Judgement said in a voice of steel, "I shall strike thee down into the fire." Cedrith looked to him in terror; despite his pain, the youth was hefting his iron-tipped staff in both hands.

The necromancer turned to look on Judgement with a kind of petrified delight. "Ah, the spry little monkey who destroyed my Makine. I shall attend to you and your paltry threats presently, be assured."

"And here…" his gaze swept now over Cedrith on the ground, "one of the Eldest, a great mage no doubt come to your assistance? Sibling," he taunted, reversing the customary form in insult, "tell me your name and training."

Cedrith felt literally dragged to his feet, and managed to say, "Cedrith Fellareon, I am… a sage."

"Of course, those busy drones scraping together flecks of dung from the corpse of your nation, all these long years. I salute you. You may call me Eldest, assuredly." He turned back to Natasha then, with no more heed to Judgement or Cedrith than if they had disappeared.

"Now, queen of the bugs, the time draws close and though I've waited nearly four thousand years my patience is not unlimited.

Choose one of the Hopeward's treasures, and I shall reward you with release in death."

"Choose not," Judgement said again, definite and defiant.

The tall mage clenched a bit then as if his neck had a tic, and his voice dropped to dangerous tones. "Choose, or I shall slay your companions and it will be horrible to watch. Afterwards they shall serve me for hundreds of years. You will be responsible for their agony, and have you not borne enough such guilt for one evening?"

"He means evil," Judgement again dared to interpose. "His plans, of all, must be frustrated." Cedrith was agape now, and as the evil mage turned back to face the Man in Grey, the Elvish sage cried out and fell to the ground again.

"Insect! Have you any notion whose wrath you are invoking?"

"Aye, I know well," said Judgement with deadly calm. "Thou art the liche Wolga Vrule."

The mage actually flinched, completely discomposed. Hearing his name seemed physically painful. "You– how do you know my name?"

"From your first foe, the learned mage Exeter Polanquan, whom thou didst murder."

Now the liche shouted in surprise, and lurched to the edge of his dais, forgetting Natasha for the first time. "I forbid you to speak that name again!"

"Aye. Names are important," Judgement responded laconically.

"So, you waded through the tortured ravings of that madman Fanem, but it avails you nothing. Come here, insect, and take the gift I offer."

The liche extended an imperious hand, and Cedrith felt he could never consider resistance, spell or no spell, had it been stretched toward him. Yet the Man in Grey never budged. Anger flared on the face of nightmares, and focusing his fingers, Vrule said, "COME!" in his voice of command.

Judgement simply took a wider stance and held his staff at the ready, saying, "Nay. Comest thou to me."

At this, the undead master threw his head back and roared in frustration. The grey youth nodded then, glancing to Cedrith, saying, "The rules constrain him."

"You mean… he cannot come down from there?"

"Until a choice is made, sooth."

"So that is why he wanted Natasha–"

"Aye, but more."

The liche had lowered his head to glare back at Judgement, and now raised his scepter threateningly. "I cannot yet step down, fool, but do not believe I am incapable of destroying you." He barked out a series of syllables, and the last thing Cedrith saw clearly was his friend diving to one side and farther away from the dais. As Vrule pointed, the place Judgement had been standing exploded in blackfire. Cedrith was blinded at once, and could only hear sounds for several endless moments:

The loud, staccato crackle of the sorcerous flame, which made itself felt on his skin as pain rather than heat. Cedrith scrambled on hands and knees to get farther away.

Vrule cursing volubly in another tongue, Judgement gaining his feet and running.

Natasha crying out a warning.

Another syllable of magic, and a rush of energy passing close by; Cedrith briefly saw a flare of reddish lightning cutting through the darkness. It must have impacted something solid behind him for he could hear the grinding burn of it striking.

Vrule: "Come out, coward! You hide behind treasures of which you have no comprehension."

Judgement: "Mayhap you will choose, then, necromancer. Destroy one of these pillars here, it may crush me as it falls."

Several more bolts being cast, a gasp of pain from Judgement. Each time, the flare of the spell overhead was sharper; now Cedrith thought he could discern shades of lighter black, sparkles of color, and the deepest tints of purple imaginable as his vision cleared.

He was huddled near one of the pillars closer to the dais, and on instinct scrambled to the other side of it from the liche. Judgement was still alive, shifting further away and putting as many obstacles between himself and Vrule as he could; his free hand clenched his side, which sparked blackly around the fingers. Cedrith was stunned at the young man's courage; he still quailed just to hear the liche's voice, yet Judgement was defying him. A small part of the sage felt envious, for he would have liked to spend his final moments doing something useful. One hand touched the rucksack he was still dragging, and a tiny charge of possibility pulsed through him.

"Enough idiocy. Come out now, insect, or I end the healer's life in agony."

There was a short pause, and Judgement called back, "Or I do, and then once dead, ye do the same. Ye have said so."

"Come now or she dies sooner, and you only later."

"Sooth, we all die, whether I obey thee or not. Say something interesting."

"Dung-eating beetle! Do you dare make demands? What then?"

"Say thou wilt not kill her."

"Not?"

"Mine life is easily worth less than that, I trow."

"Judgement, no!" Natasha cried, and then urgently to Vrule, "I accept your gift, kill me now but spare my friends."

"Achk, the nobility sickens me. Cease this prattle. Choose."

"No," Natasha said calmly, and Cedrith, peering round the pillar now, could see her again. "I am done with choosing or deciding for others. I will not."

"Then you are of no further use to me, white queen. Prepare to serve in the life hereafter."

Judgement stepped out from behind the pillar that held an enormous black suit of plate armor. "Hold!"

Vrule stopped with his hand halfway to Natasha's unresisting face, already webbed with scars.

"What is it, dung-monkey?" he sneered. "Say something interesting."

Judgement took a step forward, free of the pillar but within diving reach. "I shall choose, if ye wish it. In return, thou shalt swear not to harm my friends."

The small part of Cedrith, wanting to protest this sacrifice, was completely overwhelmed by the rush of desperate need, reaching out to grasp this unseen chance to be saved. The tears started in his eyes, and it was shame and anger at himself, more than anything, which drove his hand under the flap of the rucksack, feeling and searching for something, anything with which he could make a statement.

The undead mage on the dais was pausing now, and a flicker of interest crossed its visage. "No doubt, you have many friends, young monkey."

"Thou seest the sum of them here with us."

"One must not commit to a vow carelessly. Still, this seems acceptable. I give you my word, no harm shall come to the queen or this Elf, if you choose a treasure from the Hopeward."

Cedrith's voice choked in his throat as he tried to warn his friend. Judgement stood with one hand on his staff and the other holding his side. His face, as ever, was a mask of resolution.

"Swear in the Ancient tongue."

"What? You dare!"

"Swear in the tongue which forbids the lie, Wolga Vrule."

Again the monster flinched at the sound of his name. "Who are you? What manner of man-child have you brought to my presence, white queen? I would have your name, before… we complete our business."

Judgement straightened as if under interrogation. "I am Solemn Judgement, third son of Final Judgement. A student. And I remember my father's face, Wolga Vrule. Dost thou?"

Contempt, pain, anger, and a shade of something else made war on the liche's face for several seconds. Judgement was merciless, saying again, "Swear, Vrule, and I shall choose for thee."

Ripped from his decayed lips in a loud, booming scream came the word, *"Promissar!"* The echoes rebounded from the crystal dome and ran erratically between the columns of treasures. Cedrith stopped rummaging in his shock, unable to trust his senses. The ancient liche had bound himself not to harm him or Natasha. But…

"Judgement! He did not swear to spare you."

The youth nodded calmly, looking directly at his foe.

Vrule spat, "That, I would never do. Wait another thousand years, but I should never have promised that. Choose, boy."

"Natasha, come down from there," Judgement said. "Thou art free." The healer looked in wonder at her captor, who made a derisive gesture affirming her liberty. She stepped back down to the main floor, and Cedrith stood to join her. Judgement pointed to the arch marked with the symbol of Hope, saying, "Best ye stand there, and be thou ready to go when yon portal opens." With a glance back to the dais, he added, "I trow, 'tis little sense in tempting this fate." He turned to pace up the row of treasures, stopping to examine certain cases before moving on.

Natasha gripped Cedrith's arm painfully hard, and the tears had started in her eyes again; good signs, the sage thought, better than her drained passive resignation. Her eyes followed Judgement as if any moment she expected him to disappear forever. Desperately,

Cedrith flogged his mind for an escape. Perhaps if the youth chose from the podium closest to the portal and then fled…

Judgement paused by a cylinder bearing an ornate golden staff and turned to the dais. "What is the precise manner of the choosing? Are there words to speak?"

"You simply choose, dung-monkey. The magic of the Hopeward will sense your true intent, and the crystal will release it to you. Come now, with such a name, this task should not be beyond you."

Another pause, while Judgement paced to the top of the row, looked at an enormous red gem, and a silvered helmet chased in amethysts and sapphires. He looked at Natasha with sober compassion, and then addressed another question to the liche.

"Why did you not make Eddoran choose?"

The healer gasped, and Cedrith marveled at the boy's intellect. Vrule shrugged.

"Or any of the corpses from the plain below, insect. The undead are beyond choice. The mage, indeed, was an interesting case…" Here the necromancer's face showed an avid light of animation to discuss his handiwork. "Having taken mortal wounds, but wearing that gewgaw he had found, created a fascinating sort of between-state. I could compel his body through necromancy after only a few days; thus he was dead. Yet his mind, oddly, remained his own."

He laughed drily, enjoying Natasha's discomfiture. "Oh I tried, you may be certain. I positioned him before the cases and applied, shall we say, varied brands of pain. But he resisted me. An undead cannot choose, suffice to say."

"Nor yet can thou," Judgement returned, "as the scriptures make plain: *'those who enter may choose'* and *'the remaining one will then also choose'*." He studied a moment, looking directly at an empty case. "Which, then, will be your choice?"

Vrule just stared imperiously down on the youth with great attention and hatred.

"Judgement," Cedrith said, "perhaps if you choose the one… the choice of Vrule, it may work to frustrate, I mean…" But he could not see any real hope of this course. "Take the helm!" he said impulsively, "and don it immediately, it may protect you." Neither Judgement nor Vrule offered any reaction to this advice.

The sage's hand inside the rucksack touched the Mien, and his heart jumped. But without training, neither he nor the Man in Grey could move or speak while wearing it. Cedrith and Natasha remained where they were, nearly in the middle of the hall and only a few steps from the dais. The sage heard a voice telling him to stand by the portal, and be done with this adventure at the cost of his friend's life. But another voice could not be overcome: protect the boy. His hand continued rustling in the rucksack. He tried to do it unobtrusively, but there were so many pockets and inner chambers, he was groping blindly with no idea how it was set up.

The youth trod the path between the pillars several times, examining each one but in no order the sage could follow. The longsword without a sheath was a matchless piece of workmanship, and he studied it a long time; Cedrith thought of Nador's shop and saw that the youth was trying to understand the fastening of the blade to the tang. He almost thought the choice was made then; but Judgement straightened up with a slight shake of the head and moved on. Cedrith found he was breathing only shallowly, between the suspense of his friend's choice, and the end of his life which must follow, as well as his own quest to search the sack without notice.

Abruptly and smoothly, the choice was made. Judgement stopped and pointed to a podium on the side behind the ruined white statue, inside a crystal cylinder wherein lay a single leather gauntlet. It was somewhat shorter than the one Judgement wore, handsomely worked in leather with silver studs of metal on the back-hand side; the symbol of Hope on both the palm and the reverse declared its nature, though it seemed thoroughly unremarkable.

Vrule, following his hand eagerly to the spot, erupted into a terrifying peal of laughter. "That! That rag of hide is not even magicked, you fool! Put here no doubt as a ruse, or to placehold a later submission which never occurred. Yours and welcome."

"Judgement," Natasha cried. "Why?"

Judgement continued to hold his arm towards the crystal which before their eyes began to melt away. "'Tis in my thought that it be less powerful than any other item here, thus my burden of releasing it into the world is decreased. Also, 'tis a left-hand gauntlet. I need a replacement."

"And," Cedrith cried with a cracked laugh, "it is of course grey."

The crystal walls had disappeared and the Man in Grey reached in to take and don the gauntlet. It seemed to fit his hand well, and despite the ruin of his scars he flexed his fingers in it easily. Nodding his head, he bowed so slightly to the dais. "Go now," he said to Cedrith and Natasha. Behind them, the portals to both arches shimmered with golden radiance, and Cedrith, now this close to home, felt such a wave of anguish that he nearly passed out in Natasha's grip.

But the horrid voice spoke again, crying "STAY!" and they could not move.

The liche walked in stately fashion to the edge of the dais, and hesitating a moment, put one foot down to the first step. Realizing his success, he pealed a long call of wicked joy and triumph, and Cedrith felt the pain of it through his being. Natasha cried out and shrank back, but unable to move, and Judgement reacted as if battered by a strong wind.

"Forsworn!" he shouted. "Your word was given."

"Nonsense, monkey, I have done nothing to harm these two. Observe." The liche stepped over to the two and thrust his hand again at Natasha's face with great energy. It stopped an inch from her scars as if he had slammed it into a wall; he rebounded his arm and remarked, "That actually hurt."

Yet he was clearly in a gleeful mood, aiming his scepter at Cedrith for good measure as if to blast him with sorcery. Nothing happened, and the monster shrugged, laughing vilely at his own defeat. "I merely require that they remain to watch your demise, to know that I shall take a servant with me to the earthly realm. Reflect on that, white queen; enjoy your future years, Sibling, in this knowledge.

"But first, the remaining one will also choose." Advancing with unseemly haste to the end of the same row as the gauntlet, he paused before the case with the oblong ruby-shaded gem, the size of two human fists and faceted unevenly yet grotesquely symmetrical. Extending his arms as if in welcome, he intoned, "Now, my ally, I fulfill my vow, made all these years ago to you. The Eye of Kog, captured by our enemies, is free by my choice. I send it now to the world above. The Bolt of the Arbalest is loosed. Follow, and rule, and destroy!"

Even as the crystal case dissolved, the gem itself winked from view.

"It is done! Kog the Earth-Demon is freed from his prison, as am I. The masters of Hope delayed, but could not prevent, the victory of Despair. The central kingdom is ours to reclaim, and much more will be mine, when I have completed my researches."

Cedrith could see, as he realized what had happened, that streams of *miasma* were issuing from all three of them now, even the Man in Grey, at the liche's words. The force of chaos itself returned to the Percentalion was unthinkable; it was unfair, he thought, without the heroes to protect us what ruin would be visited upon the world. The light in the chamber became its dimmest yet, until the gleam of Vrule's scepter-gem seemed like a dread beacon. The dark figure advanced on the youth, and Cedrith cried out to be witnessing his doom.

Judgement took his staff in both hands now, and as his new gauntlet touched the wood, the iron-tips and straps flared with argent reflections. The liche hesitated a moment then, still grinning. "Well, well, a Silver-Grip. Seems the old rag had a little magic in it, after all."

As the monster came in range, Judgement went on the offensive, thrusting hard. Vrule blocked with the iron scepter, and Judgement gave ground as the monster advanced. "Now, how to effect this," he mused to himself. "We were content to blast him to ashes before, but now we have need of the body intact… more or less."

Vrule casually lobbed a bolt of ebony force, and as Judgement dodged it, reached to touch him with his off-hand. Judgement barely blocked the attack, so much easier to launch than a punch, and staggered away gasping at the pain in his side.

"Come, monkey, you are already hurt and your time, unlike mine, is not unlimited. Die and become useful; perhaps I shall leave your mind asleep. Come to me, embrace the darkness."

"But light," Natasha murmured, "the light is greater than the darkness. Judgement, light!"

Dodging behind a pillar with a dark green tower-shield, Judgement drew breath and cried, *"Luxar!"* Cedrith looked to see whether a point of illumination appeared next to him, but instead it seemed as if the entire cavern lightened, just a little. Vrule stopped in place and looked overhead in concern. The *miasma*-mist was thinning. Judgement stood forth in full view with the holy symbol around his neck glowing brightly, held up his staff in both hands and shouted, *"Luxar, Luxar simis Solar!"*

A concussive force slapped Cedrith from above, and he heard a sound somewhere between a blazing fire and a roll of thunder. The entire width of the crystal ceiling, a half a league across, erupted into brightest golden light; the thick clouds of *miasma* beneath it literally boiled away. The entire center of the Hopeward-world was bathed in a column of purest light, as if the ceiling were a prism for the midmorning sun.

Wolga Vrule screamed in horror and fell to the ground, covering his head with his robed sleeves. Natasha was driven to her knees, but turned her face up to the light with eyes tightly shut; the lattice of scars disintegrated under the sheer force of the radiance.

Cedrith felt dunked in energy, drowned by vigor, a measureless quantum of elation that his frame could not long hold. Light was everywhere, the new medium of their atmosphere, its own reason for being. He realized the crystal was not tons of weight inadequately suspended from falling; it was floating in a rising atmosphere, barely held down by the rock walls around it. The sage did not drown, but instead heaved his lungs harder, taught them to breathe something thicker and more meaningful, more life-giving than mere air. It took all his energy to breathe in, but he felt he could sing back out.

Judgement advanced on the liche as he staggered to his feet; the monster created a patch of blackfire to counter the light nearby, but it was beaten down and put out within moments. He summoned a cloak of darkness, solid shadow that moved with him, and met Judgement in combat with a snarl of bestial rage. Judgement's wound, created by blackfire, was healed and he had the same vigor in his step that Cedrith felt. Whirling his staff with skill, he feinted twice and landed a solid blow on the monster's midsection whilst his scepter was still raised. Knocked back, the liche staggered on atrophied limbs as Judgement rained down alternate blows in rapid succession.

Astoundingly, the youth was abusing his elder by sheer physical speed, not heavily harming the monster but keeping him continually off-balance and unable to summon the concentration for a response.

Cedrith laughed aloud, treading on his elation like a warm bath; was there even a chance…

"Enough!" roared the liche, and as the shadow-dimmed scepter flashed redly, the ground all around the two combatants exploded with mystic force. Both were thrown to the ground hard as enormous chunks of the stonemetalearth came ripping up four and five feet high. Two of the podiums tilted dangerously towards falling. A rain of anonymous bits came down, clinking on crystal and pattering off people. Judgement rolled to his feet while Vrule muttered syllables in an unknown tongue, rising now wrapped in a much heavier cloak of shadow. Only the wink of the scepter and a pair of crimson eyes could still be seen as the monster clambered over the wreckage.

"Monkey! Insect! I shall leave no limb connected to another! I shall tear your heart living from your chest and make you eat it before you die! Your bodiless spirit shall be bound to me for all time." Vrule reinforced his threats with a bolt of sorcerous force, which seared the air just past Judgement's head. Cedrith felt his spirits fall, but Natasha rose and shouted.

"Here! Judgement, over here! He may not harm us!"

Feinting an attack, Judgement fell back to a point just three feet in front of his two companions. Vrule raged and cursed from within the advancing cloud of shadow, for now a bolt aimed at his enemy would risk breaking his word. Still he was near-impossible to see; the light was everywhere, bouncing from objects and hitting the humans like a wind or a wave. All points in the chamber were filled with light, but none of it radiated within the cloud of shadow. The two opposites existed in concert, but could not mingle. The spiked scepter lashed forth, and Judgement's block was barely in time. His counter met only empty air, and he fell back to avoid being plunged into darkness. The scepter came out again and again, like the strike of a snake, forcing the youth back and at last evading his block, driving a spike into his side.

Judgement cried out and fell as the mace came free with a thick sound and doused in his blood. The shadow containing Vrule stepped right past Cedrith and Natasha, and his path to the stunned youth was now clear. "So it finishes boy; prepare to exist forever."

Cedrith could never recall how he managed to react as he did. Terrified, mystified, he was quite sure his mind lacked the ability to move. His hand still rummaging within the pack came across something hard and covered in cloth. Ripping it free, the sage brought it smashing down into the shadow, a pass in the dark. He hit something solid, heard the glass break, smelled the acrid odor of mingling liquids.

The cloak of shadow lifted at once, and revealed the screaming liche watching the stump of his hand melt into the dissolving ruin of his scepter, before the entire arrangement, rod to wrist, fell to the cavern floor where it popped and hissed and sank beneath the surface. Vrule screamed and screamed, incoherently and with a shock and anger well beyond pain.

Judgement managed to lever up onto his knees, panting and stunned. The liche turned a gaze upon Cedrith that dissolved his joints, so that he fell to the earth next to his friend. The sheer baleful weight of that ancient hatred made Cedrith believe that no vow could possibly protect him. But the promise had been made, though Cedrith had not so sworn. Vrule turned back to Judgement and seized his tunic-front with his remaining hand in a grip of bone.

"Yew fhool," he raged incoherently, with a voice that now seemed to come directly from his decayed mouth. "Iee hav mur thin enuf powuyr lef to duhscryoy un unsek lyk yew." Clubbing Judgement with the stump of his arm, he released him briefly and reached with his lethal remaining hand to seize his face.

But as he did so, the youth managed the words, *"Auxillis horac periculo, Areghel."*

The light did not become greater, the cavern no smaller. Yet Cedrith sensed the same Presence he had on that day in the Guild. And Wolga Vrule did more than sense it.

"Awrugul!" the liche shouted in fear, looking behind the three to a point high off the ground. Cedrith dared not turn his face, but was helpless to do otherwise, and did. At the edge of the Hopeward, standing on the mesa-top and reaching nearly to the bright ceiling above, was an armored king in full regalia and with a surcoat bearing the symbol of a fist against the sun. Fully forty feet high the king of the Percentalion stood, and the righteous fury on his face bore down on his foe as a storm at sea.

"Vrule, I have waited long to face thee since the day this ward was created."

"Ney, not wen Iee haf cum so klows!" His words, uttered in fear with such a horrid lisp, were worse than his former tone. Once there was an air of erudition and composure to the liche; now he was exposed as a rotting, dried bundle of potent hatred. Staggering away from the summoned Hero, Vrule reached the opposite arch, marked with the sign of Despair. "Butt fowr noyw, let this curst playss klowz wif miee deepahrchur. Iee shul yet win viktoree, unsek. Wee shul meeyt ugen." Hugging his ruined arm to his chest, the liche shambled through the arch and was gone.

The three mortals turned at once to face the enormous being of light standing behind them. Areghel loomed silently and stared at his summoner for a time. Without words, he raised his arm and pointed meaningfully at Judgement, who nodded as if accepting a charge. A timeless second later, Areghel was gone. The bath of light began to settle back to a more normal level, never growing as dim as it had been under Vrule's tutelage, but below the thickness where mere breathing was such a chore.

The three came together and simply embraced all around for a long time. There were moments of tears and release, and stretches where neither Cedrith nor Natasha could stop laughing, whereas the Man in Grey did neither but looked on his friends with eyes drinking their fill.

"My friend," Cedrith began, and then thought better of it. "Guildsman Judgement, you have managed to save our lives despite the best efforts on all our parts to throw them away. I thank you, and if my fiancée will still have an adventurer for a husband, then I thank you now on her behalf. I for one am most grateful that I shall have the chance to find out."

"The archway will not outlast the dawn," Natasha said, "and we have certainly used most of the night, though it seems like days. You must go."

"What?" Cedrith cried. "Natasha, all is well now, you must come with us. Let us your friends help you to bear your grief, though I–"

"No, friend Cedrith, it is not that. I no longer wish to die." She put her hand to her face, where only the most faded trace of one or two pale scars remained. "I stay because I must. The Hopeward must remain open."

Cedrith was mystified, but Judgement nodded. *"The remaining one will then also choose, and the sides will change thereafter."*

"We thought it meant the third person accompanying the pair who entered," Natasha said, "but Vrule gave away the game as he left. He said 'let this cursed place close with my departure.' Or tried to." She suppressed an hysterical giggle. "The sides must change, and one must remain until the next night of opening, or else it will be as the scripture says, *'without one remaining the doors cannot admit another.'*

I am the Healer of Conar, one of the noble class Judgement spoke so harshly of. The obligation lies on me."

"On me, rather," Judgement said brusquely. "For I was the one who released the evil of Vrule into the world. And of Kog, if we can trust his word. Mine is the fault, I should pay the penalty. And I, unlike you, Guildmistress, can live another fifty years."

"No," Cedrith said, with his heart sinking back to his stomach, to have come so close to his life and love. "It must be me, for the passage of years will not slay me. Perhaps Kia will wait," he finished weakly, with a small smile.

"Silly men!" Natasha cried, with arms akimbo, looking back and forth at them as if they could not add two plus three. She waited a moment, and finally said, "And what will you eat?"

Cedrith felt a shock to realize the force of this, and Judgement could only counter gamely, "What will you, milady?"

Natasha's face went calm again, as before she sacrificed herself to Eddoran, and to Vrule. "I shall endure," she said quietly, and without another word she raised her hand and donned the Mortal Coil.

Cedrith could see that Judgement's jaw, like his own, was gaping. His crawling horror to see the ring on her finger was beyond words. Fifty years was a substantial stretch, even for an Elf; that this human woman, in the prime of her life, would shoulder the burden was unthinkable. He reached for her hand, but could only hold it tightly, instead of trying to draw it off as he was sure he intended.

Her face was calm again, and without tears; she even smiled bravely on them both, saying, "One must be at peace to endure." And Cedrith recognized then, the gift Telhol had given to his most devoted living follower.

"I shall return to you," Cedrith promised, "after I have told the world of your courage, Natasha Ioki. I will make sure the crowns and staffs of all the nations know, and I shall point the sages to this trove of knowledge you have unearthed. Every detail of the ways across this accursed place I shall tell them. And in fifty years, if I have not perished, I swear I shall be there on the theater stage, to show them the way." He paused for breath, and added, "I may even learn to sing."

The healer laughed aloud again, and hugged him hard as she used to do. That is when Cedrith felt the tears wash over his own face, and he stood back unable to contain his thoughts for any more words.

She faced Judgement with a look of infinite tenderness. "You, wondrous lad, I have ill-used you. Your talent, your destiny are so far beyond my abilities, it was wrong for me to try to keep them to myself. For that, consider me justly punished. I beg you to hold no hatred to me, though you might deserve to."

Judgement for answer thumped the end of his iron-shod staff upon the ground, raised it and slammed it down again harder, churning up the rockearth. With a face of fury he lifted his staff and threw it as hard as he could in a random direction. It bounced, skittered, and rolled to the edge of the mesa, and only by the sheerest chance exited the Hopeful portal, disappearing from sight completely. The boy's loss of composure continued as he clenched his hands violently and tossed his head.

"There be no justice here!" he raged. "Ye struggle, and strive against the secrets kept so jealously, and whyfore? That thy world might slumber on unaware of yon blasphemous, irresistible powers toiling patiently to o'ercome us all? Whither thy Heroes in this? Certes, Areghel should come, after Alendic has died, and Eddoran, and the Eye of Kog already released. Not before! Must needs they have vessels for their use, e'en as the enemy seeks to do? Who would revere such distant, calculating powers?"

The storm of words fell on Natasha as if she were personally responsible. Her gentle smile never altered, but her tone was sad when he finally stopped. "You are wrong to be so angry, young Judgement. Had I all the years I planned, to try and teach you, I'm not sure I could answer your complaint. But I urge you: seek not always to resolve your troubles with force. Do not hate, if you can. Above all, do not become like that which you hate. No goal, not even justice, is worth that price."

She kissed him then on the cheek and hugged him more gently. He stood stiff as a board, as usual, but when she stepped back he bowed low, taking up the hem of her long dress and pressing it to his lips in reverence.

"Solemn Judgement, a gift for your birthday," the healer said, pressing into his right hand the bag of heating stones. "Use them when you find yourself in a cold place, and think of me."

Cedrith was stunned to see the tracks of tears on the young man's face. "Teacher," the youth said, "I too shall be here when yon gate opens again. And should… should the worst befall, I shall bring to thee the mastery needed to protect thy body from the curse of undeath. I shall wrest this secret from mine enemy, or I shall perish in the attempt."

Natasha nodded solemnly, and the sage realized she was already slowing slightly as the effect of the Coil took hold. Natasha ascended the treads of the dais with slow, measured steps. Once there, she was beyond the power to leave, and the matter was done. She turned as her two companions started towards the Hopeful gate. "Cedrith, I release you from your vow as promised. Speak as freely as you wish of the matter from this day forward. Fare well in Hope, both of you. May the Law and its Peace protect you."

At the golden portal, Cedrith could only nod in response, but Judgement spoke with determination: "Teacher, until we meet again."

⊕⊕⊕

Hollinsfen's inhabitants had been fairly fortunate, for folks trapped in the Percentalion. A small hamlet of some four hundred or so once lay in the far southwest of the kingdom practically in the lee of the Marble Swords. The people could still see those mountains to the west on most days. The gentle valley they lived and labored in was generally free from the worst of the weather; and incursions from chaotic creatures, though horrifying, had been brief and few. Hollinsfen had little in the way of wealth that any thinking being would want; most likely it had not even counted as one of the hundred castles, in the forgotten days. Its people worked hard, though not desperately; they asked little more from life than life. Those who sought adventure had left, a few each year, and were never heard from again; those who remained behind feared them all dead, but hoped that no news was good news.

Six from the field party disappeared at once, when the crevice opened beneath them. They fell screaming into the depths of Hell as the gigantic Earth Demon climbed out on three limbs the size of tree trunks. Looking back down towards his fiery home leagues below, Kog contemplated for a moment how rare a pleasure it would be for his minions to have the physical bodies to torment. Then the monster looked about at his kingdom for the first time in centuries.

Such law! Kog immediately sensed the remnants of mortal order, in the ground, in the air, in all the energy of the surface domain once under his rule. He felt disgust and anger that the strictures of the human world still held such sway even over himself for now. The demon gazed at his own dark red, horny trunk with three legs, sensed his massive jaw and arm-sized tusks; he could feel, above his gaping snout, the crater where once had been his second eye. He actually had to exert his will, to extrude extra arms or change his shape in any way. The land was far from the shifting catastrophic void he wanted, but that would change now.

The world was too cold, and all about him lay a stain of order and reason, taming and regularizing the earth; "crops" he remembered, was the mortal word. With a moment of sustained desire, he ignited the land all around him for a league, and the smell of burning wheat, wood, and animal flesh began in some small way to soothe him. The screams of panic and pain from the humans were sweeter still; but not too much, not too soon. Kog grinned as he decided to practice the patience that Vrule always counseled, at least for a time. Scores of humans perished in the flame-wave, but plenty were left.

The walls of the human town were another offense; wishing himself closer to them, Kog was there, and with arms grown for the purpose he began to tear them down like a child who has been told not to. Throwing great chunks of wood and stone, he aimed for fleeing people until he tired of seeing blood and bone in this way. Some few were actually brave enough to stand a moment and throw weapons at him, usually men in defense of their families. Once the walls were completely down, Kog turned his attention to these bravos. Holding them motionless with a casual thought, he made them watch as he slowly ate their loved ones from the extremities in, and then grasped the offenders by head and crotch, turning them inside out to view the last, despairing beats of their own hearts.

Kog disported himself in this way for an hour, until nearly all the humans were dead. The flames, having no further fuel to consume, began to die down, and he needed to extend another flicker of will to maintain them magically to the height and heat he desired.

One of the last survivors, a young female fleeing from ruin to stump, caught his eye, and Kog recognized that she was one the mortals would consider attractive, though somewhat young. The thought fired another kind of flame inside him and he extruded a hooked limb as long as needed to draw her to him from where she hid. He mildly enjoyed her screams as he made her watch him hatch the needed organ from his middle, and then lowered his scorching hot self onto her, into her.

The puny laws of the mortal world, which declared she must die from such heat, such hollowing, were easily put aside by the lord of chaos itself. She would live, in agony, and quicken until his progeny was ready. Kog deliberated briefly as he thrust, and decided the gestation would be four days this time; where he would be by then he had no interest in knowing. Indeed, he might not recall what he had just done, so far in the future. But one day, he knew, a demonic being would appear with enough strength to challenge him and some of his own manic confidence, to think it could succeed. Kog was sure to implant in his seed the fatal flaw required to secure the failure of that desire, and then masked its embryonic mind against discovery, as was his usual custom.

Kog dropped the smoldering torso of the woman to the scorched earth beneath him, left there to subsist purely as a vessel for his issue, and then its first meal. He chuckled to think it would be his eldest child, his heir, as had dozens before him. Plenty of time, after the death-fight coming, to create another for his amusement.

Having established the kind of world he liked as far as he could see, Kog extended his mind to view the rest of his kingdom. Certain threads of chaos, indeed, were taking satisfactory root; but everywhere, everywhere was the pollution of order and it angered him. Towns, pieces of road, a core of stability to the weather, the orderliness of procreation from the lower species; the insult of Areghel's line still held sway in scraps and pieces all around his rightful domain. Kog suddenly realized he had fallen into the unconscious habit of breathing, as other living beings did in the world; he shouted with rage and a wave of flame rippled from him in all directions. More willpower needed, then, to cut off this impulse; already the Earth

Demon tired a bit of just existing on this plane. *His* kingdom! There was a great deal of work to be done.

He extended his mind further, searching for himself, freed as promised by his servant Vrule. There! Very far away but within the bounds of his kingdom, across many slices and blobs of order that still survived, necessitating he travel to it physically. His empty socket ached with the loss. But something else: the demon's massive will also detected points of stinging, painful light, even at this distance; scattered, tiny but eternal, works of the ancient Enemy. On their own, they emanated a hateful reason and logic from their creation; anathema to him, they would be taken and melted down in the fires of Hell.

He willed himself nearer to the crevice; even now, it started to close under the influence of Law, and Kog was bored of the effort it would take to hold it open permanently. Nothing should be permanent: one day soon, his momentary whim would be the only reality. For now, though, everything took effort. He extended his will again, this time to summon servitors for his bidding from the world below.

His ears curled with pleasure to hear once again the destroying howl of the Dogs, and they were there, each much taller and heavier and faster than a wolf, with varying talons, fangs, horns, but the same deep ember eyes and triple legs. The pack crawled and leapt about him, trying to bite his legs and each other in their grateful fury. Without word, Kog slapped them down and directed their snouts to the mind-path he had detected. A small group of mortals, moving with laughable slowness across his kingdom, daring to harbor a treasure beyond their ken. The hounds caught the scent of Law and Order their master showed them, and with an enormous baying from their many throats as one, raced off with loping strides to hunt.

Kog watched them go, and on a whim conjured a black-storm to go before them. Just a harbinger of the atmosphere he would provide for any survivors in this land, once he resumed his throne. For that, the Eye. He turned again and moved away from the smoldering ruin that had once been Hollinsfen. Kog could not decide how many such survivors there would be, across his kingdom. Not many at all, assuredly. But plenty of time to decide, and then change his mind, later.

⊕ ⊕ ⊕

Cedrith passed the most miserable day of his life after returning from the Hopeward. The reports he made, on paper and in person, passed before his senses in a dull aching haze; he must have described the events themselves eight times before he was done and no image, no statement or word, remained in his mind three moments longer. All through the Guild and across the city once again to the castle, the sage moved and reported, signed and spoke; once again his hand was wrung by many folk of rank, all of whom seemed to think he had performed a heroic deed. The Sages Guild Master, Lord Constable, many healers and knights were there, and he was fairly certain he'd even heard the voice of the king. How many times, he faintly wondered, had he won praise during his sojourn among the Men, and when had it been less deserved, further from his own merit? They let him go at last, and without consciousness or volition he found himself back in his room, at some nameless time after sunset, with the entire night before him.

He got no further in his writing than the date and address of a letter to Kia, and no closer towards sleep than lying on his bed. Almost he wished he were not an Elf; perhaps a Man's need for sleep could have rescued him, but without a wound he knew he could stay awake forever, and probably would. Mere desire and fondness for sleeping would not suffice to bring the relief he needed from memory. The loss of Natasha, worse than dead now and sundered from all the world by her own sacrifice, abashed him, shamed him, hounded his mind as it seemed to slow time to a crawl.

Cedrith never slept, but at some point he became so wrapped in reverie that the change to his room arrived unnoticed, like another mystery. Fighting tiredly to focus, he finally realized something new was in his line of vision: over by the door to his cell there was a square of paper on the floor. Rising and stooping, he noted even before he opened it, the seal of the scales of justice that his friend had adopted. There were two packets; the bottom one, addressed to him, had a second line reading, "To be delivered in the case of death" which had been crossed out. The second, identically addressed, was subscribed, "For reading at the recipient's earliest convenient moment." Where, Cedrith wondered, did the man find light grey paper to write upon? With a tiny smile, he broke the silver wax seal and read.

Eldest,

I leave with the tide. If you would say farewell, meet me at the harbor. I Hope you will always know that I am in your debt, and I will strive to be worthy of the good regard you have shown a stranger and outcast. You may see and hear strange things of me in future days, or more likely nothing I do shall earn any notice. I doubt at all events I shall ever return to Conar. But I go as always remembering my father's face.

Solemn Judgement, Guildsman of Sages

Another parting. Cedrith stood for some time with the letter in his hand, and as he looked around his cell he realized that everything in it, all the Guild, the entire City of Wonders, had become distasteful to him. To think that the mysterious and confusing young man whose letter he held represented the closest soul to his own remaining in this entire kingdom… his mind just brushed past the thought of Kia and he felt a longing next to tears.

He would leave tomorrow, he resolved without realizing he had done so. He briefly scanned the title and abstract of the second packet, seeing a few facts on an obscure Conarian noble custom called sanctuary, allowing even one accused of a crime to prove his worth by a special penance. Pondering this but not yet wondering why Judgement should send it to him, Cedrith moved to get his cloak, and headed down to the harbor.

He walked the quiet enormous streets alone, in silence and perfect safety. The lamps were down to a fraction of their light, and not a soul came within hailing distance. The city slept and the sage paced along in peace; the vast stretches of stone and glass suggested some colossal stage, and a new play ready to begin with dawn. The thought of the world as a theater, which before might have amused the sage, now chilled him to the core. Why should he be the center of all adventure, here in the midst of a million souls? Did such things happen a score of times every day? It was natural to doubt, but Conar was so incredibly… *big*. How many others might suffer the loss of a friend today, in anonymity?

After a long, quiet time of hearing his own footsteps and smelling more and more of the sea-air, Cedrith emerged from the final street-corner to see the harbor lying before him in the light of Unal and the stars. The lower moon had long since made its second ambit, which he knew meant that dawn was near. As he glanced about trying to recall the area where Judgement's boat moored, Cedrith could see some activity even at this hour, as a few of the day's fishermen and some other sailors were up and about. To the northern side of the harbor where the larger ships docked, there were small boats moving to and fro from a wonderful white brigantine, fitted out for a voyage and now taking on the final passengers and supplies. Moving generally in that direction, Cedrith recalled that this vessel was bound for Novar, taking settlers and provisions to folks in the colony of the north. A hard life still, nearly two hundred years after the trip that modern hero had taken, but the Sage had heard some speak of the cold, frontier land with admiration and enthusiasm.

Life was an adventure there. Cedrith couldn't wait to get farther away from a land where adventures were possible.

He took the wrong turning so lost in his mind, and came out on a pier with a splendid view of the harbor, but far above and somewhat removed from Judgement's quay. He hadn't seen his companion here for two weeks or more, so absorbed had they all been with their separate researches, and he was surprised to see the boat in such trim. Even to a lubber's eye, it was clearly remade and fit for the sea: Cedrith had never thought why Solemn would undertake such work, except to be near something familiar, but now he felt the stab of apprehension. Leaving, for where? At sea there would be no letters, yet this tiny boat surely could not sail far. He had no idea, and as he saw the lithe form of the Man in Grey, stripped of his boots and cloak and standing in the water to one side of the skiff, his disquiet rose into panic. He called out, without much aim, and began to scramble down closer to the harbor's edge.

Judgement turned at his hail, and seeing him, waved once and then held up his hand to stop him where he was. Disheartened, Cedrith obeyed, and waved weakly in return. He noticed the boat was already pulling at its mooring line, straining with the retreating tide to be away and off into Landfall Bay. Judgement seemed ready, as he always did, but remained outside the boat in water over his knees. Cedrith knew nothing about sailing, but to his eye the man was simply puttering, and as he was unused to the practice, not doing a very good job.

Following his occasional glance, Cedrith looked to the right, farther north across the harbor, and saw there a curious procession led by the noble youth in white. He entered the water and waded out to his chest in the low tide, holding his arms to the west, as Cedrith had seen before when coming down to watch him with Solemn. Perhaps his friend was waiting to see this one last time before departing. Judgement had pointed out the man's entourage before, in the first days of his suspicions, and Cedrith could see them now: noble house-men with badges of green and gold, standing at the street's edge and down to the middle of a pier here and there. The ship's bell rang on the brig to the north, signaling the all-aboard and warning nearby craft that it would soon set out.

In the dim light of pre-dawn they all watched as Pron Dedicar endured the tug of the tide and faced the west in a sign of... what was it Judgement had said about this act of devotion? With a small start, Cedrith realized he had never said, and before he could wonder why, he felt a second, much stronger chill as he recalled the abstract of the paper he had been sent. Sanctuary, a way to atone for a crime; the man's life was in danger after all.

Looking back, he could see Judgement had boarded his skiff and cast off, with the general pull of the tide taking him westerly. The current from a city waste-pipe pushed him a bit north, somewhat closer to the noble youth, and before Cedrith could realize it, Judgement had pushed the tiller around and put up half the sail, using wind and water to swing back nearer to shore, coming between the pious man and his audience. For a moment, Cedrith's view was blocked, and when the skiff hove clear, the youth was no longer there. Cedrith could see two hands gripping the port side as Judgement sat there for all the world like a statue of a helmsman.

The noble entourage lurched into action, with men crying out and rushing down to the water's edge. Hundreds of silver pieces of fine uniform were stained with salt that morning, as men floundered in the surf and threw their hats and cursed. The Man in Grey sailed on, easily outdistancing them all and keeping his boat's shallow draft above the tide-line, angled now towards the brig. As the skiff veered just past her anchor-lines, Judgement stood and heaved a package neatly up and over the rail; behind his skiff, Cedrith could now see the white-robed youth dripping wet and clambering up the anchor-hawser to where sailors hauled him aboard. He saluted the ship's captain, who nodded and handed him the package; at the same time, the brig loosed her lines and began to move in stately fashion out of the harbor, following a small skiff now running with the tide and sail fully set. In the stern stood the Man in Grey, looking only ahead and ignoring all signs of anger and wrack and Hope left behind him.

Cedrith saw one of the nobles coming back from the surf, with his sword drawn. He suddenly slammed it flat against a dock piling, snapping it off at the hilt and throwing that into the sea in a fit of fury.

Cedrith on the dock felt so full of emotion he could not at first react. At last, he started to sing, because it was that or burst; he sang an Elven tale of love-waiting, one he often tried with Kia when no one else had been listening, and which seemed to him was not a complete loss on the ear. Cedrith sang it as loud as he could, to the west, to his lost friend, to any who would listen, as the tears ran streaming down his face. He stopped when he became hoarse, but stayed on the pier until the constables came for him. He knew now, why Judgement had said so little; he could answer the Mensor truthfully and the Law would remain unbroken.

He saw Judgement's skiff leave the arms of Landfall Bay where it picked up a sea-breeze that gave the craft a stern kick. On the starboard side, the brig rounded the cape and turned north, with a good wind to send her; behind him, Cedrith felt the light of dawn starting to reveal the City of Wonders, in its dazzling stone and glass, even as the invisible folk who lived there fully roused to the day, and its news.

Cedrith knew that Conar would never see Solemn Judgement again. A quiet, accidental death in an alley was the only fate that awaited him now. No one had bid him a formal farewell, or spoken the words meant to match those he had heard on his entrance: "Go in peace, travel in safety, live in Hope." But he fervently wished them upon his friend all the same.

Footsteps approached from up the pier. "Sir, you were a witness, I must ask you to accompany us," said a voice accustomed to command. Cedrith turned then, and saw the Captain of the West Guards with two men behind, and some of the entourage close by. Only three months ago, the Elvish sage from Mendel would have seen the man's badge of office, known him for a guardsman and a noble, and thought of nothing else. Now, honed by his experiences, Cedrith noted the patch on his surcoat: five swords this time, arranged hilts-in like a star on the field of gold.

"Are you here officially, Captain, or is your interest more personal?" Even as he mouthed the mild effrontery and watched the captain stop with his jaw open, Cedrith felt a jolt of excitement. Calmly, he turned back to view the skiff on the open sea. Already a mere blotch on the western horizon, Cedrith strained to see if it too would turn north, towards the colony and adventure. He wondered if there, perhaps, Judgement could find a measure of peace and acceptance.

"Sir, you must come with us. If you know the man in that small craft we have many questions."

Cedrith felt the firm grip on his arm, and nodded to forestall them. "One moment, if you please, Captain. I am praying here."

His arm was released at once, and Cedrith murmured quietly to the Hopelord of Men. "Conar, hero of justice, look down kindly on your servant who has risked all to keep your Law. He journeys now into danger; please guide and protect him. If he wills it, send Judgement south, to Mendel. Recall to his mind what I said to him of the great libraries and stores of learning there. South, lord Conar, please."

For several long moments, it seemed nothing changed with the spot on the western sea. The skiff seemed to hold course for the west, fleeing the rising sun and heading out into the endless ocean. Cedrith feared the Man in Grey was seeking home, or death, by returning the way he had come. Then he fancied the spot might have become a little longer than before; had it turned? Another moment, and there could be no question: the spot bobbed and floated to the left, and disappeared around the southern end of the cape, lost to view. South, along the coast that ran with the Marble Swords. Pirate seas, and the kingdom of Mendel, were several weeks' sail away for a small ship, if it could even make such a journey unscathed.

With a smile, Cedrith turned then to face the guards. "My thanks for your courtesy gentlemen. I am quite ready to accompany you now."

⊕ ⊕ ⊕

Treaman looked down at the wheels on his feet, back at the oncoming pile of stone, and then over at Haltar confidently striding naked as his naming-day to one side. He was holding just a tent-pole where his bastard sword should be, and was sharpening it with his punch-blade as he walked.

"What should we do?" Treaman asked him, feeling as if he had been in this conversation before.

"You'll know," Haltar said almost gaily, and Treaman wanted to strangle him, or perhaps breathe fire all over him.

He tried to yell, "What do you mean? I've got wheels for feet, you great oaf!" But the call of the trumpet drowned everything out, and when he tried to ask about that, it blew again. His wheels went over a large bump and he woke up.

The air inside the wagon was close, and the others were just beginning to rouse. Treaman felt a shock run through him; it was impossible to tell from the tight-set wagon walls how much time had passed, but he felt instinctively that they had slept much of the day away. The party even forgot to discuss setting a watch; they hadn't slept this soundly since Trainertown's drunken safety. He sat up and walked to the back, steadying his body against the tight turn. Opening the rear door, he staggered back from the rush of full daylight;

probably afternoon, late. But of course trying to orient under these conditions was worse than hopeless.

He fought back the pain in his eyes, and grinned to hear the shouts of dismay behind him as the others came awake in the sunlight. The wagon was describing a tight curve, the next mule team following in its trace less than twenty paces back. By now the caravan was nearly in a ring and Treaman could see the other wagons ranging back in an ever-gentling arc as they joined the circle turn with remarkable precision. Already, riders were moving into the interior as it formed, and Braja had planted a large stake in the center, which the drovers used as a marker to set the perimeter. Everyone knew what to do and was running to it with military urgency. Braja's marker-stake gave way to a much larger pole extending fifteen feet high, draped with thick ropes drawn to each wagon as it came to a stop and hooked on its corners. The first two wagons, already fully set with wheels spiked down, began to unfurl long sheets of material down the ropes to the center, forming the start of a tent.

"What's going on?" Treaman shouted to a drover in passing with a keg in his arms.

"Storm coming," was the only response, and others who approached to belay the party's wagon had nothing to add. Treaman watched as the drovers of the next wagon unlatched the complex mule-yoke with heavy metal pins. This allowed the center-pole with attached yolks to rotate square to the body of the wagon. The drovers turned the mules to their left so that the fifth wagon rolled up almost close enough to touch. The team stood inside the circle now, covered by the tarps going up.

Partway across the circle, he saw the large wooden pen being manhandled on rollers into the lead wagon through a large door on the inside; six men heaving to, yet it moved as if full of rocks.

The woodsman caught an acrid tang as the wind shifted, much more powerful than what he remembered. Jumping down to look out and away from the wagon-circle, he saw an enormous boiling mass of cloud bearing down, filling the clear sky with bulbs of ink; Treaman felt the same sense of urgency now, but with less idea how to help. He leaped back into the wagon to report.

"We are certainly in the right place," Mhoral declared as everyone took turns at the outer viewports watching the mammoth cloud bank roll in. "That rain is going to really sting."

Haltar did not disagree, but his face looked unwontedly worried. "Hate being cooped up like this. Without a tavern, that is."

{*"Hungry!"*}

"Coming, great and mighty dragon," Treaman drawled as he opened the cask in his pack.

{*"Hallah want to fly and see."*}

"Hallah should stay and eat. Storm coming."

{*"Hallah not afraid. Hallah brave!"*}

"Yes, but also hungry," Treaman mused while petting his voracious friend. The sudden onset of the storm, with some kind of hard hail against the wood and steel of the wagon, made everyone jump in alarm. The hammering was so loud they had to shout to hear. Bildon jumped to the viewport and rashly stuck his hand through. He screamed at once and fell back in to the floor. His palm was bleeding, both front and back, from a tiny hole less than the width of a nail. The party hovered by to tend him.

"Straight through, like an arrow," Treaman whispered; Linya handed him some bandages and salve. Mhoral rammed the viewport closed and put back the pin. They could all hear the shouts, brays and other confusion of the caravan as random drops sifted through the banners of tarp. Several voices continued to bellow distant orders, most in a language that Treaman did not understand.

The hail passed in just a few moments, replaced by a deluge of the fat, foul-smelling rain. The caravan, after this initial surprise, seemed to settle down and wait.

A knock on the wagon door preceded the hooded form of Pelian, draped in a thick cape of tarp, which he doffed and hung on a hook as he entered. Standing with his hands behind his back, the small thin man looked them over with a terse expression; his gaze flicked once to Hallah sleeping atop one of the boxes on the left, and then to Haltar.

"You must forgive me, I am largely unfamiliar with the ways of adventurers," Pelian began with clipped formality. "Is it common that you should leave one of your party behind, or was it your plan to have the caravan followed?"

Haltar, who had been sitting on another box with his legs stretched out, now stood up in shock. Furrowing his brow down on Pelian, he said, "We are a party of five, sir. I can have no idea what you mean to say."

"No further subterfuge, if you please!" Pelian snapped, shedding what thin pretence of civility he maintained. "I can forgive you some caution, and you should grant me the courtesy of desiring to safeguard my secrets. The penalty for disobedience to the laws of the caravan, is expulsion. Do you wish that at this time?"

"The laws of the caravan, as we have been told but never heard," Haltar responded with some heat. "I tell you we have no one else in our party."

"And thus you would have me believe that a man survives alone in the Percentalion, with no pack on his back and no weapon in his hand."

"Excuse me," Linya said forcefully, "are you saying there is a man out there alone? In this storm?"

Pelian shrugged. "He stopped as we stopped, and does not deign to approach. It would appear he has taken shelter under an outcrop. But if he suffers, that is not on my conscience."

"Yes," Mhoral hissed, "I would gather there is not terribly much weighing on your conscience."

Pelian surveyed the Elf, unhelmed with his pale scars very visible, and his face bent with either fear or disgust. "I do not answer to you, sir."

"Nor we to you," Haltar asserted forcefully. "I notice you have not supplied a weapon as I asked, though we have bargained with you in good faith."

"Faith!" Pelian barked with a laugh. "Letters of credit, you offer, with the signature of a man who has no home, if that name is even yours–"

"My name," Haltar said with his murder-grin, "is not a trade good like the items in this caravan." He waved an arm behind him at the boxes and reached meaningfully for his punch-blade. "You would find the price of further insult to it rather high. Eject us if you will, sir, by which I mean, if you can."

Pelian regarded the group now with open hostility, yet none of the fear Treaman might have expected from being in such close quarters with five opponents. When the urgent knock on the door came, Treaman jumped, but the merchant did not. A soldier in chain and helm thrust his head in the door to say, "The rain is ending, master."

"Send a detachment to bring the follower here. Two guards for this door, and lock it. When the other is found, bring him here as well."

The merchant stepped to the door, and Linya quietly asked, "Haltar?"

He held out his arm and shook his head. "Not yet; he has been our host."

“Very wise,” Pelian said. “There is no need for bloodshed, but when the rain has stopped all of you will leave. All six of you,” he added and glanced again briefly at Treaman. What the woodsman read there made Hallah crouch back and hiss.

From the distant direction the storm had come sounded a shattering din, the voice of clamour and hatred that only needed to come closer to kill. Everyone in the wagon jumped in alarm as if attacked, but Treaman kept Pelian’s eye and saw that only they two had heard it before. The call of the spotter came down, followed by a trumpet from wagon one. Pelian hesitated only a moment, and then backed out through the door.

“We can help you!” Haltar yelled.

“I can defend my own,” Pelian snapped, and then stepped out of sight. The portal slammed, and the bar slid across; now the wagon seemed very small indeed.

“Mhoral, Bildon, look outside. Linya, you and Treaman guard the door.” Haltar bent down to push a box to the opposite side for Bildon to stand on. They unhooked the ports and looked out. To that side, the storm was clearing sooner, and the halfling and the Elf stared for a long moment. Treaman could hear the sounds of activity all throughout the caravan, shouted orders, clanks and creaks, shakes to the outside of the wagon as something was bolted on both the front and back.

“We are carked,” Bildon said decisively.

“What?” Haltar demanded. “What’s coming?”

Mhoral turned back and said simply, “Everything.”

Treaman and Haltar barged up to take their places; in the early dusk, Treaman saw the ragged trailing edge of the storm still passing overhead. Behind it, another cloud was coming, a dark mass filled with flapping wings and the distant cackle of panic. Reaver-birds, by the thousands, and below them the plain was boiling with oncoming flesh. Treaman saw wolves, pantherlike felines, elk the size of horses with antlers on the center of the back; spiders bigger than dogs, low-buzzing winged insects, and two or three spindly creatures with legs taller than a cottage and bodies shaped like grasshoppers; shambling furry beasts that alternated between two legs and four as they ran, great packs of them and some with tree-branch clubs in hand; a dozen garruk or more sprinkled between the menagerie, running with fervor to the attack; horse-like creatures with fangs of tigers, some with snakes riding their necks, or perhaps attached to them; more and more beasts, a myriad of mayhem. As he watched, Treaman heard the howl again, closer, many throats baying pure hatred and death. From within the caravan, a single call answered them back; Treaman was sweating again.

Linya took her look, and cried aloud at what she saw. The sound of the bolts drawn back preceded the opening door, and two men climbed in. They stopped when they saw the group, but had no weapons, so Haltar waved the party to stand down. Through the open door, Treaman discovered the hinges along his wagon had been put to use. False-sides everywhere had been flipped down or across, linking the wagons on the outside wall into a twelve-sided fortress. The tarps were still rolled out, and horsemen waited at two gaps, with drovers ready to open the gates between wagons on a moment's notice. Fires were lit, supplies laid out, one tent clearly marked for access to the wounded. Pelian's voice called "Braja!" followed by something unintelligible; the Nubian appeared in the doorway, exchanged a brief look with Treaman and then slammed and bolted it again.

One of the two men in the wagon drew a key on a chain around his neck and hunted among the boxes. Unlatching two of them, the pair withdrew identical contraptions dominated by a thick wooden stock. As they hauled them to the outer ports, levered out the arms and dropped down the iron support bars, it became clear they were enormous arbalests.

Bildon ran forward to crouch between the ports, and the men gladly accepted his help handing them quarrels as thick as a thumb to load into the stocks. Latching the noses beneath each port, the men cranked hard and the arms came back under the force of the pulley system built into the handles. Then they peered out the ports at the approaching armada and began to fire.

{*"Hallah fly."*}

"No, Hallah stay with Treaman."

{*"Hallah fly, fight bad birds."*}

"No."

Linya was looking out the inner port, describing the reaction of the defenders from within. "They are moving like Conarian Guards out there. Birds overhead, I can see them between the tarps, Lords of Hope, there are thousands. The defenders are firing bolts, and flaming bombs of some kind over the wagon walls." The wailing, roaring, screeching, chittering and dying around all sides grew cacophonous. The two arbalesters inside the wagon cranked and fired continuously. The wagon lurched gently as a body of some kind fell against it, but Treaman heard no chopping or stabbing sounds as of a garruk trying to break through.

Too quickly, the sounds of battle began to fade, though the massive plural cawing of the reaver-birds did not diminish. The group inside the wagon heard scattered snatches of conversation from some in the defense. "Moving around… moving off… running…" The pair of bowmen were sighting for targets but not seeing anything; their conversation, like most of what called around the caravan, was in the Southern tongue and Treaman could only pick up the occasional word that sounded similar.

"They didn't really attack us," Mhoral said wonderingly.

Haltar walked to a port and the bowman there yielded the view. "The garruk have pulled back, out of bow range, a few here and there. But the other beasts are gone."

"They weren't attacking," Mhoral said again. "They're beasts of chaos, we've seen them kill each other for an extra bite of food. They were fleeing, from whatever makes that howling."

As if awaiting a cue, the horrific baying erupted, with the same hatred and power, but now Treaman sensed a note of eagerness as well. Like hounds getting closer to the covert. "They want something here," he said, "something in this caravan."

The roar sounded again, and both the bowmen stumbled back in fear; one clutched his chest heaving, cried out and staggered to the ground at Treaman's feet. The woodsman bent down, and saw blood coming from the mouth and ears, eyes glazed in shock, the breath going from gasps to high-pitched wheezing croaks. Then the man went still, eyes open and a face of horror. Haltar leaped to the viewport, glanced out and drew back at once.

"Hell dogs," he said with a heavy voice. "More than ten. And the garruk are charging in now."

"We need to get out of here," Bildon cried, a most unusual opinion for the Stealthic to voice.

"Grab that weapon, cover the door," Haltar ordered, while the other man, clearly petrified, still returned to his port, aimed and fired. Treaman struggled with the crank of the other but got it cocked, and Bildon tossed them each a quarrel. The man loaded, aimed, paused, then fired, but dropped his weapon to hang against the wall by the latch. He stepped forward like someone in a trance, his face thrust full against the viewport.

Above the sound of the attacking garruk and the shouts and orders from within the circle, a single baying groan of malice crested again. The bowman stiffened, and gave out a rising scream with his face jammed against the port. Haltar reached and pulled him away; in place of his eyes were only two smoking pits, and the man fell backward dead and stiff. Haltar closed the ports and slammed the pins.

To the inside of the wagon circle, Treaman heard a horrific crunching, smashing sound, and a lone bay of recognition, hatred and freedom. Men shouted with urgency, the twang of heavy bowstring was heard from the inside wall, and the orders of Pelian drowned under the screams of horses. Haltar shouted to stop Bildon, who had moved over still more boxes from the inside wall to get a step up and unpin the top hatch. The halfling had just enough height to reach it, and the square hatch swung down too high for him to jump out.

"We need to see what's going on!" he shouted.

"You cannot risk it," Haltar bellowed back impatiently.

"Oh, and you could! You're too big to fit out the hole. I'll run to the back, unbolt the door for you."

"Stay here. Wait. The defense may hold."

It was an unfortunate choice of words. The howling sounds were all around them now, as more wood tore and broke. Men and women began to die in agony. Treaman imagined there was at least one breach, maybe more; no longer able to hold their enemies at crossbow length, most of Pelian's people had no armor or shields. The horsemen looked like retainers, but there were less than ten of those. Judging from the whinnies of agony, they were all dismounted by now. At least one large creature was loose inside the perimeter, probably Pelian's "lead beast."

Treaman risked another glance through the viewport, and caught a glimpse of several garruk charging a place to his left, with weapons in hand. Behind them, an enormous black beast on three legs prowled the boundary, ruby-eyes glowing, sniffing the breeze. Treaman knew what had killed the arbalester, and slammed the view port shut. Then he noticed Hallah was missing.

"Hallah! Hallah!" He looked to the top hatch, still open, and his heart went cold.

{*"Hallah fly! Hallah see!"*}

Treaman concentrated, and at once had a vision of soaring and turning over the ground at a speed that made his stomach flip. There was danger and exultation in the flight itself, but he never quite forgot how hungry he was. Reaver-birds clouded the view at all times, but in the patches between, there were chits and flecks of vision. The flock had descended on the caravan, ripping out most of the tarps. Treaman saw horses torn in pieces, fires spreading and two wagons ablaze, mules loose kicking everything close to them, people fighting a few garruk, and several enormous black three-legged dogs prowling the interior and exterior of the caravan, shrugging off arbalest bolts and sniffing, sensing. The sights were distant and at an unfamiliar angle, but the screams and the ripping sounds came to Treaman from the ground, muffled yet closer. He became dizzy with the horror, and it was several seconds before the left half of a particular corpse registered on his mind.

"Pelian's dead," he muttered. "They're in the caravan, searching."

"This wagon and its contents now belong to us," Haltar declared. "Search these boxes, find a weapon, whatever we can use."

The key from the dead drover was used on chest after chest. One had another arbalest and quarrels; most were stacked with narrow clay jars, in turn filled with trade-goods. Bildon cried out, "This one, under the rest, is different."

Indeed it was, a long massive trunk made entirely of metal, decorated very densely with symbols and images but holding no apparent keyhole or hinge. "Bildon, down boy. Linya," Haltar said in the tone of command. Mhoral pushed other boxes and corpses to the sides while watching the door. Linya bent to murmur a few words gesturing at the chest, and abruptly sat back on the floor with an exclamation.

"There is more sorcery either in or on this box than I have ever detected before."

"I do love a challenge," Bildon replied, warming his fingers and stepping forward.

Treaman saw through Hallah's eyes. The reaver-birds were thinning, as they settled on a wide variety of corpses below. Occasionally one flew at Hallah, and he saw up close as she seized and bit off their heads with great satisfaction. He bent all his strength to urge his friend to stay up high, to eat later; for the most part she was indifferent to danger, but Hallah did prefer to stay away from the three-legged hounds without his help. It did not appear that any of them had been killed or seriously hurt in the fighting; one had a large iron-banded collar but was now sniffing and poking around the wagons with the rest. Most of the garruk had died, unable to deal with the defense tactics of the caravan; some few were looting and making off with items that for them were the treasures of a short and violent lifetime.

"Ho!" Bildon exclaimed. "This symbol depresses a bit. This one too. What do a bird and a scales have in common…"

"Constellations!"

"Ah, very good thanks, Linya. The zodiac in order, then? Maybe too easy."

"Can you just hurry it along a little?"

"Certainly, mighty one, why bother with poison or a blade trap on a box as obviously worthless as this one. Here, help me turn it toward the wall."

Treaman saw the hell dogs circling further from the far side of the caravan, gradually closer to his own. Each pursuing its separate path, barking and biting at each other whenever they came in contact, yet they all were coursing towards the green-trimmed wagon below Hallah's sight.

"They're coming here," he reported. "There are eight of them, maybe ten. Nothing seems to have hurt them so far."

"Bildon, tonight if you please."

"Oh, it's no trouble at all, Haltar, I'll just prise it with my dagger sure."

"Perhaps in order of the symbols."

"What?"

"First Water signs, then Air, so forth."

"Alright, so, um, Dolphin, ah, Serpent?"

{*"Hallah see man."*}

On the opposite side of the caravan, through a breach in the walls between two wagons, a man casually stepped through dressed all in black. Evidently unharmed by the toxic rain he was indeed carrying no weapon. He surveyed the carnage, looking for either loot or survivors; Treaman sensed he was making no noise as he moved, yet the hell dogs suddenly whirled in his direction. A bone-chilling howl tore from all their throats at once, and the loner stopped but showed the same concern as a man on the street hearing a stray cat hiss. He cupped his hands and called out to both sides, seeking survivors to assist.

"We are here!" Treaman screamed, and the party looked up in annoyance until he explained. The four of them, except Bildon, shouted and banged on the walls, but Treaman could see the howling and the thick wood prevented any sound from getting to the ears of the man in black. Then the hell dogs overwhelmed him.

Treaman could not see the man for several seconds, but everyone heard a distant cry of monstrous pain. From close quarters, the man was fighting, and in the growing darkness Treaman could see his right hand was glowing with mystic power. One beast, then another, fell under his assault, while on all sides the snapping fangs and shovel-sized paws of the hell pack missed him by fractions. Incredibly, he mounted one of them for a few moments, enticing the others to wound it in efforts to bite him, then dismounted with a kicking attack that stunned another.

He moved from fire to wreckage without hesitation, always using the obstacles to advantage him and confound the enemy, as if he had set them there beforehand. Any scrap or item that came to reach was immediately deployed as a weapon; one dog momentarily stumbled from the assault of a cooking kettle, another took a meat-fork in the mouth and growled in frustration before it could spit it out.

"…Turtle, Ferret, Fire-Ant, there. Nothing, cark me with a crossbow bolt."

"Forget it, a bunch of gems aren't going to help. Get ready to break out of here."

"I know I can do this!"

"It's probably trapped a dozen ways, we've got to survive now."

"So close. Wait, by the month it was last opened. Start with Fire-Ant, then–"

"Bildon, I'm ordering you!"

Treaman saw, beyond belief, the man in black had slain four of the hell dogs and wounded two more. About six were left to harass him, and they fought with insane fury. Leaping atop a wagon and taking a moment's respite, the man called out again twice more. Treaman ran to the open top hatch and screamed, though the disorientation of seeing from Hallah's eyes made him dizzy and he had to sit suddenly on a box. From the flying view, he felt his heart sink as two of the dogs cocked their ears and started to turn back towards his wagon; but the man in black evidently heard nothing. The other hell dogs were climbing up the back and front boards, so he smoothly jumped down on the outside of the caravan and began to move away. The rest of the pack smashed through the breaches to follow.

"He's going," Treaman said in a deathly tone. "Some are following, two more are coming back for us."

"Mhoral, you and Treaman carry one of the arbalests. When we get out, set it up and see if you can hurt one of them. Linya, I don't think fire is going to harm, and I don't have any advice for you. I'm going to stand in front and hold them back as long as I can; perhaps that sleep spell you talked about before."

Linya nodded with a grim face, white and drained.

Mhoral shouldered the arbalest after cranking it to cocked, and checked his flail and other weapons with his helm already in place, visor down. The dark eye-holes looked towards Treaman, who was still a little sick, and the woodsman cut off his other-vision to get his bearings. Standing, he said, "I'll be alright."

"Bildon, we're leaving, you're on your own."

"Got it," the halfling announced, as he pushed a final symbol while standing atop the box and reaching over with a single finger. Lightning-fast, he pulled his hand back as a brace of darts whooshed out to embed in the wall of the wagon. Bildon cackled in glee, jumped down in front of the chest, levered up the lid with his dagger while standing back, and bent in the middle to avoid a whishing blade that snapped across. Laughing with maniacal triumph, he flipped open the lid. The rest of the party abandoned the door to come back and look in. The box was filled nearly to the rim with very long, flat clay bricks, identical in size, each one sealed at the top and marked with Pelian's sign of the hoarding squirrel. Bildon carefully reached in for one, about as wide as his hand could span and heavy enough he needed both arms. Breaking the seal, he removed the top like the lid of a jar and poured out gold pieces by the score.

"Why bother?" he said in wondering disappointment.

"Linya, detect for magic again," Haltar ordered, and she obediently cast the spell.

"Nothing. Wait. Nothing. No, there's something at the bottom, maybe." Everyone unpiled the stacks of clay, and Mhoral broke open another to find handfuls of semiprecious gems and stones, as good as currency in many remote towns.

"Yes, that one," Linya said pointing to a container a layer up from the bottom. It was identical to the others, except the seal and lid were fake, only clay impressions. The two hell dogs howled outside, and Treaman for a moment thought he would perish like the arbalester, from a stopped heart. They were close.

"We have to mind the doors," Haltar said urgently.

Linya reached for the container, but pulled her hands back in pain. "That clay, it is different," she declared. "Something about it…"

"Boss?" Bildon breathed as he gingerly took up the clay without pain. Haltar looked to the door, the top hatch, and Bildon, then nodded. Bildon carefully raised the clay container up, then brought it down against the lid of the chest. It cracked, and most of the top came away, revealing the hilt and pommel of a longsword.

Outside the wagon, the baying of the hell dogs resumed instantly, constant and urgent and destructive. Linya screamed in pain, Mhoral fell to the wagon floor. The outside began to lurch as the monsters rammed and clawed at the wood. Recovering though breathless in fear, Bildon reached and chipped away some more of the clay shell, exposing a design on the gold-trimmed sheath that looked like a mountain surrounded by clouds. Haltar, bracing himself, reached for the pommel and drew out a hands-width of sword. At once the wagon flared into radiance, from the shine of a blade like a slice of the noonday sun.

⊕⊕⊕

to be continued in "The Eye of Kog"...

THE PLANE OF DREAMS

A standalone novel from the Lands of Hope

In the southern empire of Argens just roiled by the rebellion of Yula, a band of adventurers returns from the Shimmering Mindsea bearing enormous treasure and minus one of its members. The Tributarians, unaware of the growing threat to the waking world, embark on separate plans. But the spirit of the hero lives on in all of them, as their good deeds have consequences beyond their original intention. Will it be enough to avert the peril they have unwittingly brought about?

This first novel-length tale set in the Lands of Hope features a complex world and intelligent, dedicated characters whose actions entwine over distances and beyond their own comprehension. Like any world worth living in, the Lands have humor, mystery, horror and action to delight and entertain the reader.

SHARDS OF LIGHT BOOK I:
THE RING AND THE FLAG
A Sword and Sorcery series from the Lands of Hope.

Newly-graduated imperial officer Justin is convinced he has no future, and hearing the details of the secret mission he's assigned for the Emperor won't change his mind. Civil War threatens the North Mark. Justin must race against time to form a company, and lead his men into the center of the web; but what happens when his loyalty to the Empire means the death of those who follow him?

SHARDS OF LIGHT BOOK II:
FENCING REPUTATION

A Sword and Sorcery series from the Lands of Hope.

When the elven lords, preachers and merchants of Cryssigens need wrongs righted without clues, they look for the stealthic Feldspar to solve their problems. But the legend without a face is hard to find: and when Feldspar takes a commission from the most famous, and beautiful, priestess in the city, he finds problems of his own piling up, and is forced to choose between Hope and safety.

To be continued with "Perilous Embraces" & "Shards of Light".

www.ingramcontent.com/pod-product-compliance
Lightning Source LLC
Chambersburg PA
CBHW030551310726
48979CB00011B/2109/J

* 9 7 8 3 9 5 6 8 1 0 2 7 5 *